ICE

AN ADVENTUROUS JAMAICAN LOVE STORY

R.D. HEMLEY

DISCLAIMER

This book is rated MATURE and is intended for audiences 18 years or older.
The author does not support or condone all actions played in the book. These
actions are strictly for entertainment and plot development, and might be
triggering. These actions include: Acts of violence (graphic), profanity, detailed
sex scenes, substance abuse (alcohol and marijuana), attempted domestic
abuse, attempted sexual abuse, short mention of physical child abuse
(flashback scene) and gore/torture.

This book is narrated in and along the lines of standard English and Jamaican
Patois (acrolet, mesolect and basilect forms), as well as a very light amount of
Spanish (with translation).

If you are a surface reader – Put the book down.
If you are impatient as it relates to character development – Put the book down.
If you are a 'pick me' – Put the book down.
While there is ample smut, if that's all you seek – Put the book down.
Everyone else, welcome to my rollercoaster of unconditional love.

Trust the process.

FOR THOSE SEARCHING FOR THEMSELVES WHILE ROWING THROUGH THE
PERILOUS WATERS OF LIFE.

&

FOR THE PRE-TEEN WHO PICKED UP A NOVEL AND IMMEDIATELY KNEW
SHE WANTED HER NAME AT THE BOTTOM AND CENTER OF A
BOOK COVER.

FOR BELLE TEAM, YOU GUYS ARE MY BACKBONE.
TO MY BESTFRIENDS, MY PARENTS, SIBLINGS AND LAST BUT DEFINITELY
NOT LEAST, MY HUSBAND.

Author's Website: rdhemley.com (Link to author's social media can be found there)

01 | Company

RYLEIGH

"Toni me literally no deh pah that. I just want to finish up this term to get a change of environment," I shrug, while keeping my eyes glued to my phone.

Peer pressure anuh fi the weak

"I'm ready for UWI girl, me no have the time," my opposing protest to Toni-Anne who came with a message from Dalani, continues.

I've known Toni for a while now through a mutual friend, and to say we've grown close is an understatement. Being the only one from my friend group that came back to 6th form, I was no doubt a loner for the first month of lower six, until she transferred. We deh ah upper six now, so check how short that is? A year and some change and is like mi know her from diaper days.

Love the gyal bad to bad

"Claim him a pree you from 5th form and because you did lock down, him no make a move, but since unuh end up in the same form class, him a shoot him shot," she continues to play matchmaker. All this while her hand is in mine, aimed at convincing, while her eyes are glued to the corridors.

Her man she look for enuh.

"Toni weh me just say girl? Rest nuh. Me literally just exit an almost five year long relationship as a young gyal. From second form the boy have me a hold him hand like we glue together," rolling my eyes, I pull my hand from hers. "Besides, Dalani ex and you nuh friend?"

"Me? Me and Ghale anuh friends. My parents know her parents and that's it," she giggles knowingly.

Mhmmm... Frenemies dem enuh, and she wah give me the girl man fresh outa the knot.

Man, man, man. Everyday cannot be about man.

I want to heal and just get on with university. Dalani is sweet and would be a great distraction from my breakup but I'm just not with it right now.

I take a moment to scan the room, allowing my eyes the freedom to dance around while trying to find comfort in the freshly painted beige walls. When that fails to comfort my mind, I avert them to the windows– the dusty white windows. Outside is a relaxed mango tree, without a decor of the fruit itself and stilled leaves. Then and only then, is when I find some sort of calm.

Bwoy, nuh breeze nah grace we pon the hill today?

"See yah think 'bout him deh!" Toni squeals, pulling me from my thoughts.

"Propaganda!" I pull back in jovial shock. "Now sshh, Mrs.Dawkins a come nyam off we head right now," I add, before slightly nudging her towards her desk.

Watching as she drags her chair away, I take her in. Five feet, six inches of dark glowy skin, and her facial structure, coupled with her slight athletic figure? A BEAUTY and I mean that in the cockiest way.

Mrs. Dawkins enters the classroom, causing me to snap my head away from T' to her. The small group of us that are present for registration stand to greet her. Yes, that's how we have to greet the teachers here.

Instead of carrying out the tradition, she waves for us to sit.

"Guys ya'll know better. I'm never with the cult greeting," she laughs. "Ry' do you want to lead today?" her smile as radiant as ever.

Mrs. Dawkins is heavily pregnant by the way, so myself, Toni-Anne, Dalani and Muuch take registration, handle the announcements and conduct devotion alternatively these days. Today though, I'm not up for it... but I can't say no to her, can I?

Chalk it up to my people pleasing tendencies.

Sigh...

I hesitate to stand before walking to her, and guess who I spot from my peripheral? Dalani, springing to his feet.

I– ummm?

He's heading towards the front of the class, as am I– both of us walking to the sound of Toni's giggles. He makes it up front before me, grabs the register from Mrs. Dawkins and looks at me. Feeling slightly uneasy, I turn away, only to meet Ghale's eyes. She's staring between us and back at Toni repetitively with her lips pressed in an awkward smile.

Hope she nuh badda think say me wa–

"Ry?" Dalani's voice cuts my thoughts.

He's tall and fair skinned, with a low cut. He has to be at least 6ft2" because I'm 5ft6" and with my Wallabee, I'm an extra inch or two... and he still towers above me. His eyes are big, bright and brown with lashes too long for him to even know what to do with.

A so God love give man long lash

"Ryleigh, do the announcements and I'll take registration. Me a keep you company today 'cause man seet say you never wah get up," he continues, voice deep and thrilling.

All the boy teeeeeth them nice. Mighty God of Daniel

"Me good enuh, but cool you reach already," I shrug with a 'matter of fact' attitude.

He moves to hand me the announcements and while glimpsing around, I catch Ghale mouthing to Toni. Snapping my head to Mrs. Dawkins, I make sure she's distracted before I look to T' and it's as if she can feel my stare of disapproval because her eyes meet mine almost instantly.

"YOU KNOW WAH YOU A DO," I mouth to her. Without a trace of remorse, she laughs lightly just before burying her head into her phone.

"Antwoin," Dalani starts the call. He's able to move through registration in less than two minutes, making life easier for me.

"You didn't say Ghale's name," I pose the obvious to him.

"Me see say she deh yah mon," his retort comes hushed.

"Alrighty big boss," my response comes just as quiet. "Today all recently chosen prefects will have a meeting at the library," I hop right into the announcements.

Upon finishing it, I convince Toni to lead devotion with me.

• • •

It's now our lunch break and since we don't have a class after this, myself, Toni-Anne, her brother Jordanne and Mariah are chilling under the tree nearest to the technical drawing block. We chose that tree as ours since it's out of the way, with easy access to the football field, the auditorium bathrooms, fountains and the cafeteria.

"Ry' yuh a follow me go wholesale today?" T' questions with my hands in hers, rubbing them softly.

You woulda think we play fi the rainbows to how we behave, but she's just clingy

"Yesssss T'. Me affi buy some gummy worm too 'cause me wah join you on the second form block a morning."

I swear, when we just started selling for the fun of it, it was thrilling, but these days it a give part time job and di doll tired.

"Okay Ms.Prefect. You nuh know selling illegal?" her brows quirk up in question with a mischievous grin on her face.

Then me nuh must know

"She must know Toni," Jordanne interrupts, looking up from his phone. "Them girl yah more calculated than you think," and I don't know if he smirked at me in a flirtatious way or a gibing way.

"Danne you no have yuh own friends bredda?" Toni fires back.

"Hah! funny. My friend dem yah before yours. Man dem and me no have the same class still. Say that to you when me farwud but you too busy a look out fi Josh," he's speaking to her yes, but staring directly at me.

Mariah laughs out, causing Toni to slap her shoulders in efforts to shut her up.

"Nobody nah look fi no Joshua," T' giggles, trying to convince herself more than us.

"Ah if you say so," is all Jordanne mumbles. He's normally jovial and talkative, but today he isn't that way at all.

In an effort to push his behaviour to the back of my mind, I pick up my phone, and lo and behold, I have a text from the devil.

<u>Folan:</u> Babe?

Lan what is it?

<u>Folan:</u> Miss you ☹

Anuh you lef me say me itch up under man? Lol.

<u>Folan:</u> A wah me hear B. Did vex.

Folan that was 2 months ago, try to stick to your decision.

And with that, I lock my screen, only to look up, catching them all staring at me. Jordanne chuckles– his smile not reaching his eyes, before he looks away. Toni and Mariah both shift closer to me just in time to offer comfort while my eyes begin to glisten.

"Need fi block him don't? One gyal cannot be a yam forever after all," my words cause genuine laughter– lightening the mood.

"Girl a you alone can sad and find joke 'bout yourself enuh," Mariah giggles and in that same breath, I watch Jordanne stand.

"Mah liff up," he announces before sauntering towards the auditorium.

"A wah do your brother today T?" I genuinely question.

Her response is a simple eye roll before she says, "Me yah ask? I never know wah wrong with that boy yet!"

I think I know exactly wah dweem but–

Jordanne cannot be sad over me not wanting to date him. Yes, I've known him way before I knew Toni, or even got close to her, but I still would like to protect mine and her's friendship from any harm possible.

Dat bad?

A duppy dem set pah me today? Folan text me outa the blue fi stress me, Dalani up under me skin and now Jordanne who is supposed to be my friend, a dash straight passive aggression my way.

Thought y'all said men were less dramatic than women?

Grabbing Toni's hand, I lead her and Mariah to the parking. I already secured us a pass to leave school early today since we have no more classes.

To the gummy worms we go!

02 | Consent

RYLEIGH

It's the following morning. Jordanne pulls into the school's parking lot and before the car comes to a complete stop, Toni is out the front door. We're late and missed the small time window we had to sell our sweets to lower school.

As I'm about to exit the car, the back doors lock with a click.

Sighhh… Seet yah now.

"Jordanne open the door. Mi wah go sell before general devotion start," my words barely audible.

Toni-Anne somehow realizes I'm not with her and turns to look at us. Her eyes meet with mine, and that's all she needed to read my mind. She steps off, walking over the rocky pavement to get back to us. I roll the window down and hand my bagged worms to her. She looks at Jordanne, who's in his phone again today, before looking back at me.

She know enuh

"Thanks bubba," I verbalize my gratitude. "I'll be right behind you."

"I got you," she smiles, but nothing else on her face does. Di doll hate dis and I do too. The moment she found out that when Jordanne has his episodes, he only speaks to me, she started to feel… left out?

To this day I'm not sure how her and I just met in person last year. I mean, we couldn't have because I've avoided every invite to his house like the plague, fi years.

Mummy never deh pon that

J' and T' lost their dad while Jordanne was driving him home almost two years ago. His dad called him drunk and told him to take the car while his mom was asleep, to pick him up. While descending the Ocho-Rios leg of the toll, he lost control and the car flipped a couple times. His father was not strapped in… and didn't survive. J' blames himself for not telling his mom about the call or not realizing that his dad had released the seatbelt to vomit through the window.

"Jor–" I start but get cut off by the sound of the locks flying open.

"To the front Ry," he says in a low, barely audible tone.

"J' we can talk from here. You know you can't blame yourself fo–"

"Ryleigh this anuh 'bout Dadz and you know that," he cuts me off again– this time smiling sarcastically.

I look towards the school gate, not knowing what to say. "Jordanne I can't risk it with you, our friendship spans years and–"

"Bredda easy with the excuses. The friendship fucked already because we already had sex Ryleigh. You ride me off and now you only speak to me when we're in groups?" his eyes now suddenly depicting hate, causing me to sink into the seat.

Why is he not understanding that yes it happened, but I don't want it to go any further?

"Girl can't talk all of a sudden," he laughs. "Ry' I've loved you for years and I accepted that you were in a relationship but then that night... Ry' ah you call me fi come to you enuh. You cried to me, you told meee say you wah do certain things... and then you *ghost* me di entire Christmas break bad head. Me fi act like nothing happened?"

"J'," I mutter.

"Jordanne me name still," he mumbles.

"JORDANNE SHEER," I retort with a slight scoff. "I was going through my breakup and I came to talk to you. The sex neva planned."

"It was the second time Ryleigh," he fires back, staring at me in slight disbelief. "Yah forget who took your virginity last year or no?" this time he smiles and for the first time it meets his eyes.

"Behave J'..." I giggle, "that wasn't planned either."

"Nothing was planned but I got consent each time. Can all call it begging if you wah... on your part too," he chuckles and the chuckle turns into contagious laughter somehow– pulling me into my own laughing fit.

The laughter dies down and after a minute of silence, I speak.

"Jordanne, you know I was with Folan for years... and even though me and him have never done anything sexual, I love him for real. Yes, me give him the go ahead fi have sex with other girls 'cause me know how man stay and yesss, I still got jealous when he was sloppy, but–" I pause, to fix my face in a screw after realizing my words.

"Yammy-leigh," he chuckles.

"Yummy-leigh to you though," I retort.

Another minute of silence settles around us before he breaks it.

"Me nuh want you feel like me nuh understand the before aspect enuh Ry," he almost whispers while tapping the steering, "me fully understand that but your boy left, and you same one say if there was any reason for him or you to leave and unuh actually stop deal, you woulda consider our ting.”

I look away… and I don't know but I'm starting to feel butterflies.

Not now please.

Relax girl it's Jordanne, you like him

“Ry’ we nuh affi public if a that yah medz pon… Know you no want Toni know and me nah push that pon you but mah mek you know a you me want and ago always want. So do your healing yes, but don't ignore me, especially after wah gwaan.”

While staring at me, he holds my chin up, forcing our eyes to meet. His hands move to the hem of my skirt, causing me to freeze. He slides it under, and I welcome the feel of his gentle fingers– my body no longer apprehensive. His hands move even further, and I hear him hiss lowly when he encounters the roadblock that is my tights.

Pulling closer to his ear, I whisper, “Slide it down J’,” coercing him further by leaving a soft wet kiss on his neck. Without a second passing, he slides the tights and my panties down simultaneously, before slipping his finger inside.

“Fuccckkk Ry’,” he groans while slipping another finger inside.

I lull my head back at the feeling– while thanking God his car is tinted.

“Ryleigh, practice nuffi say nothing to me weh yuh no mean… yerr?”

“Mhmhmm,” I moan in agreement.

“Words babe, use them,” he breathes.

“I will… pra–”

The sound of the morning bell breaks through my bliss.

“Wah peak or?” he whispers into my neck.

Wahm to him? Him know we cant't cum through penetration

We've also been here for like less than three minutes…

… And it's like he read my mind, because he starts moving his thumb to circle my clit while his lips find residence on my neck. As if commanded, I start releasing on his fingers– reeling and shaking against the reclined seat. If you think that's crazy… I'm given less than a minute to come back to earth before he slowly slides his fingers out, inserting them into his mouth.

Love this boy… bad.

“Go to devotion,” his words pull me from my admiration. He then hands me the sensitive wipes. I take it, hoist my feet and begin to clean.

He finds this funny.

“Laugh and see if me nuh slip you in right now,” I raise a single brow at him with my head to the side.

“Easy,” he continues laughing while holding our stare.

“Mah leave now. You ago wait till you… ummm, till you lil friend subside or?”

“LITTLE?” he laughs out– on top of his voice too.

Right then, I realize he's back. He's okay, or at least for now.

I grab a bottle of water from the cup holder and attempt to exit the car.

"You nuh answer me Ry," he says, so much under his breath that I almost missed it.

"I'll come see you later today J'... remember you sister a dead fi we go the new froyo and bowling place later."

"Ah," he breathes.

I exit the car fully to walk across the pavement. For a prominent school them people yah sure no care 'bout them parking lot. My eyes spot my form class, walking in a queue towards the auditorium and I run to meet them.

"Me sexy form prefect!" Bert shouts.

I signal to him with my fingers on my lips. He smiles before repeating the action while cocking his head to the side.

"Bert you nuh affi compliment me, me ago keep your phone regardless," I state.

"Ah, but you know you sexy fi real though right?" he continues.

"Bert, please nuh make me affi write you up again. Just relax and get back to the line," my response falls harsher than I intended. I'm not usually strict with them, but when I am, I am.

As I'm about to pick up my pace, I feel somebody brush my shoulders. Snapping my head around, I spot Dalani. He's escorting his form class to devotion as well.

"Maamz," he calls lowly.

A who and him?

"A me yah talk D– I mean Dalani? Nuh maamz me," I roll my eyes.

He smiles before winking, all while continuing his walk towards the auditorium.

'Bout maamz. Hate the word

Moments later I'm watching my students line up in their section to the back of the auditorium. The next thing I know, Jordanne is behind me as if he's my very own ghost.

"D... I mean Dalani," he mimics my voice.

"Stop eavesdrop nuh bad man," I whisper before looking around at him fully.

He smiles before holding his hand in the air to signal surrender, while walking backwards to the stairs that lead to the wings of the auditorium. I shake my head before snapping it back around where I catch Dalani staring at the interaction between us. Turning my head from him, my eyes connect with Ghale's.

What is it wid mumma?

Toni-Anne slaps my ass and I spin around. I knew it was her just based on her smell. The girl nah lef her YSL cologne.

"We a leave early again today. Wah reach the bowling alley by 4pm, so you know that a really six," she explains.

If organized was a person, it would definitely be her. She continues to babble, but I'm now zoned out, thinking about what happened in the car earlier.

"Girl stop think 'bout Folan. Yuh hear weh me say? Your worm them sell off. Dalani bought them all and tell me fi go get you from the parking lot, but I know J' might've been depressed about daddy so I didn't come."

I laugh internally at her assumption.

Depressed 'bout supm weh anuh fi him... 'bout daddy

"Why him wouldn't want me in the lot with Jordanne?" I pose my query.

"Guess him just did wah talk to you before devotion?" she suggests.

Or him see we a talk when him a park?

Why him a keep tabs pah me? I've literally made it clear to everyone that I'm not looking for anything right now. Ever since Folan got the sports scholarship to study abroad, I've literally been surrounded by sharks.

For the entirety of lower 6th form, we were trying to make long distance work... until somebody sent him a picture of me seated beside Dalani at a local fashion show. Me say di boy lose it after that– claiming that he knows D's intentions.

I would normally fight to prove my innocence, but I was tired of doing that. For the entire year prior to that, I would have to be Facetiming him 24/7, giving him access to my location and sleeping with him on the phone.

Possessive if you ask me.

Is it bad that I'm relieved it's all done?

03 | Group Up

JORDANNE

Toni-Anne is whining about me not being ready before 4pm but nobody neva mek me know we a leave before the last session today. Usually Ry' would say something but she hasn't said a word to me since devotion this morning.

She's back to ignoring me and I can't help but think she's going back to how things were in December. Me really nuh have the time fi focus pon alla this though.

Since my dad died, I've been in charge of every single thing he left, and I mean every single thing– legal… and not so legal.

Deven wah medz that right now

I look down at my phone to check if she at least texted me to find out if mi ready and… nothing. Pushing that to the back of my mind, I start moving towards the kitchen, where I know Toni is waiting for me.

"Ina the kitchen bad man?" I blurt my thoughts while watching her re-do her hair.

"Lowe me nuh Danne," she rolls her eyes without interrupting her task.

Ignoring her, I move out the house and towards the car. The subtle vibration from my phone grabs my attention and I look down to see Ryleigh's call. Instead of picking up, I let it ring a little.

Yeah we learn, cyaa seem too desperate

After some seconds, I pick up.

"Hellooo?" she sounds annoyed, "mah call you from after two bredda. Wah do your phone?"

Almost immediately I realize I have my business cell instead of my personal phone, causing a hiss of frustration to leave my lips.

"Jordanne? Me just know anuh me you a hiss your teeth after?" she scolds. "Fool you fi pay attention to your personal phone sometimes too enuh," her tone shifts from slight seriousness to humour.

"Ba– Ryleigh," I correct myself, seeing that Toni's now walking towards me. "Me ago grab it now and buzz you back."

"Was calling earlier fi ask if you did wah leave early, but Toni say you got the memo. While ago I needed you to choose my fit... Gonna send them now."

"T' mah go grab my other phone and farwud. You can drive go today. Mah be your passenger princess or wah unuh call it," I laugh lightly while ending the call with Ry'.

"Serious-serious?" she doesn't wait for me to confirm, instead she jumps into the driver's seat and buckles up. I shake my head with a smile and walk back to the house, heading up the stairs.

I make it to my room just in time to see my personal phone going off, so I move to grab it.

Mine: Pick one. This? |attachment|
Mine: Orrrrr?? |attachment|

I find myself staring at both pictures. The first is a mid-thigh jumpsuit like thing– full black, skintight, cleavage out. I like it but...

My eyes drop to the second option. This one is an oversize type of pants with a crop top. Dah one yah me rate more, given who ago deh 'bout.

 Another few seconds pass before I find myself staring at the first picture way too long.

Fuck... Nuh know how much longer I can do this hide and seek, almost-deh-nuh-really-deh supm yah with her.

Jah Jah.

Mine: J?!

**Black jumpsuit if it was just us but the work
man pants since u lil man a go too.**

**Mine: So the black jumpsuit it is. Thanks
bestest! ♥ ps: it's called a cargo pants sir.**

**So the work man dem call
it too loool.**

I'm not laughing at all... Bestest she call you bro? Just bestest, no acknowledgement of me insinuating Dalani is her little man.

I shake my head at the realization.

Thinking of that, I go to contacts to give him a call.

• • •

TONI-ANNE

I pull in, park and watch as my brother texts my best friend. I don't understand how they think I don't know. The entire school knows if you ask them. A blind man can see their chemistry and I think that's why Folan chose to leave instead of completing his last school year.

I'm waiting for one of them to say somethingggg.

Or maybe me too nuff?

I laugh to myself, looking up just in time to see Danne look at me, but before he speaks, I do. "Ago call Ry' and see if she reach before we go in, but in the meantime take me picture," and with that I see him mentally groan.

Meee duh business.

I wait for him to exit her chat. I've been staring at their message thread as it reflects in the window– unable to make out words completely.

These two

When he closes his screen, I decide to ring her and what do you know? She picked up on the first ring.

"Baby me inside long time!" she shouts above both the music and voices of strangers.

"Okay... J' ago snap my pics and then we come in."

"Aighttt! Never know him make up him mind fi come," she lies without missing a beat.

I roll my eyes...

A affi my best friend 'cause what a gyal lie man

• • •

RYLEIGH

I wanted to go meet them outside but T' told me to stay so we don't lose our favorite section.

Dalani is here and so is Mariah, Muuch, Joshua and his friend Ryan. I've been sitting beside Dalani since we got here– slightly uneasy but still here.

My mind goes to the memory of losing Folan because of this same action... but I start to remind myself that I couldn't have lost what was barely mine. The boy was for the streets, the houses and the cars– no joke.

My phone goes off and I look to see that it's Toni sending pictures.

**<u>Sexy Bitch</u>: This good or me need fi
send fi u? |attachment|**

Story post?

<u>Sexy Bitch</u>: Duhhh.

**Looool. You good. Hurry up come
take Mr. Mase from beside me.**

**<u>Sexy Bitch</u>: Him friend a come in with
me now so him nahgo pay you no mind.
Lol you know dem in love. Me a wait pon
him fi done him spliff.**

Dalani and Jordanne are not close friends at the moment, but we all roll in the same group here and there. They used to be close, until Mr. Sheer died and J' withdrew from everyone. They've never been the same since and it's almost been two years.

I snap my head up when I hear Jordanne coming in with the jokes. He's such a different person in a group setting– always the clown, making us laugh.

Dalani decides to draw closer to me for one reason or the next, but I stand to hug Toni, so I can move and not make it awkward.

"Di girl nuh wah hug you forever T'," Jordanne chuckles before pulling me from her into him. "You good?" he whispers… but because I'm only focused on the smell of his cologne, Mariah gets to speak before I do.

"Mom and dad dem enuh man," she squeals while Muuch nods in agreement. "Just mek it official 'cause nobody nuh blind," her tone now comedic.

Toni shakes her head at the suggestion.

Yeah, she's feeding into the rumors for sure. I need to talk to her so she knows nothing is official or will ever be…

Jordanne releases me to move to the ball rack, picking up the blue one for himselffff, knowing it's my favorite. He knows I'm going to throw a fit if me cyaa use it and still gone do dat. As I'm about to, Dalani hands me an identical blue ball from the rack in the section beside us.

"Thank you," I look up at him, grinning from appreciation.

"C'mere," he mutters, pulling me to the lane entrance. He holds my hand to help me bend and step correctly. I follow through, releasing the ball steadily. It rolls away at a mighty speed but is still able to stay straight. We watch it roll to the end of the lane and all pins fall flat.

I spin around in excitement and hug him!

During the hug my eyes land on J', prompting me to pull away. I watch as he walks off simultaneously to the froyo section… even though he's next in the line-up to bowl.

Toni shakes her head before grabbing me and leading us to the bathroom.

"Ry' me love you but when unuh ago stop?" she asks, "is either unuh ago deh fully or unuh affi stop the games."

A young lady exits the stall and leaves without washing her hands.

Nasty

Toni closes the main door behind her before walking back to me.

"Wah you mean T? Me and Dalani no in a nuttin. We're not even dating," I retort.

"Not fucking Dalani Ry'! Jordanne me a talk!"

I pull back, shocked by her tone and pitch.

"I've been trying to get you to just talk to Dalani instead of J' because I know you're not healed and nuh ready fi settle. You ago hurt him and I don't want him to go through more episodes without you by his side or possibly caused by you yourself… So just stick to Dalani please me a beg you."

Huhhhhhh? I take a few seconds to look at her, realllly look at her.

"You cyaa talk?" she questions.

"T' I like your brother I do, yes… but I promise you nothing serious is going on or will ever go on. Me try explain this to him but each time I do he falls back to not speaking or being his fun jovial self. We used to good before Folan leff but ever since he did, I think J' expects me to be with him outright but I–"

"Ry' you know yuh love play victim though?" she cuts me off and once again I'm left shocked. "Me know unuh affi do supm extra, me feel it in a me bones. Jordanne only ten months older than me so we grew up like twins. I know him and me know him nah make up a scenario in his head Ry," her eyes soften when they meet mine.

Just from both her statements, I'm already at the brink of tears but I don't want her to assume I'm trying to play the victim, so I fight them.

A stall door flies open revealing Ghale herself.

"So Toni you really a try set up Ryleigh pah Dalani and you know me no over him?" she starts off hot.

Oh?

"Ghale, Dalani does not have an ounce of interest left in you. Let it go nuh. Rest, abeg," Toni speaks, clearly annoyed at this point.

"And Joshua no have no interest in you either. Yet still… you rise," she retorts, laughing out a little too loud for Toni.

Di next thing me see ah Toni phone, moving past me and heading to Ghale's face. Before I can comprehend what's happening, a dem that pon the floor.

I grab Ghale away from T' and Toni takes the opportunity to deliver more slaps to her face.

It doesn't take much time for the commotion to be heard, causing a set of knocks to present itself at the door. Just by the sound of them, I know it's Jordanne. A millisecond later I hear Dalani's voice followed by Mariah's.

"A cyaa fight Toni and Ryleigh a fight to pussyclawt?!" Mariah screams– being the extra personality that she is.

"NO!" we both stop to shout. Ghale takes this opportunity to push Toni against the vanity.

Her head hits the granite and... blood.

I fucking lose it at the sight of my friend screaming while holding her head. Ghale rushes to the door, releases the latch and it flies open... but before she can leave, I yank her back by her hair, swinging her to the ground.

Nuh bother wid it Ryleigh, is the last thing I hear my mind say before I lose all rational thoughts.

What feels like seconds later, I'm throwing punch after punch, and I can feel Mariah trying to pull me away. I ease back and she falls from me. My head props up when Mariah stumbles and I notice Jordanne lifting Toni to bring her out.

Good.

"Ry?" Toni calls, and that's when I release Ghale, allowing her to stumble to her feet.

I move off while gently pulling the hem of my jumpsuit down, when I realize Dalani is back with a tall guy holding a bunch of keys. I'm assuming he went to him to get the door open. His eyes move to Ghale who's now sobbing while holding her stomach.

What happens next is what's interesting though. Di boy move him hand to him waist.

"Try that nuh..." are the words that fall from J's lips before he can even pull.

04 | Decision

JORDANNE

I watch as Dalani moves to Ghale.

"Just reflex that bredda… Wah happen in here Toni?" he asks looking at her a little too fucking long for me.

Man no plan fi pick up him woman? Ghale.

"Your woman disrespectful as fuck!" Toni speaks from her post on my shoulder.

That's my sister but mi know a she start it, otherwise she would be crying right now, but she isn't, so she's satisfied with whatever went down.

"D' Ghale in deh a listen to our convo and come out come approach Toni 'bout her setting you up with me. She felt some type ah way and ago say Joshua no want T'. Then by me turn a them that a fight. I tried to part them but when we paused to tell you guys what was happening, she push T' ina the vanity," Ry' explains, tone laced in annoyance.

"So why the door did lock?" I turn to Toni, and just then, Joshua appears at the door.

"Who no wah who?" he asks, while reaching to take T' from my shoulders.

"Apparently you no want me sister killa," I make it clear before handing her to him.

With her legs around his waist and her hands and head over his shoulders, she looks at me, and I know to let it rest. Before anything else, he takes her out of the bathroom.

"Ghale we had a good relationship weh mi feel end pon some good terms. Why yah provoke Toni?" Dalani queries, while helping Ghale assess her bruises.

Ain't no way my sister a help him get Ry'…

"You ended the relationship, mi neva agree to that," she protests and for the first time since the door opened, I feel bad for her.

We a impede pon a private conversation killa?

"Ghale we nuh fit ina each other... Is like a triangle a try squeeze into a square and it just n–" he's explaining himself but before he's finished with his statement, I lead Ry' outside to give them some privacy.

Hope she see say a wasteman

We get back to our section and Mariah is now explaining what happened, with Muuch and Ryan as listening ears– like she did dedeh.

"And a so Toni box-box up the gyal," she mimics. "Me hear WUPLASHHH cross face. Me a say no man a plantation them a run in deh. Emancipate Ghale mah beg yuh do," she laughs.

Girl yah a real joker.

Whole time Mariah was behind the door unable to see just as me and Dalani were.

"Unuh still wah play the rounds or unuh wah get di froyo and cut?" I ask, only because I can feel Ryleigh's palm sweating in mine.

"Home..." Toni-Anne makes the choice, her eyes meeting with Ry's. The unspoken communication between them baffles me every time I see it.

"Ah cool. Joshua bring T' home... Ryan you can ride with Mariah if you no wah wait pon him and Dalani must ago see to Ghale," I delegate the rides.

"I came with Dalani," Ry' decides to remind everybody. It takes every muscle inside me to not seem bothered by her statement.

"Hmmph... and you're leaving with me," is all I offer, causing Mariah to giggle from a distance.

Girl deh ears clean enuh

"Cool me ago tell him bye," she says, walking off towards the restroom. My eyes immediately drop to her back, then her waist, then her a–.

I'm pulled from my thoughts by Toni turning my head to hug me, "Lata Jordanne," she mumbles. "Let her be big brother. Ya'll will come together when the time is right."

I tighten our hug before pulling away, to watch as they all walk to the exit. Ryleigh exits the restroom, prompting me to pick up her things from our section to meet her at the door.

"Me ago mek you, do you," is the first statement that leaves my thoughts when I get to her while opening the door.

She steps out, looking towards my car.

"Yeah me still a bring you home tonight," I confirm the question I know just popped into her mind.

She moves to my coupe, ignoring my initial statement completely.

Sigh...

The ride home is silent. Half the time Ry' is gazing through the window and the other half she's scrolling through Instagram stories.

We pull up to her gate and I put the car in park. Taking a deep breath, I look over at her, just in time to see her swipe away from my grid. She feels my stare and breaks the silence.

"Why would you say you ago leave me alone?"

"Say me ago mek you do you," I make it clear.

"Same thing," she scoffs.

"Ry' all now you no mek me know your decision and me honestly can't do the best friend thing no longer. I haven't been with anyone since last summer when you... when we– but you get weh mah try say?" I try my best to express myself.

"I do J'... but I just don't want the friendship to suffer if any feelings change along the way. Your sister knows something. I don't know how much but imagine if we have a big disagreement and she's caught in the middle... or we, as in me and you, argue and can't fix it, then boom we become strangers."

"Then we no re-meet Ry' and try again," I laugh, but almost immediately realize she's serious... "Ryleigh what if none of that happens? Why we cyaa just try and see where it goes? Promise if me ever start lose myself like a mad man me pull the plug and save we friendship. Cool?"

Truly

She looks outside for what seems like two minutes but really was just two seconds.

"Jordanne what if we have sex on the low as... friends with benefits? I don't want to be tied into another relationship right now. I want to date and see wah out deh, but I also don't want to have sex with multiple men. Sooo, ummm, since you're the only one I've ever done that with, I wanna continue. Can we explore that?" her tone now covered in plea.

Don't even think 'bout it bad head

Fuck she mean? Date? Explore?

"The fuck yah suggest Ryleigh?" my brows twist in confusion. "You wah emotionally attach yourself to next man and just fuck me? And me fi watch you go pon dates and live you maddest life?"

She shakes her head.

"Yuh nah listen! I DON'T WANT TO BE IN A SERIOUS RELATIONSHIP RIGHT NOW. ME DID INA ONE FI YEARS," her eyes now wild, "wid zero benefits and a shitload of trauma!"

She moves to open the car door, but I lock it.

"Ry' relax," I realize what's about to happen and decide to calm her down. "Relaxxx babe."

She's breathing heavy and if me coulda shoot Folan me shoot him years ago, but she loved him and I can't break her heart in any way, shape or form.

A deep sigh leaves her lips and the next thing I know is she's on me.

Siiiiclawt...

I can already feel the wetness between her thighs, which makes me wonder, how long has she been turned on?

Reclining the seat, we fall back and she captures my lips in a kiss. My fingers find the seam of her jumpsuit and I rip it.

"You ago buy back me thi–" I silence her by slipping my middle finger into her wetness.

She swings her head back, giving herself permission to grind on it.

"Buy you anything you want when you want it Ry," I whisper.

By the looks of it, her eyes are about to roll out of her head. I move my thumb to her clit and bring her head back down into a kiss. She moans into my mouth, and I use my free hand to find her nipple.

She pulls back, but only to start unzipping my pants.

"Nahv no coverage Ry," my words don't get to settle before disappointment warps her face.

Jah know...

"Morning after? Pull out?" she suggests.

"You took one less than a month ago," I remind her.

"Jordanne it's two per year safely. A new year now," she breathes.

"Nuh think a so it work Ry," I actually laugh out.

Ignoring me, she moves down, and in less than a millisecond my dick is at the back of her throat.

Girl yah ago mad me

Might even mad already.

My thoughts are interrupted by her doing the thing where she hums, and I try to grab her head up...

... but she doesn't budge.

She's definitely trying to get me to fuck her... and a dat she ago get.

Naturally.

05│Decision Part TWO

JORDANNE

My phone is going off while connected to the car. My eyes shoot to the radio screen, wondering why the fuck Dalani woulda call right now?

Could be dat supm wrong with Ghale?

Cyaa move though, Ry' have me in a trance.

I look down and her eyes meet mine. She takes that as her cue to move allllll the way down to the root of my dick.

Jah Jah God...

Feeling my toes curlllll to the max, I try to grab my phone to disconnect the call before answering.

She realizes and giggles.

Well, this is going to be hard.

I mouth to her to 'BEHAVE', hoping she'll listen.

She's facing me, completely unaware of who's calling. I successfully disconnect it and answer. Instead of obeying my earlier ask, she uses this as an opportunity to move to the tip, swirling her tongue around.

My breath hitches.

Thissss giiirlll

"Ye?" I finally muster up enough breath to answer Dalani.

"Yo just a make you know me never did ago pull earlier... Reflex fi real," he explains.

"Yuh good man," my words fall sharp.

"Me like her dawg, and me know a yuh best friend or sister type thing... and you say she off limits but me nahgo play wid her. Me actually serious."

All the words trying to surface are stuck in my throat, 'cause Ryleigh busy ah try prove a point. Me know she no feel me fi deh pon no call while she's in action.

"Bad head tomorrow we reason," I say before clicking off the call.

Somehow, I find the DO NOT DISTURB button and just like that, I'm back in a trance.

"J' I want it," Ry' kickstarts her plea.

That voice

Jah know...

"C'mere," I help her on top. She decides to look directly into my eyes while holding onto my dick knowing tha–

"Consent?" she questions… but before the word fully rolls off her tongue, I sink deep into her.

Coulda cry.

The feeling? Ethereal.

She moves her left hand to my throat while her right hand cups my balls.

Cyaa survive this. Me nahgo survive this.

She then moves to the tip and I see when she smirks before moving up and down, careful to stay at the tip of my dick and onlyyyyy there.

I've been inside her for less than thirty seconds and me feel like me ago bus, swear.

"Relaxxxx J'..." she whispers, and even the fucking whisper sends chills down my spine.

I decide to focus on my breathing and just let her do her.

Moving her hand from my balls to hold the headrest for support, she rides me for what seems like a millennia, and as I'm about to release, she hops off.

"Not yet," she breathes, so low I almost missed it.

She climbs to the back and I follow. She then positions between the seats, facing forward towards the windshield before resting her head on the center console.

Bumboclawt killa just go home. Don't go in

I whisper a quick word to God as I enter her from behind, "Please Jah guide me through the slippery wa–" but I'm cut from my prayers when she starts throwing it back.

Fuck...

I'm dying to take control like I'm used to, but I don't want to with her. Not Ryleigh. I love how commanding she is in her element.

Folan wah see this

Fuck Folan!

The thought of him annoys me, causing me to grab her neck, pulling her up to meet me. Burying my head at the back of her neck and behind her ears while my left hand finds her clit, I slam inside her just to hear her screams.

"Jor– fuccccckkkk... Jordannnnnnne!"

"Quiet," I manage to get out. In this moment I decide to take control from her.

She wah control the nature of our relationship. She wants to control who we tell, when we see each other, when and how we communicate and now how we fuck?

'Naaah,' I mumble to myself before smiling.

"Why yah be so difficult?" the question slips while I tighten the grip on her throat.

"Jor–danne… ple-please," her pleas fall out as moans.

"Ryleigh Stacia Stevens, make it easy fi me and just answer," I breathe.

She whimpers.

"I'm scared," she mutters.

"Nuh affi fraida me Ry," and with that I shove her head back down before slapping her ass cheeks repeatedly.

She keep on a underestimate me because I've shown her my vulnerability.

Fuck that.

I slam inside her again, my fingers not leaving her clit. She clamps down on my dick trying to pull the cum out of me, but I pull out– using it to slap her ass cheeks.

"J' I'm sorry," she whimpers.

"Ah," is my only response while slipping back inside her, slowly. The anger leaves my body almost simultaneously and I'm now able to give her slow strokes.

Dat is it

"OooOoooh … Myyy God, Jor–" she groans. "Cyaa live without it."

"Yuh wah do that enuh. Neva suggest that babe," I remind her, my voice now hoarse.

I inhale sharply, realizing I'm about to cum, but I need her to do that before I do.

"Ryleigh, I need you to let it go. Tell you the last time, it's not pee."

"Okay," she breathes and with just that, I can literally hear the liquid gushing from below.

My dick is now drowning while Ry' is unraveling beneath me. I don't move my hand from her clit, just enjoying how weak she is to me.

I pull her up and put her to lay on her back before moving between her legs. Placing her feet on my shoulders, I press them back to her while I sink deeper– meeting her for a kiss.

"One more time," I whisper my request.

"I can't, Jor–"

"One more time and this time without clit play," I cut her off.

"I can't Jordanne," she finds her voice to protest… and I cock my head to the side.

Holding her feet together, I watch as her pussy clumps together. Spreading them open again, I sink it, repeating the sequence of actions just to tease her into torment.

"Jordanne just fuckkkk me!" she screams.

Is like she no remember ah her gate we deh. Ms.Janette love me still so if a dirt a dirt.

I grab her knees, push her legs apart and deliver fast, steady, deep strokes. Within minutes she's flooding my car again.

The girl this weh say she can't cum through penetration? A smile creeps onto my face, realizing I just might have found the formula to solve that issue.

I'm on the verge of my own release, only able to get 2.5 more strokes in before I try to pull out. As I try to, she grabs me and pulls me down with a smile.

Yo?

"Ry'..." I barely get out.

My orgasm is already sucking the strength from my being. Mi just nuh have the energy fi move.

Giving up, I release inside her. Her smile grows from subtle to a full on cheese.

Weakness forces me to fall into the nook of her neck, and I whisper, "demon."

She giggles before hugging me tightly.

"Weh me ago tell mommy say 'bout me crotches weh tear out?" she asks, sending me into a laughing fit, a reallll laughing fit.

That's Ryleigh Stevens for you.

I love her but this has to be the last time.

06 | Decision Part THREE

RYLEIGH

I'm now at the grill searching for my keys, when I notice mommy has cut the lights on. Jordanne is in his car with the window down, waiting for me to get inside. He relaxes when he notices mommy opening the door and I finally am able to open the grill.

I watch him ease back and I know he's putting his gun back safely in his waist.

Wish we coulda sleep out don't?

I'm only 17– eighteen this coming September but regardless, my mom has never allowed me to stay by J's or him by me, at all– minus that one time I tried to use the dumb 'group work' excuse.

Unuh know the lady stand up and watch we the entire time?

I've still never been **inside** his house even after Toni and I became friends. She on the other hand has been here a million times over.

Don't get it wrong, mommy loves Jordanne and the way he is with me but she says she won't be the one that creates a space for us to do anything we'll regret and her young gyal pikny nah breed pon her.

Memba the pill a morning

I will...

"Good night Mr.Sheer. Thanks for taking her home in one piece!" she shouts to J'.

He honks his horn before speeding off with Alkaline's – My Side of the Story, blasting.

"Wah do Jordanne tonight Stevens?" my mom asks– her eyes fixed on my clothes.

"Him good mommy, probably wah go check if T' alright."

"Wah wrong with T' and what's wrong with your clothes?" she touches the shirt J' gave me to wrap around my waist.

"Toni nuh take up herself a fight gyal and now her head buss... and my crotch ripped while I was bowling," I answer her questions.

She lifts the shirt, "Me tell you wear the cargo 'cause a whole heap a movements fi bowl but you no listen," she's almost gloating.

"Mommy rest nuh... Me ago bathe, sleep a kill me," I turn away, heading to my room.

I actually don't have an ounce of sleep in me right now. My mind is set on the image of J'. The memory of my hands running over his waves straight down to his back. He's a tower of silky smooth chocolate, with slits for eyes and succulent lips atop his perfectly aligned teeth...

Sigh...

Snapping myself out of the flashback, I start thinking. I want to FaceTime Toni, I want to check on Dalani and I need to find out if Jordanne is okay with what I suggested.

Annnnd we have to sleep 'cause school a morning?

Yeah that too... Sleep, yes.

• • •

I glimpse at my phone to catch the time– 9:45pm.

"Okay girl as long as unuh know wah unuh a do and you no stress him," Toni speaks while ironing her uniform for tomorrow.

"We'll see. It's only a suggestion," I mumble while wrapping my hair and looking at my teeth.

I should pop my retainer in tonight.

Earlier I explained all my feelings to Toni and she listened and understood. I wish her brother could do the same, but him feelings ah cloud him judgment.

"Danne nahgo wah share you but if unuh choose fi do the friends with benefits thing and he agrees, at least he knew the terms beforehand and can't blame you. Me nuh wah affi pick sides," she whispers the last few words of her sentence.

"Why yah whisper?" I look down at the phone that's propped up to the corner of my bathroom vanity.

"Sound like you man walk past me room," she giggles.

"Me ago call him 'cause me wah go sleep by ten," I mumble while dragging my bonnet on.

"Ah me ago call Joshua and ask him wah Dalani say 'bout the fight honestly," she pauses, "cause weh him tell you earlier too politically correct. Danne say him claim a reflex."

"Yeah him say a reflex fi real 'cause him never know wah exactly a gwaan. Him just see Ghale on the floor and blood on the vanity."

"Them traumatized and fulla PTSD fi young boy eeh?" she roars out in laughter.

"Real!" I join her cackling. "Come offa me phone mek me go find out how my personal life ago move forward."

"Bye bitch, love yuh bad," she smiles. We blow our kisses and hang up.

I pick up the phone and walk to lay in my bed. I would normally keep my robe on if I had another call to make but it's Jordanne, he's seen it all. Clicking on his name, I wait for him to answer while I snuggle up against my pillows.

He answers, "Ryleigh… Deh pon?" eyes directly on my cleavage.

"Up here J'. Eyes up here," my lips forming a slight smirk.

"Hmmph wah'pn?" he smiles.

"You didn't give me a clear answer Jordanne," I remind him expectantly.

He hisses and ends the call.

Excuse me???

As mi start think fi ring him back and classsss him, my phone goes off.

JBae: Listen to mi Ryleigh.
JBae: Me nah… matter of fact, me
cyaa sit down and watch you live your
maddest life and me just a get covered up in private.

I sigh… before texting back.

Jordanne you're not listening so me ago try again.
I need time to heal. Folan have me itch up pon him
like glue fi years, a take bun after bun under the
guise that because I was a virgin it was fair.

You were there for most of it. You know what it did
to me. I'm not saying we will never be together,
what I'm saying is I'm not ready right now. I'm not using
you for sex, I just started to have sex and I like the
feeling, that's all. I don't know if it will feel like that
with anybody else but I'm not willing to do nuttin with
nobody else.

Please know that I love you too much to jump into it
while trying to figure out who I am and what I want.

He doesn't reply to my text for over ten minutes. The empty wait causes my heart to start pounding and my palms are now sweating bullets.

JBae: Cyaa dweet babe. I can't,

**and that's why me hang up cause I can't
say no to your face or voice.**

My heart sinks and I don't know what to type as my reply.

**JBae: Ryleigh a from earlier me a pre fi cut you
loose full time. Can't be your friend cause me nuh
wah hear bout none a you dates or ntn. I wish you
the best tho. I love you and will love you for life.**

Can I call?

He doesn't grant me a reply and my text doesn't get a double tick either. Him cyaa serious? I start typing again just to make sure.

Jordanne?

Lol stop d ramping. U need fi stop the playing.

Oh?

Ok kl.

Less than five seconds later I see Toni's text flash across the top of my screen.

**Sexy Bitch: Danne say me fi call u but I'm on
the phone with Joshua. Wah'pn?**

Instead of replying, I click out of her chat because I'm physically unable to. My hands find my water bottle and I practically throw the water down my throat, grab my AirPods, cover myself from head to toe with the comforter and click on the song I heard him playing when he drove off earlier.

The song starts booming through my pods, the lyrics resonating with me wayyy more than I expected them to.

More minutes pass with the song now on repeat. I hiss and stir, trying to fall asleep but the lyrics keep hitting home.

• • •

TONI-ANNE

The tension in the car is THICK. Tooo thick fi a Wednesday morning at 7:45am. Ryleigh is scrolling through Dalani's instagram while Danne a drive like a maniac.

I offered her the front seat today because I wanted to lie down and work through my cramps. Might as well I didn't, 'cause them deh two seconds away from killing each other.

Glimpsing at her phone as she scrolls through Dalani's page, I wait for Danne's reaction. He keeps 'checking his mirror' but I know it's to see what she's looking at.

 I watch him move to turn the volume up on the one song he's been playing since last night. His hands are now tight around the steering while he sits up, rocking and singing to only certain parts of the lyrics.

I watch again as he bobs his head while pulling his spliff from the cup holder. After taking the longest pull, he starts attacking the lyrics again while sinking the gas pedal.

Ryleigh? She's still staring at her phone, trying her very best to come off unbothered.

I–

You know me cyaa take the problem though?

Danne starts attacking another section of the song again before he breathes, filling the car with smoke. Him nah give up? Trying to annoy her this way is crazyyyy... but genius. Mi affi give him dat 'cause me can see her jaw a tic from yasso.

Ry' snaps her head up to look through the window. She picks up the lyrics that seem to resonate with her and start singing when she realizes he doesn't sing certain parts.

"Wonder why it so easy fi you get up and leave?" she starts off loudly, *"Sometime me get too close to people weh nuh familyyyy, thinking them ago stay when eventually them ago leave!"* she basically screams before hissing her teeth and looking back at her phone.

Then unuh watch drama

A this me did a run from how long now enuh. I roll my eyes and decide to get comfortable 'cause dem nahgo stop.

Jordanne laughs and continues to sing what he feels is important in the song while turning on the road to our school.

"If you no like the bredda then why you give him you number?" he smiles, cocking his head to the side.

Ryleigh hisses.

Jordanne puts out his spliff all while parking perfectly.

Ryliegh exits the car before it even comes to a complete stop and Jordanne cracks his neck before popping a mint into his mouth.

Pulling my cologne from my bag, I decide to spray myself and keep it in my hands to spray some on Ry'.

Cause me know she stink a weed and jump gone

"T'..." Danne calls in an eerie but all too familiar tone.

"You affi start drive go school now good?" and I know not to protest but...

"Why?" I still find the courage to ask.

"You wah go school with this level of tension every morning Toni-Anne? And you no wah up your driving skills now?"

"Alright Danne, whatever. I'll drive my car and pick her up myself. Know that's the main idea you're trying to get across," and with that I hop out and run to Ryleigh, hoping I can spray her before she gets near anybody.

See it very clear say dem two yah ago be a problem, whether them end up together or not.

07 | Let Go

RYLEIGH

It's our lunch hour, 1:20pm to be exact, and I'm sitting at our usual spot under the tree. Mariah is telling us a story I'm yet to hear the words of due to being zoned the fuck out.

Joshua is laughing at the top of his lungs and T' is now in tears.

Muuch has her mouth going around from a cheese patty while laughing. She looks up to see Mariah mimicking the dance she saw at the bus park this morning and just like dat the doll start choke.

Mariah doesn't stop her story though, "A so the man grab up the likkle gyal and dash her in a the bus and do him victory dance enuh," she continues while cackling.

Her eyes move to me and I quickly force a smile, masking my horrible mood.

"Them conductor yah think passenger a property enuh. Me say the girl uniform blouse soil up just 'cause him no want her take the other bus," she adds– holding her stomach while tilting over from cramping laughter.

A loud bang drags my eyes to Joshua. The boy a beat the desk while Toni a beat him shoulder.

Soon from now the Dean ago come run unuh and call we friends bad company Ms. Prefect

"Unuh quiet down nuh. Lower school no have lunch and a fi dem block this we deh pon," I whisper dramatically.

I might have made it worse, seeing as now everybody is now trying to stifle their laughter– causing even more noise.

I finally start laughing genuinely when I catch Mariah hold her legs together to run to the bathroom.

"Look weh you cause Ryleigh," Joshua barely creeks out, "Niagara Falls now enuh."

Moving over, I slap him, "Stop nuh."

On those last words, my eyes catch a glimse of Dalani walking alongside Jordanne and my first instinct is to bury my head in my phone– not quickly enough to not see when Jordanne shakes his head.

"D' a come," Toni decides to whisper to me.

I don't lift my head because I just know Jordanne wants to see my reaction.

"Ryleigh," Dalani starts, "Pure Maths session after lunch?"

"Cool," I mumble with my head hanging and my eyes glued to my phone screen– just jamming away at the weather app.

"Ah. Text you when me free up? Gonna check on my form class. Man them find phone down deh."

"Aight," is my only response before looking up, only to see Mariah, Joshua and Toni all staring at me with small smiles.

Dalani moves off and as soon as he does, Joshua speaks, "The man no need no help in a Maths enuh Ry," he laughs.

"How you know that?" Mariah and Toni question simultaneously.

"We can never be perfect. Practice a practice sir," I retort, and with that the bell goes off.

We all stand, knowing it's time to head to the auditorium.

"Above Juici we ago or pon eh stage?" Joshua seeks confirmation.

"Above Juici," Toni makes it clear to him.

We start climbing the stairs and get to a point where we can see the stage, the wings to the side, the auditorium floor and the exit doors leading outside. Upon exiting the stairs, I plop down on the first chair I see before grabbing another one to throw my feet up– in efforts to save it for Dalani.

Mariah, Muuch, Joshua and Toni move further towards the back so dem can do dem usual laughing in peace, without any echoes that might disturb our study session.

I pull my phone out and shoot a text to Dalani.

I'm upstairs auditorium when u ready.

<u>Dalani Mase</u>: Actually, was about to text you.
Jordanne a stay with mi class for me this
session so me free now.

Jordanne hates to sit in with classes. I guess it's better than sitting with us now? Okay… I guess.

Than sitting with youuu

Ignoring my mind, I type a simple 'OK' before sending it to Dalani.

After only three or so minutes, I look down to see him already ascending the stairs–his destination set to the chair beside me.

"You wah do today genius?" he smiles.

"Up to you enuh Einstein," I giggle and I can already hear Mariah mimicking us while they all chime in to laugh from back there.

I take my feet down and he takes a seat while pulling a desk in front us to share.

• • •

We're now minutes into our session but my mind is being attacked with thoughts. Deciding to say what I've been thinking, I lift my head from the pages to look at him.

"Me know none a we no need no more practice yerr? Especially you."

He laughs out genuinely before saying, "Did a wonder how long we did ago keep it up enuh, Jah know."

"So what's the actual motive? Everyday Toni tell me say you say this and you say that 'bout me but you've yet to approach me straight up."

He leans back and smirks while his eyes find me, "Ryleigh anybody can see that I like you but you're my friend's 'favourite female friend' as him call it… and you know mine and his friendship set a way from last year or so. Never wah approach you and fuck up uzimi… and you and you li– your boyfriend," he corrects himself, "did too tight, so me no bother put no chat to you."

"It's giving prey," I mumble.

"Tell Jordanne and him say you nah leff you man dem time deh. Now that you guys aren't a thing anymore, me a apply all the pressure I can from early before nobody else sweep you up," he smiles tapping the desk with his index finger.

My mind is skeptical about his advance, so I take the opportunity to observe his eyes. They hold desperation and… lust?

"I'm still not ready for anything serious Dalani," I whisper, connecting our stares.

"I didn't say I was either. Just exit a relationship with Ghale, which was almost as long as yours. Just thought we could keep each other's company while we work on ourselves?" his lips now curled up in slight mischief.

I keep my eyes fixed in his direction. I can see him yes. I can hear him yes… but listening? No.

Nahgo lie to you, the only thing on my mind currently are the three times I've had sex with Jo–

Girl?

I can't control it.

The thought pulls a giggle from my mind.

"You find joke in my approach?" he questions.

"No… a supm me remember," I continue my happy smile.

"So?" he pushes.

"So… yeah I guess. I want to date while figuring out who I am without Folan or any-body else, so we agree on that at least," I make my answer clear.

"Ground rules?" he suggests.

Without hesitation I start, "Respect is number one. We might not be serious but re-spect me while we date," now raising my pinky to signal the first rule.

"Alright boss," he salutes jokingly.

"Secondly, you need my consent to do almost anything to me. PDA needs consent along with any other physical touch behind closed doors, if we even get there cause–"

"Suuur–" he tries to get his response out, but I cut him off.

"I like to go on actual dates, since we're dating and I don't want to always plan them."

I look away for a second before turning back to him. Another smile creeps up onto his face but this time it pulls a smile from mine too.

"We do not post each other and we do not answer to rumors whether good or bad about us as a unit," the fourth finger pops up to signal the fourth rule of course.

"Is a contract?" he laughs.

"Can call it that yes," I chuckle.

"Lastly," I add, "I would like to date other people. This nahgo be exclusive," and with that he shakes my hands. "I won't be sexual with any of you until I pick someone to be exclusive with so clean up your thoughts from now."

"Okay Ryleigh. May the best man win?" he laughs and I find myself giggling.

"We can go get ice-cream after school today then?" his eyes now glued to me.

"Great start," I smile even more before hearing the bell.

Grabbing my phone, I text Toni the details and wave to everybody before he leads me out the auditorium.

Less than three minutes later we're approaching his car and I've come to realize he's on the phone, thanking Jordanne for sitting in with his class. I then move to the passenger door but his hands get there before mine, opening it on my behalf. While hopping inside the first thing my eyes land on is the Audi sign to the center of his steering wheel.

I relax my body before taking a long, deep breath, noting how fresh it is in here.

My mind flashes to how Jordanne's Benz always and I mean alwaysss smells like weed. Only one car mi know him keep fresh and that's the Porsche. I smile, thinking about how serious he is about that one car.

Dalani is still on the phone outside, so I take the opportunity to check Instagram. My fingers find what's on my mind– a picture of J' and I last year when we were in New York. The thought comes to delete it but knowing it's a joint post, I decide to archive it– so the notification doesn't trigger him.

I then scroll to the Christmas post I made when we finally made up a few weeks ago and I forced him to wear my cute Santa hat. We were back to not speaking two days after that, as is common with us these days, but I've never gotten to the point of wanting to remove pictures. I'm just not that girl, but this time I just feel like this is it and I don't need reminders.

Staring at the post for a while, my eyes linger on his jawline.

His slight smirk.

His relaxed eyes...

"Consent to kiss your cheeks?" my reminiscent memory is cut short by Dalani entering the car with a question.

If him gimi the 'ick' one more time!

I nod and he plants a light kiss on my right cheek before we get going.

The ride to Cold-Stone ice scream spot is fun so far. We're able to bounce our thoughts off each other. It's so refreshing. No baggage, no old emotions, no nothing, just vibes.

• • •

JORDANNE

I pull into the garage at exactly 5:21pm. Watching as the shutters come sliding down, I shut the car off.

My thoughts move to them. I know Dalani will date her and I've convinced myself I'm okay with it. Earlier today mi give him the 'go ahead' weh him desperately think him need. I even suggested her favourite ice-cream spot and flavour.

Grapenut or pistachio

Know she ago love dat...

Weh mi therapist say? Giving her space to find herself won't do us any harm?

"Skulli!" my voice comes loud while walking from the garage into the kitchen area.

"Yo boss?" he mirrors my pitch and tone.

"How the meeting go today? Wah the man dem a say?" asking only to gauge whether I need to show my face more or not.

I have to get Dadz business dem in order but the team affi in order before anything else. Dalani's father was my father's righthand man and since his son and I had our disagreement, he hasn't been very supportive of me taking over.

"You're home," my mom greets me as she walks over to the stove.

With that, Skulli exits the kitchen without a word.

I don't know, but ever since Dadz died, him and Sue can't seem to stay in the same room.

Shit weird

My mother turns to look at me before handing me a piece of beef to taste, but before mi even put di ting a me mouth, she reads my mood.

I stay silent, before backing away and swiftly moving towards the stairs. "Mi nuh wah medz dat right now Mum, please."

"I'm here when you're ready Jordanne!" she shouts. "You can't bottle your feelings like your father did, we see how that ended!"

The last sentence causes me to pause, turn and look at her. Before saying nuttin outa anger, I spin, move up the stairs and to my room before heading straight to my shower.

Deh so me can clear mi thoughts.

Call Ryleigh

Naahh… I'm leaving her be, remember?

I take the coldest shower, exit the bathroom, get dressed and move to my balcony. Picking up my phone, I scroll through the roster of girls I stopped talking to last year when Ryleigh and I… yeah.

My dick stirs just by the thought of what we did, but I dismiss the memory almost as soon as it comes. Continuing my scroll. I come across Emily's name and just like that I click to call. Leaning back with my spliff in my right hand and phone in the left, I wait for her to pick up.

"Hi baby!" she shrieks.

A smile creeps across my face

Still have it yute

08 | Duties

JORDANNE

I roll over to the sound of my phone going off. At this point, I'm not sure why I use alarms anymore because my body will be up at 5:30am every morning regardless.

I open my phone, and my mind takes me to only one place– her Instagram. She went out last night and my emotions are back to square one after seeing the pictures.

Block her

People ago talk 'bout that.

Ignoring my thoughts, I start moving through her posts, stopping when I get to the one I like. It's the one of her lying in bed just before she left. The camera is angled downwards so the view is aerial. The tone of her skin is my second favourite thing about her– olive. My favourite is and will always be her eyes. The way they pull me in, the way they tell her story and sometimes ours… I love the way her lips pout even when she's not the least bit angry…

… and her light freckles? The way it's the perfect amount, grouped in the perfect areas. Moving from that post, my fingers toggle down her grid, only to find that the two with me are gone. I smile at the revelation, but nothing amuses me.

Throwing the phone down, I grab my business cell to call Skulli.

He answers on the first ring, "Boss?"

"Shift the meeting to 30 minutes from now."

"Think you say a ina the night you did wah see we. Done tell the man dem–"

"Skulli… Just listen to me nuh man, 30 minutes," I repeat calmly, cutting him off mid explanation.

I'm in the mood right now.

Ryleigh mash up you medz?

I roll out of bed, suddenly happy. The shower welcomes me and I get in and out within ten minutes– my clothes on in the next five.

By now I'm making my way down the stairs, two at a time.

Eat nuh bredda

Moving to the refrigerator, I grab a fruit plate. Mum preps them days before because I tend to eat fruits in the morning instead of the eggs and all that other shit.

By 6:25am I'm out the door. My eyes scan all the cars before my mind sets on driving the Range. I hop in and pull out, heading down Jack's Hill. It's early, and a **Saturday** morning so when I hit Barbican it's a breeze, no traffic.

The car slows to a stop in adherence with the redlight and I glimpse the clock– 6:28am. Shifting my head back to the road, I floor the gas all the way to Hope Pastures, taking all the back roads to avoid any traffic build up or any more traffic lights.

At 6:38am, I'm pulling into the safe house.

First thing me spot ah Skulli car, parked perfectly to the right of the property. Only two other vehicles are here, so I assume everybody else parked on different streets and walked here to not cause attention– like I ordered.

I've told them time and time again, I'm not my father so the sloppiness nahgo work. He used to have them all park here as if over fifteen cars parked at one house wouldn't draw attention from the neighbours.

Under my lead, dem affi wear 'active fits' and pretend to be getting in their morning or evening cardio while running here. Myself, Skulli, Mr.Mase and Ramone are the only ones with print access to the gates and are the only ones who should approach in a vehicle.

Today I'm extending that access to Dalani.

I walk in to see everybody grouped up and talking. The sound from the door as I slide it open prompts silence.

On my walk to the front, Skulli greets me with the details of everyone's concerns. I move to the elevator that leads to the basement with him on my heel. I get inside, press my palm to the access pad and a few seconds later the door dings open, revealing the basement.

While stepping out I mumble, "Skulli, me a 18 ina August enuh killa. You can stop being overprotective now."

"Hear the likkle youth weh me know before him born," he laughs.

Once ah just we, di overly serious façade always gets dropped. Skulli know mi inside-out, even more than my father himself. He's been there through my darkest times and for the greatest blessings.

Mi appreciate him

Dropping my thoughts, I step towards my office, sit and bring up all the files that my dad left which clearly states I would oversee every single business... fully. All are signed and stamped by a witness.

Naturally

I spend a few minutes scanning each one to make sure my argument is solid and the transfer goes smoothly.

"Get eh two a dem please," I look up for Skulli but notice he's halfway out the office already.

My eyes stay fixed on the cameras until he gets to them. The look on everyone's faces when he picks them out, remind mi just how I felt finding out initially.

Man dem did expect Ramone fi ina di hot seat but Ramone was only working with me to find out details. Skulli couldn't do it because everyone knows he's loyal to me.

A few seconds later the elevator door dings, and I spin my chair to face the entrance, awaiting dem and dem reaction.

"Wah this bro?" Dalani walks in confused.

"Have a seat nuh… both of you."

They look at each other before sitting. Skulli steps to the corner, his eyes not leaving us an inch.

"The man them phone secured?" I ask him.

"Yes boss everybody phone ina the safe and the doors are sealed, no way in or out.

Beautiful

"So Mr.Mase… Dalani…" I look to each of them, "I become 18 in August and in the documents I have here, clearly says that I will hold full responsibility and ownership of all Sheer assets. We both know wah **all** mean, but somehow, you're trying to find a loop-hole fi say it only refers to the legal assets?" I cock my head to the side, feigning confusion.

Dalani's eyes grow wide, staring at his dad in even more confusion.

"You have been trying to seek out recruits from myyyy team to support your coup?" I continue.

"Yuh father and I built everything from the ground up! The man dead and ago leff everything to you? Dat nuh fuckry?" he looks at Skulli, seeming to be searching for agreement.

"Danne, a must mistake dis," Dalani cuts in.

I chuckle, pull for my spliff and light up. Two full minutes of silence later is when I decide to speak.

"Who agreed to help you," I ask, holding eye contact.

"The man dem weh know weh me a do right!" Mase stands.

Skulli pulls his Glock and steps to him.

"Weh yah do Paul?" he asks in disbelief– Dalani now standing between them.

I shake my head.

"Relax Mase… I already know the three weh agree. Ago handle them after this," I assure him while rocking back even further into my chair.

"Dalani," I add, "all accounts for your dad except his personal accounts are now yours. Shipments and transport are also now your responsibility, along with laundering. Yuh can manage alla that?"

"Not while I'm fucking alive bad man!" Mase shouts.

Skulli pistol whips him causing another round of shouting to spill from his lips, but this time it holds the tone of pain.

"Dalani?" I ask.

"Ye- yess, sure," he agrees right then and there to take on the roles.

"Good, then we're done here."

I stoop to help Mr. Mase up but not before whispering, "the next bloodclawt time you try undermine me, you ago know why my father leff everything to me and not you. Duh fuck up bad head," I smirk before releasing him to walk off.

"Dalani yah farwud or wah?" I question, not looking back. "Skulli you know wah fi do already."

The moment the elevator door closes, Dalani drops his pretense. After all, he was the one who told me his dad's plan. Dat just unfortunate still 'cause I will never trust a man weh snitch pon dem own fucking father.

This the nigga dating Ry'?

"Never wah Skulli lick him still. Weh him ago do with him now?"

"Just ago bring him home, nothing special," I smile. "Farwud. Time fi have some fun wid the three musketeers."

The door opens and the team is still silent. I start moving through them as they create a path for us to get to the front.

"Nipple, Drugz and Piper step forward," I speak calm and clear.

Drugz tries to move to the exit.

Paw and Slyme grabs him and starts dragging him to me while Nipple and Piper step forward willingly. In that same moment my phone buzzes and I see that it's Mumz.

My mother will always pick the rarest moments fi link me.

"Mum?" I answer.

"Ry' is here and she's angry," she speaks, and I can almost hear the smirk in her voice.

She loves it when Ryleigh behaves like this. Claim it ah di only way she gets to see me like her vulnerable little six year old munchkin.

Her exact words… munchkin.

Ryleigh is where? The house? Like weh we live-live?

Know she well vex if she find herself deh so.

I place my silencer on the gun with the phone between my shoulder and ear, to put metal between the eyes of all three men.

No torture, no nuttin killa. I'm almost angry at skipping that part.

The mumbling starts throughout the crowd and with that I hang up to call Skulli.

"Change of plans," I start as soon as he answers, "bring him upstairs and explain to the team. Did affi cut it short... Ry' deh a me yard and we know she's never been there before... so."

"Ah boss," are the only words he offers.

"Paw, Slyme... mek sure dem clean this up," I wave at the three lifeless bodies. "Dalani gwaan buil until Skulli reach up with your father," I delegate while moving to the exit.

The next thing is to call Ryleigh. Shouldn't even a call her from the work phone but–

She answers on the second ring, "Weh you carry Dalani gone Jordanne!?"

Cyaa dis she mek we leave the meeting for

"Ba– Ry' weh you mean?" I question, now genuinely confused.

"You know me can't ask over the phone so when you reach. I'm here with your mom in the library," she hangs up.

• • •

RYLEIGH

"You sure you don't want a fruit plate Ryleigh?" Mrs. Sheer asks, smiling at me and if I didn't know any better, I would think she enjoyed me screaming at Jordanne just now.

We're walking from the library where she insisted on showing me baby pictures of J'.

"I'm okay, I can't eat this early," I turn down her offer.

"Okay my dear. I just want you to feel comfortable coming back," she laughs. "In all the years you and mi son a par you've never been here, not even for Toni," she reminds me.

I laugh a little at the word she chose. Lady say 'par'.

"Yeah, mommy strict when it comes on to me visiting houses, that's her thing," I start explaining but become distracted by the sound of an engine.

Sue notices the sound too.

"Well okay my love. Let me give you guys some privacy," she whispers while walking away– disappearing up the stairs.

He swings the door open with a wild look in his eyes. "Ryleigh? Weh you mean weh me bring Dalani?"

"A that me ask...WHERE. DID. YOU. BRING. DALANI?" I repeat it slower this time.

"Weh di man say me bring him babe?" and I can see that he regrets the last word as soon as they leave his lips.

"Hope Pastures!" I shout. "Him send me a text say unuh a meet a Hope Pastures earlyyyy this morning... J' me know wah dideh... Wah you do to him? Me see you watch me story them as them post last night and I know how you stay... I swear if you do him nuttin Jordanne I–" before I get to finish, he starts laughing– uncontrollably.

Everything funny now?

"Ryleigh lower yuh voice, Dalani good... Call him and see for yourself. He should have his phone by now," he states while shaking his head.

He moves to sit around the island and with his elbows bent and his palms holding his face, he stares at me while I call D'.

"Dalani? You okay? Been a call you since I woke up to the text," my voice falls soft.

"Yeah babe me good. The phone did just secured while me sort out some stuff with Jordanne. You good?"

I release a sigh before shooting eye daggers at Jordanne.

He scoffs.

"Yeah me alright, I'll see you when I get in. I took the Infiniti to the gym by the way," I add.

Jordanne laughs.

"Ok babe. I'll be a little while so you might get in before me... later."

"Lata," I end the call before screwing my face at Jordanne who is visibly amused.

"Unuh a date or unuh a common law man and woman?" Jordanne blurts out, "bout gym... and you ina the gym clothes too," he continues, now shaking his head.

"Shut up Jordanne. I was scared."

After what he did to Folan? I have all right to be.

"Yeah Ry' 'cause me a the worse right?" he hisses.

"Neva say dat," I scoff.

"You nahfi say it. So, you tell Janette lie fi sleep out with Dalani but fi years you couldn't even come here in a broad daylight?!" his eyebrows now forming a knot of slight anger.

"I can control myself around Dalani so yes... We got in late and stayed up talking for hours. I fell asleep and when I woke up, him gone and the text say Hope Pastures... so–"

"I'm sorry J," I try to apologize, now recognizing the slight hurt in his eyes.

He doesn't respond, he's only looking at me deadpan.

After a few more seconds of silence and his piercing eyes, I say, "Okay I'm about to go," and move past him to bend and grab a room temperature bottle of water.

When I stand from bending, he has his hands on either side of me while holding onto the island. Knowing if I tried to protest I would fail, I give in– both of us now waiting for his move.

"Ryleigh you really a do we this?" he asks and the look in his eyes weakens my heart.

"J' a you stop deal wid me remember? Gave Dalani your blessing?" I cock my head to the side. "I know you told him where to take me and which ice-cream flavour I liked... No possible way him coulda be so on point."

He smiles, looking down at me– watching me talk.

"I wanted you to be happy but last night me change me mind bad head."

"So you want to do the benefits thing?" I ask.

"Ryleigh rest that. Me wah you be me woman, MY WOMAN... Me no want you pah no date bredda, no study session, no fucking ice-cream run without me," his voice climbs an octave.

A sound distracts us, causing us to look to the stairs as his mother descends it.

"Ryleigh aren't you about to catch the gym before the Saturday morning rush?" she asks, and I thank God for her because I can't keep having the same conversation with J'.

"Yeah I'm leaving now," my words land as a mumble that probably only I heard.

J' pulls back and raises his hands in surrender. I walk off and I can almost feel his eyes on me.

Exiting like this is pulling at my heart, but I have to stick it through.

• • •

JORDANNE

"Yeah I'm leaving now," she mumbles, so low I almost miss it.

I pull back, raising my hands in surrender. She turns to walk off and the only thing I can do is watch her leave.

Cyaa believe she serious yo.

"J' you're gonna lose her if you keep speaking to her like that," my mother offers.

I look up at her, unable to hide the hurt and disappointment soaring through my body. Mi almost sure the pain is plastered on my face.

"Lose her already Mum," I mumble.

Lose her already...

09 | Same Feeling

RYLEIGH

It's been over **three months, April 22nd** to be exact and Dalani and I have been doing well. That plan I had about dating others? Yeah, it was proven futile.

You're just a lova girl

Indeed.

I tried to date two other guys but none of them held up to my standards or could keep me interested long enough. Dalani and I made things exclusive yesterday evening just before he dropped me off at home.

Me need fi tell Toni she... and Jordanne

Jordanne and I haven't been speaking a lot anymore. The friendship I was so protective of is merely a fragment of our imagination right now. We're simply acquaintances, twice removed. We only speak in group settings if there are any these days and it's often just short answers or mutual agreement. Despite alla dat, he seems to be doing fine and I love dat. When I'm not around him, he's his old jovial, adventurous self.

Him have woman too

I wouldn't say that... but yes, he's back with Emily his– I don't know what to call her.

Friend with benefits... You know? The thing we were trying to be?

"Yah look outa space so Ryleigh?" my mom pulls me from my thoughts.

Quickly masking my real bother, I laugh to shake the feeling of jealousy from my mind.

"Exam them me a think 'bout mommy," I tell her what she wants to hear.

"You already got accepted to UWI Econ though. You nuh affi fret me pikny," she smiles proudly.

"I know, but you know how I am. I just want to end on a good note."

No you wah distract yourself as much as possible

I pick up my phone to text Toni-Anne, trying to quiet my rampant mind.

T' he asked to make it exclusive
and I said yes...

Sexy Bitch: Gyal anuh you say you wah explore?

I tried Toni you see and know.

Sexy Bitch: Try harder lol. Jordanne know?

A you me wah tell him. Can't
take the problem.

Sexy Bitch: Then unuh sick stomach eeeh man. Kmt.
They are here btw.

D' no mention that.

Sexy Bitch: Memba them back to being
bench & batty. He's training Dalani for when he leaves.
Sexy Bitch: *message deleted*

T' me read that already, leave go where???

Sexy Bitch: Him did wah tell you
himself. He's going to university abroad
Ry'. Yuh better act surprised when him
tell u enuh gyal.

Kmt lol I'll try. I'm happy for him ☺

Sexy Bitch: Move yuh bloodclawt. I never
see a set a ppl annoying like you and him.
Sexy Bitch: Me a come pick you up.

I have Dalani's car. I'll come to you.

Sexy Bitch: Mine me bredda shoot
alla we dwfl

Girl lol me ago get ready and drive out.

Within the next hour I'm driving from Barbican up the hill, to Toni's house. My mom and I are originally from May Pen, Clarendon but we came to live here once I passed for High School. She said it would be easier for us to leave, than for me to travel every day. Di lady pack up alla her things and moved us and her business to Kingston, just for me.

I pull up to the Sheer's residence and the security nods before letting me through. I've been coming here more often since February to tutor Toni for her CAPE exams.

Neva know anybody coulda hate Accounts more dan me.

Swear

My phone buzzes.

**<u>Sexy Bitch:</u> Saw you pull up, the door open
and my room door open. Doing my face.**

U say u ready enuh gyal.

<u>Sexy Bitch:</u> And you believed? Back ah di class.

I laugh out loud and exit the car. We're supposed to be taking a break from studying today to take a day trip to Ochi.

Noticing that Muuch and Mariah are already waiting at the gazebo, I signal to them that I'm going inside.

"Alright we out yah so a gwaan shell dem yah," Muuch responds– knocking back a mango.

Mariah agrees by nodding but is more focused on her vlog. She's not allowed to vlog inside the house, so I guess that's why they're out here.

I open the front door to the foyer and move to the path of the stairs. The house is open concept so I can already see Dalani in the kitchen looking through a pile of papers.

I walk over and give him a small kiss on his cheek, "Hi baby," I whisper.

"Ryleigh, think you woulda deh pon the toll by now," he smiles while drinking me in.

"We ah wait pah Toni," now turning, I notice Mrs.Sheer walking by.

"Know mi hear my favourite girl," she smiles at me.

"Hi Mrs.Sheer, you look gooood today."

"It's Sue, Ryleigh. My name is Sue and me nuh dolly down every day? or whatever you kids call it?"

Her statement pulls laughter from everybody, and she shrugs as if not caring about causing cackles. I turn back to Dalani, giving him another kiss to his forehead before excusing myself to go to Toni's room. I get there and open her door only fi notice she nuh deh nuh weh near done wid her makeup, orrrr her hair.

"Aye gyal you know you ago late fi you funeral?" I laugh out from complete disbelief.

"Nuh call dung no death pah me girl. Me soon done man, nah do nuttin heavy," she smiles.

"Mhmhmmm," I mumble to myself.

"You talk to Jordanne?" she goes right in for the kill.

"T' me just reach," I retort.

"Well go now. You need to tell him before D' does and he needs to tell you about him leaving 'cause see I already blurted it out," she whines, now applying setting spray.

She has a point… Not protesting, I step back to leave her room and she giggles before turning her music up.

Now walking down the hallway to his room, I start admiring all the art and just the overall architecture of the house. The ceiling is so high and Sue has dressed the walls with the finest, most appropriate art. Another beautiful part of the house is the flooring; up-stairs is dark wood and they are very well kept– no scratches or smudge.

Coming to a stop at his room door, I open it.

"Jordanne?" I call lowly, my tone skeptical.

"Balcony," I hear him say.

When I get there, he's ending his call with Emily.

"I have to say something to you," I look at him while leaning against the balcony door, not trying to go an inch further.

He looks up at me, "You made it official with Dalani?"

"He told you?" my eyes drop from him to my fingers.

"Your eyes did Ryleigh…"

"And you're leaving for college? Thought you wanted to stay here for university?" I remind him, sounding disappointed.

He chuckles, "To the room Ryleigh," and with that we leave the balcony– out of view from the gazebo where Muuch and Mariah are waiting.

He puts out his spliff and sits on his bed while I stay standing at the foot of the bed.

"Ryleigh going to school abroad is just an overall better opportunity for me in terms of my major. The engineering program at Columbia Uni–"

He tries to extend details but I cut him off, "I understand J'… I would just have wanted to know… first," my voice now soft, meek.

"Wanted to see it through without thinking about staying here for you."

Oh?

"I'm happy for you and Dalani," he brings the original topic back.

"We only made the decision yesterday," I explain.

"That good," he says bluntly before standing to pick up his charger from the floating shelf I happen to be nearest to.

My eyes snap to a charger that's literally already on his nightstand and my body reali–

"That's all you came for?" he asks, cutting my thoughts while peering down at me.

I swallow, trying to calm myself by blinking. He offers me a lustful smile while I try to step back… Now you see why we avoid each other?

"Okay," he trails off, throwing the charger to his bed.

I don't move…

The door is inches away and he moves his left hand to lock it while his right hand is already at my nipple. I inhale sharply and he moves his left hand to cover my mouth.

"Be quiet yuh *exclusive* partner and my friend is downstairs," he breathes, in a very deep, very lustful tone. In the next second, he falls to his knees, flipping my left leg over his shoulder before I feel him shift my panties– his tongue now circling my clit.

Girrrrl?

10 | Same Feeling Part TWO

JORDANNE

"Be quiet. Your *exclusive* partner and my friend is downstairs," I say to her, struggling to keep my composure.

I kneel and grab her leg over my shoulder to gain access to her clit. She sighs and just by that, I know I don't need consent to move further. Using my fingers to shift her panties, I cup her with my lips. She inhales sharply at the single action.

Pussy dripping and she say she come fi tell me that alone?

Smiling at how her body is betraying her, I insert a finger... deep. While bending it like a hook upward to find her spot, I feel her grip my head to hold it in place.

Perfect.

I move my tongue to her moans as they get louder and louder. She's lost to the fact that we're not alone and I take the opportunity to pull away and lift her to the bed.

A knock presents itself at the door and we both look over.

A which bumbohole?!

"Ryleigh me ready!" my annoying sister's voice seeps into my room effortlessly.

"Co–ming," she barely gets out, now reeling from pleasure.

I hold her in place just to ensure we get to her orgasm.

"Jordanne," she whispers, glaring at me.

I ignore her, now focused on covering her nipple with my mouth. The next sound that's heard is Toni hissing and her footsteps leaving the door.

"Jor– J' stop," she whisper-shouts.

I'm pulled from my thoughts to look at her, trying to read her expression. She flips around on all fours, ass up and her head down. Her cover-dress is still on and tangled just above her breasts.

No time's wasted. I release my dick and sink into her.

"Fuckkkkk," our voices share the same expression– hers a little louder than me.

I grab her by her neck before pulling her up to meet me. Using my fingers to gag her mouth, my free hand moves to her clit before circling it.

She starts shaking, unable to fight the feeling much longer so she allows me to take control.

Lovely.

Less than four minutes later we're undone, both falling forward. I start trailing kisses down her spine while I take a moment to recover.

Immaculate quickie. Jah Jah

"I have to go," she reminds me.

"Dat good," my response comes hoarse.

"Ry' come nuh me wah go downstairs go take pictures but D' ago ask fi you," Toni's voice is back at my door, whining.

"Ago bathe T', be there in ten," Ryleigh tells her and with that she moves to my shower.

She's out in five minutes and dragging her dress back on. Failing to fix her hair, she opens the door, looks back at me and mouths 'Lata'.

Not sure weh she mean by that but I'll take it.

Unuh a go back to square one bredda

• • •

RYLEIGH

Pushing the door to T's room, I look at her. Her face is holding disappointment.

"Toni no start," I whisper.

"Me no say nothing, unuh must know," her lips now pressed in a flat line.

"Ready?" I ask and she gets up and exits.

"From 'bout twenty minutes ago," she retorts, now moving towards the stairs.

We get to the living area where she hugs her mom before saying, "Mommy we a leave now."

"Babe, mahgo call you," I reassure Dalani, while keeping my distance.

"Two from the team ago with unuh right?" Jordanne asks from the balcony, causing me to jump from slight fright.

Sue looks at me and back at him, before releasing a giggle knowingly.

Shame a killll me!

"Skulli will be at the front and Paw at the back of their line," Sue assures him.

"Ah," he mumbles, all while disappearing into the shadows.

Toni and I exit with all the food Mrs.Sheer prepared even though we told her we'd just stop and get something. With her being a chef, she just wouldn't allow us to leave her house without some type of food.

Mariah and Muuch run up to us asking to choose their pictures. They've been all over the property snapping pictures for Instagram from what I can see.

Muuch shows me her favourite.

"Michelle Tashirrrr Egar! You come right out!" I move the phone to T's eyes.

Muuch is in a full white monokini with a sheer pants to cover it. She might thick but the doll thick in all the right places. The white sits perfectly on her dark skin and she has a cute little orange visor to top it all off.

"Barbiiiieeee," Toni sings when she sees it.

"Unuh extra sah!" she laughs.

Toni then shows me Mariah's pictures.

"Yeah gurlllllahhhh," I shriek, "no this cyaa look so good right away?? No filli?"

"Rightttt awayyyy!" we all laugh out simultaneously.

When we're all sobered up, they hop into the car. Mariah's driving us girls since she's the one with a license. Di rest a we under 18 mlovve. Mariah became 18 in March and we never got to celebrate her day. Today we ago do dat, but she nahv a clue.

Paw is the last to pull out behind us, and with that, we head towards Ocho-Rios.

• • •

Valiant's Speed Off is blasting through the car speakers and we're all screaming it word for word. Muuch most of all has been singing it while adding hand gestures to match the lyrics.

My main duty right now ah fi get content for Mariah's vlog. I snap a few videos for my story as well but don't post them because the Sheer family is strict about live location.

As we pull in, I notice Jordanne's car and instantly remember getting a text to distract Mariah so they can speed past us without her noticing. Mi never did even affi do dat, she distracted herself by stopping to pee. Yes, roadside pee.

"Then dah car yah look like yuh brother own so?" Mariah questions as she pulls into the villa's parking lot.

"Look the same yes but you know the choppa dem full up yah so Range might common," Toni laughs.

We get our stuff and exit the car. I'm left with the task of stalling Mariah which proves to be the hardest job ah Jamaica. Muuch and Toni went ahead to check on everything inside, just to make sure everybody and everything are present.

"Girl come nuh you look good," Mariah whines.

"I want more pictures, just a few more," I plea, pouting the best I can.

She rolls her eyes and continues to take them.

"Okay mek me see them," I ask when I notice her growing agitation.

They look good, all of them do but I'm still waiting for Toni's go ahead. As soon as the thought dances across my mind, a text from her lands on my screen.

<u>Sexy Bitch:</u> Come down to the pool.
<u>Sexy Bitch:</u> |attachment|

> **Cuuuute! Coming now she a**
> **get miserable lol.**

<u>Sexy Bitch:</u> U man know how fi take
pictures though (Dalani me a talk lol cause
the way how yah move u nahgo know which
one) Murdaaaaa (rest yuh front!)
<u>Sexy Bitch:</u> |attachment|

> **Picture ate! No call you 'sexy bitch'**
> **fi ntn enuh T! Me a come slap u batty!**

I look to see Mariah walking away. "Wait nuh gyal!" I shout at her while grabbing my purse to leave too.

We get to the entry way leading to the pool and I run in ahead of her, signaling to everybody that she's here.

"SUUURRRRRPRISE!!!"

"Watch yah and a come me come fi lay down and nyam enuh," she laughs out.

I take a moment to look around. Everything's just as in the picture T' just sent. Huge balloons thrown in and around the pool, number balloons of one and eight. There's even swan floats, enough for everybody to indulge... and it's all pink.

I love it.

Muuch and Toni runs up to hug her and when they're done, her father Skulli, hugs her– lifting her off the ground.

"Daddy ah you plan this?" she asks when he puts her down.

"Jordanne and Toni mostly, but a me do the ground work yes," he smiles.

"Tell her say mi pocket burn nuh," I hear Jordanne laugh. We make eye contact and I quickly look away to scan the poolside for Dalani.

I find him staring at me from one of the chairs, so I move towards him and for the rest of the night it's us.

• • •

It's almost 11pm and the party is getting raunchy. Almost everybody is drunk, including me, while the elders are upstairs playing dominoes. Well, except for Mrs.Sheer. She's behind the food stand clearing what's left away.

Some of our friends from school are chilling by the pool and a handful of girls are dancing.

Emily is here just say that

Yeah she...

She's sitting in Jordanne's lap while he blows circles of weed smoke over her head. I take another shot while looking at them, then my song comes on. Joshua is the DJ and mi know him know wah him a do.

Wild & Wikid by Armanii comes on and I move to Dalani's lap.

I move to straddle him while holding onto the pool chair behind his head. My mind tells me to start twerking and that's what I do– now staring into his eyes while he puffs his spliff, singing along to the lyrics of the song.

He grabs my throat and I throw my head back to grind on him. The lights are very low but every time it flashes our way, I can see that Jordanne is fuming.

I smile and spin around to give Dalani a clearer view.

Of what?

He holds my waist while I continue to twerk and grind against his lap.

'Set it deh so mek me knock it!' the lyrics blast through the speakers as Joshua replays it for the third time!

I attempt to put my hands on the ground to give him an even better view, but this time somebody pulls me up.

"Weh yah do dawg?" Dalani's voice comes clear.

What's happening?

"You nuh pre say she drunk fam?" ... Is that Jordanne's voice?

Jordannnnnnne

"She looks like she's just having fun babe," I hear a female's voice.

Emily?... Babe she say while ago?

"Ryleigh get up," J' repeats himself.

"Bredda she a buil with her man. Wa'ah di problem?" Dalani emphasizes and I finally look at what's really happening.

Jordanne is actually angry while Dalani is confused and annoyed. Toni is on her way over to us and Joshua is doubling over with laughter.

I brush my hands together just before Toni pulls me away from them.

"Dalani no answer me certain way bad head. Me can get dark too. Yuh can clearly see say she drunk and you sit down a enjoy that shit?" Jordanne speaks, a little too calmmm.

He sees that I'm leaving the pool side and decides to waltz over to Toni and I. Muuch and Mariah are now busy handing me water and bread rolls.

"The bread ago suck up the liquor," Muuch whispers.

"And the water fi sober you up too," Mariah adds.

"I'm okay," this is why me can't bother with Jordanne. Why him draw down crowd pah me like everybody else no drunk?

"She good?" Skulli asks, walking down the stairway.

"Yeah, me a bring her upstairs," Jordanne assures him.

He then takes my hand from Toni to lead me upstairs. I watch him grab a towel from the powder room beneath the staircase before wrapping me.

"Text me," Toni requests before they all exit the entryway to rejoin the party.

A minute later, J' and I get to a room towards the front of the villa, away from the noise.

"Why you leff Emily? Why you so concerned 'bout little old me?" I ask him while laughing, before gulping down my water.

He shakes his head, walks to the bathroom and the shower comes on almost immediately.

"C'mere," he waves me over when he's back out– already stripped down and is no doubt ready to help me do the same.

I stay put, but he moves to the bed and lifts me. We get to the shower and he starts removing my two piece. I'm in and out of it but I feel when the warm water hits my body. Shortly after, I can feel soap on my back. He spins me around and rubs the soap over my breasts.

I gasp.

No… No, no, no.

Smiling, he pulls me under the stream with him and the comforting feel of the water sends me *out of it* again. Within minutes I feel him dressing me in what has to be a shirt. With my head woozy and my body now too heavy for me, he lays me down and covers me with a blanket.

He then places a kiss on my forehead, and I ask him, "Aren't you staying?"

"I'm going to the next room Ry'. Nuh wah cause problems for you and Dalani."

"Stay with me," I demand, and surprisingly he doesn't protest. Instead, he gets under the covers with me and with that, I slip into my dreams.

● ● ●

7:45am

A knock wakes us both and immediately I come to my senses. I fly up and look over at him.

He's unbothered. Let him go back to sleep nuh lady
"Ry?" I hear Dalani's voice, but I don't reply nor do I move.
You mean you don't know if we should move or reply

11 | Tipping Point

JORDANNE

She springs up looking at the door.

"Ry'?" Dalani's concerned voice makes it beyond my room door to us, pulling nothing but annoyance from me.

You check pah you woman boss?

Emily good man...

Ryleigh looks at me but doesn't make the slightest movement or sound.

"Open the d–" I try instructing her but before I get it out, she throws her hand over my mouth.

I laugh, 'cause is a mad woman this if she think him no suspect say mi in here.

She flies up and runs to the door. I watch her take a deep breath before she opens it just enough to slide out– only wearing my shirt. Realizing the situation, I laugh to myself even more, knowing I won't lie about what happened last night. We nuh do nuttin and she's the one who asked me to stay.

Personally, I feel like him fi know who she feel safe fi sleep wid while under the influence.

I chuckle to myself.

My phone buzzes, and in that same moment I hear their footsteps leaving the door.

<u>Ryleigh Stevens:</u> I' told him I was in the room
alone and that you left after making sure I was okay.
So please stick with that J'. Please ☹

I stare at the phone in disbelief.

Jah Jah

Dat good. Do unuh ting

Laying there staring at the ceiling, I start to feel my emotions becoming a whirlwind. My breathing is next, it becomes ragged, so I start feeling for my spliff.

It no dedeh bad head

Fuck me bring her up here fah? When her own man did ago make she drink and gwaan until she pass out.

I close my eyes to organize my thoughts and not slip into any flashbacks, but before I can, I'm captured by what happened almost two years ago.

FLASHBACK

"Take off the bag," I instruct Skulli.

He drags the bag from Folan's head and I watch as his eyes flutter open. We're at the safe house in Hanover because I'm yet to be able to leave our villa here since my father... passed.

"Jordanne?!" he asks, looking up at me surprised.

"Drip that yah look pon right now. Jordanne gone pon a small vacay," Skulli laughs.

I don't indulge.

The nickname 'Drip' came from my dad's associates within the team. During my training I wouldn't be satisfied until blood was dripping from my opponent– whoever it was at the time.

"Whichever name you prefer killa," I look at him while humorlessly smiling.

"Why you have me yasso dawg?" he asks, frantically looking around.

I chuckle.

Kinda man this Ry' mek try put him hand pon her?

"How was the ride?" I pose my first question... but he stays silent.

"Yow answer the man and mind me put one in a you precious knee," Skulli barks.

If I were him, I would listen 'cause dem man yah no love nuttin more than playing wid hot metal.

"Lo– long," Folan mutters, still looking confused.

"Okay," I grab a chair, spin it and step over it to sit while holding the top rail to the front– facing him. "Mek we get to the point then."

I continue, "So you convince yourself say you have the right fi try take advantage of Ry' when she been a tell you say she no ready fi a certain step?" I ask, carefully watching his eyes.

"Ryliegh a me woman enuh bad man... and she say when we graduate, she woulda wah have sex. A 6th form we ago now so that did way past due," his lips now sporting a smirk.

Man brave

"So to understand you perfectly, you pin her down and try beat her up because she a you woman and you feel she owe you her body?" with my head now cocked to the side, I return his smirk.

"Me never pin her down ina no harmful way. You know how woman stay, when them say no it mean yes sometimes," his reply ticks me off.

"Waste man yah man? Danne just mek me leff one ina it," Skulli suggests.

I look at him and shake my head 'NO'.

As much as I want to kill him, Ryleigh ago heart broken and I don't want to see her like that. Relinquishing my thoughts, I move closer to him, causing him to flinch.

"Nah touch you bad man... but me ago want you do supm fimi. Me ago want you text Ry' and tell her you a leave next week. Need you fi act like everything good and you just a leave the country early because of an opportunity," I explain.

He's now looking at me with even more confusion in his eyes and a glint of doubt.

"Me no get the scholarship approval yet so–" he tries.

"Listen me nuh man. A me a talk to you enuh me don," my words fall as genuine laughter. "Just do weh me say and everything else will fall into place. Send the text. You're leaving early, you can only do a next week of 6th form and that's it... Know you have enough sense nuffi tell nobody 'bout our chat," I smile.

He looks up at me and the doubt in his eyes from earlier are gone. Paw, Dalani and Slyme move behind me to ensure when we release him, he doesn't try anything.

I instructed them beforehand to free him from the chains as soon as we were done, but to replace the bag over his head until they were back in Spanish Town– where they grabbed him.

"Skulli," I call, and without hesitation he moves to do wah we discuss earlier.

As the chains start being removed, a surge of confidence hits Folan and he says some things I'll never forget.

"Yah do all a this fi wah exactly? Yah pretend like a because me rough her up but everybody in here know ah because you want her!"

Skulli cocks his gun but I wave to him fi just buil back. "Boss... ah true you no know," he shakes his head.

"No bruises. Him still have a week ah school leff," I remind them.

"Pussy she no want you! She nahgo ever want you no matter how much of daddy's money and toys you have! Friendzone you stuck ina wasteman!" he spits.

I look at him and laugh before taking a deep breath, 'cause me know wah him a try do.

Paw and Slyme aren't pleased but they must understand that I'm more strategic than my father was. My attention moves from them to Dalani who's looking at Skulli– shaking his head.

Folan continues, "She say a years you a try get her and she nah medz you! Anuh me mek you kill you father and can't get me gyal!"

With that, I lose it. Every single cell in my body wakes up and I lift him from his chair, Throwing him against the wall.

"Release me nuh! Nuh fight like a bitch," he suggests and without a thought I instruct Skulli to take the chains from his feet as well.

He stands firm, shaking them to rid them of discomfort. I stand still in my position looking at how eager he is.

Before anything else, a di man that a run to me– attempting to punch me? I block his hand and bend his wrist back, while swiping his feet and he falls to the ground holding his hand.

Our audience of four starts chuckling.

Me nuh find it funny

"Yuh knee next enuh me general," Skulli adds.

I watch him struggle to his feet before moving towards me again. Grabbing him early, I knee him in the stomach.

"She might no want me but you nahgo have her," I whisper close enough to his ear before throwing him to the wall.

I start to walk away but not before nodding to Skulli to continue with the plan.

"Boss the man think a show him ina. Fight yah try fight to freedom?" Paw almost a scream-laugh after di man bro.

I shake my head before going towards the elevator. As the door dings, I hear a loud bang and turn to see Dalani on the floor. I pull my gun and so does Paw and Slyme.

We turn to see Skulli's gun to Folan's head and a random gun on the floor.

The one mi give Ryleigh?

I move over to Dalani who is bleeding heavily. "Yo bad head you good bredda! Keep you eye open!"

"Skulli deal with him but do NOT kill him," I add, referring to Folan.

"Yow how the man have gun this whole time and unuh no know!?" I turn to Paw and Slyme.

"A Dalani grab him enuh boss. Memba a him, him familiar wid," Slyme speaks.

"Boss a front we deh and Dalani round deh with him and did fi check if–" Paw tries to add.

"Alla unuh did fi fucking check!" I seethe.

Man dem sloppy you fuck! I don't know how my father never end up a prison. Affi clean up the team and train those with potential.

"Dalani we a carry you to 'Surgeon' right now. Keep you fucking eyes open!"

PRESENT DAY

A knock pulls me from my episode and before I can answer, the door slides open.

"Me bring you weed and some fruits 'cause me know you nahgo come chill downstairs until a time fi leave," Toni whispers while tip toeing to the bed.

"Weh Mum?" I ask.

"She and Paul gone bring back the rentals."

"And Emily?"

"Oh you remember her after all?" she laughs. "She made us all breakfast and is currently cleaning up, trying to impress Sue I guess."

"T'... we no do nuttin. Swear to G–"

"J'... whether unuh do nothing or not, the intimacy is thick and everybody can see it except your woman and her man."

True...

I light my weed and start puffing as she continues. "You and Ryleigh have to either go full time or stop full time, but the part time supm nahgo work. You need to focus on leaving for uni. Maybe then you guys will grow and develop into individuals who are ready fi handle each other."

I know this, I know all of this but...

Easier said than done. Swear

"I was done yesterday, T' a she ask me fi stay with her last night."

"She never ask you fi save her last night though, you did that on your own. You basically fling Emily offa you fi go fi her," she reminds me.

"She did drunk Toni-Anne," I try to build my point.

"She did alright Jordanne! We were all drunk and I was watching her. If she did take another shot I would've pulled her up myself."

Ignoring her, I pull on my spliff a little too long and a cough leaves my throat.

A wah kinda bush weed Toni carry come?

"You were jealous Jordanne and everybody see. Joshua play the song thousand times just fi get under your skin and you played into it."

"Dat good," I retort.

"You always say that but me come find you in here a look ina the ceiling. You supposed to downstairs a laugh after we," her eyes soften and my heart breaks a little.

"Okayyy... Ago keep my distance, up until I leave. You good with that your highness?" I offer while laughing.

"Quite so Mr. Peasant," she laughs back.

"Come eat you girl breakfast, it must cold by now. It's been hours, 'cause it look like she ina pick me competition with herself," she mumbles while exiting the room.

Women, I think to myself while shaking my head.

• • •

We're all packing to leave and I notice Mumz and Skulli just a pull in.

Can't take so long fi return couple chair enuh

I shake the thought away and turn to help Emily put her bag in my trunk. I'm letting her drive home today because she needs the practice. Everybody else in our group drives pretty well and will get their license whenever dem next birthday drop.

"Babe, I left my iPad can you grab it for me pleasssse?" she looks at me, pleading with the cutest eyes.

"Where is it?" I ask with no trace of emotion in my voice, good or bad.

"I think it's in the kitchen," she smiles.

I close the trunk and move off to re-enter the villa, to the kitchen. The first person I see is Ryleigh– searching for something as well.

I try to ignore her as I spot the iPad on the island close to where she's standing. I even grab it from my end so as to not walk around to her.

Wah she a look for so hard?

Anuh my business still…

"I can't find my fucking pills," she mumbles aggressively, more to herself than to me.

Ignoring her still, I start moving to the exit.

"Jordanne, help me push the sofa please?" she squeals, while trying to move it herself.

Jah Jah God a wah you want from me? Want me start church?

I don't open my mouth, but I move to help her push the couch back. A pack of birth control pills reveal itself and I pick it up to hand it to her.

Pills? Really? Raw sex? Really?

"Thanks!" she attempts to hug me but I step back.

"Really J'?" she asks, and I nod before moving to the exit once again. I hear her hiss but ignore it to continue the walk to my vehicle.

Entering the passenger's side, I catch her staring at me in surprise.

Cause yah mek Emily push your Range when you've never allowed her to

I taught her how to drive…

Yeahhh ina Mumz Jeep

She steps off and walks to her friends. She then says something to Toni and they both laugh, as they get into the car.

We all start pulling out in a matter of seconds.

Skulli is leading the line, followed by me, Toni and her friends, then Sue, a minibus full of our 11 school friends that could make it, Ramone and Dalani after them and then another car with 4 men from the team including Paw and Slyme.

We make it to Kingston in record time and before you know it, we're turning onto Ryleigh's street.

We all come to a stop and Ms.Janette is at the gate in seconds. "Weh me big son?" she shouts, and I know she's looking for me.

I exit the car before she can find me and notice Emily.

Ry' is now shaking her head at her mom in disbelief. Why? because she hasn't acknowledged Dalani who left his car to see Ry' off.

"Jordanne you no plan fi stop grow? Trim up and look nice like yah try thief Mariah birthday so?" she releases a hearty laugh.

I smile at her way of complimenting me.

My mom steps out of her vehicle to join in the excitement, "Janette me son nice but your daughter nicer!" they embrace each other.

Ryleigh and I pass a glimpse between each other but say nothing.

"Alright mommy me tired," I hear her say.

"Then a weh you a do fi tired as young gyal?" her eyebrows form an instant knot while her eyes find Dalani– shooting disapproval.

I laugh knowing that I prevented *that* at all costs.

"Girl dance whole night," I chuckle, causing everybody to laugh, except Dalani.

"Well alright come rest. Your dinner share already bubs. Thanks for taking her home safely Mariah!" she shouts to her from a distance.

"Jordanne don't be a stranger now! You too Toni!" she waves at T' who is looking from the car– her demeanor exuding happiness.

"Mr.Mase," her body language changes, but not in a hateful way, more of a playfully strict type of way. "Thanks for bringing her back in one piece," she adds, now rubbing his shoulders.

Dalani finally laughs before hugging Ryleigh goodbye. We all hop back into our cars and when we get to the end of her road, we disperse in different directions.

The weekend never so bad

Give it a solid 7 outa 10 based pon how me think it did ago unfold.

Less than twenty minutes later, I get home. As I'm about to pull into the garage, my phone vibrates...

It's a text from Ryleigh.

<u>Ryleigh Stevens:</u> We good?

I move my fingers to the block button but it only hovers...

12 | Secret

RYLEIGH

We good?

<u>Jordanne:</u> ......

I wait for him to finish typing, but he doesn't.
Sigh…
We need to tell him what we really wanted to tell him
I can't, he would never forgive me for keeping it secret.
At least tell Toni-Anne, but you can't keep it all bottled up
No.
I look back at his chat and his display picture goes blank. Pressing my lips flat, my eyes find outside.

"Eat your food nuh Ryleigh," mommy orders.

"Trying mommy, but memba Sue full we up," I lie. Sue didn't cook today since she had to return the rentals. Emily made breakfast but I didn't eat it.

We also stopped at the KFC drive-through on the way to Kingston, but I haven't had a bite. In fact, I left my Zinger sandwich in the car.

I should really eat.

I wish I could…

Now I've started pushing my food around the plate to at least look interested while I seek to text Lorelle. Lorelle and I were the very best of friends all throughout school. Her and my other friend who is also her cousin– Keif, didn't come back to 6th form… instead they opted to start Utech right away.

She's trustworthy… I can tell her.

Picking up my phone, I decide to search for her chat. It's been a week since we checked in on each other but don't mistake that for a distant friendship, we're very much still close.

Relle?

Dutty foot: **Gimi 5 mins.**

Within the next three minutes she's typing.

Dutty foot: **Present Ms.Stevens.**

Me ago just get straight to the point.

Dutty foot: **This sound serious.**

Kinda. So remember me tell you bout the times me and Jordanne had sex this year?

Dutty foot: **Yeah? yah scare me now.**

I got pregnant apparently and I don't Know if it was from that time in the car or what but all February long I was sick right up until early March.

Dutty foot: **Was Ry'... u say was?**

Dat me a get to. Go doctor go confirm my suspicions. The way me nearly drop down! I sat down with the confirmation until early April.

Dutty foot: **Two weeks ago that Ry?!**

So, April 8th I went back to the doctors and there was no heartbeat.

Dutty foot: **Ryleigh omg? Wah me come over?**

Yeah, lost someone I fell in love with at only 11 weeks on our journey.

Dutty foot: **Calling you rn so go in private.**

I jump up and run to my room before the tears are able to surface. Mommy became so consumed with her episode of Family Feud that she barely noticed me leaving.

Lorelle and I spoke for hoursss into the morning, just talking about everything that I've been through and what I deserve now. She knows exactly how to cheer me up in my absolute worst times.

Since I found out Folan was cheating, to that time he tried to hit me and I had to tell J'– she's been there. She's been there through the times when I gave Jordanne my virginity– last summer and was confused as to if I should keep things going with Folan or not...

She was present even right up to the time when Folan and I broke it off as soon as I started upper six. He saw the picture of me sitting beside Dalani at the fashion show in November and that was that.

You realize Jordanne is always present in your relationships?

Duhhh, that's my best friend.

We've only ever had sex with him. Weh you mean? It ah give 'we man'

I'm not ready for that step with Dalani. As me did a say before, I tried to make the long distance work between Folan and I for the entire time I was in lower six...

... but of course Jordanne hated me for almost the entire school year. He couldn't understand why I went back after he tried to hit me. When we finally ended things for good, I was back at Jordanne's feet for the second time and we had sex again.

She's been privy to all this information, and she's never once judged.

That's my sister for real.

Fast forward to January gone, it was only right to update her when Jordanne and I were at it again.

You no see a pattern?

No...

Jordanne might be the love of my life, who knows? But that day I saw Folan's face and the things I knew J' did to him, I couldn't see him as much more than my friend.

I've seen his sinister side a few times but never to the point where he would hurt somebody like that, whether they tried to lay hands on me or not.

FLASHBACK

"J' mi nuh think me need this. I don't even know how to–"

"Ry' me no in a the mood, me give you a thing use it. Skulli will teach you weh you need fi know," he retorts.

He's been so snappy since his dad died but I get it. When my dad migrated, I was the same way.

You did not just compare migration to death Ryleigh

Closest that me have...

"Jordanne I don't think he was going to actually force me into doing it," I try to defend Folan but the look that creeps into Jordanne's eyes are one I've never seen befor–, one I know not to push.

Ignoring me, he grabs his phone and I hear him call Paul. "Skulli, meeting tomorrow morning…… No not Hope Pa– Just farwud a West," he grunts before turning to look at me– eyes holding a hint of pity and disgust altogether.

"Jordanne please," I plea. "If me know you did ago snap me no tell you nuttin."

"Ryleigh a years me watch di man diss you and pretend like him a god a road and you defend him with the 'I gave him permission' fuckry!" his voice shoots up a few octaves.

My body becomes frozen. From what? I'm not even sure.

He notices immediately.

"C'mere," he whispers… but I don't move because the 'look' hasn't left his eyes.

He sighs with his eyes closed and when he reopens them half of the anger seems to be gone.

"Ryleigh, I'm sorry. Come," he pulls me into him.

In his arms are where I realize he's probably the only person that understands me through and through.

"Nah do him nothing Ry' just ago give him options," he whispers– pulling me closer.

"Okay…" is all I offer.

PRESENT DAY

He didn't keep that promise.

Folan didn't come back to school the following week and when I saw him days later, I could barely recognize him. All he said to me was dem rob him a Spanish Town and that he was going to leave for university on a sports scholarship.

I knew then and there what happened, but me nuh mek him any wiser. That same day I confronted Jordanne only for him to disregard my feelings. That was definitely the first big rift in our friendship.

It's 1am, I realize from looking down at my phone– on my way to his chat.

I notice I'm still blocked, so I move to his Instagram and…

Blocked.

He doesn't use any other social media platform, so I flip the phone over, pull my sheets and allow my tears to comfort me to bed.

• • •

TONI-ANNE

"Ryleigh we ago late!" I scream with my windows down from her gate. Big Monday morning, 7:30am and the girl cyaa come out all now.

She runs through the door with Ms.Janette bolting behind her, holding what looks like her usual egg sandwiches for both of us.

"Take the sandwich dem nuh Ryleigh!" she shouts.

"Mummy me no hungry!"

I am… Tuhh, I ammmm

"I am! Bring them come Ms.Janette," I smile and she runs to the window.

Ryleigh is busy entering the car when her mom hands them to me and tells us to drive safely. Before walking away, she tries at Ryleigh again, coercing her to eat but again Ry' shrugs it off.

Weird… Breakfast I can understand but not so many meals back-to-back. Know she leff di Zinger ina the car yesterday.

"You good Ry?" I ask as we pull off her street.

Glimpsing at my rearview mirror, I'm reminded of Danne. He tags along to make sure we're okay in the mornings while Skulli is behind him to make sure he's okay.

Yes. Is ah Chiney skip effect ina the morning these days.

"I'm good," she barely gets out.

I know she's not.

She seemed fine on the ride home yesterday but now it's like–

Now it's like I suggested that my brother keep his distance from her?

No way he actually listened though right?

Shoving my thoughts to the side, I begin to focus on the road. The ride to school is smooth and silent. When I get there, she exits the vehicle without a word other than thanks, before heading straight to the auditorium– looking for Dalani I presume.

I turn to see Danne exit his Benz.

With long strides I make my way to him, holding the question that's been lingering on my mind the entire car ride.

"You stop deal with her or supm?" I ask boldly, a little too bold for J' it seems.

He retorts with a, "Nuh wah medz that now T'."

I hiss and walk off because that's all I needed for confirmation. Can bet him go 'bout it blunt and wrong.

I wasn't even there to comfort her.

No matter how me try save them it gets worse every time…

Soon lowe dem altogether.

13 | Dissociated

RYLEIGH

While walking to the auditorium, the sound of Toni's voice starts echoing across the air. Looking back or answering her calls are not top priority right now.

Yah dissociate enuh Ryleigh

Quieting my last thought, I start moving faster– hoping she'll give up on ringing my name. While descending the steps to the auditorium entrance, I spot Dalani talking to Ghale. I pause for a second... allowing the image of her to disappear.

She's still there Ry'

Not to me...

Not after I told him I'm not comfortable with their little relationship.

My feet finish the journey of the short steps to the entrance of the auditorium, prompting me to move towards him. Grabbing his wrist, I pull him up from the lunch bench.

He's saying something but I can't hear it right now. Ghale tries to say something too, but my mind already deleted her.

"We're going to the dungeon," I say calmy. He replies but of course, I don't hear him.

We make it the dungeon entrance before we start moving down the steps to a tiny classroom that overlooks the field.

I sit down and take a breath... and only then do I hear what Dalani is saying.

"Babe say supm nuh... yuh good?" he's genuinely concerned, isn't he?

Just get it over with

"I came to be honest with you and to give you a choice of moving from exclusive dating to relationship or to stop completely," my words flow much easier than I thought they would've.

Thennn, out of nowhere, my eyes start glistening, but I catch myself.

He's taken aback by my choice of words, proven by the current look in his eyes– the look of slight confusion.

"Talk Ry'..." he trails off, shifting his hands into mine.

A sigh leaves my lips.

"So... the summer after 6B... last year... I, well Jordanne and I had sex. It was my first time and if I could understand why it happened, I would explain that to you, but I don't. Mi say that fi say it happened again when Folan broke things off with me and I went to Jordanne for comfort," I manage to get my load off.

He looks at me quizzically but I don't give him a chance to share his thoughts, instead I continue.

"In January it happened again... With proper reason that time... We were discussing becoming... uuhhh... 'friends with benefits' and... yeah," I murmur.

You know for somebody with a distinction in Comm-Studies you can't talk though

"It–" I continue when I notice him trying to speak. "It probably would've happened at Mariah's party when he brought me upstairs, but it didn't because he said he didn't want to cause problems for us," I whisper, pointing back and forth between him and I.

Instantly I feel him pull his hands from mine.

I look up at him trying to read his face but nothing is there.

Just imagine if I mentioned the quickie?

"D'?" I mutter.

"Do you love him?... and not as a friend Ryleigh, mah be serious now," his eyes now holding a hint of hurt.

"I... don't know," I try while attempting to reach for his hands.

Standing to his feet, he stares at me almost as if I've betrayed him.

Keep the baby to yourself enuh mumma 'cause...

"Ryleigh, I'm not stupid... Jordanne and I have been friends since baby days, so me know him love you more than he lets on, but me just think him never willing fi step over the friendship line so it never bother me. When I got shot because of his antics with yuh ex man, me forgive him. When him pull weh from me after Mr.Sheer died, I forgave him. When him underestimate me daily and treat me like an outcast, me let it go... But now yah say you and the man been a fuck? from last year? and it coulda gwaan again Saturday night?!"

Studying his face to figure out how I should answer, I see a familiar expression. It's the face Jordanne has when I speak of Folan.

So hate? Let's use our words

"Yes?" I mutter while trying to stand to meet his gaze.

"Ryleigh that sound good to you? The whole school think unuh did deh enuh and me defend unuh– so right now me look like a clown yute!"

I flinch.

"Bredda weh yah do?" Jordanne appears at the class door with Toni-Anne.

Dalani looks at him, shakes his head, then starts exiting the classroom.

"Yuh gov?" Jordanne asks, but instead of answering, I stay silent, grab my bag and try to follow Dalani.

Nahv the energy fi J'... Him wah pretend like me no exist then cool.

Somehow, I catch up to Dalani even though him a move like a Champs we deh. I grab his hand but–

He pulls away...

Janette send we go school fi run down man? When last you check pon you form class?

I squint, trying to quiet my inner thoughts.

"Dalani!" I whisper-shout, trying to avoid any unnecessary attention.

Now exiting the dungeon, I make it back to the auditorium and people are already lining up for general devotion. I briskly move to the door, but by this time I can see that he's already halfway to the parking lot.

Man ago him yard. Not even the security the man nah medz

I stand still at the auditorium steps, watching as he pulls out and leaves the compound.

Know you salt?

Well, I got that off my chest so...

• • •

I'm now waiting for the bell to go off as I'm sitting in with a third form class, while reading over the notes from my Econ problem set. I preferred Micro-Economics, but Macro is starting to grow on me– at the literal enddd of the term.

The last bell goes off right on schedule. I give the students instructions to pack up, say prayer and leave. As they're leaving, Toni appears at the door.

"Mah call Goose fi come get me today," I make my plans clear.

'Goose' is my long-time taxi driver. Reliable, trustworthy and a cool guy from Papine.

"Ry' wah happen between yesterday and now? Why you nah eat and why Dalani gone home?" she reels off every question on her mind– tone holding genuine concern.

"Will call you when I get home... Just need some space to recoup," my words land as mumbles while I walk past her.

Looking up as I walk to the front lawns of the school, I spot Jordanne looking down at us from the third floor.

Ignoring him, I quickly make my way to the security post out front before ringing Goose. He answers on the fourth ring.

Thank God.

"Goose you deh my way?"

"Stranger danger!" he laughs. "Yeah man me deh 'bout five minutes out, so look out fimi."

"Alright so 15 minutes then?" we laugh knowingly before I hang up.

Dropping my bag from my shoulders to the pavement, I notice when Mrs.Dawkins walks by.

"Leaving early again today Ms. Stevens?" she questions.

"Yes Miss, just wah go home go get in some studying," I smile, but I'm sure it doesn't meet my eyes.

"Dalani left earlier today too," she mentions, causing me to sigh.

"You don't have to tell me Ryleigh. I know when my nephew is off," she whispers and I take the opportunity to wipe the façade from my face.

Nahfi pretend wid her.

"I was honest with him today and he didn't respond well…"

"He's liked you ever since I've known him. He'll get past whatever it is that's bothering him about the truth and seek you out after," her words comforting.

She nah go on maternity leave?

Let's not pry.

If I'm being completely honest, I don't care if Dalani move past dis or not.

At all…

Hopping off the thought train, I watch as Goose pulls in and realize he really meant five minutes. I move to the back door before opening it.

"You know time now man!" I giggle while sliding onto the backseat.

"Easy nuh," he laughs, "you wah know a turn me turn back 'cause me see say it ago go way past 20 minutes if me go Trees and try come back."

"You made the right decision," I smile, and with that I pop my AirPods in to listen to Sza's new album.

It's a good distraction because in this moment, I don't want to care about anything or anybody.

'I guess I gotta goooo, I guess it's time to go. I gotta let you goooo' I sing to the lyrics internally while staring through the window.

14 | Send Off

RYLEIGH

**<u>Sexy Bitch</u>: Girl stop the foolishness me
a come pick you up mommy want you here.**

**Toni you know me nahgo
comfy though.**

**<u>Sexy Bitch</u>: Jordanne can only pretend
like him no want you at the sendoff.**

Toni and I have grown even closer over the past **three months.** We host endless sleep overs and girls' nights with Muuch, Mariah, Lorelle and Keif. She got accepted to UWI to pursue Marketing and we decided to move on campus together to gain some independence.

Of course, Paw and Slyme are almost always in the shadows wherever we are. I don't mind that much these days though. She comes with that, and I'll take it if I get her to myself.

You mean separate from her brother

Exactly...

Prepping for my transition to university has been a breeze since mommy has been there for me step by step– picking out supplies for my dorm room and making sure I have all the appliances I'll need.

Dalani and I decided to call it quits a week after he stormed out of the dungeon. We thought it best I take time for myself to figure out what I want to do in this life– as it regards to relationships 'cause trust me, I got everything else figured out. I also haven't said a word to Jordanne since then. Not a text, FaceTime, Instagram DM, iMessage, WhatsApp or email.

Girl

I find that's best for my mental and somehow for me and Toni as well. I no longer push passive aggression her way when I'm upset with him and vice versa.

> **lol okayyy. Only coming for Sue food n memba**
> **move in day is tmmro so me can't stay late!**

Sexy Bitch: Yessss! be there in 45 minutes!

> **Wah me fi wear?!**

Sexy Bitch: You can wear anything with
the new gym body!

I've been cooped up in my house for the past two or three weeks, avoiding all the girls' nights and sleep overs I was just raving about. I wanted to flake on this exact day.

The gym body T's referring to came by way of me gaining weight and having no choice but to join the gym because I stayed on the birth control pills since April, just for the simple fact that I have less cramps while taking them.

Less than 35 minutes later I'm almost ready.

Glimpsing at myself in the mirror, I decide to snap a picture and send to Toni for approval. I don't want to be overdressed if it's just a sendoff party.

> **|attachment| Ready! this good?**

Sexy Bitch: Perfect! Me a drive out now. Open
the group chat for once, everybody fit's in there. Soon come

I scroll to the group chat comprising of me, her, Muuch, Mariah, Lorelle, Keif and Ghale. Yes Ghale same one. We're all going to be enjoying or stressing at college together so why not?

The name of the group is "Bubbas" a cute nickname that I like to call them these days.

Of the entire group only Mariah, Lorelle and I are fair skinned. Muuch, Keif, Toni and Ghale are all chocolate coated dolls. I stare at each person's picture some more. Everybody look damn good– casual and cute.

BUBBAS

Ghale Bugali: Where's your picture?!
We haven't seen you in so long.

> **Me no take any. When me reach ☺ .**

It's so awkward speaking to her on this level but I'm trying.

Toggling from the chat, I walk to the living area where I find mommy curling her hair.

"You no ready yet?" I question.

"Little girl me a drive myself. Me no affi deh pah your time," she smiles up at me.

"Sarry, sarry," I laugh and with that I hear Toni's horn outside.

"Me gone," I bend to kiss her.

"Me daughter thickkkk," is the last thing I hear her say before I make it through the door.

• • •

Toni pulls into the garage and the music from the party can already be heard from the front lawns. She mentioned that it was being held in the guest house towards the back of the property, but why the sound mek it seem like is a big ting?

I know the guest house well– from endless video calls I might add.

We walk through the main house where I greet Mrs.Sheer, Paul, Ramone and the others. I let Mrs.Sheer know that my mom will be here soon and that she's bringing a cake.

"She tell mi yes. Unuh bring 'round these fimi," she hands Toni and I some cups, containers, ice and packs of utensils to take to the back.

"J' a leave and all of a sudden me a get overworked," T' whines.

I giggle before using said containers to lead her out. When we get to the back porch, we realize some of the patrons have taken residence here instead of inside the guest house itself. Our friends notice us and they all walk over– each one taking something from our hands to bring to the guest kitchen.

Instead of walking through the party to gain access to the kitchen we were sent to, we decide to take the route at the side of the house, and sure enough I see Jordanne snapping pictures of Emily.

No jealous feeling?

I'm good...

She's in a cute little white dress, her curly hair brought into a top knot, gold hoops rested well against her light skin tone and her little handbag clutched beneath her arm... She's posing, posing for my ma–

"Regular ass mixed chick," Lorelle whispers to me when she catches my short stare.

Jordanne realizes what's happening and shifts from snapping pictures to greeting everybody. I continue to walk to the kitchen and so does Lorelle and Toni. Lorelle because she low-key hates him for me right now and Toni because she sees her brother daily.

Sighing, I decide to just get out and stay out of my mind today.

Two or more hours later the party is in full swing. Tonight, I'll be avoiding alcohol at all costs.

No fuckry nahgo gwaan

None at all.

A familiar Squash song is now playing and my friends and I are to the side trying our best to do the dance challenge. Keif ah lead it of course, since she's the best dancer. Mariah on the other hand?

Two left feet

Joshua switches the song to Valiant's C.A.L and we go crazy! *"Cut all me losses!!!"* Toni, Mariah and Muuch sings.

"Fuck nuff man weh a crasses!" myself, Lorelle and Keif scream.

Jordanne, Dalani and Ghale find their way to us while singing the very next line.

We all group up singing on a high for the rest of the Valiant session… Just like the old times.

"Ago miss unuh dawg," Jordanne says, causing everybody to move in for a group hug.

I think about joining but realize… Naahh I'm good. Honestly, it's best to stay away.

Turning my head away, my eyes land on Emily who's now talking to Mrs.Sheer. I roll my eyes, slightly annoyed at their banter.

My vision averts to mommy and Skulli with the crew behind them singing. Seeing that everyone's busy, I decide to take the opportunity to go to the bathroom. While walking to the tiny restroom off the passage, I hear the music switch to oldies.

Party a done

Thank God 'cause I have a long day tomorrow. Some seconds later I get done peeing, wash my hands and start to admire my makeup in the mirror. My eyes drop to mi batty and me start admire that too.

I bend over to twerk it and, in that moment, I hear a round of clappers go off.

Clappers at the end of August? JacksHill?

Bringing my phone to my face, I double check the date and my location 'cause dis cyaa real…

Another round goes off and I realize those are gunshots and not nuh fucking clappers. I stoop, immediately putting my phone on silent.

"Ryleigh!?" I hear Jordanne's voice from the passage.

"Bathroom J!" I shout.

He bursts through the double doors and grabs me out.

From weh mi can see, people are running and trampling each other but he's moving through them with ease– yanking me behind him.

So strong. So protective. Sooo se–

Another round goes off as soon as we get to a weird little corner. I watch him press his palm against an access pad and the hidden door slides open. He shoves me in and I realize my friends, Mrs.Sheer and my mom are all there safe. I turn to look at him, but the door closes and I hear him move away.

Releasing a sigh, I turn to mommy.

"It's okay Ry' he's coming back," she whispers before pulling me in.

Emily is crying the loudest while Mrs.Sheer tries to calm her.

A wah do dah cow yah man? She no know fi quiet?

Right? the room is soundproof from what I remember but still…

"Toni bring up the cameras," Mrs.Sheer whispers.

T' is shaking but manages to power on the screen. We watch as the group of men we know move swiftly, taking out another group of unfamiliar faces.

"Anuh Mr.Mase that?" Muuch shrieks causing us all to pull closer as we try to confirm her outburst.

"Fuck… Jordanne," I hear Mrs.Sheer mumble before flying to the door.

"Mummy!" Toni screams but the door closes before she can stop her. I watch her try to open it, coming up empty each time. That's when I realize her prints might not have been added.

Yours have

He might have deleted them. The thought comes to my mind to get it open for T' but deep down I trust what Sue and Jordanne's doing.

"See her deh!" Ghale points to the monitor.

Everybody's head tilt to her direction, finding Mrs.Sheer adding a silencer to a gun.

A weh di rass?

I look to the second screen and see that Joshua and possibly Paw or Slyme are ushering patrons into the main house. My phone buzzes in that same instant– Jordanne's name topping the notifications.

<u>Jordanne Sheer:</u> Ry' tell Mum Mase deh yah

She see and leff. She's beside

the court.

He doesn't reply but I look back at the screen to watch as he runs to the tennis court area

"Jesus… Jesus!" Emily's cry picks up.

"Emily please shut up!" Toni screams, and for the first time I'm a little sad for her.

"Is that Dalani?" Ghale asks and we look to see him checking the men on the ground.

"Guess he's checking for life," Muuch mutters.

The main monitor starts lighting up from gunfire, causing everybody to snap to it. Skulli just clip three man in a one go and is now moving towards Jordanne who's now with his mom and Mr.Mase.

Jordanne and Mr.Mase are having an exchange while Mrs.Sheer is watching from the sidelines with her gun pointed at his head.

Everyone is focused on the action but me? I'm wondering if that's a tattoo on J'.

I don't know but supm 'bout watching him in action creates a heartbeat between my legs

Looking down at my phone, I notice it's now 11:55pm.

I'm pulled from my thoughts by the the gasps leaving everyone's mouths. My eyes find the screen just in time to see Jordanne disarm Mr.Mase skillfully before pinning him to the ground.

Did that just… turn me on???

Girlll

Skulli moves toward them and I visibly see when Mrs.Sheer breathes a sigh. They keep him in that position up until 12 midnight. It's Jordanne's birthday… August 21st, so it's all starting to make sense why he tried this tonight.

My phone vibrates again but this time it's Mrs.Sheer, telling me it's safe to exit and that my prints are still registered. I waste no time moving to the access pad. Planting my palm on the screen, the door slides open.

"Oh?" Toni raises a single brow at me. Ignoring her, I step out to start moving towards the main house.

While moving through the chilly night the sound of sirens finally make their presence.

Jamaican police ago late…

• • •

JORDANNE

We wrapped things up with the police minutes ago. Mr.Mase will be going to prison for a long, long time. Dalani begged me not to kill him and a the grace ah God keep me from pull the trigger earlier.

I'm assuming he wanted to kill me before my 18th birthday so I wouldn't be able to acquire any of the assets that are tainted with illegalities.

There is a loophole in the Trust that allows him ownership of those assets if I were to die before age 18. Every 'clean' asset would be passed to Toni and Mum so they would still be well off, but Dadz didn't think it right to leave them with the burden of the team and or anything else that has been tainted.

The way Mum handled herself tonight I'm sure she would be fine.

No doubt

I look up to observe the lawns. Everybody has left for their homes except my close friends and some from the team.

Dalani is sitting with Ghale, feeding her water.

Dramatic

Toni is in Joshua's arms staring at the stars.

In a time like this them a be romantic bredda?

Muuch, Mariah, Lorelle and Keif are laying on the pool chairs recounting the scene. Mariah of course ah add in her own details to spice it up.

Skulli and the crew are with Mum and Ms.Janette, as they hand them cups of beef soup. And… Ryleigh. Ry' is by herself on a pool chair looking at her phone.

You can check pon her now bad head

She looks up to catch me staring and I decide to take a leap and walk towards her.

"Happy birthday," she says before I can sit.

"Thanks Ry," I mumble, watching as her soft eyes meet mine. "You good? Wah stay here until tomorrow?"

"That's up to mommy," she answers swiftly before looking back at her phone.

"2:33am," she mumbles the time more to herself than to me.

"Sure she a stay still," I retort, watching her look over to her mom.

"Look so yes…" she shrugs, "guess I'll be sleeping with T'."

"She ago host Joshua."

"Then I'll take one of the two guest rooms," her eyes find mine again.

"Man dem ina that and the couch already," I smirk.

She breaks eye contact to look around, "And your second room?"

"Is for Muuch, Mariah, Lorelle and keif. You wah go squeeze up with them?"

"Me no mind."

"Ry' let me cut it short. Dalani ago take a couch after him drop off Ghale 'round the corner and your mother ago crash with Mum, me sure. The guest house is now a crime scene so you can't stay there either…" I trail off.

"I will sleep with Ms.Pat in her quarters," she retorts, and I laugh, pulling the attention of everybody around us.

"Ryleigh buil… My room we ago, me nah bite you," I mock her.

"And if Emily were here?" she asks knowingly.

"She wouldn't be," I retort, and with that my mood shifts.

"Mhmm," is all she offers.

"Ryleigh just make me know if you ago sleep out here or not," I look at her deadpan.

"Defensive much. Me affi get good sleep fi move up tomorrow so me a take you bed and you can sleep in your chair," she cocks her head to the side before smiling.

So pretty… and fucking sexier since lately.

"Ina me own house?" I ask, feigning shock.

She nods slowly.

"Dat good," I chuckle, and just like that we start moving towards the entryway to enter the house. All eyes are now on us and I hear when my mom giggles.

Mum mix up yuh fuck

15 | Symbiosis

RYLEIGH

As we walk to the entryway I hear Mrs.Sheer giggling to herself. Jordanne shakes his head, causing me to wonder, if she thinks we're really going back to square one.

Not with Emily in the picture.

Suuure

"You mother a supm else enuh J'," I whisper and look over, just in time to catch his smirk. "Wah sweet you?" I pose a question I might know the answer to.

"Just in agreement with your statement Ry," he retorts, smiling even more.

We walk down the halls and up the staircase towards his room. With him behind me, I can feel his eyes glued to my frame as I glide. We get to his door and I shift my weight while he enters his Kaba code. The tiny green light flashes before I hear the familiar click. He then pushes it open and allows me to step inside.

Since mommy has been allowing me to stay at Toni's, I'm now familiar with their household and how it's ran.

"You didn't change your code?" I look at him with my lips curling into a smile.

"Yah watch out me life so Ryleigh?" he laughs, "you alone know it and you can't enter the residence without me knowing... so me think that safe."

He's told me his code numerous times hoping I'd somehow slip into his room when his sister and I just became friends, but as we know Janette neva did a have dat.

"You know me and Troopa a big friend right?" I laugh out loud as we enter his room.

"Troopa no wah lose him job..." he trails off, holding a hint of humor in his tone.

Sometimes I forget how much he controls at his age.

I really do... He's a different person with me most of the time. Since he gained full control, I haven't been around enough to see him work, but I see how he commands any room he enters and how these grown men around him respect him completely.

I'm pulled from my thoughts by the feel of his eyes. He's just standing there looking at me.

"A wah'pn?" my eyebrows form a knot of confusion.

Fake confusion 'cause we know exactly weh him a stare pon

The weight gain.

"Been a lift?" he questions while pulling his shirt over his head.

"Yeah, I've been gaining weight from the birth control pills so I decided to start the gym and keep it toned," in the moment the words leave my lips, his body tenses.

My eyes fleet to his, holding a millisecond of eye contact before I avert them to his built.

"Oh…" he trails off.

"Jordanne don't start," I mumble while walking to the bathroom.

Need fi shower.

"Just a wonder why you deh pon pill if you and Dalani stop deal," his tone now bitter.

"Jordanne how about you keep tabs on Emily's reproductive system?" I scoff.

"You wah ina Em' shoes Ry'? Wah di problem?" he snickers.

Fada if I laugh in yah… Bright nuh bloodclawt though.

"She wants to be in my shoes Jordanne," I laugh while stripping down.

Suddenly, I realize, I have to stick to the boundaries set in my head and attempt to close the bathroom door. He blocks it and I suck my teeth.

"Jordanne let's not argue or cross boundaries tonight," I drag the hiss and he smirks.

"Ryleigh me agree to no boundaries wid you?" his eyes lingering on my breasts.

Ignoring him, I move to the shower and close the glass door.

"Why you still a take the pills Ry'? Is there somebody other than him?" he asks softly… and you know wah? Me ago quench his suspicion.

"No Jordanne. I prefer knowing exactly when my cycle is due and the cramps are less painful this way, that's all."

He releases a sigh… of relief?

The way him like behave like mi husband of ten years. That's why me prefer stay far enuh.

"Cool…" he mutters and the bathroom door closes.

I don't know if he stayed in or he went out to the room, but minutes later I'm exiting the shower wrapped in a robe I'm sure was placed here for me.

After entering the room, I realize he's absent. Deciding to not question it, I hop into bed while looking at my phone for the time, just to see that it's 3:10am.

Me ago tired tomorrow

The room door clicks open, startling me. Jordanne enters in nothing but his towel wrapped around his waistline– exposing just enough of his V-line.

I turn away quickly, causing him to chuckle.

"Ryleigh, once again, me nah bite you," he continues his laughter but I don't turn around. Instead, I bury my head in my phone and listen as he walks to his closet to get dressed there.

"You ago stay ina the robe or you need a shirt?" he queries from inside.

"Shirt," I respond, "a long shirt preferably."

Cover we batty yes

He chuckles and grabs something.

Turning around, I'm faced with him at the entrance of the walk-in closet, holding up a shirt I assume will stop at the top of my ass.

"Jordanne don't play wid me. I will stay in the robe if you cyaa give me a long shirt," my tone now clipped.

Shrugging, he saunters over to me with a smile before throwing me the shirt. Walking back to the closet, he swings a drawer open and takes a familiar panty out.

Oh... my drawer

I completely suppressed the memory of him creating a drawer here. Last year he told me that he made me a drawer and virtually added my prints to the security system. To see everything he put together be true is somewhat shocking to me. The kaba code is the same, the panic rooms are just as he described, my palm print actually works to access them and now he has a drawer filled with things I would need if I were here.

Then how do we know anuh fi Emily too?

I don't actually, 'cause you know how man evil.

Why him woulda keep the panty he took from you in a drawer with her things stupid?

Right... I shrug my silly thoughts away.

"Ohhh," I giggle a little uncomfortably, "Emily doesn't have a problem with my things here?"

Ryleigh you torment you fuck

Me affi ask. Next thing she take them carry go St. Mary go turn me ina goat.

"Em's never been here," he states, walking over to his chaise.

"eM's nEVeR bEeN hERE," I mimic him.

He drops on the chaise, releasing a throaty laugh.

I slip my panties on and pull the sheets while watching him. A moment of silence passes before he breaks it.

"Ryleigh you know ah you make Emily get access to me right?" he asks seriously.

Men are supm else

"Me nahgo answer you tonight. Just mek we sleep," I retort.

"No fi real G. All I wanted from you was to take me seriously but instead you only wah sex and dem thing deh. Then you start date me friend and wah me fuck you under the quiet? Think me coulda agree to that killa?" he laughs. "Nuttin no break me heart more than watching you with him fi months bredda and then me see you a search behind couch and is a birth control that pop out... That mean unuh did a go at it raw."

I'm taken aback by his tone and decide to defend myself right then and there. Mi work too hard to be at peace from these men for them to be having this image of me.

"Firstly bRedDa, don't blame me for jumping into a relationship or whatever you call your situation with that girl... Secondly, I went on birth control becau–"

Easy girl we can't tell him that

"... because of my cramps! Not because me a fuck nobody. I've only ever had sex with you! Why you friend no tell you say we never got to that point 'cause when I told him the real history between us, and asked him to make a choice of being in a relationship with me or walk away, him choose the walk weh route?!!!"

... And I don't care who wah hear we.

He rises and walks over to the bed. He's in grey sweatpants, that hang just below his V-line– no shirt and just the aura of sex around his head.

I watch him lift the covers and move behind me.

Boundaries! Boundaries!

Be quiet! I try fighting my inner monologue and its rules– the rules I set...

He pulls me in and kisses the nape of my neck.

Instantly a leaky pipe becomes the reality of what's between my legs and my nipples are now threatening to rip holes in this T-shirt.

I grab a handful of the sheet to try to calm myself, when I feel his mouth close to my ears. His warm breath whispers something that disconnects my brain from its sense cords.

"Open your legs," he breathes and without hesitation I fling one leg across his body. His hands are now moving simultaneously but to different areas of mine. One moves over and around my neck and the other is currently shifting my panties.

"Just say the word and me stay right yah so and miss mi flight tomorrow," he whispers... but before I can answer, he slips his fingers inside me.

I revel under his touch.

You know him leaving is best for him right?

I know, I won't let him stay but be quiet fi a minute deh please.

It's as if he realizes I'm distracted by my chatty mind, so he takes the opportunity to squeeze my neck a little harder while sinking his fingers into me a little deeper.

"Ohhh... Myy...G–" the words barely leave my mouth in a moan.

"Jordanne," he corrects me.

He turns me enough so that I'm now flat on my back with one knee pulled up. His fingers slip out and he slides them into my mouth.

I feel like every hair on my body is standing at attention while my heartbeat can be heard through my chest.

Grabbing my other knee to push up, matching the next, he moves between my legs and in a millisecond, he's circling my clit with his tongue.

I cyaa tell when last I've felt like this.

Seconds later I feel him insert his tongue while using his thumb to keep sensation on my clit. My eyes clamp shut… just from said sensation. My back arches from the bed to the maximum and I grab his head to keep it in place.

No drown him enuh 'cause I duh know weh you woulda tell Sue

"Jordaaaaanne!" I moan– loudly… too loudly.

"Mhm?" he grunts.

"Don't stop…" and before I can complete my request, one of his hands move from pushing my knees back to twisting my nipple.

Mighty Gahddd!

All type ah things start run through my mind now. Like a this him a carry go foreign? This him a give Emi–

My thoughts are interrupted by my orgasm rising.

I can't hear?

I can't HEAR!?

You can't see either enuh mumma

The pleasure is causing temporary blindness???

Am I fucking levitating?!

No idiot

My thoughts are interrupted once again by him gripping me back to his face and in less than a second, I'm watering it.

He doesn't budge nor does he stop.

"J!!! go easy– Please?" and it's as if mi shouldn't say nuttin. He moves up and flips me. Not allowing me any time to recoup, he slams into me and stays still.

I try to push up to my knees and arch my back but fail.

Mi nuh have the strength… at all.

He kneels in bed and slides his hand under my stomach to lift me towards him. I hook my feet behind his bended knees for support before moving my head down to the sheet.

"Pussy yah…" I hear him mumble, as if questioning the feel. Less than a millisecond later I'm receiving repeated slaps to my ass.

This entire time his dick has been inside me pulsing without movement.

I start moving back and forth but he grips my waist. I'm assuming he wants me to stay still.

● ● ●

JORDANNE

Me just need a moment. Swear to Jah there is no other pussy like this one, in front me.

Why she a move?

I grip her in place, preventing her from throwing it back.

Like she want it last two minutes

I slap her ass just to watch it jiggle.

She got so thick. Fuck!

You affi start now enuh

Mhm…

With that I grab my spliff from the night table and light it up.

She looks back confused.

"Be patient babe," I mutter.

She's fully melting around my dick, dripping on my sheets. Affi carry dah sheet yah with me killa. No joke.

"J?" she questions, looking back.

I take the longest pull from my spliff before putting it back on the ashtray. Gripping her waist, I start moving in and out– deep and steady.

She becomes a moaning mess.

Mine… My moaning mess.

"Yeeee– eahhhsss," she moans, gripping the sheets while struggling to hold herself together.

I grab her neck from behind and start slamming into her mercilessly.

"Jordanne! Oh My G–"

"Tell yuh already a just me babe," I smile.

This seems to annoy her so she tightens her ankles behind my knees, arches her back the deepest I've ever seen, and starts slamming it back.

Siiiiclawt!

My toes stiffen and separate from each other. I grab her ass cheeks, spreading them to see the full view of my length being ridden this way.

Pussy yah no have a flaw at all.

Want her flood mi dick right now

I snake my hands to her clit and the motion sends her legs spreading.

PERFECT.

I start rubbing her clit softly– at the same pace as my strokes.

"I'm gonna cum," she moans, and I keep the same pace and clit circulation going. Within seconds she's soaking my sheets and screaming.

Certain everybody can hear her.

My Ice...

You no give a fuck don't?

Not even one.

"Good girl," I groan while slapping her ass.

I get off the bed while stroking my dick and she climbs down, dropping to her knees. She grabs my length and moves her mouth down, taking it to the back of her throat. I stumble backwards, forgetting how good she is at giving head.

 She giggles.

The vibration from her giggle sends electricity up my toes and to my spine.

Star you a see?

Star me a see yes.

I look down at her bobbing up and down– just admiring her on a whole.

The girl pretty... in any situation.

She seems to feel my eyes and look up to meet my stare. Without another thought, I grab her hair in a pony and start fucking her mouth– feral. She moves her hand to her clit and starts rubbing it. That's when I lose it and start fucking her mouth harder.

I want to feel her again...

"Ry' to your feet," I basically moan the words.

She slurps me before standing– weakness now consuming my spine.

Before I can tell her what to do, she's bent over holding her ankles. I waste no time slipping in and as I repeat my strokes, I start to feel my orgasm rushing to the forefront.

"Ryleigh!" I grunt. I was about to let her know I'm going to cum, but I can see that she's experiencing her orgasm so–

Deciding not to disturb her, I close my eyes and let our souls intertwine.

She becomes weak and start to fall forward but I grab her and move to the bed. I lay her there and use the last bit of energy I have to get a warm rag and wipes. When I'm back, she's asleep. Taking the opportunity, I clean her with the rag before using the wipes to clean the floor where our juices lay in a pool.

I then head back to the bathroom to clean myself up.

When I'm done, I move to the bed and get under the covers with her. Hugging her, I whisper something I might regret.

"I love you Ryleigh Stevens," I breathe.

"I love you too Jordanne Sheer," she mumbles.

I smile to myself before nuzzling into her nape– placing a kiss behind her ears... and before I know it, I'm passed out holding her breasts in my palm.

16 | Adieu

RYLEIGH

I stir to the smell of stew chicken dancing across my nose.
Sue...

I know the fragrance of Mrs.Sheer's cooking anywhere.

You no plan fi go move in your things on dorm?

Jumping at the thought, I grab my phone from the nightstand to look at the time. It's 11:57am. Realizing Jordanne isn't in bed, I head straight to the bathroom to take a shower and brush my teeth, all while trying to open his chat.

Ambling about, I find it and click it open.

Jordanne Sheer: I left to take care of something with the team.

> **Ok what time is your flight? I wanna see you before I leave.**

Jordanne Sheer: Flight rescheduled for tonight. Mi send Skulli dem go move in your things with you mother. Soon talk to you. LY

> **Ok thanks? LY.**

If he doesn't do anything else? Him ago take things into his own hands.

I click out of his chat and enter the shower. Minutes later I get done and get busy in the drawer he claims to be mine– taking out sweatpants, a tank top and fresh underwear.

He really did set it up for us

So it seems, yes...

I get dressed and head downstairs with one thing on my mind and that's Mrs.Sheer's stewed chicken for breakfast.

As I descend the stairs, all eyes find me.

Everybody is still here?

Me pussyclawt.

"Rise and shine!" Toni laughs out loud and Lorelle hits her jokingly.

"As a siren," Joshua doubles over with laughter.

"Duh pay them any mind," Mrs.Sheer smiles, as my cheeks flush red.

"I made your favourite since you… had a night… and there are fried dumplings and fried plantains covered on the island if you want to add those," she points at them, still smiling at me.

If I could disappear right now I would! Open di earth now Fada.

Everybody is acting as if we no witness at least seven murders last night. Muuch, Mariah, Keif, Lorelle and Joshua are all seated around the island. I'm assuming Ghale went home last night for real.

Mrs.Sheer hands me a plate filled with my favourite parts of the chicken causing a smile to creep across my lips. Turning from her, I walk to where everybody and the fried dumplings are– to start adding to my plate.

Lorelle shifts, almost gluing herself to me. "How was your night? Sounded like choir practice up there," she giggles.

Killll me nowwwww.

Ignoring the embarrassment blanketing my body, I shove her while laughing before taking a seat on the free stool. My eyes find the floor to ceiling kitchen windows, wondering where my mother was while I was, ummm… being loud.

Instead of guessing any longer, I ask Toni the question resting on my mind.

"She didn't hear a thing," Toni assures me.

"Yeah Mrs.Sheer took her to the lawns out front along with the team when she saw you guys leave. Dem chat and drink beer straight to 'bout 6am this morning," Lorelle adds.

Phewwwww! Me couldn't manage the lecture this morning at all.

"Dalani?" I ask, looking at Toni .

"Him hear everything!" Mariah shouts, and that's when I realize they're all invested in what happened last night.

"So did you guys finally make it official or wah?" Toni queries.

"Please Jah!" Joshua laughs with his hands to the sky.

"Tell we," Mariah pushes.

"Unuh stop pressure the girl! Come frienddd," Lorelle takes my hand while Muuch, Keif and Mariah continue their cackle fest.

Both Lorelle and Toni drag me to the mini dining table across the kitchen to give them all the details, and I mean alllll the details.

"Me shouldn't even a listen to this. Me wah vomit and dead," Toni whines.

"A unuh ask enuh," I remind them.

"So is it official or not 'cause God know me can't take the back and forth and me cyaa stand Eggplant she," Toni complains while shoving her last slice of plantain to her mouth.

"Eggplantttt? Wah day a eggnog," Lorelle snorts.

"A Emily unuh a deal with so?" I query.

"Then a coulda who?" they ask in unison.

"He said all I had to do was say what I want but he didn't give me a chance to reply. Him send him finger straight up in a–"

"Mighty Gahhd! Me nuh wah hear it!" Toni screams. This pulls Mrs.Sheer's attention who then laughs and asks if any of us wanted seconds.

Me... but mi cyaa mek it look so.

The birth control has opened my appetite tremendously and that's why gym cyaa miss me.

I'm dragged from my thoughts by the sound of **his** engine. Immediately I get up to place my dish in the sink and grab a bottle of water. Less than a minute later the door opens. I don't turn to look but I can feel his presence.

I'm assuming he's moving towards me since everybody is cheesing while their eyes move to me.

I feel him spin me before placing a soft kiss on my forehead.

Murdaaaa! PDA liiiive!

Unable to control my emotions, I release a childlike giggle.

"You decide?" he whispers in my ear.

As I'm about to answer, Dalani walks through the door and I involuntarily pull away, putting distance between us.

"Mmmtchewww!" a loud hiss comes from Joshua's mouth, directing everyone's attention to him.

Jordanne looks at me for another second or two before he turns and ascends the stairs... disappearing.

Why we do dat girl???

I fake a smile and while passing Dalani to follow Jordanne. I know it seems weird but I just feel bad for D'. Because of the way things ended with us, I don't necessarily want him to have it in his face.

He heard everything last night love

That no say.

I get to Jordanne's room and he's already throwing stuff into his suitcase. He doesn't even need to pack. The house in New York is normally stocked with whatever he needs.

"Jordanne that wasn't on purpose. My body just reacted that way because I don't want to hurt him anymore than I already did," I explain softly.

He doesn't answer.

"Jor?" I try again.

"Dat good," he mumbles with his eyes set on packing the unnecessary set ah clothes.

"Jordanne duh shut down," and with that I move towards him.

He turns to face me.

"Ryleigh," he laughs, "Dalani a big man. Him know how me feel 'bout you. Told him everything after unuh stop deal. So there is nothing fi you protect him from, him anuh pikny. Him treat Ghale no different when him see you?"

Him and Ghale back together?

Wait? Told him everything? Including the quickie while he was downstairs?!

"Jordanne… again, I just felt awkward and my body reacted that's all," I try to explain.

"Do you want me to stay or not?" his eyes now soft, almost emoting a plea.

I can't let him stay just for me when he has the chance to go to an Ivy League. That would be selfish right? and I'm trying to be less selfish.

"Jordanne you can't pass on an opportunity like this."

"Ah," he mutters before moving right back to packing.

"Jordanne!" I raise my voice.

His head snaps up back to me. Turning, he moves towards me, grabbing my neck and forcing me against the wall– his eyes now sinister and his breathing ragged.

I can never recognize him when he's like this.

"J," I struggle to get out of his grip as he tightens it.

"Ryleigh, how long yahgo take me fi idiot?!" he asks, but I can't answer.

I can't even breathe.

Holding onto his hand, I try to wiggle my way loose but fail miserably. He seems to realize my dilemma and removes his hand while holding my gaze.

"Yahgo mek me be who me no wah be enuh Ryleigh. So before that, me ago cut as you say," he mumbles more to himself than me.

"Jordanne me telling you to follow through with your plans has nothing to do with Dala–"

"Girl yah ago mek me lowe her fi good enuh… Jah know," he chuckles to himself.

"Fine! Act like a fucking child and not try to listen to reason. I'm trying not to be selfish and tell you fi stay, when you can go to a university like fucking Columbia!" my voice breaks.

The crack in my voice seems to soften his demeanor… He moves to me and pulls us down to the bed.

"I'm sorry," he breathes. "Just hate seeing you care 'bout another man or wah another man think 'bout our ting. You did a lot of that while you were with *your boy.*"

Folan…

Pulling me into his hold he continues, "So we ago do long distance or no?"

Umm, I fear speaking my answer but get it out anyways.

"I don't want that either J'... I want you to go and focus on school and the uni experience while I do the same. I don't want to start anything now, and then distance ruins our fair chance."

"Understandable," he murmurs while running his hand through my curls.

"So you ago tell me why Dalani father gwaan so wid himself last night or no?" I ask while laughing.

"Story deh a fi di flight," he joins me in laughter.

"What flight? To New York?" I asked all excited– jumping from the bed.

"Yes Ryleigh. New York," his smile now bright against his lips.

"Will I be back before orientation ah UWI Monday?" I ask, just to make sure 'cause I duh want to miss anything else.

"Yes Ry' you don't have to exit the jet, they'll be coming right back after."

"Okkkkay. Can the girls come?" I shriek.

"Everybody except Toni," he chuckles a little too much at my excitement.

I smack him.

"I LOVE YOU!" launching our hug, I bring us down on the sheets.

I could get used to this. I hope whatever it is we just agreed to doesn't hurt us.

"Jordanne?!" I hear Mrs.Sheer's voice coming up the stairs.

"My room Mum!" he shouts back, and I see when she opens the door smiling at us.

"Emily is at the gate. You didn't update her on the time switch? Troopa wants to know if he should allow her in or not."

I pause...

"Let her up," he says while looking at me.

I hiss... and slide from the bed.

Anuh we man enuh, remember good

Be fucking quiet.

17 | Mile High

JORDANNE

I watch Ryleigh exit the room in anger. Her mood switch is met with me shaking my head.

"Jordanne?" Mum whispers, but I don't give her the response she's looking for.

"Mum just direct Emily to the library, mah farwud in a few," with that I slide to the edge of the bed, pausing to run through my mind.

Mum sighs before walking away, leaving me to my thoughts.

Emily no deserve this bad man

Shouldn't even start nuttin wid her from them time deh. Jah know.

Standing to my feet, my eyes scan the night table for my spliff.

Go without that fam

Need fi be less reliant on it yes, but not today.

I walk to pick it up and move to the balcony to gather my mind. Leaning back in my chair with the spliff in my mouth and the lighter in my hands, I puff– trying to get the flame going.

Just as I'm about to relax, the sound of commotion makes its way from downstairs.

I close my eyes leaning further back, hoping for a clear head. If ah nuttin important Mum will let me know.

My mind goes back to the decision about my personal life. Might affi go with the flow fi keep the peace today and let her down easy when I get there? Blame long distance?

"Jordanne!... J?!" I hear Ryleigh's voice moving towards me.

Wah'pn now?

"Jordanne Toni a fight Emily enuh, and not even Sue can part them," she spills.

I hiss and get up to put out my spliff, regretting having let Em' in. The tension between her and Toni-Anne have been high since we got back to doing whatever we're doing.

Now moving down the stairs, I spot Joshua with Toni over his shoulders and Sue shielding Emily.

"Oh them finally pull them apart..." Ryleigh mumbles from behind me.

"Let me go Josh! 'cause deh gyal yah must feel mi nah damage her today!" T' screams, kicking her feet and slapping Joshua's shoulder.

"T' buil," I speak. "Wah gwaan yah so?" I turn to Muuch who seems to be the only levelheaded person right now.

"Bwoiii Jordanne, Emily walk in and no say nothing to anybody but your mother. Then she basically bounce Toni while trying to pass go upstairs, when you mother done say a library she fi go, go wait pah you. She say she nahgo no library cause she see Ryleigh a come from upstairs and a your room deh to the way weh she a walk from."

I cock my head to the side while doing everything to keep myself from smiling.

"So Toni a try tell her," she continues while eating a bunch of grapes, "say she can't just storm upstairs like that– she has to respect the house and wait in the library like Mrs. Sheer said... and then Ryleigh go giggle," she chokes on a grape, trying not to laugh in this moment.

I turn to look at Ry' behind me.

Wah me ago do with her?

"Yeah so you no know say Emily try offa Ryleigh when she giggle and before her hand leave her side good, Toni floor her," she doubles over laughing.

"Guys none of this is funny. You guys are young ladies and fighting at the least sign of disrespect is unbecoming. Yes, Emily was wrong for not listening to my orders but–"

"So me did fi mek she lick Janette pikny?" Toni asks, cutting Mum off while Joshua finally sets her to stand.

Keeping my eyes on them, I take a seat around the island, observing everybody's body language.

Emily is now sobbing in my mother's arms next to the living area while everybody else is gathered at the stairway. Ryleigh has moved to the couch and is on her phone– probably texting her mother– with Dalani seated next to her, sipping a bottle of water.

Everybody at the stairway is trying to speak at once, defending what Toni did but Mum nah have it.

"Yeah man! Pick up fi the gyal!" Toni shouts at Mum, "me will never be right in your eyes... No gyal nah try offa me friend ina me father house and get weh," she stares at Mum with hurt in her eyes.

"Toni buil," I speak lowly. "Muuch, Mariah, Lorelle, Keif... Ry' want unuh on the flight later. It leaves 7:30pm so if unuh wah go home go check with unuh parents and get ready?" I suggest.

They all nod awkwardly before saying their goodbyes and moving to the exit.

I continue with the orders, "Toni you and mommy need fi iron out unuh issues in private. Do that now, and T'… Ryleigh want you on the flight too so sort it out by 5."

I watch as she nods and walks outside with Joshua.

Mum moves off too, trailing behind them.

My eyes then find Ryleigh, still on her phone but typing this time, while talking to Dalani.

I shake my head.

"Emily, to the library, like my mom suggested earlier, please."

With that she scurries off.

"Dalani you no have accounts fi go over before transport next week?" I glare at him.

"Ah," is his response. "Text me later Ry'," he mumbles to her, causing my blood to boil.

"Ryleigh duh leave. Soon farwud," I instruct, while watching her turn her head away to stare outside.

While walking past her to the library, I bend and plant a kiss on her forehead. She rolls her eyes, keeps her head down and sighs.

Pulling away, I look up at the library doors, dreading the walk inside. Nuh ina no relationship butttt me almost sure Ry' no want me in that room with Em' right now.

Your life or hers?

Regardless, I know what I want.

The doors squeal open and my eyes meet Emily's. Her face is filled with remorse and a hint of embarrassment.

"Emily, Emily, Emily," I start.

"Jordanne I just lost it when she giggled. I–" she tries but I hold my hands up signaling for her to be quiet.

"You tried to hit her because she had a human reaction to a situation? Bredda me no hide nuttin from you," with this I take a seat in the chair facing hers.

Let's correct that. I tell her enough.

"So you know from the jump what our situation is. Tell you we a test the waters but nothing no set in stone… Bring you 'round my family and you disrespect me mother orders and ina things with T?" I ask, waiting for her to explain her side.

"Jordanne me see di gyal a come from your side of the house when everybody downstairs. Yah tell me say anuh your room she a come from? And then she ago laugh when your sister a try tell me weh fi go," she shifts in the chair– rubbing her arms.

"Emily you've never been upstairs. Why is it you thought that would change today? Ryleigh has been welcomed in this family for years. The jealousy thing affi dead yah so."

I lean over to pour myself a drink and she watches as I fill my glass before bringing it to my head.

"Jordanne if you ago claim ah your best friend then fine, but she has way more access to you than I do… How our ting ago have a chance fi grow?" she looks up at me, basically pleading.

Grow? I smile internally.

"Em' go home. I'll call you when I land in New York," I speak, leaving no room for her to protest.

She stares at me, trying to fight her words. Giving up, I grant her the freedom to do so.

"So I won't be with you at the airport then? And when did the flight time change?" her tone now holding concern.

She no like take instructions enuh

"Yeah, I decided to change it and bring Toni and the girls on the trip. Seeing as you guys fought though, better you buil back."

She sucks her teeth, "You changed it for Ryleigh didn't you? Fuck you Jordanne! I hope she continues to choose everybody else over you," she storms off, and all I can do is shake my head.

I follow her to the living area only to catch her throwing Ryleigh a wicked stare before exiting the house.

• • •

RYLEIGH

I look at her in disbelief.

Girl yah try no try it with me a second time 'cause me nahgo leff her to Toni

I turn to see Jordanne eyeballing me with a stupid grin on his face.

"You see how you woman wild?" I ask him, genuinely concerned as to why she gwaan so today.

I mean I get say she might vex 'bout weh she ASSUUUUME happened between me and her so called man, but to skip past his mom and sister when them a tell her one thing… and then try put her hands on me???

I'm pulled from my thoughts by Jordanne's head falling into my lap.

"A bay things gwaan more while ina dah house yah enuh dawg," he laughs, mimicking Vybz Kartel.

"Yah the root cause J'. Why you never text the girl and tell her di plans change? Suppose we did end up fight fi real? Fighting ova man? Me? Nyackkk," I twist my face in a jovial screw.

"That wouldn't happen man," he laughs, "she good now. She tell me fi fuck off and gone," he's now bursting at the seams from genuine laughter.

God a watch we yerr? The girl never deserve none ah this

"Yah go home to Ms.Janette before the flight or nah?" he asks, looking up at me while playing with my hair.

"Anuh you say mommy gone drop off my things on campus?" I state, knowing my mom completed that task an hour ago and is home right now.

"Skulli tell me say them done good while now?" he grabs his phone to no doubt ring Paul.

"Relax J', mommy deh home a cook," I smile.

"Ry' you fi buil enuh... Farwud, let's get you home and back in time fi leave," he whispers before standing to pull me up and out the house.

• • •

7:00pm

We're boarding the jet and I don't know why but I'm a little sad. We're back on good terms so why do I feel this way still?

"Fix you face lady," Lorelle mutters as she takes a seat beside Keif who's snapping away.

Mariah is doing the same– collecting content for her vlog as usual.

Muuch and Toni are busy asking the flight attendant a million questions about the menu. Observing all my girls bring a smile to my face. Lorelle and Keif have blended in so well since May of this year. I hope while we're on campus and they're at UTech, we still keep the link up and running.

I attempt to sit at an empty chair to the side when the flight attendant sees and tells me not to.

Okay?

I look at her puzzled.

"Mr.Sheer requested you sit in the back lounge. You're Ms.Stevens right?"

"Yeah girlllll, Mile high!" Keif laughs and the effect of her laughter moves through the room causing everybody to cheese at me.

Jordanne walks in and does a once over at everything, "How unuh so happy already? Weed gummies onboard?"

"We weren't made aware of that Mr.Sheer," the attendant says, smiling at him a little too long for me.

I roll my eyes and he catches it.

"Dat good man. Joke mah mek. 'Cause me see everybody a grin," he replies to her while staring at me, lust written in his eyes.

My nipples start to stand, sending his eyes to them. I turn to walk to the lounge area towards the back of the aircraft, and of course, he follows.

"Unuh take time with the noise this time," Toni chuckles, "me no wah vomit mid air, please."

A set of giggles escape my lips just from weh she say.

Lock you legs tonight

Sealed shut...

• • •

We're an hour enroute and Jordanne continues to go on and on about the program at Columbia, but I really want to clasp my lips around his dick.

"J'..." I whisper, cutting him off mid-sentence.

I move my hands to his zipper and am met with a pause. Him becoming frozen causes me to laugh out. He brings his fingers to his lips, signaling me to be quiet.

Looking around I would say we're safe. The jet according to him is a Gulfstream G550 so our section has a bed almost the size of the one at home and a cabin divider with a pocket door for our privacy.

I slide off the bed and pull the door shut before looking back at him with a smile.

"Up to no good," he shakes his head.

"Correct," I cheese, hopping on the bed to straddle him. I slide my top off and watch as he slips my breast into his mouth, twirling the nipple around his tongue.

"Uh..." a sultry moan escapes my lips.

"Quiet," he whispers, while using his hands to find my entrance.

I ease back and up, allowing him to slip his finger inside. Staring at him directly, I move down to kiss him. He deepens the kiss but doesn't lose focus on the motion he has going inside me.

"I want it..." I whisper impatiently. We don't have long and believe it or not, I want to cuddle with him some more before we land.

"Ry' if we have actual sex me can't guarantee you ago be quiet," he laughs.

"Really Jordanne? Yuh nahv no faith ina me?" I look down at him with the best puppy eyes and pout I could muster up.

"Not even an ounce," he chuckles.

I move to unbutton his pants and to my surprise, he allows it.

Good... as if him no want it– hood stiffer than cadet shirt

"Ryleigh, buil nuh," he whispers, while moving his lips to my neck.

"No," I giggle and with that I try to release his dick.

It flies out standing tall and bent...

Woahhh, just wow.

My fingers move to caress the pulsing veins and without hesitation I move down to force it inside. It takes a while, but we get there.

"Jah Jah," he mutters hoarsely while I try to take the full length.

Getting on my feet, I hold his head in my palms to have him meet my gaze.

I want him to look into my eyes

I rise to the tip and perform kegels. He clamps his eyes shut and I pause.

"Keep them open J'," I move down to whisper.

"Ry'…" he groans before sinking his fingers into my skin.

A proud smile finds its way to my lips and I lull my head back, welcoming his wet lips that have now found their way to my bosom.

18 | Junction

JORDANNE

We're exiting the aircraft as I've successfully convinced Ry' to stay the night for us to go to our usual spot in the city.

She's always been a Nobu girl, a sucker for the sushi.

I watch as she escorts her friends to the back of the sprinter. Nahgo deh home fi her birthday so a night in the city will have to do. I'll have all her gifts delivered on the actual day as usual– this year a little more extravagant since she's turning 18.

Know we nah miss her birthday

Might have to enuh. The degree is rigorous as fuck.

Running things from here with the team will also eat away at my free time. Hopefully Dalani doesn't disappoint.

Skulli deh-deh still, to keep him in line

"Really?" she looks between the Bentley and I, scrutinizing the choice. "We couldn't take the Sprinter with everybody else?" she adds, looking at me while feigning displeasure.

"You lucky me even allow your friends fi farwud," I chuckle, "it's our last night together."

"Still no reason for the Bentley, you know I don't like the attention," she whines.

Women

And if me tell her go take the train ah problem.

"Ryleigh, T' ah take the girls to a VR room in Midtown and we're going to Nobu downtown. Yahgo reach back in time, no worries."

Her eyes light up at the mention of Nobu.

Can never surprise her properly enuh

"Say no moooore J'... I'm not dressed for the occasion though," she looks down, patting herself.

"Babe buil," I smile as the chauffeur directs us inside the car.

We get inside and the first thing she does is find the cashew pack.

"So leff space fi dinner nuh Ry," I laugh out.

"Who tell you me no have space?" she giggles, cashew in her mouth and all.

"Me feel that firsthand still... no space no normally present itself until I make it," I wink.

"Jordanne Jesus... You smutty beyond this life," her cheeks flush red. Her next move is looking at the driver who's now pulling off towards the immigration hub.

Love act innocent

• • •

Hours later we're leaving the restaurant to go meet up with her friends. We made a pit stop at the penthouse so she could change. Not sure why when we had a private room reserved for us, only people that saw us were the staff.

"J I want pictures pleasssse," she looks up at me with the most pleading eyes.

Nahhhhh, I can't take them to please her, ever.

"Ryleigh me ago hire you a photographer," I start my complaint.

"A you me wah take them all the time Jordanne. I don't want more people in the shadows trailing us," she mumbles while eyeing the shadow guards and with that she shoves the phone to me.

"You miserable so Ry'?" I pull her in, planting a kiss on her forehead before she steps back.

"Just start snap," her face now blushing.

I try to get her best angles, though to me all of them are perfect. I remember before she gained this weight, she would always try to poke her ass out.

Deven need that nuh more

Love dat.

My eyes are focused on her more than it is on the phone.

You literally just get her on the flight enuh killa

And in the penthouse art room, but who's counting?

"Jordanne yah take the pictures or yah eye fuck me?!" she's getting annoyed.

I chuckle and try to actually take good photos this round. I get through 31 snaps, yes I counted, and she finally wants to see how they turned out. Handing her the phone, I sigh, dreading the moment.

She looks at them. Today she's in a skintight black dress with a mid-slit up her thigh while her hair is straightened and laying on her shoulders. She just pretty bro.

"I only like this one. I look so grown and sexy," she squeals.

One outa 31?

"C'mere," holding her hands, I pull her into a hug.

The noise from the city is usual deafening but all I can hear tonight is her. She sighs in my arms and I know she's a little sad we won't be close to each other for years to come.

"Do you think we'll be like this 3 to 4 years from now?" her voice laced with anxiety.

"Nuttin cyaa change my feelings fi you babe. So a must death, or if you breed fi a next man," I joke to lighten the mood.

"We're allowed to see other people then?" she asks genuinely.

"Because me say if you breed fi a next man?!"

"A youuuu say it!" she laughs out.

I take a moment to think about it.

"No wah tie you down ina college still. I can assure you say me personally nahgo seek out somebody else and hopefully you don't. If you do, ensure him know my trigger finger friendly when it comes to you," I plant a kiss on her big ass forehead.

Mi likkle alien

"Okay so the answer is a no," she laughs.

By now our car has pulled around. We move off to hop in– set to go meet her friends.

• • •

RYLEIGH

"Mi fraaaaaiiiiiidddd!!!" I scream holding onto Lorelle.

"Jump!" Toni and Keif scream from the sidelines.

I know it's just virtual reality but why it feel so damn real?

Lorelle jumps, leaving me standing alone on this virtual ledge. I spread my hands to try to balance myself. In actuality, I'm on a piece of narrow board that is risen from the floor by only two inches. However, through the headset I'm on a skyscraper's roof, walking off a ledge.

This level of the game requires you to walk out on the ledge and jump off to meet your friends.

"Jordanne?" I whisper.

"Him cyaa save you Ry," Mariah laughs.

"Just lock your eye dem and jump!" Muuch suggests and I don't hesitate to do as she says.

The sling pulls me up when I do and I feel my stomach drop!

"Fada God a wah this! Ahhhhhh! Take me outa this bumboclawt!" I scream and I can hear them all laugh in unison, especially J'.

"One thing with you, you ago loud enuh," Lorelle doubles over laughing as I pull the headset from my eyes.

99

The assistant walks over to help me release the sling before handing me a bottle of water.

I brush my hair down and walk over to my friends. This was the last activity in their session and we came just in time to catch it.

"See why wickedness cyaa done?" I look at them all with disapproval. They continue to laugh while Toni suggests that we grab street pizza and head back to the penthouse.

Toni of course knows the residence since she was here last year when J' had Mrs.Sheer buy it. Lorelle, Muuch, Mariah and Keif are about to see it for the first time.

• • •

The elevator door dings open to the entrance of the suite and I listen to the shock exchange between the girls. Toni, Jordanne and I exchange knowing glances at each other as we anticipate the pool of questions we're about to be asked. I quickly excuse myself to the restroom to not part take in the quiz.

"Wait pah me bad man," J' says, basically running towards me.

"Unuh sick stomach," Lorelle laughs, but we know we're only leaving to escape the badgering and not to… you know.

We get to the room and I head straight to the shower before closing the door.

Cyaa take a next round

It's one bathroom space but it's split in 'his and hers' sections right down the middle.

I hear when J' walks to his shower and I release a breath.

Thank God

Moments later we both get out at the same time, get dressed and head to the bedroom. I hop on the bed, pulling him down with me.

"Yuh gov?" he asks with a small smile on his lips.

"Yeah, I'm just gonna miss this," I whisper.

"You know I'll be home every holiday they permit right?" he grazes my nipples with his palm.

"Yeah, but it's not the same. I can't catch glimpses of you at school or at your house while hanging out with T'."

"Then I'll make you *missing me* a holiday and hop on the jet to you even for a few hours… Dat good?" he genuinely asks and I laugh so loud I'm certain the entire city is on edge.

"Jordanne just how much money dem have you in charge of? To gas up a jet anuh baby money enuh," I giggle.

"In charge???" he laughs, ultimately ignoring my question.

I'm starting to think I myself might not be aware of just how well off he is.

Aside from the wealth his dad left, Jordanne has always been doing his own thing especially in real estate. His mother would buy the properties on his behalf, before he was at a legal age and add them to the Sheer family trust. He would flip them for resale, renovate them for short and long term renting, while some are left as buildings for those who have fallen on hard times– to live and bounce back at.

I think this is why he's interested in engineering. He recently got into commercial buildings and his first purchase was this one.

Yes, the entire building.

Still, that is just the tip of what he has going. For someone so young I admire him so much. I'm not sure if I could've handled it all. I rarely get to see him in his element, legal orrrr… since when I'm around, all focus is on me… but when I do, it turns me on.

Thinking about it right now turns me on.

We're wrapped in each other while my fingers trail down his chest for comfort.

"I took a picture of you at the pizzeria earlier," I whisper.

"Yeah? Lemme see it," his lips curl up in a mischievous smile.

That smiiiillle.

Sigh.

I pick up my phone and scroll to the album of him.

He takes a quick look at it before saying, "Nah this look too pretty boy. Soon as I've cemented my place properly at this school, mah colour up mi skin," he laughs, while using his free hand to twist my hair.

He attempts to scroll on further and I try to grab the phone away, but he doesn't budge. Another picture of him pops up.

"Ry' how much sneak pics you have wid the killa?" he cheeses, and I grab my phone, burying my head in shame.

No sahhhhh and look how you gwaan like you can live without the boy

"You barely use social media, so I get my fix from these," I chuckle awkwardly.

"That good babe," he plants a kiss on my lips.

So soft, so wet…

"I have to make a call," he mutters, now propping himself up.

"Okidoki."

He leaves the room and I instantly find it odd that he picked up his personal phone instead of the work cell.

I lay there a little longer but then decide to walk to the kitchen to get a bottle of water.

And fi watch the man

As I pick up the bottle of Fiji and spin to walk back to the room, I hear him mumbling in the office.

Just go back to the room nuh Ryleigh

Moving closer to the door, I try to listen to what he's saying and...

"Emily I called you as soon as I could. Mi send you a text say me land hours ago. Wah the problem now?"

My heart sinks and I move back, staring at the door.

Bet me kick down this bloodclawt and fuck him up...

Girlllah!

Bet me poison him bumboclawwt...

A sigh leaves my lips while I try to gather my emotions.

We're not together. We're not together. We aren't together.

Alright watch this. The moment I get home him ago know if we can 'see other people' or not.

I walk back to the room as quiet and as calm as I can. Releasing a sigh, I curl up under the sheets trying to force myself to sleep.

Moments later, I hear him enter the room and seconds later I feel him snuggle up behind me.

"I love you Ry," he whispers, kissing the nape of my neck.

What a wicked pussyole

"Mhm," I moan and with that I drift off to dreamland.

19 | Deceitful

JORDANNE

I alight the jet, moving quickly down the airstair to meet Skulli who is here to pick me up. The smell of Jamaica has already started tugging at my heart.

Fresh air and warm weather. Finally.

Cyaa believe it's been a year already, since I've seen her… touched her.

It's her 19th birthday today and I want to surprise her full on this year. I didn't make it back for her celebration last year, nor did I make it home for Christmas break.

Or Easter, or summer…

Yeah, I've been busy.

School is much, muchhhh more work than I thought it would be. Likewise, handling all the family businesses and those of my own, hands me a crazy schedule.

Not to mention the team

Yeah, the team.

The team is now span across all 14 parishes, cementing me at the top of the chain. A lot of people don't like that but it was my father's dream– I had to see it through.

Least me can do for what I–

Neva your fault killa

I've made quite a lot of enemies along the way but have been able to keep them all in check. Skulli has made me aware that Mase has been running things in prison and that I should quell it. I'll handle that when I get to the safe house tomorrow.

Tonight is her night.

I smile to myself as I enter my Porsche. Missed the car yuh fuck!

Surprised I allowed myself to let Skulli drive it here, but I don't have time to change, and this is what I want to drive tonight. Toni tells me that they're celebrating Ry's day at a private club here in Montego Bay so that's where I'm headed.

Last year I gifted her shares to her favourite cosmetic companies and luxury brands, a girl's trip to Aruba since I couldn't make it and her own Benz coupe to match mine.

This year I have something bigger up my sleeve that she'll be able to build and rely on for steady income.

"Yo boss, weh you say the name a di place again?" Skulli queries while puffing his weed.

"Bredda no smoking ina the Porsche. Tired fi warn you," I hiss.

Man like this man

"Tryall Toni say it name. Cost me a fucking arm and leg to rent the entire place," I hiss again.

Cyaa believe the man try smoke ina me baby

"Oh the golf club, villa place," he nods, "think is a night club 'cause mah say you invest ina them thing deh but you yourself nuh too indulge."

"Woulda indulge if a deh so T' did choose same way– long as a Ryleigh. She still vex with me from last year, you believe dat? Bay short answer replies and one minute FaceTime calls for the entire year. When me tell her me have the internship for the summer with 'Perkins+Will' she just say congrats and hang up the phone," I chuckle.

"And wah 'bout Emily?" he queries.

"Yah police tonight sah?" I look at him, laughing.

He laughs out loud, "Just wah know from now if me ago enjoy the night or if me affi monitor unuh tension."

"You nahfi do nuttin. Dat good," and with that I sink the pedal in efforts to get to the villa as soon as possible.

• • •

RYLEIGH

My party is in full swing and I'm so happy!

Girl we high

Yeah, that too!

Toni forced me into having a piece of her edible and now I'm sky high.

Me no like the feeling

That's because I'm able to tune you out...

Everybody is here. It's like T' and Mariah invited all of Kingston and half of Mobay.

I take a shot of **1942** before looking at the cameras pointed at my face. All my friends are trying to catch the moment before I blow out my candles. The DJ is blasting my favourite song of the month, and that alone a mek mi extra happy.

I blow out the candles and start singing along to the lyrics. With each line another one of my girls join me– raising our gun fingers and throwing up random gang signs weh we nahv a clue 'bout.

I look around, when I notice Toni hasn't been singing along, but then I notice she's missing.

Probably brought Ghale to the bathroom 'cause she can't hold her liquor. Yes Ghale, we're cool as fuck now.

Believe it.

I dip my hand in the cake and smack some icing in my mouth while I continue the lyrics. I spin to twerk, and my friends keep singing along while cheering me on. By now Mariah is slapping my ass while I look back smiling for her vlog.

The feeling in the atmosphere shifts when the DJ cuts the music to announce 'Drip's' arrival before bringing the volume back up.

Jordanne...

I look down from our elevated section to watch as the crowd opens to give him way. The women all seem to be staring at him in lust, prompting me to roll my eyes as usual.

My eyes then move from him to Toni who is now behind him cheesing.

Then where is Ghale?

Toni really kept this from me? What a girl good.

I snap out of his trance, spinning around to try and ignore his presence for as long as I can– averting my full attention to the cake.

"Ryleigh Stevens..."

My body shudders at the sound of his voice. It's gotten deeper and even more sexy. I don't know if it's the edibles or just my weak ass body when it comes to him, but I can feel my panties soak.

Turning around, I face him.

"Jordanne Sheer," I mumble, unable to relinquish my smile.

He cocks his head to the side and I can feel all eyes on us.

"You still vex with me?" he whispers while pulling me in– squeezing my ass.

"Yup," I basically moan.

"Sorry Love," he fake pouts before putting his spliff in his mouth to light it. "It's been a rough past year, but I'll make it up to you this year," the smoke from his lips circle us.

"Promises J' ... just promises," I roll my eyes, trying to pull away.

"Unuh get a room nuh man," Toni says breaking the tension, and everybody in our section starts laughing and vibing again.

I should just enjoy my birthday and deal with the issues later. Yeah... that's it.

The waitresses are directed by members of his team to set up a dimly lit section for just us– a little above the section we are now. He doesn't like the crowd where we are, whether it's our friends or not.

As we move to the section, I catch one of the bottle girls staring at him while whispering to her friend or coworker. I cock my head to the side with raised eyebrows, smiling at her.

She sees this and averts her attention to setting our ice bucket on the table.

Jordanne sits and I waste no time sitting on him before nuzzling his neck. He's gained slightly more muscle and is growing out his beard and hair. I hated the hair at first but I'm starting to like it now.

"I missed you," his breath hits my ear while his hand slowly finds its way up my dress.

"Ditto," I whisper, "but you upset me."

"Buil nuh babe. I got you something," he says, spinning me around to straddle him.

He hands me a box, one that resembles a jewelry box but not quite. I look at him quizzically while a small smile threatens my lips.

"What is it?"

"Open it Ry."

Not wasting another second, I pry it open and a key presents itself.

"A key?... to where Jordanne?"

"Mi heart," he giggles, causing me to shove his shoulder. "It's a key to your own apartment complex Ry."

Complex? Him serious?

"Jordanne huhhh? Stop lie," I laugh nervously, "you were listening to me rant about wanting long term rentals?"

… and here comes the tears, threatening release.

"I'm always listening Love, even on the days when I have no energy to," he replies while moving up to peck my lips.

I capture his lips and move my tongue between them. My hands move up to his head and his hands move down to my ass.

Seconds pass and I can feel him rubbing my thighs, asking to enter.

Here?

Now?

The DJ cuts on a Dexta Daps outa nowhere, and I become completely lost in him. I grab his hand and move it up to where it rests beneath my dress and he does the rest.

● ● ●

JORDANNE

She grabs my hand and leaves it just beneath her dress.

Skin smooth as ever

My dick is pulsing, and I want to sink it deep into her but I can't... not here at least. I can see that she won't mind now but when that alcohol wears off, she might...

I remove a travel size sanitizer from my pocket and clean my hands. Shoving her panty to the side as the music moves through her body, I find her clit.

Circling it with my thumb while inserting two fingers, I whisper to her, "You're going to be my wife one ah these days yerr that?"

Her response is a mixture of approval and moans.

I watch as the bottle girl from earlier tries to enter our section, but Skulli stops her.

I slip my finger out of Ry' and into her mouth. She sucks them clean, still moving to the song and I use my free hand to signal the bottle girl over.

She makes her way over and leaves a bottle. My eyes stay steady on her frame, watching as she looks down as if she jealous ah Ry'... who by the way is still dancing.

Women...

I signal for her to leave and she does, still holding the scowl on her face.

"A wah with you and her?" Ryleigh questions as soon as she's off the platform.

"Babe, I duhh know that girl from nowhere, believe me," I hold her close to me while attempting to slip my fingers back in.

She allows it and within minutes she becomes undone on the index and middle.

Wah fuck her, mercilessly

"Let's leave," I suggest holding her chin up.

"Okay I'm tired anyway. Let me say bye to my friends."

I watch as she steps down to bid her friends goodbye. Just having her so close to me after all those months has put a permanent smile on my face. She walks to the restroom, and I signal to Paw to keep her trail.

Minutes later she's back, looking like I didn't touch her... and that's when I realize...

Pictures she ago want enuh

Pictures.

I step down to meet her halfway through the crowd and we walk to the exit with Skulli, Paw and Slyme on our tail. We get outside and she says the words I've been dreading.

"Pictures?" she pouts.

"Yuh friends no take your pictures Ry?" I query.

"They did but–" she starts the whining.

"You don't like them?" I finish her sentence, laughing. "Okay, farwud."

I take her phone and start snapping. Less than two minutes later, I'm through.

"See how quick that was," she smiles.

"14 pictures in? Must a get better fi real," I chuckle.

We walk to my Porsche, and she hops in while I hold the passenger door. Skulli leaves to go back inside but Paw and Slyme stay outside on their phones. I walk around and attempt to open the driver's seat only to see a tiny woman marching towards me.

Jah Jah God

Emily?

I attempt to walk towards her, but she walks directly to the car.

Bro if she touch the Porsche.

Porsche yah worry 'bout and Ry' might destabilize we life?

I snap to my senses and grab Emily but I'm too late as Ry' is now exiting the car.

"Jorda–" she looks around for a second, "Emily?!" she shrieks before laughing lowly to herself.

"I saw that fucking story of you guys! You put me up in a hotel and tell me you nah land till tomorrow afternoon? Let me guess, you were going with her to the villa tonight and then fuck me tomorrow?" Emily screams.

Nahgo do the back and forth thing right now killa.

Her voice pulls a small crowd, and I instruct Slyme to take her home while I try to speak to Ryleigh.

"Ryleigh!" I try while watching her take her heels off to walk back to the quiet section of the villa alone.

The distance is too long, she won't be safe.

"Ryleigh weh yah do?" I attempt.

"Jordanne if you know wah me know you leave me the fuck alone," she hisses.

"At least let me take you," I suggest.

"Ayee," she laughs, "mine me tell you 'bout Sue. Better you gwaan yerr."

Paw looks at me in disbelief. Either he can't believe she said that, or he can't believe I fucked up... I close my eyes for a second before getting into my car. As soon as I sit, I pull for my spliff, before speeding off to the hotel where Emily should end up.

Sorry Porsche.

Night fucked.

• • •

RYLEIGH

"Paw me good enuh," Lorelle a come follow me.

"Boss say me nuffi leave you," his eyes holding pity.

More embarrassment. Now him have people a pity me.

"Our villa is less than half a mile. Lorelle a come walk me. It's the same property and it's secured," I frown.

I watch him pick up his phone, calling Jordanne I presume.

"Boss she deh here a say the property secured and she no wah me follow her."

From where I stand, I can hear J' going off on the line.

"Law..." is the next and final thing Paw says before hanging up to look at me for a second or two– then agreeing to my request.

I turn to the sound of Lorelle's hurried footsteps. She pulls me into a hug as soon as she makes it over.

We stay hugged for a minute before we start walking to the opposite side of the property, hand in hand.

"You ago good Ryleigh… Memba yah top bloodclawt gyal. Memba good," she scoffs bitterly.

"No know why me feel like fi bawl 'cause we deven deh," I choke up.

"Ry' no tell me no fuckry. Unuh no together in which universe? Fi unuh universe alone?! You can't date nobody else you no see that?! Anuh you and him a nyam off each other face a while ago?" she hisses. "Jordanne too secured fi mek dah gyal deh a step to you fi the second time now… You did know dem still deh?"

"No girl you mad?" I sniffle while consciously coaching myself not to cry– not right now.

"A real thing maamz a say B," a deep voice comes from the shadows.

Lorelle and I step back in fear, causing him to chuckle hoarsely.

"Me watch unuh all night and when Drip farwud mah say, ohhh a him woman this… only fi see weh me just see," he hisses. "Pretty woman like you no deserve waste treatment."

We don't respond, but instead continue walking while picking up the pace.

Think Toni say the place secured?

"How you get in? Who you know?" Lorelle questions as we walk, and all me wah ask her is if her mother never tell her don't talk to strangers.

"Mariah me know still, from the media. She invite the man dem. Did ina the section 'cross from unuh… just laid back."

"You name Rome?" Lorelle asks, observing his features.

"Yeah… Jacen a the government name if you wah check the guest list," he chuckles.

Lorelle does just that, pulling the list as I'm too disoriented to care.

"A him fi true. See him picture here too," she whispers, showing me the phone screen.

"See me nahv nothing fi lie bout," he retorts.

"Aight… Walk with we gah our side 'cause God know me a walk and 'fraid yuh fuck," Lorelle laughs.

We get to the door leading to our rooms and he daps us before leaving.

"Him body nice eh," Lorelle states and I roll my eyes.

He's the opposite of Jordanne. Fair skinned, thick, tattoos from neck to wrist, cornrows, a full beard and way too much jewelry… Fully Mariah's type.

Him look good fi real but right now every man sick me stomach. Sigh…

We enter the room and I immediately walk to the shower. This is about to be a crying fest. I swear this time I'm done, finished…Together or not, that shit was embarrassing

20 | Faded

JORDANNE

I got here less than ten minutes after leaving the party and Emily is still locked in the bathroom... even now, at 6:38am.

It would take me less than a second to free the locks and drag her out but me nahgo do dat. Need her fi feel safe enough fi come out.

"Em' just exit the bathroom. I have things to do in Kingston today," my tone now annoyed.

"Gwaan Jordanne," her words land in soft sobs.

I don't get it, I've always been honest with her about my feelings for Ryleigh

Yeah but we neva treat her like we woman?

Treat every woman good still... she no used to that?

"Affi leave at seven, so if you no free up by 6:45, me gone," my voice calm.

Really a try me best killa.

"I'm not coming out and if you leave, I'm telling your so called princess everything. She know you were here for your birthday last month? She know I was in your bed, on your dick?" she asks, sobbing hoarsely.

"Emily," I chuckle, "Em' don't make me come in by force, just open the door."

Ryleigh would never understand me being in Jamaica and not seeing her. I can't allow her to even utter the words to her– not now.

Affi find a perfect time to explain everything to her.

If she eva deal with we again

She has to, I can't lose her this time.

Nope...

"Emily I'm coming in," my tone is laced with frustration at this point.

"Okayyy. Ammo open it," and with that I hear the door squeak open.

As the door slowly swings open, she steps back to sit on the side of the tub. I move over to her while fighting every cell in my body to be calm. I place both hands to the side of her face and tilt it up, to face me.

"Emily why would you do that?" I ask, deadpan.

I feel when her body tenses and I remove my hands from her face and step back to create space between us.

She releases a sigh.

Cyaa 'fraid she fraida me?

Comical

"Emily yahfi talk before me lose me patience. Again, why would you do that?" I repeat my question.

She tilts her head and start twiddling her fingers.

"You're afraid I won't like the truth?" I ask genuinely concerned.

She stays silent... and I grow even more impatient.

"Emi–"

"Yes..." she whispers, cutting me off.

"Nahgo spiral bad head. I just want to kno–"

"Jordanne, you say we aren't a couple, yet you buy me things regularly, you've met my parents, we speak everyday... even when you're busy. The only day you got to leave the U.S you spent it with me... yet somehow, I shouldn't fall in love? or be jealous?"

"Yeah precisely... I did say, back in high school, and the summer before I left, that yes we tried, but I can only see myself with one person... and that wasn't you," I trail off, looking directly into her eyes.

Hopefully she gets it this time?

Jah Jah God. Like we lead her on too long

I'm pulled from my thoughts by her crying.

"I just thought- I- I just thought somewhere along the line you changed your mind, based on the actions you portrayed that I just listed. Do you not see how I could get things confused? especially knowing that you are nowhere near Ryleigh... So just imagine my surprise when my friend sent me those pictures and sent me stories from Mariah's insta story," she explains.

Which friend?

Focus on what she's saying

I get it but I'm used to treating women a certain way, whether we're in a relationship or not.

Honestly...

What's the most I've done?

I make sure she has pocket money monthly, her car has been updated, I've helped her open a salon space... small things that I would do for a random person if they asked and I can see potential.

Some women aren't used to that

She should be. She nah farwud from a different social class.

The bar cyaa be that low?

Bredda you also talk to her everyday

Yeah because of the baby thing...

"And the baby thing really took a toll on me. I thought you at least bonded with me over that decision," she sobs on, as if reading my mind.

Her voice breaking at the end of the statement tugged at my heart a little bit.

Jah know

That decision was solely hers though...

I move over to hold her while she breaks down.

"Emily I completely understand your dilemma and your feelings are very much valid... but understand that I thought we were sticking to our agreement when I concluded last year that we weren't going to go further with what we have now– sex and a good time. After the baby thing, I started to check in on you more out of genuine concern, not because I wanted to take anything to the next step," I try my very best to explain, leaving no room for further misinterpretation.

Really and truly, I just didn't want to have sex with Ryleigh while we go through university. I know how I am, and me nahgo want her far from me if that should be the case.

But man a man, and I still needed sex, so Emily was the next best thing. And even so, I still wasn't able to keep my fingers out of Ryleigh last night

Not even for a second

I must've only had sex with Emily around four times the entire year. Three of which I sent for her via the jet and the last was last month, when I came home to handle something Dalani fucked up.

So all of this was basically for nothing? I chuckle to myself at the realization.

Shoulda lowe har

"Emily this has to be the last of whatever it is we have going on. You know my personal number if you need help with anything, but I can't continue to hurt you... or Ry' at this rate. Dat good?" I ask, dreading what she'll say.

Me really no wah affi deal with her no other way.

"Whatever you say Jordanne. It is what it is," she sobs.

I shake my head before picking up my phone to call Paw. On the first ring, he answers.

"Need you fi carry Em' go back to Kingston," I speak directly.

"Ah, pin the location," he says, and I do just that before hanging up.

I then scroll to Paul's name to let him know plans have changed. He too answers on the first ring.

"Boss?"

"Need you fi start the meeting without me today. Paw a bring Emily go home but I haven't spoken to Ryleigh and me no know how long that ago take."

"You know me neva see you put off business fi woman though boss. A months we a delay Mase and–"

"Skulli?" I question, 'cause obviously him forget a me deh pon the line wid him.

He goes silent.

"Good… Call me when you reach," and without delay, I hang up.

Nah explain nothing further to no man.

Ryleigh comes first and right now, me certain she ago done with me forever.

The next thing I do before leaving is call room-service to order breakfast for Emily.

See weh the girl a talk 'bout yute?

A just second nature…

I order her pancakes, eggs and whatever other fuckry them have.

Grabbing my keys after ending the call, I shout my goodbye to her, as she finally exits the bathroom.

Not wasting another second, I head out and towards my car. I get around the steering in no time and before driving off, I dial Ryleigh's number.

• • •

RYLEIGH

I stir in my sleep to the sound of my phone vibrating on the nightstand. I just fell asleep, whoever it is can wait, I hiss to myself.

Cho.

The phone keeps going offfffff, and offff and offff, so I decide to look at it.

JBae……

I need to switch that stupid name.

I need to remove his name fully.

I need to block him… from my phone…

From my life…

I hiss and see when Lorelle stirs in her sleep at the sound of my annoyance.

Me nah answer him enuh

I grab the phone and activate airplane mode, turn off my bluetooth, deactivate the wifi and stillll bring the volume allll the wayyyy down.

Here we go

If you knew Jordanne you would do the same. I'm surprised he's not here wreaking havoc to see me.

Does that hurt you?

A little, but that good... as he would say.

I realize it's 7:12am and decide to go back to sleep. I only drifted off to sleep sometime after 5am this morning and my eyes are heavy. The girl's and I planned on taking a yacht out to sea for brunch later, so I need all the rest I can get.

Me nah lay down sad whole day and me look so? Crazzzzyyyy!

I pull the sheets back over my head, leaving a tiny hole for breathing, before I attempt to re-enter dreamland.

A couple minutes pass before a knock on the door wakes me again, but also wakes Lorelle this time.

"Bumboclawt man!" she sneers, dragging the pillow over her head. She was also up the entire time, comforting me, so I know she's tired.

I pat her back and slide from the bed.

"Mariah or T?" I ask.

"A Mariah... T' still a sleep," she whispers.

Then a coulda wah now?

It had to be her or T' because Muuch, Keif and Ghale are in the rooms downstairs and one thing 'bout them three deh, dem no wake before 11am no day.

Not even 8am classes them no take. Who signs up for 8am classes you might ask?

I do.

You don't even go

Sign up...

I chuckle at my thoughts while opening the door. Mariah's little self is shoving her phone in my face.

"Me come tell you before nobody else wake. Look pah this."

I take the phone and see that it's a screenshot of somebody that liked her story of me twerking and her slapping my ass... and then another one of when Jordanne was whispering something in my ear.

"A the bottle girl that enuh, weh we hire... and guess who she follow? Emily," she adds.

Her saying that makes me realize that no one made the others aware of what happened last night in the parking lot.

"Mariah you wouldn't believe wah gwaan as soon as I left the party last night," I whisper, dragging her to the balcony.

I explain everything to her causing her to become livid. She's upset she hired the girl without doing proper research but also thankful she did, because we're now aware of what Jordanne's been up to.

"So you think Toni been know this?" she asks staring at her phone.

"I don't think so. Knowing her, if she did, it wouldn't come to light this way," my eyes move from her to the majestic view of the sea.

Later ago nice bad. Cyaa wait fi drink and forget last night's embarrassment.

"The guy weh you say follow unuh come 'round ago deh pon the boat today. Me like him little brother so me invite him," she blushes.

"The good body tatted guy?" I raise a single brow at the new information.

"Jacen yeah... same one," she giggles, "him brother nice too."

"Where you know them from?" I ask genuinely.

I've learnt enough from Jordanne to know not to be at the wrong place, at the wrong time, with the wrong people.

No stray bullet nah catch the doll

And me know anuh 9-5 him do in Jamaica with tattoos up to his neck... and hair long so.

"You know a daddy carry me go wah 'Back to school' give away thing wah long time now and ah them did a host it," she explains. "Not sure what business them and daddy ina but the bigger brother is the Don for Mobay... Him hardly deh here so the brother weh me like run things when he isn't," she explains– her eyes gleaming at the last few words.

"Gun man you wah?" I laugh out loud.

"Then no you me a follow," she shoves my shoulder and we both start laughing hysterically.

Unuh ago wake Lorelle again?

"Okay cool as long as everything secured when we touch sea right up until we get home... The big brother look good so if a so the whole family look, they can all come," I double over... laughing even more while Mariah is basically screaming.

I look up to take in the view of the sea one more time before I go try to attempt sleep again, but what I see irritates me.

In the distance is a Porsche speeding down the driveway to our villa and before I can say it, Mariah does.

"Then no you man that a come? Me gone a me room," she laughs but I know she's a little scared.

I hiss and move from the balcony, closing the doors and closing my suite and room doors as well. Me just no ina the talking and the bagga lies today. Girl wah enjoy her day in peace.

I was okay for months without him.

Were you?

I was, I was starting to accept the drift. If him think him can bully me into accepting that bullshit from last night, him sick.

Heavy! and I mean heavy knocks drag me from my murmured thoughts. Somebody is mercilessly banging on the front door and me just know ah him. I grab my phone and quickly deactivate airplane mode to send a text to the group chat.

33 missed calls from 'JBae.'

I tap on the group chat and start typing.

Unuh duh answer the door it's Jordanne and I'm not in the mood. Will explain later.

<u>**Sexy Bitch:**</u> **Jesus a wah now ?**

Ask Mariah T'

And with that I turn my phone off.

Lorelle sits up looking at me.

"You no know you man if you think him a leave," she chuckles.

"Emily man mlavvvve," I say before pulling the sheets back over my head.

Five minutes or less go by and the knocking stops. I take a deep breath, hoping he left. I snuggle in, thinking mi can finally get a nap but–

Footsteps… I hear heavy footsteps coming up the stairs.

Different pairs of feet.

"Jordanne she no wah see you!" I hear Toni's voice, "me only let you in because me no want you shoot off the lock!"

"Toni-Anne buil and stay outa me way bad man," he says in the calmest, most sinister voice I've ever heard, from him.

My body shivers…

A this me cyaa badda with enuh, the wildness.

I pull more of the sheets over my head and Lorelle joins me beneath them.

"You sure you no wah just mek him talk?... You no affi care but you know Drip nah leave and me cyaa take no shot right now."

I laugh at the fact that everybody is lowkey afraid of him.

Must joke this

"Me say Jordanne if you shoot off the doorknob me a call mommy!" Toni shouts.

I hiss and slide from the bed before walking over to the door, while still holding the sheets around me. Slowly, I pull the door open and our eyes– mine and his, make four.

Toni shakes her head and descends the stairs with Mariah on her tail.

Muuch, Keif and Ghale are at the base of the staircase looking.

Where was Ghale last night?

My focus shifts when I feel Lorelle hug me.

She exits the room while giving Jordanne the dirtiest look, but he doesn't take his eyes off me. I walk back to lie on the bed and Jordanne enters the room before closing the door.

I release a sigh.

"Wah now Jordanne?" I breathe, because I'm genuinely so, so, sooo tired of the back and forth.

Literally drained

21 | Regret

JORDANNE

I enter the room keeping my eyes on Ry'. Her eyes are swollen and her face is puffy, which means she's been crying.

I hate seeing her like this... She would get like this whenever Folan would cheat...

Fuck.

Yah put her through the same thing

A breath I didn't know I was holding onto leaves my lips. Looking away, I start searching my thoughts, trying to figure out where to begin.

"Ryleigh you know I love you right?" I kick it off.

She laughs– hysterical laughing too, while looking at the ceiling.

Give her joke?

I'm serious...

"What do you want to know?" I ask, trying to pinpoint a better start to my explanation.

"Well the way me think me did know everything, start from when you born," she jokes without a hint of humor in her tone.

"Ry' I'm being serious," my demeanor depicting just that.

"I've been serious since last August," she whispers, "thought we were on the same page. You know that night in New York I heard you call her and I decided to let it go. Now I'm being punished for my stupidity."

My eyes find hers, and I realize in that moment, she isn't angry... and my father always told me when a woman is no longer angry, you've lost her.

Jah know

I had a feeling she overheard that conversation. That morning, she couldn't leave fast enough and ever since then we've been distant.

And you never think that's more reason fi see her on her birthday? or Christmas, Easter? summer? something???

Mek me kick it off from August...

Good

"Ryleigh that night I called only to let her know I landed safe because when we spoke in the library nuttin neva really resolved. I thought maybe if mi let her down easy, she would be less hurt by the fact that I didn't want to move further with her."

She giggles.

I continue...

"When you left, I called her explaining my thoughts clearly. We arrived at us just having casual sex when I needed to... if I ever needed to."

Ryleigh giggles again, this time sitting up to look at me. "Aren't you the one who said you wouldn't seek out anybody to be with Mr.Sheer?"

I look away again, finding it hard to look into her eyes.

"No man look pah me because this is the last time we'll be this close," she hisses.

My heart sinks and the reasonability I have in rotation, is now being replaced by anger.

Need mi spliff...

She no mean that when me wait pon her fi years fi move through alla her fuck ups.

Moment she gi we a chance, you fuck it up bad head

I close my eyes for a second, trying to quiet my mind.

"I did say that yes... but I also didn't seek her out," I retort.

"Hahhh murdaaaa... Fada be a fence fimi please," she laughs, but her eyes are filled with pain.

Another sigh leaves my being.

"There were times where I sent the jet for her, three times in total. Me nahv an explanation for doing any of this, other than wanting pussy. I know it sounds fucked up but I didn't want to have sex with you while we gave each other space to grow s–"

I'm cut off by her laughing. This time, it actually reaches her eyes. I step back and continue, praying to get through this as quick as possible.

She sobers up before looking at me with pure hate in her eyes.

Ignoring it, I continue, "Today she mentioned that she got confused about our agreement and started to misinterpret the things I did for her, as relationship acts. Nahgo lie, mi send her money, upgraded her car and mek she open her own salon, seeing as she doesn't want to go the college route."

The silence that sweeps the room as soon as those sentences leave my mouth, is heavy.

A tear falls from her eyes, and I immediately feel like shit.

Fuck...

"Ryleigh say supm... please," I plea– pulling closer to her.

"Jordanne if you come near me, we ago fight," her voice cracks at the last word.

Affi tell her the rest... Everything on the table, if she leaves she leaves.

"There's more," I manage to say, and she holds her hand to the sky as if asking God for mercy.

I continue, "The third time we had sex... she... got pregnant... She decide fi get rid of it because of the fear of her parents and to be honest, I didn't protest 'cause I was worried that was something you wouldn't accept when our time came."

Releasing yet another breath, I watch as she holds her chest before doubling over on the bed– crying.

Jah Know... mi nuh sure wah fi do.

Comfort her

She say me nuffi touch her...

Obeying my mind, I move towards the bed and wrap my arms around her.

She's shaking.

"Ryleigh I'm sorry... Neva mean fi cause n–"

"I was pregnant the last semester of upper six," she sobs, refusing to look at me.

I pull back slightly.

Upper six? Last term?

We had good sex that year

Mine?

"Ryleigh wah happen to the baby? Did y–" I try to ask but she answers before I can finish.

"I had a miscarriage Jordanne," her cries get heavier.

Wah exactly she just say? Why wouldn't she tell me?

We used to tell each other everything.

"You went through that alone?" I ask softly.

She doesn't answer but continues to sob.

The birth control pills

I could've been a father? Twice at that.

I'm pulled from my thoughts by her suddenly shoving me away from her and screaming.

"Coom Out! Come ouuuuttttt!!!" she shoves me, "you been a fuck gyal raw behind me back till she breed??? and ago say you never wah fuck me but as soon as you reach home yesterday ah you hand that ina me hole and if she never pop up we woulda go home go fuck right into the morning!"

She swings at me but of course I shift from it.

How she so fast?

And why me like dat?

Sexy...

"Still have supm else fi say," I murmur, attempting to grab her hands, but with each try she evades me.

"Me nuh wah hear nuttin germmmmssss!!!" she shrieks.

I have to tell her everything today.

Sigh...

"I was here on my birthday last month. Only farwud fi 'round 18 hours to rectify a deal weh Dalani fuck up, regarding securing most of Montego Bay. When I got here, Emily was already in Mobay and–"

"Let me guess, unuh fuck?" she starts with the laughing again.

I nod, observing her carefully. I won't hit her, so I have to be attentive because she's swift and strong as fuck fi no reason bad man.

She moves to the lamp placed on the nightstand and swings it at me. When I successfully evade it, she gets upset and throws it into the wall. The sound of it is enough to pull footsteps from downstairs.

Toni ago kill me yo.

"Ryleigh buil!" I warn her, trying to balance my emotions while watching her every move.

She grabs some sort of statue set from the floating shelf and throws them at my face. With each one inching closer to my head, I decide to get serious. I grab her by her hands and swing her to the bed, pinning her down in efforts to calm her, but it doesn't help.

She continues to cry, scream and kick.

"Jordanne open this bloodclawt yah," I hear Lorelle's voice and for once I'm happy it's not Toni's.

"Lorelle move me have the master key," Toni speaks causing me to look back with a hiss.

Ryleigh takes the opportunity to slap me across my face... and I turn to look at her. I'm not even mad, but I hate seeing her like this.

The door flies open, and within seconds Toni is pulling us apart. I turn to see Lorelle hugging Ryleigh while Toni is busy screaming at me. Unable to hear anything other than Ryleigh's sobs, I start to feel like shit again.

Jah know

Need the spliff now.

"Ryleigh?" I try, hoping she looks at me.

"Ryleigh?" I try again but she doesn't budge.

By now the rest of girls are at the door watching. I take my phone from my back pocket and call Slyme. He's the only one left here with me apart from those stationed in Mobay... I need him to drive me home, cause mi head nuh ina eh right space right now.

Cyaa believe alla dis.

I turn to look at Toni who has stopped trying to talk to me. With my eyes, I tell her sorry, before walking to the door. I turn to look at Ryleigh one more time before stepping through it, but she's now wailing in Lorelle's arms.

Holding my head down, I decide to leave the villa.

• • •

RYLEIGH

My friends found some way by the grace of God to get me out on this yacht today. Toni convinced me not to let J' ruin my weekend like this. Mariah did my hair and makeup, Muuch fed me, and the others haven't left my side, even Ghale.

All now me nuh know weh she did deh last night enuh

We're in full party mode and although it's hot as hell out here, we don't mind. Liquor, weed and food will do you that.

Jacen has been eyeing me all afternoon, but my mind is not with that anymore. I'm focused on myself right now.

Way me feel, me woulda join the rainbow club to rass

My heart fell out of my chest earlier today and I never picked it up to put it back in.

I'm snapped out of my thoughts by the DJ shouting my name and wishing me a happy birth weekend.

I laugh out at his choice of words.

Shake by Skillibeng and Jada Kingdom comes on and I hold the rails and toot over to start shaking. My friends gather to hype me up and sing along... You know, the usual with us. I lap my knitted skirt and continue to shake but distraction finds its way to me by the song stopping.

"One Don say money pull up fi the birthday lady!" he shouts, restarting the song.

Mariah shoves me to the middle and I don't know if it's liquor courage or the charge from the sun, but I don't hesitate. She bends me over and we start twerking together.

Seconds later I'm wining on her while she slaps my ass while singing and of course me join her– out of breath and all. She continues to slap my ass, giving our audience a real show. Matter of fact, I'm almost sure she's looking at Jacen's younger brother.

He winks at her and I pick up on another line, following her lead by gluing my eyes to Jacen.

His demeanor suddenly softens.

We finish our little twerk session and continue to enjoy the party– the Hennessy coursing through our veins.

Moments later, I start to feel sick and in efforts to not pull anybody away from the party, I stagger to the bathroom below deck myself. I manage to pee, fix my hair and give myself that pep talk we give ourselves when the liquor is about to kill us.

I wash my hands and exit the bathroom to the lounge area. Spotting a tiny fridge, I decide to check if there is water. I could get water at the bar on deck, but I need a moment to rest here.

None of the bottles are sealed, causing me to hiss.

"You can have mine," I hear a strong, deep voice suggest from behind.

Almost jump outa mi sandals

He chuckles and removes his shades.

I shake my head 'NO' as words evade my mouth. He moves closer, now towering over me.

"I insist," he adds.

Me really wah the water… so I take it and start gulping it down.

"So gun man alone mek you drop panty? Dat you say?" he laughs and I don't know why but I find it funny too.

"In the moment thought," I mumble while analyzing him.

"I see… Well happy birthday," he adds with a wide smile.

Cute smile.

"Thank you," I giggle, "my birthday was yesterday but you know how girls are, we need the whole week or month."

Why we a giggle so?

"I figured," he smiles. "Hand me your phone," and again I'm not sure why, but I do.

He types something and hands it back to me.

'The Future' is what he saves his number as and again, I'm giggling as I read.

"Do you plan on getting back to the party?" I ask, peering up at him.

"That depends on if you want me to. I came to check on you."

"Check on me?" I ask genuinely.

"Yes. Last night you were angry and today you're stumbling down the stairs alone. I felt compelled to check," his tone sweet but strict.

I swallow and suddenly I'm parched again.

"Okay fair enough," I murmur, taking another gulp of water.

"Are you enjoying my weekend Jacen?" I speak boldly, eyes finding him as he takes a seat on the couch.

"It nuh bad. If you were mine, I would have you and your girls off the island."

If I was his? Men love ownership so till.

I chuckle, knowing we were in Aruba last year, but I don't make him any wiser.

"Okay Mr.Big Shot," I whisper.

"You alright?" I hear Toni's voice and look up to see her and Lorelle at the entrance.

"Yes, I was just sobering up a little to get back to you guys. Me good now," I say while walking to them.

"Thank you Mr.Big Shot," I turn to Jacen before I start climbing the stairs back to the deck.

"You're welcome pretty lady."

His words tickle me.

Pheeeew

He's intimidating as fuck!

I like it...

Supm 'bout it.

22 | Clipped

JORDANNE

"**B**oss you good?" Slyme asks as we descend the toll.

I'm assuming he's worried I'll have flashbacks from the accident. Flashbacks are happening yes, but not from the accident with my father, it's of Ryleigh's tears mere hours ago.

You break her bredda

… And I tried to take accountability.

We made a stop at the safe house in Hanover to ensure things were in order and now we're almost back to Kingston.

"Me good man," I offer him a low response.

"Drip a years me know you enuh. You nuh affi tough it out 24/7," he suggests while sitting up in the driver's seat, gripping the steering tighter.

I shake my head.

"Me good man, a just Ryleigh," I murmur.

"You wah talk 'bout it?" he asks, his voice now laced with genuine concern.

"Dat good," I avert my attention to the scenery out my window.

He chuckles and shakes his head.

Things like this I would only feel comfortable talking to Skulli about but–

"A just the fact say me might lose her fi good," I start and he takes a quick glance at me.

"Ryleigh as in Janette daughter? Toni friend?" he questions.

I nod, remaining silent.

Feel like mi head ago explode any moment now.

"Fi some reason me just think unuh on and off, and no plan fi take it serious? Never know a to the point where it woulda affect you this much. You look like shit right now," the moment the words leave his mouth, I notice fear creeps into his eyes.

I laugh to lighten the mood… simply because his observation holds some truth.

"Sorry boss," he joins the light laughter.

"Dat good man, just wah deal wid Mase thing and head back to school," I assure him.

After this, I have to come back all the way to Mobay to leave.

It ago be a long day.

I think about prolonging the Ryleigh topic with him but mi just no comfortable a read out the status between us to no man right now.

• • •

We pull into the safe house and Slyme parks. I get out to observe my 'baby' for any scratch and or dent. None nuh present demself.

Slyme and I made it just in time to join the last couple minutes of the meeting. I walk inside with him following my lead. The door slides open at the entry of my prints, and every head in the room turns.

I nod for Skulli to continue his speech before leaning against the wall to listen. Me no ina the chatting today but my presence is needed.

"So Mase a roll with either 'Glock P' or 'Ultimate' based on the intel we gathered from the cover we have a Tower Street Correctional. So as most ah we know, 'Ultimate' is the only gang we couldn't get to yield during the take-over last December. Dalani tried again last month and dat drop through," he looks at Dalani with disapproval written all over his stance.

He continues, "A problem will arise either way but Mase linking with 'Glock P' would have a greater impact on business movement since they have access to… not important routes per se, but enough to cause trouble. If him a link with 'Ultimate' then at least we know him nahv none a that… Me ago need two volunteers fi drop a foot, go undercover and find out exactly,"

I watch as several members from the exec team move forward as volunteers, including Dalani.

"Weh yah do Dalani? Yah pretend like you fada no know him son?" Skulli laughs before looking back at me.

I unfold my hands and lean from the wall to step forward. I point at who I think should go– 'Snoop and Buckle' since they're relatively new and Mase won't recognize them.

"I can go asking for forgiveness and find out his plans," Dalani suggests, but I ignore his efforts.

"You two will go as wardens and find out every single thing. What he eats, who he speaks to, how he sleeps, his visitors, right down to the tissue him use wipe."

A bunch ah them start shouting, "Why fi dhattttt!"

Not a single cell in my body finds it amusing, so they simmer down.

"As I was saying, I want all the details and quick. Unuh can manage that?"

"Yeah man.... easy work," Buckle chuckles.

"Easy ting," Snoop agrees.

"Good. Dalani, yuh father would never trust you again and me nah risk him giving you wrong intel. You're the reason he's alive so pray this mission goes smoothly so it stays that way," and with that I turn to exit.

"Drip," Ramone calls.

I stop in my tracks.

Ramone barely speaks, so I know if he has something to say it's likely that something is going wrong in tech– that he needs my approval to address.

Turning around I signal him to the elevator. Everybody else from the exec team is heading out or speaking to Skulli. We enter the elevator and as soon as the door closes, I ask him what the problem is.

"Nahgo dance round you boss. A supm serious so wait till we reach di basement," he suggests.

How much more fuckery ago gwaan fi the day yo?

The door dings open and we move to Ramone's designated office space. It's fully secured, much like a walk-in vault. He enters his kaba code and the door clicks open. I watch as he steps in, before I follow suit.

He hops into his chair and swipes through a couple videos. He then pauses on a particular one, and the images moving across the screen sends an unknown level of anger throughout my body.

It's Ryleigh, on the yacht, stumbling down the stairs from the deck. The video rolls on further to where I see Rome follow the same path seconds after her.

My palm forms an involuntary fist.

"How long ago this?" my eyes now glued to the screen.

"No less than 20 minutes ago."

So me leave Mobay and by time me reach Kingston ah this a gwaan?

"See the boy them ina the party last night and me mek them buil enuh 'cause my little sister have enough sense fi know weh she a do," I speak.

Rome is the leader of 'Ultimate', the gang that refuses to yield. He still controls more than half of Montego Bay and I want that section of the island. I sent Skulli years ago to convince him at one of his yearly 'Back to School' drives. He was considering the option, up until Dalani was to close the deal and fucked up.

"Think the yacht party did fi phone free?" I question.

"A woman dem enuh bro, somebody ago post in real time. Somebody always slip up at these things."

Bad head me cyaa deal wid a next thing.

Me know just as much as Ramone say the man go probe me woman just now.

I pick up my phone to call Toni-Anne but there is no answer. Closing my eyes, I take a deep breath… 'cause right now me ago need three to four big head spliff.

Need fi send the troops I have ah West go warn him.

Don't start a civil war over woman bredda

Fucccckkkk!

I slam the table and exit the tech room.

• • •

RYLEIGH

We make it back upstairs just in time to catch the dancing session and Keif is already leading the routines. Every dance you can remember, and every challenge is being done.

I feel so happppyyy!

Taking a moment to just look at everybody enjoying themselves, I whisper a prayer, thanking God for keeping me 19 years. Turning around, I see Jacen climbing the stairs back to the deck and for a moment our eyes meet.

He looks over his shades at me and I smile. I then spin around as a blushing mess, only to be faced with Toni's glare.

"No," she speaks.

No what? Weh she a say?

"No?" I ask for clarity.

"Yes Ryleigh, that's what I said… anybody but him. They're not even supposed to be here. Mariah begged me to allow it," she explains.

For some reason I'm confused but there is also a tinge of anger.

"A who fah birthday? If there are gonna be stipulations about who I can look at then no keep nuttin else fimi," I sneer.

She grabs my hand and walks me to a quiet enough section of the deck.

"Ry' that's the leader of Ultimate, Jordanne's only rival gang right now. The peace is present between them but it's very frail. If you go deh so, a just more problems, for everybody," her voice hushed.

Me wah know if me a the glue fi gangs. Why I gotta sacrifice nuttin fi dutty Jordanne?

"I want to think about myself for once," I retort.

"Then do that nuh and stop think 'bout man!"

I'm taken aback just by her tone. She realizes and shifts her weight while holding her stare directly at me.

"Ry' that came out harsh but a still the truth. After Folan, you went onto this whole rollercoaster thing with J' and Dalani. Now you and Jordanne say unuh ago buil and deal after college but none of the two a unuh cyaa relax. If you ago deal with Rome, deal with him separate and apart from trying to spite Jordanne. And if you choose that route, know that there will be issues, bigger than me and you– whether him decide fi fall under J's command or not," she hisses.

I narrow my eyes at her. I can't believe this shit. Who told her I wanted that man? He's a good looking man and I like to flirt. I haven't had sex in a year and Jordanne a sling dick cross the seas but me cyaa flirt?

That she just say enuh. Are you taking an interest because of spite?

How that matter? I see a look good man, I want a look good man.

As a young look good gyal.

"Did you know about Emily?" I ask her, skipping right over the topic at hand.

"No," she mutters, "Not until last month."

I swear, all the air in my lungs are knocked out by her response and the blood from my body drains empty.

Mi bloodclawt

"Weh you mean T?" I ask while the tears threaten my eyes.

I cyaa take a next round a bawling or betrayal.

"In August I was in Montego Bay, you know, the usual weekend baecation with Joshua and I saw him and her leaving a villa next to ours. To this day he doesn't know I saw. You're the first person I'm repeating it to," she explains with clear hurt in her eyes.

I'm not sure what for, since all the hurt in the world belongs to me. I step back to create space between us before holding my head up to combat the tears by batting my eyes.

No sah… How me salt suh? and me nuh shit ina church.

I close my eyes and take a few deep breaths.

"Ryleigh," she tries, but I keep my eyes closed and continue my breath work because if I don't, mi sure me ago shove her overboard.

Swear it.

I open my eyes and a smile plays on my face.

"Well Toni, our friendship was beautiful while it lasted, I'll be on my way now," I turn on my heels, heading towards the section where Jacen is seated.

On my way over, I spot Lorelle mouthing 'A WAH?'. No doubt she saw the exchange between Toni and I and wants to know the details.

I mouth back 'MI GOOD' and she gives me a thumbs up.

While refocusing on my destination, I realize Mariah is now chilling with them. Right then, I decide to play it off as me checking on her and walk straight to group.

"Mariah you gov? You just leff we fi a new set a males," is the first thing that leaves my lips.

The men chuckle, but it's as if they're afraid to look at me for too long.

Jacen breaks the laughter by saying, "She's with a better set, you should try it."

"I just might," I smirk, biting down on my lips.

He exhales and a circle of smoke wraps his head. I move closer to him, removing the spliff from his hand to take a pull.

You know the man from nuh weh gyal?

Today I'm bold.

This year I'll do whatever the fuck I want to– my 19th year.

He smiles and pulls me into his hold. I can see my friends and the guards from Jordanne's team staring with concern, butttt mi nuh give one shit.

He hands me another bottle of water and I drink it while wrapping my arms around him.

The cover clicked open, so I know it's fine.

"Weh we ago tell you man say?" he whispers in my ear– his breath tickling my inner most urges.

I look up at him, "Tell yourself whatever you want."

He laughs out loud and that's the first time I've seen him genuinely laugh since we met.

So handsome.

"Slick, very slick Ms.Pretty," he whispers and I lean into him, watching everybody continue to party. We stay like this for the entire afternoon into the night. Just vibing off each other, eating and laughing.

The hours went by fast. We boarded the boat a couple minutes before noon and we just docked and are about to leave at 7:15pm.

Hand in hand, I walk with Jacen down the ramp.

"J?" I hear Toni's voice, and my body tenses.

Must Joshua she see.

I look up and as blind as I am, my eyes spot Jordanne, leaning on his Range, with his head cocked to the side, smiling at me.

23 | Clipped Part TWO

RYLEIGH

I stand still in my tracks, looking at him. Him cyaa serious. My brain acts quick to cover my true feelings, covering my slight fear with a façade of annoyance.

You know him nah bully me though...

"Jordanne..." I manage to say.

"Stevens..." he responds, and I watch Paw hand him the fattest spliff I've ever seen.

Jacen starts mumbling as they attempt to depart the yacht, and realize what's happening.

"Yuh good?" Jacen whispers to me with a smile.

I grip his hands tighter before replying, "Perfect."

Jordanne shifts and Jacen's hand moves to his waist. Within seconds there are multiple tiny red dots moving all over Jacen's body.

Bumboclawt

Jacen's men immediately pull their weapons.

"Just a try smoke me weed and the man a reach," Jordanne smiles.

I step in front of Jacen.

Aye gyal you think a show?

"Ryleigh you ago make me finish the spliff before you drop a foot?" J' asks, with a single brow raised and a newfound genuine smile on his face.

I roll my eyes.

"You nuh affi do nuttin you no feel fi do," Jacen mumbles, while shifting me out of aim.

"I know," I smile up at him.

Jordanne chuckles and continues to puff his weed. Toni makes her way down the ramp arguing and shoving everybody to the side, even the armed men.

"Jordanne really?" she queries, rolling her eyes. "Mariah! Muuch! Ghale! Keif! Lorelle!... we a leave the mad people dem fi kill off each other. Come!" now storming off.

I want to laugh but know better.

They all follow her onto the pier and Jordanne shakes his head.

"Ryleigh, the spliff a done..." he warns, his tone no longer jovial.

Fuck me fi do now? What happens if I stay?

After me nah stay a Mobay with a random man.

And me friend them gone leff me

I turn to Jacen and tip to get to his ears, "I'll reach out... but this no worth it."

He pulls me into a hug... a little too long.

"Unuh see how the man a hug me woman and a look ina me eye?" Jordanne chuckles.

"Then him fi live?" Slyme asks and I just now notice him exiting the shadows.

"Dead boy," Paw snickers.

Jacen chuckles and I pull away to walk off the ramp and onto the pier to Jordanne's car. The lasers don't shift from Jacen's chest or head and for a split second I worry.

"Today she did single," he holds his hand up in mock surrender while smiling, "my bad," he says before ordering his men to lower their weapons.

Even after doing all that, the sniper lights are still on his body, but he doesn't seem to mind.

"Jordanne weh alla this fah?" I ask as soon as I get close enough to him.

He drops the tiny bit of spliff left and crushes it beneath his heels, "In the car Ry'," he orders, in a tone that lets me know not to protest.

Yuh nuffi get involved with badman enuh, especially the one that makes the law.

As we enter his car the beams are lowered from Jacen's body and I watch him leave the ramp with his men behind him. He finds my eyes before waving bye, but I don't think it wise to respond.

I gather all the gleam in this world and center them in my eyes, hoping he can read them.

You know you no listen?

Affi see him again... Jordanne nahgo bully me.

"Fuck do you Ryleigh?" Jordanne's voice pulls me from my thoughts.

I don't answer. Me no have the energy when it comes to him and him wicked sister.

"You me a talk to enuh," he repeats.

"Just a try enjoy my birthday weekend. Weh the fuck do youuuu?" I throw his words back at him.

"Me leff you fi do that but you go too far yo," he hisses, looking at me disappointed.

I cock my head to the side and cross my legs to look at him.

"You must think mah pikny. Yuh and you wicked sister cyaa tell me what to do!" I shout.

He raises a brow while staring at me. The look that enters his eyes, is one I've never seen. He tenses and closes them for a quick second before he relaxes again.

I hiss.

"Why we nah drive?" I query.

"Be observant for once," his tone now laced with bitterness.

I turn my attention to the side mirrors and notice that there is a line of cars behind us. Men are entering and doors are being closed. In front of us I can see Skulli's and Paw's vehicle pull out.

We start moving once everybody gets in line.

"Mmkayyy," I whisper more to myself than him.

• • •

We drive to the villa where I get to collect my stuff. The girls are instructed to pack and leave with our line. Jordanne wants nobody in Mobay that shouldn't be here.

I speak to everybody while packing except for Toni-Anne. She doesn't say much to anybody at all and I could not care less if she wah play victim or not.

One thing me know, and a say Lorelle woulda tell me

Blood really thicker than water eeeh? Thick bad.

The ride to Kingston is silent and dreadful.

Pretty sure Toni did say him a leave from Sangster's and not Norman Manley.

I gather the courage to query, "Anuh Mobay yah leave from?" keeping my head to the road 'cause him a drive like him ago crash... again.

Low blow that Ryleigh

"I can leave from wherever, whenever... Fact say you think me can leave after weh you just pull, mek me know you no know the depth of weh you just do," he hisses.

He then flies the arm rest searching for? another spliff? But comes up unsuccessful.

I open the glove compartment to search for his stash that I know should be there. Spotting it, I pull it out and throw one at him. He grabs it and shoves it in the corner of his mouth.

"Light... " he says, turning slightly to me.

I take the lighter from the cupholder and give him a flame. He lights up and I can see him physically relax after a few pulls.

I shake my head. The substance dependency is crazy.

"Ryleigh we ago good?" he asks, eyes focused on the road– I'm certain we're clocking 190.

"That a you only worry?" now turning my attention to him fully.

Need to assess his body language.

He chuckles.

"Supm else dedeh fimi worry 'bout?" he asks, his voice now dancing in sarcasm.

"Before we start arguing again, mek me buil," I mutter.

"Ryleigh, me know weh me do fucked up on the highest level and I'm sorry. Yuh no feel we even with weh you pull just now?"

"Even?" I laugh out.

A wii crash the car with the two a we enuh

"Jordanne grow the fuck up nuh!" I raise my voice. "Yessss, yesss I basically played in your face with Dalani but I wasn't okay mentally. I took that summer break to focus on myself and bounced back. I knew what I wanted; I've always known what I wanted was you. The problem was always giving us a fair shot... I see now that, that might be impossible. We had a whole new agreement in August when you left for school and I kept my end of the bargain, so now me just feel like me supposed to get my lick back... not saying that a the reason me entertain Jacen today, but it was a big factor," I lay it out.

He stays silent as if searching his thoughts.

"Did you know your sister saw you leave the villa with Emily and didn't say anything to me?" I decide to question.

He takes a few quick glances at me, and I nod to confirm what I said.

"Yeah, that's how much you affect all aspects of my life. My own friend 'fraid fi mention nothing she think ago cause a rift between us... That sound healthy?" I sigh.

He doesn't say a word.

Yeah man

"Ryleigh," he speaks, "I apologize for doing what I did with Emily, how can I fix it?" his tone now silky soft.

"You can't," I retort.

"So what now? we become strangers?" he looks at me as we drive down the street to his house.

"I guess," I mumble.

He nods.

Minutes later we're entering the Sheer residence and the first person I see is my mom.

Mummy ago deh yah enuh

I exit the car to her running to hug me.

"Me piknyyyyy! From this morning me a call and can't get you, nuh do me that again!" she pulls me into a hug and I laugh for the first time since leaving Mobay.

"Mommy I had a long night and then as me wake them carry me gah sea without phone signal," I explain, avoiding half of the story.

"Girls!" Sue shrieks as she exits the house with a large fruit plate. "I know unuh no eat nothing sensible, come and have some fruits and water... Toni what is wrong with your face?"

"Ask yuh son," Toni mutters.

Muuch takes the plate from Sue's hand, and they all enter the house. The men follow seconds after with our bags.

"Jordanne?" Mrs.Sheer questions in pursuit of an answer.

Jordanne shakes his head and mutters, "Ting good Mum."

With that my mom and I enter the house and Jordanne and Mrs.Sheer follow. Everybody is gathered in the living area, so I attempt to go sit with them.

"To my room Ryleigh," Jordanne speaks.

Both my mother and Sue develop confused expressions. I offer them a smile to let them know it's fine, but Jordanne's aura is not helping me to convince a soul.

I ascend the stairs and he follows.

Not waiting on him I try the kaba lock but realize it has changed. I look around at him...

"They change quarterly now," he murmurs while approaching me. "Try again it's your birthday reversed."

"How corny," I smile and only realize the words are said out loud when he looks at me cheesing.

The door clicks open and we enter. I waste no time in starting the conversation because I need him to understand we're actually done.

"Toni told me Jacen is your rival?"

He nods.

"Only him no wah respect the new chain of command yes... Say him nah listen to anybody younger than him," he explains.

Sounds like him...

You've only known him a day

Still...

"Okay so if we aren't together and I'm with him, what are the consequences? Map the projections fi me."

His eyes darken and he drops to his chaise, looking at me. A moment of silence sweeps the room before he answers.

"It can go either of two ways enuh. Him can have you, decide to join and not cause issues but me sure me ago see unuh too much and get jealous then kill him, causing issues... or him can be stubborn and allow him ego fi tell him say 'cause him have you, him nahfi join, which also causes an issue... Me nuh willing fi risk either," he explains.

"So you're trying to tell me it's a no all round?" I look at him.

"Correct Ryleigh..." he retorts, "and why you think me ago like see you with him anymore than I liked seeing you with Folan or Dalani?"

"You nuh like see me with nobody though, but you wah spread you seed worldwide," I sneer.

"Ryleigh..." he signals defeat with his hands.

"Just a try find out weh you expect me fi do," I ask genuinely.

'Cause I do not know.

"Forgive me," he smiles.

"Jordanne, I love you but I can't continue. Notice I'm not even upset, I'm going with the flow and the flow a say we cyaa deh in peace."

He gets up and walks to the balcony.

I follow him to go gaze at the stars.

"Remember when I used to come school come tell you 'bout my balcony?" he looks out, "and how the sky is beautiful from there?" he asks, and my heart sinks.

"I do... You said it was the only peaceful place here," I whisper, looking up with him.

"Time really fly fast..." he trails off.

We stand there looking at the stars for a moment longer before he holds my hand in his, brings the back of my palm to his lips, kisses it and meets my gaze.

"Me ago let you go. We've caused each other and the people around us too much pain and drama. We almost started a civil war today for almost no reason at all. So whatever makes you happy Ry'... I'll be here if you need me as a friend," he finishes, pulling me into a hug.

The tears are welling in my eyes already.

This is what you wanted

It's for the best, right?

Right?

24 | Incognito

JORDANNE

She's slamming it back onto me while holding onto the balcony rail. I grab her hair in a pony, wrapping it tightly around my palm.

Bringing her head back to look at me, I plant a soft kiss on her forehead. She doesn't stop her pace and I find that impressive. Using my free hand, I slap her ass, knowing whoever she belongs to will see my palm prints.

"Jordanne... Uhhh– J!" she screams.

Ignoring her cries, I steady her movements and shift control to myself. Slipping my dick out of her slowly, I watch as the juices from her sweet spot drip down both our thighs.

She turns and moans in frustration.

"Patience babe," I smirk.

I scoop my hands beneath her thighs and lift her slowly– pulling her directly down on my shaft. She swings her hand around my shoulders, when she realizes my aim.

Pussy tighter than ever.

I love her so much...

Lost in her feel and the motion of my strokes, I find my ground by looking into her eyes. They gleam with love, lust and yearning.

"I love you," I whisper, holding her steady on the tip of my dick.

"I love– you– too Jordanne," she lets out, unable to control the deep need to cum playing in her tone.

"Cum for me Ry," the words feeling foreign to my lips.

Why?

As I proceed to bring her down on my length, my phone goes off. Ignoring it, I continue to focus on delivering her orgasmic pleasure...

... but the phone keeps going on and on... and on, andddd fucking on.

Bumboclawt man!

I turn my head to the sound, in an attempt to find it, and turn it off. As soon as I'm close enough to my cell, my eyes fly open.

Bumbo-bloodclawt

Realizing it was just a dream, I hiss loudly.

A nightmare to pussyclawt.

The same dream that's been plaguing my sheets since that night Ryleigh left my balcony.

My home…

My life…

Everywhere but my thoughts.

Fuck!!!

Releasing a deep, painful sigh, I look down and realize my dick has formed a tent beneath the sheets.

Like me a mad out bad head

Don't mistake my dreams for me not being active. I've been with a new girl every week since then, trying to rid myself of the memories of Ry'.

I took the rest of the semester off from school, just to stay back and sort things out. 'Ultimate' or rather Rome himself, has yet to agree to the chain of command. Surprisingly, we have an 'okay' trade relationship in Montego Bay. Hopefully in the new year we're able to come to a better agreement– my agreement.

Without any violence.

I turn on my side, waiting for my dick to dismount. Browsing my phone, I pull up her chat and realize she texted earlier.

Ry': Gym still?

I don't know if I can see her today enuh. Since that night when we agreed to leave our relationship completely platonic, we've stayed in contact. Things are just like years ago when we would do everything together.

The difference is the lingering history of our pain that roars its head in subtle sarcasm or blunt reminders of Dalani and or Emily every now and then.

Laughing it off always seems to work… for her. For me? not so much.

What time your exam done?

Ry': 2:30.

Cool, pick me up at 3.

Just say me can't manage fi see her today, I know

The moment I realized Ry' was serious, and I would probably be stuck here in Jamaica, unable to…

… touch her.

See her…

Feel her… I told her my license got suspended and that I would need somebody I trust to take me places, and to my surprise, she agreed.

I made it clear that I don't like Toni's reckless driving, and Skulli had his own life. When she challenged me to hire a new driver, I told her it would be unnecessary to hire and train a new employee just for a month.

A month turned into two…

… and now three.

She gave up protesting when our days became less awkward and more natural.

Did I even really let go?

Not even a little

I look down and realize the tent that was hovering above my crotch has disappeared. Hopping out of bed, I head downstairs.

• • •

3:01pm

Why yuh late?

<u>**Ry'**</u>**: I'm not late**

Both texts come in at the same time.

Connected…

<u>**Ry'**</u>**: Yuh annoying enuh me park outside.**

Just did ago kunk you fi a text and drive.

<u>**Ry'**</u>**: Come nuh man, n lock chat.**

I chuckle and head out of the house.

We work out at the safe house in Hope Pastures. I prefer using the training gym, away from the public and prying eyes.

Prying eyes, for you or her?

No wah nobody see her, ina them gym clothes deh. No shame about how I feel either.

I open the car door and smirk at her.

She hisses, "Jordanne you ago start pay me enuh. You no like nobody you mother pick fi drive you round?"

I haven't been looking and neither has Mum. In fact, my mom knows nothing about my license being gone… because it isn't.

"Ryleigh, I leave in two weeks. Me ago sort it out by then," I lie.

"The amount a strings you hold, I can't believe you can't rectify your license all now," she rolls her eyes before pulling off.

Baby miserable today.

"What's with you today?" I query.

"The one section of the syllabus weh me nuh study, a it deh a the front of the paper. Bruk vibes man," she whines.

I laugh, "Unuh deh too much party man, nah get enough time fi study."

My tone is jovial, but my spirit isn't. I wish she would stay home.

She a live her maddest life

Maddest, no joke. Other day she post a video from the club twerking and me wah pull up and light up the club with couple rounds from the AK. Swear to you.

"I have something to tell you," she switches the topic and before I can properly acknowledge it, she continues.

I turn the bottle of shake to my head.

"I've been hanging out with somebody," taking a quick glance at me, she smiles.

Why she happy?

"Yeah, who?" I ask, my tone flat.

Dead boy... just drop the name.

Jordanne buil

Maybe just bruk couple ribs?

Jordanne

"J' me nah tell you a who, but promise me not to pry? Just let it blossom and if we get serious me come to you?" she begs.

"How me fi promise that? Need fi know you safe Ryleigh," I explain.

"I am. A somebody you know and him say unuh good now, sooo..."

The wheels in my head start turning.

Me know?

Good now?

Me nuh know no man enuh.

Deciding to give it up and change the topic, before my emotions seep through my facial facade, I start complaining about her driving.

"You a drive like is a Fit me buy give you," I laugh.

"Jordanne gweh nuh," she laughs and I realize we're pulling into the property already.

I watch her exit the car, being as observant as I taught her.

Proud.

I exit after and allow us access inside. Her prints grant her access to the property and to the storage shed behind the house but not inside the main house.

Not yet...

We walk to the gym on the second floor, and I take a moment to observe her– sexy personified.

Just perfect.

"Jordanne stop watch me batty mad head," I don't know how she knows, but each time my eyes fall on her, she realizes without looking.

Connected man. Tell unuh from start

"Why?" I ask, faking innocence.

"You know why. Now come, where is the Surgeon?"

Surgeon… Surgeon is our doctor when we can't bring certain cases to the hospital and also my personal trainer.

"On him way," I respond, while shifting my rising dick– hoping it buil today.

• • •

RYLEIGH

"Jordanne was super weird at the gym today," I say to Lorelle.

I'm heading back down Jack's Hill to campus, and decided to call Relle after dropping Jordanne off.

"Maybe he's anxious about going back abroad?" she suggests.

Doubt that.

"Nah I mentioned Jacen and after that him just start act funny."

"Who you say you mention Ryleigh?" she basically screams in my ear.

"Mi nuh say him name Relle… Jeeeez, but them okay now so we no supposed to have an issue," I defend my action.

"Like you no know Drip from noweh. Just gwaan link up with the big buddy coolie boy until unuh ready fi dead, but as me nuh have no funeral clothes right now, mah beg you wait likkle fi me come back from 'work and travel' next summer," she fills my car with uncontrollable laughter.

"You see all you now," I laugh yes, but somewhere deep inside I know she is serious.

"Toni ago deh the supm tonight enuh," she whispers, and I hiss immediately.

"Weh that affi do with me now Lorelle?" I genuinely ask, my tone laced with annoyance.

"Ry' she say she sorry enuh. You can't treat her so forever 'cause you and Jordanne good again. That no unfair?"

No I stopped dealing with Jordanne intimately because of it, so I think it's fair. She was my friend… and just decide nuffi say nuttin and a laugh up ina me face.

I'm hurt, much more than how J's hurt feels.

"Me ago call you back when me a get ready," and before she protests, I hang up.

'Bout Toni. Weh she have fi do with me? Me nuh see her and stay me distance– simple.

• • •

We were supposed to get here at 12 but you know how that go already. It's now 1:02am and Lorelle, Keif and I are just exiting my car to head to the club entrance.

There are two lines.

We move to the VIP line to stand. The bouncer immediately recognizes us and pulls us around. The way we party hard him woulda affi know we. It's university though, partying is a right of passage.

GPA is still a 3.9 though. Neva shake, neva move

As we climb the steps to get inside, a text comes in on my phone.

Stillen: Where are you tonight

Meca.

Stillen: Deh Kingston tonight. A roll through. What's the PDA rule?

Ok cool, I'll be in my section. I'll let Lorelle drive my car home and we can leave together after? No PDA tonight.

Stillen: Hate this Stevens, but long as me get you to myself after.

Muah!

Stillen: Future wife.

I blush at my phone before looking up just in time to see Lorelle eyeing me. I raise my brows and she raises hers before we both double over laughing.

"One a dem night deh weh you response fimi car," I whisper to her.

"You know me love floor the beast enuh. Me nuh mind. You and Rome can go drive 'round and chat all unuh want and pretend like unuh no wah fuck each other."

"Where is your filter? Me no wah go deh so if Jordanne no know," I mumble.

"Well no think 'bout it 'cause him nahgo good with it. So either yahgo run it pon the boy or not. Anuh you say J' have a new girl every week?" she shifts her weight while staring at me– seeking confirmation.

Keif proceeds to walk to the section, leaving us.

"Yeah but–"

"But? All me a say is, stay down low and sample the Mobay pipe, 'cause once you open you mouth and try get your forever man fi accept that, wulla we a dead weh," she warns in a satirical tone.

I smile. Knowing it might be true worries me the most.

We make it through the thick crowd and to our section. Mariah, Muuch and Ghale are already there. I greet them and move to the couch to sit.

"Noooo, no, no, no," Mariah shouts over the music, "yuh nah do this tonight, open up."

She's holding a bottle of Casamigos over my head.

"You know me only fuck with brown liquor Mariah," I complain.

"No excuses tonight girl, open up!" she shouts, placing her free hand under my chin.

I open wide and she proceeds to pour, too much!

Way too much.

• • •

Thirty minutes in and me nice yuh fuck!

Keif is dancing as per usual while the rest of us cheer her on.

Masicka's Have It starts moving through the speakers and we all join Keif instead of just watching.

Gyal dem love a Masicka.

Of course, we only dance with each other when we're out. No wasteman to the dolls.

I already feel a little lightheaded, but I chalk it up to the Casamigos. Bubbling all the way to the ground, I steady myself with my hands above my head.

Lorelle screams my favorite line from the lyrics and we do a 'Hi5' while laughing from our level. Mariah stands and picks up whatever is flashing on our table.

It's our phone

She hands it to me and I see that Jordanne was calling.

Why him no deh him bed? I scroll to his chat, only to see that he texted.

<u>Danne:</u> A pass through the club with T' in a few.

<u>Danne:</u> You know me hate them thing yah so get a

bigger section so the man dem can comfy.

<u>Danne:</u> Pick up the phone.

I attempt to type back to let him know we already have the largest section so that's fine, but as soon as I start typing... I feel his presence.

I immediately send a text to Jacen

**Drip ago in my section, just find out. Not
sure if I can leave with you tonight.**

**<u>Stillen:</u> Him affi go find out tonight enuh,
bcuz I want to see you after. Tired fi a hide.**

You say you and him good right?

<u>Stillen:</u> Right, soon reach.

I'm pulled from my phone by Toni's voice, "Dolly demmmmm!" she squeals excitedly before moving to hug everybody.

Before she gets to me, I move to the couch. She notices and sighs.

Jordanne is saying something to his men, and I take the opportunity to look at what he's wearing. Full black... Black straight jeans, black long sleeve shirt with a slim gold cuban laying below the neckline and a black Prada sneaker. The watch on his wrist is an Audemars Piguet, Royal Oak to be specific and his little finger is weighed down by a square shaped gold ring he's had since I've known him.

My breath hitches.

I realize I'm staring and look away.

Less than ten seconds later, Jordanne is seated beside me on the couch.

"See how you ex bestie draw me outa me bed?" he laughs, looking directly into my eyes.

I swallow...

"You did wah come man," I giggle.

He pulls closer and moves to my neck, "you smell nice..." he whispers in the crook of my neck.

He still has that effect on me... I need to have sex with someone else.

Ughhh!

That nahgo change it. Same feeling fi life

"Me ago bathroom," I murmur to him while standing.

"Cyaa wull you liquor?" he laughs, pulling at my hand.

"How you know?" I giggle.

It's not the liquor per se, my panties are soaked, making me uncomfortable.

"Know you better than you know yourself," he chuckles, leaning back in the couch.

I stand and make my way down into the sea of people– walking through the crowd and to the bathroom where I slip my panties off, pee, fix my hair, compliment all the girls I see and give myself the pep talk.

The usual.

As I exit the bathroom, I'm faced with Jacen who's moving through the crowd. We see each other and a smile plays on his lips.

Why him stop?

I shake my head, signaling to him that we can't right now and his smile fades. He turns and continues moving through the crowd. The light flashes across us and I look up at my section to see Jordanne staring at me.

When we lock eyes, he brings his cup to his lips before nodding, as if saying, "Ah kool, me see wah gwaan."

I immediately fall into a pool of anxiety.

When I get back to the couch beside him, he's focused on the section that is now housing Jacen and his men.

"You so quiet?" I ask, trying to lighten the mood.

He looks at me with darkened eyes and a smirk, "You know why man."

25 | Incognito Part TWO

RYLEIGH

The shift in mood and the tension increase is sending bubbles to my stomach. I just... I don't even know anymore.

Do not let him bully you...

Do not let him bully youuuu...

"You mean by J?" I ask, feigning ignorance.

"You good man Ry'. Do yuh thing."

"Okay," I mumble, keeping my eyes on him.

He doesn't shift his attention from Jacen's section, and I'm not sure if I should try to talk to him now or later.

Sigh...

"Jordanne?" I try again.

"Ryleigh, you good yo. Me good, we good, them good, the world good," sporting a sinister smile, he stands and pours himself another drink.

"So you just ago kill the vibe?" I give it another try.

He looks at me blankly for a second, then walks away to stand with Paw and Slyme.

I release a heavy sigh and attempt to text Jacen.

Before I can, Lorelle is in my ear, "Ryleigh stay offa dah phone deh."

"Why? You know me a leave with him though..." I state matter of factly.

She laughs, "Ry' just buil fi once. Yes you want your own way but buil."

I do... and with good reason.

Lorelle shakes her head and adds, "You wrong but me ago support you through whatever. However, if at any point you make you man blame me fi nothing..."

They keep referring to J' as my man. From Joshua, to Mariah, right back to Troopa. I don't know how, but I have to release myself from this hold.

If we can't just be friends, while I date freely, then what's the point?

Date anybody else

I could be hanging out with a poster of somebody else and he would still act weird.

I heave another sigh.

Me ago lose my friend fi good? All because we just can't function in the same environment. My therapist told me to take baby steps and I've been trying– though I see him every other day. Maybe I need to see him every other week?

Have you ever been tired? Tired of an ongoing situationship but you can't shake the habit? Me feel like an empty bottle at this point, nahgo lie.

We need to separate from him completely

I don't know exactly how to do that. It's easier when he's away.

Jumping from my thoughts, I scroll to Jacen's chat.

He knows and isn't happy.

<u>Stillen:</u> Yuh good babe, no worry no ina our ting, just say the word and we leave.

'The word'

<u>Stillen:</u> Stevens yuh no funny lol.

We both look at each other before laughing from across the club. My eyes dance to Jordanne and he's now sitting on the single couch behind our table.

I go back to typing.

I'm serious, I'll be outside.

And with that I hand my keys to Lorelle and slip away.

• • •

The time is now 4:04am. Jacen and I are on our way to the apartment he has here in Kingston. We're on Constant Spring Road, heading to Russell Heights. The short drive is a breeze and our conversation is light and free.

Free of painful jabs or old truths.

But still missing something

"So weh you say? You have an entire complex?" he asks in slight shock.

"Yeahhh, got it only a few months ago and all the units are almost full," I say proudly.

"That's good for your age," he smiles impressed.

I switch the topic because I don't want to get into how I acquired it. "When are you leaving the island?" I ask genuinely.

"You know a right after Christmas still," his voice laced with disappointment.

"As in the Christmas next week?" I ask a little too loudly.

"Yeah," he laughs, seemingly impressed by my concern.

"When do you get back?"

"Whenever you want me to," he smirks.

Weh me hear that before... the unfulfilled promises. I don't answer but realize we're pulling into a gated complex.

Pretty sure Joshua lives here

This world of ours is toooo small.

I climb out of the car and wait for him to lead the way while I look around, taking a picture of everything with my mind just like J' taught me.

Jacen holds my hand to lead me to his apartment and for some reason a knot forms in the pit of my stomach. I don't like the feeling...

Why am I anxious?

It feels like I'm cheating...

• • •

JORDANNE

I watched her get in his car and leave less than twenty minutes ago and well... if I couldn't leave her be before... I can now. She made her choice very clear.

"Jordanne you good?" Toni's voice pulls me from my thoughts.

"Yeah, mah leave in like three hours," I decide to share my decision.

She stands, looking at me before shutting off her car.

Toni has been staying at home instead of on campus since Ry's birthday weekend. Feel guilty 'bout weh dem relationship deh now, swear.

"Leave go where Danne?" she questions, her eyes searching for confirmation in mine.

"Mahfi leave sis, otherwise me ago do weh me nuh wah do. Just ago cut and focus on school," I explain, placing a light kiss on her forehead.

She doesn't protest but instead pulls me into a hug.

My spirit is tired. I've been waiting on Ryleigh to see me for yearrrrrs... and just as Emily said, she'll continue to choose everybody ova me.

She has, again.

Is like she think me mek outa stone... I have feelings too. Then she keep on a water down me thing like me a some regular bag boy. I'm the fucking law to the streets. Off the streets too.

Girl only see me as her little high school bestie

Jah Jah.

I pick up my phone to ring Skulli. Wake the man out him bed yah now... 4:15am.

Somebody answers on the fourth ring.

"Hello?" A familiar voice comes in.

Sue?!

I look at my screen to ensure I dialed the correct number and... I did.

"Mum?" my free hand rolls into a fist involuntarily.

"Yes Jordanne?" she asks as if not realizing what's wrong.

'Sue a my phone you have' Paul's voice comes in from the background.

There is shuffling and more muttering.

"Boss?" he chips in, clearing his throat.

I think about saying something, but Ryleigh took all my fight away.

"Just come pick up me car from the airport in around two hours," not giving him a chance to reply, I hang up.

Yeah me need fi leave...

I make my way to my room and put my laptop and important documents in my duffel bag. Swinging it on the bed, I walk to the drawer she has here.

Why you still have it?

Couldn't tell you... Hopeful?

Putting the components in a travel backpack I bought for her last year, with the intention of her flying in to see me often, I shoot a text to Toni, letting her know where to find it when I leave. Hopefully when she delivers it, they put the bullshit aside and actually talk things over.

I move to the shower to rid myself of the club air. When I'm out the shower, I drag my boxers on and plop down on my bed, ready to take a quick nap. I'm surprised I made it through the night without turning to weed.

Might affi roll up a morning.

Indeed

Within seconds my eyes close down and I'm asleep.

• • •

RYLEIGH

I look at my phone to see that it's 6:20am. Jacen and I fell asleep sharing childhood stories. I learnt that he grew up poor and made a name for himself after his God-father died. He has multiple businesses abroad and intends to place interest in agriculture in Jamaica.

I like it...

He leaves his brother to handle the gang for more than half of the year because it's not something he actually wants to do forever.

His brother however, loves the power and the name.

Typical

The feel of his arms wrapped around my waist sends me smiling.

He sleeps like a baby.

I'm a little uncomfy in the couch though, so I turn to find comfort. While turning, I spot my phone and decide to check my notifications. To my surprise there is one from Toni– sent since 4:45am.

What now? Mi nuh wah deal with this… Clicking on her chat nonetheless, I begin to read… but only two words stick out to me.

<u>Toni-Anne:</u> I know we don't speak, so forgive me for texting this early. My brother is leaving today. The look he had in his eyes is the same look he had when the doctor told us that dad died. I'm not saying you should reach out, I'm just letting you know. He loves you and what you did tonight might've pushed him to the point of no return when it comes to you guys. He leaves 6:30am back to NY to chill until his classes resume. There is a bag here with everything he had for you and a folder holding info for an account he's been adding money to for you, to surprise you on your next birthday. Let me know when you can come pick em up.

Brother? Leaving? She said 6:30am?

Today???

I look at the time to see 6:22am. Knowing I can't possibly make it, I scroll to his contact and click to call but it goes straight to voicemail.

Voicemail?

I dial the work number and it does the same, so I start texting him instead.

♪ you had two more weeks before school?
how is it you're leaving today? right now?

One tick. No Display picture.

You're blocked

I send the same words to IMessage and guess what? It doesn't deliver.

The time shifts to 6:25am.

I start searching frantically for his Instagram but come up empty.

Blocked

I start laughing.

God if you're there.

I know he's leaving me for good this time… I can feel it. I can't explain it, I just can.

Jacen stirs in his sleep at the sound of me laughing in disbelief.

You fucked up huh

Royally.

It's now 6:28am and I decide to give it one last try– still voicemail.

The tears are threatening to escape my eyes and I bite my lips while trying to control my breathing. Jacen finally wakes up and looks at me. It takes him a second to realize that I'm in distress.

"What happened? yuh good?" he asks, his eyes dancing with concern.

I don't speak.

"Ryleigh?" he sits up and pulls me into his arms.

"Can you take me home, to my mother?" I whisper, trying not to allow my voice to break.

"No campus?" he asks with soft eyes.

"No campus," I repeat and with that we're up and getting ready to leave.

• • •

Jacen pulls up at my gate while mommy is already standing at the grill waiting. I called her earlier and she could hear from the sound of my voice, that I wasn't myself.

For the short drive here, Jacen has been asking if he did something to upset me. I've told him no quite a few times… but he doesn't believe.

"Ryleigh, call me when you're up for talking?" he suggests.

"Will do," I turn away from him– my eyes glossy.

The tears are less than a millimeter away from sliding down my cheeks. I fly the door open and basically run to my mom.

As soon as she holds me, I break down.

"Ry' what's wrong?"

I don't answer and she doesn't pry. Every emotion I've been suppressing since September is released… The loss of a friend– Toni. 'Cause that shit hurts just as much as any break up. Toni was like a sister even…

The loss of a… lover? friend? soul mate? in Jordanne. The loss of a child just last year… The memory of that hits me and my knees buckle. My mommy holds my weight and moves us down to the floor.

26 | Intermediate

JORDANNE

I've been in New York for two full days. Since I got in, I've been sitting at the window just watching people go on with their lives.

Feel like mine went over a cliff...

My mother is with Skulli, the righthand to my father and now to me.

Did I ignore every sign, to the point of delusion?

"Mr. Sheer?" Pat's voice pulls my attention from the window.

Sue decided to send her here to me the day after I left. Though I would much rather have my privacy, I can admit that I do need her here.

"Whatever it is, leave it on the table," I groan.

"Jordanne, from me come yuh deh a the same spot. Mrs.Sheer say me nuffi make you drink, smoke or starve yourself to death, and I have to do my job," she flashes her motherly smile at me.

I hang my head, wanting to be alone.

"Me ago eat it man," the words exit my mouth without emotion.

She leaves the room and I resume the song I've been listening for the past 48 hours. Scrolling from through the list has proven futile, since this ah the only one weh fully relatable right now.

Bredda yahfi eat

I will.

Turning my focus back to the window, I continue to street watch while trying to quiet my mind. My thoughts have been filled with regret and just overall vengeance.

Probably fi take on the gym.

Do dat

Dat is it fi real.

I stand and make my way to the home gym, walking by Ms.Pat's plate of baked chicken and potatoes.

Ago eat it later fi real man.

• • •

RYLEIGH

I pull the sheets from my head when the song I want doesn't play… 'Cause how we reach a soca? Sad songs me tell SIRI enuh.

I groan and reach for my phone, moving the wrappers of chocolate, cookies, chips, whatever you can think of eating without cooking– all present with me on this bed. I find my phone between an empty water bottle and a plantain chips bag. Pulling it to my chest, I blink as my eyes adjust to the light.

My fingers swipe to a more fitting song for this occasion and believe it or not, I start to feel a little bit better– just a little. Suddenly, I remember what I was doing before– deleting the pictures we have together. The memory forces me to click back into my albums and move to our pictures.

My eyes connect with one that was taken of us years ago. The picture that started the rumours. I smile to myself while looking at it. I think it was our barbecue that year. He hated going to our high school barbecues, but he would do it for me.

Anywhere for me…

Then look how we little and maaaawga.

Oh my God, mi hair!?

It's the makeup for meeee

The earring? No sah.

I find myself smiling…

"Ry?" my mom's voice moves through my room, grabbing my attention.

"Mmmmm?" I groan, pulling the sheets down.

"Ryleigh you ago make rat take we ova?!" my mom whines.

She's been a gem for the past two days. I've been drowning myself in my sorrows and she's allowed it– zero pressure.

She done now though

I would be too.

"Come now Ry', you affi get up and cheer up yourself," she pulls the sheet from my head and almost passes out when she sees what's under the covers.

"Ryleigh! cup and plate full the room and now you have bay garbage under the sheet. Yuh mad?!" she screams.

I sit up looking at her, unable to communicate my thoughts. Her face softens and she sits beside me– pulling me into her hold.

"Ry' you and Jordanne ago alright. I've never seen you guys not speak for more than a few months at best."

"Not this time mommy," I groan.

"What I'm more concerned about is why you felt you couldn't come to mi? You went through the pain of a miscarriage alone at 17. I feel like mi fail you as a mother," her eyes glisten– forming tears.

I don't want to talk about this…

A sigh leaves my lips.

"Mommy I know how much you tried to keep J' and I apart so I didn't think to–"

"I was never trying to keep you guys apart. Sexually yes, but not totally. Me a you mother and mi see say you and Sue son in love from you bring him come here 'bout group work, and a the two a unuh alone ina group," she laughs.

I laugh too, at my younger self.

Really thought I was doing something there.

"We still ago get ice-cream?" I switch the topic.

"But the way you a nyam yuh feelings me think you can't hold no more," she laughs and I attempt to slap her but she hops off the bed.

"Clean up in here and bathe yuh frownzy self, then we can go before night come down," she suggests, placing a kiss on my forehead.

"Cho," I groan, getting out of the mess I made.

She leaves the room in better spirits and I start collecting my trash piece by piece.

I'm suddenly in better spirits too… so I gather all the trash, make the bed and sweep the room.

Grabbing my phone, I select my favorite playlist while entering the shower. Moments later I'm out and have decided to look like I have a home before hitting the road.

A text comes in from Jacen, but I ignore it like I have been since he left me here. I'll speak to him when I'm a little better than this. I let my hair down and decide to put a set on that I've been dying to wear but haven't had anywhere to wear it to.

Staring in the mirror, I start to judge.

I love it!

Deciding to feed my ego, I set up my tripod and take a picture for my Instagram story. It's up for less than ten seconds and I already have likes and reactions popping up.

Rome_emperor reacts with a heart.

Dalani_M reacts with a heart.

Big_Muuch reacts with a heart.

Ghale.b reacts with a heart.

Ria_don reacts with a heart.

Lrlle reacts with a heart.

Keif_A reacts with a heart.

T'Don 'you look good af wifey'

I click into Toni's chat and like her statement. Still not feeling the vibe to reply to Jacen, I scroll to his page.

Bout him name 'Rome_emperor' how corny haha!

I scroll through his grid and land on a not so recent picture.

Such a cutie

I like the post, lock my phone and head out to get mommy. Lorelle dropped my car off yesterday, from what my mother told me.

"Ready mummy?" I ask, watching her take selfies of herself.

Moms

"After you," she giggles.

"Come then," I say, pressing my keys.

The car clicks open– another reminder of him. Nah get rid ah this though, might hurt but mi no fool…

• • •

TONI-ANNE

At least she like my comment, and mi nuh blocked anymore. I really want to apologize to her. Holding something like that from her, was inevitably detrimental.

"Toni, let's go get some ice-cream," Sue's voice descends the steps with her, startling me.

I'm not in the mood fi no ice-cream… Ughhh.

Work on the relationship with Mum' Jordanne's voice replays in my head.

Cho.

"Where to?" I smile, hoping it's not Devon House. Cyaa bother with the crowd.

"I-Scream," she giggles, overly happy.

Wah she up to?

"Oki, long as you drive," I smirk, and she grabs her keys.

Within seconds we're pulling out.

• • •

RYLEIGH

Mommy and I have been sitting and catching up on all the things I thought I was hiding from her.

"Yuh cyaa hide not one thing from me. Every time supm do you me know. I might not know exactly what, but I always know," she laughs while slapping her tongue around the cone.

"Anything you say mummy," I laugh, dipping a spoon into my cup of sugar sweet pain eraser.

The sugary goodness causes me to close my eyes while it covers all the emotional hurt soaring through my being. I reopen them and… Is that Sue? Just as my day a get better. Isn't that Toni coming back with ice-cream for her?

The wheels start turning in my head before landing on the conclusion that mommy set me up.

"Mommy, why Sue and Toni a walk towards we?" I question, quirking a brow.

"Really? What a coincidence. Me nuh have a clue mlavvve, but me ago run go bathroom and come back," and with that she giggles and walks off.

I watch as her and Sue step away to the complete opposite direction of the restroom.

Toni is now standing less than six feet away from our table. I wave her over and see her sigh a relief. It's awkward enough, we might as well get it over-with.

"Hi," she kickstarts the conversation, with a small smile playing on her lips.

"Hi T', when since you like ice-cream?" I ask, breaking the ice immediately.

"Yuh know I only came because Jord–" she pauses, I'm assuming not to finish his name out of respect?

I don't know exactly.

"Because of what somebody told me to do– which is work on mommy and I's relationship," she continues.

"Oh, so two ah them trick we into coming here then," I offer a warm smile.

"Yeah," she whispers.

A minute of silence settles between us before she picks up again, "Ry' I'm sorry. I had no idea he was here for his birthday, so when I saw him and her, I was just as shock as you were when he told you. I thought maybe it was some sort of plan to get to somebody since I didn't see them in the actual act… Or some sort of arrangement that you guys had that I didn't know about. You guys have had quite a few of those that I was never privy to," she gives her explanation.

"Those have never involved anybody else," I retort.

Really? We never wah date other people and still fuck him?

The memory rocks me, while Toni glares at me knowingly.

"Okay but still…" I surrender, slipping more ice-cream into my mouth.

"Yeah… I'm not trying to create an excuse. I'm trying to communicate the reason for not saying anything to either of you. I've always tried my best to stay out of it, and it did just a get well hard. Unuh annoying bad sometimes… Jordanne expected me to convince you to either be with him or wait on God knows what, while you expected me to support you wanting to be with him but not really, while knowing who he is and how him stay…"

… And I understand where she's coming from, but at the same time, she knew how much I wanted things to work out for us while he was away. I told her…

I complained to her about him not holding his promise of *'making me missing him a holiday'*. I complained about the phone call I overheard in New York that night. I complained about every single little thing he did that entire year, and when it came down to it, she kept very vital intel from me.

Sigh.

"I understand where you're coming from, especially since he and I always have some kinda new agreement without letting anybody know the exact details," I decide to keep my thoughts to myself for another time.

Right now, I just want my friend back. I miss movie nights... beach days... and her complaining about Joshua.

"You didn't come to get the bag that he le–"

"So how is Joshua?" I cut her off, "pretty sure I was at his complex the other morning," I smile, watching as her face lights up at the mention of his name.

I didn't want to cut her off but that bag he left can stay. Mi no have the energy fi go through dat. I prefer to talk about her and Joshua right now. Their relationship has always been so easy and fun loving... It's hard not to admire.

"Him good enuh, we supposed to go have a likkle din-din tonight," her tone filled with so much excitement, I can't help but smile.

We fall into easy banter for the rest of the evening.

I've missed her... really missed her.

27 | New Flex

JACEN

It's Christmas day and I'm sitting here texting Ryleigh about wanting to see her before I leave the country.

> If I don't see you today I'm not leaving.

Stevens: I'll be there man. A drop ah Toni foot first though.

> Kool, let me know when to swing.

Stevens: I wanted to drive still.

> You wah drive go all the way to Bay? Lol.

Stevens: Luv done off the highway ☺

> You can drive my car.

Stevens: Then who bring me back Rome?

> You can keep it ☺.

Stevens: BFFR you serious?

> Until I get back yes...

Stevens: Deal. 2 cars to my body now haha!

I laugh out and affi click out ah the chat. She's a sweet girl. Mi go deal wid her good. Drip nah get her back.

Yah play a risky game

She worth it to me.

I want to take her to see the family today. She's supposed to be stopping by her best friend's with her mom for dinner today as shi say, so after that we do road.

I find myself smiling at my phone, just from the thought of her meeting aunty Cherry.

Realizing that I haven't given her a time, I quickly type to let her know I'll be there at around 3pm before clicking out of her chat to call my brother. Affi mek him know fi up security and mek aunty know somebody special a pass through tonight.

• • •

RYLEIGH

Toni is talking to Jordanne on FaceTime and I'm hesitant to let her know I'm leaving.

And dem nah stop chat

I've already said bye to mommy and assured her I'd be safe since Lorelle and Keif will be behind me in my car. I might be adventurous but I'm not stupid. Next thing the man leff me a road.

Nope.

I try to signal to her that I'm leaving but she doesn't budge. Is she being deliberate? 'Cause that would be toooo soon.

"Toni-Anne," I try and her eyes finally avert to me.

'I'M LEAVE-ING' I mouth, while pointing to the door.

"Leaving to where Ry'?!" she asks out loud, causing me to roll my eyes.

I just know he heard for sure.

"Later me link unuh back," Jordanne decides to remove himself from the equation.

"Mid convo Danne?" Toni laughs, and I attempt to leave.

Jacen has been at the gas station off the foot of Jack's Hill for a while now. That's as far as Jordanne permitted according to Ms.Sue. Guess that's fair enough, not wanting him to know much of his personal area.

"Ryleigh," I hear Ms.Sue's voice, "Slyme is coming with you ladies," she smiles, cocking her head to the side.

I look to her, then back to Toni, then to my mom, and back to Ms.Sue.

Is like from you tell one, you tell all

"I'll be okay he doesn't have t–" I try to explain but is cut off by the voice on the phone that I thought was gone.

"Bus head," he speaks, referring to me, "listen to Mum... Toni me gone," Toni's phone call ends abruptly and I'm left standing there just annoyed at everybody.

Why me fi listen to Ms.Sue, or Jordanne at that?

The annoyance of the never ending control starts getting me riled up... but then I remember my therapist saying not to stress over the things I can't control. Since whatever Jordanne say or feel is law, then whatever.

As if him no have like half of Mobay under his governance already.

I hiss, lowly.

Why me need Slyme behind we?

"Okay," I nod and turn on my heels to head out.

Shooting a text to Jacen, I let him know I'll be there in less than five minutes. I walk out the house towards Lorelle and Keif who are in my car outside the gates. I wave at them excitedly before stepping out.

"Where is Slyme?" I turn to Troopa.

He walks out of the security post and looks around. The sound of a horn outside the gate distracts us both and we look to see that it's him.

Oh... Why it seem like him been ready?

I nod at Troopa, leaving him a smile as I step through the small gate and walk towards my car.

"Gooooodzzzz!" Keif shouts.

"Big farrid yuh did ago take forever?" Lorelle asks, feigning distress.

"Couldn't interrupt Toni fi tell her me a leave. She was on the phone with such man," I roll my eyes, only for them to start screaming from laughter.

"Bet him send somebody," Lorelle cackles. "Man cut gone a whole week now and still know the runnings."

"Yeah you no see Slyme car behind we," I hiss.

"Then look how God answer me prayers, me say whole morning me 'fraid. Bubble guts nearly kill me before me reach yah."

She scores a laugh from each of us with that one.

"Ayeeeee ayeee," we hear coming from behind us.

Then no Mariah that?

"Mad gyal tappi noise ina the people dem good-good neighborhood," Keif hushes her with her hand hanging through the window.

"Ryleigh how you no tell me you a leave? Daddy just say you gone and me run come down yah," Mariah shrieks.

Mariah spends Christmas here every year, due to her father being Skulli.

"Honest to God me never know you serious Mariah. Toni ago vex enuh," I look at her while she's prying my door open.

"Then me business? Me wah go see me baby! I nah miss a trip," she giggles while popping her gloss.

I laugh inwardly.

Then this move from me visiting Rome, to Lorelle accompanying me, to Lorelle inviting Keif so she isn't a third wheel and now Mariah wanting to see her little north coast beau. I wouldn't be surprised if Muuch and Ghale pop up outa the woodworks right now.

We jump at the sound, of Slyme's horn.

Murdaaa, the man ready enuh!

Lorelle grabs the steering and floors the gas pedal, causing us all to jolt backward into our seats.

"Aye gyal a so you drive me things when me no in yah?!" I turn to her.

"How you mean? Me and it in loooove," she chuckles.

I laugh at how happy she is, I might have to get her, her own, once I go over the books from the apartment complex.

Just a few minutes later, we pull up to the gas station in Barbican and I see Jacen's Benz parked and waiting. I hop out of my car and walk towards it. The door to the driver's side flies open before I could touch it and I slip in.

"Hi cutie," I cheese.

"You ready fi the mess I call family weh me about fi drop you ina?" he asks jokingly.

"Fully ready, and ready fi bun off road," I giggle, before lifting my foot from the brake.

I notice he has a car before us and one after us. Lorelle moves behind the vehicle that trails us and Slyme stays behind her.

A line of five vehicles pull out at once– our destination set to the second city.

• • •

We get to his aunt's house and I notice how humble it is. He must really like me to trust me enough to bring me here.

I like that.

We walk hand in hand through the gate with all eyes on us and I mean allll.

His aunt breaks the silence with a, "Nephew yuh reach!" pulling both of us into a hug.

She's a chubby Indian lady, in her mid 50's maybe. I learnt when we had our child-hood conversation that his parents died when he was around three years old, so his aunt and Godfather parented him. When his Godfather died, he bought his aunt a house out-side of the ghetto, but she refused to leave.

He comes here ever so often to check in and to give back to the community as much as he can... I just love it.

"One yah pretty Rome, natural browning, batty siddung," she slaps it and I jump from fright

Mighty Gawd

The yard roars in laughter.

"Get her some soup fimi please aunty," Jacen commands and she doesn't hesitate.

"You friend dem shy?" he whispers in my ear.

"Not even a little. I don't know why them no come in."

I signal them into the yard and Mariah is the first to step off. Slyme nods but stays leaning on his car, smoking his weed. I figured he wouldn't join, but still. My eyes find the four other guys standing guard with him and I shrug before turning back to Jacen.

Unnecessary Jordanne

"Pretty girl see the soup here and some extras for your friends," her demeanor is so welcoming and sweet.

I take a cup of what I think is mannish water and so do my friends. After taking one sip, my mouth becomes a paradise. Jacen seems to notice and smiles at me.

"Yeah man, Ms.Cherry cooking that fi you," he laughs. "Come, we ago upstairs go chill out."

I follow him to a back porch on the second floor where it seems only he has access to. We're overlooking most of the community and he takes the opportunity to tell me more about his exploits as a boy. We spend about an hour laughing at the stories we remember from our early lives.

Long after, music starts at the front of the yard, where most people are and we decide to go back down since the rest of his family might be here too.We move down and he introduces me to a few people. Surprisingly, I remember some of the faces from my yacht party.

I look to locate my friends and realize Mariah is in the arms of his brother– Ruse, while Keif and Lorelle are halfway through their plates of food.

Everybody good man

"Wehm deh?" a female's voice breaks the peace.

Almost everybody turns to look at Jacen knowingly. He shakes his head and averts his eyes to where the little bodied woman is shoving her way through the tiny crowd. She comes to a stop in front of us, eyeing me from head to toe.

"Wah deh gwaan yah so Rome?" now waving her fingers a little too close to me.

Haha! Dem ago mek we fight a Bay? And then yuh ago hear say a ova man

Better me did stay home.

I glance at my friends to see that they're all now standing, paying keen attention to what's happening.

So is Slyme.

"Easy yuhself Stace. Tonight anuh the night fi embarrass yourself," Jacen looks down at her, and that's the first time I'm hearing his voice take that tone– a deep, no-nonsense tone.

I shift my weight to my other leg and she looks at me before smiling.

"Nuh worry pretty girl, him ago use you and skip you out too," she laughs.

"Only one a we a idiot," I mumble, but too loudly.

"Weh you say gyal?!" she blurts out, moving closer to me.

If she bad

In the blink of an eye Mariah, Lorelle and Keif are behind me while Slyme starts to move to the yard with the other men, cautiously.

"You too close to me woman enuh Stace. Either you relax and eat some food or you affi go leave," Jacen commands, holding her tiny shoulders to move her out of range.

We must have 'fight me fi you man' pah our forehead

No sah, life funny eeeh?

"Yuh see you son wull day Rome?" she asks loudly.

The crowd mumbles.

Son?

SUN OR SON?

I dart my eyes to Jacen who shakes his head.

"Jay deh a me yard right now Stace. For a mother you need fi keep better tabs pah your child."

She hisses and rolls her eyes.

"Stace no mash up me nice Christmas party," Ms.Cherry smiles at her but it doesn't reach her eyes. "Jay is with the nanny at Jacen's. Me just FaceTime him too, him deep ina him game. He was here earlier with me until Jacen drive out," she explains while holding her hands to lead her to the back.

I take the opportunity to smile at Jacen.

Start call him Rome from now 'cause him a fall already

"Do you want to explain?" I ask, my tone now sarcastic.

"Do I have a choice?" he tries to play it off.

"No. You leave tomorrow so I need to hear now."

My mind prompts me to find Slyme, only to spot him on his phone.

Bloodclawt man

My friends have moved back to where they were chilling, while Jacen's now walking me to his car where he claims it's quiet and private. I don't know which explanation him coulda have fimmi because me nah be no 19 year old step mother enuh.

Madness

Crazzzzzzyyyyyy.

28 | Saved

JORDANNE

"She good now, like them gone talk," Slyme continues, after disrupting my meeting to let me know Ryleigh continues to make stupid decisions.

I tap my index finger on the side of my glass, wondering if I should refill it or not.

"No seem like she did know enuh," he adds after my silence is prolonged.

"She nah do no research man, but she say me nuffi 'pry' so mi leave her fi do her business," now bringing the glass to my lips, while removing the phone from my ear to the desk.

I tap the speaker icon.

Can't continue trying to save her from herself

"Done know the man have a yute good while now, but a her choice that still. Long as everybody good and no trouble nah mek, we good... Me affi get back to the meeting with Snoop them."

"Ah, mii shout yuh if anything else pop up," he assures me.

"Nah mek she handle her business, just make sure them safe if nuttin pop off weh well serious."

"Ah," Slyme's voice comes through the speakers.

I click to end the call before shaking my head. Standing up from my chair, I start to pace my office– the list of things I have to deal with, floating across my thoughts.

Intel on Mase and what next to do...

Ryleigh just being Ryleigh...

Paul and Mum...

My classes...

Trade issues with the Venezuelans...

The few properties that have failed closing inspections because the man dem wah scrape money and cheap out the thing.

One thing after the bloodclawt next. Dadz woulda livid!

Walking to the mini bar, I pour myself the fourth glass of whiskey since I've been in here.

Is this a switch from one substance to the next?

Alcohol fi weed? Just might be…

I walk back to my chair deciding to clear my mind of all things except Mase.

Sending the signal to Ramone, I sit back and wait for my monitor to come to life. In less than a minute it does, with Snoop and Buckle both on the other line ready to tell me everything they've gathered over the past couple of weeks.

Minutes fly past and I decide to end the call.

Weh me just learn a while ago detrimental. People ago dead and a that me neva want…

Picking up my phone, I call Slyme to let him know to get the girls out before twelve midnight.

I lean back in my chair and chuckle, finding the new information amusing.

• • •

RYLEIGH

Supm bout this explanation yah just sit down pah me chest. It nah add up and a 1 me get inna Add Maths so supm no right.

"So she went missing for some time after high school and when she was back, you had a son?" I ask, ensuring my eyes meet his.

The question wasn't how or when she got pregnant enuh. It was how me just a know him a father after weeks of talking.

And why she feel comfortable enough fi step to we

'Cause we all know if the child is under five, the relationship is still alive…

He starts to say something but, I cut him off, "How old is he?"

"Four soon to be five."

Same thing

He's 23, which puts us back to 18… minus 9 months? So he would've been 17? Give or take some months… but she left after graduation… Graduation a normally May, June? and she came back with a 4 month old the following July?

Somebody check that fimi…

I start giggling and he looks at me in confusion settling on his face.

"Jacen, you said the last time you guys had sex was the Easter before graduation? If you're not lying that puts the birth at November-January, depending on full term growth, so how she come back with a 4 month old July?… Yah lie to me? 'Cause I don't miss a timeline, never have, never will," I say proudly.

He taps his fingers on the steering, searching for an appropriate answer but comes up empty.

"Hmph, you're ly–" I attempt to say something else but there is now a tap on the window.

It's Lorelle.

I roll the window down to look at her with a questioning smile.

"Slyme say, say ummm… such man say fi wrap it up."

Excuse me?

I look at my phone to see that it's minutes to 11pm.

"Me affi leave in a couple hours anyway," Jacen says, keeping his gaze ahead.

"I'm staying until you leave…" I turn to him, sporting my signature smile, watching his demeanor change from tense and worried to relax– with slight happiness.

Without saying a word, I exit the car and walk back to where my friends are gathered.

Then what a way you willing fi look past the lies

Be quiet…

"Yuh good?" Mariah asks, searching my face for genuine hints.

"No, me know him just lie to me and carry me 'round bay corner, but see 'cause me no have sex fi a year and adddd, anything the boy say a it me a work wid."

My choice of words sends Keif almost on the ground laughing. Mariah and Lorelle hold each other, humping while creating fake moans.

"Then me give unuh joke? Memba from me leff New York, as a yam, me no take no more pipe, up to noowwww as a faithful yam. So me no willing fi give up this one yet," I laugh, while shaking my head left to right frantically.

"Then you plan fi be 'Aunty Ry' to the man son?" Lorelle questions.

"And enemy number one to Little Miss Anansi," Mariah adds.

"See it clear say unuh nah understand. The pipe me say me want and that's all me a collect, me no say nothing 'bout no iPad addict."

They all start laughing again.

While they sober up, I pull them all into a hug, extend my goodbyes and walk back to the car.

"Ready?" Jacen asks.

"Ready babe," I offer him a reply, moving my hand to hold his.

• • •

JORDANNE

"Mah board now so me supposed to be there by 2:30, 3ish," I say to Skulli.

"Ah me ago deh a foot."

"Good," is my only word before hanging up.

I board the jet and the first thing I notice is what the attendant is wearing. Did not know they had a gentleman's club version of the uniforms. She notices my stare and bites down on her lips. I offer her a small smile before moving to the lounge.

Can still remember how I enjoyed this lounge with Ryleigh. Hmm… anuh supm fi forget.

I sit down, picking up her favorite brand of cashews, deciding to have a few before I take a nap.

• • •

2:30am

When I hear instructions to strap in for landing, I jump up. Moving to the chair across from the bed, I sit down and strap in.

Within thirty minutes, we land in Montego Bay, and a sinister smile creeps across my face.

Mek we do this nuh

• • •

Skulli and I pull into the safe house near Rose Heights. I notice how there are no vehicles lining the streets, drawing any unnecessary attention to us.

I smile like a proud father.

Man dem with it man

Slapping my prints on the access pad, the door clicks open and I enter. More than 55 men and five women are standing around waiting for my go ahead. My top team from Kingston is present, along with those stationed north-west. I spot Surgeon standing to the corner, packing medical kits in case we have any injuries tonight.

Bullet proof vests, guns, corresponding ammunition, maps and a host of other equipment are being passed around too.

Being satisfied with the current order of things, I decide to speak. I usually leave the chatting to Skulli but tonight is personal.

"So everybody know the plan, but not everybody know the details… Over the past year, more recently the past three months, certain things have been revealed to me about my father's passing and a coup I thought I handled, not knowing the depth of it," they all start to mumble but I raise my hands, signaling silence.

"Mase has been moved to the Richmond Farm prison in St. Mary. The north-east team was sent earlier to eject him and bring him to us. Whoever will be here when he gets in, leave him alive… we need to speak. For the rest of us that are going to handle business here in Mobay, let's get the ball rolling."

"Law…" Skulli approves.

"Lawww," they say all at once.

With that, myself and a team of no less than 40 leave the house in groups of four.
Night yah ago be a night to remember.

• • •

RYLEIGH

"Uhhh," I moan as he plays with my nipples.

"Yuh flawless," he groans and moves his head down to cover my right boob in one swallow.

I take the opportunity to look at the time on my phone– 4:43am.

I decide to go for it.

Might as well

Holding his head, I direct it between my widened legs. He doesn't hesitate to shift my panties and start tongue fucking me, but I want clit play.

This has to be quick.

"Clit," I moan, grabbing his hair before raking my fingers through.

He doesn't protest, instead he gobbles it up gently. Releasing it, he starts moving his tongue up and down at a steady pace.

Hurry up!

I look at my phone again to see, 4:45am.

"Fas–terrr," I moan, and he lifts me, positioning my entrance closer to his face.

Before that movement is done the door flies open.

"Rome!" a young man screams but before he can say anything else he falls to the ground.

Rome and I look at each other before I swing off the bed, pulling my dress down. Next thing I know, Jordanne enters the room.

"Ryleigh me hear moaning enuh," he almost says it as a question– throwing a pistol at me.

I hiss while catching it.

What a boy ears good.

"A me make you take forever? You said 4:30 the latest," pulling my hair into a top knot, I look at him, but he doesn't shift his eyes from Jacen.

"So you did ago fuck him if me neigh reach in time?" now with his nostrils flared, holding a tighter grip on the Mac-10.

"Just a one headas, retribution fi Emily... and the new girls every week," I smile.

Jacen is now in complete shock but doesn't move, as he's half naked and unarmed with Jordanne's gun pointed at his skull. I watch as Jordanne snakes his hand around to check if the silencer is screwed tight.

"Pussy duh even think 'bout it," he stops Rome from trying to shift.

"Ryleigh?" Jacen looks over at me, but I don't look back.

Now anuh the time fi we sorry fi him

"Say nuttin to me woman again and me done everything right now," Jordanne sneers.

I adjust the gun in my hand and walk over to him.

He places a kiss on my forehead and says, "You did well babe."

I hiss internally, upset at the fact that mi nuh get me lick back– not even cum.

"Move in," J' speaks again, still keeping his focus on Jacen.

A group of men I've probably never seen, move into the room and start restraining Jacen. My head involuntarily turns away, while my heart is swallowed by a tinge of sadness. I actually liked him, until Jordanne called me via Ramone's weird ass encrypted line on that day after Toni and I made up. He told me what he found out and what he was going to do, with or without my approval.

I offered to help, and at first he wasn't having it, but then he came around to the idea when I suggested it would cost less lives lost. We spoke until the sun came up that morning, about trying again... on us. I told him I would, under the condition that he goes to therapy to work on himself, as I've been doing since September... and maybe sometime in the future we could 'go together'... and we left things there.

It was not until **earlier tonight**, when Ramone connected us, that he told me he connected Mase and Rome in an even more interesting way than we initially thought. Mase is the Godfather Rome kept saying was dead.

Imagine...

Look how me nearly go full on deh with the man super enemy. Whole time I thought it was just an ego trip. Let's all just blame my stubbornness.

"C'mere, let's get you home," Jordanne mumbles, pulling me from the room and down the hallway.

As we move down the hallway, my eyes spot a shocked Skulli.

I offer him a smile, knowing he never expected to see me of all persons here. Jordanne normally tells him everything, I'm not sure why he didn't tell him this time. I understand why everybody else had to be in the dark but him?

We need to ask, what's with the rift between them

We exit the hallway, and I start to see bodies piled up.

My skin crawls...

Jordanne must've sensed it and decided to pull me tighter, moving us faster to get outside. We get into an unfamiliar car, and just like that we're off to wherever 'home' is in Montego Bay.

The villa?

The house?

The apartment?

I haven't a clue.

"So yuh really did ago mek the man jook you babe?!" Jordanne starts again.

"Jook Jordanne?" I laugh at the word he chose, "yuh no think that fair?"

"Ryleigh me tell you me nuh have sex with the girl dem enuh," he glances at me.

"And me never did ago have sex with Jacen either. Head, like you said the girls gave you," I smile cocking my head to the side.

"Jah know? We never even together at the time…" he mumbles lowly but I catch it, turning my whole body to glare at him.

"Ah, Ah, buil, buil," he laughs out loud.

Shifting my body back towards the door, I stare out the window, just watching as the road moves.

Two more minutes and me woulda water the boy face

I rub my shoulders at the thought before releasing another giggle while bringing the seat back to relax, since I'm not sure how long this ride will be.

What a night

29 | Mission

JORDANNE

It's been less than five minutes and she's already asleep. I swear, once she gets around me, she either sleep, eat or argue.

Pulling into the safe house, I dim my headlights and decide to leave the car in the driveway instead of the garage.

I can't stay…

My phone has already been going off from Skulli wanting to know why he was left out of this leg of the mission. I had no reason, it was just between me, Ry' and Ramone for obvious reasons.

The weight of Ryleigh in my arms pull me back from my thoughts.

Girl heavy yuh fuck

Can't wait fi–

Focus

"J?" she stirs, her eyes fluttering open.

"Babe?" I mutter, focusing on trying to figure out how to get my palm on the code screen with her in my hands.

She continues to say something, but I ignore her to throw her over my shoulder– since she wake and decide fi buss ears.

The sun a come up enuh bredda

The time window is closing.

"Jordanne I could've walked, you out here a struggle," she giggles.

The door clicks open and I sigh.

Now you affi tell her we a leave

I bring her all the way up the stairs and into the master suite, ignoring her protests for me to let her walk.

"Ryleigh me have something fi deal with a Hanover before daybreak. I need you to stay put until I get back," I speak firmly while putting her to stand.

She rubs her eyes while yawning.

"Weh you say?" she questions– her voice decorated with drowsiness.

"Ago deal with something and come back," I repeat, this time placing a kiss on her forehead.

"Jordanne, me one nah stay here. Why you carry me come fi leff me yah so?" her argument is digging into my time.

"Ryleigh just do wah me say fi once. Mah be back before midday. Ramone ago work from here and Slyme should be back from Kingston any minute now to be here with you until me drop back a foot… You know the place fully secured so what's the real issue?"

She rolls her eyes.

"I don't know, you have a habit of leaving women in houses to go see other women," her lips now pressed into a sarcastic smile.

Yuh nah live that down enuh yo

Jah Jah.

"Really Ry'?" I think about not explaining shit to her, because I don't have to with anybody else, but… it's her.

I hiss internally. Why she no just listen? The trust cyaa still broken after what we just pulled.

"Yeah really," she retorts.

A heavy heave leaves my lips.

"There is something else happening right now. I can't tell you the details, but I have to go meet up with the team. Affi mek it to West before sun ripe outside so please just understand."

She tries to say something but I continue, "Keep your phone off until I'm back and if anything go wrong, the elevator is to the back-left of the hallway on the first floor. Your prints have been activated for this location. Press 'U' for underground, enter the code I gave you earlier and stay there. DO NOT USE YOUR PHONE until I'm back, Ry' not even fi scroll IG" I hold her gaze.

She shouldn't even involved ina the first place. She should be as far away from this side of my life as possible. I saw what being involved did to my mom and in turn her relationship with Dadz.

"Ok… I guess," she shrugs, trying to hide the worry in her eyes.

I decide to soothe it. No worry no fi deh pon her brain.

"Me ago good man, the riskiest part of the job done," and while pulling her up for a kiss, I realize just how much I've missed her.

• • •

RYLEIGH

"Me ago good man, the riskiest part of the job done," He pulls away with lust in his eyes.

Ryleigh that's love

"Mek sure you get back, on time too," I nudge him, feigning discipline.

He laughs and shakes his head, pulling out his phone that's been going off for the last ten minutes.

Unuh ago tell me anuh woman?

"Skulli... Mah meet unuh there......Yeah...... Everything get take care of? Ah...... Swing past the main then and me just join the line so we drive down together...... Ramone and Slyme...... She good man...... North East team reach and secured 'bout an hour ago...... Dat good... A drive out now."

That sound like woman to you? Yuh fi shame

Can't shake the trust issues, but I'm doing better at least.

I watch him pat himself down for his keys before taking my hand. He kisses the back of my palm, eyes finding mine.

"You remember the shower routine I told you about?" his eyes search mine for confirmation.

I do remember.

"Yeah but I can shower normally right? I didn't have to use the pistol," my tone holding a hint of disappointment.

He smiles, reading my expression.

"No, do it still, no chances," he commands, and I nod.

He then releases my hand and exits the room. I grab all the things I'm supposed to use and head to the bathroom. Before stepping inside the shower, I strip, and ball my clothes up to put into a ziplock bag like he told me.

My favourite dress.

Ramone will know what to do with it.

Trying to switch my thoughts from being anxious to relaxed, I step into the shower, allowing the warm water to flow from the top of my head down to my toes.

You feel bad don't you?

I do... I feel bad for Rome. I just know Mr.Mase had a bigger part in this. Jacen will have to bear the burden of death while Mase gets to just stay in prison. Finding out he had a son tonight is making it even harder.

But I have to understand these things if I want to be with Jordanne, right?

Right???

I don't know, something about it isn't sitting well with me. According to him I should just trust him. He didn't even want me involved at all in the first place, so let me be quiet.

• • •

JORDANNE

I pull into the line of cars right on time. We should get to our destination in no more than an hour, hour and five minutes max.

… And with how all a di man dem drive, dat might chop ina half.

I laugh to myself.

Hope them buil and nobody no get pulled over fi speeding. Cyaa risk dat.

Within fifty minutes we're all on location. I exit my car and walk over to Skulli who is now glaring at me, his face filled with unanswered questions.

Have some questions me wah ask him too…

"Boss the East team say him a make a fuss," I hear Paw's voice.

As me reach a supm killa.

"Eeeh? Mek him continue then nuh, we a wait pon the son," I smile, knowing Dalani is less than ten minutes out, according to Ramone.

I need to hear what exactly him, Mase and him long lost God son Rome have fi say.

I need details…

Of those involved…

Who sold them intel…

Who the mastermind is…

My mind a say a Mase but something 'bout it a say Rome and then a tiny feeling a shout Dalani– so mek we see.

Walking to the elevator with Paw and Skulli on my heel, I spot Surgeon coming up the steps from the storeroom.

"Everything good?" I ask.

"Yeah man, him did unconscious for a while but me… revive him, if you wah call it that."

Paw chuckles and Skulli smiles in approval.

But me? I'm not in the mood today. This is very personal to me.

And yuh wah done and go home to you woman

That too…

I access the code pad, we enter and press the button to our floor– each person taking a corner of the elevator for themselves. There is still tension between Paul and I… and I think Paw just realized it.

"How the man dem so quiet?" he chuckles lowly, looking at us both.

"No know why Skulli so quiet," I laugh, but nothing about it exudes humor.

He tries to say something, but the ding of the door interrupts him and I exit without another thought.

"Prison neva enough fi you?" Mase blurts out as soon as I come into his view, now pulling on his restraints.

He's tied up, stretched at all four limbs, head hanging to the side. I'm surprised he had the strength to say that to me.

He looks a mess.

Ignoring him, I grab the chair directly in front of him. Spinning it to the entrance, I take a seat wanting to see the exact look on Dalani's face when he enters.

Paw and Skulli are standing in their respective corners.

We wait for less than a minute before the elevator dings open to reveal Surgeon, two of my guys from the Mobay post and the big man himself, Jacen.

Haha!

Ahh kill him just fi even thinkkkk 'bout me woman.

Mi heart... My world...

Yeah you in love we get it. Where is Dalani Mase Jr.?

Hmmm...

I take a quick glance at my watch to see that it's now 6:40am.

Man ago mek Ryleigh argue with you 'bout the time enuh

Affi wrap this up quickly. I look at Paw who shrugs knowingly.

"Ramone say him due anytime now boss," he assures me, causing me to avert my attention back to Rome who is being chained up the exact way Mase is.

He's not protesting at all.

The sound of the elevator brings my attention to the entrance, and I turn just in time to catch the look on Dalani's face.

His eyes move to me and I smirk. He tries to press the button to go back up but–

"Bad idea dat chief," I laugh, and that's the first time I've found something funny all mission.

Paw and Skulli are with him in seconds, taking him to his restraints.

Yeah man, string dem up.

Beautiful

I smile while eyeing them, just admiring how all three of them are helpless and at my mercy.

"Alright, time fi some fun. Me woman a wait," I chuckle.

30 | Mission Part TWO

JORDANNE

The door dings open again and I'm happy to see Snoop and Buckle step in. For a split second I think about how they accessed the elevator but then I remember Ramone added a few trusted members just until the mission is over.

Supm else deh pah me mind...

Few other things actually, but that one thi–

Focus yute

"So gentlemen, I have a few questions I need answers to, just for clarification. If you're thinking about lying, I suggest you don't. Paw is eager to remove limbs and Skulli ova yah so, finds all this as entertainment."

"My guys Snoop and Buckle here, gathered enough info to let me know that this plan started before Dadz drop out... Nahgo tell unuh wah me know, so start think from now. Anybody wah volunteer to speak first?" my eyes find Rome.

Dalani shifts...

Mase spits blood and pulls on his restraints.

Rome doesn't move.

"The man a wait enuh," Skulli walks over to Mase.

I swear him hate him on ah next level.

A moment of silence goes by, stretching my patience thin. Realizing I still have my bullet proof vest on, I decide to take it off. Rolling my sleeves up, I start pacing back and forth, fighting the impatient thoughts in my mind.

"Unuh ago make me pick somebody?" I ask, but don't give them a chance to protest. "Jacen? me feel since you did so bold these past weeks you woulda run chat first?" my tone now laced with the drug of vengeance.

Have a mind just torture them without questions, but I need to know if anybody else was involved.

Mase shuffles and I look to him... In that same second his head falls back down. Irritated by that action, I nod at Surgeon. He moves to rub a substance I don't know enough about at his nostrils. The effects of it are shown by Mase now reeling and screaming.

Seconds pass while I wait for him to relax... and when he's finally calm enough, I ask, "Ready now?"

"Your father...... Sheer... did a plan fi cut me out, both me and the man 'round deh suh–Skulli... 'cause him find out him a dig out you whoring mumma."

I pause, just to ensure my emotions don't play a part in the decision. Certain him say that to dig at them, with the assumption I'm clueless.

It would've worked had Ryleigh not pissed me off with her likkle idiot man. I wouldn't have called Skulli dem hours deh when him off duty fi drop me a no airport.

God reveals all, no joke.

Skulli's hand moves to his waist, but I shake my head in disapproval.

"Continue," is the only word that leaves my mouth.

"When me find out me tell Paul and I don't know weh him do or say, but weeks pass and Sheer no deal with none a we. Me of all persons, weh never involved ina Sue slackness... Days after, me ago over the books and find the new arrangement. As soon as you became 25 you would take his spot and if he were to die before that, all control would go to you at the age of 18," he spits again.

I keep my eyes on him.

Everything matches the intel so far.

"... but if you both were to die then, I would assume the role. No man no wah no teenager at the top rank in the streets."

Paw snickers at his follow up statement and Skulli hisses his teeth.

I glance at them and back to Mase.

He continues, "So me bring him out fi a drink a Ochi after him call and a vent 'bout you mother. Easy thing fi get to the brakes once him park up. Neva know you woulda survive that. Understand say me and you father a come from primary school days and the man did ago cut me outa supm we built together," he ends.

Rome laughs... First reaction dat outa him.

"You wah go next?" I lend him the attention he clearly wants.

"Lie him a tell," is all he says before hanging his head back in place.

"Speak then," I suggest.

"A the son. Before you even take over, I was open to the idea of falling under your command until my God brother here, convinced me otherwise. Man say you soon ago deh a foreign and you focus deh more pon woman than anything else... Say yah teach him the books, routes and inner security, so if mi hold out and no take your deal we can take over together. Man say him go after you woman but him girl did a get jealous so him switch plans. Say me fi get into her birthday party and him ago make him girl send pictures to somebody name Emily. The night of the party me barely see the Ghale girl, but somehow the pictures reach Emily anyway… A wah day me a hear say a Ghale let her ina the property," he gasps and I signal to Surgeon to get him some water.

Pusssssssyyyyyclawttttt

The man whistle enuh… Big snitch, I smile to myself.

Connect…

Connecttt…

Connecttttt…

A cloud of silence settles around us– disbelief plastered on everybody's faces.

Dalani act like him ah idiot but him sensible

Jah Jah…

Surgeon starts feeding Rome from a small bottle of water. He takes a moment to recover, and I move from standing, back to the chair.

Rome picks up, "All me did affi do is get Ryleigh fi like me, and them say you would be off your game or leave. So said, so done. You left… the problem was I started to actually like Stevens."

My brow quirks up in that same breath. Is a nickname him have fi me heart?

Her surname dat bad head

Still…

What he's saying is connecting all the missing pieces. It had to be Dalani, nobody else has that much access to fuck things up at this magnitude… but Ghale? Ghale is a fucking surprise.

"Me father raise you from you idiot people dem dead off and yah sell we out right now?" Dalani's voice is laced with the sound of hate.

"Me deven rate none a unuh. A long time Cherry a tell me unuh a fuckry. Nah give up my life fi unuh. Me have mi yute," he hisses before weakness forces his head back to hanging.

I laugh out and I mean really laugh.

Mase really think him did ago get weh with this? Even if they had killed both me and Dadz in the crash, Sue is a force to be reckoned with– worse a Skulli a speak fi her now.

Ridiculous plan and execution

"Man dem pathetic," I chuckle.

Not knowing if I should kill Jacen or not… I start pacing around the room, trying to quiet my sinister thoughts. The intel says that Mase had his parents killed and it doesn't sound like he knows.

Should I tell him, is the real question.

Jah.

Him have a son, break the cycle

Going against all the cells in my body, I turn to Paw before saying, "Release him."

"Fuck you mean Drip???" Skulli's voice comes across the room.

The tone of his question sends me over the cliff I've been hanging onto. I walk over to him, grab his throat and bring him to the wall.

"Stop fucking undermine me and just listen," my fingers firm, venom coursing through my veins.

I don't care how open my parents' marriage was, Sue and Paul wrong fi weh dem do. Realizing my anger has grown, I release him and move away. Paw moves to release Rome and I instruct Snoop and Buckle to get the anchors.

I need Ghale here. If it takes all morning, Ryleigh affi go understand.

"Where is Ghale?" I ask, glaring at the great Dalani Mase.

Junior or Senior?

Both at this point.

None of them come up with an answer.

"Skulli bring the toolbox," I smile.

On my words, he moves to the tiny closet towards the back of the basement. In less than a minute he's back with said box.

"Leff it deh so," I point to a small table off to the side.

By this, Paw and Surgeon are tending to Rome while Snoop and buckle are back with the anchors. They move over to the Mase's and a confused look graces both their faces.

I would be confused too.

"Weh yuh girl Dalani?" I repeat, picking up a scalpel.

This should be fun...

"She no ina the island," the father's voice barely makes out the words.

"So if I were to call my heart right now, and ask her to ring her, she would tell me she was abroad?" my smile now even wider than before.

"No," Dalani finally speaks up.

"Wow, you're back," I chuckle. "Sooo, weh she deh?"

"Mi nah tell you dawg," he mumbles.

I move towards him.

Obviously them think me have time fi waste. Is a miserable woman deh ah the house a wait pah me killa.

I take the scalpel and run it along his wrist. He stifles his screams but the veins popping out his forehead speak for him.

Drip... Drop...

"You have less than thirty seconds to tell me where she is, before you pass out. It only takes two minutes to bleed to death from a radial artery cut, you decide... twenty seconds," I smile, cocking my head to the side.

"Here! Here! She deh yah!" the father shouts.

I snap my fingers to Surgeon who walks over to Dalani– his eyes now fluttering.

"Thank you. Cyaa guarantee he will live though," I mumble to Mase, whose feet are now being connected to a block of iron.

Perfect

"The son too, whether him make it or not," I add final instructions to Snoop and Buckle.

Mase starts mumbling something, but he's too weak to speak aloud and I'm too impatient to care.

I turn to Skulli, "Find supm do with Rome until I'm back here later tonight. I'll make a decision when I get back."

 He nods but says nothing verbally.

"Where exactly is Ghale?" I ask the father.

"The post in West Village, the town house. This idiot never wah leave her a Kingston," he spits.

I assume he's willingly offering more information, thinking I'll grant one of them mercy.

"Good! Less time wasted for me," I chuckle. "Surgeon cut the fuckry, we both know you can't save him with just stitches. Me wah go home within the hour... Sorry Mase but me no willing fi save none a unuh. Thanks for the info though."

I don't know where he gets the energy, but he spits at me almost having it land.

Nothing me hate more than that... I walk over to him and deliver a punch directly to his windpipe– certain I broke it.

The impact have him a gulp and a gasp.

"Skulli when the anchors are fully attached, bring Buckle, Snoop and two others with you to sea. Go as far out as you can and make sure yuh stay for an hour after dropping them in. Slyme ago get Ghale and bring her here."

He nods.

Man nah talk fi the rest a the day?

I wanted them both to be dumped in alive so them can fight fi them life while they drown but Dalani pissed me the fuck off.

"Skulli, when we reach Kingston tomorrow, me need fi talk to you and Sue. Dat good?

He nods again...

With that I turn on my heels to find my way upstairs to the shower.

Time fi go to me baby...

... and rest my brain until Ghale reach.

31 | M.I.N.E

RYLEIGH

My eyes find the wall clock for the millionth time since I woke up. This time it's saying 11:57am which means, Jordanne might not be back in time.

He said midday right?

Ryleigh the man has three minutes

Two minutes, 57 seconds…

I decide to walk downstairs. Earlier I fell asleep after handing my clothes to Ramone and heading back upstairs. I slept like a baby, regardless of what I saw earlier today.

Crazy right?

I get to the kitchen…

Nobody.

I move to the living area…

Nobody.

I walk to Ramone's office, and surely enough, there they are– playing FIFA. They don't even notice me. The men left here to protect me, don't even notice my footsteps.

I turn to walk off.

"Him soon reach Ryleigh," Slyme speaks, without looking up from the game.

Oh?

Ramone laughs, "The man call me thousand time."

I smile while suddenly becoming conscious of what I'm wearing. It's a basic cotton shorts and top, but my ass keeps eating away the shorts.

I should get newly sized house clothes.

Why?

For you know, when I have visitors?

My head pops around, following the sound of an engine pulling in.

You ago bruk you neck fi man?

My man? Yeah.

I find myself smiling and I start thinking of things to do, to not seem like a creep. In that same instant the sound of footsteps startle me.

It's Ramone. He looks at me and we both double over from laughter.

"Wah kinda joke yah give me woman Ramone?" J's voice covers the room.

"Inside joke boss," we both start laughing again while Slyme exits the office, trying to look just as busy and as serious as Ramone and I just were.

"Me hear the game from outside man… Slyme from you drop Ghale a in deh so unuh deh a play match?"

Ghale?!

Slyme tries to explain but both Ramone and Jordanne start laughing immediately.

"Unuh fuck off," Slyme chuckles.

Today would be the first I've heard him say more than two words in under 24 hours. Nah, I'm being extra but he really doesn't talk a lot. Paw is the funny one and Ramone is the corny type… while Skulli is much older and much more serious.

We need fi ask why J' and Skulli a behave so

I will.

Jordanne puts a duffel bag down on the kitchen counter before saying, "Ryleigh…" while biting down on his lips.

Before I get a chance to respond, he lifts me onto the island.

"Mek we cut," Ramone suggests to Slyme, "the West Village town house empty," he continues.

"Nuh know why unuh still present," Jordanne chuckles.

Ramone grabs his keys while laughing and they both end up out the door before Jordanne can stick his tongue down my throat.

With our bodies almost merged, I realize how fresh he is and pull away…

He reads my eyes.

"Ryleigh don't start. I took a shower on location because I didn't want to wait when I got to you. I've been waiting a year and four months," he explains.

Who?

Him?

Be for real right now.

"No IIIIIII've been waiting a year and four months. You've been waiting four months and who knows, maybe only two weeks," my eyes now almost rolling from my head.

He doesn't answer.

Therapist said to leave the blows in the past

Fuck the therapist… but fine.

He attempts to say something but I fear killing the mood, so I pull him in for another kiss. Tracing my hand down his shoulders, I quiver.

He's built so nice, so firm, so stro–

Before I can finish my thought, he's grabbing at my blouse, trying to pull it over my head. Our breathing becomes ragged, replacing the silence in the house. In the next second, he is tugging at my shorts. I lay back on the counter and tilt my pelvis up for him to pull them down. He rips them off in less than a second, throwing them over his shoulders.

"Open," he groans, barely audible.

I do as I'm told.

"Wider."

 I spread them further.

"Wider," he repeats, and I decide to swing them towards my shoulders.

"Perfect," he groans.

I smile.

Halfway through that smile, he ends up between my legs, chowing down on my sweet spot. I hold onto my ankles for dear life, welcoming the euphoric feeling.

With what's happening now, we can never host in this kitchen, can we?

He realizes I'm stuck in my thoughts and speeds up his tongue movements.

"Woahhhh… oahhhaa… J–orrr–dannnne," my moans send us both into a frenzy.

He inserts two fingers at once, dragging a high-pitched squeal from my lips. I missed those fingers. Big, long, clean fingers.

He bends them upward and it hits my spot.

"Jeeeeeesuuuuuuusssss!!!" I scream.

"Jordanne," he comes up to say.

I shove his head back down and can feel when he smiles against my lips.

The pace of his fingers slow, he twists them carefully and starts to move his tongue in a vertical motion. He swipes from where his fingers are stuck at my entrance, all the way up to my clit… and back…

… and forth.

And back,

… anddddd fooorthhh.

"Fuckkkkk," I moan, arching my back while holding his head steady.

My toes start curling and my eyes hit the back of my fucking head.

Jesus, mercyyy.

"Aaahhhh yeahhhsssss," I reel under his hold as my orgasm moves through my body.

My legs start to shake and I release my ankles. Like reflex he catches one of them with his free hand and holds it back. Looking up at me, he continues to swirl his perfect tongue back and forth. Each time I get close to the edge he slows the pace, as some sort of punishment.

"Jordanne please," my plea comes out croaky and my eyes find him.

He holds my stare while still eating away, raising his brows as if to say 'please what?'

"Please… make me cum," I manage to get out.

All my senses are now leaving… all except touch. He stops completely, still looking at me, so I search his eyes for what he wants. We haven't had sex in so long, I don't remember the cues.

"Please… J'… let me cum in your mouth."

You would think I entered the code to one of his panic rooms the way he moves on command. He brings his fingers back up and to the roof of my pussy, hitting the spot that turns on the flood pipes.

I start wiggling, fighting the sudden urge to pee.

It's not pee

He slaps my ass, as if to reiterate what my subconscious just said… and just like that, I'm spraying.

• • •

JORDANNE

I slap her ass, knowing she's resisting the pull of the squirt. She gives in… and just like that, she creates a waterfall.

That's my girl.

"Good girl," I come up to whisper in her ear.

My shirt is soakedddd. I look down at her, noticing she's seconds away from dreamland. Swinging her up and over my shoulders, I decide to bring her up the stairs.

"Babe, what happened?" she questions when we get to the top of the staircase.

"You knock out," with a smug grin on my face, I continue to the room.

"I can sense you smiling," she giggles.

We get to the room and I waste no time.

"Same position, I want to see it," I demand.

She doesn't hesitate, swinging her feet back towards her face while looking directly into my eyes.

Woahhh

I can just look at it and know it's going to be the death of me. I start stripping but she gets impatient and starts rubbing her clit.

Wow

WOW

Wowww…

Shoulda pray before this.

"If you wait another second, I'll fuck myself," she whines.

I chuckle.

While moving to the bed, I'm careful not to brush my dick against anything for fear of an explosion. Di ting rock hard and by the looks of it, the veins are about to pop.

Hovering above her entrapping figure, I slide in… but regret it the moment I do. To buy even more time, I pull out and start using it to beat her clit. She moans from frustration, while holding onto her nipples. Just the sight of her is bringing me to heaven. Me need fi look away, think 'bout something else…

I try to do just that but fail.

"Jordanne?" she questions, and I snap back to reality.

I slip inside her again, this time she pulls me down to her, holding me firmly in place— no escape. She brings her legs around my waist before lapping them together. I move to capture her nipple and I feel when her walls grip me, sucking my dick into her paradise.

My body shudders and a moan leaves my lips.

The raw sense of pleasure forces my head up, and I look, to find her squinting.

"Look at me," I instruct, sinking deeper— but moving at a very slow pace.

In…

…and

Out…

She looks at me for a second then breaks the stare.

"Look."

"At."

"Me," each word accompanied by a stroke.

She's a shaking mess but I want to pull the orgasm out of her gradually. As I slam into her slowly, her juices sing their own song while creating their own spring.

Slippery.

Slippery as fuck!

I catch her almost breaking the stare while I go deeper— begging for her to try me but she doesn't.

Good, I smile.

"Jordanne, I can't handle the edging," she moans, her eyes glistening.

Me baby…

"Yes you can Love…" and with that, I ease up but not out. Her legs set me free and I find her clit with my thumb.

"Oooohhhh myyy–" she shudders, clamping her eyes shut before coming to the end of her moan.

"Look at me Ry," I command and she flies them open.

Continuing at the same slow pace while rubbing and stroking, I admire her juices. They keep flooding my dick while dripping on the sheets and I don't know what it is, but I find that beautiful.

Wanting more of that show, I quicken the pace on her clit, stopping the strokes altogether, with my dick still inside. Her walls start clamping me, just like I knew they would, while I bring her to her climax.

Love that.

"I'm cummmingggg!!!!"

"I know baby," my smile now present while I hold the stare…

… And with that, she becomes undone. Her climatic shudders are one to experience. The entire experience itself… Her walls convulsing, the moans, the gripping and her warm juices set to drown my dick.

● ● ●

RYLEIGH

I've missed him so much.

I love him so much.

I want to have his children.

A wah do you girl?

That was goooood.

He's a little too smug for me though. I watch as he eases out and I know he's about to suggest a backazz but I want to ride, so I slide from the bed not caring where my juices land.

"Lay down," I smile.

He cocks his head to the side and I nod to confirm what I said.

"Yeah," I speak again.

He gets on the bed, lying flat while resting his hands behind his head. With my eyes set on him, I hover for a second before deciding on reverse cowgirl. It gives him the view of a backazz, but with the feel of my control.

Yessss

Holding his dick myself, I slide down slowly to the beat of his moans. As soon as I get to the root, his hands move to my ass. Climbing to my tippy toes, I begin a slow ride.

Up and down…

Up and downnn…

I get to the tip and go around.

"Fuck Ry," he groans but I don't give him the chance to recoup– I'm back down to the root taking all his length in one go.

"Bumboclawttt," he hisses in pleasure.

I throw my head back and sit there rubbing myself. The wall mirror in-front us reveal my devious actions, causing him to pull my hair and slap my ass a few times. Moving my hands from myself, I move down to grip his ankles. When I have a firm grip, I find a comfortable momentum.

This is how I'm making him cum today...

I look between my legs at the sight of him going in and out and it turns me on.

"Ryleigh, I fucking love you," he grunts.

I love him too.

"I love you too J'," I moan, now picking up the pace.

When I get to the tip, I stay there, riding it from that distance. He starts losing his mind and I'm enjoying it. His breathing has even become more ragged...

He's near.

I pick up the pace even more while slamming it down on him– wanting to pull it out of him. In an instant, my waist is grabbed and that alone sends us both over the edge.

We become undone together, moaning all types of 'I love yous.'

I fall forward and he falls back. We stay like this for a minute before shifting to find our way to the shower.

• • •

We had another round in the shower... and phewwww, I'm drained.

I climb into bed beside him, ready to cuddle for the rest of our day.

"Slyme dem a bring food," he breaks the comfortable silence.

"If I can stay up to eat it, I will," I cheese at him.

He kisses my forehead before pulling me into his arms.

"What's with you and Skulli? and why is Ghale here on Boxing Day?" I ask what I've been meaning to– not wanting to forget.

"Ryleigh how you fasss so?" he laughs. "I'll tell you when we've slept and eaten, promise."

"Fair enough," I yawn, nuzzling into his chest.

Within minutes, I enter dreamland.

32 | Leap

RYLEIGH

We're on our way back to Kingston and he's only told me Ghale was involved in Mase's plan. Ghale enuh… imagine that.

Me say my spirit never wrong yet.

He refuses to tell me how he got Mase out of prison or what he did to him, his son or Jacen. Jacen… I keep telling him I don't think he was dishonest for most of the time, but he keeps ignoring me.

Chalk it up to his jealous tendency.

Yuh easy fi sorry fah too much

I just don't think a son should lose his father. Call me dumb or whateva.

"So why did you send for Ghale?" I glance over at him. He's speeding home with Slyme on our tail as per usual.

"I won't give you any details on anything else babe. Just rest it," his tone flat.

"Jordanne did you–" I turn completely focusing all my attention to the driver's seat.

"Ry'… me no hurt females, so no, she good. She won't be an issue anymore though. You can sleep wid dat your honor?" his words laced with sarcasm.

"I don't find you funny," I retort, rolling my eyes.

He laughs.

"Wah sweet you?"

"Love when them roll back like that," he smirks, bringing his eyes back to the road.

"Pay attention to the road and stop watch people woman," I joke.

He doesn't laugh…

Murdaaaa! Too soon, too soon

I quickly change the topic to something he would like, "Do you think we should tell everybody at once?" I ask, my fingers now finding the curve of his biceps.

"Tell everybody what?" he asks, barely audible.

"Say we deh Jordanne," I snap, as if it could be anything else.

He immediately starts laughing and I mean lauuuughinngg, to the point where I pull down the mirror to see if I have clown makeup on.

Wah him problem?

He's almost crying at this point.

"Why yah laugh?" I query, needing confirmation because I'm truly clueless.

"Yuh funny. You think people no know? But if you wah keep a town hall meeting then sure," he smiles while sobering up.

I roll my eyes, again.

"But we only start talk couple days ago… last week. I owe it to Toni at least, and Lorelle hate you like poison right now me certain."

Tapping on the center console while digging through my thoughts, I try to explain my thought process.

I feel him glance at me and I avert my attention back to him.

"Dat good, just no think it necessary. Trust me when I say everybody know we never did ago nowhere ina life without each other," his smile grows even wider.

Him have a point.

"I still would like to let everybody know the new wavelength," I repeat my thoughts in similar words.

"When would you wah this 'press conference' held?" he's still smiling at God knows what.

"Tonight, the sooner the better. I don't want to answer any questions when we walk to your room together," my tone switches from slightly stern to gleeful.

Watch the girl weh take 470 years fi realize she want the man

I find myself smiling.

"Can I use my phone now?" my hands already digging through my bag to find it.

"You coulda use the phone from me touch back Ry," he chuckles.

Like him did gimmi a chance…

I decide not to voice my thoughts this time. The memory of us melting into each other sends shivers down my spine. Ignoring the gnawing feeling caused by the flashbacks, I pop my phone out, power it up and toggle my way to send the group chat a message.

9 missed calls from mommy…

145 messages from Bubbas…

230 Instagram notifications…

I ignore everything except for the group chat, on the basis that Jordanne told me he made my mother aware I was with him when he left me at the house to go do whatever he did this morning.

Only reason why ah 9 calls and not 90 with a police report

BUBBAS

Almost home, weh unuh up to ina
the boxing night yah? link up
at Toni's?

Sexy Bitch: Mariah and Muuch done deh yah
already, them no live noweh lol.

Muuch: Me deh yah more than you, a my yard. Nuh
Russell Heights yuh live with Josh?

Mariah: File get read enuh man looool that's why
mi nuh throw stone in yah.

Sexy Bitch: STFU looool a campus me live!

@Dutty Foot @Keif???

Dutty Foot: Mah come yes. Just pick up Keif
ina you nice vehicle, go get some fish.

Mek sure when me get it back gas
in deh bitch.

Dutty Foot: Looool and money a drop offa you and
you man? Yuh wishhhh.

About that... lol later me talk to unuh.

Sexy Bitch: Side eye...

Muuch: That sound so?

I decide not to reply and instead text my mommy.

Mommy me soon reach back, ago ova
Sue, want you there.

Mummy Luv: Me deh yah from evening Ry' a do
Sue hair. So when you land.

I smile to myself and Jordanne shifts his attention to me. For a minute I forgot he was there. He shakes his head knowingly before fixing his attention back to the road.

Another text comes in from a new group I don't know about, "Drama" is the name and the participants are Keif, Lorelle and Mariah.

<u>DRAMA</u>

<u>Mariah:</u> Yuh and Jacen good?

That me have fi tell unuh, you couldn't wait?

<u>Mariah:</u> True me no hear from Ruse since morning.

I decide not to reply… Ruse, Jacen's younger brother. I don't know if he was involved in Jordanne's mission or not, but I know not to say a damn thing.

<u>Dutty Foot:</u> Yeah me did just ago call you so if a later a later.

<u>Keif:</u> Later me down ina the fish.

Ah, love ya'll.

• • •

We're pulling into the garage and my anxiety hits out of nowhere. As if connected to me, Jordanne faces my direction, reaches over and places a soft kiss on my lips.

"No worry nuh ina it," and with that I start cheesing– lips turned up from ear to ear.

Slyme and Ramone are already halfway inside the house. I spot my car so I know Lorelle and Keif are here already too.

Jordanne walks around and opens my door.

Princess treatment enuh

I giggle out, like a fucking 12 year old.

Stepping down and out of the car, he closes the door and locks it, and we make our way to the entrance– hand in hand.

Breathe…

Breathe……

I'm grown, so why nerves a kill me?

He attempts to open the door and my grip on his arm tightens. He stops to find my eyes. Nothing is said but the comfort I get from just his eyes is enough for my nerves to stop dancing.

Pushing the door open, we enter and notice everybody off to the left where the living area is, staring at us.

Joshua is here too… I know if he's downstairs, then so is Toni-Anne.

"Yeah man me win the bet!" Joshua jumps up, holding his hands out to Muuch.

"Which bet?!" Toni asks, staring at them both, who are now arguing as to the confirmation of what seems to be my and J's relationship status.

Murdaaa, the people dem bet pah we to rass. The realization sends a giggle from my mouth. Cyaa believe dem something yah.

Jordanne shakes his head and walks over, leading us to the far couch. My mom and Ms.Sue... or Sue– I'm still trying to get used to just calling her Sue, are CHEEEEESING. The meeting really neva needed fi real.

Slyme, Skulli, Paw and Ramone are now off to a corner drinking amongst each other.

As Slyme and Ramone reach so?

"Wah gwaan yah so?" Lorelle inquires, "me swear Jordanne deh foreign," she continues.

"Me too girl," Mariah looks around, her face plastered with guilt.

She's the one who accepted Jacen and I more than anybody else– since she likes his brother.

"The man is a PJ owner, in and out when him feeeeel like it," Keif says and I don't know if it's her tone or her gimmicks, but it sends us all into a fit of laughter.

We sober up to the sudden sound of Jordanne's voice, "Baby wah keep press conference, so she get a press conference," he shrugs, pulling us down to the single couch.

Everybody's eyes shift to focus on us. All their faces are sporting smiles, except for Toni. Her face holds a weird expression. It's like she's happy but confused, simultaneously.

She ago vex the most 'cause me always a hide things from her, putting her in the weirdest position

Anuh like me did allowed fi say nuttin 'bout it this time...

"Sooo..." I start, while playing with my fingers, "Jordanne and I have ummm... decided to ummm... you know."

"Decided to what? Say it else Muuch nah gimi me 50 gran," Joshua pleads.

T' slaps him before pulling him to sit.

"We decided to be boyfriend and girlfrie–"

"Man and woman," Jordanne corrects me.

The entire room starts laughing, including Skulli and them.

"That's it?" my mom questions.

"Yes," I reply, wondering about the relief that's settled on her face.

"Me think yah breed enuh me pikny," she laughs, "then a who never know you and Jordanne ago deh back?" she finishes her statement still laughing.

Sue laughs out while hitting her and they both stand to walk to where the other adults are.

"So why it look like a me know last?" Toni questions, staring at us both.

I look to Jordanne who seems annoyed by the question.

"Nobody knew. I was actually with Jacen for real, but something happened and I decided he wasn't what I wanted," I explain, holding her piercing stare.

Lorelle looks at me knowingly and I offer her a small smile while shaking my head 'NO'.

"No, it's not the baby mother. That would've ended it yes but that wasn't it."

"We nuh need fi know no more. Run the funds Muuch, neoowww," Joshua interrupts me and the room goes into a laughing marathon again.

Jordanne pulls me in and kisses the back of my neck, causing me to shiver. I pull his hand around my waist for more comfort. Cyaa believe we're here, finally.

Toni catches my attention when she gets up to leave the room. I attempt to follow her but Jordanne stops me.

"Say your true feelings, just like you did with me that night when we spoke, otherwise she nahgo understand," he suggests, tone soft but compelling.

I stand up to follow her and he stands too.

I look at him quizzically, but he doesn't offer me an explanation.

"Mum, Skulli... Library please," are the only words that leave his mouth, landing with bitterness and causing obvious discomfort amongst the two.

I decide not to pry and continue to make my way to the lawns outside where I can see Toni taking a seat.

Sigh, a it this...

33 | Amends

JORDANNE

"Mum, Skulli… Library please," I speak, carefully assessing their body language. Sue hands her cup to Ms.Janette and walks off before Paul.

He glances at me for too long a second.

I hold his stare, giving him time to adjust and move to the direction of the library before me.

Just wah get this over with

We all make it to the library and Mumz is sitting to the corner where the shelves are, just staring at nothing– lost in her thoughts. Skulli takes a chair closer to my desk and sits while tilting himself back.

"So?" I take a seat, suggesting someone starts.

"Jordanne it was a long time ago," my mother kickstarts her explanation, "that night you called and we were together, was a like a relapse."

Think me coulda sit through this but she just start and me wah leff already.

"Mase told him how Sheer found out Suanne… him more concerned about that," Paul tells her.

They exchange knowing looks.

Paul releases his locs and Mum shifts in her seat.

"Me want it from top man, so she good," I say to them both.

Really wah know how everything start and how me just a pick that up after Dadz pass. I chose to ignore too many signs.

"The day your dad found out was probably the worst day of my life," she starts over, and I swear Skulli just hiss him teeth…

… Under him breath.

I shoot him a look, asking him to test me but he spins his chair, directing his attention away from Sue.

Man a behave like a bitch so tonight, a wah?

Jah know.

She begins to tell her story in detail.

FLASHBACK

"Suanne, why you make me come here if you no plan fi tell him?" Paul asks, with waves of pain and disappointment in his eyes.

"Paul... Sheer look like somebody fi play with? You have to give it time."

"Time wah Sue?" he says cutting her off, "how long now me know you? Before Sheer right? You never tell him back then and you nahgo tell him now," Paul sneers.

He's looking down at her with nothing but hurt bouncing off his shoulders. She shifts her weight and attempts to lighten the mood with a kiss. He doesn't move but instead allows her to deepen their kiss.

With their tongues playing swirl sweeper and hands searching for intimate areas of pleasure, Sue's head lulls back as Paul finds her neck. A moan slips from her lips much like Paul's finger slipping inside her bra to cup her breasts.

They forget where they are and welcome their inner urges.

Paul moves back to Sue's neck, shoving her down on the desk, disregarding the stationery scattered all over. Her head falls back, allowing him more space to kiss on. As he leaves wet kisses along her neck, the pleasure forces her eyes open.

"No don't let me interrupt unuh at all," Robert's voice comes calm and clear, enveloping the room.

He's leaning at the entrance, with his head cocked to the side, putting fire to his Cuban cigar.

"Boss–" Skulli stands, pulling his locs back into a ponytail.

"Robert I– we were– you weren't to be back until–" Sue stutters, trying to make herself presentable.

"Relax Sue, yuh ago need fi relax fi get out your words... wife. Relax so me can hear exactly weh yahv fi say."

Paul attempts to say something but is silenced by Robert taking his gun from his waist.

"Robert!" Sue pleads.

"Sue talk quick nuh man. Time is money and unuh a waste my time right now," he finishes his statement while walking to a wall safe to retrieve something.

"Sheer she no happy," Skulli picks up, meeting Robert's stare.

"And me hire you fi make her happy?" Robert retorts, with his eyes narrowed at them both.

"Nuh say that but she express herself to me daily and as humans... well. You know me know her way before you so the hurt me watch you put her through no sit well with me," Paul tries to explain– his hand slowly reaching for his weapon.

"Get yuh. So Sue yah complain to man daily 'bout we marriage? Think you happy? You lift a finger in here? You head hurt you 'bout nothing? You ever hungry?" Robert asks now tightening the silencer around his gun, all while still puffing the cigar from the corner of his mouth.

"Nobody said that Robert! Did you ever ask me if I wanted an open marriage? If I want to smell different women's perfume on you nightly? If me wah suck you hood and imagine you a sink it ina somebody else? No, you just opened our marriage and I went along for fear of you leaving. Well, it wide open now and me let in Skulli, so wah now?" Sue sneers, walking closer to Robert.

"There she is... the little ghetto gyal from Spanish town," Robert laughs.

"Robert say weh you want. If you dish it you take it," she hisses.

"So Sue, that's what I am? Just a dish you a serve back to Sheer?" Paul questions.

"Like you no see, Sue ago always be mine so if you think she did ago leave me fi deh with somebody that moves on my command, you no know deh gyal yah," Robert laughs proudly.

He then pulls and starts to release a thick cloud of smoke from the cigar.

"No Paul, I've grown to... love you," Sue basically whispers.

Robert's smoke release is cut short by him coughing– surprised at what his ears have recorde... in his house... in his library.

"Fuck you say while ago Suanne?!!" Robert tries to move towards Sue, but Skulli blocks him.

"Sheer no put you hand pon her again," he looks at Robert deadpan, tone final.

Robert looks him up and down... before laughing– the most hearty, devilish laugh.

"Ah you know wah, mek me leff yah so."

PRESENT DAY

"He walked out that night and didn't come back for two weeks," she says, looking at me. "You remember? I told you guys he went to Venezuela for business."

I have gotten up from the desk, soon as I realized she was talking about being in the library.

Need my own house... like right now.

"So you know Mum from when?" I direct my attention to Skulli.

"School days," he answers and I cannot hide the slight shock on my face coupled with a smirk.

Wah this remind you of?

I laugh to myself.

My father was ruthless, yes but him right hand man?

Sue… Jah know.

Remembering that Mum was the one who introduced them, sends bells ringing in my head.

"So unuh did have a thing in school?" my eyes find them both.

"No," – Sue.

"Yes,"– Paul.

"Den me no know man. Mum why yah lie to me?" I ask, looking at her.

Why she feel fi omit things?

"No want it seem like me never love you father because I did. Paul and I didn't have anything in school. Heee had a thing for meee," she turns to him.

For the first time since I pulled them into the library, Skulli smirks. "Never give me the chance Suanne."

I laugh to myself taking a mental note of the moment. The universe wicked fi this.

Mirroring how you and Ryleigh could've ended up?

Nahhh… She woulda be mine if me did affi kidnap her.

"Hear wah, me ago lowe unuh," I move off, "came in here with the intention of firing Skulli but that clearly nahgo stop unuh."

Mum's smile widens.

Jah Jah.

"And Mum, me need my own place, sort that out before Easter please. No have the time to do it myself with all the inspections that went left with the commercial properties."

She nods and I give them another glance over before leaving the room.

Cyaa believe nothing me just hear bredda…

Leaving, I walk to find my woman and my annoying little sister.

Hope them a work it out…

• • •

TONI-ANNE

"So yes again I'm sorry but I couldn't say anything this time for real," she explains.

I pause to analyze what she said but that's not the explanation I want. I completely understand why she couldn't say anything. A mission is a mission. I've seen my father keep my mom in the dark about those, so she's lucky Jordanne told her.

"Toni," she calls, pulling me from my thoughts.

"Ryleigh, me not knowing about last night was fine but why am I second to everybody?" with my eyes focused on hers, I search for answers.

She tries to speak but I cut her off, "I'm second to Jordanne, I get it, y'all were friends before you and I, and unuh in love and so on. I'm second to Lorelle, and don't even try to say I'm not, because I am. I'm also second to you in Jordanne's life... now more than ever and I feel like I'm second to him in my mom's life as well... So you tell me, what is it about me?"

"... I try to do things for everybody, plan things for everybody, my house is the hang out spot for everybody, I go above and beyond for everybody and as simple as you ago Mobay and wait last minute to tell me? But Mariah get fi tag along? Keif? Honestly Ryleigh, if the basis of our friendship was you getting to know Jordanne's sister you could've said that," I end my monologue of raw feelings...

... and she says nothing.

See weh mah talk bout?

I attempt to stand and leave but she pulls me back in place.

"Toni, half the time I feel like keeping you at arm's length because at the end of the day that's your brother. I can't freely express what he does to annoy me without thinking it might come off disrespectful to you. I can see how my naïveté might have led me to think that you were trying to control what I do, to benefit your brother, but I see now you were trying to protect me– all while toggling between us..."

"...We leave people, not just you... people overall, out of our relationship most of the time because we never really know exactly what it is, when it is. You get mi? ...And you letting me know you knew about Emily just rub the wrong way, still does..." she ends, releasing a deep sigh.

Still does? Sigh...

Know me shoulda tell her enuh, but the way she is, she woulda blow it up and I wasn't sure what J' was doing so I stayed out of it. I could've lied and said I didn't know when she asked, but I didn't. That should count for something.

"I just wanted to stay out a unuh thing. As mi say, I didn't know what your agreement was at the time. Looking back, I should've said something to you... I'm sorrrrryy," I say, feigning a pout.

She pulls me in and we laugh while hugging each other.

"I'm sorry too sexy gyal. Promise to tell you everything before them all happen."

We laugh even louder at that.

"Pull up this," I hear Jordanne's voice and I roll my eyes.

"Jesus Jordanne, see her yah, take her, take her!" I hiss jokingly before releasing her.

She stands and falls seamlessly into his arms. My eyes are glued to her shorts for a second before Jordanne speaks and they avert to him.

"Wouldn't believe weh me just learn. Nah advise nobody fi go back ina the library, especially 'round the main desk," he chuckles.

"Wah?" Ryleigh asks, looking at him with nothing but happiness shining from her eyes.

"Sue and Skulli," he says in a low tone, spewing exaggerated disgust.

Me know supm did ina supm the way them ever missing. I'm the eyes of this house… things barely miss me.

Damn right

"You said you were gonna tell me enuh," Ryleigh whines, looking up at him.

"When we go upstairs me give you the full details Ms.Inquisitive," he retorts.

With that, she tips up and kisses him. I find myself staring at her nipples through her top and–

What was that?

I DON'T KNOW!

I don't know…

I blink rapidly before standing to leave.

"Me gone find Joshua," I swallow, forcing a smile before walking back into the house.

What the fuckkkk was that Toni?

Me say me nuh knowwww!

34 | Baby Steps

RYLEIGH

"So tell me, how did that affect you?" she asks, her face holding an unreadable expression.

Hoping to avoid the question at hand, my eyes start searching the room to connect to something, anything but her. It's been **two weeks** since telling everybody what Jordanne and I decided on doing but–

How it affect you girl?

How did that affect me?

I–

"Ms.Stevens, how did your father leaving you and your mom, to live in another country, offering no communication, affect you?" she repeats, this time with empathy written in her eyes.

I–

Four months coming here and we're yet to make a real breakthrough. What is she doing wrong? Or ah mi? Me cyaa fix?

You keep holding back

I can't put the feeling in words!

"Take your time," her voice creeps through the cold room.

My eyes find the shelf she has, that's decorated with thick spined, serious looking books... My fingers find each other, and the twiddling starts.

"I felt, betrayed? Unworthy? Not enough? Less than?" my reply comes out a mutter.

She writes, but she says nothing.

Sometime me wonder, if me a waste me time with dah woman yah. Four months, me supposed to fix up now and happy?

Happy within myself...

Happy with him...

"Do you feel like that has led you into seeking validation from the men in your life?" she pushes– crossing her legs while looking over her tiny red glasses.

A who and her? Who a seek validation?

Me?

I laugh internally… Please, definitely not me.

"Excuse me?" deciding to voice my opinion, I narrow my eyes at her.

"Do you feel like this leads you to seek va–" she tries to repeat.

"You know after four months coming here, we've gotten nowhere?" my words now bitter.

Instead of offering my question any attention, she starts taking more notes on her little notepad.

I hiss, lowly.

"Ms.Stevens did you find my question offensive?" a flat nonchalant tone is what she decides to wrap her words in.

"How yuh mean? Mi did tell you me a run backa man?"

Realizing the pace of my breathing has picked up, I inhale deeply to find the ground beneath my feet. Why dat piss me off so?

We both fall silent for a second or two before she starts adding even morrrrre notes to that damn pad.

"Okay let's try something else," she suggests. "Do you look to Jordanne for support, in any way, shape or form?" her bright eyes now piercing me.

Holding our stare, I start digging deep for the appropriate answer.

That's the problem, you nah be raw

"I look to him for… love," again my words fall out low and weak.

And stability…

Loyalty…

Validation?

Approval even.

"So that's a yes," her sharp voice breaks my thought process.

I look away at the clock, dreading how much time's left.

Four minutes? Oh!

Thank God.

Ryleigh

"And when are you the happiest with him?" she digs even further.

"During se–" my throat locks, before ending that statement.

Cyaa tell the woman a sex a give me the most peace

She writes again…

I want to burnnn that notepad.

We no reach my miscarriage, the whole relationship with Folan nor Jordanne's disloyalty, and these are all things I can talk about. There are still things I can't share, like what he does that he conveniently hides 95% of. Ghale being missing, what I saw that night in Mobay or even how I haven't seen or heard from Jacen despite Mariah saying he's fine.

My eyes find the clock again– 4:59pm.

"Me ago leave, I have to meet somebody," I blurt out while grabbing my bag to exit.

"Ms. Stevens we still have a minute left," her tone dipped in disapproval.

"See you next week," I share my farewell while halfway out the door.

• • •

JORDANNE

I haven't said more than two words at a time since I've been here. Ryleigh wah me go therapy, so that's what I'm doing… but wah the sense if half of the things me cyaa share?

Weed better than this.

Neva lie

"Mr. Sheer," she calls, looking at me.

I raise a single brow at her in question.

"You agreed to having too much on your plate for your age?" she tries to will a response from me.

"Mmhmm yeah," I agree.

"These, things would be? School? Women? Friends?" she tries to dig.

Finding her amusing, I start to chuckle.

School? That ah the least. I fly back tomorrow morning, a week late, already behind and dat still ah the least… believe me. Try my house being raided by the police or Ruse trying to start the very war I've been trying to avoid for years, as payment for what I did to his brother.

Wasteman

How about Ryleigh not seeming to be present in our relationship or Skulli and my mother being public as fuck. Try still having distribution issues with the Venezuelans.

And dem man deh no play

School a definitely the least.

"Yeah man, a school. School stressful," I offer her the best answer– hoping the hour I have here is already over.

Bringing my wrist up to check the time, I notice it's in fact over.

Dat is it

Coming here for two weeks and all this lady do is strip me with her eyes. Swear to yuh... If Ry' didn't choose therapists in the same building, I would go smoke for an hour and pick her up after her sessions.

I've been taking her everywhere just to maximize the time we have left before I leave again.

Now that I'm leaving tomorrow, I can get away with that– the no therapy thing.

"Do you hold school as a priority or do you thi–"

"Mah liff, we can do the online session supm you suggested next week. Ago collect me woman," I make my next move known, not giving her the opportunity to protest.

While exiting the room, I lock eyes with the receptionist. She offers me a smile while biting down on her lips.

Ina me bad days me woulda kill it.

Hear the man. Bredda we a 19

Neva know age have nuttin fi do wid it.

By now my feet are gliding the stairs to the floor where Ryleigh does her thing. I can now see the office suite she goes to but I don't see her waiting there as the usual.

No see Slyme outside either...

I get to the end of the flight of stairs, only to hear, "Gimi yuh wallet!"

My hands move to my waist involuntarily, but her scent moves with the wind to tickle my nose.

"Ryleigh you wii dead enuh," spinning around, I pick her up.

"Me tell her enuh boss, and she say me too coward," Slyme chuckles.

"Like yah feed pah breadfruit. Me did need your voice, if I said it then him wouldn't frighten," she laughs and I take the opportunity to put her down.

Finding the nook of her neck, I whisper, "How was your session?"

"Fuckry..."

"Same... so why we nah quit?" my face now nuzzling her neck.

My dick stirs...

My hands find the hollow above her ass and–

"It's supposed to get better from what I hear. We need it Jordanne, before we can start go together... You promised," her tone whiney.

I did, yeah, I did.

Bloodclawt.

Did she suggest it when we were fucking?

No, just when we think we did ago lose her fi life

Yah, dat mek more sense.

"Okay, let's go. Too many eyes a gather yah now," I whisper in her ear.

Pulling away, I hold her hand in mine and start moving to the parking lot with Slyme on our heels.

"Drip?" a female's voice seeps through my thoughts, pulling me back to reality.

Who this now?

"Jordanne?" the voice repeats while the woman herself is looking me up and down.

Government name???

How she look so familiar?

I blink.

She look like the week five girl. Week five was a rough week. That was the week Ry' was in the club twerking. Shoulda just pull up and spray the club... honestly. But no, I wanted to handle it differently. Now look, is a woman weh look like she ago cause trouble.

"Slyme," I call, because me nah have another argument with a next woman in front her.

Slyme takes the woman's hand, leading her away from us.

"Alright Danne! Hope she know how fi please yuh!" she shouts, looking back at us.

I don't give her any extra attention. Instead, my eyes find Ry' who is somehow halfway to the Benz. Shaking my head, I follow her lead while making sure the doors are open before she attempts to get in.

She love argue 'bout that too

A frustrated sigh leaves my lips as I hop in. Her eyes stay straight ahead, not shifting once to drill me with any questions... so I decide to let it be.

Maybe we safe

Mmhmm...

"You know wah funny?!" she starts, keeping her head forward as I glance at her re-peatedly.

Fucckkkk.

"Babe, you know 'bout them so–"

"Wah funny to me is that nobody, noooobody at all can get close to you... but sur-prisingly, every woman can get within four feet when a me and you," she laughs.

Weh she mean?

I can't control public spaces.

Deciding not to bring that thought to the surface, I keep my focus on the road.

"Weh that tell me say is, Slyme and alla dem no get no orders fi mek sure say no woman no step to you, or at least in my presence!" her voice is at its very peak.

Very top...

Loud...

She no have a point?

She does, me just never think 'bout it that way. The man dem already affi a scope out certain place and faces. Now I'll have to add past females to the list– half of which me no remember.

Yuh remember Ms.Week five man. We used her for week six and seven

Jah Jah.

The memory jolts me back to the reality of Ryleigh's voice.

"Yeah yuh cyaa talk? Me no get how unuh man love allow unuh woman fi confront me??? A wah so? Me look nice and quiet?" she giggles but without a hint of humor.

She's getting angrier than I thought she would.

"Babe, you know Emily had access because of Ghale the second time. The first was my fault, I admit. Just now my only focus was you. Me no know the girl enough fi see her from a mile and cut… and when you ago say 'unuh man' weh that supposed to mean? You want me take responsibility fi Jacen baby mother too?"

Now turning at the stoplight just before the last street to our home, I step on the brake a little too sharply.

She looks at me as if I'm crazy, "Alright kill me off," she hisses.

Shaking my head, I tighten my grip around the steering. I don't want another thing on my plate. All I want is peace from her.

Yuh give her peace?

How yuh mean?

"Fi the head of all things, crime… them sure nahv no respect enough fi care if you have a woman or not. Them supposed to know and understand not to step to you in certain situations or at alllll. Me too mature now fi fight but don't mistake it 'cause me wii liff up a gyal if she try touch me instead of dealing with you, the man. That's why me always walk weh," her words land bitter.

I smile.

Not sure why but I do.

"Yuh nahfi worry 'bout that again babe. Fully get weh yah say and I'll make adjust-ments to the perimeter," I state, focused on pulling into our garage.

When yah tell her, her name is on the deed?

When she asks? Or try to move out…

We've been here nine days and she threaten fi go back a campus four of those nine days already.

Before exiting the car, I turn to her and plant a kiss on her lips.

She moans.

Me baby…

Pulling away, I whisper, "Nobody else, I promise…" but when my words fall out, she rolls her eyes.

I get out and walk to her side, freeing her. We walk to the entryway and I watch her enter the kaba code for the front door.

My eyes avert to her ass.

Sexy…

"You have classes tomorrow?" keeping my eyes on her ass, I ask my question.

She shifts her weight while forcing the heavy door open.

"Afternoon hours, yeah. Switched it when you told me you were leaving early tomorrow."

"Oh, dat good," my tone holding slight disappointment.

She turns to look at me in question. I smirk, and she immediately picks up on what I'm suggesting.

Yeah man, all night tonight.

• • •

RYLEIGH

We both took showers, cooked, well I cooked us roasted chicken and baked potatoes; and now we're on the couch watching TV.

I have to hand it to Sue. In less than a week she had this house ready for him. Impossible for others but I assume when you're paying full-funds-immediate it's different.

The design is immaculate. The walls imitate a stone like structure, flowing into floor to ceiling windows, allowing a lot of natural light inside. The interior design itself is breath taking and suits him well– neutral enough for all genders to enjoy.

It's not the typical bachelor pad type of decor, which I expected, seeing how his room was back at Sue's.

This house has the feel of a home.

I love it.

He's been on his phone for a while which gives me the opportunity to grab mine. With the intention of texting T'... since she's been avoiding me forever. I toggle through the notifications and the first thing I notice is that my Instagram is going offfff.

Why? I haven't posted in a while.

Clicking on one of my notifications, I realize that I'm tagged in a story post. It's from his page...

"J'... wah you do?"

Just from the sound of my voice, he starts smirking.

He has a string of pictures of me on his story. I pause to look at one that has a queen emoji and my heart starts racing. Mi cyaa take the legion of botheration weh 'bout fi drop down pah me. His Instagram is empty, except for a post of him and his dad when he was younger, so him posting me will draw attention. A lot of it too.

Him post we when we deh high school, wah the issue?

That was a joint post that I initiated. High school different... he's now different. Almost everybody knows who he is now, and what he's responsible for.

I stare at the post... my eyes locked in on the time tag.

14 minutes ago.

14 longggg minutes ago?

The boy ina me lap a post ago weh enuh, and I've been consumed by the movie.

I'm not sure why I have a problem with it or even if I really do. I just know the publicity is making me nervous.

"You don't like them?" his voice sweeps the room.

I look down at him, "I do... Just that now everybody knows... as in everybody," I whisper.

He laughs.

Putting his phone down, he pulls me down for a kiss that I return it without thought. The kiss ignites my urges and my nipples begin to poke through the shirt he gave me earlier.

Noticing my heavy breathing, he sits up and flips me onto his lap to straddle him. I can't tell where we haven't had sex in this house, but I know it's about to be the third time on the couch.

"I love you, just know dat?" he slaps my ass and the feeling averts my attention from my thoughts to him.

All the wonder and worry from his posts exit my body and I slip down from straddling him, to my knees, between his legs, all while trying to release his length.

35 | Foreplay

JORDANNE

I watch as she falls to her knees, keeping her eyes matched with mine. She pulls her hair into a pony, careful not to break the stare.

Pretty

Her hands brush my thighs, pulling a deep breath from my lung. She smirks and begins trying to free my dick again. She's successful this time.

It springs out and up prompting her to wet her lips.

Sexy as fuck!

My chest rises and falls, awaiting the comfort of her mouth, and throat…

She props her body up, settling on her ankles in a stoop position before reaching to the couch for support. I take the opportunity to admire her face.

Before I can take her in fully, she takes me in, pulling my mind back to the present.

"Ssiiiiclawwwt Ry," I curse, as the walls of her mouth vacuum my length.

She wastes no time, moving it to the back of her throat. Realizing it won't all fit, she takes a deep breath… and that action slowly creates space.

The tip of my dick enters an unfamiliar terrain.

Fuck a gwaan?

Throat this mi ina?

"Ry'… go easy," I whisper, but she ignores me and instead swallows, which brings my dick further down.

Looking down, I realize there is no length left exposed.

Bloodclawt.

She takes another breath and pulls me out slowly, allowing all the saliva created to flow free.

My toes curl into a ball…

My knees fall weak…

... and me deven stand up bredda.

Without granting me a second to hold the pleasure together, she starts bobbing her head up and down at a steady pace. Her lips stay wet and the feeling of her tongue swirling around my tip every few strokes is sending me to heaven.

My hand finds the couch cushion and I squeeze it, searching for something to reduce the tingles running up and down my spine.

"Babe–Go–Ea–" my words are cut off by her popping me out– replacing her mouth with her palm.

Jah Jah God

She smiles up at me, realizing her effects.

Demon.

A pool of pre-cum presents itself at the tip of my dick and she uses her thumb to swirl it around, driving me up the couch.

"Fuck!!!" I shudder while moving back into the couch.

She didn't like that... the shift in her breathing tells me she didn't like that at all.

She holds my knee with her free hand before asking, "Yah go J?" all while sporting a wicked smile.

My hands find the cushion again, squeezing it for dear life. She starts to envelope her mouth around my dick, while keeping her hand at the base– spinning it to create more friction.

I'm almost sure there are tiny little insects crawling all over my skin.

Nerve endings live!

I shudder again while taking the deepest breath. Holding that same breath, I peer down at her technique. She has added both hands to the mix while still sucking at the tip.

I get lost in the feeling, only being pulled back to life when I feel all sensation pause.

The Fuck?

I open my eyes to see what's causing the delay, only to find her towering over me.

"Stand," her eyes now glossy and filled with plea.

Doing as I'm told, I stand and start removing my shirt when I notice she has removed all her clothes.

Flawless

She drops to her knees before my shirt is over my head and in one swallow, takes me to that unknown terrain at the back of her throat again. This time she doesn't move... instead she holds it there. I feel a vibrating sensation and realize she's doing that thing again.

That thingggg.

Electricity shoots up my spine and I clamp my eyes shut, using my toes to keep me grounded.

She ago kill me before tomorrow

When she's satisfied with the result of her evil doing, she stops. Her next move is grabbing my hand and placing it to the back of her head, granting me permission to fuck her face.

Gladly.

Hmmph...

Gripping her hair– full roots through my palm, I send her head down to the root of my dick. She rocks her neck to create movement as soon as she gets there.

Bumbo-Bloodclawt

"Babe," my word leaks out as a moan.

The fuck a gwaan fi real?

The grip I have on her hair falls loose and she grabs my hand, putting it back.

I smile inwardly. Weh me ago do with her?

Me baby.

I can see how eager she is to please me.

Love dat.

I decide to tighten my grip on her head, sinking my dick to where she seems to like it. She moans and I watch her hands find her nipples. The sight of it hardens me even more than I thought possible. In that same breath her mouth tightens, sending my senses into a frenzy.

My strokes continue, pulling out to the tip each time before sinking it fully after. It goes on for a few more seconds before I start to feel my end approaching. She realizes this and out of nowhere comes a fresh round of wetness, springing from inside her mouth.

"Bumboclawwwttt Ry!" I hiss, quickening the pace– hard and fast.

She chokes a little but holds on to my legs for support while recovering. I watch her utilize her nostrils to usher oxygen to her lungs. Her eyes find me, granting me the permission to not slow down.

This motion goes on for a while until I can't help but let my orgasm run free. I try to pull back to cum on her boobs like we always do, but she holds me in place.

Wooahhhh...

Nahgo even fight her, me nuh have the strength.

She slides back just enough to create room for my cream... and I–

I–

I become undone in her mouth...

... Shaking.

Tipping...

Almost screaming like a fucking bitch

Just when I thought it was over she continues to suck...

No!

No. No.

NO–NO... Nooo.

"Ryyyleigh Go eassssiii nuh," I let out, my knees almost buckling.

She pulls away smiling, just before she swallows.

Pussyclawt

"Tell the gyal from earlier nobody cyaa top me... 'Bout mek sure *'she'* can please you," she rolls her eyes and walks off to the direction of the powder room.

I fall to the couch, taking deep breaths.

Need fi recover...

... but I can't tell if she vex right now or not.

The sound from the TV reminds me it's still running and I suddenly find it annoying.

"ALEXA, TURN OFF T.V."

"OKAY."

With that I struggle to my feet– dick in hand, deciding to move to the bathroom to find her.

36 | Night Before

RYLEIGH

I watch as he struggles to the bathroom. Fighting to keep my laugh in, I grab the mouth wash to gargle. I'm not used to the taste of semen, but I expected it to at least be salty? Instead, it was just warm and sticky sliding down.

Don't know what that's about.

"Ry?" his voice creeps into the powder room.

"J?" I answer, keeping my focus to the mirror.

He moves behind me, meeting my stare in said mirror. We hold it, for no more than a few seconds before my laugh finally comes out. Throwing my head down, I quickly release the mouth wash.

"Yah laugh so Love?" he asks, narrowing his eyes at me.

I lift my head, continuing my giggles.

"Just a remember how yuh behave," the laughter forces itself out of me even more.

He smirks before saying, "Mmhm, the night nuh done yet enuh."

I spin to face him, eyes meeting his dick.

He lifts my chin and we look at each other for what seems like a decade before I pull back just enough to mouth, 'LOVE YOU'.

Within seconds his tongue is halfway down my mouth– my jaw still tight from our previous shenanigans.

Well tight...

I halt the kiss to open my mouth, moving my jaw up and down to release the tension.

Jordanne starts laughing.

"That sweet yuh? Mr.Couch Climber?"

This sends him into even more laughter. He then pulls me into his arms, leading me to the stairs.

"We affi go link Sue dem before I leave," he whispers.

A heavy sigh leaves my lips. I wanted to be alone with him. Am I selfish? Him have a family so me nuffi hog him time right?

You do too. When last we see mommy?

Outside of the daily FaceTime calls? I can't remember.

"Okayyy..." I mutter and he picks up on my disappointment.

Stopping just as we get to the top of the stairs he says, "A after eight Ry', we'll be back before 12. When since you turn house rat?" he genuinely asks.

Since we basically moved in duhhhh. Now I'll have to leave this paradise of a home to go back up a dusty UWI.

Ughhh!

"Let's shower," he offers, interrupting my thoughts– leaving no room for me to voice my opinion.

At least you'll get to see Toni

Yeah if she no deh a Joshua. Can't understand why she been ah avoid me when we left off on such a good note.

Weird ass energy...

• • •

We're out the shower, and I head into the room. Something tells me to check the time and– 8:50pm. Then how me fi ready ina ten minutes?

"You can do it," his voice startles me as he enters the room.

Him a read mind hard from wah day yah enuh.

"You think I look fine even when I roll out of bed, so mi nahgo take no time limit from you," I retort, rolling my neck at him.

He shakes his head, "Ten minutes Ryleigh or you drive yourself."

"But you know me blind!" I shriek.

"Wear your glasses for once or be ready on time. Your choice dat babe."

I hiss my teeth, and he ignores me to enter his closet. Ignoring him right back, my feet start taking me to... my closet? The closet? I don't know– the closet that seems to be mine, and immediately release my robe. Slipping on my new favorite seamless panties, I take a look at myself in the mirror.

Need fi go back a gym but Jordanne insists I wait until the one here is finished.

Controlling much

These days I don't contest him. I've come to understand why he is the way he is.

Yuh no feel like it get worse though?

Yeah, but–

My thoughts are interrupted by the sight of my favorite shorts. Now how the fuck did he get these here? As soon as my thought is complete, I realize how ridiculous it sounds.

It's J', of course mi shorts deh here. Grabbing it, I pull them on before going further into the closet. A white top pops out at me while I sieve through the racks.

Perfect!

Deciding to just ruffle my hair and rock the messy look as is, I exit the closet. Makeup? I don't think I have the time. To confirm, I look down at my phone.

8:58pm, Ugh!

I run to the vanity section and start moisturizing my face. Seconds later the dabbing of light coverage foundation across my cheeks finally comes to an end.

In case them a be cute, 'cause one thing with Sue, she ago turn any get together into a full blown party.

As I apply the last coat of lipgloss to my lips, I hear his footsteps. Jumping to my feet, I move to meet him at the entrance of his closet.

He smirks and I smile.

"Was that hard?" he asks, peering down at me, the intensity causing me to lose my balance.

"Yes it was…"

"C'mere," he pulls me in, "Slyme dem downstairs," and without another word we head to the living area.

When we get there, I decide to grab a snack from the kitchen. Feel like I've lost weight these past few days.

Jook too much

Yeah, sex and sleep isn't a good combo… for my weight at least.

I grab my snack and lean over on the island, watching him on his phone. When he finally notices me, he mumbles, "Ready?"

"Yeah."

Throwing his phone at me before walking off he says, "Before you ask."

I look at the phone to see a picture of myself. Whole time me think the boy a text– I could've posed.

"Me neva want no picture today," an appreciative smile consumes my face before I move off, jogging swiftly to get back to him.

He pulls the Porsche key from the entrance bowl and I decide to bother him.

"Thought we were for special occasions?"

"We?" he questions, looking back at me.

I laugh, "Yeah me and the Porsche."

He laughs out.

"No, only the Porsche. You go everywhere with me," he chuckles and I get to him just in time for him to place a small kiss on my forehead.

Love him…bad to badddd.

"Smart answer Drip."

Yuh wouldn't believe the amount a butterflies ina the doll belly right now.

"That name isn't for you. It's Mr.Sheer, Mrs. Sheer," his words dripping in love.

I giggle like a school girl as we exit the house. I spot Slyme sitting in his own car directly in-front the gate and wave at him before moving to J's car. I hop in and he closes my door before walking to his side.

I'm gonna miss it here…

So tell him yuh wah stay… Wahm to yuh?

Seems pushy, I don't know.

Pushing the thought to the back of my head, I bring my focus on getting to Sue's. I hope Mariah is there since she a clearly Sue step daughter now.

<u>BUBBAS</u>

Who deh a big yard?

<u>Sexy Bitch:</u> **Anuh me yard yah call big yard gyal? Muurdaaa dwfl!**

Same one lol! You stepsister dideh?

<u>Mariah:</u> **How you mean if me deh yah. Is a room me want now loooooool.**

<u>Sexy Bitch:</u> **From me know you, you basically live ina the guest room though.**

LOOOOL watch sister's quarrel.

<u>Mariah:</u> **Don't feel left out. Memba yah her sister in law and my wah? Step sister in law?? Dwflll**

<u>Sexy Bitch:</u> **Kmt**

<u>Dutty Foot:</u> **No me a buil back tonight. Me and Keif deh yah a finish up U-Tech assignment.**

As school start? UWI would never! The
lecturer no come until week 2 lol.

<u>Muuch:</u> **Ova So-Sci yesss not Law, yuh bright.**

Either way.

<u>Keif:</u> **Me did tell dutty Lorelle fi mek we wait and go UWI but noooo.**

<u>Dutty Foot:</u> **Couldn't do a next year a we high school.**

215

Me almost reach @SexyBitch

I wait a second, but Toni doesn't reply. We're almost there anyways so I'll see her inside.

• • •

We pull in and I wave to Troopa.

"Me ago thief you put a the new house enuh. I miss you!" I shout as we drive in.

He laughs, while fanning me away.

"Ryleigh mine me leff one ina the two a unuh," Jordanne chuckles, and I don't know if he's serious or not but I decide to laugh it off.

'Cause a must joke. Me and Troopa buddy-buddy fi real but… I don't know, that man funny as helllll.

Jordanne parks and exits the car to walk to my side.

The usual…

I get out when he opens the door and we head inside– hand in hand.

• • •

The 'get together' is in full swing. Mommy and Sue are handing out kebabs. Slyme, Paw, Skulli and Ramone are seated playing dominoes. Joshua and his friend Ryan are working the sound.

Surprised J' finally allowed Ryan here. I'm only used to seeing him when we all go out together. Last time I saw him was at the bowling alley. He notices my stare and waves at me, I wave back, and Jordanne pulls me in closer to him.

Really?

Toni and Mariah are seated next to the fire pit drinking what seems to be sorrel beers.

"Mah stop a the man dem," Jordanne tells me.

Oh, he was just getting ready to say bye for a while, and not being possessive… Okay.

"Okay me ago link mommy and me gyal dem," I share my plans while getting up on my tippy toes to kiss him.

I walk over to my mom who's busy gathering ice for the igloo.

"Mommy long time no see," I hurl myself into her arms.

"Yessss you find husband and dash weh you mother," she squishes me, "memba a me and you when him did gone," she chuckles, holding her focus to the bag of ice that she now has hanging off to the side of us.

I help her to lift it into the igloo where she pierces it, setting the cubes free.

"Him a leave tomorrow, I wanted all the time with him until dem get Spring break,"

"Yuh no affi explain to me. I was young too and me know nuttin no nice like young love," she assures me, now brushing her hands in her apron before holding my chin.

"Mommy you hand cold," I laugh while trying to pull away.

Sue joins us saying, "Daughter in law, cyaa see you again? From you get house you dash weh this one?"

Not she a try put me name pon the man place before him.

"Jordanne new place comfy bad, nah lie. I'll be here more often when him gone man."

She gives me a look that I'm unable to read.

I shrug.

She turns, her eyes now searching the backyard, then stills when she spots Jordanne. Turning on her heels she walks directly to him. I watch as they seem to go back and forth, but decide to go talk to my girls instead of prying any longer.

"Mummy me ago ova the sound yah so," I announce, giving my mom another hug.

"Alright goodz. Me and Sue ago deh yah so a chat when she come back."

With that I turn to walk to Mariah and Toni. When I'm halfway to them, Toni walks away...

A weh di–

Pretending to not notice it, I continue walking towards Mariah.

"Stepsister in lawwww!!! Me know we did ago be family one sweet day enuh," she laughs, pulling me down into a hug.

"A wah do T'?" I immediately ask, "she only text me one word replies from when... and she can never FaceTime anymore or nothing. She say me do her supm?"

"No girl, she no mention nothing, but she and Joshua a argue nuff lately so maybe a that," she shrugs.

Okay I get that.

Me love take out my man problem pah people too.

• • •

For most of the night I only see Toni when she comes to speak to Josh or to grab a drink from the bar. Jordanne decided to join the domino game and hasn't paid me any attention since.

Men...

My eyes drop to my phone screen, only to realize the time is now 11:15pm. Rass, unuh know me ready though.

Yup

"Yes girl. A wah go upstairs go give me spoogy some phone sex," Mariah stretches to the sky as if reading my mind.

I laugh out at her statement. Girl yah a sample.

"Who that now?" I decide to play the fool.

"Ruse, who else?"

Jacen's brother... Jacen... Should I ask? I look up to find Jordanne and it's as if he can hear my thoughts 'cause as soon as our eyes connect, he mouths, 'SOON COME'.

I offer him a small smile before turning back to Mariah.

"Him brother okay?" I decide to ask her despite everything in me yelling not to.

Her eyes widen and she grabs me closer, "Girl him did get hurt bad-bad, and now Ruse a say him can't come back a Jamaica," she whispers– pity plastered in her eyes.

I–

"Wah kinda hurt?" I prolong.

Ryleigh

"Girl them beat him to the point where he was unrecognizable. Him a get a lot of surgery now though according to Ruse and with time him supposed to okay again."

I shudder.

Drip...

"Mariah," I hear Jordanne's voice behind me.

He's not close enough to have heard what she was saying... but knowing him.

"Yes little brothurrrr?" she laughs and he hisses, while still offering her a smile.

"We a leave," is all he says to me.

 I stand, hug Mariah and walk off.

My mind drifts to Toni and I look around to see her helping her mom pick up plates from around the yard.

"Babe meet me at the car?" my words find Jordanne.

He stops, turns and looks at me, raising a brow.

"Toni me ago say supm to," I offer him an explanation.

He nods and I turn to walk towards her before she can move.

"T' wah di problem now?" I sneer, looking at her deadpan.

"Wah you mean Ryleigh?" she decides to act oblivious– her lips pressed in the most forced smile I've seen in my 19 years on this earth.

"You know weh me mean. Me think we did good? Yah avoid me like me have a contagious virus or supm."

She laughs.

"Mah avoid you yes, but not because of anything that happened between us or to our friendship. Just supm me a try figure out and when I understand it, you'll be the first or second to know," she explains.

My eyes soften and suddenly I feel bad.

Yes because not everything is about us

"Are you okay?" I hold her shoulder.

She brings my hand from her slowly, "I'm okay Ryleigh. I'll speak to you when I'm ready."

"Okay, fair enough, but stop avoid me to such an extreme degree," I laugh to lighten the mood.

"I'll try," she smiles... and I'm not sure, but she seems... off.

Hope she good.

Without saying another word, I walk away, deciding not to dig any deeper. Moments later I get to the car and before I can touch the door J' flies it open from the inside.

Me man sweet...

I hop in and immediately grab the water I was drinking on our way here.

"The house is yours Ryleigh," is what I hear next.

A cough leaves my mouth, bringing with it a mixture of saliva and water. Weh him say? Which house?

He sits there staring at me, just waiting for me to get it together.

"Which house J?" my words caught at the back of my throat.

"The one we've been staying in Ryleigh," he offers while pulling out.

I could've stayed in one of my units enuh.

"When yuh did ago tell me?" I genuinely ask.

"When you try leave or do supm extra," he chuckles while using his free hand to search the center console.

Weed him a look for enuh. Him must have a new car on the way 'cause he doesn't like to smoke in the Porsche. He comes up with a freshly rolled spliff and drops it between his lips. He then leans toward me and I already know what to do. I take his lighter and help him light up.

Deciding that though our journey home is short we should still have music, I connect my phone to his car. Scrolling to Popcaan and Toni-Anne's - Next To Me, I click on it and turn the volume all the way up.

His flight leaves 5:30am and this is just the song I want to listen to right now– it's fitting. I start singing Toni's part as he puffs his weed. He looks over to me before smiling and bringing his seat a little further back.

I don't know why, but that just turned me on.

Taking his spliff from his mouth, I take a few pulls. Handing it back to him, I start singing, *"Don't know where we'll goooooo."*

I continue my car karaoke, having absolutely no regards to me not being able to hit a note if my life depended on it.

He joins in surprising me, *"The love we have is never ending, tell mi how yuh feeling"* the smoke from his lips circle us.

I giggle and continue the next line. My heart is just so happy and my spirit content. We've come a far way from screaming that one Alkaline song at each other in high school.

Thank God

I love him...

"Want dah moment yah last forever," I hear him murmur.

My heart sinks, and I lean over to leave a wet kiss on his cheek. I'm not ready for him to leave.

Sigh...

Reaching back to replay the song, I take the spliff from his mouth again. We can't make it last forever, but we can make it last a while longer.

37 | Deep

RYLEIGH

We get inside and before the door closes, he's all over me. Starting to think he brought me to Sue's to delay his recovery.

I smile.

Smart choice.

I'm pulled from my thoughts just by the heat of his breath against my ear.

"When me sink it, don't run," he whispers.

My breath hitches… my nipples perk up, the hairs on the back of my neck stand tall and the lady between my legs decides to start dripping. By now the effects of the few pulls I took from his spliff are mildly present. My senses are heightened, and he knows…

Grabbing my neck while releasing the door shut, he moves me straight to the foot of the staircase.

"Ryleigh," his voice comes out laced in lust and animalistic desires.

"Mmhmm?" I manage to mutter.

"Look at me."

I peer up at him through my lashes.

He tightens his grip around my neck and I can feel my juices gush forward, ruining my perfectly dry panty.

He moves down closer, licking his lips.

"Tonight, you don't come until I tell you to," he orders, leaving no time for me to protest.

Releasing my neck, he starts to undress me– starting from the shorts.

Why me ina shorts? Should've been a dress.

I'm so horny!

My breathing has become heavy and he notices, but only offers a smile.

I attempt to help him pull my top over my head and immediately regret it.

"Don't make things worse for yourself," he smirks, eyes glistening with what must be evil thoughts.

I'm not sure if it's the high or me, but I love how demanding he is. I feel him lift me in one motion before bringing me to the top of the stairs to sit.

"Legs apart," his tone serious.

I move my legs apart and watch him undress himself, standing only a few steps down from me. He's still able to tower over me regardless of where he's standing. Looking up at him from this distance, is about to make me cum. Just the view of him is–

My eyes follow along the muscles that line his chest…

… his arms.

His abdomen…

That V-line…

My tongue finds my lips to offer them hydration. I take a deep breath, watching him watch me. My eyes move down to the natural curve of his dick.

The length…

The veins…

The smooth pink head…

The feel of more juice leaking from my pussy lets me know I'm ready. If him take a step up yah him slide enuh.

I smile to myself at that last thought. High yuh fuck!

The feeling dancing through my body sends my legs to meet but before they close, I hear his voice, "L E G S … A P A R T."

Startled, I look up at him just in time to see his jaw tick.

"I was just trying to suppress the feeling I–"

"Ssshh," he lets out.

I swallow my words and watch as he moves down to me. Here I am thinking we were going to make love here, on the stairs, but he picks me up, this time bringing me to his closet.

The journey from the top of the stairs to the closet felt like a flight. It's like I'm unaware of what's happening but also hyper aware of my skin against his. I take another deep breath as he lays me down on the closet island, not caring about the few things he has laying there.

My eyes land on a very wide, and tall mirror to the front and another just like it to the side of the closet. Suddenly I realize his motive.

Wait! Maybe mi shouldn't call him no couch climber

He steps away from me, stroking his dick while admiring my pose. I can see the head of his dick riddled with pre-cum, as blind as I am.

He picks up on my impatience from the pace of my breath because his next words are, "Say tuh you earlier?"

I roll my eyes which leads him to chuckle.

"Don't cum until you say suh?"…whatever that means, 'cause me a cum when me ready.

He smiles as if reading my snarky thought, then moves behind me with little to no sound. I stay still, deciding not to look back, watching him through the mirror. He slides a drawer from the island open and I watch him pull out a blind fold.

I–

I avert my attention from the mirror, snapping my head around to meet him.

"J? Wha–" I try to ask but my question is cut off by a simple gesture from his hand, signaling silence.

I–

He walks over to me and places the blindfold over my eyes and suddenly my sense of touch and sound have skyrocketed.

The weed is doing its jobbbb

He pulls me to the edge of the closet island and what I feel after sends my screams throughout the house. Jordanne sent his dick all the way up to a place I didn't know was there. My hands go into slight panic, searching for sheets to grab like I usually would, but they come up empty.

No bed, no sheets

I feel him move down and I hook my fingers into his back, trying to replace the missing feel of the sheets. The warmth of his skin on mine is another feeling in and of itself.

He stays still inside me… awaiting my recovery it seems. When my breathing subsides, he moves to my ear to say…

"I should be able to wear every piece of clothes in here with the memory of you cumming, stained within them."

I– ummm.

My thoughts have left the building.

He doesn't seem to notice or care, instead he starts moving in and out. First slow and steady, then at a more rapid pace…

… and ohhhh my Godddd, that sppppotttt!

"Jor–dannnne," I moan hoarsely.

The only response I get is him taking one of my boobs into his warm mouth. His hands find my legs, resting them around his waist. In one lift, I'm up and lapped around him.

I wannnnnaa see

"I wanna s–" I try, but the next thing I feel is when he lifts me up all the way to the tip of his dick, only to slam me right back down.

"Fuck Jordanne!" my scream ear shattering– hoping to calm his pace.

It doesn't though, it doesn't calm him at all. In fact I think I made it worse...

He brings me up again but this time it's coupled with a question.

"Why yah ask 'bout Rome?" his voice seeps out, laced with venom.

My eyes start dancing behind the blind fold, searching for an answer I can't seem to find.

Ummm...

Cyaa help you with this one

"Ryleigh?" I hear him ask while bringing me down, "yahgo mek me ask twice?"

My mouth falls open at the feel of his dick caressing my insides.

I don't know...

You were concerned or curious

"I–" I try to voice my thoughts, but the words seem to be stuck in my throat.

He uses this opportunity to move his hands from my waist, placing one across my back and up to my shoulder while the other holds my head.

Like a baby...

He moves me back to the island before removing the blind fold. My eyes fly open, blinking multiple times while adjusting to the light.

"Stand," he orders me.

Obeying him, I try to stand but struggle to find my footing. He moves behind me, grabbing my hair in one hand, arms in the next. Without using any hands to guide his dick, he forces himself inside me from behind.

I shudder at the raw feeling, my head now up and my eyes on the mirror. Our eyes meet and I suddenly feel intimidated.

Letting my head fall, I look away.

"Look at me," his tone now stern.

I find his eyes in the mirror again and he tightens the grip he has on my hair, pulling my head up a little further than where it was first.

"Again, why yah ask 'bout Rome? When mi tell yuh a ting already."

When my answer doesn't come, he starts moving in and out of me. The strokes are long, deep and hard– repetitively hammering my G-spot. I don't have control of my hands to grab anything, so instead, my walls grow tight around him. Gripping his manhood inside me only makes the feeling more pleasurable.

"Oh my Go– Jor– da–" I breathe, trying to follow his rule of not cumming until he grants permission.

"You find words of pleasure, but yuh cyaa answer man question?" with that he releases my hands.

Watching him bend, I realize he's pulling out a drawer positioned just below his knees. He lifts my right leg, resting it on the open drawer before snaking his hand to my clit.

Fada God

Looking at my reaction in the mirror, he smirks.

"I was just curious," my answer comes out of nowhere.

"Bout next man?" the pace of his strokes increasing.

I reel under the feeling.

Me cyaa bother enuh

Weh him wah me say? That's really it me just wah know if him alright.

"Jordanne drop it. You know I'm a curious person," I retort.

"Too curious," he says, grabbing my neck from behind.

Seeming to have dropped the question like I suggested, he starts focusing on his strokes. The more he rubs my walls, the weaker I become... The wetter I become... The more ragged my breathing becomes...

He notices that my body is asking for a release and mouths the word, 'NO'.

I must've thought he mouthed, 'CUM' because before his lips are finished expressing his thought, I grab the sides of the closet island, screaming for dear life while watering his dick.

•••

JORDANNE

She's shaking beneath me, enjoying the orgasm mi tell her fi hold on pon. I watch as she realizes I didn't grant her permission.

Impatient all round

"Did I tell you to cum?"

"... No," she whimpers, no doubt regretting her choice.

I slap her ass and help her up with my dick still inside.

Wish me coulda live ina it

Jah Jah.

I move us down to the closet chair, taking a seat. Her legs find the hook of my knees and she bends forward, resting her hands on the mirror.

That ah go be a memorable smudge

I find myself smiling at that thought.

Lifting her waist, I start pelting steady strokes to her center.

"I'm gonna cum again J," she whimpers after the first minute or two.

That was quick... I still don't want it to end.

Her pussy feels like...

Like...

... like the first pull you take in the morning. Like releasing the trigger in a boy weh ah annoy me fi months...

Like the first sip of Hennessy after a stressful day.

Comparisons yah nah do her no justice

I don't know, the feel of it is just satisfying. Not even the physical feeling, just di energy it a give off.

Jah know

"Ahhhhhhh!!!!" she screams, her voice jolting me back to earth.

She starts throwing it back– her way of letting me know she's ready to be filled. But I don't want to stop…

Wah live in deh.

Deciding to allow her release, I grab her waist, pulling her closer to me. Squeezing her ass cheeks while delivering fast rounds of strokes, my own orgasm makes its way to the forefront. In less than two seconds all nerve endings in my body, direct their energy to my dick.

"Ry," I manage to get out… but she doesn't give me the time of day.

Girl busy a fight her own orgasm for the millionth time.

Me baby…

Moving down to her ear, I whisper, "Flood it," and just as I instructed, she starts squirting.

Bloodclawt

On command? … and that's how I know she's mine. Always has been and always will be. The sound of her scream brings me to the edge. My cream shoots to the forefront of my dick before settling inside her warmth.

A quick chill runs down my spine as she reaches for the hand I have holding her waist– pulling me down to her again.

I don't hesitate on leaving kisses on her shoulders… She's perfect.

Enough reason fi kill Rome

"C'mere," I groan, slipping out of her while lifting her to her feet.

She stands, looking at me with nothing but love in her eyes. I gently take her hand and lead us out of the closet and into the bedroom.

•••

5:00am

I stand there with her in my arms, my eyes glued to the airstair. If I could convince her to join me, I would.

And what would she do about school?

She doesn't even need school.

Bad head buil

Okay she could do it online while with me?

And you get to have a normal college experience while she does what?

Better than her twerking in the club, on a random Thursday night.

Fuckry.

I hiss at the battle playing out in my mind and she looks up at me.

"Sure yuh nuh wah farwud?" I ask, my eyes hoping for a yes.

"J'... be fair," her smile soft but her eyes tell me her mind's made up.

She's always been stubborn. My mind drifts back to me getting her the Benz Coupe to match mine and her giving it to her mom just to get herself a Range– just last week too. That's not even the real issue. I like when I have everything under my control, even her... but I can't control her, and dat ago stress me brain while I'm away.

"Dat good, but if you change your mind," I smile, masking my true desire.

"I won't," she tightens the hug we've been in.

... And for a moment me feel like lift her up, throw her ina the jet and call it a day.

Hmmhmm, swear to you.

"Mr.Sheer?" the attendant's voice comes from behind us.

Not giving her my attention, I pull Ry' in even tighter.

"Go to school babe," she whispers.

Ignoring her command, I pull her in for the last kiss. She deepens it, sending my memories into a frenzy. We haven't slept all night, instead we used the time to move through rounds of intimacy. The quick flashback brings a smile to my face that I know she can feel within the kiss itself.

"Mr. Sheer we have to get going now," the attendant's voice breaks our kiss.

Fuck do dah woman yah?

Pulling away from Ryleigh, I look up to her and ask, "Yuh like you job?"

A look of embarrassment sweeps across her face and Ryleigh slaps my chest.

"Jordanne be nice!" she whisper-shouts. "I love you, now go to school. I'm cold and tired."

"Must tired," I smirk.

She giggles out before tipping up to plant another kiss on my forehead.

I beckon to Skulli to come take her... and as she leaves with him, I mount the stairs. Stopping to look back, I watch her enter the car. She waves at me as Skulli pulls off and I sigh, watching as the vehicle disappears.

Walking to my seat as the crew locks up and ready themselves for departure, my mind settles on only one thing...

... Her asking about Rome.

38 | Get Away

RYLEIGH

It's Good Friday and the girls, Sue, my mom and I are packing for a mini staycation in Negril. Everybody else ago Ochi but we want to be outa the way, you know.

"Ry' mahgo ring yuh back," Jordanne's husky voice comes through the speakers.

"Cool..." I mutter, picking up the phone from where it was propped up against my jewelry box.

Since January, before he even left, there has been a disconnect between J' and I that I can't quite put my finger on. I've been consistent with my therapy and some of the things we've been unfolding, has been causing a rift.

I'm not sure if he's been consistent with his sessions or if he even goes at all. These days he's snappy and angry, with a hint of possessiveness. I mean, I knew how he was from the start but that shit has multiplied.

We're supposed to go to our first session together online, sometime next week, but...
Sigh.

I decide to fix my hair in a pony before dragging a simple swimsuit on. **April** isn't a good month for me and hasn't been since– since that.

The house is empty, cold... and as much as I love it here, I wish Toni would come stay with me until J' gets back. She stilllll hasn't told me what all that was back then but we've been hanging out more, finally.

Staring at my reflection in the mirror, I smile before deciding to call my mom.

She answers on the third ring.

"Mi pikny," and I can hear the wind from her car.

"You soon reach?" I query, forgetting to mask my emotions.

"Turning on your street, how you sound so?"

"Just no feel good," I whimper.

"... MHmmm, you think you–" she begins to ask but I quickly shut it down.

"No mommy, I'm still on the pills… Just that I–" I start but stop, "me alright man just did up too late last night," I find a quick excuse to hand off.

"Mhmm, you just mek me know if you need me fi come stay with you after this weekend," her tone now serious.

I force a giggle to lighten the mood.

"You nuh reach yet? Remember alla we a go down ina three cars."

"Ry' me just say me a turn pon your street. The car nah fly."

Another call comes in and I realize it's Troopa. Yes, I was able to have my own way and have him moved to our home instead of Sue's

Bruk bad

Whatever I want…

"Mommy Troopa a call, me wii see you in a few," I state, switching the call before she could continue to drill my true feelings to the surface.

"Troopa?" my voice emitting actual concern.

"Lorelle outside."

"Troopa you nuh affi call me fi Lorelle or Toni, just let them through each time," I laugh.

One man cyaa so strict.

'Me tell yuh! open this man!' Lorelle's in the background arguing.

Within seconds I hear the car roll in and soon after the doorbell rings. I move down the stairs, with my little carry-on, ready to start our weekend and forget about my issues.

I open the door and she hurls herself at me.

"Me look okay? Me affi promote the hair, it too much?" she's way more concerned than she needs to be.

"Yuh good Lorelle and when since you turn influencer?" I ask, feigning happiness.

"Since me no wah pay millions fi likkle braids. Mariah gave me her link," her eyes take me in, "why you look and sound so?" she asks, eyeing me from head to toe.

I snap my head away because I know I can't lie to her. Anybody else but not 'Relle.

Sigh…

"It's April…" I murmur, pulling at the straps of my bikini.

Her eyes soften before she pulls me into a hug.

"It's Okay Ry' we ago carry you go forget about it. Once we exit crosses Town, you nahgo feel so," she assures me while trying to lift my spirits.

I offer her a small smile.

"You spoke to Jordanne about how you're feeling?" she asks, searching my eyes for confirmation.

"No, why?" I ask, peering at her.

"Cause him text me say fi make sure you good this weekend, so I was expecting you to be down, but not this low," she explains– eyebrows knitted in concern.

I smile... and for the first time a weight is lifted from my shoulders.

He remembers...

... And cares.

My smile grows into a laugh.

"You loooovvve out sah. As me mention the man name you fix? Mercyyy," she doubles over in laughter.

We both laugh until the sound of an engine presents itself outside.

"Mummy that enuh, come," I drag her and my luggage out.

"Only you and Lorelle deh yah?!" mommy shouts from her window.

"Yes, the rest a come with T' and Slyme dem!" I shout back.

Lorelle offers to lift my luggage to mom's car.

"Weh yours?" I ask while following her.

"Wah? Me plan fi naked all weekend. I have fresh panties in my crossbag right yah suh. See," she holds up her tiny bag.

I giggle before shaking my head and stepping off. Live she ago live ina robe and swimsuit whole time.

We get to the gate and Lorelle throws me my keys. I might as well say her keys at this point though. I can't go anywhere without Slyme anyways so what's the point of having my car 24/7.

The thought sinks my mood again...

We hop into mommy's vehicle while waving bye to Troopa.

"Ah, see unuh Monday," he waves back.

• • •

Exactly five hours later we get to Negril.

Me batty numbbbb

Pheewwweee, my God mi batty stiff. I can't wait to get out and stand.

Lorelle was right, soon as we left Kingston, I started to feel much better. The fresh air and lush trees alone did most of the job.

We pull into the little boutique hotel that's rented out completely, only because Jordanne intervened, saying he wasn't taking any chances.

"Girlsss," I hear Sue's voice as we exit the cars.

We all turn to find her waving us over to help with her pots from the trunk of her SUV.

"Sue wah chef deh yah enuh," Skulli reminds her– shaking his head in disapproval.

By the way they speak to each other, it's easy to tell they've known and been in love for years. Watching them now, I don't know how we miss dat.

Minutes later we're all inside and scoping out who gets which room.

"Mi feel Ryleigh fi get the master suite since a fi her man money spend!" Lorelle argues.

"You just wah the nice room 'cause you know she ago pick you fi sleep with," Keif laughs.

"It's whatever for me," I mutter.

"Me agree with Keif," Toni adds her two cents.

Mariah thinks we should do a raffle for the rooms so she can add it to the vlog. I like the idea, and mi nuh mind whichever room I get.

"Raffle me say we a raffle," she silences everybody.

I smile to myself, watching her write the numbers down. It's 4 suites, 7 bedrooms in total with 8 bathrooms, 2 big kitchens, a nice pool and a section of the beach that's just for us.

"So since a 7 bedrooms, Ms.Sue and daddy ago take one, Ms.Janette a take one and Slyme a take one," she says while setting up her camera. "That leaves 4, so the 6 a we affi go split. Whichever number you grab, whoever grabs the same number ah you room-mate."

By now she's done writing numbers and is busy rolling papers– shaking them in a temporary pouch she made from her head scarf.

"You first," she turns to me.

I dip and come up with #3

She goes around the room.

Muuch picks #1, Keif picks #2 and Mariah herself picks #4. Nobody has a roommate yet so she goes to Lorelle... and she picks #2.

Pheew me ago get me own room?

Yesss!

Toni-Anne is last to pick and she picks... #3. Well that was a good thought while it lasted.

The look that sweeps her face confuses me and I let my emotions speak before I think, "A wah... Me no good enough fi sleep with?" I try to read her expression.

"Just did wah me own room fi call Joshua," she laughs.

Oh! I completely understand that.

I giggle, because room or not me a call my man fi sure.

"Okay so Ryleigh get the big suite 'cause unuh done know how that go already... Your sharing nahgo bad 'cause the beds far apart," Mariah giggles while running off to her room.

Her and Muuch are the only ones with their own space. Have a feeling she rig the game enuh... How she nah share?

I smile at myself, realizing she definitely did.

"Pool?" I ask, looking at everyone left in the living area.

"Pool and pics?" Lorelle suggests and with that we all leave our stuff in our respective rooms and walk down to the pool.

In less than ten minutes all pictures are taken, since we don't really want extra 'pro' looking pictures this time around. We all just want to enjoy our trip and be present.

Everybody sends what they have to the group chat just to make it easier to pick and save.

I take a look.

Mariah body great and I love her slides. Of course she still took her picture serious, it's her job. My big batty, shorty-poom-stick browning. My eyes find Muuch's picture next and she thick and sexy as per usual. So me love when a thick girl look nice and clean, very comfortable in her skin. My eyes then move to Keif's picture. She's such a beauty... It's always the melanin for me when it comes to her, Muuch and T'.

Lorelle like myself didn't want any fancy flicks. She took a picture of her hair for the salon to repost and that was is... but T???

Toniiii?

Whew, gyal prettyyyyy! I actually click in on her picture just to look more. The prettiest, and me not even a exaggerate.

My scroll ends at my picture. I was already in the pool trying to drown out my feelings. I didn't do a great job at hiding my mood at all– it's written all over this picture. Shrugging I upload it to my story anyway, after ensuring no unique location marker got caught.

Less than ten seconds later, a direct message comes in from a profile with a handle I don't recognize. It seems we have communicated before because the chat is there but the space is empty.

Huh???.

I can't remember un-sending anything... to anyone on Instagram. I click on the profile to investigate but it comes up empty. Deciding to ignore it and move back to my page, I notice a green circle has popped up around their profile picture in the story feed section.

Close friends?

Being the 'nuffy' that I am, I click on it... and immediately recognize **his** tattoos. Panic sends my body into slight shock, causing my fingers to click the fuck out of the story. Shocked out of my mind I look around and my eyes meet Lorelle's. Deciding to not say anything, I lock my phone and go back to swimming.

Nah chance it a Bloodclawt.

39 | Miscommunication

JORDANNE

"Ry' mahgo ring yuh back," I say, getting ready to end the call. "Cool..." she hangs up.

The disconnect is evident between us. Normally we coulda fix it through sex but since we're miles apart, that's not an option.

She keeps asking me about my therapy sessions... the ones I haven't been going to.

Just nahv the time skull. This one course a kill me.

Mathematical Methods of Engineering

You know when you think yah top man, until yuh reach a certain point in your degree and realize yuh affi actually take it serious? Affi actually study?

Deh so me deh.

But that a just school alone. Me have other obligations too. I've managed to get all the properties in order, get Ruse to agree to fall under command and stop try start a mediocre war weh me nuh have time fah... and I've even accepted that Sue is in fact with Paul and nothing cyaa change that. Everything except the issues we've been having with the Venezuelans and the JCF lingering around my family home every now and then according to Mum, is under control.

So therapy is the least of my worries.

How yuh finally get the girl we been want and a fuck it up, again?

Nah fuck it up intentionally, just have a bagga shit a gwaan right now.

"Jordanne?" Lizzy nudges me.

I look back to face her, and realize I've probably been staring out into space... again.

"Lizzy?" I retort, quirking a brow at her.

"The problem Jordanne. Did you get to the conclusion?"

I look down at my booklet and realize I haven't even started.

"Distracted," I mumble, offering her a tiny smile.

She rolls her eyes and asks, "Is it Ryleigh again?" and for a split second I think about telling her that assumption is disrespectful.

But I don't... Instead, I ignore her and move to my spliff.

"You can't smoke that in here," she reminds me, but I've been smoking here since freshman year.

"It good," I pull, hoping she'll shut up for a second.

She doesn't, instead she goes on about something happening to somebody who smoked in their dorm room. I drown her out by taking deep long pulls and within minutes my mind is cleared.

Therapy cyaa do dis.

Yuh never gave it a chance

More minutes later, I'm going through the booklet with ease. When I get to the last question, I ask her to match her answers to mine and surprisingly they're all the same– give or take some steps.

"We should reward ourselves don't you think?" her voice pulls my attention to her.

Since I got back, she's been trying to get me out to mingle and actually see what college is really like.

Mi nuh know still... Ah just nuh my ting. The bagga people and noise. Only Ry' can drag me ina them thing deh... Miss her yuh fuck. Maybe me fi go home? But naaah, she just complained about her space, forcing me to bend my rules. I've granted her everything, except traveling without Slyme.

... And she still no understand that. Maybe me fi carry her go work so she can see who she's actually with fi real.

Nah, keep her from it as much as possible

All Troopa me give her, and me deven like how them laugh up with each other either.

"You keep blacking out, let's go. There's a party going on in the lounge," Lizzy drags me up from my desk.

I decide not to protest.

Maybe me need fi go mingle fi real... Do some networking.

• • •

The party is now in full swing.

I've decided to stay in my corner while observing everybody. Dem people yah party different. I've seen at least six different types of pills being passed around. Plus mushrooms...

Infused weed...

Coke even...

Jah know. Wonder who a dem supplier?

Don't add another thing to your plate

Just wah know.

"Smiiiiile for my camera," Lizzy shoves her phone in our faces.

"No cameras Lizz."

"I won't post it, promise," she whines.

Her innocent eyes and smile brings me to do what I feel will be a mistake. I go along for the hell of it anyways. Offering her the most genuine smile I can, she takes the picture. It's university, I should make memories right? before I'm back to a life where I can't do that as much.

She snaps the picture and shows it to me.

Me woman ago kill me

Probably but… it's an innocent picture, babe ago know that.

Cyaa get her offa my mind.

Deciding to soothe my thoughts, I step out to call her but she doesn't pick up. Know she ah enjoy her weekend though, so I don't give it another try. Instead, I ring Slyme, just fi mek sure everything gov.

He answers on the first ring, "Boss?"

"She good?" my question falls out and immediately I regret it because–

"She good Drip," he laughs out loud, too loud. "You know nuttin cyaa gwaan and me and Skulli present. The West team surround we too as per your instructions."

I chuckle.

"Ah kool. Just a check 'cause she no pick up."

"Wah tell yuh say dem out yah drunk as fuck ah dance with each other," he laughs again.

Hmmhh sound like dem yes.

"Ah tell Ramone link up before Sunday," I remind him, signaling the end of the call.

I hang up with a satisfying smile and feeling before heading back inside to sit in the same corner I was earlier. Noticing Lizzy is no longer there, my eyes start searching the room for her. I find her having an argument with a random, and the sight of it drags a hiss from my lips.

Jah know, mi fi ignore it don't?

My jaw ticks and I realize I can't leave her to argue with a group of guys. Walking over to them, I grab her arm and pull her from the small crowd.

"Who the fuck are you?" the voice of the main guy asks.

I quirk a brow to look at him, not offering any explanation.

"Nah 'cause who the fffuckk is this nigga for real though? Ya'll know this guy?" another one sporting a ski mask asks while looking around.

The room goes quiet.

I smirk…

My knuckles haven't had some fun in a while and if I were to get suspended, I could go home to mi woman wid proper reason.

"Just deh yah fi mek sure the girl I came with drop back home safely," I realize how sunken my voice is and how warm my blood has gotten.

"Oh Bob Marley! It's Bob Marley everybody!" the main guy laughs, grabbing Lizzy.

I hold her steady and connect my fist to his nose. He stumbles over a few chairs, coming back up with an instant nosebleed.

Hmmhmm... Him will buil back next time.

The others move to me but I lift the hem of my shirt, just to show them it's a bad idea. I don't want to pull, but I will if I have to.

"Lizzy, we a leave," I muter before pulling her to the exit and out the party.

"Well that went well," she laughs... but I don't find it funny.

"Come on Jordanne lighten up. You handled yourself well," she giggles.

Dah girl yah a sniff the white lady enuh.

Fi sure yute

Ignoring her behavior, I lift her to my shoulders and walk back to her dorm. We make it there in less than five minutes and I deliver her to her house mates. When I'm satisfied she's safe, I leave to walk back to my dorm.

• • •

RYLEIGH

"Mi ago bathrooooommm!" I scream to them, and with that I stumble to the restroom nearest to the pool.

One ting with me, me ago wah piss after liquor.

Before peeing, I grab some paper towels to get my phone screen dried enough to check my notifications. There are a few, but the only one I care about is the one from him.

Me love out fi real enuh.

One hundred percentttt

His missed call stands out the most, so I decide to ring him back and of course he answers on the first ring.

"Yuh good?" his voice groggy– he seems to be pulling himself from sleep.

"Yeah just checking in. See yuh missed call."

"Yeah man, just did a check in. You no say nuttin from you reach," he explains.

"Neva ina no good mood. You know how April is for me..." I trail off.

With that I hear him sigh, "You wah me drop ina the place?" his suggestion throws me off guard.

"J I'm okay I promise."

A minute of silence passes before I speak again, "Go back to bed, I'm going back outside."

"Cool... Ryleigh?" he calls, "know we nah communicate properly fi a while now but promise me you'll stick it out until me reach home?" his words trigger my anxiety... a little bit.

"I will," I offer him as much comfort in my words as I can.

"Good, love you more than you know... and don't sink yourself into depression thinking about supm weh anuh your fault. Enjoy the rest ah the weekend."

Instantly my lips turn up into a smile. I really wish he was here for real, but if I so much as mention it, he'll drop everything for me.

And we no need that

We don't.

"Good night Mr.Sheer," I whisper.

"Goodnight Mrs.Sheer," he whispers back, and I smile before ending the call.

Not the fucking Mrs!

Ughhhh! Me love di bwoyyy.

With everything he said at the top of my mind, I use the bathroom in the happiest mood possible. Approaching the mirror, I tap the soap, rub it in and wash my hands. My phone starts vibrating and I click open the notification without thinking twice... but what I see next knocks the wind out of me.

It's a picture of Jordanne and a random girl. She's leaned over on him, smiling with her tongue out to the camera. And him? He's smiiiiiiling too...

Yeah? I giggle.

Yeeeeaaah???

Say no more then. Say nooo moooore.

I click the phone shut and look at myself in the mirror.

Yeah?

Yes girl yes

Mi fi call him back?

Who tagged me? Why would this person tag me?

Be calm, you don't know the situation

And dem so cozy???! Wah else me need fi know? I snap my phone back open and click back to the profile. Before anything else I screenshot it. Immediately after that, I type, **'Cute'** and click send.

Deciding to go back to the party and not say anything to anybody until maybe tomorrow, I head out. Me nah go down this road with Jordanne again enuh.

Bwoiii I don't know

No but why this Lizzy person tag me?

I plop myself down in one of the pool chairs before going back to the notification… but it's gone.

Ina two seconds?!

I scroll back to my screenshot and look at the name again… Heading to my search bar, I type the name in and click on the profile that's now private.

Watch purpose

Realizing this person knew what they were doing, I laugh out– no traceable humor. It's private but I can see that he's the only mutual we have… and he only follows like 65 people.

Now how the fuck yuh miss when him following go up by one?

I don't know.

Observing her bio, I realize she goes to Columbia too. There's a Nigerian and British flag sitting up there too.

I toggle to Jordanne's chat and decide to send him the screenshot.

|Attachment|
Ya'll cute af ☺

"A wah?" I hear Lorelle's voice above me.

Clicking the phone shut, I look up at her before saying, "Nuttin, just a video. Me feel extra tipsy," I switch the topic.

"Giiiiirlllll the Henny have me a wayyyyyy," she drops down on the chair I'm in.

"AAAAAAYYYYYYEEEEEEEEE!!!" Mariah screams at us, "unuh getttt up man! Unuh can rest a morning."

Lorelle and I look at each other, laughing at how fucking loud she is.

Nevertheless, we stand and walk back to the pool bar… and for the rest of the night, I forget about the post.

40 | Boils Down

TONI-ANNE

"We're getting ready for bed– Ry' and I… and I'm thinking about switching rooms with Lorelle for real, but knowing her, she nahgo stop ask why until I explain. She's leaving the shower…

Naked.

I snap my head away not wanting to cause myself that feeling again.

Not now.

"Toni why yah act like you fraida breasts? You no have two pah you chest?" she questions.

If dah girl yah nuh go put on clothes!

"T'?" she mutters, and I don't know which switch flips in my mind, but I decide to just lay it out.

"I think I'm bi," I mumble.

She immediately holds her boobs.

"Bi like bicycle? Or bi-sexual like the flag team?!" her eyes dance with questions.

Somehow she makes me laugh…

"Sexual Ryleigh," I smile, before grabbing the nearest robe to hand it to her.

She takes it and slowly throws it on while watching me as if trying to figure out if this is another one of Mariah's little YouTube pranks.

"Weh di camera?!" she laughs, but my face stays blank.

"You're actually serious?" she continues while tying the robe.

"I am," my eyes find hers.

"So that's why you've been avoiding me? Why would you avoid me? You could've said something, you know me no business," she reassures me, while plopping down on the bed.

I hold my eyes to hers, hoping she reads them and I don't have to explain. The room falls silent for a few seconds.

"No... Say a lie... You like me don't you?!" she laughs. "Mi know me was a goodaz enuh but not this gooood," she doubles over.

"Gyal shut up nuh, yahgo tell the whole place?!" I join her cackle fest with genuine happiness.

And this is why I think I like her.

Ah just the energy.

"Tell Joshua me a tek him gyal," she continues laughing. "But seriously I don't think you like me. I think you're discovering your feelings for women and I'm just the closest you have to a perfect relationship with one."

… And until she said that just now, I haven't thought of it from that angle. Could be true but why does she turn me on?

"Maybe," is the word that chooses to leave my lips.

"Trust me you'll figure it out. Anuh me per se… Not saying me anuh the best gyal you ever seeeee and know," she laughs, "but those feelings can get confused."

She's laughing-laughing at this point.

What a dutty gyal, I join another round of her contagious laughter.

"I hope so," I giggle. "So me fi stay pah your bed or?"

"Not too much bitch," she snorts, "find yourself pon the second bed ova deh so. You lucky me no make you switch rooms but you know we friends nahgo stop ask a wah."

She right 'bout that.

"Right, Right," I nod.

She offers me a warm smile.

"And Ry'…" I turn to her, "don't tell J'."

Her laughter picks up again.

"Yuh know the boy say you did a look pah me though. When we a talk on the lawns and me tell him say him a idiot," pulling the sheets across her torso, she stares at me trying to suppress her smile.

Fuck.

Nothing duh pass that boy. Him worse than daddy.

"Still, I'll go to him when I'm ready, like I came to you," I explain.

"No probs," she shrugs, before wiggling herself further into her sheets.

With that I throw myself on the bed across from hers. I pop my AirPods in and start trying to force myself to sleep.

That's off my chest…

Pheew

●●●

JORDANNE

My alarm goes off and I grab my phone to shut it off.
Exactly 6:45am.
Releasing a yawn, I toggle to Ry's chat.

<u>Mrs.S:</u> |Attachment|
<u>Mrs.S:</u> Ya'll cute af ☺

Fuck this me wake to? Really?
I forward the picture to Lizzy.

|Attachment|
Fuck this Lizz?

<u>Lizzy MME class:</u> Jordanne I can explain.

Quickly.

<u>Lizzy MME class:</u> I didn't do it my homegirl did, stg.
When I woke up and saw that she replied I deleted it.
I was drunk, you know that.

Who reply to wah Lizz?

<u>Lizzy MME class:</u> She replied saying 'cute'. I'm sorry
my hg thought we were cute and pulled that shit.

So how the fuck she find Ry'
page if you did so drunk?

<u>Lizzy MME class:</u> I kinda mentioned her. They
kept pressuring me to get with u so I told them you
gotta serious gf and showed them her page. I've known
her page since you tagged her earlier this year b4 coming
back from the semester you took off, the story posts.

Get yuh but hear wah,
the study sessions done.
The hanging out, done.

<u>Lizzy MME class:</u> Jordanne it wasn't me.

And me say me get yuh but
them ting deh done.

She continues to type but I decide on ignoring her. Ryleigh already warned me 'bout
the access weh other women have to me, now this.

I hiss my teeth. Jah Jah.

Laying back in bed, I start contemplating calling her. Doubt she up but, I try anyway. Clicking on her name, I give her a ring but of course, she doesn't answer...

Bumboclawt.

I attempt trying again but get cut off by Ramone's call.

"Early rise," I speak first.

"Early rise. Skulli say link up?"

"Yeah, on the encrypted line," I explain.

"Ah... mah pull that up now," he says.

Hanging up, I hop out of bed and move to my desk, opening my laptop. Within a minute Ramone is on the line.

"We have a lot to talk about, concerning the Venezuelans. Skulli a deal with JCF so me nahfi too worry 'bout that."

"Cool, shoot," he gives me the go ahead, rocking back in his chair.

"Gabriel a say some stacks come up missing but me sure everybody double checked before flying down. So things must've gotten fucked up on the ground in Guyana. Ago need yuh fi send the routes in detail. The pilot info, the runner dem info, every fucking thing basically... 'cause we continue to lose off this route. Mi can't continue send a certain amount and when confirmation pull, stacks missing. Money a tilt."

"Everything did good before we send over the cash, so is either Gabriel a gi we pill fi swallow or somebody on the ground a pinch," Ramone offers.

Only explanation that fi real, and mi really hope anuh Gabriel a lie to me. Woulda affi go above and beyond fi prove that.

And den yuh affi go kill him and draw down a whole country pah yourself

If a so a so...

"Get them to me by tonight," I instruct, leaving no room for objection.

"Ah," he agrees and before his gesture is finished, I hang up.

Ry'... my mind reminds me of my personal issue. I look at the time to the top right corner of the screen to see 7:05am.

Ago try her again

I do as my thoughts suggest, but come up empty. Toggling over to Skulli's contact, I ring him, but him nuh answer either.

Man lock down and off him game killa.

I move to Slyme's number and like always, he answers on the first ring.

Man deserve upward ranks and a raise

"Early rise," his voice comes clear across my phone's speaker.

"Early rise," I murmur, barely audible. "Wake her please."

"Ah, dem just go sleep though," he tries to explain.

"Important. Wake her now," and with that I hang up.

Man a tell me say? When me clearly say wake me woman
I hiss, my frustration now at its peak.

• • •

RYLEIGH

I stir from my sleep by the sound of the room door banging lightly.

A hiss wrapped in annoyance comes from my mouth. If anuh Muuch a try wake everybody fi go eat Sue breakfast, then I don't know.

"Ryleigh," I hear Slyme's voice, and jump up immediately.

I look over to Toni who got woken up too, but is now dragging the pillow over her head.

Me likkle LGBTQ... XYZ.

I smile to myself while attempting to slide off the bed.

"Ryleigh! Yuh ago mek the man fire me?" Slyme's voice seeps into the room.

"Me a come," I offer lowly... and suddenly I remember I sent **him** the screenshot.

I hiss, loudly this time.

My feet take me to the door and I open it, taking the phone from Slyme.

"Keep it, him ago call," he lets me know before walking off.

So him couldn't call pah my phone? Wah him have fi say so? If him come with the work bullshit again, I swear.

I walk back to the bed before crawling back in and before I'm even relaxed, the phone goes off.

"Yes Mr.Bachelor, what happened?" my tone snarky.

"Ryleigh, buil," he starts, his tone serious.

41 | Outside

RYLEIGH

"**B**uil offa wah exactly J'?"

"The picture innocent," he starts explaining.

"Yeahhh? It look innocent to you?" I retort… and the line goes silent for a few seconds.

Mhmmhm.

Innocent and goodie tag me like she have supm fi prove? More while me wonder if them give my man the least amount a sense when it come to gyal. If anuh Emily, is a random girl outa road, now it's a random girl from school.

No sah, free for all?

"Lizzy a just somebody me study with most times. The girl mek me farwud a wah party, me see she take out her phone and snap a picture and me mek it gwaan. She get ina wah little thing with some man and me pull her weh and mek sure she reach ho–"

"Alright Superman, when since you start mingle?" I cut him off.

Me no wah hear it, I just don't want to.

"Ryleigh, believe me, the picture innocent."

"Mhmmhm… If you see one come to you phone look the same way, memba it innocent," I mumble more to myself than him.

"Fuck you say a while ago?" he sneers.

Wait… That's the very first time he's used that tone with me. The anger skating from his voice to my ears send shudders around my skin.

Girlllll

"Yuh know yuh no know who yah deal wid more while though?!" his voice comes across dripping in hate.

I lower the phone from my ears.

Toni flies up and looks over at me.

I–

"Try nuttin and me put you and whoever you pick to sleep. Stop fuck 'round me medz bredda."

Hear yah?

"Oh? So yuh can continuously put me in fucked up scenarios but as me mention nuttin you ago kill, yahgo kill, yahgo kill. Well fucking kill me 'cause me nah back. Pussy stop play with me feelings 'cause me nuh affi deh yah so yerrrr? Why the girl tag me? A so you have perfect explanations each time some bitch pulls a stunt and a so me fi swallow them??? Me must get a yam tattoooo? Tell me from early," I let out– my breathing now heavy, and my hands shaaakingg.

Me fraid yuh fuck! But I have to say how I feel. Can't be with somebody I can't talk to. He releases a deep but deadly laugh– drawing tingles from my stomach just by the sound.

"Hear wah, do yuh ting."

"Defini–" and before I finish the word, the line cuts off.

MMMMCCCHHHHTTTTTTTT!

I hiss while looking at Toni. I can see that she wants to pry but my face tells her to leave it alone.

Tired ah him ways man. Tired…

• • •

It's the afternoon and we've all decided to head out and do some site seeing. While walking down the garden path from my room, I encounter mommy and Ms.Sue– just Sue, struggling to take each other's pictures. I grab mommy's phone without any explanation and start snapping.

My mother she wid her hourglass, 'light bright' self. Today she's sporting a roomy jean pant and a cute top that stops just above the waist of the jeans, exposing less than an inch of her waistline. She has her natural hair out today too– her curls looking as juicy as ever.

Sue? is another story. She's in a short tweed dress that houses three asymmetrical colors, while her hair is pulled back into a low bun. I love how her dark skin sits against the vibrant colors, the doll angle.

"There," I shove the phone to mommy, "cause unuh ago try take pictures all day."

"A the one trip we get fi come pon enuh Ryleigh. We want to store the memories," mommy giggles.

"Right! Take mine too," Sue giggles, now bolting towards the hammock off the side of the property.

I walk to meet her while she poses– her smile almost to her ear.

"Mrs.Sheer yuh no look a day over 16," I joke.

"Just Sue Ryleigh and nuh swell me head enuh," she laughs while taking the phone from me to look at the masterpiece.

Cause if I can't do nothing else, me can snap a picture

"Love it! Let's go before Paul dem start complain," she turns before walking back up to the pavement.

Following her, my eyes scan the beauty of the property for the millionth time since I've been here. The next thing I spot is Muuch, Mariah and Keif hopping into Slyme's open Jeep. Toni, Lorelle and I hop into mommy's coupe and Paul and Sue take his Trackhawk.

Muuch and Slyme have been all buddy-buddy since yesterday but let me mind my business.

We head down the strip just looking for cool spots to stop and check out... and nice little restaurants to sample.

Like authentic tourists

We pull up on a little shack like, fruit stall, not too crowded but enough for us to conclude the fruits are good. All three cars pull over and we hop out, ready to dig into the coconut guy's cart.

"I'm a pineapple girl enuh," Muuch complains, looking at the bags of pineapple that seem to not be yellow enough for her.

"Eeeh?" Slyme laughs.

He doesn't normally talk but he's been light this entire trip.

And look how a Paw me did wah come

"Cokenat me want," Mariah walks over.

"Picture yah look enuh," Toni laughs.

This sends myself, Lorelle and Keif into a laughing fit, because we all know it's the truth.

"Nuh that's why she run go ina the open Jeep, fi vlog it, but look pon her hair now," Lorelle laughs out– slapping poor Keif.

"Like a in deh dem hide Bolt money," Keif adds to the cackle fest.

I giggle and move to the mangoes.

Mango season no start good yet and them have them big ripe one yah? Country nice enuh. While picking up a few, I hear Ms.Sue's voice directed at me, "Pick up more if you want me to juice or slice them up for you when we get back."

"A now she ago eat them Suanne, yuh no know Ryleigh. That wii eat a bucket by herself," mommy chimes in.

Everybody laughs out, including me.

"Me ago pick up extra yes. Me no love the juice but you can add them to my fruit plate."

Within a few more minutes, we get what we all want before moving to the side of the cars.

Everybody's now busy doing one thing or the other. Mariah is having Toni take pictures of her holding her coconut... Muuch and Slyme are sharing a bag of pineapples... Ms.Sue and Paul are halfway through a slice of yellow melon...

Lorelle, Keif, mommy and I have decided on mangoes– stretching our bodies away from our hands to make sure we don't get the juice on our clothes.

What a life

Another set of vehicles pull over to the stall and a group of guys and four girls hop out. The last guy to exit, is tall with alotttt of tattoos– sporting a ski mask.

Me know him a bun up

He catches me staring and I look away, continuing to eat my mango.

Man look like him just a come back from the deepest, darkest prison

Moments pass and I'm now busy trying to source water to rinse my hands– since mommy them done it without me getting a chance to wash my hands.

"You can use the igloo water pretty girl," the guy that owns the stall suggests.

"That ago freeze up me finger man," I offer him a warm smile.

"You can use my water," the scary looking guy speaks– keeping his eyes on me.

Then how man can offer me water so? Me give off thirsty?

I look down at his hands, but there is no sign of a water bottle. Snapping my head back up to him, I quirk my brows in confusion.

"Bring the water from the car Peppa," he shouts, and another even scarier looking guy moves to the car, bringing back a small bottle of Catherine's Peak.

Not offering my words, I take the bottle and rinse my hands away from my feet, careful not to splash it.

"Yuh stush, Town yuh farwud from?" he chuckles.

I take slight offense to the accusation and say, "May Pen me born and grow..."

Why yah tell the man yuh business?

"Anuh play pen. Mi like that," he smirks.

"Tanx fi'eh waatah," my rural accent takes course, determined to make my point clear. Me is not a Town girl...

Girl we deh-deh over eight years

Making a note of that thought, I decide to plan a trip to visit my family in Clarendon.

"A little supm a gwaan pon the beach lata, if unuh wah step?" he hands me a flier while observing my friends, who are engrossed in talking.

I take the flier and slip it in my deep dress pocket.

"Bad head we a cut," I hear Slyme's voice behind me.

He never calls me that but I'm smart enough to know that he doesn't want to use my name around strangers.

"Tanx again Mr?" I pause for him to give me his name.

He doesn't, instead he looks at Slyme and says, "Welcome, princess."

I turn to move back to where everybody is standing, but Slyme meant what he said when he said it's time to leave. Because of that, we all hop back into the respective vehicles to continue our tour.

• • •

"I don't know me feel like we fi go," Mariah suggests, holding the flier from earlier in her hands.

"Yuh know we can't go without the man dem and Slyme done say a yah so a the pree fi the rest a night," Lorelle mutters.

"Slyme a focus pah Muuch," Mariah blurts out... and we all laugh.

"Me wah go but going alone seem cayliss as fuck," my eyes find Mariah's.

"YOLO girl. Me a 20, the bigger one, mah make the decisions," she retorts.

"Okay but we a bring Toni," I demand.

"T' nahgo deh pon this. She nah disobey we brother," Mariah pushes.

"WE brother???" myself and Lorelle laugh out.

"A wah? A long time me want a family," she cackles.

I take the flier from her to really look at it.

Fuck it. Might as well

• • •

It's 12:18am and Mariah, Lorelle and I are sneaking off to this beach party. I'll send my mom my location when we get there, if we can even find it. Hopping into my mom's car, I shove the gear to neutral, allowing it to run without sound.

Mi know the shadow guards won't question mommy's car leaving as much as they would with anybody else's.

"Turn off the headlight!" Lorelle whisper-shouts.

Obeying her, I flick them off while watching the mirrors as we roll back. Mariah has the gates opened and I successfully make it off the property. Lorelle hops into the front and Mariah carefully closes the gate– ensuring the slam from it being automatic isn't loud.

She completes her mission and hops into the back seat. With that, I kick it into drive and we're offffff!

"Woiiiiii Slyme kill yuh a morning!" Mariah laughs, pulling my hair from the backseat.

"Slyme yah worry 'bout? Her man ago crucify we, stay deh nuh," Lorelle corrects her with a hint of seriousness in her voice. She love the excitement too but is always the voice of reason when it comes to stupid shit like this.

"Well we out already enuh, cyaa turn back," I giggle, sinking the gas pedal, pushing us back. Tonight better nice enuh.

Better!

42 | Outside Part TWO

RYLEIGH

I park the car along the road where everybody else is parked. As I'm perfectly getting in line a knock comes at the window.

"$250 park mumma, $250 and nobody no touch the beast," a random guy bargains.

I hiss and wind my window down, to gain a better view of how close I am to the bushes, 'cause you know girl kinda blind.

"$250, me have change," he repeats his service offer.

"Me no have no cash pah me," I sneer, keeping my focus on lining mommy's car perfectly.

"Eyih!" Mariah's voice comes out covered in annoyance.

I glance back to see her handing him a $500 bill.

"Watch it twice as hard!" she warns him.

"Tanx mumma, 'cause you friend ah front nah pay me no mind."

"She busy," Mariah counters, and with that he walks away, leaving us to go annoy other people who are now trying to park too.

"One a dem man deh ever present," Lorelle laughs.

"And dem nah watch nuttin enuh," I chuckle while putting the car into park, before shutting it off and exiting.

None of us know where the fuck we are, so we decide to follow the crowd and sound of the music. We walk a short path to the beach and what I thought would be just a small beach party is actually a big event.

No wonder everybody dress so serious

We make it to the entrance and attempt to walk in, but the security asks for our names or an invite.

"We only got a flier," Mariah tries to explain.

I stay quiet...

"Yeah a guy gave her the flier, he didn't say his name," Lorelle adds.

He looks at me before raising his eyebrows in skepticism.

A wah? Me need fi ina designer or supm?

"Unuh have the flier? It's not a flier, it's an invite and it's one per person... so."

"Peppa!!!?" Mariah's voice breaks the conversation open.

Then look how the girl store up the man friend name. She dangerous enuh.

I smile to myself at her determination.

The guy, Peppa? looks over in slight shock. I wave at him, and he walks to the entrance.

"Ohhh, a Chief people them elder, let them in," he shouts while beckoning us over.

Mariah is the first to model past the barriers, then Lorelle. I follow them closely after, offering an apology smile to the security.

Peppa or whatever him name, leads us to a small section for ourselves.

"Unuh a drink?" he asks.

"Yeahhh," Lorelle answers, handing me a surprise.

"Quiet girl from May Pen, yah drink?" he looks at me.

"Whatever them want," I murmur.

"Ah, mah send ova a bottle girl and unuh say weh unuh want. Put it pah Chief tab," and with that, he disappears.

"Ahhhhh!!!" Lorelle and Mariah both shriek... but me? For some reason, I'm unimpressed.

We're only in a tiny corner with our own table nothing fancy. Either way I'm here to enjoy myself without the prying eyes of people I know, not for the extravagant elevated section.

•••

The party has picked up full speed. Looking down at my phone, I notice it's 2:13am. Shock forces me to quickly send my location to mommy. Shoving my phone back into my purse, I whisper to Lorelle to accompany me to the hookah stall since our bottle girl hasn't made it back yet. She agrees, saying she wants to make sure I pick blueberry and not no watermelon.

I laugh out knowing that was my intention.

"Mariah secure the table, we ago get the hookah weself," I shout over the sound of Masicka's voice.

Lorelle grabs my hand and we move through the flashing lights across to the hookah stand. We get there and start ordering what we want, "Two hose and six tips, blueberry mint!" I shout.

"9k!" the attendant shouts, "when it done we bring it. Which part unuh deh?"

"Left of the DJ booth!" I tell her while grabbing at my purse to pay.

Lorelle looks at me, rolls her eyes and looks back at the attendant to say, "Chief bill it fi go pon!"

This girl, I shake my head.

"Oh alright!" the attendant starts writing it down.

Lorelle turns, pulling me away to the side.

"Girl a come we come fi enjoy weself. Why yah move so shakey?" she glares at me.

I laugh at how different she is under the influence. Before this she was warning me about Jordanne. I'm about to give her my reasons when a slim dark skin girl with full curls, walk up to us.

"Top man say me fi call you ova," she taps me on my shoulder.

"Who that? Me no know nobody from here..." I trail off before turning back to Lorelle.

She walks off and Lorelle continues to scold me about being 'stuck up' since the trip started yesterday.

"Lorelle you know me no like this mon–"

"The Don send fi you," a male voice interrupts our conversation.

At this point, I'm already annoyed at Lorelle which causes my tone to shift when I answer him. "A one Don me know and me certain him no deh noweh yah so. I'm not leaving. Tell whoever say me deh a the table ova deh so to the DJ booth," I spin around to grab Relle.

We walk back to our table where we find Mariah snapping flicks of herself. I hope she know nuffi post nuttin till we leave.

"Make sure you no post that," I remind her– my voice still laced with annoyance.

"Girl no service deven out yah so," she laughs.

Her saying that prompts me to look if my location delivered to mommy.

It didn't... just my luck.

I start to worry but manage to push the thought to the back of my head.

Let's just get through the night

"A wah a happen?" Mariah is staring away in confusion.

My head props up to look around and I notice a sea of men moving through the crowd.

"A ova yah so dem a come?" Lorelle asks, looking at me.

How me fi know? Must a money pull up ago gwaan 'cause you know dem man yah love depressive song. The sea comes to a halt before us and parts, revealing the guy from the fruit stall earlier today.

He moves to our table and says, "Two people me send fi you enuh May Pen."

I look to Mariah who is shocked, and then to Lorelle who looks like she's about to make a run for it.

"Yah the so call Top man?" I query.

"If them wah call it that, yeah," he accepts the title– holding his hand out.

I look down at it, refusing to take it.

"We a move unuh to our section, me just reach," he clarifies.

I swallow and my eyes move from his outstretched hand to his face.

Peppa steps forward and says, "Come man, him no always this serious."

His words lighten the mood, and I take the guy's hand. Chief, I remind myself... Chief. I look back to ensure Lorelle and Mariah are behind me. Yup, they are. They're hanging onto Peppa while the sea of men closes us in.

This serious though

I'm somewhat at ease though, knowing that my man is top command to whichever man feel like them a 'Don' anywhere across the island.

A smirk comes across my face.

As I move to the elevated section, the sea breeze hits my skin, and I look over into the crowd. The men below us look pleased, while the women seem curious. I take a few steps, moving myself to the back and out of view. Taking a seat while rubbing my hands, I look over to my friends. They're already selecting which bottles of champagne they want for themselves.

"You cold?" Chief's voice tickles my ear.

"A little," I whisper while nodding.

"Want a blanket?" he asks... but I decline.

Di rass him fi get blanket from?

Man prepared.

"Neva know unuh woulda farwud," he continues.

I laugh lightly before saying, "Yuh no know my friends."

"Weh the rest?" he looks at the fact that it's only half of us here.

"Them did 'fraid," I lie...

... But I really want to know if me fi 'fraid or not.

"Them no have nuttin fi scared 'bout. Me unuh a roll with enuh man," he chuckles, "ah assume you never 'fraid?"

"Nahh, know fi hold me own," I lie– finally meeting his eyes.

We fall into easy conversation after this for a few minutes– in which I share as little as I possibly can about myself. Him no hard fi talk t–

Before my thought ends, my phone goes off, and I see that it's Slyme. There is also a string of missed calls from him and mommy. I just got service? Maybe because I'm now elevated, they're just popping up.

Fuck.

Fuck.

Fuck.

I get up and walk to Mariah, showing her the phone. She stands, blanked out...no words from her mouth for the first.

Lorelle turns to look at my screen too, "Jesus no answer, mek we cut."

I nod in agreeance. We enjoy weself enough. Mariah nods too, agreeing for the first time tonight. Walking over to Chief, I decide to thank him for the night and let him know we're leaving.

I start explaining, but get cut off by his words, "Nah man, me just reach. You mommy ago understand, gwaan relax fi a next hour?"

"No man, we ready fi leave too," I counter but he smiles, ignoring my comment.

Knowing that Slyme will be here any second, I try to explain further.

"Ry!" Lorelle shouts my name... and when I look over the barriers, another sea of men are moving through the party.

Yeah man, then J' nahgo kill me fi real now?

"Wah gwaan?" Chief asks Peppa who has just ran up the steps to inform him of what's happening.

"Man dem fully strapped say them come fi a Ryleigh," his eyes find me.

Chief turns to me and I hang my head low.

"A yuh name so don't?" he chuckles, "Yuh good or you need we fi step?" he asks, seeming genuinely concerned.

"Me good me know them... well few a dem."

He chuckles again before saying, "Leff you number with me."

"Me will find her, mek she liff," Peppa suggests, and with that he concedes.

As I move down the few steps, all eyes are on me. The music has stopped and if I coulda bag mi face, I would. Slyme's eyes meet mine and he tucks his Glock back into his waist. Everybody else keeps their guns pointed.

Cocked and ready...

Skulli grabs Mariah and starts asking if she mad or deh pah molly.

"Daddy we did alright," she protests.

Lorelle is holding onto my hands, as we all exit the venue.

"J' deh pon the phone enuh," Slyme says to me.

I stare over at him...

I–

All the blood from my body shoots to my head and I get an instant, pounding head-ache. We make it outside and I can see mommy, Sue, T', Muuch, Keif, and Skulli. I hang my head even lower this time.

"Ryleigh!" mommy's voice lands clear, "duh frighten we so again! Unuh a big woman, do not sneak out! We think them gone with unuh!"

"Mommy me send the location," I whimper.

"We didn't get the location until minutes ago Ryleigh and no tracker is in her car. Is after three now enuh," Ms.Sue sounds worried.

"Yeah boss, mah give her the phone," I hear Slyme... and mi know a my judgement this.

My breathing increases and my palms become sweaty. He hands me the phone and I hold it to my ears, refusing to say the first words.

"Ryleigh, weh mi say to yuh earlier?" I hear the lethality within **his** tone and decide not to answer.

Wrong decision.

"Ryleigh weh the fuckkkk me say to yuh earlier?!!!" he repeats and right then, I decide to answer.

Walking away to the side and out of the view of everybody, my mouth falls open.

Breathe...

Breathe...

"St-stop ramp wid yuh-wid yuh medz?" I whimper.

"So how the bloodclawt me call and yuh missing????!!! Explain that fuck to me Stevens, 'cause right now mah pre fi come mek you explain it in person."

"Mariah say–"

"Duh blame nobody enuh... Tell me wah your thought process, how you think you can deh wid me and do weh you feel, like people no know a yah me weakness Ryleigh?!"

"I–"

I can't figure out what to say... I can't talk when he's like this. Tears start welling my eyes just before I notice Toni has walked over.

"Ryleigh, you know wah? Mek it done... Better me lowe yuh and you can get as much space as you want... cool?" his tone cold.

"I– you, mi nuh–" the tears fall from my eyes but my words keeping stumbling over each other.

I want to explain to him that I just wanted to have fun, coupled with being upset, but how much time mi ago use the same excuse?

Sigh

"Fucking immature and me nahgo deal with it, so after this, you take as much space as you want... Dat good?"

I still don't answer. My words are trapped by regret.

"Give the phone back to Slyme," I do as he says...

Toni embraces me, her arms like a comforting blanket.

"You good?" she asks, "Why you never carry me, me woulda take the blame."

That statement pulls more tears from my eyes. She pulls me in closer, before walking me over to the cars.

That's when I overhear Slyme saying, "Ah... mah hear yuh... cool."

Just from that, I know he just got orders that I don't want to hear right now.

"The genna change him mind!" out of nowhere we hear Peppa's voice.

I snap my head around to pinpoint his position. Slyme pulls his gun immediately and the sea of men that came with him surround us.

The next thing I see is Chief stepping forward, "Mi no like the fact say unuh mek she a cry, along wid the disrespect infront a me people."

"Bossy better you sit out dah one yah," Slyme suggests.

"Peppa just make me know say a Drip woman… and since me come back fi the top command, me feel like this cyaa done so, you get me?… Weh you think Peppa?" he asks, looking at his short friend.

I peak over to see that the sea of men from inside the party are now behind them.

"Duh mek you ego start no war," Skulli speaks from beside us.

"Mek she come back come enjoy the party and leave when she ready… and everything ago good," Chief suggests.

Slyme laughs, "The man weh yah underestimate nahgo like that at all."

I'm getting super fucking nervous.

God please mek them relax.

"Mah give unuh couple seconds still," Chief pushes.

I hear Skulli hiss before saying, "Long time me wah kill dah boy yah and him daddy. Fuck it," with that, he shoves us to the cars and the rounds start going off.

We all make it to the car almost trampling each other, still being shielded by a small group from the team. I know all the cars are bullet proof, so we hop into the closest– Skulli's Trackhawk.

Sue makes it to the driver's seat and my mom gets in the front passenger. We start backing out and I look back to see that Paw is behind us with the rest of the girls in his vehicle.

When him reach?

Be more observant Ry

By now people are running from the party to their cars, creating absolute chaos. The rounds keep going off and due to the crowd and the small pathway to exit, we get stuck trying to leave.

"Everybody heads down!" Sue instructs.

We oblige, holding our heads down, regardless of being safe in the car. A rapid set of rounds go off and–

Mariah screams out and I look to see Skulli hit the ground.

She flies the door open on impulse, running to her father.

"Mariah!!!!" I scream.

43 | Outside Part THREE

RYLEIGH

"Mariah!!!"

"Ma–" I give up trying to repeat when another set of rounds go off.

"Lock the door!!!!" Sue shouts.

I've never seen her this serious before. Her hands are in the glove compartment, and I already know what she's looking for. I hop out of the car and slam the door shut, just like she said.

She neva say come out idiot gyal yahgo kill we?

My mom screams while trying to open the door again, but Sue locks it, refusing to let anybody else disobey her orders. I spin away and run low towards Mariah, who is now on the ground wailing at her dad's side.

"Daaaawwwddddyyy!" she cries, her voice lost in the sound of chaos.

Stooping down to help her, I watch as the life drains from Paul's face.

"Mariah come bacccckk to the car!" I whisper-shout.

"Me nah leff him yuh mad! A him alone me have!" she screams, wiping her tears with the back of her hand, that's now slathered in blood.

I look around to see that most of the men from Chief's team are down. My eyes move across the pasture to find Slyme. He's clipping everybody from behind a tree, one by one.

Immaculate aim.

"Fuck unuh a do?" I hear Paw's voice hovering above us.

Thank God 'cause I don't know

We don't answer.

Mariah keeps crying while putting pressure on Skulli's chest wound.

"Why unuh leave the car?" Paw shouts, keeping his focus on our surroundings.

Neither of us offer him an answer.

Skulli coughs and Mariah starts wailing even louder.

"Him ago good Mariah, farwud me affi get unuh to safety. Surgeon deh pon him way to the safe house," Paw explains.

So we're not going back to the boutique hotel?

Like yuh no see wah gwaan yah so

A bullet flies past us, a little too near... before connecting to Peppa's knees. Another hits his shoulders before he tumbles. I watch him fall flat to the ground, hitting his head.

Mi pussyclawt!

"Carry them back go the bloodclawt car Paw!" Slyme shouts, and I realize that those bullets belonged to him.

Him communicating that to Paw, gives away his position and another set of rounds head towards him. Paw hisses before grabbing Mariah and moving down to get her back to the car. I follow his lead, staying low while trying to be as observant as possible. Looking to my right, I see when a group of men usher Chief into a van and it speeds off.

I hiss. So alla this a did fi wah? Fi him prove some kinda point?

We get to the car in time to see Sue exiting, with what I think has to be an Uzi.

Bumboclawt...

Paw throws Mariah onto the backseat. She's screaming and kicking at a wild rate but Toni grabs her and pins her down while I get in.

My mother clicks the door shut and starts praying.

Sue comes to my window and points to the driver's seat.

'LEAVE' she mouths– signaling to the steering... and with that, I climb over into the driver's seat.

Everybody is out of it...

My mom is in mid prayer worship, Mariah is a messss and Toni is just about ready to knock her out. I look back and realize Paw is not back to his car that has Muuch, Keif and Lorelle and in that moment I decide not to leave.

My fault them even reach out yah a look fimi, so how me fi leave?!

Hmmph

I think about hopping out to bring them to this car, but I recognize that's just another stupid decision. The sound of the shooting quiets for a minute and I look to where Slyme was to see both him and Paw leaving to run to Skulli.

By now the venue is empty, the lights left on flashing and the aura is just eerie.

Like a bad dream...

I realize Paw and Slyme are lifting Skulli with Sue just behind them– pointing her gun in all directions. From what I saw that night at the 'send off for J'... I hope nobody tries her in this moment.

They move by me and my blood runs cold as I catch a glimpse of Skulli's eyes rolled over.

God please let him survive

They get to Slyme's Jeep and throw him in. Sue hops in the back, lifting his head and fanning him with what seems to be the flier we had left in our room. I watch as Paw runs to his car, hop in and starts it. That prompts me to start Skulli's Trackhawk and although it's big, I should be able to handle it.

We speed off smoothly for a few seconds until we get further along the roadway... and stop.

Wah we a stop fah now?

For a moment I wonder about the reason, then I remember mommy's car is parked along the side where we left it. I watch as Lorelle hops out of Paw's car and into the coupe, almost immediately starting it and swinging out of the parking spot to line up with us.

Pheew!

All four vehicles are now speeding along the roadway. My mother has now come up from prayer and is simply sobbing beside me. Mariah has gone silent as Toni rocks her, while feeding her a bottle of water.

Sirens are going off in the distance, but I already know the police in this country is simply for decorative purposes.

Stepping on the gas, we fly back in our seats to end up less than three meters away from the Jeep in front of us.

• • •

Tyres screech and we all park, running inside the house I'm unfamiliar with. According to Paw, we're in Hanover which I know is not very far from where we were staying in Westmorland.

"Use your prints!" Sue screams, causing my head to snap back at her.

My prints??? I can't remember ever coming here.

Have you ever needed to be present for him to add them?

"Only Paul and I have prints and since my hands are covered in blood! Use your prints now Ry! Him a bleed heavy," she shrieks.

I move to the access pad, slamming my palm across the monitor. The door clicks open and they rush inside, laying Skulli on the dining table.

My ears pick up more tyres screeching outside and I look to see what or who it is. It's Surgeon... He jumps out of the car with two women carrying loads of medical equipment. Deciding to hold the door wide for them, I watch as they rush in.

"Keep him head up Sue!" is Surgeon's first instruction.

He cuts him out of his shirt and starts cleaning the area. He then lifts him to observe his back before saying, "It went through."

Mariah starts crying again.

"That's a good thing Mariah," Sue looks at her, offering comfort.

Minutes pass and Surgeon's still moving through the steps to get Paul back to us. The floor is swimming in his blood and by the looks of it...

My eyes finally start to glisten.

The reality of the moment is settling in.

"Okay him stable enough. Help me bring him to the medical room, him need blood."

I watch as they lift him carefully to a room down the hall. Deciding to stay, I walk over to my friends.

We all sit in silence on the sofa waiting for somebody to wake us from this nightmare. What should've been an exciting weekend filled with memories has quickly become a horror movie.

• • •

I watch as the sun rises, nobody has gotten sleep. I've been googling home blood transfusions all night to add comfort to my mind.

While tapping through google, I feel Slyme move to me.

"You no plan fi sleep?" he asks, staring at me with a mixture of concern and disappointment written in his eyes.

"I couldn't even if I wanted to... Know me shouldn't leave the property without unuh, and yet still me go," my head hangs in shame.

"Mi used to unruly as a teen too. Seem weird fi say since I'm only 22 but between those days and now, the change evident. Unuh ago wah do things weh no make sense sometimes, which is understandable, but yuh affi understand the family weh you ina," he explains, keeping his eyes on the sunrise.

I stay silent, taking in the view myself.

It's calming...

"It's never the case where me go look fi trouble enuh Slyme... Jacen found me from what I was told and this man just offer me some water fi wash me hand, that's all... Little deeds like those aren't supposed to hold this level of consequence," I shift my weight onto my left leg.

"How you mean Ryleigh? Understand say Drip is at the top... so whether you come from Jungle, March Pen, Farm, Flanka, Matchez Lane, Canterburry, Grants Pen, Webb Lane, August Town, Cassava Piece, DeLaVega, Salt Spring... me can go on and on... each parish, every single trade, murder, punishment and law affi go through him... So you might think you can just go about life freely, but people know you, especially after the posts. So when you see man like Rome step to you and Drip say buil offa that, you affi trust him 'cause them man deh intention is always fi get to him through youuu," he breathes, averting his attention from the sunrise to me.

I turn to look at him.

"Look pah tonight," he continues, "Skulli a mek me know earlier say a recognize the boy recognize Sue and pull over just fi see who him can talk to. Just so happen say him talk to you but him woulda try invite anybody else just fi cause problems. Bingo him bingo when him realize who you be and a that make him come back out with full ego tonight."

His words connect a lot of dots and clears a lot of my vision. Here I was thinking mi just salt, whole time them a try get to me man.

If he even is my man anymore

The thought sinks my heart, and I look away from Slyme to my toes.

"Keep you head up man. Skulli go through worse than this, him ago pull through. As fi Drip," he laughs out, "mi no know weh you ago tell him say. Try mi best stall him until we find you but we just couldn't pinpoint your location fast enough, even when you mother find the flier."

"That good, him say it done before anything did even pop off fully so..." I mumble, looking back at the sunrise.

He doubles over in laughter.

I look at him confused.

"You know Jordanne, but you obviously no know Drip at all... 'bout done," and with that he walks away.

I move over to Mariah whose eyes are now red and puffy, emitting pure pain and regret.

"Come," I whisper, pulling her into my arms.

She releases her weight on me.

Rocking her from side to side, I try to comfort her cries, nonverbally letting her know it's not her fault and that Paul will come back to us.

God nah do we so...

He's like the one father figure here for almost all of us.

44 | Reflect

RYLEIGH

I wake up to the sound of Sue moving through the kitchen. Mariah isn't with me any-more though.

I pick up my phone to see what time it is– 10:50am.

My heart starts pumping through my chest because I know what's to come next... Jordanne. Man say it done so me supposed to good? No?

"Hi Ry' Skulli was up and well. He should be resting now and the girls have all show-ered and are on the balcony eating. Do not go downstairs or to the basement until I say so... The guys are having a meeting."

She watches as my eyes search hers to ask the question I fear to ask out loud.

"He's downstairs," she says clearly.

"Okay," I mutter.

"Come and eat before you do anything else," she suggests, offering me a soft stare.

Mi no hungry...

"I'm not hungry," I voice my thoughts.

"Eat Ryleigh, everything is going to be fine," she hands me a plate of banana pan-cakes, with scrambled eggs and bacon.

I take the plate, deciding not to put up a fight.

Sigh

Minutes pass and I'm simply playing around with the food. I decide on putting it into the microwave before heading to the rooms to find the shower. When I pinpoint the room that the girls' outfits from last night are sitting in, I enter.

The bathroom is within the room, so I close the door and saunter to the shower. Five minutes later, I'm out with no clue of what to put on.

I decide to search the drawers.

Must your place. Call T' and ask

Nuh ina the mood fi talk.

Finding a pack of white T-shirts and some sport shorts, I decide on throwing them on. Plopping down on the bed, I take my phone and move to the group chat.

BUBBAS

Unuh good?

MariahLuv: Much better now, Sue drunk we off with food and daddy was up.

Sexy Bitch: Weh u deh?

The room weh me see unuh things ina

Dutty Foot: Bring a charger, we on the balcony.

MuuchLuv: Yeah Sue say we can't leave from upstairs.

KeifLuv: And me nuh mind, the man dem downstairs scary

Somebody come get it.
Me no feel good, a go back go sleep.

Dutty Foot: Ah mah come.

With that, I lock my phone and roll over onto my back...

I hear the door click open.

Thinking it's Lorelle, I say, "A run you run come round yah gyal?"

The room falls silent... and the door clicks shut. I prop my head up to see that it's Jordanne.

Instant anxiety consumes my body.

My eyes follow him as he pulls a chair and sits directly in front of the bed, his eyes not leaving me. We both look at each other, words failing to exit either set of lips.

I–

"You wah tell me wah you did a think?" his voice comes across deep and clear.

No nonsense.

"I just wanted to go out, I'm not sure how else to say it," I mutter under my breath.

He takes a moment to observe my tic. I twiddle my fingers, waiting for the scrutiny. He leans back into the chair before knitting his fingers through each other and bringing them to his chest. I watch his eyes grow narrow as they shift from watching my fingers, to meeting mine.

"Ryleigh...weh yuh want from me?" he asks... and if he's not staring directly into my soul, then I don't know what he's doing.

Suddenly I'm lost for words.

"Talk no man 'cause me deh pon the brink ah evil, so the distraction weh yah offer no needed."

Woah...

So I'm a distraction now?

Coooool... Cool, cool, cool.

"Okay mek me just say exactly how I feel and have felt for years," I decide to start.

He sits up in the chair, pulls his spliff from God knows where before lighting up. I roll my eyes, knowing he's trying to calm himself... There is no way me aggravate him this much.

"We've been friends since like... mid high school right? You said for almost all of that time you've loved me but I was right there watching you move through almost the entire female population like nothing... Watched you move through couple other schools and women weh leff school long time too. When I came to you about my ex, you would disregard anything I expressed, saying I didn't deserve it when you were doing the same thing to other women."

"Ryleigh duh compare me to your ex," his voice swallows the room, sending a small chill down my spine.

"Weh none a that have fi do with last night?" he asks, cocking his head to the side with confusion plastered across his face.

"Yahgo make me finish my thought?" I look up at him blankly.

"Do yuh ting," he chuckles.

I hiss, internally.

"Watch you do alla that and when my ex left school you wanted me to what? Take you serious? Certain you would treat me no different, so I didn't think to take our relationship further than what it was, sex and laughter. Yuh say me pick your friend and yeah you can crucify me fi that but me did just a date and see what was out there, instead of taking that time for myself like I should've. Recently in therapy, I learnt that that's a habit of mine."

The mention of my therapy sessions seem to throw him off... but I ignore it.

Continuing, I say, "So when them little incidents here happen with you, I slip back into thinking maybe I'm just not somebody who people will choose not to ruin. The Emily thing, was heart breaking and me no think you realize all now because we always fuck and cover up the wounds. You with the different girls each week hurt, even though we weren't together at that point or whatever, and now a random girl tags me in a cozy picture of you and her?" I breathe.

"All a that just throw me for a loop, more time me just feel fi spite you but somehow it always turns out way worse than I intend and last night was one ah those nights."

He takes the spliff from his mouth and rests it in the ashtray next to the chair.

"Ryleigh, my coping mechanisms are just that, coping mechanisms. If me end up a go through things and the one person I always feel like talking to, I can't talk to, the next answer is always sex or weed and there is only so much pussy and weed out there," he argues, holding our stare.

I don't budge.

"If you feel like the things you see me do, me woulda even think fi do that to yuh then you no know me at all… Mi never lead on no woman yet, each of them knew exactly wah them did a sign up for. Yuh say me no realize the heart break from the Emily thing but you no realize the continuous heart break weh you issue me almost yearly," he pulls the chair closer to the foot of the bed.

I pull back a little from intimidation.

Ry' babe, relax

"Mek we go through them… First you say you ago leff you man and this and that because the feelings you had for me were hard to ignore… That no happen all now enuh bus head. You go back to him afterrrr me take you virginity of all things… Me mek that slide same way…

… Then you say unuh leff and yahgo give we a try and whole time me put off every meaningful relationship I could have had because wah? You…

… We fuck again and then you just stop talk to me completely, only fi you pop up back like nothing happened and then ask if we can be fuck buddies???"

I roll my eyes and attempt to say something.

"Wait… mek me finish 'cause you nah play victim today," he breathes.

I raise my brows at him and he nods, confirming what he said was correct.

Victim???

No bother vex just mek him talk

"Then Ry' all of a sudden yah date me friend??? Yet every chance we get we fuck? And then you had a miscarriage and me no know until ah whole year and add later?" the ticking along his jawline lets me know he's getting angry… so I fall back onto my back in the sheets.

Him laying it all out like this puts a lot into perspective.

"And still," he continues, "stilllll me end my relationship all to still not be in a relationship with you but to WAIT on us to finish college together. And yeah, I promised to not go seeking out nothing but me just never wah me and you fall back into the cycle of sex without a foundation so me send fi Emily. The logic fucked up but it made sense to me at the time… Just remember after how many years, a just since January you finally agree to an actual relationship with me."

A knock comes at the door and we both look at it.

"Who?" he asks, seeking confirmation.

"Slyme… Thing them ready so we a pre fi cut now."

"Ah mah farwud," he says, rising to his feet.

He then looks to me, "I haven't been to therapy since I left Jamaica. When me drop back yah so we finish this conversation and see wah ago happen fi this," he points back and forth between him and I.

"Okay," I mumble, throwing the sheets over my head.

That went much smoother than I thought.

The conversation no done yet enuh babes

I whisper a prayer for him and everybody leaving the house because I know exactly what's about to go down.

Sigh…

I fucked up.

45 | Correction

SLYME

Mi decide fi send a text to my favourite girl right now... She's been on my mind all morning, all weekend if me a be fully honest.

Ah step now.

<u>Muuch:</u> Careful muah!

In one go, I close the the phone and throw it back to the bed.

No personal devices on this mission.

Descending the stairs into the crowd of men, I watch as Ramone decks everybody in earpieces to keep in contact with each other.

Man cool yuh fuck

"One tap to speak, two to get off the radio completely," he walks around explaining.

Cyaa believe Drip a do this ina broad daylight.

Him wah make sure everybody get the message since him been a try be reasonable from him take post, but everybody a take it as him being too lenient. Have a feeling say them ago regret that. People see him as young, inexperienced, too caring even, but from what I've seen, the man just a try calm him demons. When him get ruthless it's not easy for him to snap back.

Man cold

Double him father...

"Everything packed?" Drip asks, staring at me while I slide my vest on.

"Yeah, everything ready boss," I offer up a clear response.

"Ah..." he steps to the middle of the living area to address the men. "The man dem outside already know how it ago come dung, so who in yah so me need unuh fi execute accurately, no fuck ups, no sorry fa. Kids, old women and pregnant women off limits."

Man nuh give a fuck 'bout a regular woman... Tell unuh enuh, the switch nuh regulated.

Jah Jah.

I decide not to ask or mention it to him.

"In and out in less than 30. Anybody get stuck after 30, leave them, whether a me or yourself. Don't fuck it up fi nobody else or else yahgo wish you did stay instead of make it back to the trucks late, believe..." he smirks.

The room falls silent except for Ramone's typing.

"Unuh get dat?" Drip checks in on the team.

"Lawww..." they all repeat.

"Law," I add myself.

"Outside," he says, stepping out of the house with the pool of men behind him.

I wait for them to leave before I speak to Ramone, "You notice how him cold fi dah mission yah?"

"Man tired a the fuckry. Chief pick the wrong time fi fuck 'round. Watch you head out deh."

"Wrong time him choose yes," I chuckle before leaving.

When I exit the house I kid you not, there are over 700 bodies getting ready to leave.

The man pull every foot soldier from the central and west side of the island

I pull my Jesus peace from beneath my shirt, kiss it and hold it up to the sky.

This ago grimier than me plan fah

Let's have some fun, I think to myself while smiling.

Hopping into the Jeep with Paw driving and Drip on the back seat, we head out, following the vans in front with a few behind us. Not even ago try count it bredda. Is just ah million a we yah man... We're all decked in full black with smoke masks to hide full facial structure and skin colour. Drip might be angry but him still nah leave nothing to chance.

Man say pullover and kerchief ah fi common criminals.

I chuckle to myself, and it pulls his attention.

"Fuck do yuh Slyme? Yah laugh-laugh from you step outa the house," he questions, sounding muffled from under the mask.

"Just ready fi clip wings boss," I lie.

"Continue lie to me and see if yours no get clip," he chuckles, causing Paw to laugh too.

In less than 20 minutes we get to the foot of the hill leading to Chief's garrison. Trucks have stopped along the way, leaving some men on foot at different posts to await orders.

The vans move up the hill, driving slowly.

It's no later than 2pm and the sun is beeeeeeaming, children are playing, women are getting their hair done and the sound of a church choir rings throughout the air.

My body shudders.

I know the moment I pull the trigger my mind will be lost to evil, and so I whisper a prayer to God.

"Fada pull me out of deep evil, when my spirit forgets mercy, grant it to who deserves it. Leave room in Drip's mind for peace so he can find his way back from his evil as well. Protect the team and most importantly, mek dem boy yah know nuffi stir up this man again, Amen."

"Approaching target's perimeter," Buckle's voice chips into my earpiece.

Start it start

"Clip everybody within the perimeter," Drip's order comes clear, his voice flows hoarse– lacking all logic and humanity.

I clamp my eyes shut and when I reopen them, I feel like a different person.

The first round of gunshots go off...

Beautiful, I smirk.

Drip shifts and before I can stop him, he hops out of the moving Jeep, clearing about four guys playing Sunday football on a field to the right of us. I follow him and clear four more, and before we know it, men on foot join us, clearing all 22 men involved in the game along with those watching from the sidelines.

"Remember the aim of the outside perimeter anuh necessarily fi kill but to wound," Drip's voice comes through the earpiece.

"When we close in then we start take lives," he repeats while hopping back onto the Jeep.

I follow, ensuring he's covered if anything.

"Murdaaaaaaaa!!!!!" a lady cries, running from a small shop to the side of the road.

Before I can pinpoint her, Drip puts one to her knees and she falls, rolling down the hill, only stopping at a chopped branch off the side of the dirt road.

The screams of everybody else watching are barely audible, with my mind lost in the mission, the earpiece and the mask. More women start running downhill, scattering their things as they seek cover.

A group of our guys march past us heading to tighten the perimeter before we make it there.

"Boss we spot the target," Buckle's voice come across.

"Leave him fimmi," Drip responds immediately. "Turn every fucking thing pass the bar ina strainer. Every house, every car and anybody caught in between."

"Except the women and kids?" Buckle tries to confirm.

Drip doesn't answer.

"Except the women and kids the man say that earlier," I confirm, hissing to myself.

Six automatic rounds go off simultaneously.

Bumboclawt

I twist my neck, releasing the tension, knowing it's time to hop back off the Jeep and move to Chief. Drip is first to hop back off the Jeep, while Paw exits the passenger seat and positions himself through the open roof, with his favorite toy– the M134 machine beast.

Sweetest gun me ever hear sing

I watch him slip his spliff to the corner of his mouth while throwing the excess length of rounds over his shoulder– steadying himself for fire. A group of Chief's men exit the house, firing at us... but the pre-stationed snipers from various roofs, start taking them out in one sweep.

I watch as Drip steps over the bodies and pushes the gate open. Moving behind him carefully, we sweep the front yard. Two young girls hold their hands up in surrender and we nod at them to leave. Without hesitation, they take off down the street that is now riddled with bodies.

"15 minutes!" Drip calls the time.

"Copy," a wave of different voices respond.

"First floor cleared," Buckle's voice chips in again.

"Slyme, we ago clear the second floor," Drip orders.

'READY?' he mouths, putting up his thumb, then index, then middle finger to count us off.

We move off on three, slowly going up the stairs.

•PIIIIIINNGGG•

A bullet ricochets from the metal railing onto the stairway. I look up quickly, spot the trouble, and clip the guy that fired. He falls over the balcony, crushing a glass table just below.

The sound of the crash triggers Drip.

"Slyme, easy with the noise," he mutters.

Before his words settle on my thoughts properly, six shots are fired at us and one hits me. I start falling, but Drip catches me, breaking the fall to lay me down. That's the last thing I remember before I hear Buckle's voice hovering over me.

"The vest it lick, see him wake deh," he announces– voice dancing in amusement.

Bumboclawt

Nah lie, that was a little peaceful.

The death supm...

I open my eyes to see Drip smirking while holding Chief who's stripped down to his boxers.

"Yuh no miss much you were out for less than two minutes. Ketch the pussy a try jump through window," Drip laughs.

I quickly scan everybody's role. Everybody's standing guard except for Buckle who's sweeping the scene to make sure the rooms are all empty.

"Shit easier than I thought," we both laugh while I get to my feet.

A set of sudden gunfire goes off and we look at each other confused. Everybody should know we have the target and to get back to the vehicles. I look at my stopwatch... Five minutes, that's all we have left in the window.

"Yo me nuh know wah that but five minutes to the trucks and outa this. Fuck everybody," I tap my earpiece to remind them.

"We under attack. Most ah the man them gone back to the truck and a fresh set a man just come cross the ball field a fire wild shot," Paw's explaining.

Chief smiles and before it reaches his eyes Drip gun butts him– one upside his head and the other to his throat.

He starts gasping for breath, but Drip doesn't stop.

"Boss! We affi leave!" I shout, trying to pull him from drowning in his evil... But di man nah stop, him just nahhhh stop.

Ryleigh woulda annoy me fi the rest a her life if me mek him get trap yah so.

"Jordanne!!!" I grab him away from Chief, who is now battered and bleeding.

"A mad man!" Chief barely grunts.

Before the man save him strength fi beg fi him life?

Jordanne spins back, raising his boots to land a kick straight to his chest.

"Pussy this a the first and last yahgo see daylight," Drip spits before aiming his gun.

Without hesitation he puts two to his knees.

"Pleaaaaaassse," Chief groans– his voice barely there.

It's a scene to see. He's toppled over with blood and saliva dripping from his mouth– still gasping for air while holding his throat. Drip laughs, before I watch him add two to each of his shoulders. He falls flat this time, face forward, while trying to drag himself away with dead limbs.

The sight of it amuses me.

I look down at my stopwatch again... Three minutes.

"Drip a 30 minutes Ramone say him can keep down the JCF system fah enuh, we affi liff."

He doesn't budge.

A thought pops into my mind as he puts another shot into Chief's thighs, and spine, while standing over him.

"Weh Unuh deh?! Me clear the new set a man dem and ah go back ina the passenger seat now, farwud!!!" Paw shouts.

I watch as the last set of men leave the house, running to the vans and downhill to the trucks.

"Ryleigh ago need you back enuh boss, and mi no wah she annoy me fi life..." with that, I see the hold he has on the gun loosen.

His chest rises and falls rapidly, and after a few seconds, he releases a round into Cheif's skull.

"Fi Skulli," he sneers while stepping over the body and to me. "Minute and 30 seconds!" he shouts across the earpiece.

Oh now him know time?

Jah know, I shake my head in disbelief.

We bolt down the stairs and out of the house just in time to see Paw driving to us.

He slows down without stopping and we hop in.

The tyres screech, dust blowing in the rear as we speed down the hill and out of community.

"Boy Drip make Satan take him ova in deh Slyme?" Paw asks, glancing back at us while laughing.

"And look how me pray fi him? A one name bring back the man," I laugh.

"Shut the fuck up," Jordanne joins our banter.

I look back to see women finally running to the bodies of their sons, fathers, lovers, brothers, cousins…

Beautiful…

Word will spread of what happens when you fall outa line wid Drip.

One Law…

Drip Law…

Simple…

46 | Worth It?

RYLEIGH

I've been lying in bed for the past hour. Even though most of the men left earlier, Sue still suggested we stay on the second floor until it's time to leave.

For the entire time, Jordanne's words have been replaying in my mind, *'Continuous heartbreak weh yuh issue mi almost every year.'*

Every year?

Be honest with yourself, every year fi real

Deciding to ignore my subconscious, I slide out of the bed and move to the door. Exiting the room, I saunter down the hallway recounting my steps from earlier to find the balcony where my friends are.

As soon as I bend the corner, I pick up on Toni's voice, "Speak of the devil! Sleeping beauty, you ready fi come relax you mind?"

They all giggle, and I start wondering to myself, if I'm the only one holding a heavy heart.

"Watch how me woman eye red," Lorelle whispers, with an over exaggerated pout.

"You Okay?" Mariah steps forward.

"Me alright, you?"

"Yes me good. Daddy ago recover, Surgeon say it sure," she offers me a small smile.

My eyes avert to the gate at the entrance of the property and lingers there for a moment.

"Sue say them soon come back," Muuch explains after noticing my stare.

Then my mind easy fi read sah

"Yeahhhh 'cause you no stop bother her bout SSSSSLLLLLLLLYYYYME," Keif laughs out, sending myself, T', Lorelle and Mariah into a laughing frenzy.

First time me a laugh from after two last night.

We sober up and Toni starts asking us exactly what happened.

"Girl Ry' show me the flier and me decide say we ago, you know me do anything fi the vlog," Mariah explains– her face laced with regret.

"Mi beg the gyal dem no go enuh, but Mariah determined and Ry' she just wah go fi one reason or the next," Lorelle shakes her head.

Hello?

Like when she reach she never down ina it too.

I decide to take a seat beside Muuch, whose eyes still haven't left the gate. Toni looks over at me knowingly, having heard the argument yesterday morning between J' and I. In that moment I decide to let the others know what happened. Pulling out my phone, I bring up the screenshot of J' and whoever the girl is. It takes a moment for them to realize before they all take turns looking at it.

Toni is the last to see the picture.

"Lizzy?" she asks… and we all look up at her.

"You know her???" I query, feeling triggered by the fact that she knew about him and Emily last year.

"I know of her… She a like the only person him study with. You know him no mingle with people at all," she goes on to explain.

"Oh," is all I manage to get out.

"Wehm say 'bout it?" Lorelle questions, staring at the picture as T' holds the phone.

"Say the picture innocent…" I mumble.

"Look well tight to meee," Keif whispers, sticking her hand around Lorelle to take the phone from T' just to get another look.

Muuch gets up and joins her in the zoom fest.

"Why she lean down pon him? And she look too happy, too comfy… Watch him smile, I never see J' smile so unless a with y–"

She's cut off by Toni taking my phone from them and handing it back to me.

"How you see it?" T' asks.

I raise a brow at her, because how dat matter?

Keeping that thought to myself, I decide to respond with, "The lady tag the doll mlavvveee," my response falls out in a wave of humorless giggles.

"Tagggggggggggggg????" they all ask in unison, including T'.

That was my reaction too.

"Yes sahhh, the lady make sure me see… and J' wah say it innocent," I continue my empty chuckles.

"Yeah she do that intentionally. Me cyaa pick up fi Danne pon dah one yah," T' mutters.

"Pick up fi him too much," Mariah sneers. "We touch road 'cause me see say Ryleigh sad from before we leff Town, and it became even worse Saturday afternoon, now me know why. Regardless a wah happen with daddy, going to the actual party mi nuh regret at all. She did need some cheering up," she turns to me, offering empathetic eyes.

A part of me is happy to hear her in good spirits.

"If you know weh me know you stay outa them business," T' mumbles to herself, but Lorelle catches it.

"Weh that mean Toni?" Lorelle peers up at her, seeking answers.

"Yeah, wah that supposed to mean?" Mariah doubles down on the open question.

I release a sigh, knowing exactly what T' is trying to say.

"Yuh ever see them leff completely? Or even deh completely? No... Things like this ago happen because Danne a who him be. So every time wah gyal try offa him unuh wah she run go mingle with people a road? Or leff? Only fi go back???... Mariah a you same one encourage her fi link up with Rome dem. Sometime me wonder if none a unuh mek one," with that she rolls her eyes and sticks her head into her own phone.

"A who and her?" Lorelle laughs.

I start getting into my own head about her statement but get pulled from them by everybody shouting at once.

"Unuh done!" Keif's voice breaks the loud chatter.

"Toni is right," is all I say before getting up from my chair to lean my body against the balcony rail.

Everybody falls silent, averting their eyes to me.

"Eye dem just open wide as to who Jordanne really is. If he was anybody else me coulda play childish games but because he's... yeah... as soon as me do supm a big problem. A shoot out we ina last night enuh," my eyes now dancing between each of them.

"Right," T' cosigns.

"So him get fi just get way with whatever all the time?" Mariah asks, looking at Lorelle who is looking at me– studying my body language.

I release a heavy sigh...

Shrugging my shoulders I plop back down into the chair.

"None a unuh nahv no sense," Muuch says still staring at the gates, "Ryleigh just affi be less cayliss with what she does to try to get his attention or spite him for whatever reason... Running off to the nearest man available no make sense 'cause more than likely the man know you man. It's Drip, who no know him?... And Jordanne just affi communicate with you more about that side of things 'cause you obviously clueless... T' you do pick up for him a lot... The access weh woman have to him is ridiculous 'cause no man no have that type of access to him. Him woulda never make a man snap a picture of him with them head pon him shoulder, so the picture cannot be 100% innocent... simple," she finally turns to us.

"Them a come," she adds, pointing at the distance.

We all look to see a set of vehicles in the far distance speeding towards the house. My heart rate picks up and my palms instantly start sweating.

• • •

"Weh she deh?" I hear **his** voice from where I'm rooted on the balcony.

"That a my cue," Lorelle laughs lightly while leaving the balcony… and just like that, they all get up, leaving me to J'.

"Ryleigh!" I hear his voice creeping up the stairs.

Deep.

Hoarse.

Angry.

Horny?

Which mood this him ina?

I couldn't tell you.

As I'm about to open my mouth to answer, I see when he gets to the top of the stairs. His eyes meet mine, sending a wave of panic throughout my body. The look in his eyes is not the look I want to see either. I watch him lift his vest off, pull the gloves from his hands and walk straight over to me.

"Jor–" I attempt to say his name but he grabs my throat, pulling me into him.

"No wah you talk right now," he breathes.

I look over his shoulders to see if anybody is there to save me, but the place empty mlovve.

"Mum them ago collect unuh things from ova so and the man dem a cut. Skulli affi move to where Surgeon can offer him better care. So unless a Slyme, Paw or Ramone yah look fah, you deh pon you own," he smirks cocking his head to the side.

I think about rolling my eyes, but mi know better.

Unable to get my thoughts out, I hold his hand– begging for release. He doesn't budge, instead we start to move. I watch without air as he enters a room I didn't notice was here before. When the door clicks open, he drags me to the shower– hand still around my throat.

Drown him ago drown we

My breathing picks up. He notices and releases his fingers from around my neck causing me to fall over the vanity– gasping for air. He looks down at me with narrowed eyes and a face riddled with disappointment.

Sigh

I watch as he strips, putting his clothes in the same biochemical-waste bag that I had put mine in the morning after what happened in Mobay.

"Strip," he speaks clearly– his tone warning me not to hesitate or argue.

I strip down…

"To the shower Stevens."

I want to let him know I literally showered less than two hours ago but I keep my mouth shut. Deciding on stepping into the shower, I grab my hair into a pony. He pops up in my peripheral vison, as he uses packets of a special liquid to cleanse his hands– the same packets he instructed me to use after the incident with Rome.

When that step is done, he lathers his hands with regular hand soap up to his elbows. The movement of his fingers slipping in between each other sends a throb to the forefront of my clit.

I–

Catching myself as he rinses the soap off, I continue to bring my hair into a pony. Before I'm finished, I feel him lift me, throwing me up against the shower tiles, with his hand once again around my throat. His free hand moves to the buttons beside my head and the shower comes alive– immediately steamy. The warm water starts creating a mist around us that ripens my nipples to the point of slight pain.

"Today me almost agree fi kill woman and kids," he speaks, in a tone I don't recognize, "that's the level I get to when it comes to you."

I'm unable to respond but I feel when my pussy does it for me.

"So tell me… weh me fi do 'bout that, 'cause that can't safe fi nobody," the look in his eyes now deadly, lethal even.

My breath hitches, and I try to look away.

The emotions running through my nervous system right now are fear and raw lust. I don't understand the mix but I'm unable to battle with either.

He moves his free hand down to my entrance and I watch as he feels the wetness leak from the deepest parts of my loins. A smirk makes its way to his lips, and he shakes his head before forcing two fingers inside me. I inhale sharply, grasping for all the air that wasn't available when his hands were clamped too tight around my throat.

"Answer mi Ry," he sneers.

"Mhmmhm? I–you–I don't–know," I breathe the words between each stroke of his fingers.

He isn't satisfied with my response and slips them out to shove them into my mouth. I clasp my tongue around his middle and index finger, meeting his eyes all while moaning.

"Fuckkkk," he groans in frustration… and satisfaction.

I slip his fingers out of my mouth before spinning around, arching my back while pushing against the shower tiles for support.

"Weh me ago do with her fi real?" his question is posed to himself.

Before his words land safely, he shoves himself into me without mercy, hitting the very top of my walls.

Like yahgo dead after all

If a from this? I'll take it…

47 | Resolve

JORDANNE

The hold she av ova me Killa? Wicked. Soon as me slip it in, I no longer want to address the issue at hand.

Focus bro

We should finish our conversation from earlier.

Yeah

Yeah man dat ago gwaan...

While moving deeper into her– hitting that sweet spot, she screams my name.

Sigh...

Fucking sexy...

Deciding to not prolong the sex at the risk of losing myself in her and forgetting the reason I'm angry, I pick up the pace. Keeping a steady grip on her waist, I move us directly beneath the warm stream shooting from the overhead shower.

"My hair," she whimpers, but I ignore her to focus on delivering my strokes.

She realizes I'm not slowing down and finds her balance by grabbing at a set of the soap holders that are stuck to the corner of the tiles. They fall, since they aren't built into the tiles.

I smile.

She gives up and decides to spread her hands to either side. One reaches the shower glass while the next falls on the shower tiles.

Good enough

Releasing her waist, I decide to find intimacy in holding her breasts instead. Her hands fall from bracing at the sides and she loses her balance, but I pull her into me, keeping her steady. The back of her head hits my chest and I tighten the grip I have on her breasts.

I start pulling out of her slowly, only to return my dick full force.

"Jordanne!!!!" she screams, her voice wrapped in pain.

"Sssshh," is all I offer her.

Cyaa gauge my mood right now so it's better if she stays quiet.

Her hands start searching for balance again, but I don't give her that privilege. Balance hands her control and if she gains control I'll lose to her sexual tricks.

Demon…

Bredda mine yuh kill Ms.Janette daughta

I smile at the thought.

Her moans start getting louder– less pain more lust…

See? She good.

"Babe," she cries, and the word tugs at my heart.

No… Noooo bredda.

Closing my eyes, I hold onto to what she did last night. I try to focus on my current emotions while still delivering raw slams to her center. The anger resurfaces and I hear when she screams, grabbing onto my hand meekly.

Finding my vision, I realize my dominant hand is back around her throat while the other hand holds her in place via her breasts. My head is now buried in her hair and somehow her tiny feet are swinging above my ankles.

Yah lock off her breath killa

I loosen my grip for her to find her feet but just enough to hold her in the same position.

"Please duh kill me," she whines, reeling under my continuous strokes.

Ignoring her plea, I continue my movement.

In and out…

In…

… and out.

The feel of her walls tighten around my dick, telling me her body is reaching its peak. I hold the same pace… same motion, same grip around her throat, and watch as she becomes undone.

Duh lose yourself badman

I try to hold onto the thought my subconscious brings, but I can't help the feeling. My own body is about to find it's max and all mi wah do a tell her say me love her.

Kiss her…

Eat her out…

Give her a family…

Give her the last name…

Cyaa win dah battle yah… Pussy hypnotizing.

The pussy manipulative. Di ting a hold me hostage killa.

Jah Jah God

In the moment I take to listen to my thoughts, Ryleigh uses that same time to perform kegels around my rod.

"Bumboclawt," I let out... involuntarily.

The feeling of my orgasm moves from the tip of my toes straight up my spine and back down to my dick, not stopping until my soldiers have settled in her.

"Hmmpphh," is the last thing I groan before my body falls weak.

•••

RYLEIGH

Nuh know why but mi feel like him fuck me with the least amount ah feelings a while ago. No kissing. No words...

Not like we been a communicate anyways.

I hiss my teeth internally at the realization.

Disconnection during sex tooo?

So yuh know it bad

The sound of him exiting the bathroom pulls my attention to his direction. I watch as he rubs a small towel over his head– drying water from his hair.

Dreading what's next, I decide to say, "Just say it."

... 'cause.

His head snaps over to channel his focus in my direction. I swallow as the look he had in his eyes earlier has returned. Trying my best to hold the stare, regardless of him being intimidating, I pat the space beside me, signaling him to take a seat. He ignores me to move to a tiny closet in the corner of the room, where I watch him get fully dressed.

Why?

I haven't added a piece of clothing to my body since exiting the shower. Feeling self conscious all of a sudden, I pull the sheets to my chest. My thoughts try to move me to get up and drag my clothes back on, but I decide not to.

He finally exits the closet and comes to sit on the edge of the bed– almost as if we're strangers trapped in a movie scene.

Wah this man?

Why him a move wide?

"J... you ago finish the convo from this morning or?" I snap.

He doesn't answer. Instead, silence envelopes the room. I give up and throw myself down, laying flat on my back, facing the ceiling.

Me really cyaa badda.

I hiss lowly.

More silence…

… And even more silence.

Almost 15 minutes later, he breaks it.

"Decision yah a prove itself harder than mi anticipate," his voice comes out throaty.

Decision… What is he talking about? But before I can voice my thoughts, he continues.

"The way you are naturally, mi can't change it and me no wah change you or you change yourself for me and then you end up resent me. So me just ago go ahead and give you all the space you need… permanently."

I sit up blinking, trying to gather what he just said.

Huhhh???

"Jordanne weh you mean, permanently?" my voice falls out with cracks.

His chest rises and falls, before he turns to me.

"We try this already and we never really leff. This time mah mek it be fi good… You were right, we shoulda just stay friends 'cause now we can't be friends after this either."

I smile.

Why him a ramp with me?

Just pay attention to him eyes, how them full a pain, he's serious

Realizing my subconscious is right, I hop out of the bed, keeping myself wrapped in the top sheets. Moving to where he is, I stand directly in front of him.

"Jordanne… be clear. I– mi nah understand weh yah try say enuh," I breathe.

He cocks his head to the side, allowing me into his thoughts. My eyes meet his, and I realize he's serious. My heart rate picks up and my skin becomes heated out of nowhere.

"Jordanne I'm sorry about last night, I just wanted to go have fun… I'm not having a good month and the picture–"

"Ry," he cuts me off, "the picture isn't the problem. Yuh nuh like my boundaries, yuh no like the security dem behind you, you complain 'bout di lifestyle more than anything and because ah that, you a put everybody in danger constantly… Yah mek me do things to people weh me not even wah do B," he hisses.

B???

My eyes dance left to right, searching his facial features– looking for a hint of humor, but each time I come up empty.

 He's serious.

I giggle… nothing is funny but it's what I do in uncomfortable situations.

Not after him nearly fuck we kill we moments ago?

"Is this because of what happened to Paul?" I ask, holding the most pathetic tone I've ever heard myself express.

He stands… and pulls me into his arms before resting his chin atop my head.

"Nahv nothing fi do with Skulli, we don't work... as a couple... and I can't be your friend," he expresses his thoughts clearly before placing a kiss on my forehead.

Shockkk, shock is taking over my body... and my stomach is becoming upset.

All cold sweat start wash me

"J?" I question one last time while burying my head into his chest, "I'm sorry," I whimper, and I can already feel my tears flooding his shirt.

I have more to say but I can't get the words out. Feel like me throat a lock up. What the fuck is happening? He doesn't offer me words... nothing. Nothing but comfort for the pain he himself is inflicting. Realizing how fucked up that is, I pull away.

"Ry'..." he trails off, when I speed off to the closet, grabbing another random outfit.

Right now I don't know who fah things me about fi put on, but I pull a big ass shirt over my head and grab the shorts I had on earlier.

"Ryleigh, yah go?" he questions, "You know the place? Relax man," his tone spewing annoyance.

Ignoring him, I pick my phone up from the bed and call Lorelle while exiting the room. She answers on the third ring.

"Hel–"

"Come back fimi please! Pleeeeease," I plea with my voice cracking.

"Okay, Okay. We did just a leave the place, mah come back," she assures me, holding concern in her tone.

"Come alone... thanks," I hang up, granting her zero explanation.

His footsteps are heard behind me and I decide to move to the balcony without offering him any attention.

"If you ago hate me dat good, but one ah we did affi make the decision."

Me really feel like fight him, but we know how that woulda done.

I hold onto the rail, squeezing the barrier, fighting my tears, biting my lips, just waiting to see Lorelle in the distance.

● ● ●

We've been on the balcony in silence for more than twenty minutes, when I finally see mommy's car coming down the pathway.

Moving past him, I head down the stairs.

He stays less than a meter behind me all the way to the living area, where I spot Paw and Slyme staring at us. Their eyes hold questions of course, but none of them ask.

I open the front door, walking to Lorelle who has decided not to enter the property. The walk from the door to the gate isn't short, and I can feel him behind me every step of the way.

I shake my head.

While slapping my palm on the access pad for the side gate, I look back. He's rooted on spot behind me, watching as I leave...

Snapping my head back to Lorelle, I exit and slide the gate shut.

Deciding to use the backseat instead of the front passenger, I hop in– careful not to look back at him a second time. Lorelle has chosen not to pry and I appreciate that because I would rather not cry right now.

As the car leaves, I turn to look where I left him standing. He's still there, rooted in the same spot, watching as I leave... The tear I was holding onto rolls down my cheek and I decide to bring my legs up, laying down in the fetal position.

You missed your pill yesterday and today

"Relle?" I call, "any pharmacy we come cross, you stop," is the last thing I say before drowning myself in thoughts of regret.

48 | 'Of-Age'

EXACTLY TWO YEARS LATER

JORDANNE

Man dem a move suh?" Paw chuckles, pouring more Henny into his cup.

"Like yuh born a rum shop so bad head?" Skulli counters.

"Man wah drink fi the whole Jamaica," Buckle laughs out.

Laughter erupts on the side lawns at the last statement and a small smile creeps across my face.

"Yo mah go fi Muuch," are the words that exit Slyme's mouth while everybody comes down from the high of laughter.

Muuch... She's been around often since her and Slyme started to take the ting dem have serious. Realize them ina supm from two years ago, but now them a move well official.

Wish that was you huh?

The thought of having a seamless and loving relationship crosses my mind but the thought of– Never mind...

I push the thoughts and feelings to the back of my mind.

Two years... Two years since we've said anything other than 'Hi and Bye' to each other while in passing at Mum's little 'get togethers'.

Two years enuh skull... 730 days.

Jah Jah

Lighting my third spliff on the third hour, I nod at Slyme, granting him confirmation to leave.

Neva take up back the therapy thing but me really a think 'bout it now. Past two years I've been changing, more bad than good.

I was able to complete my four yearlong degree in three and a half years–

Three if you don't count the semester I took off

–by completing semesters in the summer. I've been in Jamaica since early February, getting all the plays in order to move back… part time.

Part time, yes. Six months here, six months there.

That's good all in all, but mentally I'm not doing well. I've murdered a ridiculous amount of people… The number? I've lost count of. My weed and liquor intake are lethal, my temper is beyond short and the women? The women I've managed to damage along the way, I'm sure will come back to haunt my off- spring.

So me pray me no get a girl

The interruption of my thoughts come by way of Joshua finally testing his audio boxes. Over the past months, he's been taking the DJ thing very seriously and recently asked me to invest in an event idea he had. Nice likkle all inclusive, exclusive event.

Love the idea, so me drop couple bricks.

Mhhmhm.

"Soup?" I hear Mum's voice and look up to tell her no.

If Sue no do nothing, she ago serve soup enuh.

"Suanne the men no wah no soup, carry food come feed dem," Ms.Janette giggles.

Regardless of Ryleigh staying away since I've been here, Ms.Janette has been here every day, and every word she says, all her mannerisms and the glint in her eyes reminds me of Ry'.

MMMCHT.

"Food we wah yes," are the only words that leave Ramone's mouth.

Tuning everybody out, I get up and move to the gazebo while lighting another spliff with the one I have now that's almost done.

Minutes later, when the new spliff goes out, I decide to go to my old balcony. It alone gimi peace anyway… and mi can't smoke a next spliff fada…

• • •

RYLEIGH

Pressing my hair down to make sure none is out of place, I look at myself in the mirror, admiring how much more toned I got since last summer. These past two years really shaped me into a different person, a better version of my younger self.

I graduated in October last year with first class honours, holding my bachelor's in Economics and International Relations. Since then I've taken a more physical role in over-seeing the apartment complex. I've been delegating the duties to a board I hired with the help of Sue here and there… I finally gave the Range to Lorelle, who still to this day thanks me every time we ride in it together. I also went ahead and switched out the Benz coupe I had given mommy for a G-Wagon and turns out, she loves it even more.

… What? I had to, not just because of the memories it holds from Jordanne, but the memories it holds from that weekend in Hanover.

Since January I've been working at BOJ as a Currency-Officer. As indecisive as I am, I sent out a general application just before graduation and this is what I was chosen for. The aim though, is to become a Compliance analyst and or an Economist.

Has always been the dream

My phone goes off and I see T's contact flash across the screen.

Sexy Bitch calling…

I slide to answer and her loud ass voice breaks through my speakers, "How me land a mommy and yuh no deh yah?" she questions.

"Me about fi drive out, yuh extra so?" I giggle.

"Ah, me a go back upstairs until one a unuh land. Me just done get some PR videos fi Joshua ting and Slyme say him gone fi Muuch."

"Mariah dem deh-deh?" I ask genuinely, since she told me she was joining us with a guest she refuses to tell us about.

"Say she a come yes. Yuh hear from Lorelle and Keif?" her words laced with concern.

Keif was in a car accident earlier this year and so we weren't sure they would make it 'cause one thing fi sure… Lorelle nah go no weh leff her cousin, especially if a sick she sick.

"Yeah Lorelle say them a drop in."

"Ah, link me when you outside beb," she says before hanging up.

Jordanne

The thought of him pops into my head out of nowhere, and the feeling of anxiety comes alive in the pit of my stomach.

Uggghhh!

I've managed to keep it cordial with him whenever I would see him at Mrs.Teathers' little family events, but he's been back for months now and doesn't seem to be leaving anytime soon.

Thought his degree was four years? So he would be finished this June?

I know mine was three years but for sure bachelor's abroad span four years no? I shake the curiosity, replacing it with Sue's new name… Mrs.Teathers.

Suanne Teathers.

I'm still not used to not calling her Mrs.Sheer … and every time it slips out, Paul looks at me as if to strangle the memory of her old name out of my mind.

I find myself grinning at the memory of him arguing with me about it once.

Man love a Sue

Deciding on getting a picture of myself, to send to Lorelle, I move to my hallway.

I live in one of the apartments on the complex now because I haven't been back to the home Jordanne had bought for us since what happened in Hanover happened.

Yeah…

Toni let's me know he doesn't go there either, but Sue keeps it up by sending cleaners, and gardeners from time to time. Anuh my problem still… He could sell it and keep all the profits for all I care.

If yuh say so

I'm serious.

"Len… can you snap a picture of me please?" I beg, batting my eyes at him.

He smiles, shakes his head and takes the phone from my hand. After three tries he gets the perfect picture… well, good enough for my memory only. I haven't posted on social media since the breakup and I don't feel the need to. These days I use it to simply watch stories and support Mariah's and Toni's content.

Love the short hair

Me too, I agree with my mind.

I cut my hair the day I completed therapy… I still go from time to time but she took me off the once per week program early last summer, and then I moved to twice a month. Now it's whenever I feel the need.

Yahhh…

"Thanks baby," I look up at Lenard, tipping to plant a kiss on his forehead.

Len and I met at a conference last May, that I went to learn more about real estate and where the market is going. I was so comfortable being on my own and focusing on my goals that I didn't really pay him much attention at all.

Other than the occasional advice here and there, I never really communicated with him. He's much older and I've never thought about dating anyone more than 5 years my senior. That quickly changed when I saw him in Mexico while on my solo birthday trip last year. I thought it a sign and decided to actually listen to his interest. Safe to say, he won me over and since September 30th last year, he's been handing me nothing but peace and good sex.

Ehhh… I mean

Be quiet.

Shaking the doubt from my mind, I decide to ask him, "When are you leaving?"

"Two days from this. I have a meeting in Hong Kong. You're free to join me," he smiles.

I offer him a smile right back.

Last night was the first night he's spent in my apartment and I'm already ready for him to leave. Not that I hate his presence, I just love my space.

We basically lived with Jordanne though?

That was a different point in my life, and for most of those four months he was at school. The woman I am now likes her space and will always put herself first.

"Regardless of the Easter holidays, I still have work... the central bank does not rest," I smirk, giving him another kiss on the cheek. "I'm about to leave, let me know if you decide to stay another night or not," I say, before leaving clear instructions for him to adhere to.

"Okay Miss.Bossy," is all he says when my list ends– his tone satirical.

• • •

Lorelle you reach?

I type the text to Lorelle before pulling up to the Sheer residence... or Teathers? I duh know.

"Pretty round head," Troopa laughs as I bring my window down to ask him where to park.

"VIP garage Ry'. Yah act brand new so? Everybody else park a road," he says before pressing the button to release the gates.

"Ah knock knee, no say a word," I laugh, rolling my windows back up while watching him double over into laughter.

**Dutty Foot: Girl me reach bout 3 minutes ago
and dutty Troopa ago say me fi park outside. Him
nuh like me enuh!**

I laugh in disbelief. It's either he really hates her or he has a thing for her and wants to see her walk past him up into the yard each time she's here.

I come to a park and exit my Coupe.

Upon exiting, I hear T's voice, "Meee??? love the short hair! The boss bitch aura, the tone up body!" she shrieks.

"Easy no rainbow warrior, yuh nahfi shower me with compliments. We no wah Kelly grab me a road!" and we both scream buckets of laughter while walking to the lawn where the 'get together' is in full swing.

Mek we go find your mother 'cause she gwaan like she live yah

Walking closely behind Toni, I start to feel eyes on me. Multiple sets of eyes as is usual when somebody new enters a space. I've learnt not to let that feeling intimidate me anymore and I don't... buttt... I can feel a specific set of eyes.

His eyes...

I snap my head up to the balcony and sure enough I see him peering down at me.

Shirtless... exposing all his new arm, chest and neck tattoos...

Joggers hanging from his hips...

Two different bottles of champagne in each of his hands...

Jesus

The throbbing that picks up between my legs is ridiculous.

He doesn't break the stare for a second, and I don't either. My throat runs dry, and for a moment it's just us.

With a raise of his brow, darkened eyes and a wicked smirk, he mouths the word, 'HI'

I–

"Come nuh gyal!" Toni shouts, not realizing what's happening.

Her words cause me to snap my head away, focusing all my attention on finding my mom. I haven't seen her in days and I'm ready to tell her about Lenard.

Mmmcht

Be quiet!

49 | My Era

RYLEIGH

I duh know why mommy feel like she a young gyal. Since T' took over her social media, every living second I have to get her pictures taken. I can't lie though, the salon has picked up since she hired Toni for marketing. Her customers are no longer just stay at home moms from upper St.Andrew; she has tapped into early millennials and Gen-Z.

Love that fimi nice madda.

"Come no Ry' me wah go back rounda the lawn. I was just speaking to a potential client."

"Lawd mummy, see it here. Look, me done…" I retort, handing her the phone.

The genuine disinterest plastered all over her face while she observes the picture, lets me know that T' is really holding her against her will for the content.

I find myself smiling.

"Me have supm fi tell you enuh," I say, hoping this new topic of conversation will keep me out here longer.

I do not want to go back to the lawns to sit under his stare.

"What is it bubs?" her eyes soft… and searching mine.

"Nothing to worry about mommy, I just met someone," I get it out with a stupid smirk plastered on my face.

She pauses in slight shock, looks me up and down and says, "Some… one?"

I swear to you, my mother does not like anybody for me… Nobody at all.

She like J'

That a fi her business.

"Nuh bother with it, he's a nice guy, software engineer that dabbles in real estate, lives in London but is here in Jamaica for long periods at a time," I begin to explain, watching as she shifts her weight while folding her arms to look at me.

She nuh trust man enuh

"How long you know this fellow? And how old is he?" her forehead creases from concern.

I heave a sigh.

"He's…… he's 29," and before I can tell her how we met, she's shouting his age back at me.

"Twenty-nine!!?? Ryleigh you're twenty-one!" she sneers.

"Twenty-two in five months!" I snap back, rolling my eyes.

Know me shouldn't tell her nuttin though…

"Weh a man eight years older than yuh ago talk to you say likkle gyal? Mek certain him nah try groom yuh! Weh yuh say unuh meet?" she asks, disregarding my initial attempt to tell her.

I hiss, loud too.

My patience is growing weary and I think for a second to end the conversation and walk back to the lawn. That thought quickly dies though…

Yuh no wah see the man?

Not at all.

"The conference I went to in May of last year… and then again in Mexico. His name is Lenard McPhaw, he's really kind and sweet. We've been dating since Mexico and I just thought you should know. Yah act like we ago get married or supm," the words leave my lips a little more harsh than I anticipated.

"Yah big woman enuh Ry' but me have more experience in this life than you so me affi skeptical. Soon as you ready, I want to meet Mr.29 year old British… Weh you say engineer and real estate whatever him be. I would like to know his intentions, thank you," and with that I smile.

I know she might come off miserable, but her intentions are always pure.

Pheeew! Now that that's over.

Go back to the lawn

"Come mek we go back," mommy mumbles before walking away… but I stand rooted.

Mi wah go home

If me never wah see Muuch dem, God know me leave… I can always invite them over for a girl's night anyways right?

Yeah

Mhhhmm.

"Me ago leave…" are the words that roll off my tongue.

Mommy snaps her head back in confusion, "What? How long me no see you? From last week Sunday. A Good Friday, take yuhself and spend it with me and no mek me stress out… See Lenard a take you way already," she fake pouts.

I giggle at her theatrics.

"I just feel a little anxious… so better me go home," I hold my choice– looking at the distance between where we are standing at her car and the garage where my car is parked.

She saunters back to me and grabs my face in her palms, searching my eyes for answers.

"Is it Jordanne?"

My body suddenly riddles with a feeling I don't like.

"I… I just want to leave," I whisper.

She releases my face and offers me a comforting smile.

"The last time you bottled your feelings and didn't tell me, it almost broke me as a mother, don't do that again. You're grown but you're still my one baby," her words tug at my heart in the most painful way.

Sigh…

"Mommy… I don't trust myself around him, I don't want to relapse. The peace I've had for the past two years has been so good, regardless of how rocky it started. Mi cyaa badda with that again… Jordanne tend fi turn me ina somebody weh just jealous and vengeful," my lips release my true thoughts.

"I know that feeling, I had the same feeling with your father. When he left it was painful but needless to say, it was probably best for us both," she sighs.

The mention of my father adds more unease to my already uneasy body. I shake the thought away and decide to hug her.

"You have to face him though Ry'… Sue is my friend, his sister is your best friend, Muuch is with his right hand… The entire circle is connected, you can't live like this for life. Start by trying today and eventually yuh wii alright," she pulls away to look at me.

I take a second to think about taking up on her offer, when I hear Mariah's voice.

"Ryyyyyyyyyyyyyyyyyyy!!!" she screams, "from one good body to the next yuh nooooiiice."

Her bubbly personality instantly shifts my mood.

Maybe you can get through the day with her now

I look behind her just noticing that Slyme is driving in with Muuch. There's also somebody still at the security post waiting, but I can't quite see who it is. I watch Troopa pick up the phone and I already know who he's calling.

"A Ruse, him no wah let in Ruse ina me owna yard and daddy done say J' say him can come so me no know why Troopa a bhave so," she complains while winding her neck around.

I laugh at her movement.

Troopa nah mek J' clip him fi stupid decisions. I laugh out again from that thought, a little too loud and she joins me unknowingly.

Muuch walks up to us, asking for Lorelle and Keif. I let her know they're on the lawns and she offers us a hug, takes my mom's hand and saunters off. It's not until Mariah falls silent that I realize why Muuch did that.

Jordanne is exiting the house, walking directly towards Mariah and I.

"A him alone?" his voice comes across.

He has a shirt on now…

What a way you notice

"Yes and Troopa a gwaan the most. Why you come out? Yuh no normally come down fi simple things like this," she giggles, looking back and forth between us.

This girl is something else.

He ignores her and walks to the gate… and me? Meee? Wah run gah me car and speed weh.

I watch as Jordanne and Slyme hover Troopa, who is searching the hell out of Ruse. Minutes later they all walk back to where Mariah and I are standing.

Mariah hugs Ruse as he says, "Ry' yuh up?"

"Yeah," is all I offer him as a response.

Mariah then drags him away to the lawn, with Slyme right behind them. I attempt to walk away but Jordanne whispers my name. My nipples perk up and I immediately fold my arms to hide them.

Today ah neva the day nuffi wear a bra

I turn around to look at him, offering him none of my words.

"Yuh ago avoid me for the entire time me deh here?" he cocks his head to the side– the weed aroma pouncing off him.

"Never know you did a plan fi stay. You no have school and dem thing deh?" my query brings a smile to his lips.

"Done school December… Still have to graduate with the bunch in June though."

He notices my confusion and goes on to say, "I did semesters in the summer."

Oh…

Two years of only 'Hi and Byes' and suddenly he wants conversation? Ughh.

"Okay me ago back to T' them…" I trail off before turning to walk away.

"Dat good," is all he says.

Surprisingly, he allows me to leave.

• • •

Everybody is either drunk, high or just happy on life. Not me, I gave up heavy drinking months ago. Watching how happy everybody is brings my mind to Lenard. I can't wait to be able to invite him to these things.

Be fucking for real

I giggle at the stupid thought.

Deciding to walk to the kitchen in search of a sorrel beer, since I drank all the ones from the igloo, I pull myself up from the chair and slowly move to the kitchen.

Yesss, yes… I said 'heavy drinking' not light beer…

Sue has made a few changes to the kitchen, so I'm having a hard time finding the fridge. She has somehow blended it into the cupboards and every time me come here, me no remember a which one.

"This one," **his** voice causes me to jump from fright.

"Relax killa," he laughs.

The room is dimmed, only allowing moonlight in from the large windows.

He moves past me to get to the cupboard, and I can't help but notice how his muscles are carved to perfection, even beneath the shirt. Opening the refrigerator, he pulls out what he knows I'm looking for before handing it to me. When the cold glass bottle touches my skin, so does his fingers… and a sigh leaves my lips.

He moves closer to me closing the space between us.

The throbbing, the uncontrollable throbbing…

Reaching across and over my shoulders he says, "Just a grab a napkin…" in my ear.

Me ago dead in yah

His breath tickles my ear and my breath hitches. He moves back, holding the napkin he claimed to have wanted before looking down at me with a smile.

"Nipple dem a betray you babe," his voice crawls all over my body.

I quickly fold my arms across them and watch as he licks his lips.

Yeah me affi leave

I hiss and turn to exit the kitchen when he says, "So you and Len good?"

Bumboclawt

Now how? You know what… mi shoulda know. I swear to you, nothing in this country no slip this man.

"We are…" I turn to look at him.

Nuh leave we fi a leave the kitchen?

He walks over to me without saying a word.

Before I know it, I'm against the island with both his hands to the side of me. He lifts his head to hold my gaze and stares at me for what seems like a millennia, before he takes a deep breath… and walks away.

I watch as he disappears up the stairs.

That's why me no come yah enuh man

I hiss my teeth.

Yeah I'm going home… With that I pull my keys from the little key rack at the entrance of the kitchen and head to my car.

50 | Loose

JORDANNE

I move back to the balcony deciding to let her go.
She looks, happy?

Different…

Regardless of how I feel, if she happy with the square she happy with him.

A we leff her enuh

Neva have much of a choice deh so still… Don't think we woulda even be acquainted choosing to continue the walk down that path. But Lenard? After Ramone done dig him file, he came up clean. Squeaky fucking clean.

Know she no like that

Might be settling, but if settling gives her peace then dat good.

Nah wile her

I pick up my 6th spliff for the day and take a seat, looking down at Sue's guests. Mariah is wrapped in Ruse's arms, Muuch in Slyme's, Mum in Paul's, T' in Joshua's…

Kelly deh?

A smile pulls at my lips…

Cyaa believe the one Joshua have two woman fi himself. Generation yah serious yuh fuck.

Our generation bus head

I don't know how T' convinced him to go along with that. Me personally couldn't share my woman, not even with a next woman bredda… Nope.

Leaning further back into my chair, I see when T' notices that Ry' is leaving. Her head snaps up to me and I shrug, feigning ignorance.

Nuh do her nothing fi she leave…

T' pulls out of Joshua's arms and bolts to Ry' who is busy speed walking to the front of the house.

They both stop and the body language spewing from them tells me T' is trying to get her to stay... but Ryleigh isn't having it.

Closing my eyes I take a long pull from my spliff. Maybe me fi give the therapy thing a next try?

Humph

The thought of trying that again is interrupted by my phone going off. I look to see that it's Ramone. Man yah no take a break from work?

I shake my head before sliding at the screen to answer, "Ramone..."

"Drip, same issue from last time a pop up again with the V dem enuh," his voice comes across the speakers muffled.

"Yehh?" Is all I offer.

If mi a be honest, mi not even ina the mood fi listen.

See her one time and yuh no wah focus pon work again?

Work and school got two full years of my life... And now? I might be ready to fix myself... for her...

Say she happy with the square but her body a say supm else.

"Boss? Yah listen me?" Ramone's voice cuts in.

"Yo, yeah hear wah. Just ago leff some pon the floor a Taboo. That will at least lift few bags offa we without a paper trail. So farwud round 1 O'clock and we go treat the ladies," I give the instructions– hanging up before he gets a chance to respond.

If mi a be real, there are many other ways to get rid of the marked cash but me have a soft spot fi hard working women and nobody works harder than the pole dancers... in my opinion.

And you know Ry' nah skip the chance fi go Taboo

Precisely...

Finally getting to my high, I pull myself up out of the chair. Six spliff it a take me now fi get to even the lowest point of my high? Jah know.

When I look down, I notice T' has somehow convinced Ry' to stay and she's now standing with Lorelle and Keif next to the gazebo. Troopa neva did ago let her out stillll... but good job to T'. Smiling, I decide to move my post downstairs.

● ● ●

RYLEIGH

Me ago regret this?

You good girl. Act like a big woman

I quickly send a text to Lenard, letting him know not to wait up any longer since he decided on staying the night. T' them decide dem ago Taboo and you know who nah miss that, fi love, money or maturity.

We love a pole spinner

Love see them tricks bad to bad.

"Yeah man just make Cory mek him wife know the pre," Slyme's voice comes across the lawn.

We've all decided on going except for the older folks. All Troopa get a bus, since the night shift security came at midnight.

"Me cyaa wait fi drop bricks ina gyal draws side," Mariah shrieks, sending us into laughter.

"Leave dem ting deh to me," Kelly giggles.

Kelly is soft spoken most of the time but when she has that alcohol in her system? Di gyal no leff nuttin fi rest pon her mind.

"Ready?" Ramone asks, handing out four duffel bags to respective parties.

Slyme gets one.

Joshua gets one.

Ruse gets one.

And... is he walking to me?

"Drip own," he explains while smirking... and I notice everybody's giggling.

I think about refusing it but there is nothing I like more than throwing money at women who are busy being majestical in the air. Feeling a little self-conscious, I take the bag and avert my eyes to the gazebo. With the little courage that the edible T' forced down my throat earlier gives me, I lay my eyes on Jordanne, squinting them in faux disapproval.

He smiles, puffing what has to be the 900th spliff since I got here this evening. It's a wonder him no overdose.

All a this and I have to finish my reports to hand in first thing Monday morning

My thoughts are interrupted by Ryan walking out of the kitchen and towards us. I swear, I only see this man once every six months. Averting my eyes to the parking lot, I notice Surgeon with his own duffel bag.

How much money them a leggo tonight so?

"Ready," Slyme says clear enough to get everybody's attention, and with that we all move to the cars... and by all I mean, Muuch and Slyme...

Ruse and Mariah...

Kelly, Joshua and T'...

Lorelle, Ryan and Keif...

Ramone, Paw, Troopa, Snoop and Buckle.

I move to join them in the pilgrimage to the cars when I hear Skulli's voice.

"Yo mad head, farwud likkle bit," he shouts, I assume he's calling to Jordanne?

I continue to waltz to the cars when Jordanne says, "The new Porsche Ry," his voice only audible to me.

I stop in my tracks, thinking about protesting but deciding not to. The back and forth weh that might kick start, mi nuh ina… anymore– not at this age… and me just deh yah fi enjoy the rest of the night nothing more, Right?

Suuure, if yuh feel better with dah talk deh

Standing at the lawn chair nearest to the kitchen, I watch as him and Skulli go back and forth.

Love dem new relationship

In the weirdest way the dynamic has shifted from Paul just being his righthand worker and convenient father figure, to him being a full fledge father, granting guidance and advice to J'– from what Toni has been telling me. I can see that in play now, right before my eyes, as I watch how Skulli's face crinkle with concern and slight paranoia.

Not sure why he's worried, by the rumours I've heard about J' these past two years, I'm certain he'll be okay.

Nobody no wah them head leff pon a spike ah them lane entrance

I still don't know if that one is true… Don't know if I want it confirmed either.

A shiver runs down my spine and the sound of multiple engines roaring to life pulls my attention to the front garage.

"Ready?" J's voice pulls me from thought.

"Ready," I mumble, handing him the duffel bag.

• • •

As we pull onto the Taboo premises, I notice that we're the only set that's allowed to park on the actual grounds of the club. All other cars are routed to the parking lot a few meters down. Constant Spring Road at this hour always bring back fresh memories from second year. That was a lit year in college. Taboo was the after spot for every single event and now it's rolled over as tradition in the family.

"My stash," Jordanne's voice grabs me back to reality and without a second thought, I fly the glove compartment open, removing his stash of weed.

"You smoke in this one?" I ask, turning my head to face him.

"First time mah bring it out," he responds lowly.

His voice has become deeper with the years… and is it me or does he talk way less also? Like him no say more than five to six words at a time

Weh yuh wah di man say?

I watch him exit the car, tucking his gun into his waist as he moves around to my side. He flies my door open and holds my hand, helping me get up from the car.

The new Porsche is a Taycan so it's much lower than the Macan he's had for a while. I've seen the Taycan prices… splurging, are we?

Grabbing his hand to lift myself to my feet, I whisper a low, "Thanks."

"Girl! Yuh ready?" Toni's voice comes across, breaking the tiny moment of tension.

My savior dat

"Right awayyyyyyy!!" I laugh.

"Right awayyyyy!!" all my girls respond.

We make it to the entrance, disregarding the line at the front door. I stop, thinking I have to get banded, but J' slightly pulls me from my stance.

"Yuh no need no band," he whispers.

See? Five words at a time.

We all make it inside and I already know what section to walk to. There are already strippers and bottle girls waiting on the wing section just in front of the stage to the right. The DJ announces the arrival of 'Drip' and the crowd shifts to make us a pathway to the section.

His hand doesn't leave mine.

I can see the strippers whispering to each other, ready to find themselves in our section at some point in the night. Slyme, Muuch, Paw and Snoop mount the steps first before taking their posts in the section, followed by J' and I... then everybody else after.

I move to the corner of the couch, knowing that's where he'll want to sit.

It's like muscle memory

"Noooo," Mariah screeches, walking over to us before we get to take a seat. "Danne yuh cyaa get her wull night. We ago throw money," she giggles.

"Dat good," is all he says before bending to whisper in the ear of the bottle girl that's been waiting for orders.

My eyebrow raises in... jealousy? But I catch myself and move to the center and front of the section wid me best gyal dem.

● ● ●

It's 3:15am and we're down to the last duffel bag of cash. The section is swimminggg in money. The stage and floor below us? Riddled in USD singles, 20s and 100 bills.

I've had maybe four shots of Azul and another gummy edible, so I'm loose at this point.

Mi love this yuh fuck!

Lady Saw's 'If Him Leff' makes its way through the speakers, bouncing off the walls and back to our ears.

My team becomes a choir and we start screaming the lyrics. Mere milliseconds later I feel when a stripper bends all the way over in front me. I'm taken aback by how big her batty be. No mannn!

T' and Lorelle notice and start laughing like fucking hyenas while watching my facial expression. Since I'm the one with the bag, I release a brick and put a lump of 100s in the string of her panties. She starts shaking it more and I don't pretend shy, me slap dat!

Dat is it

Yeah gyal skin clean.

The music goes low and the lights dim, pulling everybody's attention.

"Ladies and di deep pocket man demmm... To the stage right now, closing the perfor-mance section of the night issss... Diamond!!!" the MC announces.

I don't get the chance to listen to what he says next as my curiosity pulls my head to the stage. The audience falls quiet and only one stage light is left on– pointing directly at her.

"Fix yuh rass face!" I hear Kelly, and I know she's talking to T'.

Gyal jealous beyond this world. I don't know how them and Joshua work.

I laugh lowly before quickly bringing my attention back to the stage. A Dexta Daps song cuts on and I watch as Diamond swings herself up and around the pole.

What a gyal good

The ease at which she moves around the pole is mind boggling. She gets to the roof and starts hanging from the beams at the top, swinging her head in circles. My hand finds the duffel bag and I start showering the stage with cash. She notices and hooks herself back unto the pole– dropping in one single motion to almostttt the floor, with her legs still wrapped around the pole and her head angled to me.

My favorite move

I throw more cash at her…

She swings around the pole a few more times before she climbs it, only stopping midway. The next thing she does is flawless. She holds her body inches away from the pole and sky-walks around it all while keeping the rhythm.

Jeeesshh!

Two other women enter the stage and I already know it's about to be a tag team. The slimmer one climbs the pole first, then Diamond… and then the pretty, thick, dark skin one that was here just now.

They mount onto each other, spinning and performing tricks I've seen before and some I'm just seeing tonight.

This goes on for a couple more minutes before they dismount and exit the stage.

That was a show!

Only half of the money is left in the duffel bag, and I have no clue what to do with it.

"Lorelle come throw this me ago rest me foot," I say to Relle who has been lit for every second since we made it inside.

"Me will know wah fi do with it," she giggles.

I watch as she hands everybody we came with a brick, until the bag is empty. They all move down from the section and to the stage sides.

The strippers are not really doing much right now. They're basically just dancing instead of performing– seducing the men on the sides to get their last round of cash before the night ends.

I grab a bottle of water from our table and walk to Jordanne, who has simply been sitting and watching us enjoy ourselves with the occasional stripper dancing in front of him throughout the night. He doesn't take lap dances. According to him, him no know who the girl dem rub pon before him.

Man terrible so till

And I love it.

Plopping myself onto the couch beside him, I hear when he asks in a concerned tone, "Yuh good?" while bringing his cup to his lips.

"Yup," is the response I offer him while bringing the water bottle to my lips.

"So you and Mr.Boring?" he smiles, but I watch how it doesn't reach his eyes.

"Jordanne, don't start. Just realize today that yuh probably ago ina my life forever but me nah do the back and forth with you about anybody I choose to date. Me go above and beyond this time fi make certain dah man yah no know nothing 'bout crime unless a cyber."

"Get it right too," he mumbles more to himself than to me.

"Weh yuh mean?" I ask, looking at him.

His eyes pull me in under the lights before he admits...

"Had Ramone run a check. Man only have speeding tickets," he sort of hisses in disappointment.

But is like dah man yah mad? Problem if me date a nice man, problem fi date a gunman.

Problem fi anybody but him

When a him leff me?

Anger starts climbing through my veins... but I decide to not let him have me relapse. Mi come toooo far.

"Okay," I whisper, holding his stare.

"I like the hair," he smirks, eyes filled with admiration, and for a moment I feel like it's two years ago all over again.

Pull yourself away from this right now sista gyal, 'cause yuh still love di bwoy

Kartel's 'Bet Mi Money' cuts on and I decide to dead the conversation him a try have right yah suh, right now. The song reminds me of the night of his sendoff years ago. I remember that night to this day... and not because of the murders I witnessed.

Ignoring my very clear subconscious, I climb over, straddling him in the closest way. My dress rides up, stopping just above my hips, exposing me only to him... and I watch the shock take residence all over his face.

I duh know if ah the liquor, the edibles or just me relapsing but me just feel fi dance and dance with him. Snaking my hands around to the back of his head before cupping it in my palm, I hold his stare and start moving to the lyrics of Kartel's song.

Ensuring that I'm directly over his length, I start grinding. His hands move from my waist and up to my hair.

Me likkle bald head!

The feel of his hand sends blood rushing to my clit and the throbbing immediately starts. Before the first verse of the song ends, I start feeling his dick harden beneath me. Refusing to stop, I continue, while watching him fight the temptation of touching me the way he wants to.

The song comes to an end and I immediately pull myself from him. I stand and look down to the stage where everybody is, only to spot Lorelle slapping a random stripper's ass.

Them no tired?

I peak at my phone to see that it's now 3:55am, so I toggle to Len's chat.

I'll be home before sunrise. Muah!

He doesn't reply as I expected, so I click my phone shut before bringing the screen to darkness.

"Ready?" I hear and feel Jordanne's voice behind my ear.

"Ready..." I offer him a soft response.

Him see yuh text?

Nahv a clue, but wah it matter?

• • •

"Yah go?" I ask, as I put the last piece of jerk chicken into his mouth while he drives.

"Yuh yard... the rightful one," he answers, offering me a quick glimpse.

See wah you put yourself back ina?

"Jordanne..." I avert my eyes to him, "just carry me to the complex, Lena–"

"Bredda who give a fuck 'bout yuh man?" he laughs, but without humor.

See dem sump yah now? Nah wile him 'cause me nah argue with a soul. Not tonight at all. The car ride falls into silence all the way to pulling into our home. I watch as Slyme's car turns back as we enter the premises.

Not even realize him did deh behind we

Jordanne pulls into the garage and shuts the car off– walking around to my door to get it open. The likkle ride from the club to here mek me realize me gone yuh fuck. The lady head lift off.

Holding my hand, he pulls me out of the car, locks it... and we walk to the living area hand in hand. Looking around, I realize nothing has changed. Sue really has kept it up. Feeling comfortable, I move to the kitchen like it's second nature. Jordanne follows me as I wobble to the pantry.

Lady yuh know if food deh yah?

It's Sue, food ago deh yah like a decoration.

My eyes meet a cinnamon roll and I pick it up. Wasting no time, I start devouring it.

J' chuckles... and I decide to ask what's funny.

"Just you," is all he says.

I throw him one and watch as he adds cheese to it, warms it, allowing the cheese to melt and then devours it.

Minutes have passed and we're both on the kitchen floor moving through fruit plates Sue has created.

"A swear to yuh, them fresh. She come here every Sunday evening come do her thing, sometimes ah she and Ms.Janette," he assures me.

I make note of how much he's talking again. Much less tense and intimidating than he was earlier. It's as if he's his old high school self.

I like that...

"So she a do this fi two years? And unuh never think 'bout selling it?" I open my mouth for him to feed me a single green grape.

My mouth clasps his fingers for a little more than two seconds and his eyes shoot to me. His whole demeanor darkens, and I can feel the sexual tension that was just created from that one touch.

"Yeah... Me tell her me no wah let it go still..." he mutters.

"Why?..." I whisper.

Ignoring my question, he moves into me, capturing my lips into a kiss. I hesitate for a second but then decide to let it be. The kiss is deepened, and I feel when he pulls my tongue into his mouth.

WooOOooah.

Kissing him is nothing new, but tonight, the feeling is foreign.

He leans back, slightly shoving the fruit bowls away while I climb on top of him. In the same moment, he slips my very thin panties that are already soaked to the side.

He doesn't insert any fingers but instead focuses on my clit. The feeling sends me in overdrive. There is nobody that knows my body like Jordanne.

Absolutely no one.

A single finger is slipped inside and my spirit leaves my body. Moans start spilling from my lips and I start grinding on his fingers. My orgasm starts rising to the peak and I can't believe me ago cum so quick.

The fuck a gwaan?

He seems to pick up on the motion and forces another finger inside, hooking them upward this time.

Fuckkkk

My spot…

Shuddering, I lull my head back and let him bring me to the peak of pleasure. The pace he has going on my clit picks up and that's all it takes to send me over the edge. Within a minute, I'm screaming and shaking above him.

I fall from my peak but he doesn't stop.

"Jorrrrdannnnnneee!… Oh–Ohhh–my–God… stoopppp–stop-st-st–" the words leave my mouth in pieces.

Jesus.

Jesuss…

Jeeesuss…

"Relax babe… I'm here. Let it go," he starts coaching me.

"Ryleigh… let… it… go," he repeats.

My breathing picks up as he talks me through finding my second high. He keeps his motion and pace, and I'm forced to cum back-to-back, this time squirting all over him and the floors.

"Good girl," he praises, just before my body falls weak– forcing me to lay on his chest.

"Woulda fuck yuh right now… but me nah share you… so clean yourself up and go home to you man."

Wah?

My head barely lifts from his chest before I voice my thought.

"What?" I look down at him.

"Bad head, anuh yuh say yah get home before sunrise?" he asks, and I turn to see that the sun is indeed rising.

Fuck…

Deven surprised at him reading my text.

Pulling myself up, I step over him and the fruit bowls to head to the bathroom. When I'm done with my shower I give Goose a call.

Moments later Goose is at the gate and Jordanne is seated in the couch, in fresh clothes.

Our couch, Our house

"So… what now?" I ask, searching his eyes.

"You fi tell me that Ry," he peers up at me.

"Last time me check youuu left and me nah–" I stop myself from finishing the sentence.

Nah join back dah circus yah a bloodclawt

"You know supm, bye. Mek T' drop me car at the complex please," I spin to exit the house.

He says something that I don't stop to listen to.

While walking to Goose's taxi, I shoot Lenard a text. While looking at the time, I see that it's 6:13am.

Hey baby! I got a little too drunk and spent the night at Lorelle's. On my way home now. 🖤

Clicking out of the text box, I enter Goose's car.

"Long time me nuh see dem girl yah," he laughs.

"Easy no Goose, you know when you get rich you affi switch likkle," I laugh out, and just like that we fall into easy conversation– catching up on what has happened in our lives since I left high school.

51 | Toying

RYLEIGH

"You made breakfast?" I ask, walking to plant a kiss on his shoulder. My knees don't have the strength to help me tip and kiss his lips.

"How long have you been up?" I throw out another question.

"Just since six, when I realized you weren't in bed. I was gonna call but then I saw your texts, how was the girl's night?" he asks, while tossing the eggs around in the bowl.

I slide myself onto the stool around the island and start peeling back a banana.

"Good we had fun, went to Taboo and stop ah Lorelle as you know," I whisper, biting the banana.

We barely get out dah lie deh sista gyal

With his focused fixed on the mixture he says, "Oh... you don't look like you had a lit night. You look... fresh, like yo–"

"Yeah," I cut him off, "I took a shower before coming in to help with the hangover."

He falls silent... and so do I.

The kitchen stays silent until he slides a plate with French toast on it and a side of blueberries.

Weh mi wouldn't do fi Sue stew chicken instead ah this

I smile, getting ready to create space in my tummy to eat his breakfast, even though I ate earlier with such man.

"All this time mi never know you can cook," I giggle before biting into the toast.

It's surprisingly so good!

Watching the genuine smile spread across his face, I tip up to actually kiss him on his lips this time.

"Is that Tom Ford?" he pulls back in confusion.

Tom Ford?

Tom Ford???

"Tom Ford?" my eyebrows scrunch up in as much confusion as his.

"Yes... the cologne... you have a faint smell of it lingering on you."

And look how me baaaathe and scrubbbb

I force a tiny smile before I mutter, "Must be from Lorelle. She loves perfume, men's cologne too, she collects them," I lie through my teeth.

With that, I stuff another piece of toast into my mouth to give myself time to recover if he has another question and...

... he does.

"Come with me to Portland today?" he suggests, and as the words leave his lips, I thank God it's not another question about my misdoings.

Portland... I love Portland.

Man dem a dash yuh favourite things at you this weekend

I have to finish my reports for Monday. Easter Monday or not, I have to turn them in.

Virtually

But still...

"I have to work... and," I try to protest but he cuts in.

"Ry' it's my last day with you, allow me to take you there. You can bring work with you," he smirks.

I watch as he removes the apron before bringing himself to sit and eat his toast.

"If mi wake up and feel rested, I'll join you... What's the latest we can leave?"

"10:30."

I look at my phone to see that it's already minutes past 7. Then I would have to pack. What a lucky thing me nah no hair fi stress me, I'll just bring my favourite frontal.

"Okay I'll be up by 10," and with that I scurry off to my room, dialing Lorelle to fill her in.

Cause the way you throw bay lie ova the lady yard

Wah else me did fi do???

• • •

JORDANNE

Pulling into the driveway of the safe house in Hope Pastures, I see Skulli standing at the entrance. He's about to access the house when I shout at him, announcing my arrival.

While walking up to him he says, "Wah do you man. Mi nuh must see say a yuh?" he chuckles.

"No know enuh. Yah get old up yah now, might can't hear or see," I laugh.

"Thing them clear?" he asks.

"When we reach downstairs we go ina dat."

"Man serious so man?" he chuckles.

"Nuttin new," I laugh.

"So you get back yuh woman?" he asks… and almost instantly, my mood shifts.

When dem ago stop say 'get back'? Deciding not to answer, I move inside and towards the gathering.

"Ahhh so that's a no," Paul laughs, and I turn to look at him with the deadliest glare.

He holds his hands up in mock surrender.

"Man dem," I hail, capturing everybody's attention.

"Lawww…" they greet me clearly.

Without any further hesitation I get straight to the point, "As the leaders of all the posts, mah expect unuh nuffi drop di standard. So why me affi a clean up unuh mess myself?"

No one offers an explanation.

"Miself mah talk to?"

Still no answer…

Cool.

"Slyme who responsible fi south central collection?"

"JJ on behalf of him father, Jerome," Slyme speaks clearly… and my eyes avert to JJ.

"So young yute? Yuh know the ropes and the protocol 'cause mi know you father wouldn't leave you fi oversee things if not. Wah happen? Why the cash never launder in time? Twelve bags never launder and me coulda barely leggo four last night… So tell mi weh me must do with the remaining eight?" I raise a brow, offering him a sarcastic smile.

I already know exactly what to do but mi wah hear him solution.

Just wah intimidate the youth

See myself ina him man but him shakey, need some tune up.

"Boss me nuh really know how them miss up. When we ship off the first batch everything did good. By we reach the last set, me leff fi a minute and tell di man dem done it… When me drop back, everything load and we good… Say me a do a sweep before me leff just fi mek sure the warehouse empty, and me find dem ina barrel… Man dem weh did a pack and ship, chained up as you ordered… just a wait fi your next instruction."

Heard this story before through Slyme, but I wanted to hear from him myself so mi can read him body language.

"The Venezuelans ago need dem money regardless and it affi go come outa my pocket? Wah you suggest me do 'bout that?" I raise my hands to signal question.

Mek we hear him plan…

"You can cut my budget fi south central and mi fund it myself for the whole month," he suggests.

Skulli chuckles.

I smile too… The man think twelve duffel bags can fund the entire south central Jamaica fi a whole month. Somebody need fi show him the books.

"Yuh hear dat Slyme? A whole month di don say enuh," I laugh while looking JJ up and down.

A few of the other leaders join the laughing match. My left hand goes up, signaling silence before I move closer to him. The closer I get, the more intimidation settles on his face.

And that anuh my intention enuh

Tapping on his shoulder I say, "That was less than a week's worth of cash… Yuh good, it no shake we, but you need fi do frequent cleansing within your team."

His shoulders drop from relief, but he says nothing.

"Yeah mon, 'cause your team a mine and me no wah no thief 'mongst me, cool?" I hold my hand out for him to shake.

He hesitates before shaking it and the minute he extends his hand for me to shake it I pull him in.

"Next time yuh fuck up, big or small, your father a get you delivered to him in pieces as a nice package," I whisper.

While releasing him, he nods before moving to the back of the room.

Hate carelessness

And that's why I couldn't be with Ry'…

"On to other things… Ramone? Catch dem up pon cyber 'cause some man still a use them work phone do weh dem nuffi do," I glimpse at Slyme who has been calling Muuch from every mission.

Man gwaan like a first him a get girl.

Say you wouldn't call Ryleigh with it nuh

When I was younger maybe… now? Nah put her ina that spot.

Ramone steps to the front and starts talking while I move to Skulli.

"Mek we talk ina the basement… need yuh advice," I say to him and by just my eyes, I know he knows I'm ready to talk about Ry'.

• • •

RYLEIGH

"Plum? Ryleigh…" I keep hearing a male's voice lingering in my dreams.

"Hmmmm?" I mumble.

"We're here," comes Lenard's voice, jolting me from my dreams.

I snap my eyes open in excitement. This is my first official 'baecation' and I intend to live it uppp– all if a just 24 hours.

Lifting my seat, I stretch over to him to leave wet kisses along his face and neck– just to show my appreciation.

Meee? love this fi you

The villa is beautifullll. It's hidden and quiet, smack in the middle of nature.

Mosquito

That ah the least.

"Glad you're happy baby, nothing pleases me more," he pulls away to exit the van.

He then walks around to my side and opens my door, taking my small 'spenanight' bag from me. Hand in hand we walk down the path to our suite. When we get there, I simply cannot believe the view!

Breathtaking

Minutes have gone by and I'm still rooted in my stance, just taking it all in.

The chirping of the birds...

The river rushing downstream...

The wind ruffling the leaves...

Just the fresh air...

Peace, So much peace.

Len just left my bag on one of the chairs before leaving to ensure we have access to the Wi-Fi. Deciding to snap a picture for my story, I take my phone out. I upload it using my data and click my phone shut.

No time fi waste, me wah go see wah the property have fi offer right nowww! Apart from the suite's mini infinity pool.

Moving down the hall, I find the bedroom and decide to change into my bikini. It's a simple brown two piece that melts into my skin effortlessly. Admiring the fit, I rub my hands across my chest.

My boobs have gotten bigger... hmm

Taking my wig from my bag, I drag it on and use my spray to glue the front down.

Good enough, but let me use a scarf to tie it down

As I tie the scarf, I hear Len's voice.

"Come, let's get your pictures out the way so we can enjoy the rest of the day," his sweet sultry voice fills the room, but does nothing for my body.

Cho.

"You know yuh woman?" I laugh while handing him the phone.

"Woman? So it's official?" he peers down at me.

"Well, I told my mom about you..." I whisper, holding his gaze.

The news sends him happy... and he scoops me up into his arms before spinning me around.

I giggle out from the pure affection.

"Len come nuh man," I whine, "let's go, remember I have to work later tonight."

Hopefully I can use the work as an excuse to not have sex. I knowwww what you're thinking but no, I'm just not in the mood...

He throws me over his shoulders and moves us to the balcony. About a million pictures later, I finally find two that I like.

"There, yesss, those two," I shriek.

"Alla dem look good to me enuh Ry'... cyaa blame me," he defends his skills.

"You'll learn. I had to teach Jor– Jorissa just the same... but anyways, share the WiFi with me," I save myself before he thinks to ask who the fuck that is.

I toggle to my settings, just to make sure the WiFi connects to my phone. When it does, I slide to my Instagram again– quickly getting the two that I like ready while ignoring the previous notifications.

Seeing how cute they are, I decide to make a post with one and leave the other on my story. I haven't posted in two years, so this should be a good come back.

Wonder if nobody know dis villa?

Ago post regardless, I look toooo good.

I drop my second picture on my grid and watch as the likes and comments pour in. For a few minutes, I manage to ignore them as they pop up... until one catches my eye.

MMMCHHT.

I move to delete it but users have already started to like it.

Them quick yuh fuck

Me know it screenshot and reach Pinky already too.

Jordanne, weh me ago do with dah man yah? Why would he comment the 'perfect sign' emoji.

As I keep refreshing, more likes pour in, more replies fall under his comment and my DMs start getting crowded. A specific reply pops up under his comment that makes me laugh out a little too loud.

Pamela65: "Then unuh a never besties a High school? A yuh take the picture?"

A long time Pam fass enuh, and she no change at our big age.

Turn off the comments

Why me neva think of that earlier?

Toggling to settings, I quickly turn off the comments. Not sure why, because me certain somebody screenshot it already. Lenard doesn't use social media that often but he's still a cyber guy. I don't want him to see the number of likes Jordanne is accumulating under mi tings.

Nuh know how yuh woulda explain dat

"Yah smile so?" he asks, picking up a bag I assume is packed with things we'll need for the river.

"Nothing. Mi ready, let's go," I giggle and loop my arms into his.

We get down the steps and start walking the path to the river, when my phone vibrates.

Maybe Jordanne...

Realizing who it is, I let the phone ring to the end before I quickly find the data option and turn it off.

Not now Satan

Tightening the grip I have around Lenard's arm, I start thinking about the peace that he gives. The relationship has been so easy and understanding. No control, no possessiveness, no nothing to give me any form of anxiety.

That's not boring to you?

My therapist says peace is often mistaken for boredom and ah she mi a work wid.

No better way to spend my **Saturday.**

52 | Who Else?!

PAUL

"Yah hear me? Yuh can't push violence to her all the time. She anuh one from the team. Mek she make her own decisions and if it's meant to be she will come back," I explain, but Jordanne just a pre stubborn.

Killa want back the girl

"Nah… She's not fully affected by me anymore. Har body? Yes… but her mental? No… Mi feel like if me wait longer she ago stay with dah bredda yah and me affi go end up kill an innocent man and help her mourn," he stares at me, deadpan.

I immediately start laughing.

Weh di man just say?

Jah Know.

"Yo yuh cyaa serious?" my words slipping through the laughter.

"Me serious. Feel like leaving her was a mistake… She good now yes, and me proud ah dat, her head deh pon her body but it deh pon it a little too good," he chuckles and I watch him bring the lighter to his spliff.

"So yuh no feel like unuh ago clash more now that she's been through therapy and have a steady medz?"

Taking the lighter from him to light my own spliff, I study his face for the truth in his coming response.

He hesitates… for a second or two.

"Mi ago try that again. Me just need a therapist who ago understand say them cyaa repeat or report nothing weh me say… else a dirt. But at the same time, me no wah threaten nobody yuh get me?" and with that he stands, pulling his phone from his back pocket.

We've been talking for hours.

Every event him and dah girl deh go through has surfaced and she's really been there for everything and vice versa. I can't pinpoint why them nah get it right.

Couldn't pinpoint it with me and Suanne, either so me deven surprised

I watch as he scrolls through his phone for the millionth time, looking at whatever Ry' posted.

"Jah know," he mutters, with a torn look on his face. Torn between different ways he should handle this whole situation.

To me, Ryleigh man seem like a good option fi her. Him stable and nah cause no problems, but mi nahgo ever say that. Whatever mi son feel right, just right...

Yeah

"Work pah yourself bad head. Ry' nah exit your life no time soon. A one family, if you prove to her say yuh can buil and wull serious medz, she might drop back in. Just like how she a prove to you now say she can keep her head pon her body. A simple ting."

"Mek a therapist sign ah NDA and have a nice talk with them 'bout what happens if them even dream 'bout reporting nuttin."

Watching him, I see when he slides to her contact.

Him hear nuttin me just say?

"Yuh hear me sahh?" I ask, looking directly at him.

"Hear everything. Mahgo set it up man, call mah call her now," he holds the phone up to his ear.

Certain Janette tell Sue say she deh way Portland

"She deh way a–" I try to tell him but he finishes the sentence for me.

"Portland... Yeah, mi know," he quiets me by holding a finger up.

I chuckle... Mi must off my game fi real. Why me think him wouldn't know that?

"Ring out," his tone disappointed.

He then redials.

"Portland enuh. Maybe she no have service," I suggest... and he looks at me before shaking his head in disagreement.

"Phone wouldn't ring out," are the last words he says before I watch him hit the elevator access pad and hop in to go back upstairs.

"Jordanne, anuh Portland yahgo?" I question, but he ignores me, only offering a smirk just before the elevator door comes to a close.

Them young people yah.

Dialing Sue's number, I hit call and she answers on the first ring.

Wife dat

"Paul, I was just about to ask what you want for your **Saturday** dinner, steamed fish or jerk salmon wi–"

"Sue," I cut her off, "call Jordanne and talk him out of going to Portland. I'll explain things when me drop in but just tell him not to go... and steamed fish sounds good."

"Okay mah start dat. Weh me one boy up to now?" she asks, disregarding me telling her not to pry.

"Sue me just say me ago explain when me drop in... A Ryleigh," my words come out with humor because she really coulda wait till me reach home.

A heavy sigh comes across the speaker followed by, "Ah, let me call him right now," and with that she hangs up.

Not even a 'love you?' or a 'Lata?'

We ago fix that man... and my thoughts pull a smile to my lips.

• • •

RYLEIGH

"I'm hungry," I mumble more to myself than to Lenard.

It's 4:24pm on this nice **Sunday** evening and all mah think 'bout is mommy nice shelly rice and peas, with some baked chicken, fresh veggies and a side of mashed potatoes. We left Portland two hours ago– just in time to get back to Kingston, so he can catch his flight at nine.

Mi really no know wah do me, because I ate a biggg seafood platter just before leaving, and I've been snacking on a bag of sugarcane the entire ride.

Jesus the gym is taking a toll on my appetite and me coulda eat so from morning.

"Want to stop and get something now or you can hold out and we get something in Kingston?" Len asks, pulling me from my hunger thoughts.

"Kingston is fine," I mumble, while digging through my bag for the peanut cake I bought in traffic.

He glimpses at me and chuckles, causing me to giggle too. While pulling out the peanut cake, my hand brushes my nipple and I wince at the tenderness plaguing them.

Woahhhh...

I really prefer being on birth control because my PMS week is always a struggle, not to mention the actual week of my period.

Ughh!

And mi know a lie nasty Adam tell pah Eve mek we get dah wicked punishment yah enuh. That's why me cyaa like man... Toni have di right idea going.

With the peanut in one hand and my phone in the next, I rip the plastic with my teeth and start munching down, all while scrolling to the 'FLO' app to see when exactly my period ago keep.

Looking at this month, I realize I have like two more weeks...

30th it ago start. Dat no bad

So these are ovulation symptoms? 'Cause PMS don't start till like the week before.

The 'ups and downs' since coming off the pills have been a rollercoaster. Sometimes my cycle is heavy, sometimes it's light. Last time it was very, very light… but it still lasted the five days, so I don't even know.

Whatever yah man, hungry a kill me

Shoving the thoughts to the back of my head, I recline the seat and decide to try a nap until we get to Kingston.

Can't believe the peanut cake done by me finish look pah the dates.

Drop ina wah corner a me teeth

Sigh.

• • •

It's now 6:07pm and we didn't stop to get anything to eat because mommy said that Sue was going to send food, since she has extra today… and Len is saying he'll just grab a salad at the airport.

And me???? love my mother-in… Sue's cooking.

Bringing my window down, I signal to the security that it's me. He immediately allows us to drive in and I start packing all the things I have scattered in Len's van.

"Ago miss you," he mutters, looking over at me while pulling into the parking lot.

"It's only a couple days," I smile before leaning over to kiss his cheeks.

Our weekend was fun, and you know me no do my reports? I'll have to stay up all night completing them to get them in by 9am tomorrow.

"I'll miss you too," and not even a full second after the words leave my mouth, I spot a Range Rover to the back of the lot.

Shrugging my thoughts to the side, I pull away from Len to pick up my charger…

… because mi know few of my tenants have Range, so.

When I look up, Len is already out the car and walking around to my door.

Nice body

I bite down on my lips, while watching him open the door.

"Yuh nuh affi follow me up enuh. You can go pack and be on time for your flight," I smile genuinely.

"No I'm good. If I miss it, I'll buy another ticket. Come, let me bring this," he takes the bag from me before holding my hands.

We enter the elevator together and move all the way up to my floor while having easy banter. When we get to my door, I slap my key card against the locks and push the door in, all while smiling with Len as we recount how mi nearly drown off yesterday.

Because the lady cannotttt swim good and the way me jump offfff!

Murdaaa!

Before Len is able to enter, I smell him– Jordanne.

Mi pussyclawt

My heart rate picks up, forcing me to stand rooted in the doorway.

"Why you stop?" Len queries as he pushes the door wider– now able to see Jordanne seated, on my island, eating in the dark... gun on counter.

He doesn't acknowledge us, and I snap my head to Lenard.

Len pulls at his waist, but Jordanne's voice comes clear before he can complete the action.

"Nuh do dat killa," he chuckles... and I look to see him turn a bottle of water to his head.

Before Len can say anything, I speak, "I know him," my words hushed.

Lenard's face softens.

Jordanne chuckles, again...

... and I roll my eyes internally.

"Nice to meet you Lenard, I'm Jordanne," he hops off the island to walk towards us. "My mom, who's her mom's friend... sent me with her dinner," he explains while completely ignoring Lenard– his eyes locked with mine.

My breathing picks up.

"And you come ina her place just so?" Len's tone is skeptical.

"Well–" Jordanne starts but I butt in.

"Mommy probably gave him the key. Let me walk you back down to your van."

"Nah mi good," Len declines, raising his eyebrows while keeping his focus on Jordanne, who is now back at the island eating again.

I hiss at his actions, loudly this time.

"So the whole friend group like Tom Ford?" Len asks, and all of a sudden my brain picks up.

The apartment has the scent that was in question yesterday, courtesy of Jordanne being here right now.

"Coincidence," I mutter...

... And for the third time, Jordanne chuckles– a little bit too loud this time.

"Call me when you're boarding and when you land," I brush it off, tipping to kiss Len's lips.

He looks over at Jordanne again and back at me.

"Yuh sure yuh good?" he asks, louder this time.

"Yeah, I'm okay," I assure him before throwing myself into his arms.

We hug for maybe three seconds, before pulling away to allow him to leave. I step out the front door and watch him walk all the way to his car, for fear of Drip having somebody out there to kidnap him or supm.

Glad yuh know

He pulls out and beeps his horn as he leaves. I walk back into my apartment to find Jordanne now eating my fucking apple.

"J' weh di fuck duh you?" I ask, walking over to the kitchen area.

"Hear say you man a starve you, so me just farwud and save the day... You no like that?" he asks, sporting the dumbest smirk I've ever seen.

Mi nuh like man enuh!

"Jordanne, what do you want?" I ask nicer while opening my fridge– not looking for anything specific.

Just affi keep my eyes off him before the lady between my legs betray me. He stays silent for more than ten seconds and that's when I look to him. Staring at his arms, I wait for him to answer my question... 'cause me and him know anybody else coulda bring me dinner.

"You... I want you, but besides that, mi ago want you eat, shower and we ago link a therapist," his tone spewing seriousness.

My eyes have never rolled so far back in my head as they're doing in this very moment.

Mi eyiiiaaaaaatttte dah man yah!

Girl please

"My therapy is done. You want me to do it with you? Why? Mi nuh understand," I sneer.

He moves from the countertop to a stool, continuing the devour of my apple.

"I didn't go years ago, as you know. Nuh because mi never wah go, but because things weh bother me... I can't really say much about them. But now me just add a therapist to the payroll so we can go," his eyes have changed with this statement– from the spite that was in it earlier to genuine plea.

Two fucking years too late.

Aye! He gets me sooo angry... and them emotions yah only mek me think illogical and make bay careless decisions.

"J' I have reports to do that will take me into the morning. Plus, you have to complete individual therapy before you even think of doing anything with me there," I retort.

Rolling my eyes, I grab the apple from him. Me one green apple the boy wah done off. Biting into it, where he left off, I listen as he laughs.

"Okkkayy, take you apple, man deh nah feed you... and yesss, I know and I'll try to do both, so eat, shower and let's go. She'll be at our house at 8, and me can help yuh do yuh little report when that's done," he smiles, cocking his head to the side while focusing on how I'm digging into the apple.

I sigh.

Walking over to the food, I open the container, realizing it's Sue's curried goat and white rice. The excitement that moves through my body is evident and I hear when he chuckles.

Rolling my eyes at him, while tucking a fork full into my mouth, I say, "I'll be there if you need me to be but I'm pretty sure you have to do at least a few sessions alone before we can try to solve any issue between us… And mi wah yuh know this no mean nuttin, me nahgo stop link Len."

I watch as he smiles at me, bringing his hands up in surrender.

"Whatever yuh say Ry'. Deh wid who yuh want…" and just from his tone, I know he's making a mockery of my love life.

Hissing my teeth, I dig down into the plate of food while he moves through his phone.

Weh mi say me do? Eyyyiiiatttte him!

Bad, bad.

53 | A Start

RYLEIGH

Still no understand why she couldn't come to my apartment?" I hiss while packing all my work materials into my bag.

He takes a quick look at me, with the same stupid smirk from earlier.

"Maybe mah kidnap you neatly?" he gives me an answer, causing me to raise my brows in suspicion.

He laughs lightly.

Mi believe him

"Real medz, me just prefer she know one property and if we were to get back together, she would've already known our address," he makes a point.

"Your address," I scoff, "and you have high hopes eeh?"

He ignores my newfound attitude and takes my bag from me. My attitude has been on and off all night. I just can't seem to keep the needle steady when it comes to him. This minute I'm laughing at his snarky remarks or his smutty jokes, next minute I'm suppressing my sarcasm that's always marinated in mistakes he's made in the past.

Because I did a lot of dumb shit too

But anyways...

After a silent ride we finally pull in and I notice there's a new security guard standing post.

"Wah happen to Troopa?" I genuinely question.

"Ryleigh you wah Troopa guard Mum dem place and your place one time? A one man enuh," his tone housing a hint annoyance.

I laugh to myself, remembering how much he hates the type of relationship Troopa and I have created.

"Just a askkk," I mumble, all while still smiling.

"And a yesterday mah tell Skulli say you head screw on enuh. Like me did wrong," are the words that leave his lips.

I watch as his smile widens for the millionth time since I found him on my kitchen island earlier.

Wah really sweet him?

"Wah sweet you? You've been grinning since I saw you," I jeer, turning my torso towards him.

He ignores me, holding the grin on his face while exiting the car. Deciding to open the door myself to hop out, I turn to take my bag from the backseat. Holding the door handle, I watch as his eyes widen at my simple action.

The door opens and I step out.

"You start open doors now? Drop yuh standards?" he chuckles.

There hasn't been an hour where he hasn't said something jokingly rude about my love life.

Swear

"Actually, I still don't touch doors, but you're NOT my man... so you know mi affi do it myself," as the words fall, I watch as his eyes darken and the grin disappears from his face.

Instantly I regret my choice of words.

We're not even supposed to be petty

But anuh the truth? He isn't...

He turns to walk off when I try to say, "Me lie?" and before I get to continue my point, he turns around and walks back to me. Looking down at me, he lifts my chin, allowing my eyes to meet his.

"Ryleigh, wull medz... 'cause mi no have none ah dat right now," releasing my chin, he turns and walks to the front door.

Now why would you say that?

He's been low-key rude all night though.

Rubbing my arms from the night chill, I saunter to the front door behind him.

• • •

We've been at it for less than a minute and Jordanne is already arguing with the lady.

"Mr.Sheer, you paid me to do a job, allow me to," her tone crippled by displeasure.

He takes a seat to the opposite corner of the couch, staring at me.

"I already told him he would have to complete individual sessions before doing whatever it is he wants to do," I retort, focusing my attention away from them both.

Looking around, I kind of miss it here.

Kinda?

Not that I hate my apartment, I just love the feel of a home– always have.

"Just fix it," Jordanne snaps.

"It's recommended to go that route yes, at least a few... But persons have previously done both simultaneously," she explains while picking up her tablet.

I look over at him just in time to see him sport a gloating brow raise.

Mmmcht.

"Ms.Stevens you authorized transfer of your notes from your current therapist. I see that they just came in," she speaks despite browsing.

She continues her quick review of my files, occasionally glancing up at me and back at Jordanne. He's been quietly tapping away at his phone, waiting for her to get to the point.

I need her to start soon, I have a lot to do.

She clicks the iPad shut before saying, "I have an activity."

Jordanne's head snaps up from his phone in confusion, and I smile at his reaction. I know these, and mi sure he's not going to participate.

"Kinda activity?" he breathes.

Standing, she pulls two blank pages from her folder and hands them to each of us.

"I need you both to write down how the other has wronged you or hurt you in any-way. Don't hold back at all if you want this to work," and with that she steps back, retaking her seat.

I do not want to tap into those memories. Me just nuh wah dweet.

I look to my right and... Why J' a write already? Me do Mr.Man nuttin?

Rolling my eyes at how eager he is, I pick up a pen from the end table. My next instinct is to tap it against the paper that's now folded in two for support– since I'm too lazy to find something to press on.

Minutes pass and we're scribbling away. I come to the last point I can remember and write it down. As I'm about to lift my head to see if such man's list is complete, I see him lay his pen down.

"Since you both seem to be done, I need you guys to switch," she orders, with an unreadable expression plastered across her face.

"Switch?!" I shriek, my words play out shock riddled.

"Yeah, the switch part no sound effective. We a try avoid the arguments," Jordanne explains.

"You guys have to trust me," are the last words she says before taking our sheets, switching them for us and moving back to her chair.

Turning Jordanne's paper around, I realize he has quiiiiite a few points.

1. No medz me fi years while I made my intentions very clear.
2. Promised me a fair chance then went back to her ex.

3.Going back to the same ex that shot my friend, almost taking his life. (Same ex tried to abuse her)
4.Cutting me off after sex.
5.Being with my actual friend. (Same one that got shot)
6.Dating somebody who she know no like me just for spite and for the entire team to see.
7.Almost repeating that very same mistake with somebody even more dangerous, that I had to fix. (same situation almost cost my step dad his life)
8.Never apologizing until the moment I broke it off.
9.The miscarriage. (Hurt the most)
10.Overall just not listening or trusting my lead.

Why him ah act like me did know weh Folan do? He kept that from me.

I take my lips between my teeth, forcing my words to stay in.

His feelings are valid

His feelings are valid…

His feelings are valid…

I guess.

Releasing a deep sigh, I look at how he's reading mine. I only had 6 or 7 points, so mi know it can't a take him so long.

• • •

JORDANNE

This is my third time reading her points. My list ah state specific situations and her list is a mix of situations and my character traits.

Jah know?

-Only shares half of his life with me.
-Disregarded my feelings about what he did to my ex.
-Cheated!
-Lying by omission.
-Disrespectfully possessive.
-Uses violence as a way of intimidation.
-Too accessible to every bitch it seems.
-Acts as if my actions aren't triggered by HIS actions.

Girl say 'disrespectfully possessive.'

Haha!

"Really?" I ask, nearly inaudible, but she hears when the word leaves my lips.

"Yessss really. Why yah act like ano way down me know wah happen with the shooting?!" she snaps.

Either way, I hiss ... and just as I'm about to answer, Terry takes the sheets from both of us.

"No arguing. Now that you both have a clear idea of the hurt, you'll know how to work through it... By just browsing Ms.Stevens' files, I can see that you guys have been working around every issue, but all that does is fester."

Me coulda tell myself that. Mah pay so much money fi she say weh me sure we both know?

"Sometime a just the only choice, since three quarters of the time we no ina no relationship anyways," my tone now clipped.

From my peripheral I can see how tense Ry' is right now. Neva want the night play out like this.

"Yeah and the one time I gave you anything close to it, somebody breed and yuh have the nerve fi vex 'bout me keeping my miscarriage a secret?" she spits my fuck-up back in my face.

Her words are icy and I can feel them pulling me to anger.

"Ryleigh," Terry basically whispers, "you don't have to revert to anger. Just as you expressed your feelings, so has he."

Real...

"I fully understand that but–" Ry' tries but Terry shuts it down.

"We sometimes only turn to the most familiar emotion, which for most persons in our society is anger. You guys have to go through the hurt, work through the betrayal and maybe then, if done right, you might have a chance at a clean slate."

Mek sense

I look to Ry' and she looks at me– smiling, before she rolls her eyes.

"I guess," she shrugs.

"So I'm gonna leave if that's okay with you Mr.Sheer? I'll be back every other evening at 6," Terry reminds me whilst gathering her things.

"Appreciate it doc, dat good," I stand to shake her hand. "Not a bad start."

"You're very welcome. Now I have to be on my way since you pulled me from my late night client," she laughs, but her eyes display nothing but fear.

A little intimidation neva really kill nobody. She good.

Ryleigh walks her to the door and if I know her well enough, it's to ask questions she doesn't want me to hear.

Ignoring them, I take the opportunity to hit the shower.

• • •

RYLEIGH

"How a your job and me better at it than you Ry'?" Jordanne chuckles, turning his screen to me, showing his completed report.

It's now 2:33am and we've been at it for a while.

"Ensure when I go through, there are no mistakes," I hiss, feigning annoyance.

"Yuh ago waste you time a do that. We no make academic mistake," he smiles, the bright and warm smile that drew me to him in the first place.

This is how I like it to be... If we could keep it this way I might think about tryi–

Helloooo?

Lenard? I remember him.

As if reading my mind, Jordanne says, "If we get through the therapy then? 'Cause yuh say you nah leggo offa you T-square," his tone laced in jealousy.

Aye, the disrespect for Len is crazzzyyy.

And we nah defend him?

I mean me defending him nahgo mek J' stop, we know this.

"Nah make no promises. We see how that turns out each time we do. Maybe just focus on getting through this first?"

"So yahgo in therapy with one man and in a relationship with the next? Yah killa enuh," he laughs and I'm happy he's making light of the situation.

I think he underestimates Len. Sure, Jordanne has a hold on me because he's been in my life forever and knows my mind and body better than I do... but Lenard came to me at a time when I really was just starting to be at my best, and he was able to not shift that peace.

He added more peace to what I'd already created– and mi love dat.

Okay, but do we love him?

Be quiet.

So J' can take it lightly, but I just might not want this for real– it's just too much.

Always has been too much.

"So for the two years we've been apart you haven't been seriously looking for anyone? You had this plan of coming back, all this time?" the thought came out of nowhere and before I could suppress it, it was out my mouth.

His head snaps up from the laptop and to me. His face softens and I can see that he's thinking about what to say or how to answer.

"I mean, I've seen or heard of a few girls in rotation, the usual," I roll my eyes.

But he doesn't budge...

Because that's not it

"Ry'… " his soft whisper almost missing my ear.

I pause, knowing that tone and what it comes with. My fingers stop typing, but I keep my focus on the screen instead of turning to him.

"I'm actually with Lizzy," his words sting.

Que?!!

Cyaa be the Lizzy weh tag me?

At present I want to be angry, I want to fight, to scream…

Shit and vomit, everything

… but I remember how to find my calm in situations I might not like. And why would I be angry? If I'm literally with somebody else. I steady my breathing and try to work through my thoughts, but each time I try to justify him not telling me about her, I get angrier.

Disappointed.

A just the same fucking cycle wid him. It's been yeaaarrrrsssss… of the same thing.

"Ryleigh?" his voice brings me from my thoughts.

Closing the laptop, I turn to him with questions as my ammunition, instead of the anger boiling in the pit of my stomach.

"So what are we doing? That's the very same girl that tagged me… One can say causing me to get angry and go di beach party, only fi Skulli nearly dead, only fi yuh leff me? So correct me if I'm wrong but, the bloodclawt yah waste me time fah?" I sneer, clearly getting my thoughts across, with the least amount of anger I can.

"We just start deal like November, before I came home… Coming back to you was never the plan, it wasn't. Did really try stay away… Did wah see you move on and be, happy? I tried… and I could make it through when I would come home for five days max, but since January, mi realize that can't work… and seeing you out with Lenard? Cyaa mek it rest."

"And before you start, I actually am about to dead things wid Lizz before I ruin another woman."

Yeah suuuure. If lying by omission was a perssssonnn.

Nah give him an inch more of a reaction.

"At this point Jordanne, whatever you say. Just have it ina you head say we might not come out of this together, but at least we'll be healed from each other," I mutter with all seriousness.

'Cause if him keep on a do the same routine from high school and college and a expect different reactions from me, him affi mad.

Mad Bumbo-Ole

Getting up, I decide to walk to the kitchen. Fun and joke aside, me hungryyyyyyy yuh fuck! Mi no know wah happen to Sue dinner. I ate every grain of rice and every piece ah goat meat. This is about to be my fourth snack for the night.

This is ridiculous now.

As I remove a fruit plate that I know would be prepped and ready, I hear his footsteps behind me.

"Why yah eat like yah prepare fi go ina hibernation?" his tone is jovial but his eyes harbor seriousness.

I hiss... I already know what he's assuming. Him and Janette ah the very same.

"Must a eat fi two," I deliberately say, knowing I'd get on his nerves.

His body tenses and I watch his face change into something I don't like.

Take back the joke right nowww

"Jordanne, I've just been eating more since lifting heavy at the gym and mostly because I came off the pills," I explain.

He walks over to me... and I pull back...

"Why would you stop taking the pills if you ina relationship same way?" his question blunt, while he stares down at me.

His figure stands tall and I slowly slip a strawberry into my mouth, peering up at him through my lashes.

I–

"I wasn't with anybody so I decided to give it a rest. I'll be back on them starting next cycle," my tone is one of uncertainty and my words fall weak.

He looks me up and down before taking a slice of kiwi from my plate.

Biting it, he says, "Yeah... do dat."

I watch him walk out of the kitchen and up the stairs...

... and I know he's back in one of his moods. All 'cause the lady hungry? And stop take pills while she was single?

Cho

Making my way to the couch I pick up the remote. I roll my eyes and plop myself down, pulling my knees up for comfort. Deciding to toggle to Apple TV, I put on the first series I spot and get lost in it.

Work is at 8am tomorrow

The weekend was short but eventful... bad.

54 | Gradually

RYLEIGH

"**B**abe it's been two days, mi give yuh long enough killa," Jordanne's voice comes clear, echoing throughout the master bathroom.

Cyaa even answer him right now...

Another wave of weakness sweeps my system and I grip the rim of the bowl, throwing my head forward.

Pussyclawt me feel like we ago dead sista gyal

It's been a **week and a half** since we had that therapy session, and I don't know how or what got me sick, because we've been cooped up in this house ever since. I can't be pregnant, I know that. I had my period less than three weeks ago. There is no way I would be having morning sickness this early?

My thoughts are cut by my insides rising to the roof of my mouth and landing in the toilet before me.

"Ryleigh, mah call Surgeon or him nurse them if you no comfy with him... or you can just let me bring you to the doctor like I've been saying since Tuesday gone," his plea is wrapped in the softest tone.

I remember this tone from the night of Mariah's 18th birthday party.

When we did drunka than the man dem ina bar a fortnight

I try to stand, and I feel when he releases my hair from the pony he's been holding it in. Moving to the vanity, I stoop and start to rinse my mouth out.

It's been a bloodclawt week...

From having sex every day 'round the clock... and I do mean everyday 'round the clock, to falling ill like two days ago and throwing up my insides since then. Dem supm yah why you nuffi give bun enuh man. First time me see it fit fi partake ina the sin and seet deh, God a plan fi purge me!

Sigh...

Lenard doesn't get back until tomorrow.

Him and me period due same day eeh?

I plan on telling him I'm just not ready to take things serious and I need time for myself– let him down easy.

Jordanne and I have finally decided to commit to the relationship we can't seem to run from, no matter which end of the earth we are or how long we're apart. I haven't been back to his sessions but according to Terry, he's keeping an open mind. Stubborn still, but open to discussing his emotional trauma.

Love dat

"J," I mumble while ambling to the tub, "no wah waste di time go today. If I don't start my period tomorrow, then I'll take one of the four million tests you bought."

I watch him shake his head, watching me struggle because I refuse to have him help me 24/7. I lift my leg, trying to climb into the tub while he holds me steady.

Warm baths have made everything bearable. I push through the weakness and sit, the water swallowing my limbs. He slips in behind me and I lay my head on his chest before picking up my phone. Scrolling to my FLO app, I tap it open to stare at it again.

Three hearts recorded between the 11th and the 17th, all belonging to Len.

Seven hearts recorded from the 20th to the 26th, all belonging to Jordanne.

Ovulation took place on the 19th, that's the Monday after Portland… and my period is due tomorrow, the 30th.

I keep racking my mind with the details. I can't be pregnant… nahhh. I'm fine, my period is coming tomorrow bright and early.

Yeah, tomorrow for sure.

"And if you're pregnant?" Jordanne asks, in a tone I don't recognize, at all.

"I'm not pregnant… I'm certain I'm having some kinda withdrawal from cutting the pills cold turkey," I defend my theory, "fi real like I've felt like this before but it neva last this long."

He doesn't answer, so I scroll to my search window, pulling up the gazzilionth search I found that supports my theory.

"See!" I whimper, bringing the phone up to his face.

"Bredda dat deven say .org or .edu, nuttin valid… Google just a support your search. So as mi say, Surgeon ago farwud tomorrow evening…" his tone lets me know not to protest.

Sigh, fine. Might as well prove him wrong.

"Yah talk to your boy tomorrow? In this condition or?" he adds, now taking my phone from me to rest it on the board before us.

Know him no wah me go to him but I just think it's best I say it in person? I owe him at least that.

"I will, he deserves that. Not everybody can break things off with people over FaceTime," my comeback emitting pure sarcasm.

The boy really gave Lizz a simple FaceTime call. Ting lasted less than a minute.

The way we affi go pray we no get a daughter, or even a son at this rate

I giggle at my thoughts, thinking about how many persons have caught strays from just us trying to prove points to each other. Skulli literally caught a real bullet

"Lizz good, she probably always knew," he mutters, snaking his hands around to my boobs.

Comfort…

I slide down further into the water, allowing it to stop just below my lips. The illness that's been plaguing me for the past two and a half days has finally subsided, or at least for the moment.

•••

<u>**Following Afternoon**</u>

JORDANNE

"Yeah it a get worse still, so me ago need you now. No wah hear weh she have fi say," I explain to Surgeon who is somehow on Ryleigh's side.

"Me can check for other things but a fi her choice 'bout the test. Me can't force dat boss," he retorts… and for a second, I think about being violent.

Nah do dat still…

"Bredda just reach nuh man," is all I manage to say.

I hang up before he offers a reply and turn to look at Ry' who is rooted in bed, curled up in a ball. She couldn't even make it to the bathroom to throw up this time. I had to get her a bucket.

Standing at the foot of the bed I peer down at her. If stubborn was a person. Whether she pregnant or not she really need fi figure out what's wrong.

Deciding to call her mom, I pick up my phone to find her contact.

"Jordanne," Ryleigh's voice lands on my ear, tugging at my heart.

She sound weak bredda

"Babe?" I move closer to her out of concern.

"Don't call mommy, know a that yah do. I'll take whichever test you want but mommy ago blow things outa proportion."

I raise a brow at her request. She a read mind now?

A small smile tugs at my lips before I respond, "Dat good. Surgeon on the way… So all mi did affi do ah threaten yuh with Janette?" I scrunch my brows and a chuckle breaks through, causing her to smile as well.

"Shut up," she manages to say, and I can see that she's still weak.

Deciding to join her in bed, I pull the covers and slide right in front of her– pulling her head onto my chest.

"Mine me vomit pah you," her words are timid and barely audible.

"Ryleigh wull medz... and rest. Surgeon soon reach."

• • •

45 minutes later, Surgeon and one of his nurses are standing in the bedroom.

"So you willing fi take the pregnancy test too? Boy Drip bully yuh?" Surgeon laughs, looking at me.

I throw my hands up in mock surrender and Ryleigh nods.

"Him blackmail me yes, can call it that," her voice sounding less weak after the nap.

"Okay so the nurse ago draw blood. We ago do general blood work and a hormone test since you say you've been off the pills since January. How long were you on them?" Surgeon asks, signaling to the nurse to get what she needs to draw blood.

I avert my eyes to Ry' as she answers.

"Since I was 17, so four years plus? Almost five," she answers while Surgeon takes note.

"Was there a reason you went on them?" he asks, glimpsing at me.

Man yah?

"Yeah, I had bad cramps... but I–" she starts twiddling her fingers and I know she's uncomfortable, but David needs to know.

"I– umm. I had a miscarriage and when I went to my gyno at the time, she suggested a contraceptive method since it was an unplanned pregnancy... When I realized it made my cramps better I just stayed on them," she heaves a sigh before finding my eyes.

I offer her a comforting look.

She nahfi feel bad

The nurse comes back and orders her to sit up. She does, but refuses my help this time.

Stubborn

I watch as the nurse pierces her skin, and the blood slowly fills the tiny sample bottle. She pulls that away before attaching two more bottles– one after the other.

"Okay, 4.5 years is long for oral contraceptives. Anuh like is a IUD or so. The hormone shift normally causes withdrawal when you suddenly stop. In some people it's very bad and can look like this... To rule everything out though, do you want to take the pregnancy test?"

She looks at me and back to David.

Man ago feel we bully her fi real

"Yeah, might as well," she mumbles.

"Cool, we'll test your blood. It'll tell us if you're early-on, faster than the urine test... and fi ease dah one yah mind," he looks to me, "you can take one ah the hundred tests me just walk past. They're just as good as the strips we use," he explains to her.

The nurse is now adding a bandage to the spot on her forearm where the needle was. I watch her nod at David's instructions, while the nurse helps her back down.

"Get some rest and try eat and drink nuff fluids," Surgeon instructs before asking me outside.

"Mek we chat out yah so," he waves me out.

I don't offer a verbal reply, but follow him closely. We exit the room and get to the top of the stairs, away from the room door– while I watch as he scrolls through the iPad.

"Doubt she pregnant but it's not impossible. Ago try me best mek the lab know fi rush the results so you can have a clear answer by a morning."

I run my hands over my face.

'God me no link yuh as often as I should but please...'

"No like see her like this killa. Swear," I mumble, keeping my focus forward.

"Understood. It no seem chronic so you can take that outa your mind. Know yuh like do dah overthinking ting deh," he offers me words of comfort.

I don't respond, instead I turn and look to the room door.

"Man dem ah ask fi yuh still– Slyme and Ramone specifically. Say dem cyaa see Drip from last week. Bay one-one phone call dem a get," he laughs out, and manages to shift the mood.

I laugh genuinely before saying, "Mi no wah no man a look fimi enuh. Deh home with me woman fi a while."

"Man lock down like never before," he laughs out, too loud.

I hit his shoulders.

"Come outa me place and go find out wah gwaan with mi girl."

"Nuh say ah next word. Will send the results to her phone. If she wah share it with you she will."

"Mi yuh work fah or she?" I chuckle.

"She a di patient enuh boss," are the last words he says before descending the steps.

I watch him get to the end of the stairs and hear when the nurse exits the room. Watching her as she makes it to where David is before they both leave, I turn to go back to the room. Walking back to the room, I prepare myself to hear what Ry' has to say about taking the home tests.

Mi just need fi know

... Or else, mi can't sleep tonight and me need fi sleep. Nuh sleep from she sick Tuesday gone– nothing more than an hour at a time at least.

55 | Gradually Part TWO

RYLEIGH

It's been three minutes... and I'm scared to look. Me say if it positive me roll down the stairs. Straight down the stairs too– take myself out this wild equation.

Cayliss

Sigh...

Taking another minute to look at myself in the mirror, I observe how pale I am.

"God, is this punishment for sleeping with Jordanne the minute Lenard left? You know my heart. You know I just want to wait for him to get back before nuttin... and you know more than anybody say Drip tie me. Please nuh mek me breed. Please, please, please."

Who tie we?

"Ryleigh stop talk to yourself and come outa the bathroom," Jordanne's tone startles me. It's clear, deep and fucking intimidating for no reason.

I breathe and turn the first test over... only to see...

||

Weh dat mean???!!!

Jesus!

Jesus, Jesus, Jesaaass.

I move to the second test and turn it over...

||

I immediately start to laugh. Then nuh must joke this? Deciding to ignore those two, I turn over the ClearBlue, 'cause me need fi see it in writing.

"Ry'?" I hear his voice as I look at the ClearBlue test.

NOT PREGNANT.

But the other two a show clear lines? Dem fully positive.

"Stevens!" Jordanne shouts, and I decide to answer this time.

"Mi almost done Jordanne!" I shout back, grabbing another one from the bag– one similar to the two that are positive.

I duh have no more urine leff ina me enuh

Opening the box anyway, I take the test and muster up as much pee as I can. A good flow streams out, and I hold the stick steady, while hovering over the toilet.

Minutes pass and I can hear Jordanne at the door tapping away at his phone. Deciding to look at the stick, I move to the vanity… slowly turning it over.

||

You know mi cyaa badda? Now one look slightly thinner than the other.

Watch confusion. Him ago kill we, show him the negatives first

My breathing picks up and I pull the cupboard and quickly take my anxiety pills.

Breathe, I tell myself.

No but you no know if that pill can take during pregnancy

Well…

Opening the door, I find Jordanne looking at me, specifically at me holding all four tests in my hands.

"So?" he asks raising a brow, seeking confirmation.

I don't know.

"Nuh know," I mumble, handing him all four.

"Yuh cyaa just dash yuh piss stick dem pah me enuh Ryleigh," he laughs.

I don't… Glad him find things funny.

Give him a second

So said, so done. Less than a millisecond later, his laughing comes to a halt.

"Which one you take first?" he asks, and I point at the ClearBlue.

"ClearBlue first, then the others weh a show positive… and the last one that's showing only one thick line I took after you call mi out," I explain.

He doesn't answer but I watch his eyes grow narrow, staring into my soul.

God, me prayer nuh reach?

"Hear wah… mek we wait pah David," his tone now low, while handing me the tests.

"David?" I ask as I take them.

"Surgeon Ryleigh, who else we woulda get the results from?" he hisses, and I know from his newfound body language and tone, he's upset.

I decide not to press and just let him be.

Walking to the room, I pick up my blanket, deciding to move my post to the couch where it's nearer to this food and fluids thing weh Surgeon say mi fi deh pon. As I slowly descend the stairs, carefully holding onto the rail, I hear the front door slam shut.

Continuing my down climb, I decide to ignore that too and walk to the kitchen to grab a banana. While peeling it back, I move to the couch, listening as the sound of his car's engine roars to life.

Him a gwaan the most

I hiss and plop myself down on the couch. With the banana in my left hand and my phone in the right.

Sliding to contacts, I decide to call Lorelle. She answers on the third ring.

Mi gyal

"All hail the First Lady," she says and my mood immediately lifts.

"Yuh wouldn't believe how me salt!" I start off.

• • •

JORDANNE

Speeding through the streets, only stopping for red lights, I grab at my phone to call Slyme. The phone rings to the fourth, before he picks up.

Cyaa tek how the man dem fall in love and stop answer pon the first ring enuh.

Yuh any different?

"Law… You come up fi air?" he laughs… and my mood calms a little. A chuckle slips from my lips and I grip the steering while tapping my index finger.

"Need yuh fi send your woman go stay with mine fi couple hours, four max."

I hear him shuffle and the line goes silent for a while. When it re-opens, Michelle's voice comes across the speakers.

Yuh woulda dead before you call her Muuch?

Mi hate the name yuh fuck.

"Wah yuh do me friend now Drip?" she asks and I must say, of all her friends, Michelle a the only one weh drive some sort ah fear ina me. She serious yuh fuck.

"Easy nuh genna, she sick and me did affi leave fi go meet somebody so me need you fi run over. Yuh deh the closest," I explain, and I can almost hear her smile.

"How yuh know me deh yah with such man," she giggles.

"You can go?" I reiterate the initial topic.

"Already a drag on me clothes Mr.Impatient. I'll be with her in five minutes," and I just now realize the extra shuffling and how muffled her voice sounds.

She's getting ready, no hesitation… Me baby have good friends.

"Ah cool, me ago drop back in, 'bout 6, 6:30 the latest that good?"

"Coulda 6 a morning, that good," she laughs and before she's done, I hang up.

Dutty style

Cyaa fix it.

I release a deep sigh before picking up my spliff from the cup holder.

Need it…

Truly

Moments later I'm with Surgeon pulling into the lab near Crossroads. Looking at the wave of people walking around, I remember how much I hate public spaces. The parking lot and the premises of the lab are empty but the streets are full.

People fi stay home enuh. Jah Jah.

"Yuh know yuh serious though Drip. Me tell you wait and a that you couldn't do? Yahfi remember say I work outside of you and me no wah burn no bridges within my industry."

I chuckle, genuinely… 'cause the man funny fi real.

"Surgeon, is just a test result me need enuh. Yah behave like mah go in deh go spray," I laugh even heavier.

He pushes the door to enter, and I follow.

"I've seen what you can do, especially when it comes to Janette daughta. If them say we can't get the results right away then what?" he asks, his eyes portraying real concern.

The man cannot really think mahgo do supm psycho fi some test results. A 'cause me just basically grab him and throw him ina the car fi come down here?

I rub my chin, pretending to think up a storm, "Then we convince them," I wink.

He hisses his teeth.

Haha! Man miserable so?

"Take a seat mek me deal with it," he points me to a set of chairs before walking to the back.

The lab is quiet, apart from shuffling in the back. The lights are very bright– ting a give horror movie… and the smell in the air is of medicine and disinfectant.

Deciding to focus on the second task I want done no later than today, I give Ramone a call.

He answers on the first ring.

Dat mi a talk 'bout

"Laww," he goes first.

"Law… Him land?" I jump right to the point.

"Yeah boss, tracking him to the house right now," he shares.

"Ah, just make Skulli know say man fi deh a him foot fi pick him up before him can exit the vehicle good… out of camera sight."

Ramone laughs.

"Know that already boss, on it," he assures me, just before hanging up.

Ending the call before me? Man dem a learn.

Minutes pass before Surgeon is back with a blank look on his face.

"I sent the results to her," he mumbles, walking right past me while swinging the door open to leave.

I jump up and follow.

"David, duh mek me slip into darkness. Wah di results?" I mutter in question, and I can already feel myself slipping.

He takes one look at me and hands me the hardcopy.

Good.

I grab it and my eyes start swinging across the paper. Blah blah blah... Blah blah blah... Ryleigh Stevens, blah blah... specimen, blah...

NEGATIVE

Bumboclawt

God me owe you some time big boss... 'cause if she did ever breed fi dah square deh, I don't know who woulda have more sins... me or Lucifer himself.

"Boss?" Surgeon calls to me, breaking me away from my thoughts.

I drop my smile, just now realizing how wide it is. I enter the car just as he does, keeping the results firm in my hands.

"She has higher than usual levels of hCG so you might wah look into what medications she's taking. She never mention nothing earlier today," his tone concerned.

I wonder for a second if I should share that information with him or not. Since him love say a 'her' decision.

"She a take some Valium for her anxiety, every now and again. That's the only thing I know about," I explain.

"Bingo, unuh coulda just say that to me from earlier," he hisses.

I laugh out loud.

"Bredda mek me drop yuh off a yuh car. Me have supm else fi deal wid," I suggest, glimpsing back and forth between him and the road.

"Nahh, mek me car stay ah the office. Yah pussyole! Yuh pick me up and no wah carry me back a me yard. After work hours now, mi nah sit down through this traffic."

Watch how the big man a complain? I slip into a frenzy of laughter.

"Ah fish, mah drop yuh a yuh yard," I chuckle, stepping on the gas.

• • •

RYLEIGH

"Girl anything coulda possible but a just to how mi neva ready," I smile, looking at my results for the trillionth time since getting them earlier.

Prayer deh reach enuh girl

Reachhh! God never did a sleep.

"Yuh never ready or you never ready if a did fi Lenard?" Muuch asks, staring at me with a stupid grin on her face.

Murdaaa

When mi say my mind easy fi read it easy fi read.

"None ah them. Mi never ready fi no baby overall," I lie.

She rolls her eyes and says, "Eeehh, yuh nah convince a soul."

What a way as me see the results me feel better? No sah, your brain is a hell of a thing enuh. I hope I've been through the worst of the birth control withdrawal because me tired fi vomit. Tired, tired bad.

I'm about to get up to grab a bottle of water when I hear multiple different engines. I move to the window immediately knowing it's Jordanne.

"Noooo man! Yah pikny? Weh yah run go like a patty them carry come from market fi yuh," Muuch laughs and I basically scream with giggles.

Why dah girl yah no lowe me man? Mi frighten fi my man, especially like how he's myyyy man now. Like mine-mine, fully.

I watch as Slyme and Paw exit a car. Jordanne exits his, and Skulli exits his Jeep with...

LENARD???!!!

MI PUSSYCLAWT

I move back from the window but not soon enough for Jordanne not to see me. He sees when I pull back and smirks.

"Michelle!!!" I whisper-shout, "why dem out deh with Lenard?" I grab my blanket and bolt up the stairs as fast as my weak limbs allow.

I don't make it halfway before I hear J's voice.

"Ryleigh, bring yourself back down yah so. Yuh owe this man a conversation," his words drip in humour and venom simultaneously. I've never understood how he's able to do that.

Devil

Fuckkkkkk!!!

Squinting my eyes shut, I stay in place. Maybe if I stay here, they'll go away.

I hear when Slyme starts laughing at the top of his fucking voice. Cho, I can't help but smile, while opening my eyes. When I turn around, they're all staring at me.

Sigh, I guess I gotta go...

Slyme takes Muuch and they move to the back porch with Skulli and Paw.

Jordanne takes a seat on the couch and says, "Unuh can use my office... Ten minutes tops... and Ry', don't test it."

I swallow and bring my blanket over my head, only leaving space for my eyes and nose. When I get to Lenard, is the only time he speaks.

"What's going on Ryleigh? Man dem refuse fi say nothing to me 'bout why mi deh yah. I was gonna go to your apartment after settling in. If it's because I wasn't answering yesterday I–" he tries to explain but I start to feel bad.

Ughh!

"Jesus Len–" I cut him off, "follow me to the office. I'll tell you everything."

I point to the office for him to go before me. When he moves off, I turn to Jordanne and shoot him a deadly glare. He removes his gun from his waist, cocks it and places it on the end table. Looking directly at me, he mouths, '10 MINUTES'.

I don't know why I smile but I do.

Turning around to walk to the office, I start wondering how the fuck mi fi explain all of this to Lenard... in ten minutes.

Sigh.

God if me pray again, me a ova dweet?

Girl, just hurry up

Be quiet!

56 | Gradually Part THREE

RYLEIGH

It's been exactly eight minutes and I'm not even halfway through explaining myself. Len is seated, while I pace back and forth trying to align my words as best as possible. Mi no wah tell him no lie...

... But I also don't want to give the idea that what we had was a joke, because it wasn't.

Sigh...

"So yuh feel mi fraida him? Yah mek the man manipulate you into supm weh nahgo work?" his words spew hate and jealousy, as he watches me go back and forth.

Slowing my pace, I decide to address his response.

"Manipulate? Lenard, mi no think yah understand mi fully... I've loved him for most of my life. Why would you want to be with me if mi wah somebody else?" I ask, coming to a pause to stare at him.

He stands to face me.

"Because... I– love you... and if he's the ex you told me about that just couldn't get it right, me disappointed. The man look like him a born criminal. How do you plan on doing life with somebody like that?" his face plastered in confusion.

Be for real. How long him know me? Less than a year, love who?

I watch his eyes dance left to right, searching, pleading even... for an answer satisfying to him...

... but mi no have it.

I really don't, because what do I really know about Jordanne's day to day? I vaguely know he's into shit but what kinda shit exactly?

"See," his voice drags me from deep thought, "Yuh don't know. Him have supm ova yuh? Is he blackmailing you? What is it?... Yuh no affi stay here, we can live in London like we always talked about. Travel Europe and Africa together," he whispers softly– holding my chin up.

I look at the genuine love in his eyes.

For a moment I think about it… A moment too long, because the door slowly creaks open and I know it's J… well, Drip by the aura I can feel oozing from the doorway. I pull back and Lenard looks up.

Jordanne doesn't utter a sound, but leans against the door frame while watching us.

"I promise you I'm okay. I've known him forever. This is my decision," I whisper.

He tries to pull me into a hug but, mi know better.

"Yah push it," J's lethal words part us even more.

Turning away from Len, I decide to walk to Jordanne. Before I can throw myself onto J, Paw and Slyme walk in. The feeling I get in my stomach tells me to warn Jordanne.

"No bother with the fuckry, him nah do nothing," I look up and over at him.

He smirks…

"Wah kinda person you and Surgeon think mi be? I have control… most times."

Like when?

I hiss and he laughs out this time. We move off and I look back, taking a quick glance at Len. Paw and Slyme a explain supm to him that I can't hear.

I want to hear

Jordanne notices and softly pulls me away, placing me in front of him.

"Mi feel bad, guilty," I groan as we walk to get to the foot of the stairs.

"Nuh guilt no ina it killa. You know this did ago happen fi days now."

"Not like this," I retort.

He doesn't respond, instead he lifts me and I find myself giggling.

Look how unuh ruin everybody life and just a ready up fi live happy?

My eyes roll internally at how my mind only refers to my actions in third person when it's time to blame.

• • •

"Weh yuh wah know?" he asks, as if him no know weh mi no know.

"Everything," I mutter, watching him as he chops the onion. "Nuh know how yuh say we a friend how long and me just a know you can cook."

He keeps his eyes on his task, but I can see his smile.

"My mother is a chef. Me head couldn't so tuff genna," and with that he starts throwing all the chopped herbs into the skillet.

My man

My body tingles and I have to quickly remind myself that I'm too weak fi nuttin gwaan right now.

I watch him stir the green herbs for a bit before he gently scrapes the veggies into the pot. He then moves to the carousel organizer that houses the frequently used powdered seasonings and starts picking what he wants.

Grabbing what I think is garlic powder, he sprinkles it in and stirs. Seconds later I watch him bring a piece of carrot to his mouth for tasting, causing my body to fill with heat.

How me one horny so?

You woulda think mi celibate fi years, when we really only haven't had sex in three days...

He grabs a fork and stabs at the pan, picking up a piece of broccoli this time. I watch as he slides it from the fork before moving towards me. As if on cue, I open my mouth and take the tiny piece of vegetable onto my tongue, not forgetting to lick the sauce from his fingers.

He pulls back and raises a single brow at me, causing me to snort.

"Mah try feed yuh and yah try fuck me, Jah know, young girls these days," he quirks his brows even more with faux concern.

His little dramatic response causes me to move from snort-laughing to straight on choking. Grabbing my water bottle, I try to sip some to move whatever went down the wrong section of my throat, but he adds to my misery almost immediately.

"Think you neva have no gag reflex enuh," he continues and before you know it, di wata a come back up with the laugh.

I raise my hand, signaling for him to stop, but he continues.

While grabbing a napkin to hand to me he says, "Sloppy" and winks.

Unuh cringe

We deserve to be.

Cleaning my mouth and the area on the counter I spat on, I start to think about what I want to know for real. As he removes the steamed fish from the oven and start pulling them from the foil, I decide to voice my thoughts.

"I want to know the day to day, the books, the legal, the illegal, all the safe houses etcetera," realizing he paused to look at me I continue. "Important people I should know and people I should stay away from."

"Woulda want you stay away from everybody," he mumbles, and for a moment he seems serious.

I narrow my eyes at him.

"Jordanne," I scold, 'cause me and him nahgo play the overly possessive dolly house.

I've been working from home this entire week because apparently my job is not in an ideal location?

"Joke, but the things you're asking for comes with being my wife... " he trails off, cocking his head to the side.

Helloooo?

I'm literally just about to become 22, then me coulda mad? Move this nuhhh.

"Cyaa talk?" he asks, now placing my plate in front of me.

"You asked me what I wanted to know, I stated such, now you a say that comes with another status," I shake my head.

The food smells so good! Bredda if there is anything else in this world I love more than my mother and the man in front me? A food.

... And food that he cooked? Tie up!

"It easy enuh, just take my name. Access granted after that," he declares before bringing a bottle of Tropical Rhythms to his mouth.

"Yuh cyaa serious? We're 21," I laugh while shoving another piece of fish into my mouth, followed by a group of veggies jammed on my fork.

He doesn't laugh... but I can feel his stare.

Di man serious!

"You're serious???!" I shriek, and he nods, offering me no amount of access to his emotions.

"Jordanne–"

"Yah plan fi leff?" he asks, and by the tone of his voice, I know to search for my response properly before voicing it.

Sigh...

My eyes find the food before me and I start poking at it for way of a distraction.

"Talk nuh mon," are the words that leave his mouth next.

"I'm just saying, wi young. You young especially... Yuh wah get married at 21? That's a lifetime commitment, so young..."

"If you say the word young again... Ry' I'm not saying you have to get married to me right now. I'm saying if you want access to information like that, then being my wife would be best, because me granting you that access gives you no room to leave in the future... My mother asked for the same thing when she got tired of being left out and ended up regretting it when she wanted to leave and couldn't. Mi no wah that fi our thing, no forcing you to stay just because you hold too much information. Yuh get mi?"

His words put everything into perspective.

Cyaa testify against your spouse either

Makes all the sense, but him couldn't possibly believe me woulda give up information if we were to ever break up?

"So in essence, you don't trust me enough to make me privy to certain information because of the fear that I would what? Use it against you if we were to ever break up?" I ask, just to clarify.

To manipulate

"Precisely… nuttin no hidden ina weh me say, so stop try spin it," he holds the stare I initiated just now.

I release an animated chuckle, knowing we're on the verge of an argument.

"Okay Drip," I mutter bitterly.

He stands, bringing his plate to hover over the bin, only to dispose of what remains of his meal. I raise my head and watch as he moves to the sink. A thought comes to my mind and I decide to voice it because why not?

"So what would I be able to know now? Being your untrustworthy girlfriend," I press my lips in a straight line, forming a sarcastic smile.

"Ryleigh, rest it," he mutters.

Well…

Me must live with man and watch them live a double life, that I know nothing about? Cool.

Just marry him

Mi nah married a soul fi get likkle information outa them, mmcht. I find my eyes rolling as I stand to follow the routine he did earlier.

Garbage bin…

Sink…

Wash…

Rinse…

Set to dry…

By now he has left the kitchen and gone to the couch, since we planned on watching a movie before bed. I waltz to the office to find my blanket exactly where I left it earlier. Memories of the look on Len's face earlier floods my mind. He would never hold anything from me, he taught me so much more than Jordanne has and somehow, I didn't choose him.

My phone vibrates and I suddenly remember I have friends and a life outside this house.

'Cause we lock down fi real

I don't even know when Muuch left but me know she did affi leave with Slyme.

BUBBAS

Dutty Foot: Hello? Group supermarket
tmmro as usual?

Sexy Bitch: Unuh know me no serve no purpose
there but yes.

Mariah Boo: Count me in. Me need some things fi

Ruse fridge, that boy only stock him Mobay fridge.

Muuch Boo: Ago ask Liam.

Keif Boo: Askkkk??? Fi go right up a Megamart deh so?

Muuch Boo: Yuh know how Slyme dem stay.

> Tell mi about it ugh.

Sexy Bitch: Oh yuh living Ms.Ryleigh??

> Did sick, think Muuch or
> Lorelle tell you.

Sexy Bitch: Yahv me number just like dem.

> Okay?

Muuch Boo: Dolly did sick weh fr. A her
man call mi mek me know.

Keif Boo: Wah time tmmro? Same 5?

> Works for me.

Dutty Foot: Me too.

Mariah Boo: Me 3

Muuch Boo: If the man say yes that good.

> T'???

Sexy Bitch: However it come dung, free wul day.

Reading her response, I click out of the group chat and decide to call her. After 15 minutes she's all caught up on what's been happening and we're back to normal again.

Me? love di gyal... but the lady miserable bad.

Deciding I've spent enough time in here, I saunter to the couch where Jordanne is now sprawled out, going through his phone with the movie on pause just five seconds in.

We him a wait pon enuh

Me realize.

When I get to the couch, I drop myself between his legs, slowly snuggling up against his chest whilst bringing my blanket to cover us.

"Yuh good?" he asks.

I nod.

"You good?" I return the question.

"Mmhm," is all he manages to say before resuming the movie.

I love it here

We're now halfway through the movie and I'm screaming at the actors and actresses to do what I want.

"Babe a just me and yuh enuh, dem cyaa hear yuh," he laughs.

I hiss, "Me just cyaa bare fi watch fuckry," I complain, picking up my phone.

Jordanne's hands move up and around my chest, from under my boobs. Ignoring his touch, I click my notifications, which takes me to my direct messages on Instagram.

Stevens.
You just ago leave me pon seen?
Me know you know a who.
Know you never have much choice in what
happened, much like myself, but mi know
our ting did real and me want it back. Ring me byrd
when u can. 773-850-8229.

Woahhhh

I almost throw my phone but instead, I click it shut and slap it back beside me. My breathing picks up and I just know J' ago notice.

A few seconds pass and he says nothing.

If him no say nuttin, we nahgo say nuttin?

Why, me mad? When I get up from here, I'll just block Jacen, simple.

Jordanne's hand moves again, this time to bring a gummy bear to my mouth from the pack we've been sharing.

Relief washes my skin.

He didn't see... Phewww!

Thank God.

57 | Clean Slate

JORDANNE

"**M**um nuh argument no ina it, send back the man nuh man," I hiss. Why Sue wah gimme a fight ova Troopa?

Man deh must have the greatest personality on the island. Ry' only likes him and to be honest, I only trust his judgement when it comes to securing my space. Him and him little team good.

"Is you want him back or Ryleigh?" she questions.

"Ry," my answer blunt.

The line falls silent for a second.

"Fine, wouldn't get him back if a did just you."

Jah Jah… Two of the most important women to me a give me the biggest headache ina the **Saturday morning** yah.

"Ah Mum, if that make yuh feel better. Just make him know fi drop a foot a morning and thereafter," I hang up, knowing my point is clear.

Spinning the office chair to face my desk, I see when the door slightly pushes open. Her head peeks around and she immediately starts batting her lashes.

Supm she want now enuh

Mhmhm…

"What is it Ry?" I raise a single brow while bringing my attention back to the monitor.

She steps in and walks to my desk.

"Soooo, we have this thing where, every Saturday we all go to the supermarket together, and if we don't need anything we go get our nails done or something just to catch up–"

She's babbling…

Somewhere in there, must be a question.

"Who is we? and what are you trying to get across?" my eyes find her, looking up from where I'm rooted. I still have like a million contracts to sign before 6pm today and she a tell me 'bout nails and supermarket.

The house is stocked.

Her nails coulda do fi real though

I zone back into her babbling just in time to hear her say, "–ask permission to go 'cause me know how unuh stay."

I pause to peer up at her again, "Fi go where?"

Cyaa supermarket she a ask permission fi go.

"The supermarket. Are you listening?" she rolls her eyes.

I smile… Her rolling her eyes reminds me of one thing and one thing only.

Yeah, that.

"Calm down big farrid. Why you need my permission fi go supermarket? Just go. The shadow guards know their job. Two years has changed nothing in that regard… Two to three will be with you at all times unless you're with me," I explain, all while continuing to browse the contracts– zoning her out again.

She says something else but mi no hear…

E-signature…

… First sketch.

… Another E-signature.

When mi ago done this Fada?

"Jordanne!" she shouts, pulling me from focus, "me only in here fi less than five minutes enuh. Mi a talk to you," she whines.

Sigh.

I lock the screen and swing my chair to the side of the desk before pulling her into my lap.

"Yuh want baby?" I lend her an ear, not forgetting to grope her breasts.

"I want to drive the Porsche," she whispers shyly, smiling up at me for added convincing.

"Sure," I respond, and my lips find her forehead.

Her nose…

Her lips…

Her neck…

"The Taycan," are the words that leave her mouth and… mi cyaa believe.

Siiiclawttt

"Ffffuckkk noo. Yah mad?" my head shoots up to look at her.

She jumps out of my arms and lands on her feet.

"But–" she tries to protest.

"But nothing. Yuh wah drive me baby go supermarket?!" I glare at her and I mean really glare at her, to see if I can find any trace of coke lingering around her nostrils.

'Cause a must coke she deh pon fi real.

Affi be dat killa

"Megamart, where else do I go? You no trust me fi drive it go nowhere far... and I don't go out in Kingston, so," she mutters, pouting excessively.

Mad woman this

I take a moment to think about her reasoning...

Jah, me weak to her. Fact say me even a think it through.

"Yuh can drive it tonight, I'm taking you somewhere," and before my sentence is complete, she grabs my hand into a handshake.

"Deal!" she squeals, now grinning like a happy child.

I shake my head.

Women...

"Yuh no easy enuh Ry," is all I say before sliding my chair back behind the desk and unlocking the monitor.

She bends and kisses my cheek.

"Thanks. I'm taking the Macan to the supermarket," her giggles like music while she looks back at me.

I shake my head again.

Ginnal dat enuh

My ginnal though.

"Do yuh nails too," I suggest under my breath... but she catches it.

"Excuse???" she laughs out loudly. "Gimi your card and yuh can run them orders deh."

Without hesitation, I take my wallet from my pocket and remove both my licenses before throwing it at her. She catches it while sporting a genuine look of surprise on her face.

"Yuh no serious?" her eyes widen– all 32 teeth showing.

I am. Why would she think I'm jo–

"Ryleigh gwaan no man, me have things fi sign," I smile, knowing I just made her the happiest she's been all day.

"Alright big bossss. Them have pin?"

"Most nuh use pin and those that do, ah the first four of the kaba code for whichever quarter we're in, backwards," I inform her– not looking up from the contracts.

She doesn't respond, and I must say that's the fastest I've seen her exit a room that I was in.

Like we affi give her the wallet more often

I chuckle at my own thought.

● ● ●

RYLEIGH

"Mi bredda get saaaawwffff," T' mocks, now watching me exit the Porsche.

I laugh, carefully closing the door. It might be the lesser of the two, but he still loves it.

"Yuh bredda been saaawff, just not to anybody but me," I proudly smile before hugging her.

We pull away and I turn to look where Lorelle is busy parking.

"Batty big so!" Toni picks up on her mockery– holding her palms apart to show how thick I am.

"Gwaan nuh! I haven't eaten properly in like three days but before that? Mi did a nyam like a chichi," I laugh out, practically screaming.

A group of girls walk by and one in particular gives me the dirtiest look. Me nahgo act stush and quiet fi please dem enuh, so better she walk gwaan.

"Dolly demmm," I hear Keif's voice and turn to hug her.

Lorelle makes it to where we're standing and I hug her too.

"Muuch no reach all now?" she asks.

We shake our heads no. She never did confirm if Slyme would let her or not. It's giving prison...

Yuh did affi ask too though?

Let me have it, jeez.

"Mariah a come from Ruse new apartment so she–" before T' gets to finish her statement, Mariah honks at us pulling our attention.

Big fat AMG

Love it!

It takes me a moment to realize who is in the front seat next to her– Ms.Cherry, Jacen's aunt... Yup, from the Christmas dinner.

Guilt roots me in spot as I watch her park, and they exit the car. Nuh even know why me feel so. Jacen was the one dating me for the sole purpose of getting to J', but still, I can't shake the feeling.

They walk over and of course Mariah starts making her rounds.

"Tight ooooolezzz!" she hugs us one by one. "Sorry Ms.Cherry," she turns to apologize when she realizes her words.

"That alright pretty mama."

"Pretty girl!" her eyes find me, but before I can respond she pulls me into a hug.

So she no have me up? Thank God.

Moments later we're all at the food court area waiting on Muuch, who called to let us know she was coming.

Probably barely a survive the evening traffic

Pulling Mariah to the side, I decide to ask her what's been on my mind since she pulled into the parking lot.

"Why she come?" I whisper.

"She know wah Ruse like fi eat. Memba me come fi stock the man fridge. Me text you but you no read phone and dem thing deh. And no, the lady couldn't make no list," she rolls her eyes.

Oh… Me really need fi read messages fi real now man.

"Yuh stepbrother nahgo like it," I mutter.

"Yuh and Michelle sick stomach eeh? Everything unuh man nahgo like," she giggles lowly.

I let out a hearty laugh while turning to see Muuch, who's finally walking towards us. She gets to us and we all swarm her, showering her with hugs, kisses and compliments.

A few people look at us but none for too long.

When we've sobered up, we each grab trolleys and baskets to go off into the world of processed foods.

• • •

It's now 7:15pm and we're just exiting the people dem place. Wah chat we chat and gwaan the most, only for most of us to only exit with six to seven items. Mariah is the only one with boxes full of grocery. I told everybody to rack up the bill since I have such man's cards, but nobody was in need of much.

Paid for everything regardless.

Before moving to our respective vehicles, we partake in our usual group hug. Another minute or two post, we start pulling out, one after the other.

Deciding to call my nail tech to begggggg for a last session squeeze in, I connect my phone to the car. Dialing her number, I drop the phone in the cup holder section, 'cause dem police yah nahgo ticket me.

Crazzzzyyy.

Tashawn's voice blares through the car's speakers, causing me to jump.

"Tash, is a spot me a beg enuh," I speak, pausing to await her response.

"Girl like you me love hear call enuh! Me just did ago lock up but come. Me know my tip ago well nice when we done," she laughs and I can't help but laugh too.

I do tip heavy, because me just love a hustling woman, nuh know what it is.

• • •

The traffic wasn't bad, so I was able to get to Tash's by 7:45pm and the fill was finished by 8:35pm. The traffic to my house however is devil sent.

I think about taking the Constant Spring route but bwoyyy. Nowhere will be better, me might as well be patient. I hiss, tapping my fingers against the steering.

Minutes go by before I'm on the road to my house and it's exactly 9:10pm when I pull in… exhausted. Duh know where Jordanne was planning to go but he's going to be angry.

Parking perfectly, I grab my grocery bag and walk inside.

"J'!?" I shout, seeking an answer.

Nothing comes.

"Jordanne! Are we still going somewhere?" I shout for him to hear.

Still nothing.

Deciding to go to the kitchen, I kick my slides off and walk over. The grocery bag is rested on the island and I move to get a bottle of water.

"Ry…" his voice comes soft but scary.

I jump, spilling water down my cleavage.

What a man like this.

"Yuh cyaa this jumpy," he laughs, pulling me into him while taking my water.

"You were in the gym?" I ask, just now noticing his clothes and how sweaty he is.

"Correct," is all he offers before pulling away.

"We still ago somewhere?" I throw another question at him.

He starts ascending the stairs, "Yup, be ready by 10:30. Our reservation is at 11, when the restaurant section is closed to the general public."

10:30???

"Ten thirtyyyyy!???" I shriek to myself, while looking at the time on my phone.

It shows 9:16pm.

I dash up the stairs, passing him at high speed. He laughs of course, but I ignore it.

Affi get my hair together

Thirty minutes in and I start to regret having cut my hair. Mi spray it down and gel it down so tillll– to get it into a high pony.

Jeeshhh!

Looking at how it still is in the mirror, I give up.

"This affi do enuh," I mutter to myself.

Can't fight it no more.

Another hour and a half goes by, and by now we're about to be seated in the restaurant off to a section far away from the bar– that's still going by the way.

I like it here

Didn't notice how nice this place was. The girls and I have been to the bar section before but never the actual restaurant. A sharp pain around my ankle drags me from my memory. I've only been in this shoe for 20 minutes and already my feet hurt.

God if me a get old just say that.

The host comes back to say that the table J' wanted is being cleaned and set. I look up at him and I can tell he's not pleased. Before he can say anything, I butt in...

"That's fine. We'll wait a bit more... Can we have drinks while we do?" I lighten tension.

"Sure Mrs.Sheer. The entire section is open to you guys. We're just setting the table that has the view and it's taking longer than anticipated," he explains further.

I'm taken aback by the name he used to address me but decide not to correct him.

"What would you like?" he asks, his eyes glued to us.

"Midori sour," I respond.

"Balvenie, neat," Jordanne adds.

"No problem. Your waitress will bring those over in a minute," he scurries off.

Jordanne quirks his brow at me when he walks off.

"What?" I decide to take the oblivious route.

He says nothing, only offering me a smirk.

Moments pass and the waitress is here with our drinks. I take mine before it hits the table, just to taste test, all while swinging my legs at the instant sourness.

J' and I go into a minute or five of chatter– catching up on our day and the past two weeks overall.

"Your table is ready," the host's voice pulls me away from the conversation.

Well that was a short wait.

Jordanne holds my free hand to help me up, and we walk over to our table.

• • •

It's been a great dinner, we've talked about all that we've been up to for the two years we've been apart. We've talked about what we both want to do with our future, we've even talked about kids... and the concept of family overall.

Currently though, we're exiting the restaurant, and as we do, I start to feel how much my liquor intake has settled in my system.

Wheew...

I really have to commit to giving up liquor.

"Yuh good?" J's tone now holding concern as he opens the car door.

That he didn't allow me to drive like he promised

Ughhh, when?

"Good enough," I whisper, plopping myself down in the passenger's seat.

Woahhh... The lady nice yuh fuck. I giggle, and search for my phone to play music before he gets inside. Mi cyaa listen not another badmind and wicked friend song. I toggle to Bayka's - 'She Like It' and start bobbing my head.

He pulls out of the parking lot and speeds off.

We've been off for less than two minutes and I can already feel him taking quick glances at me while I sing the lyrics.

When mi say me nice? Mi niiiiiccce!

Yuh drunk

Maybe enuh.

We come to a stoplight, and you know what my mind tells me to do? To reach over and release his belt. So a dat me deh pon right now.

"Ryleigh," he groans and I feel when the car moves off.

The man nah stop a the stoplight fi nothing more than a second ah night time

Ignoring him, I pluck the button open and pull his zipper down.

"Ry, if we crash weh yahgo tell mi say killa?" his hot breath hits my ear and the side of my neck.

His voice...

My nipples are the second to acknowledge my feelings, since my panty has been a pool way before we left the restaurant.

I put my hands inside his pants and feel... His dick is rock hard... and di boy a play like him no wah me bring the hood tuh my tonsils.

Liquor a walk ina we

Be quiet.

"Mi no say nothing Ry," he chuckles, and I realize I might've said that out loud.

Deciding to pretend that never happened, I pull his length free– watching as it springs forward. Without a second thought, I clasp my lips around it and begin to move down... all the way downwwn.

"Bloodclawt yo," he hisses, but instead of his words deterring me, they give me motivation.

I pull up to the tip of his shaft and circle my tongue around the smooth pink head, before jamming it to the back of my throat again.

"Fuckkkk," he moans, and I feel the car jolt forward.

With that, I hold onto the edge of his seat and start bobbing my head up and down at a steady pace.

"Ssssssssss," he lets out. That's the sound I know he makes when his toes curl.

Lovely.

Let's see if he can get us home safely with his dick lodged in my mouth.

58|Clean Slate Part TWO

RYLEIGH

Let's see if he can get us home safely with his dick lodged in my mouth. The thought pulls a smile to my face.

We might crash

Doubt that, he won't put a scratch on his precious 'baby'.

He pulls his gun from his waist and places it on my seat? Or somewhere to that side— me cyaa see. Deciding to make things even harder for him… and on him, I move my lips to the base of his manhood before gargling.

"Bloodclawt gyal yah," he moans, releasing a full breath of air.

This sends me into overdrive, causing me to pull my mouth back to his tip while gripping his length with one hand. I use this hand to create pleasurable friction while making slow oral love to the tip. This continues for another minute before I feel the car swing, signaling a sharp turn.

Ouuuu! Okay this is exciting now

His moans are nothing but music to my ears, I can feel his body fighting to multitask. His foot keeps switching from the gas to the brake pedal at timed intervals. His breathing is ragged… if me never know better mi woulda stop and think asthma a kill him.

Liquor courage really gets me goooing, because the next thing I do is grab the hem of my skirt and pull it to my chest.

Might as well mi neva badda.

The car swerves for a few seconds, sending his dick to rest at the roof of my mouth. I feel when we come to a sharp and sudden stop, and I decide to peek up.

Di man park enuh.

He looks down at me and before I can continue my tease, he pulls me up, forcing me to straddle him. The car is small and there isn't much room for what I think he wants to do.

"Jor–" I try but he silences me by popping my already provocative top open.

My breasts spring free and he immediately pulls me down, popping one into his mouth all while sliding his seat back. The feeling of his large hands take residence on my ass cheeks, sending me into a reel.

"Jordanne, somebody ago see," I snap my head around.

"And wah else?" he comes up to say, finding my eyes.

He doesn't give a fuck, does he?

The look in his eyes is one of pure lust and me??? Mi love dat. I giggle and find his neck, to start eating at it. His dick brushes against my inner thighs and the feeling sends a shock wave throughout my body... Before that feeling comes to an end, Jordanne's hand has already moved from cupping my ass cheek to massaging my insides.

Mighty Gahhddd...

The hold I have on his neck is interrupted by an involuntary moan. Taking a deep breath, I close my eyes and try to calm down, focusing on the pleasure his finger brings.

Good with him finga, sharp shooter

"Pussy so wet Ry?" he groans the question, but before I can offer a response or mere movement, he rips the panty open.

If dah boy yah mash up a next piece a me things–

He slips his finger out, silencing me. He then uses it to rub my clit, coating it with all the juices dripping around freely.

"Mhhmmm," is all I manage to breathe.

This cyaa realllll... Mi feel like me wah enter the boy skinnnn.

"Ahhh!" I scream, snapping my head up from nuzzling his neck.

His dick is now lodged deep inside me.

No warning...

No soft entrance...

Just forced inside.

Without giving me time to adjust to the feeling, he grabs my neck softly before taking a nipple into his mouth.

"Dripppppppppppuhhh," my moan is sultry, muffled and laced with eagerness all the same.

Noooo... A dem supm yah why me cyaa leff di bwoyyy. The feeling is, UNREAL!

I– I coulda cry real tears.

"iiiccce," he responds, releasing my nipple from his mouth to stare into my soul.

For a second, I think of what he's referring to but decide to ignore my thoughts.

When mi say I don't know if a me, or the endless number of cocktails I had earlier... but I don't break our stare, instead I take the opportunity to hold onto the grab-handle with my right hand and the rear view mirror with my left.

Up and Down...

Allll the way up to his tip... and downnnn to the base of his dick.

I continue this movement until he's too weak to keep his hand at my throat. He drops it to my waist and I drop mine to his shoulders– closing the space between us. He starts to buck his hips, thrusting all the way inside me, creating sounds of soft claps and wet taps.

I–

"I–" trying to get my words out, I try to steady myself, but he won't stop pounding... and pounding.

"I–I'm–gon-gonna–"

"Words babe, use your words," he coaches me, in a smug tone.

I just–

Deciding to give up, I lull my head back and let my orgasm fill my mind and soul. My walls clamp tighter than I think they have ever before, sending him into what looks like shock.

"Pussy yah must mad mi," I hear him mutter, while I'm on another planet, dancing with the God's of pleasure.

While climbing down from my high, I feel his thrusts start to become uneven and I know that's his body's way of reaching its peak. I look down at him, deciding to move to his ear to talk him through it.

"Yessss... don't stop," I whisper, watching as my words take control of his soul.

"I love you... Now cum for me," I continue, "fuckkkk mi like you dessssserve ittt..."

His breaths are now heavy as fuck.

I move from the nook of his neck to face him, moving my hands to his throat– something I haven't done to him since high school maybe? When I grip it, his eyes fly open... filled with a sinful glare and raw pleasure.

I smirk and hold our stare.

"BREED MI," are the last words I get to whisper before he shoots, filling me up with his cream.

Yessss

His face falls between my breasts, and I rub his head– a giggle escaping my lips.

"Yah Satan first daughter," he mutters, releasing heavy breaths.

And him a Satan first son, me nah ask

Dat mi know.

We stay like this for a moment before I try to get to the glove compartment for wipes. He realizes what I'm trying to do and takes over. Pulling it out, he hands it to me.

I immediately feel a tinge of jealousy.

"Why yahv wipes in here? Feminine at that?" my tone now sharp, my brows raised by skepticism.

"Ryleigh nuh start. Me and you know nobody can't enter this car. Me ask T' fi wipes Taboo night and a this she give me," he defends.

Mhmmhm, me affi go confirm dat.

Hoisting myself up, we do the routine we used to do when we were younger. He places the sheet of wipe in his palm and cups it where he thinks the excess semen will fall. When I dismount his dick, the juices fall on target and we get to cleaning up.

Halfway through getting ourselves together, I notice a blue light flashing.

Wah dis now?

Before I can say anything, he lifts me to my seat, closes his zipper and drops his spliff under the car mat in one swift set of movements. His gun is on my seat and without him telling me what to do, I force the things I have in my purse into the armrest console before forcing his Glock inside my bag.

He looks at me and back at his side mirror.

I avert my eyes to the mirror on my side and watch as the officer walks over to us.

Dat man know exactly wah did a gwaan

He gets to the window and my heart is now almost out my chestttt.

• • •

JORDANNE

I glance at her, and I can see that she's nervous. Mi no bother tell her the gun licensed… Baby gone ina protection mode. Maybe I really should tell her how things work.

Yah think with yuh dick now?

I find myself smiling internally.

Affi tell the man dem dis. The girl real yuh fuck.

The offisah boy gets to my window, and I wind it down.

"Goodnight Offisah," I offer him, holding a cynical expression.

"Goodnight. License and registration please," di man gone right to the point.

I chuckle.

Man no address mi woman or tell me why him flash me. Mi fi step outa the car and gun butt him few times well.

Mi support dat

I look to the glove compartment and Ry' is already deep inside it, searching for my papers.

Another chuckle leaves my lips.

She finds them and hands them to me, with nothing in her eyes, other than fear.

My face softens and I try to offer her the comfort I can't verbally. She receives it and I watch her relax.

Good…

Handing the officer my papers, I decide to ask him, "Why the check?"

"Well I see a suspicious car, on an empty property, after midnight, movement clearly taking place inside… ago take a look," he explains in a very demanding tone.

Fair enough.

He moves through the papers before he says, "Step outside the vehicle for me please, Mr.Sheer."

Turning to Ry' I mouth, 'SOON COME' before flying the door open and stepping out as per the officer's request. We walk to the back of the car, where he begins his routine speech.

"You know this is private property right? And I'm sure the owner wouldn't want a random vehicle parked here after hours," he starts but before he can continue I decide to dead the conversation.

Nuh too have the patience fi this.

"I'm the owner of the property, so dat good," I satisfy his concerns– now watching the shock settle on his face. "If you need proof I can pull up–"

"No need fi dat," his words fumble out while he clamps his pen back onto his uniform.

"My ting is, yuh never ask that, you just assume–"

"Somebody radio it in mi boss, so me just assume say–" he cuts me off, againnn.

Man yah ago mek me lose it

"Yuh assume wrong enuh. As a police officer, yuh need fi ask the proper questions. Anything coulda happen to you tonight," I retort, taking blatant note of his badge number.

"A threat that mi boss?" he asks… and I find it funny how him tone move from authoritative to 'mi boss'.

Dem police yah.

Shaking my head, I ask, "Is there anything else?"

"Who is the young lady to you?" his head snaps back to the car.

"My wife…" my voice clear, "we were heading in from a dinner date and got… carried away."

He smirks.

I offer him a chuckle.

"If she can confirm that then we good. Any heavy drinking from the driver?" his eyes are now scanning everything but me.

"None at all," I lie.

"Okay," he points me back to the car.

I hop in and buckle up. Ry' has her seat belt on already.

The officer walks to her window… knocks and of course she brings it down…

"Good night," she says offering him a smile.

Nobody should see that smile, but mah mek it rest.

Really yute?

Really.

"Can you tell me where you guys were coming from?" he asks her, seeking confirmation.

"We had a late dinner," she confirms, all bubbly and sweet.

Di girl this weh just a whisper all kinda things ina me ears? Jah know.

"Well okay Mr and Mrs.Sheer. Have ah safe drive home," he knocks the roof of my car.

Bet me shoot him fi dat. Pose the man scratch me things yo?

Jordanne buil

He walks back to the police vehicle and I pull off the property.

Ryleigh falls silent for a while but I decide to break it.

"Mi gun nuh illegal enuh Wonder Woman," I laugh, offering her short glances.

She turns to me and slaps my shoulder.

"Jordanne yuh couldn't say supm!" she shrieks, "mi nearly piss up. Wicked drankro."

I let out a hearty laugh.

"You all sober up," I point out, still laughing at her.

She hisses before saying, "People like you send up blood pressure!"

"Humph," I scoff, still holding onto my smile– this time stepping on the gas pedal to get us home quickly.

Need fi know who call that in just now

"Tomorrow me show yuh two pre… but only on the legal side a things, dat good?" I ask, keeping my eyes on the road.

"That's perfect," she giggles, reaching over to plant a kiss on my cheek.

Love her fi real…

No joke

59 | Clean Slate Part THREE

RYLEIGH

The roasting feel of the sun against my skin forces me to finally open my eyes. Looking across the room, I notice that Jordanne is the one opening the black-out curtains.

"Yuh torment?" I groan, voice a little more than groggy.

My eyes drop from his busy hands to his built... Shirt off, joggers hanging from just below his V-Line.

No enuh, resttttttt yuh front

I went to bed with cramps and I can't figure out if it's from all the sexual drilling or from my period finally being ready to make an appearance.

Could be both.

"Wah happen? Yuh tired?" he looks over at me, smiling knowingly.

I giggle and he sits on the bed, his hand finding my thighs.

"It's only around 7:20, but yuh say you wah know things? So mah grant you that wish."

The way me tyad, me really a think 'bout skipping out. But I can't do that. It ago look like me no serious don't?

Sigh...

Pulling the sheets from my body, I sluggishly slide from the bed before heading to the bathroom– leaving him seated in spot, staring at my departure. I smile, looking at how mesmerized he is in the mirror.

"You eye full?" I ask, pushing the bathroom door open.

His head snaps up and he realizes my focus is on his reflection. Smirking, he gets up from the bed.

"Yuh womb full?" he narrows his eyes at me.

"Shame fiiiii killlll mi," I shriek, feigning shock and embarrassment.

A throaty laugh exits his mouth just before he moves at me.

Nope! Not today devil. I swiftly move into the bathroom and close the door, turning the lock immediately. I hear him try to spin it before laughing out even louder.

"Get weh," he says between chuckles before the sound of his footsteps leave the room.

You know me a start fi understand say me one cyaa manage dah man yah. Nooooo, I can't be going at it every day. Nahgo have no belly bottom by the end of the year.

By the end of next week mlovve

My thoughts put a tiny smile on my face, just before I step inside the shower.

The time winds down to 8:30am when I finally get downstairs. J's waiting at the island, consumed in a phone call.

"Nah… tell them everything for today get push, mahv supm fi deal with, and tell Ramone mah try link him from before day and all now the man no link me back… Joke ting di skull deh pon…"

That tone…

See this is why I need to know his influence through and through. Still no understand how him can talk to the big man dem so. There is no wayyy.

'READY?' he mouths to me, holding the phone away from his ear. I nod while moving to the fridge to get bottles of cool water.

Yuh eat?

I stand rooted at the refrigerator door, now looking for something to eat as well. I browse for a second before his voice consumes my attention.

"Ms.Pat made breakfast," he informs me, pointing to the microwave.

All Ms.Pat him thief from Sue yard? Good 'cause I'm not one to cook every day.

I move to the microwave and notice the food is in tupperware. Looking back at him, I realize he's staring at me, as if waiting for me to notice that I have to eat in the car.

He signals me over all while still deep in conversation. I move to the drawer to get a fork and before you know it, we're out the door. Noticing that he doesn't walk to the garage, I start to wonder what the motives are, but before I can ask any questions, he offers me an answer.

"Slyme outside the gate," he assures me, and with that we walk to the side gate to leave.

He opens the back door to Slyme's Jeep and we hop in.

"Kinda emergency tour ting a keep boss? Who a di new employee?" Slyme turns around to ask.

Jordanne releases a low laugh, while using his chin to point at me.

"Nothing special, just a carry Ry' go show her two things ina the day yah."

Slyme looks at me quizzically and then back to J', before he chuckles. He does a double take when he sees me opening the dish.

"So Ms.Pat no send breakfast fimi?!"

A laugh escapes both my and J's lips at his shock.

One thing with Slyme, him ago eat.

"Yuh can have mine," I offer.

"Eat yuh food Ryleigh," Jordanne shuts it down.

"Yeah... eat you food. We wouldn't want you fall in love with me 'cause we shared breakfast," Slyme laughs contagiously.

Mocking Jordanne is crazy

I practically start choking at his statement because of the look on J's face. When jealous did a gi weh, dah man yah definitely push weh everybody and grab the full supply.

Jordanne shakes his head and goes back to his phone– making another phone call.

"Law... Yeah Skulli... 'bout 15 to 20 minutes...... No know weh Ramone deh... Hmmm send a man go check fimmi... This is unlike him," his conversation is clear and I watch Slyme's facial expression change from the rearview mirror.

His eyes move from light and welcoming, to dark and cold.

"Ting good?" he asks, referring to Jordanne.

Jordanne doesn't answer verbally but they speak through their eyes. Whatever was said, Slyme is in full agreement because he nods.

Minutes go by and we pull up at the exact building we were at just hours ago– getting lost in each other. The memories bring heavy butterflies flapping around in the pit of my stomach.

Jordanne notices and smirks.

Us having a fresh shared memory is a feeling I can't explain right now, it's just... ughh. I love him.

"Farwud," he takes my hand as we both hop out of the Jeep.

I look over to the back section of the lot, that looks like it's still under development to see Skulli standing to the side of one of his many vans.

"Boss say a yah so the tour start," he smiles at me as we walk closer to him.

I take notice of how he has his locs down today. He usually has it in a top knot.

It really is a day off for them, for the most part at least

The next thing I notice is his crossbody bag. Mi just know him have him piece ina dah bag deh.

"Mek me talk to yuh," Jordanne speaks, pulling him to the side.

Seconds later they start going back and forth over something that seems serious. While I'm busy trying to pry, Slyme comes into view and hands me a helmet.

I look at him confused...

"Boss say yuh fi wear it, 'cause the building no done, and yuh head bald," he laughs, forcing the helmet over my treacherous hair.

I washed it while showering earlier and was able to slick it down with some mousse before leaving– but the way it dry and look bad same way... It's growing back and now at the awkward stage, and to be very honest... mi tired ah it.

"Farwud," Jordanne or should I say Drip shouts, because he doesn't sound like the man I know in this moment.

Something is off but mi nahgo badger him with questions. The building is empty today, but I can see that construction takes place every day. The floors are covered in dirt, random broken pieces of tile, tools, ply, pipes and wires.

"Watch you step," and I look up to see J' holding his hand out to me.

Grabbing it, I step over the tiles. Slyme and Skulli are way ahead of us, chit chatting about what they think the place will look like when it's complete.

"So why yuh never say a your place last night?" my mouth starts with the questions.

"I did, just not to you," he retorts.

I scoff.

"What's it gonna be?" I pose a second question.

"Business center," he mutters.

What is wrong with him? He's normally overly chatty when it comes to new business adventures or anything regarding his degree.

"What's wrong?" I decide to just ask. I've been wanting to since the exchange between him and Slyme in the Jeep.

"Why you ask?" he stops to pull me closer.

I peer up at him to say, "Really? I've known you forever, just tell me."

His lips curl up into a smile that doesn't reach his eyes.

"Ramone missing…"

I pull back in shock… Weh him mean missing? Like missing-missing? or nah answer him phone missing?

"Like missing-missing???" I voice my thoughts.

"Send some man go check him house and he's not there, with signs of forced entry," he expounds, now rubbing his temple.

"And yuh deh yah a show me empty building?"

"Neva wah cancel yuh thing. Done wake you up and everything, nuh certain nothing bad happen so me a give it more time," he explains.

Just as I'm about to tell him that decision is stupid, I spot Slyme and Skulli moving quickly towards us.

"Drip!" Slyme shouts, while Paul looks like he's ready to go to war.

"Mariah," Slyme continues.

Mariah wah?!

"Mariah wah?!!" I go into instant panic.

I notice that Paul doesn't stop when Slyme stops to explain to J' what's happening.

"Sue can't get to her and yuh know she no miss Sunday breakfast no day. Paw go check Ruse apartment and none a dem nuh dideh. Ruse nah answer him ph–"

Before Slyme's statement is complete, Jordanne grabs me and we're moving to the door.

The panic has now consumed me completely, and I try to remind myself that nothing has been confirmed. Maybe everybody phone just nah work and them gone a country or something.

Ryleigh please. We can be anything, but yuh see right now? Be fucking for REAL

We get inside the car and this time Jordanne is in the passenger's seat, instead of in the back with me. None of them have said a word since leaving the building.

I pick up my phone and dial her number.

Straight to voicemail.

This cyaa real

That girl does not miss a call. A coulda after three ah morning, she's picking up.

Moments later we all pull into the family home and Sue runs to Paul.

"She just nah answer! She always answers. Paw say the apartment empty and some things turn ova!" her words send my blood running cold.

Everything is happening so fast.

God plea–

Jordanne's phone goes off and everybody goes silent. The few people that know his personal number are all here standing, and the only other people that have it are... missing.

He looks at it before his eyes find Paul. Before Paul can say anything, J' holds his hand up to silence him, putting the phone on speaker.

"Mariah?"

The person on the other line laughs...

I know that laugh...

"A Rome man, she good."

Instantly me limbs go numb...

60 | Clean Slate Part FOUR

RYLEIGH

"A Rome man... she good."

Instantly my limbs go numb.

"Sometime yuh nuffi make certain people live," Jordanne breathes, and I watch his demeanor change from slight concern to sinful...

Vile...

Vicious?

Just a wave of darkness.

Snapping his fingers to Skulli to get his attention, he mouths something to him, prompting Skulli to enter the house.

"Mi not even come pah dat. That was warranted but yuh mek mi bredda switch camp. The one family me have? Cyaa live with dat," Rome's tone is lethal.

Jordanne's eyes become venomous and I know now that if I tell him about the direct message it won't end well. I swallow and start to move towards the side of the house to try and find my mother. I know she's always here on Sundays, but how is it she's not at the front with everybody else?

'STAY' Lorelle mouths to me from beside the gazebo and for some reason I listen, planting myself just before the pathway to the courts. From where I stand, I can see everybody clearly, and they I.

I look to Jordanne who has now fully transformed into Drip.

He smiles genuinely when he says, "Rome, listen me good, just drop off Mariah. Her father anuh somebody fi joke wid... but you know that already."

The smirk that creeps across his lips tells me all I need to know.

Toni shifts her weight and holds onto Joshua, while he holds on to Kelly.

Mi just cyaa understand the dynamic

Now anuh the time, me a try figure out what the fuck fi say 'bout the DM.

"Me either," Rome chuckles, "tell we woman me say 'hi'... and that I saw that she read the messages before she run the block."

Jordanne's eyes shoot to me, and whatever amount of control or calm he had just went out the window. All other eyes shoot to me and when I say all, I mean everybody, every person from our circle, even Ryan.

I become cripple... Cripple right on spot, watching him move to me.

Everybody is trying to say something, but I know he can't hear it, because I can't either. The emotions have made us both deaf in this moment. The difference is my emotions are, fear, anxiety, panic...

... and his seem to be anger, anger and more anger.

The fact say me not even deny it right away already lets him know that Rome isn't just lying fi throw him off him game.

"Drip!!!" I finally hear Slyme's voice from... behind me?

When him reach so close?

Jordanne doesn't stop and my legs want to move but my brain has disconnected.

"Jordanne fucking Sheer!" Sue screams and that's the first mi actually hear the lady cuss badword.

Jordanne still doesn't stop; he's walking slowly but directly to me. Seeing as my limbs have given up, it makes no sense to protest right? Just as he's about to grab me, I hear Skulli's voice coming from the balcony.

"Jordanne... the violence," he speaks, with not much power or volume. Surprisingly J' stops, less than a foot away from me.

"Exactly!" T' hisses loudly, "You know if the man a tell lie? Him know your weakness."

See how the lady a put out her head pon di block fi we?

Swallowing, I look up at Jordanne's cynical expression.

I can hear Rome's breathing on the line...

I look to the phone and back to J'. Mi no need fi explain nuttin, me so sure him ina me thoughts a dig it up as we stand here.

"Man a talk say Ryleigh?" he questions, through gritted teeth.

My eyes shoot to my mom, who's just now coming from either the backyard or the side lawns.

Jesus.

"I– uhmm. He–" I start.

"Quickly!" Jordanne says clearly, his words stinging at my skin.

"Jordanne–" I look away from him and to my fingers, "him just DM me on Instagram that's all. Mi no reply and I blo–" before my statement is done, the air that's supposed to be freely flowing to my lungs has been cut.

My eyes find his and mi no know wah really a gwaan. Everybody is shouting and mi just a try find mi foot dem.

"Jordanne! Leggo mi pikny!" my mom screams, running to us with Sue on her heels.

He ignores them and hands the phone to Slyme, "Yo mek sure unuh get back Paul daughter, use the east team, mah go with the north team fi Ramone."

I can't see what Slyme is doing but I know he accepted the order. What I can see is when Sue grabs my mother, trying to calm her down.

I– I cannot breathe...

Mi cyaa fucking breathe!!! No mi never know the day woulda come weh him a try choke mi outside of sex. My eyes start fluttering and something clicks within, triggering the memory of Folan trying to force himself onto me.

His grip tightens as I try to free myself by pulling at his hand.

One fucking DM!

One fucking DM and him ready fi turn pah me!

Maybe we shoulda block him and tell him?

"Yahgo bring me to the point of no return," his words drag me from my thoughts. He pulls me closer and moves to my ear, "Stop bloodclawt play 'round wid me yerr? Mi watch yuh read the fucking messages and no say nuttin... Say me nah look into it because mah try fall back from the possessive thing like weh Terry suggest... Say mah trust yuh fi come to me if a nuttin or nobody serious and a this gwaan? A Rome contact yuh and you no feel fi say nuttin?"

Tears start to roll down my cheeks as I look over his shoulders to see my mom crying in Slyme's arms, while Sue is being calmed by Skulli. He notices where my attention is and drops his hand from my neck before turning to see what's taking place.

"Yo unuh liff up! Me gi di man dem ah order! Like unuh wah mi kill Rome myself and come back come kill unuh!"

I'm busy coughing and gasping for air.

Somehow T' is now at my side with water, forcing me to drink it. Nah drink a ting, nuttin me body nah allow me fi do more than bawl.

Sighhhhh

"Ryleigh drink di supm, Mariah ago alright, Paul have the location."

I–

Forgetting everything he just did, I hold onto T' and use my eyes to find him.

Girl?

"JOR-danne," I try to shout but it fades before making its exit.

"Jordanne," I try again, this time Toni beckons Lorelle over.

I see when my call reaches his ear and he hesitantly stops to turn and look at me. I find my feet and decide to walk to him.

"Ry," Toni calls, trying to stop me, but I ignore it.

She hisses her teeth, pure frustration beaming from the sound... and mi cyaa wrong her.

He stands still, watching me until I get to him.

"I'm sorry, just never think mi fi bother you with anything me coulda just block out. I love you. Affi tell you that before you go do weh yah do."

We stand there for a moment trying to read each other. Well him, trying to read me because I can't find a trace of emotion in his face.

No love...

No hate...

No anger...

Just cold empty eyes... on a cold empty face.

Instead of replying, he looks me up and down... twice, before handing me his personal phone.

"That's why me no jump ina people business enuh mlovve," Kelly laughs out and I'm assuming she's shading T'.

Jordanne hops into his Range and starts to pull out of the yard. Troopa flies the gate just quick enough for him not to slam into it.

His face wasn't showing the anger but his actions certainly are.

• • •

JORDANNE

If a did anybody else mi bruck dem neck, believe.

Cyaa understand weh this girl have over me. The love? Yeah sure, but what the fuck else? I sink the gas pedal, trying to close the gap between me and the team. We're all going to the safe house to equip ourselves. Bwoy Rome think him smart by allowing the call to go over a minute. Any sensible criminal know that open doors to your location.

And any experienced criminal know say once them no end the call quick, it's a set up. Luckily me experienced enough. Done tell the man dem fi send some decoy bodies go draw him out and deplete him likkle thing before them go in.

My main focus is on Ramone. Mi cyaa lose him... We a come from too far. Mariah ago good, Skulli no play 'bout her, so mi affi have Ramone back to di fullest.

Dat is it

I finally see Skulli's van and decide to slow down.

• • •

"So that's the plan. Still no know which leg Ruse a stick to, so careful," I say to Slyme as he slides his vest on.

"Mek sure you can pull yourself from the darkness when mi no dedeh enuh. Know you and Ramone a come from prep days but just leff some a the emotions and come outa it clean enough."

Him right. Me and Ramone go prep together yes, then split up fi go high school but never drop the link. Neva ever affi question him loyalty either, not once.

Leff me fi wonder how Rome know fi hit all the key points. Is a mystery how him no get to Sue or Toni although Dadz train dem up almost as much as he did me.

Maybe Ry' need that. Sometimes I forget she kinda new to this…

… certian things mah expect her fi just use her common sense still.

Jah Jah.

Why she woulda hide the fact say somebody like that a bother her? Whole time mah say is a random nigga. Fight myself fi no look into the phone number or username, day in, day out.

She did want the bothering?

She did a plan fi reply at a later date? Cyaa wrap my head 'round it.

Probably just trying to keep the peace

Jah Jah God.

"Boss?" Slyme calls and I realize I've been having my internal conversation a little too long.

I look over at him and he hands me my vest.

I smirk.

Well, well, well… Last time me affi join a mission myself was two years ago. Everything in between me go fi dem myself, get them fi drop a foot before the torture or simply send Slyme go end it.

Today, I get to play.

"Drip," Slyme calls again.

Man annoying so today?

"Yuh look likkle bit toooo evil right now bro. Mek mi come pah your mission," he suggests and I chuckle.

Man no believe me can pull out myself.

Haha! Can you?

"Easy no killa, me good man. Skulli yuh fi mek sure you can pull out today," we both laugh.

Turning, I look down at all the men preparing for the assignment. Surgeon is sliding vests onto his nurses and explaining the usual to them. Buckle and Snoop are loading ammunition into duffel bags for men who are lined up. Paw is standing by the exit puffing his spliff.

A just fi him way of preparation dat.

Truly

Another set of minutes pass before we start to pour out of the house and into the vehicles.

"See you on the other side a di rainbow," Slyme bids his farewell before driving off with his team.

I turn to find Paw who's putting out what is his second spliff.

"Farwud," is all I say before hopping into the van. Seconds later he's inside and around the steering.

"Ready fi take boy points enuh," he laughs, pulling a small smirk from me.

"Castleton way," I instruct and without hesitation he brings the van to life, spins it into the direction of the gate and speeds out.

The men on our team will meet us along the way.

Less than an hour later we pull up to an empty building off the side of a river, according to the cardinals given to us by Ryan. Hopefully him correct. Ramone has been training him for the past six months and him swear up and down say the man skills no bad. Dat will be proven today, 'cause a straight bush this yah so.

"A wah kinda riva party the man send we boss?" Paw chuckles.

I chuckle, taking note of the surrounding area. He goes on to say something else, but I raise my index finger to quiet him.

Just hear a sound come from the abandoned house. Stepping slowly, I signal to the men to surround the building.

"Nobody should leave it," I whisper-shout.

They gather and move in synchronization, jogging to different posts around the house. Paw and I walk over to the entrance and surprisingly, the door is open. I use my boot to shove it further open, revealing what lies inside. The outskirts of the building woulda fool anybody, but the inside clearly shows somebody has been living here.

I slowly step in, followed by Paw and six other guys from the north team. They know how to clear a house, so I don't have to give further instructions. Looking around, I notice female clothing and products laying around what seems to be the living room– that seems to be in use as a bedroom currently.

Ignoring that, I move to the kitchen, using my gun to open the cupboards– one by one.

"Boss the stove still hot," Paw points at the grill above the burners.

Before I can walk over to see for myself, I pick up shuffling coming from a tiny room off the kitchen.

Washroom, or what used to be

The muffles grow louder as we move closer. We get to the door, and I signal the count of three on my fingers to Paw.

"… 2… 1," and on that, we kick the door open.

"MMMMhh!! Mmhm!" Ramone mutters, his mouth gagged with some form ah cloth.

I grab a knife from my boot and cut it loose.

"Ghale!!!" he shouts and before he can continue, I cut his hands loose before handing him the knife to do the rest.

Without instructing Paw, I move to the exit. Upon leaving the house, I catch a female silhouette on the ground, hands behind her head.

But it's not Ghale...

It's–

"Em?" I whisper more to myself than out loud.

For some reason mi wah laugh and cyaa laugh. Weh di fuck a gwaan? Kinda dolly house Rome have the girl dem a play? I turn to look if Paw followed me, only to see him holding Ghale by her arm, yanking her to where Emily is kneeling.

Pussyclawt Killa. Joke this

This time I can't control the laughter. Cyaa this me bring out the north team fah.

"Let mi guh!" Ghale sneers at Paw, spitting for it to land in his face.

He shifts and it misses him by less than an inch... and I kid you not, if the general order wasn't 'Not to harm women' she woulda pick up a bullet. He hisses and shoves her to her knees beside Emily.

A few men join Paw to keep them grounded by pointing their weapons at them, while I make a call.

"Mah go fi Ramone," Paw states, stepping back into the house.

The guys surrounding the house move to break formation, but I signal to them to keep it.

Cyaa be too jumpy. Nuh know which other woman di man might recruit fi come play Roman's revenge ina bush.

Skulli answers on the first ring, "Law."

"Lawww, unuh have him?" I quickly ask.

"No."

"Fuck you mean no?" I sneer.

"Man just neva dedeh Drip," his tone blunt, voice lacking emotion. "Me have Mariah beside me and her likkle man tie up ina the back," he continues.

Running my hands over my head, I turn to see that Paw and Ramone are exiting the building.

I hiss.

"Yo just bring di brother to the basement and get everything Mariah know and report to me. Mah drop in ina the next hour," I instruct, hanging up before anything else is said.

"Oyi yuh!" I call to Ghale, "start talk now," I shove my gun to her forehead.

I was less angry when I thought Rome would be in my hands by the end of the day, but now? Mi nah promise nobody dem life a bumboclaaawtt.

As Ghale is about to speak, Paw interrupts, "Ramone a say him have an idea as to weh the Powa Puff Girls' leader deh enuh Drip."

I chuckle at his choice of words.

No matter which frame of mind me ina dah yute yah ago pull a laugh from me.

"Wah dat?" I ask, looking to Ramone who is aimlessly soothing the bruises riddled across his body.

"Deh back a Bay," he suggests.

"Dat would be stupid," I retort.

"Di man want back him territory, and as with any other clan, some people no rate Ruse or the fact say him yield to you. Easy prey dem deh fi di man slide back in. Memba when mah do me weekly check me see a strange number call Ruse couple time. Each time it last less than 30 seconds."

Ghale shifts and I sink my gun further into her skin.

"Go easy," I mutter a slight warning to her.

If she move again me might pull, swear to yuh. I'm becoming agitated as the seconds fly by.

Ramone continues, "Yeah so, before me ask, Ruse come to me a say Rome call him and say him wah come back a Jamaica, just fi see him son in person. Me pass the news to Slyme 'cause mah say me have him location at all times if nuttin fi gwaan me call you myself. Last night me see the man on the move outa Chicago and mah try give you the encrypt call but Slyme say you nuh deh 'bout...

... Jump ina the car fi come tell you in person and by me spin so, a two bredda dat a throw me ina them van. Yah so me wake up to them two idiot yah a play house," he points to Ghale and Emily.

A heavy sigh leaves my lips.

"Tie dem up and mek we liff up from yah so," are the last words that leave my mouth before I signal the men to break formation and head back to the van.

"I didn't want to Jordanne. I was blackmailed!" Emily shrieks and before I can offer her any reaction...

... Paw says, "Aye Bubbles! no talk to di man! Keep yuh mouth shut and accept yuh penalty."

• • •

It's another hour and a half before we get to the safe house in Hope Pastures. Rome is on the loose still, so I need every piece of information everybody has gathered today and days leading up to.

"Mi never tell yuh no come back Ghale?" I ask, staring at her feeble body, hooked up to Ramone's homemade electric chair.

"Dat a before mi know say yuh kill Dalani!" she shouts.

"So you woulda prefer him kill me?" I smirk, holding her stare.

She doesn't answer, instead she pulls on her restraints and rolls her eyes. I move over to Emily.

"Em' how you get ina it?" I ask, genuinely curious. Emily isn't somebody to partake in anything of the sort.

"She! She said if I didn't somebody name Rome would kill my parents," her innocent voice brings a smile to my face.

Cyaa believe I even thought of the possibility of maybe calling her last year, before Lizz and I became a thing. If all it takes is somebody to threaten her parents for her to join an aimless plan against me, then how that woulda work?

Fuckry

"And yuh believe her? Just so?" I quirk a brow at her.

She nods but says nothing else.

"Paw!" I yell, "get as much info outa them as yuh can, mahgo talk to Ruse."

Stepping away from the torture chamber, I move to Ramone's vault office where Ruse is seated, still rocking his restraints. Skulli and Slyme are with him already, badgering him with important questions.

I break the chatter when I ask, "The back and forth deven necessary. Why yuh brother leave the apartment fi we find unuh so easy?"

"Mi keep on a tell di man dem him leff right after him end the call with unuh," he explains, and I know he's being genuine just by his tone.

"Let's hope fi him and your sake, you nah lie. Me have a team a bring Stace, and JJ to my family house as we speak..."

... And all eyes in the room avert to me.

Mhmhm

Yeah man, certain plans me no disclose.

"Man no tell me nuttin," Slyme chuckles.

"A mi teach him enuh," Skulli laughs.

I internally smile at them both, knowing my father is the one who taught me to keep certain things to myself until I need them. Much like the fact that I saw how the DM shifted Ry's mood that night on the couch. Neva get a chance fi see a who, and convince myself not to look into it but–

Fuck!

Ry'....

Ms.Janette...

Mum...

Now that I've sobered up from poisonous anger, I can clearly remember the look on her face when my hands wouldn't leave her neck. The shouts from my mother. The screams from Ms.Janette.

Affi apologize yute

Like she did. I really need to open up to her– give us a clean slate.

For the trillionth time

"Yo wul it down... Me a go back home fi make the call. Him son probably reach," I say to them while turning to leave.

When I get upstairs, I switch the van keys for the Range keys while dialing Buckle.

• • •

Moments later I'm entering the family home to see that Buckle's van is present.

Dem reach man.

Parking out of the way, I exit the Range and head inside. Mariah is surrounded by everyone except Sue who is now knee deep in preparing dinner. They all stop to acknowledge my presence, but my focus is on one person.

Ry'...

Mariah gets up and runs towards me.

Yo she see you as her blood enuh killa

Realize man.

The force she lands with stumbles us back.

I laugh before saying, "Yuh think you dead duh?"

"Yuh fuck!" she cheeses, covering her mouth after realizing Sue and Janette are present.

Ms.Janette... Sigh...

She pulls away and I ask Ms.Janette to the library. Sue looks over from the kitchen and shakes her head in disappointment.

Valid.

Ms.Janette stands to her feet, and we both move to the library.

"Mek mi kick it off by saying I'm sorry," I go first.

She looks at me before moving her arms from being folded below her chest to akimbo.

This cyaa good

"Jordanne yuh know me love you, and me prefer yuh ova anybody else fimi daughta, but when you ago put you hand pon her, a deh so me draw the line. Unuh cuss, unuh leff, unuh do all kinda things to each other but keep dem hand deh to yourself," she warns, looking me directly in the eyes.

My face softens in remorse, "Nuh know wah kinda hold she have ova me Ms.Janette. Can't control myself when me feel like she a frig me ova again, or if somebody a fuck round her. The same level of anger surfaces every single time. Nah give yuh no excuse... Weh mi do wrong anyway yuh look at it, just a mek yuh understand wah drive me to that point earlier."

"Mi know, but as me like fi tell her, me have more experience in this life than you guys. Unuh young and the love is raw, try fi garner it into something controllable, otherwise unuh just ago continue behave wild, get me?" she offers words of wisdom while moving her hands from her hips.

"Understood," I offer her a small smile.

"Next time you put you hand pah me pikny, Sue cyaa go wul me," she slaps my ear.

"Easy nuh Ms.Janette," I chuckle, holding onto said ear.

"Now come, you mother a panic cook and you woman no say a word from she hug Mariah earlier."

I sigh, again.

Apology tour dis now enuh bad head

Say dat like a joke.

• • •

I've apologized to Mum and here I am walking over to Ry' who looks so out of it. I don't have much time... Buckle has Stace and JJ in the safe room at the guest house to the back.

All eyes are on me as I walk to the couch where she's seated. I hold my hand out to her and she looks up at me but doesn't take it. Instead, she stands and allows me to lead the way to the side lawns.

Mek it quick killa

"Ryleigh I'm sorry," is all I manage to say.

"Jordanne, I think you triggered my trauma... mi nahgo lie," she breathes.

Jah Jah God.

Words fail me and so I try to pull her into my arms. That fails as well, since she pulls back. I look down at her figure and realize she's shaken.

"Ryleigh, me have supm fi do right now... What you did was dumb and what I did was even more stupid... but we've been good. Mi honestly cyaa promise you say if we slip back into old tendencies me ago stick it out, so give me the chance to offer you a clean slate for the last time... I'm sorry."

"I know you are. I just can't shake the feeling... it reminded me of Fol–"

"Duh finish dah sentence deh," I quiet her.

She breathes before she continues, "Maybe it's time for me to join you and Terry?"

"Maybe," I say, trying for the second time to pull her into my arms. This time she allows it.

We stay like this for at least five minutes before I'm able to pull myself away.

I place a soft, wet kiss on her forehead before letting her know I'm going by the guest house to the back of the property. She tips up to kiss my lips, and something from inside the house falls.

We both turn to look and realize everybody has been staring at us from behind the large glass windows. They're now pretending to do anything that makes them look less guilty.

Joshua start wipe Sue glass window with him hand dawg.

We both laugh out loud when we see Mum walk over before slapping him and pulling him away from her things.

"Soon come link you. You can go to my old room if you no feel like talk to nobody."

"Never need your permission fi that but cool," she giggles as she walks back inside.

A smile makes its presence known on my face, as I watch her leave.

Back to business

• • •

As I slap my palm on the access pad to the safe room, the sound of a happy child greets my ears. When the door clicks open the first person to speak is Stace.

"Wah dis bout?!" she asks, rolling her neck.

I don't offer her a reaction.

Nuh worth my time

I move to the child who is no more than 8 years old. I bend to pick him up and she shuffles but Buckle grabs her.

"Weh unuh a do with me son?!" she screams, "Ruse no tell mi nothing 'bout this!" she continues.

Her tone is pushing me to physically shut her up but I won't.

God, gimmi the patience.

"Bring up the screen," I say to Buckle and watch as he puts the codes in for the encrypted call, that should mimic Stace's number.

The line rings for a few seconds before Rome picks up.

"Stace, a wah now, mi deh pah mi–" he's driving but pauses when he realizes it's my face on the screen, cheesing at him.

"Big bossss," I chuckle, "yah drive up and down ina my country without permission?"

"Drip... Lowe mi yute outa this," he almost begs, face plastered in fear.

"How me fi do that and yuh no gimme no choice bad man?" I retort. "Right JJ?" I ask while placing him down.

"Right!" the boy replies.

This makes both myself and Buckle laugh.

"Tell daddy you want to see him," I instruct him in the softest most playful way.

"Daddy, come see me. It's nice here, they have a better version of my game!" he shouts excitedly at the monitor.

"Yuh hear dat bus head? Farwud man, mek we have a chat," and with that I watch as he locks his steering, I'm assuming to spin the car around.

I chuckle at his actions.

"Hope Pastures, before midnight, or else yuh son ago grow with me," I smirk, hanging up before I can hear his pointless protest.

"Farwud we ago dinner," I say to Buckle and Stace.

Her facial expression moves from fear to utter confusion.

Good

We ago wrap this up but a time fi everybody take down some a Sue food.

Truly.

61 | Content

RYLEIGH

"Is that so Ms.Stevens?" Dr.Drew questions, spinning his chair around to finally face me.

Dr.Richard Drew is the head Economist here at BOJ. He's what you might call, snobby? Born to a lower middle class family but worked his way to the top of his field and now thinks he is the pinnacle of Jamaica's financial system. Only ten years older than me as he likes to brag.

If he's the pinnacle, then him affi be the worse, 'cause di way everybody a thief and get weh.

"It would only be for a few days, I'm certain my calculations will be done and sent over before I leave," I mutter, twiddling my fingers to fight back my anxiety.

The people pleaser in me has not died... at all.

Me a work from last year and never take a sick day, a personal day, a vacation day, nuttin to rass. Jordanne is not having an excuse for his birthday weekend, so dah man yah better tread lightly.

"IFFF... if you leave Ms.Stevens," he scowls.

I hiss, but luckily he didn't catch it and if he did he's showing no signs of such. I open my mouth to speak but he holds his hand up, willing silence.

"Ms.Stevens, aren't you up for the open slot on the reserve managers team?" his bushy left brow now raised in question.

"I am..."

"Then how does one expect to compete? You already have less experience than your competitors and now you want to have less hours in office?"

I–

Maybe him a talk the truth enuh. Them already have it fi say a 'cause me a woman, and they need gender diversity why I'm up for the role anyways.

"Dr.Drew it's a typical weekend, I'm only asking for the Thursday and Friday of the week before, and the Monday of the following week," I decide to stand my ground.

Proud a yuh

I have my own employees, and one ting me do is give them time off. Him think me need this? I just want to do what I love in peace.

With all the frustration going through my head, I manage to hold my face pleasant.

"If you can have your calculations to me by Wednesday," he stands, hovering above me, all six feet and four inches, "then I'll consider it," he picks up his folder.

"Consider?" I push.

"I'll give you the days Stevens, nuh push it," he mumbles.

Mi no know wah take over me body but I hurl myself at him, hugging him tightly.

"Appreciate it!" I giggle.

He takes his index and middle finger to press into my shoulders, scraping me off his towering body, like gum stuck to a nice shoe side. Immediately I realize how compromising the position might look, and gather myself.

He cocks his head to the side, "Ryleigh, duh do that again. They already think I give you special treatment," he starts leading us to the door.

"Maybe show them my numbers, so they can actually see say anuh back a di class me par," I hiss and exit.

He laughs, making the love-hate relationship between us even more evident.

The day winds down to 4pm and we're just about wrapping up closing procedures. To the public the bank closes at 1pm, but we usually have to stay until four– sometimes up to seven, just to get everything in order for the following international business day.

My phone goes off and without looking at it, I know it's Jordanne. A sheepish smile makes its way to my lips while my insides spin.

Sliding at the screen, I answer without hesitation.

"Mr.Sheer," I whisper, in the sweetest voice I can muster up– seeing as sleep a kill me.

And hungry tuh girl

"Love, yah get in before five?"

I drag the phone from my ear to double check the time– 4:03pm.

"If there is no traffic on the way to pick up JJ," I respond, waiting for the instructions I know will follow.

He chuckles, "You insist on playing mother, why yuh no just mek me fat yuh up?"

Not this again...

I roll my eyes playfully, before switching the call to video, while packing my stuff to leave for the day.

"Ryleigh, you can't find," he pauses, "looser clothes wear go the people dem place?" his eyes glancing at the phone that seems to be propped up in the famous cup holder now.

"Jordanne please nuh start... and I just think Junior shouldn't have a bunch a different criminal a pick him up after school, stability is good."

For eight days in **August,** they have all the new students going in for orientation purposes. Each one is accompanied by a seasoned student, to help them with the ins and outs of their new environment.

"Bay criminal used to pick me up..." Jordanne's voice wavers off.

"And look how that turned out," I laugh.

This makes him laugh out, only hissing when he's had enough.

"A dis ting yuh deh pon enuh. Just reach home before five please, I have something for you. Wah give you personally but you know I have things to do them hours yah daily."

I hate that we live in the same household and barely see each other. I leave at around 7:30am in the mornings and get back in at around 6pm on a good day. Likewise, he leaves at 5am to do God knows what, gets back in at 10am maybe, leaves at noon, gets back in sometimes in the evening to try and catch me or JJ... all to leave again until 8 or 9pm.

It no done...

... Then spends hours in the home office before crawling into bed, somehow still having energy fi beat out me back.

"Okay, I'll try," I mumble, convincing not even myself. I can't make it from here, to Ardenne Road and to Jack's Hill in less than an hour.

● ● ●

It's 4:35pm when JJ flings himself onto the backseat of my car, slamming the door.

Mi must kill him

"Good even-nin Ms.Ryleigh," he mumbles out of breath.

"Just Ryleigh Junior, just Ryleigh... How was it watching table tennis?"

"Good but I–I want to play," he whines.

I giggle, looking at my mirror to see if Slyme is behind us still. He obviously is, but I have a double-checking obsession going on right now.

Giving crazy

He honks at me to go and I pull out.

"Yuh soon get fi play man," I decide to speak words of encouragement into the child as my mother would to me– when I wanted to dance, to design, to join debate, to write essays... anything me wah do she say me fi try.

JJ goes silent and I hand him a pack of fruit snacks, a mini Shirley biscuit and a CapriSun, all in hopes he doesn't ruin the backseat like he always does.

Then look pah me at 21, with Stace pikny, a play mother.

Couldn't do dis and beat me

Couldn't! I giggle to the Tiktok reference.

Moments later, I'm pulling into the garage and before I can shut the car off, JJ fly di door and gone already. Not even a thanks, see you later– Garbage left right there on my leather interior.

Pikny deh no appreciate me enuh.

I frown and exit the car, mumbling to myself about his behavior. When I look up, I'm met with Jordanne's warm eyes.

He smirks from where he's standing before he says, "If him a did yours, you coulda slap some sense into him buttttt, you wah wait on the second coming of Christ, so no get miserable."

This sends me into a frenzy of laughter.

"Comedy a yuh hobby?" I ask, deliberately brushing past him, extra hard.

"A just di facts," he chuckles, grabbing me by the waist before I get to stomp off.

He pulls me in and plants a kiss on my lips, wiping away the stress from the day I had. I melt into his hold, wishing I had the discipline to become a housewife. If I was granted that trait, I wouldn't spend a next day Downtown.

As if reading my mind, he pulls my chin up to ask, "When yuh ago just stay home?"

Never...

Ever...

"When I've accomplished all I've wanted," I murmur, not wanting to break the peace by going over this dream of his again.

"I need you Ry'... You can't keep an eye on all the businesses while working for somebody else, and you definitely can't become privy to what's illegal if you are," he breathes.

I pull back to look at him properly, "How long you know me?"

"Too long," he chuckles, knowing I'm about to crash out.

"So weh yuh mean say me–" I start but he cuts me off by covering my mouth with his palm.

"Alright alright, rest it," he laughs, pulling me to the back of our home.

Ms.Pat comes and takes my bag from me, with JJ just behind her, blowing the CapriSun packet to maximum capacity.

If him buss it in yah me kill him!

Jordanne realizes my growing concern and moves, yanking it from his tiny hands.

"Bredda, not ina her house. Is a mad woman when it come to dat."

Junior smiles and says, "Okay, me ago play PubG," before running up the stairs two at a time. Ms.Pat takes off after him, yelling at him to take a shower first.

I sigh, shaking my head at the handful he is at only 8 years old.

Almost nine

Deciding to rest my thoughts, I follow Jordanne's lead to the backyard.

Which business him wah discuss now?

I'm on top of all the books I'm privy to, the accounts are doing fine… So I have no idea what he could 'have for me'. He slides the doors wide open and we step out. To the left I see nothing. My eyes dance in confusion. That's where we normally set up to host or just to chit chat about the week.

Confused at what I'm to see, my brain moves my eyes to the far right, just beyond the outdoor bar… and I see it.

"A lie yah tell?!!" I scream, releasing his hold to run over.

"Believe," he laughs.

I run to the quad bike, dragging at my pant knees, to give myself room to climb on.

"Ahhh! I just mentioned I wanted one last week?!" I look at him, trying to figure out if my little statement alone compelled him into buying this.

"I listen and observe… 24/7. You know dat," he smirks, moving over to plant a kiss on my forehead.

The same kiss has moved to nudge my clit into throbbing.

"Every girl wah bags and you wah bike???"

"I want bags too sirrrr, yuh bright."

I start looking at how thick and smooth the terrain bike is below me. Rubbing at the sides, I start to imagine how my weekends will play out. I've always longed to be able to go out, somewhere away from the city to ride ATVs, camp, bird-shoot and the list goes on.

Mi grow up a country, unuh know that already so any piece of adventure excites me.

Noticing how deep I am in my imagination, Jordanne says, "Just duh kill off yourself, that's all mah ask."

I laugh while pulling him in for a hug, before I stand, tooting my ass up to twerk while mock riding and swerving.

Girl

No 'cause Lorelle and T' wah seeee this! We outside enuh.

He laughs watching me, before his phone goes off and ruins the mood.

Ughh! Work.

He answers without a second thought while stepping away. I watch him speak… as not my Jordanne, but their 'Drip'. When he finally ends the call, I shoot him a knowing stare.

"Mahfi liff," he states clearly, walking back to me.

"I know," I whine, barely audible.

"Spain… so I'll be later than usual tonight," he adds, and I hop off the four-wheeler carefully, to walk him to his car.

I watch as he moves through the house and to the front porch where Slyme meets him before they walk off together.

Leaning at the door, I watch as they leave. Maybe I should be a housewife, I would see him more.

My lips curl up at how dumb the thought is, because the devil would definitely find work for my idle hands.

Nah ask Crise

• • •

I spin the combo again since it didn't work the first two times. This is the last time, and I've become agitated...

... Nervous.

Fearful as fuck.

My fingers move away, as I spin to the last number and hear the wheels click open.

Fada

A heavy sigh leaves my lips.

Siiiclawttt... mi no learn enuh man. What am I doingggg?

As I twist the wheel, the door cries. With all the strength I have, I pry the big vault door open and like clockwork, the stench hits my nostrils forcing me to pull up my mask.

Jesus

Tip toeing to the victim who's chained up and hanging on for dear life, I screw open the water bottle I brought.

"Hmm," he stirs.

Ryleigh mek we leave nuh!

I have to help, if even a little...

"Hey, I brought you water," I whisper, bringing it to his mouth.

He gobbles it, barely getting much down his throat– half of it is now on the floor.

"Stevens, him– ago– kill you," his voice weak, shaky, more fearful than mine.

"He won't. I brought soup too," I figured that's easiest for me to feed him since his jaw might be broken.

Jordanne really do a number pon him.

"Is JJ–" he tries to ask but I hush him by shoving a spoonful of red peas soup to his mouth.

"Ssssh he's okay," I whisper.

He blinks up at me and I can see the tears he's holding back. I'm on the brink of flooding my eyes too.

Mek we gah we yardddd

I hurriedly feed him the soup, right to the bottom of the medium cup before offering more water. When I see that he's full enough, I move away, wishing I could clean him up...

... but I know if I do, J' will notice, like he notices everything.

"Mah leave," I whisper, turning away.

"Thanks," he barely grunts, voice sounding so defeated it cracks my heart.

Before my tears can leave my lids, I offer him a nod and rush out, pushing the door shut and spinning the dials back to the exact numbers I found them.

Jesus me cyaa do this again enuh...

Yuh shouldn't start from first!

I have to talk to Jordanne... There must be some part of him that can find a better solution.

I really hope so, if just for Junior's sake.

62 | Torch

JORDANNE

Twisting the doorknob to our room, I find her sleeping, peacefully. The peace I can only wish for when I go to sleep. It's been months and we still haven't found out who exactly was helping Rome.

He won't say a word no matter how much mi bring him to death's door and back.

Di man serious 'bout informing yuh fuck

Mek mi start think him know me no wah kill him because Ry' wouldn't like that, since JJ would be fatherless.

Hissing, I move to the bed where I find her stirring. Before coming upstairs, I used the shower downstairs to rid myself of all things torture. Lifting the sheets, I slip behind her while mindlessly moving my hands to her breasts.

Love them.

She shifts and mutters something I fail to hear. Planting a kiss at the nape of her neck, I move my hand down her thighs.

"Jordanne mi say no," she mutters, scooting over to create distance between us.

Think the girl a sleep.

Jah know.

I laugh, pulling her back to me before whispering just behind her ear, "Go back to sleep."

Minutes pass and mi cyaa sleep...

People under the Mobay camp no with me or Ruse and me cyaa figure it out. More while me feel like line them up and just start spray until somebody talk, but that senseless... according to Terry.

Terry... I can say now that she's good at her little job. I've been less possessive, more understanding, less viole– Okay maybe not less violent per se but... yuh get me?

Jah know maybe going away next week is what I need. Just need fi clear me head and maybe a solution will present itself.

My fada woulda know exactly what to do. It woulda cause unnecessary blood shed but it would still get the job done.

Sometimes dat unavoidable

I continue moving through my thoughts, before Ry' turns to face me. Still slightly asleep, she pulls me down and into her bosom.

My favorite place this.

A smile finds my lips and I revel at the thought that she can feel my unease even while she sleeps... and knows exactly how to comfort me.

Heaven...

Before I know it, I'm knocked the fuck out.

• • •

My eyes fly open on cue, no doubt it's 5am. Me deven need no alarm again killa. I turn carefully, trying my hardest not to wake her. She's a light sleeper, that loves her sleep.

Pre sunrise, I like to take myself to the gym for an hour before leaving to meet up with shipment– just to sign them off myself prior to departure. When that's done, I move to the main safe house to have meetings, clearing up anything that needs to be handled and delegated to the team. That usually ends around 9:30am. After such, I normally make my way back home to shower and have breakfast before going into office to oversee the legal things.

All commercial real estate...

Residential real estate...

The construction company...

The freight forwarding company...

The restaurants...

Yacht rentals...

... and more recently, the multi crop and animal farm.

Despite the fact that I've appointed a board to each, and have put in place proper systems to keep them running without my micromanagement, it's still a lot. So when mi say me need me woman, me need her.

She can use her brains on my side, but instead she wah give it to the government. Imagine if I used the knowledge from my degree fi go work fi somebody?

Just no understand her...

Yuh don't have to

Her stir pulls me from my thoughts and I quickly leave the room before disturbing her anymore.

Mi affi inna her good graces today because today is the day me feel like mah end dah bredda deh life.

Mhmhmm.

Time boils down to a little before 7am and I've decided to cancel the meeting with the team today. The only people here are myself, Slyme, Surgeon and Paw.

Need some one-on-one time with the general.

After checking to see if the turn knobs are on the numbers I left them yesterday, I start spinning away at the combo. The door cries before I pull it open.

Stepping in, I waste no time moving to him.

"One don," I hail him, stooping to where we lowered him last night.

"Hmmph."

"Need fi have a talk wid yuh man to man," I rise to my feet and walk over to the control.

Rome is hooked up to a pulley system, where the chains that are holding him up have been pierced through his chest via hooks. Each time the system brings him further up, his skin pulls. A few times we've pulled too fast and too high, causing his skin and muscle to rip.

Today might be one of those days.

I look at him, eyes swollen shut, six of ten fingers left, body riddled with small but deep flesh wounds and burns, blood stained lips, drooling... I could continue but I'm not here to observe the damage done.

Deh yah fi the info

"So months later, yuh still no plan fi tell me who ina the camp a shake?" I press the button causing the pulley to lift him.

"UUhhhhhhhhhhh!!!"

Ignoring his scream, I let the pulley roll for an extra two seconds. It comes to a halt, forcing him to hang from the skin on his chest. No groaning today? He's too defeated to even protest.

Beautiful...

"Talk nuh man. Me tired a the games," I huff, walking over to him, stopping just before where he hangs.

"Ki– kihhll me."

"You no know how much me wah do dat," I hiss.

Moving to the blow torch, I notice a single... pea?

Which one a di man dem have the stomach fi eat in yah?

Jah Jah.

Shaking my head, I set the torch off. Rome starts reeling at the sound, not realizing or caring that the more he reels, the more his muscle and skin will tear from the hooks.

"Ready?" I ask, looking up at the broken man hanging almost lifeless.

"You go– kill– me anyway," he cries.

"Right, right… but me can grant you a less painful death in exchange for the information… and say you don't tell me, right here, in this moment… me still ago find out, starting with your brother, whether him loyal or not then Ms.Cherry, yuh baby madda, the people in the community you love so much… Somebody affi talk. Since you wah be hero, mah suggest you do the talking."

With that I bring the torch to his feet, causing him to drag against the hooks.

The left hook breaks from his chest, leaving him hanging from the right and by now the skin on his feet are pulling back from burns.

His screams fill the room and when I move the torch from beneath his feet, the second hook breaks, causing him to fall– landing in a ball.

I hiss, from frustration. Affi just end it. Four months of wasting my days just to find a 'peaceful' ground.

I move towards him and stoop, hovering over his body, while I screw the silencer to my Glock.

"Peh," he breathes, and I almost feel sorry for him.

Sorry? Haha!

My thought causes me to chuckle before I use my foot to shove him on his back.

He coughs…

Dah bredda yah?

"Peng and anybody, weh… wehFallUndaHim."

"That did hard?" I ask, hissing from even more frustration.

He coughs again before he says, "J–J."

I press my gun to his forehead before offering him comforting words to carry him into the next life.

"Junior ago good," and I can almost taste the venom in my words.

My fingers find the trigger and I don't hesitate to pull it.

Stepping back and out I call to Surgeon.

"Clean it up," is all I say before turning to leave.

Slyme looks at me and I nod, letting him know I got the information I needed. My next move is to the safe house shower, after disposing my clothes.

Just another day

• • •

RYLEIGH

"No because yah gimmi the days or not sir? I have to tell my ma– I have to let involving parties know if I'll be available or not."

Whether me get the days or not, I gotta go to be honest

"Stevens, yuh come fi stress me? Didn't I email the confirmation this morning?"

My eyes find him, no doubt displaying my shock.

After mi no check nothing. From me come me a try finish my numbers before next Wednesday so me can leave.

This weekend I'm hosting the girls. Junior will be with Stace for the weekend under heavy supervision by Sue's… and God know me need it 'cause the little boy RUDE.

You can't fix your daddy issues by filling the gap for that little boy Ry'

I roll my eyes, ignoring the wicked thought that has broken free in my mind.

"I didn't check my email. Some of us are busy crunching numbers to keep the country afloat," my words sounding a little more serious than I intended.

"Why the attitude? Like yuh wah me tek back the days?" he chuckles now moving to the exit.

"Thanks."

"You're welcome, enjoy your weekend!" he cheers before we part ways to our cars.

I can see Slyme waiting for me to pull out and I wave. My mood has been lifted at just the mention of the weekend. I haven't seen my girls all week and me ready fi drunk and tunova ina the house while spilling all kinda tea.

All kinda files, All kinda rub out.

Linking with them at home is like the live version of our group chat. Mi excited bad-ddd.

Bad, bad, badddd.

• • •

When I get home and don't see Jordanne I immediately call. He's normally home on Friday evenings at this hour, but not today.

I bring the phone to my ear, waiting for his voice to come across the speakers.

"Love," he picks up and his voice alone sends bubbles to my brain.

With a smile too wide, I ask, "Hi, where are you?"

"On my way to the second city. Ms.Pat did fi tell you that," his words send me into a sulk.

Without responding, I move to the fridge to find something to munch on. My eyes land on a chocolate bar and I grab it, ripping at the wrapper.

"What pulled you away from date night?" I query.

"Business… Babe you know we can't have this conversation like this. When I get there me mek Ramone hook we up, dat good?"

"That's fine," I say, chomping down on the chocolate. "Remember I'm hosting the girl's tomorrow night, in case you're thinking of switching date night to then."

"No sure if me a drop back before then, so you safe," he chuckles.

I love his voice…

I love his laugh…

I love him…

Me love outttt!

Then why yah feed Jacen?

'Cause me heart weak!

My thoughts shift my mood, and I move from the kitchen to the closet upstairs, stripping out of my work clothes. Jordanne stays on the line, silent, like we do when he has long drives or is abroad without me.

"Yah strip?" his voice startles me.

"You have camera in yah?" I shriek.

He laughs, "Easy, mi just know you movements."

I move to the phone, switching to video call, but realize my mom is calling.

"Mommy a ring me, call me when you're there from Ramone's line... Be safe."

"Always... Love you more than life itself."

"I love you too Jordanne," I whisper, emitting the sultriest tone, before ending the call and picking up my mother's.

"Mummy, weh yuh deh pon? Me hair wah–"

"Likkle girl me call fi hear 'bout you day not fi you tell me your dry head wah do."

I laugh out loud while stepping into the shower– putting her on speaker, ready to complain about Dr.Drew and everybody else down a BOJ.

•••

It's 7:45pm and I'm heading to the safe house like I usually do. About ten minutes past that time, I pull over on the street next to the one the house is on. I grab the soup I bought and start pacing to the next street.

I get to the gate, making sure I'm staying within the cameras' blind spots. Nervous and out of breath, I slap my hands on the access pad and the electric gates pull open. Slipping in, I press it shut before it gets a chance to completely open.

Moving quickly, I land at the front door before giving myself access. Staying to the walls, I move to the elevator before hopping into that too. Feeling safe since there are no cameras beyond this point, I breathe a little. As it moves to the basement, I pull my mask over my mouth and nose, not wanting the stench to hit me when I pull the vault doors.

When the door dings open, I walk out and put the soup on a tiny desk to the side. It takes me a minute to memorize where the numbers were left, before I start spinning in the codes.

Left pass 3 times…

25.

Right pass 2 times…

05.

Left pass one time…

50.

I breathe, comforted by the sound of the clicked handle. It's open.

First Try!!!

Gripping the bar firmly, I drag it open, ignoring its usual cry.

Mask yah must a work good today, I duh smell a thing while me drag it open.

I pull the door wide and… nothing. It's back to normal, holding clean floors and a few stack of boxes.

No Jacen…

No stench…

No blood…

No faeces… Nada.

I stand blinking for a quick second before I step back, closing the doors, setting them at the dials I found them. I grab the cup of soup and decide to head home.

Maybe that's why he's heading to Mobay.

Hopefully Rome finally said something, and we can all move past the stress.

63 | Group-Chat Live

SLYME

"**Y**esss Liammm!"

I watch her throw her head back while I thrust my stress away. Move mi hand dem to her breasts and start caress the nipples.

Instant grip from her walls.

Fuck, feel like me ago pop.

I start to slow the strokes, coming to a complete stop a few seconds after. Sliding my dick out, I use it to slap at her entrance. When I'm satisfied, I move down, sinking so deep into her, she screams while using her nails to hook me in place.

Tell dah girl yah no mark me skin enuh

As I ease up to warn her, my phone goes off.

Muuch Killa 🖤...

Bloodclawtttt.

I stand, leaving my dick lodged inside Toya, while I slide to answer Michelle.

"Princess," is the word that leaves my lips, while I press my palm against Toya's lips, making sure she knows to stay quiet.

"Why yuh camera off?" Michelle asks, wearing an unreadable expression.

"A deal with a work ting," mek we go wid the simplest answer.

"Yuh a work today?" she whines, "knowing me no have my car with me and I want to go to Ry's girls' night later."

Neva memba dat.

Jah know

"Wah time?" I ask, watching as Toya rolls her eyes.

I move my hand from her lips and to her clit, summoning more pleasure, knowing it'll take her senses away.

Nuh ina the long argument after this.

"I want to go from ina the evening hours, so mek me know if T' fi come pick me up or nah."

"Mah dideh man. 4:30 good?"

"Perfect," she cheers.

She then attempts to hang up but I decide to say, "Love you enuh girl."

"I know," she giggles before moving back into the screen, "love you off too Liam."

A smile creeps across my face as I click to end the call.

Mi feel… guilty?

I peer down at Toya who is handing me the deadliest stare.

"Wah now?" I ask the obvious while picking up the pace of my strokes.

Her answer seeps out as a moan and I move down to lift her– spinning us around. Lying flat on my back, I allow her to ride me to heaven.

Yah supm else enuh bad man

Know dat…

• • •

RYLEIGH

"Mariah come offa the phone no girl, you attached to your man more dan anybody?" I breathe, trying to grab her phone from her hands.

The sound of Ruse chuckling at my complaints, comes across the line.

"No stop wid me lady. Alla we know if yuh man call right now you drop wi. Nah askkkkk," she rolls her eyes, and the entire room starts laughing, including me.

She talk enuh

Toni-Anne is here with Kelly, both sitting at the far ends of the dining table that's now riddled with games and shot glasses.

Know this big rass table would come in handy one ah these days.

Lorelle is forcing herself to eat a slice of Pizza-Hut pizza, since she swear di only pizza that should be eaten is Dominoes. Muuch and Keif are the only ones with a cup of liquor in their hands. We're halfway through the night and I'm ready for everybody to play 'Fingers Down'

People business yuh wah ina

Then no must dat.

I move to my phone that's connected to the surround sound and press pause, successfully gaining everybody's attention.

"Finger's Down!!" and the way I say it, lets me realize I'm tipsy as fuck.

Lorelle quickly stuffs the last bite of pizza in her mouth, brushes her hands, grabs her cup and moves to take a seat at the table.

"Alright babe me gone," Mariah whispers to Ruse, ending their call while moving to the table as well.

I pick up another bottle of Appleton, bringing it to the table, with nothing but mischievous thoughts in my head.

"Alright 'cause a long time unuh no drop unuh business a floor... Be honest too!!!" Lorelle sneers while glaring at us all.

I laugh out, knowing she's just as tipsy as I am.

"Ten fingers on the table," I start, "unuh know the rules already. Pull a finger in if you did the deed, keep them up if you haven't, take a shot if you plea the 5th and if you lie about anything and more than one person at the table calls you out, you have to chug your mixed cup... Mek wi start."

"Which side we a start from?" Keif asks and I point to T' who's at the head of the table.

"Mistake yuh mek," she laughs, looking at Keif, "mi nahv nuttin fi hide."

"Fingers on the table man," I laugh, and she slaps all ten of her fingers on the table while eyeing me.

Kelly asks her the first question, "Have you ever liked anybody at this table?"

The smile drops from my face and my eyes swing to T's fingers. She bends her left pinky while saying, "You're at the table Kelly."

Her and her brother are one and the same! Lie in very cute ways

I giggle and look to Lorelle who is now asking her, her question. This goes on until it gets to me. The way me loopy I don't even know how to put my words together. She has answered all her questions with ease. After all, di girl is an open book.

Weh mi can ask that would make her drink?

I take a sip of my mixed drink before asking, "Have you ever liked anybody at the table, ouuuttside of Kelly???"

Yuh wrong fi dat

"Murdaaa! That me shoulda ask!" Kelly laughs, but quickly stops when she realizes T' took a shot.

The room goes silent as she slams the shot glass back to the table. I drag my eyes away from her when I realize she's sending eye daggers my way.

"A me don't?? Me just know a meeee," Lorelle shrieks, breaking the tension.

"Easy girlll. You're absolutely not my type," T' jokes, lifting herself from the head seat.

Lorelle plants herself in the seat and completes her questions, taking three shots and avoiding any chugs. Kelly goes after, followed by Keif, myself and then Mariah. Mariah was the only one to admit to everything, avoiding all shots.

Muuch is the last to go, and we're all drunk and delirious at this point.

Laughing and slapping the table, T' asks her the first question, "Have you ever had a threesome? Regular day that fi me but mi wah know if you eva?!"

We all basically start screaming at her latter statement. No sah dah gyal yah wicked bad! Muuch too jealous fi them supm deh.

Or so I thought because…

… to our surprise, Muuch pulls her finger in from the table.

"Murdaaaaaa!!!" I scream, turning what's left from my cup to my head in one go.

Lorelle staggers over to me while laughing. With tears in our eyes and almost no breath, we start mixing ourselves more drinks.

This cyaa real. Michelle?!

"Wid whooo?" Keif screams, breaking through all the laughter and chaos.

"Anuh so di game go Keif!" Toni and Mariah shout in unison.

Yeah man, dem gone too.

Gone, gone, gooone.

"Alright!" Keif laughs, "mek me phrase it better. Have you ever had a threesome with Steven?!"

None of Muuch's fingers bend inward, so we know anuh Steven!

"Slyme?!!!" Mariah shouts quizzically, widening her eyes at poor Michelle.

Muuch laughs before she says, "Anuh so di game go either!"

"Girl!" Mariah doubles over, "have you ever had a threesome with Slyme?"

Muuch brings a shot glass to her lips and when mi say the whole room drops to the floor screaming.

"The shot no mean yes!" I try my best to defend her.

It no mean no either

Mammaaa!!! Then a so Muuch active. But how this sweet everybody so? Dem know wah kinda man Slyme is.

Jordanne a di same type ah man

Jordanne better no tryyyyy me!

Lorelle's eyes swing to me and that's when I realize I said that out loud.

"Girl it no dat bad," Muuch defends her decision.

"Tell her nuh," Toni laughs, chomping into a spicy wing from KFC.

"Me wah see the girl!!!!" Mariah runs over.

"So the game done?" Muuch laughs, standing from her seat.

"Gyal gwehhh nuh! No more games, straight gossip 'bout fi take place now," Mariah retorts playfully.

I shake my head, hoping Muuch know she no affi show dem her business.

And we wah know too?

Mi wah know yuh fuck!!! Haha!

We all stagger to the living room floor, just before the T.V, where Muuch pulls out her phone and scrolls to Instagram. She pulls up the girl's profile and I immediately recognize her face. Weh me know her from? Coulda swear me see her a give me bad eye a Megamart months ago.

Maybe anuh she still.

I make a mental note of her handle @toy-yah, promising myself to look at it when I'm sober. She's pretty, BBL look fresh, is ah dolly masah.

Lorelle looks away when she says, "Muuch yuh betta dan meeee. That's why me nahgo have no man enuh 'cause me cyaa do dem supm yah."

Murdaaaaa! Mi no like Relle style enuh mannnn

"Mi and you girl, me anddd youuu," Keif cosigns before slapping a Hi-5 shake with Lorelle.

Mariah hisses, "Unuh stop judge."

"You woulda give Ruse?" I ask, and before the words fall from my mouth and settle properly, she says…

"Yuh crazzzzzyyyyyyyyy??? Ruse wah threesome him go look dat without me, and try no mek me find out 'cause is a six bloodclawt sum me a do and video it go send him."

"Bumboclawwwwtttt!" Keif screams.

"Mariah double it to rassss!!!" Toni laughs.

The only person quiet in the room is Kelly. She looks as if she's about to pass out from liquor induced sleep.

"Kelly you can go sleep ina the guest room, it's past the kitchen, down the hall, to the left," I direct her.

"Thanks girl, 'cause me did just ago drop yah so and mek sleep be freee," she moans while rubbing her eyes.

"Mah come wid yuh," T' hops up from the floor and holds her before pulling her in the right direction.

"Please mah beg unuh, if unuh ago rub front, strip me sheet dem when unuh done," and with that Toni flips me off, disappearing into the shadows.

"So unuh ready fi Joshua event?" Muuch asks.

"Yeah girl," Lorelle answers first, "know how long me no go wah decent party. A just work and home, work and home."

Lorelle has ventured off into the world of nails. She doesn't actually do nails herself, but she has her own salon with over eight technicians. She recently spoke about adding a lash technician and a waxer, just to make the beauty bar somewhat of a one stop shop. Between that and working for Digicel, as a communications director, she doesn't have much time.

"Me know that ago nice, the way me see T' ah angggggle the marketing. Everybody a talk 'bout it and a just the first staging," Mariah glees.

I smile.

A wave of proudness just take ova me body so.

We're all coming from the same school, only dreaming of half the success we have now. We always knew Toni would be okay but for the rest of us, we were a little worried about getting stuck in low paying 9-5s, without the freedom to enjoy our twenties.

We barely have freedom Ry'

Me can get it if me want it though, and so can they. That's all we ever wanted.

My phone vibrates in my hand and for a second, I wonder who's calling me at this hour… but of course it's–

Mr.Sheer 🖤......

The smile that lands on my face is wider than the width of my head. I quickly slide to answer, and his face pops up on my screen.

"Love, you good?" he asks and I can't find the words to answer. Instead, I'm all smiles and butterflies.

He notices and shakes his head, smiling back.

"Yuh gone enuh. Liquor a rule you right now," he chuckles.

Glad him know

Without offering him or the girls a word, I sprint up the stairs, not knowing how I made it to the top without falling. I can hear that he's having a side conversation with somebody, so I take the opportunity to quickly strip and hop into the shower.

He stays on the phone doing what he does, as we always do. When I get out the shower, instead of going to the closet to get dressed, I go there to entertain him.

"Are you in private?" I ask, knowing he isn't.

"No babe, the man dem out yah with me."

"Get yourself some privacy," I pout, propping my phone up against the shelves that hold my bags, before climbing onto the closet-island and spreading my legs for him to get a full view.

"Ryleigh," he says, but before I can answer, the call ends.

I laugh, knowing how agitated he must be right now.

Moments later the phone rings again and I slide off the island to answer it, only to climb back on, giving him his view.

"Babe, now? Really?" his words dripping in a mixture of lust and pain.

"Well I thought you would be back before girls' night ended. I don't want to wait till tomorrow," I whisper, moving my hands to my center.

"Jah know," is all he says before I start circling my clit.

Let's go

64 | Ibiza

RYLEIGH

Hope Dr.Drew him know me nah stay today enuh.

It's the Wednesday morning before we leave for Ibiza and I want to make sure all is right before we go. Jordanne and I leave tonight, while everybody else comes in on Saturday morning.

Then mi coulda excited so?!

Tapping my hands on the steering, I pick up the lyrics of Jada's song, Dickmatized.

7:55am and a this yah mek we listen???

Ignoring my subconscious, I sing out on the top of my lungs! My hands find my cup with the likkle mint tea, just so gas no take me up. I pick up on my favourite line before thinking say Jada must have me file.

My singing is abruptly cut by my phone ringing. My eyes make it to the screen and–Ramone? I find myself reaching out to answer, before glancing back to the road.

"Stevens," his voice comes slathered in concern.

My mood immediately shifts, and my stomach becomes uneasy.

"Ramone?" I whisper in even more concern.

"The line is safe. Couldn't wait till you reach back from work because the boss ago reach home by then."

Weh him mean?

"Is he okay?" I ask, slowing down with the traffic.

"Him good, this is about you," his tone unreadable, heightening the bad feeling weh ina me stomach.

Then a wah me do dats we affi talk on the private line?

"So me a do the check them last week," he kicks it off in a cold tone, causing my skin to populate with goose bumps. "Why were you at the safe house every evening for the past week?"

I–

I don't say anything...

Cause why wouldn't they check to see who gained access by prints idiot gyal?

The car behind me honks and pulls me from my state of shock, causing the tea I was sipping to spill– pah me fucking white top at that.

"Ryleigh me cyaa help you if yuh no talk enuh sis."

"Ramone... that's all you saw?" I ask, slowly driving.

"Yes, but Drip ago wah know why and easily me can tap into things and find out," his words send chills down my spine.

Talk early this time

"I–mi did a bring... soup," I manage to stutter out.

"Bring soup?" he questions, confusion evident in his tone.

"Soup, yeah," I almost whisper.

"Did this soup happen to be red peas, 'cause the man a ask everybody who eat ina the vault chamber... and nobody nah own it. Only few of us had access while Rome did in deh."

I can already feel the tears welling my eyes.

I literally can't tell you why I did what I did. I just didn't like to see it. Might as well him never show me or tell me nuttin. Mi nuh know a lot 'bout that side of things but if that's how it always is, I duh know if me heart can manage.

Then let's stick to the legal aspect of things

Sigh.

"I'm sorry, I'll let him know when I get in later today," I murmur, barely audible to even me.

"No Ry', him nahgo look past this one," he says, sending my heart fluttering. "Hear wah, mahgo search fi anything else and wipe it. I'll take the blame for the peas too... Anything else you wah tell me?" he asks.

No, that was it...

... and that will be it.

"No, that's all I did..."

I hear him shuffle before he says, "Okay, ina the lata–"

"Ramone," I try, before the call ends, "is Rome Okay?"

The line goes silent for what seems like forever. Jordanne refuses to talk about it until he gets back, and his one-day trip to Mobay turned into five days.

"Ryleigh... talk to Drip 'bout that... Lata," he sighs, hanging up before I can pry anymore information from him.

I stay rooted in my car, listening to some gospel, until five minutes before start time.

Ignoring the stain on my top, I walk inside. Figure say if me just a drop off my numbers and leave, then me no need fi wipe out nuttin.

• • •

So much for just dropping off my calculations. It's four hours later and I'm just leaving. I look for Slyme's car, but I don't see it.

Strange

My eyes dance around the lot before landing on Jordanne's GLE. A wave of mixed emotions washes my skin, but I mask it as much as I can. I wave at him and to my surprise, Slyme steps out, waving me over.

While I walk towards them, Slyme says, "Throw your key. Boss want you fi himself today."

I gulp, and throw the keys, remembering to mask my emotions.

Ramone got we

I hope.

Before I touch the door, it flies open and his smile is warm and inviting.

"Wife… wah do yuh shirt?" his brows form a knot of confusion, and for a moment I forget what caused the stain.

"Oh, me tea drap panni dhis mawning," I explain while getting in.

"You have the Clarendon accent. Weh you nervous 'bout?" he inquires while wrapping the steering to get us out of the lot.

"No nervous. Probably 'cause me just did a talk to me cousin," I lie, twiddling at my fingers.

He looks over at me, eyes finding my fingers, forcing me to stop. His eyes then move to mine for a split second and then back to the road.

"Cool…" he trails off, 'causing me to sink in my seat.

Me cyaa take di pressurrrrrre

Deciding to find a change of topic, I say, "How was your trip?"

"My trip was work babe. How was living without me?" a smirk now forming on his face.

Finally, Pheeew!

"Horrible. Do not leave me in that place alone with JJ again!" I roll my eyes.

"You and Ms.Pat no make one," he laughs.

"None a we no have your voice. A dat alone him fraida."

Jordanne grins, turning up the music while picking up his speed.

• • •

JORDANNE

"C'mere," the words leave my mouth as a whisper.

She's been in a weird mood all day.

Hope she a breed

Woulda love dat.

Pulling her to my chest, I slide the windows up for her to see the view. It's ridiculously beautiful. She climbs over, eyes still puffy from sleeping the entire flight. As we descend, the sunrise becomes more and more breath taking.

"Babe," she breathes, holding her head to the window

"Love?"

"Then place pretty so?" she giggles.

"Yuh live a paradise and a ask dat?"

"This is differenttttt," she admires the view, finally perking up and...

... the phone. Me know man.

I watch her take multiple videos and pictures of the scenery. Baby nah leff nuttin fi when we land.

"Get back in the seat. We have to stay buckled in for landing," I whisper, rubbing the small of her back.

She pouts and moves to her seat. Within minutes we're on the ground and I can almost taste the excitement beaming from her body.

• • •

"Mr.Sheer?" the villa manager greets us while handing us cocktails, "I'm Estelle."

Ry' gladly accepts and attempts to chug it before I squeeze her in, signaling for her not to. She was drinking champagne earlier, at a speedy rate, so no more until later.

She receives my signal and sips only a tiny amount.

"We're aware of the party members arriving on Saturday but for now the entire property is for you two," Estelle smiles at Ry'.

"Thank you," Ryleigh giggles before we follow Estelle's lead.

I've been here before of course, but not this specific villa. Wah experience supm for the first with her.

"No man. Dah place yah just keeps getting better and better," she's in awe.

"Babe," words finally leave my lips since we entered the property.

Her head snaps to me in question.

"Ago make a call," is all I say.

She nods, moving back to Estelle who has been giving her a mini tour. I make my way to what I assume is the living area and dial Slyme.

• • •

RYLEIGH

He's laughing… constantly laughing and handing out jokes. I love him this way.

Guard down…

Happy…

Vulnerable… All around loving. Just cyaa shake the feeling of Ramone having to cover for me. Then mi affi share such a secret with Ramone for life???

Sigh.

I think of something and before I can stop myself from saying it, the word vomit begins.

"Rome tell you nuttin? JJ has been asking to see him. I know he can't but–" I look up from my food just in time to watch his smile fade.

I–

"Rome good… moved on to a better place."

"Okay…" is all I say, searching for a topic switch.

To a better place? Well I guess that's good. Must've brought him to Mobay or back abroad.

"So how you feel big man? Last week we were 15 and now you're about to be 22," I giggle, bringing my fork to his mouth.

He takes it and locks his eyes with mine. My nipples perk up instantaneously.

He chews and swallows before saying, "Feel di same to be honest. Been playing big man for the last half of my teenage years anyway."

Hearing his tone makes me kinda sad. He really has been a grown up for a while. Duh know if that good or bad, but I wouldn't want to have lost my teen years to so much responsibility.

"Duh worry, I'll make sure you act like a child all weekend long."

"Long as that involve fucking you, no problem," his statement causes me to choke on my wine.

Dah boy yah!

"C'mere," he holds his hand out for us to leave.

I don't hesitate to lift, and the food dem deven half. The night wind hits as I stand, causing me to shiver. Jordanne pulls me into his arms and off the ground. I can't say how much I've been drinking exactly but I duhhh know myself from the tree ova deh so right now.

None at allllll.

Before I know it, we're inside our villa… I think. Yeah we're in our villa. I just spotted my suitcases.

Seconds, or minutes pass, I duh know rasta... but I know I'm sprawled out on the bed. I can hear water running from, the bathroom?

I duh know either

Jordanne's footsteps and his sweet manly fragrance moves back to the bed. In one swift movement, I'm at the edge of the bed. I hope he knows, we don't need the foreplay, I'm already wettttt.

"Been a wait six long days fi fuck you," his voice comes low and warm along my ear.

I take a deep breath, knowing I'll be sensitive to his every touch with the level of liquor swirling around my blood stream.

He leaves a kiss on my neck before moving to the top of my boob, then swirling his tongue around my nipple...

Moving over and down to my navel... he stops.

Why him stop?

He picks up again just above my clit, ignoring the actual fruit. He then starts leaving kisses along my inner thighs– now moving further down my legs.

Aye, if dah man yah suck me toe dem me a scandal him fi life enuh

I realize that I'm giggling out loud and quickly stop. He grabs my waist and I feel myself lift from the sheets.

The boy have a piece a strength fimi.

Mammmaaa!

He swings us around, planting himself just below the headboard. Knowing what he wants, I move my body up, holding onto the headboard with one hand, while using the next to find his dick, slipping it in myself.

A heavy moan escapes his lips, and I swing the hand I used back to the headboard for support. I scoot up to the tip, and that's where I start my ride.

Riding him like there's no tomorrow, I keep thinking about how cute our child would be.

Noooo 'cause the baby woulda nice.

No more liquor for us. You're yapping through sex

His hand reaches up and holds my breasts, preventing them from bouncing. He whisks my nipples between his middle and index fingers on both hands and that action alone causes me shudder.

"You're so wet," ... I barely make out his words. He's right though, I can suddenly hear the wet slaps as my ass meets his pelvis.

"Mmmmm," is the only moan that slips out of my mouth. I'm too busy breathing, focusing on riding him.

Cyaa get tired...

Duh– get– tired.

I keep repeating the words to myself. When I feel like he's had enough of this pace, I come down to my knees while pressing against his chest and resting my head in the crook of his neck.

He loves that.

Tooting my ass up, I start to ride again, but slow and intimate this round. His hands start to move from my waist to my ass, worshipping my skin while I bring him to the clouds. He slaps it! One cheek after the other. I should be used to it but the feeling sends me to a place weh mi cyaa explain to unuh right now. I hook onto his neck, sucking it, knowing it'll bring out his inner demon.

"Ry!" he shrieks.

Yeah, that me wah hear.

• • •

JORDANNE

"Ry!" I breathe.

She do that fi spite enuh. Mi have her ticket man, nah wile her.

I squeeze her ass. It's the only thing keeping me grounded right now. If me let go, me sure we ago levitate killa.

No joke.

Deciding to take control from her, I start meeting her mid stroke, bucking my hips.

"Jor–danne!" she screams, sending the happiest smile to my face.

"What's wrong babe?" my tone now feigning concern.

She hisses lowly.

Pausing the strokes I scoop her up and off, only to flip her onto her tummy, pulling her legs slightly apart before sliding in from behind, slowly.

Siiiiclawwwttt… Mistake me mek bredda. Position yah deadly.

Leaning down, chest facing her back, I lace my hands into hers and lay small kisses down her spine while working in and out.

"Fucccckkkkk," she shudders.

Ignoring her, I continue pouring my love into her. Feel like if we never become one before, this time we are.

"Babe," she whispers… and I already know what's about to happen.

"I'm c–"

"Ssshh," I cut her off before continuing at the same pace that brought her to her peak.

Steady…

Firm…

Deep…

Within seconds she's shivering beneath me, walls clamping my length. When she climbs down from her high, I turn her around. Without a moment wasting, I spread her shakey legs. My eyes watch as her juices flow down her entrance and I take the opportunity to rub my dick along her folds– occasionally tapping it on her nerve ball.

"J," she cries, "stop teasing."

Always so impatient... but if a that she want... Almost immediately I obey her orders, slamming into her while moving down to capture her lips. She releases a moan into my mouth before wrapping her legs around my waist.

Trap...

A the signal this fi breed her?

Ignoring my subconscious, I lose myself in her hold. The feel of her hands rubbing my head, as our lips lock and my pulsating dick is lodged in her gum, causes me to lose all thoughts– Good or bad.

If mi no know nuttin mi know dah pussy yah ago be di death of me.

We continue like this for well over a few minutes before I stop fighting the feeling, allowing it to consume me.

A mere millisecond before I shoot, I pull out, emptying on her stomach and breasts. She smiles and, in this moment, I've confirmed, mi cyaa live without her.

• • •

My eyes rip open at the sunlight. Nuh sure what time it is here but I'm certain it's 5am in Jamaica. I look to wall clock to see that it's 11am. Can't tell when last my eyes have stayed shut beyond 6:30am killa.

Grateful for the time away

Ry' stirs before sitting up, looking like a zombie. Know dah look yah, baby have a hangover.

I chuckle and slide out of bed. "Good morning," I offer her.

"Good morning big buddy," she giggles, holding her head, I'm assuming in attempt to soothe a headache.

Before moving to the breakfast that was left outside our room, I snap a picture of her for my own eyes. I love how thick she's gotten. Dropping my phone back on the bed, I move to open the door, finding the breakfast exactly where I ordered it to be.

Bringing the cart in I say, "Farwud, come full you belly, nuh want you miserable today. We have things to see."

Reluctantly, she turns and starts picking what she wants from the cart.

Nuttin like spoiling yuh woman bad head

No other feeling like it fi real..

65 | Ibiza Part TWO

RYLEIGH

It's Saturday morning and we're about to leave to catch the vintage train tour. Today is his actual birthday and I actually can't wait to reveal my gift.

Mi must get him fi shed a tear.

We've been carefree and happy since getting here and mi love dat. Not one time have I seen his eyes darken, or his body tense from any troubling thought.

Well other than at the dinner when I asked about such man

We've done so much already, leaving me to wonder what the hell else is left for us to do when the rest come in today. We've done the private sailboat...

Spanish cooking class...

Hot Air balloon...

Toured the ancient castle... It's giving honeymoon and I can't say I hate that.

"Ready?" he asks, looking at me, seeming more excited than I am.

Nooo, then me never know all it takes for this man to be the old him was us leaving the country. I see my best friend in his eyes now, and not who he's becoming... or already has become.

Drip?

Drip...

Dragging the last piece of clip-in extension from my roots and throwing it to the backseat, I turn to him and say, "Long time."

Without a second thought he speeds off, heading to the site where we're supposed to board the train. The scenery is nothing like I've seen before. The landscape is lush and rustic, but if you peer down to the shore, it's beachy and island like.

Best of both worlds.

Jordanne turns up the voice of Masicka and finds himself a cigar. Trying to tame my hair that's fighting with the wind, I turn to him, only to admire his built.

"Diss e' family, close range ina yuh face rock yuh chin," he kicks it off.

Few lines later he starts again, *"Gyal a lef from work fimi buss di stocking,"* he bobs his head this time while releasing a smoke cloud.

If yuh know J' you know he only sings the lyrics he can relate to and nothing else.

Di boy really buss we stocking couple time well fi true

He's sporting full white cotton slacks and a long sleeve white shirt, whose brand name I can't pronounce. On his feet are male Ferragamo sandals and on his wrist is his AP. Around his neck is nothing but his Cuban link, studded with diamond dust. I watch him puff the smoke from his lips while he sings along to another Masicka song.

The boy nice enuh.

The sun has full access to the convertible, allowing his dark skin to reflect warm rays around him. If me never know him a the devil himself, me woulda think a Jesus righthand man.

He glimpses at me as if feeling my stare and I bite down on my bottom lip to quell the growing feeling at my core.

He quirks a brow before he says, "Nipple dem ago always betray yuh babe."

I scoff, covering my now hard nipples.

"Drive and stop pre me," I giggle, picking up my phone to take pictures of the scenery, knowing I can't post until we leave.

Ughh! Mi wah maddddd the gyal dem right nowwww.

"Ova deh a fuck me with your eyes, and wah me focus pon road?" he chuckles, pulling the cigar from his mouth to place it in the ashtray that seems to be built in.

If anybody did fi find a luxury, vacation convertible, with a built in ashtray, it would have to be this weed head man beside me.

Swear.

Moments later, we pull into the spot designated for tourists. Without waiting for Jordanne's lead, I hop out of the car from excitement and head to where everybody else is.

The mixture of different accents pique my interest and I move to start asking everybody where they're from. Before I could open my mouth to make conversation, Jordanne's hand is pulling me away.

"Anuh our stop this," and me swear me see him almost laugh.

Country come to town! Mi one nuffi shame so.

Without protest, I hold his hand and he leads me down a lonely path, where I can see the vintage train. I notice that the group of people that were at the top of the trail are now coming down.

Then why the boy say a the wrong stop

"So why yuh gwaan like me cyaa read Spanish?" I snap my head to stare at him.

Before he answers, the tour guide approaches us, handing us each a gold band.

"Sheers?" he questions and Jordanne nods. "Come with me," he continues, accent thick.

He leads us to an empty train-car at the very back of the train, decorated with fruits, finger food, wine and what seems to be empty canvases for painting.

My man, my man, my man, myyyy man!

I turn to look at Jordanne who is handing the guide a stack of Euros.

"Not you treating me on your own birthdayyyy," I giggle.

"Not you thinking we were gonna mingle with everybody else," he tries to mimic my voice, and mi almost choke pah me own spit.

I love when he's like this.

Tipping up, I plant a kiss on his lips and he takes the opportunity to grab my ass, lifting me into the cart.

• • •

We spend upwards of an hour on the train looking at the view, trying to draw the horizon, while melting into each other.

Jordanne, completed his drawing minutes ago and refuses to reveal it. I've been struggling me nah lie… 'Cause how me fi draw and the train a move? And him a–

"Mhmm… J' slower… I can't focus," I moan.

His fingers have been up my skirt for the past five minutes, but I really, really, really, want to finish this painting.

He moves down to my ear before whispering, "Fuck the painting, the ride soon end, ride me."

I wave the paint brush around, signaling a 'NO' to him, since my words are nothing but breathy sighs. His fingers pick up pace and I hear when a phone goes off…

His phone.

Cho

"Slyme?" the tone he uses to pick up is covered in annoyance.

No 'Law' today?

"Yeah dat good, Estelle should be there…" they go off into more conversation, while he brings me to my peak.

Impressive, the way he focuses on both tasks, not giving either less attention.

Coming down from my high, I pull his hands from between my legs. He looks at me and smirks. Feeling self conscious, I pull my dress down and cross my legs. Looking over at him, he smiles and turns his canvas around revealing a stick woman with a very big forehead.

"YUH THAT," he mouths, careful not to interrupt the call with Slyme.

My mouth falls open and I try to grab it from him. He laughs and moves away while I roll my eyes in faux disgust. The train comes to a stop right where we boarded, and I immediately find the bathroom.

Really wah pee

I do my business and exit, to find him standing guard at the door.

"Coulda just squirt pah me hand," he laughs.

"That was real pee fool! Watch it frah yah so," I giggle moving past him while having absolutely no sense of direction.

"This way Love…"

I turn to the sound of his voice before following his lead back to the car.

● ● ●

When we pull into the villa, I spot all my girls and all his friends including Ryan. Sue, Paul and mommy are also here.

A festive weekend this shall be

Jordanne opens my door and I run to my mom, hugging her before hugging Sue and my girls.

"Big man," Skulli's voice comes clear, "One up pah yuh strong."

Jordanne daps him up and the others mumble different ways of saying happy birthday to him, without actually saying the words 'Happy Birthday.'

Jamaican men.

My girls all tell him happy birthday and extend 'Thank yous' for the trip.

T' doesn't partake, instead she rolls her eyes at him and says, "This is the only day, I have to accept that I'm not an only child punk."

He hits her shoulders before saying, "Adopt dem adopt you, so gwaan run chat."

They both fill the entrance with genuine laughter. After sobering up, we all move inside. J' and I move to our suite, while Estelle extends a mini tour to the newcomers.

Love it here

The night winds down and by now we're all getting ready for dinner. My nerves start to kick in when I realize I have to give him his gift before leaving.

Knowing us, we ago too drunk after.

Well, me mostly.

I move to my carry on and start digging through for the box before he exits the shower. Really wanted to do this at dinner but the dinner includes everybody and me no sure how him ago react.

And me wah see the real emotions… not the bitten back ones

I clear the bed, shove all our suitcases into the closet area, pull the curtains and dim the lights.

Best dat me can do before we go.

Seconds later, he exits the shower, rubbing his towel over his head, while another is wrapped loosely around his waist.

"Hi," I whisper, smiling at him sheepishly.

He pauses, bringing the towel to his shoulder before saying, "Wah yuh up to?" eyes full of skepticism.

I almost laugh at how worried he looks.

"Have your gift."

"Yeahhh?" he smiles, pulling me to him with a smirk.

"Not that Jordanne!" although I do want that...

"Then what?" he questions.

Look how di boy mek it look like a bay pussy me wrap give him a year time.

Murdaaaa!

I bring the box from behind me and he takes it, giving me a puzzled look.

"Just open it..." my nerves dem nuh built fi this.

Watching as he unlaces the ribbon, I twiddle my fingers. He opens the box, looks at me, closes the box and plops himself onto the bed.

Rass...

"I–" I begin to start explaining myself.

Maybe him nuh like it

"C'mere," he whispers, dragging me down into his lap, before showering me with 'thank you' kisses.

"Yuh like it?" I ask, needing to hear the words.

"Love it... Your heart is so pure."

I become a smiling fool just from his words and his raw display of appreciation.

He pulls it out of the box and stares at it for what seems like a millennia. It's a tennis chain, with a pendant carved of his father holding him as a baby. On the back of the pendant reads:

"Always Holding You"

-Law

"That's not all," I whisper and watch as his eyes find mine.

Could be me but the boy eye shine. So we a get a tear?

"I got the land you've been looking at in St.Elizabeth for the farm," I start, reaching for my phone to pull up the title.

His eyes go wide, "How you get that? Me offer the man sooooo much money and nuttin."

"I have my wayssss," I laugh. "The root of my family is from Sainty. My great grandma moved her offsprings to Clarendon, but we still stay connected with those who are still in

Sainty, you know this. So when you say near Pedro Plains, I went to my grand uncle and he's a friend of the owner so me ju–"

Before I can finish explaining he's on me. Then him really ago fuck up me hair!?

Yuh wah stop him??

No.

Shutting off my internal battle, I give in to his 'thank you sex'.

• • •

Minutes later, we walk down, knowing we're late. As I descend the stairs, a wave of guilt hits me, when my eyes meet my mother's. Sue giggles before motioning to me about my hair.

And you know me try me best fix it.

Sigh.

"Yah tell me say unuh couldn't wait till after??!!" Joshua laughs, causing the room to erupt in deadly laughter.

This boy duh change enuh.

"Yuh chat too muchhh," Kelly snaps, trying not to laugh herself to death.

"Come take yuh picture girl," Lorelle says grabbing my hand while pulling me away from Jordanne. He shoots her a death glare and she rolls her eyes before saying, "Yuh have her fi two whole day!"

"It's his birthday," Keif laughs and when I look over to her, I notice Muuch and Slyme are having a heated argument to the corner.

Deciding to ignore it, I try to focus on posing for my picture...

... But the way me foot dem weakkkkkk.

She snaps a few and let's me know to check the group chat, where she sent everybody else's. I toggle to the group chat to collect my pictures while waiting for our ride.

BUBBAS

<u>Dutty Foot:</u> |attachment| Mariah yours!
<u>Dutty Foot:</u> |attachment| Kelly! yuh dat!

<u>Sexy Bitch:</u> Look how me woman nice! Crying!

<u>Mariah Boo:</u> Now me understand how yuh bend up like noooogle sista gyal lol!!! Kelly pretty yf!

Dutty Foot: Easy with the chatting till me send all pics. |attachment| Keif your own yah!

Keif Boo: Watch how the best picture a without me shoes. Mi tell yuh wait till I got them.

Dutty Foot: Crop yuh foot and shut up. |attachment| Toni-Anne!

Sexy Bitch: We appreciate you sisturrr!

Kelly: Prettiestttt baby!

Dutty Foot: |attachment| Man wife!

I look at my picture and laugh before typing.

Look like me just do a quickie???

Mariah Boo: And doooo!!! why u ina shades a night? and your hair messy lmao!...

Sexy Bitch: Watch the lady foot dem. Spin outtttt!

Not too much on meeeeee!!!
Muuch you take already?

Muuch Boo: ... ...
Muuch Boo: I'm not in the mood.

Finding that funny, I look up from the phone and find her sitting alone nearest to the exit. I decide to walk over to pry. She loves to take pictures, especially on vacation.

Supm no right.

As I get up to walk off Jordanne pulls me into him, "Ride dem outside," he announces loud enough for everyone to hear.

"Take the shades off," he flicks them, holding the most obvious smirk.

"But mi makeup mash up thanks to you," I shove him slightly.

He laughs out louder than he has this entire trip, catching everybody's attention. Minutes ago he was fucking my face and the way how eye water come a me eyes and fuck up my full face beat, I had to wash it all off. Now me face naked and him a tell me 'bout take off shades.

"Take it off," he grabs it and holds it above his head where he knows I can't reach it.

"Yuh coming like crosses!" I sneer before storming outside to meet the ride.

While walking out, I hear him choking on laughter, causing a smile to appear on my face.

Bumbohole

Real bumbohole.

66|Ibiza Part THREE

MUUCH(MOO-CH)

Sitting on the couch, I look over at everybody taking part in the early morning karaoke. The aroma of Sue's cooking has filled the room, since she decided to take over from the chef, disrespectfully.

Surgeon is trying his best to take the floor from Ry' and Jordanne, who are now on their third song. They've been so good this weekend, makes me a little bit jealous.

They deserve it

They do...

The time frame of them being together gets blurred a lot. Everybody has it they've been together since college or high school but in reality, they've just gotten a chance to live within each other, since April.

Four months...

... So if I'm comparing them to Slyme and I, who've been together and solid for two years plus, they're a baby couple. Don't get me wrong, we all know their history goes deep, but it's always been on and off.

Just no know wah do my man these days

For months Liam has been begggggging for a threesome and I finally gave in, thinking it would be a one time thing, and now? Now him wah do it again, with the same bitch!

Sigh...

Starting to think he just wants to fuck her.

With all the recent problems we've been having, I can now understand how Ryleigh kept going back to Jordanne or how he kept going back to her, no matter what they did to each other.

But is that what you want?

I don't know... They look happy now?

My eyes find them. They're now on their fourth song, with Ryleigh screaming at Jordanne to sing the lyrics even if he can't relate, but as usual, he's not having it.

"Do you remember girllll, I was the one who gave you your first kiss," Jordanne wails.

None of them can sing for shittttt but dem nah give nobody else a chancccce.

I smile at the show.

She continues with the next line before shoving the water bottle mic to his mouth for him to pick up the lyrics, but he doesn't. This causes her to hiss before singing it in her best male tone.

"Now another brother's taking over but it's still in your eyes."

Toni grabs the remote and changes the song to Alkaline's, My Side of the Story and as soon as the intro starts, they leave the floor.

"A wah?!!! Unuh no wah sing dah one yah?" T' laughs and I can't help but think why they wouldn't want to.

Averting my eyes to Liam, I watch as he taps away at his phone while smiling.

What a way him happy

I've been trying to tell him what I found out, but I want us to be in a good place before I do. A heavy sigh leaves my lips, catching Ry's attention– everybody's attention really.

Fuck, she ago question me

• • •

RYLEIGH

Since T' she decide fi kill the mood, Jordanne and I are sitting in the couch, watching the lames try to top our karaoke session.

"Booooooo," J' laughs, mocking Toni who is giving her best performance to Ashanti's, Foolish.

I start to laugh but my eyes meet Slyme and how happy he is tapping away at his phone while Muuch is on the single chair sulking.

Wah this fada?

Mek me stay outa people business

I turn to help J' boo his sister but I hear when a heavy sigh comes from the section of the room where only Muuch is. Everybody turns to look at her... She forces a smile, in an attempt to show us she's fine, before going back to staring outside.

Me cyaa take this no more. She's not like this. Deciding to get up while ignoring J's deterrent squeeze, I move to her.

"Yuh good?" I peer down at her.

"I'm... okay," she mutters, not even trying to convince herself much less me.

I hiss and grab her hand, pulling her outside. We walk to the poolside, and I take a seat on the first chair I see all while pulling her to the next one.

"Talk," I encourage her.

"I don't know if I'm ready," she barely mutters.

"It's me... I've been through enough not to judge," words of comfort slip my lips, hoping that will win me her trust.

She leans all the way back in the chair, focusing on the clouds through her lightly dimmed shades. I watch as she calms herself by taking a few deep breaths.

A coulda wah so?!

"I'm pregnant and he–"

Mi bumbo pussy bloodclawwwwwwttttt... pussy bumborasssss.

My mouth drops to the floor and my body stiffens from shock. I shouldn't be the one to give advice on this topic, it's a trigger for me.

Last thing me expect enuh. The way Muuch is team 'rich aunty'

"He keeps asking me about another threesome with Toya and me just no wah dweet again," she continues, while I'm literally still frozen. "It did fun but mi no wah do it again, and a not even because me pregnant 'cause I don't plan to keep it anyway–"

"What?" I snap my head to her.

"Yeah, I'm not ready, but me at least think him fi know so somebody can hold my hand through it."

See now, because of my miscarriage, I'm very... verrry biased when it comes to things like this. Di way how my loss was involuntary, me no understand how people do it willingly. But her body her choice?

Right, 'cause anuh me ago carry it fi her

"Bwoiii, mi nahgo lie to you, him no supposed to force yuh fi do nuttin yuh no want enuh... and... and–and like if yuh no ready fi the baby, yuh just no ready," I force out.

I literally just gave the most useless advice, didn't I?

Muuch heaves another heavy sigh.

"Michelle... on a real, if yuh no ready that's fine. We're young and a your good womb and good hole. If Slyme can't understand and support you in this decision or the threesome one, him can go. 'Mount a man DM me 'bout you when me repost your pictures is ridiculous. So him can gwaan if him want."

Knowing him might kill she and the man?

Knowing full wellllll.

A tear falls from under her shades and I move in to hug her.

"A wah? Unuh okay?" Toni asks while walking over.

All the girls except Kelly are behind her, holding concerned expressions. I wave them over while patting Muuch on the back.

"Mi say if a dutty Toya issi man!" Mariah sneers, pushing me away to hug Muuch herself.

"Weh you mean?" Muuch asks, removing her sunglasses to wipe at her leaking eyes.

"Ohhh," Mariah pulls back. "Uhm, wah day me repost you picture with the gifts Slyme gave you and she reply to the story with the laughing emoji dem. Me no say nothing 'cause mah say sometime people finger slip and send off the reaction."

"Yuh yourself not even believe dat," Lorelle hisses and Keif nods.

Muuch looks at me and I offer her soft eyes, hoping to give her the encouragement to tell them what's going on.

Maybe dem have better advice than me

"Wah did her handle again?" Lorelle asks, pulling out her phone but before anybody can pinpoint it, she says, "Never mind, me find her."

"Active ina Slyme follow list," she adds while tapping away.

Mere seconds later she shoves the phone to Mariah.

"No mek me vomit ina this," Mariah laughs. "Wah this???" her gesture theatrical, while passing the phone around.

I take the phone and look at it. In this picture she looks way less appealing than when I first saw the page. The body is giving botched, the outfit is giving stripper, the only thing she really has going for her is her smooth dark skin.

I just might've been drunk that night fi real

My eyes drop from the photo to her comments and guess who in deh?

Nooo, then Slyme bold nuh bloodclawttttt! My blood starts to boil and something leads me to click on a specific page that I saw commenting too.

@throatgoat77 'Only person better at chomping than me'

I toggle through the profile looking for a face picture but a bay back way batty pose. Gyal yah nahv no face card? When I finally get to a picture, it hits me…

Then nuh likkle miss week five this??!!!! A weh di bloodclawt a gwaaaaannnn?

That was two years ago, nuh bother with it

My eyes dart to Lorelle before I hand her, her phone. I stay silent and watch as Muuch calms down. I'm not sure if I should tell her I know Toya's face from eyeing me at Megamart months ago or…

No wah mek she feel any worse. Cause that would mean she know Muuch before Muuch know her.

Deciding not to, I listen as she shares her news with the girls. As soon as the words leave her lips, all the bickering and chatting comes to a pause. All their eyes are now filled with concern, but mine?

… Mine are filled with questions.

• • •

SLYME

Drip slides me a glass of whiskey.

Know di man ago question me now enuh.

"Why everybody surround your woman except you boss?" he asks, raising a single brow at me.

Most times me nuh fear him, but in this moment, I do… because if nuttin no clear to mi ova di years, Ryleigh's happiness being compromised make di man go mad, and if Muuch no happy, Ry' nuh happy.

Jah.

"We no good fi couple weeks now," I pull the glass to my mouth.

He chuckles, "Unuh cyaa good if yuh no leff Toya alone."

Of course him know say me still deh deh so.

"Good while now mah watch you do you ting enuh big man. Tell yuh leff dem gyal deh 'cause she and one a di girl dem me used to rotate a friend."

"She just–"

"She just wah bredda? Mi tell yuh easy pon a thing and yuh refuse fi listen," he shakes his head and averts his eyes to the girls outside passing around a phone.

"See that? Can bet mi life a find them find the girl page… and if me know my woman, she ago find the girl friend and put it together. All mi want a peace ina me house and within the team enuh skull," he looks back at me, holding a cold expression.

"Mi and Michelle just nah click and me need an outlet fi do mi ting."

"Bredda go the gym. Yuh older than mi enuh," he hisses, standing to pour us another round.

"Weh di man dem a chat 'bout?" Ruse walks over.

I duh like a bone ina dah yute yah.

Turning, I chug the fresh glass of whiskey while Joshua, Skulli, Paw, Ryan and Surgeon all start walking over to join the liquor talk.

Jordanne changes the topic to, "Man dem ready fi later?"

"If a war a war enuh," Skulli laughs.

"Old man, better yuh go warm up and stretch from now. Do couple jumping jacks and some yoga stretch fi yuh back," Paw chuckles.

Man yah man? I laugh, realizing my mood has become lighter.

Ryleigh has Estelle transforming the back yard into some kinda obstacle course ting. Apparently, we'll be shooting water guns at each other– ladies versus gentlemen. She say she want the boss heal him inner child– do things him neva get fi do as a yute.

Rate dat.

Know Muuch ago full fi her gun wid piss water

I laugh at my own thought, knowing she's not far from doing supm like dat.

While the men talk and plan their attack for later, I look outside to notice Ry' deep diving into a phone screen. God you know me always come to yuh, duh mek she stress the boss if she find nuttin, please.

• • •

JORDANNE

I watch as Ryleigh tries to hide behind the fake rock, leaving her feet in view. Ignoring her, I shoot at Toni who is now running to take cover with her. None a dem no mek half ova that bumbo... except T'.

Toni is the one keeping them all alive at this point. The mode of attire are white jumpsuits, so that when the water that's diluted with red dye hits, there's no mistaking it.

Once you dead, you dead

Suddenly I feel water shooting past my face. I dodge and fall back, ensuring my white overalls nuh turn red. The spraying comes to a halt, and I take the opportunity to peek around my rock.

It's Michelle.

"Slyme! Yuh woman have it out fi we, move from mi rock bredda!" and before di man can protest, me push him out.

He rolls into the open with a hurt expression, "Di man betray mi!" he shouts, running for cover.

Fucking lucky.

I chuckle, leaning down to get a proper view of who's left in the game. Once we get down to two males and two females, it's every man for themselves, according to Ry's rules.

I notice it's myself, Ryleigh, Toni, Muuch, Slyme, Paw and Skulli that's left.

Paul tries to move off to the flag but T' takes him down. I bite back my laughter, knowing she'll take that as motivation to come after me. Everybody pon the sidelines ah dead wid laugh, as Skulli hisses and walks off.

Slyme is next to try but the girls shut him down. I watch as Muuch moves from behind the rock they share and starts spraying him mercilessly. The red dye ah decorate di man jumpsuit, and just when I think she's done, T' and Ry' joins her– emptying their guns on his frame.

Di man nah get a chance.

Paw uses this opportunity to shoot Ry' and by reflex, my hand moves me to shoot him, and even Slyme, who is already under attack.

"Drip weh di fuck!?" Paw shouts.

"Sorry bad head! A reflex!!!" I shout back.

Everybody is in an uproar, laughing at how quick I took them down from just them painting her overalls red.

Game or not, nobody nuffi hurt her

It's only myself, Toni and Muuch left at this point. I stay behind my rock, deciding to take them both out before moving to the flag. When I lift my gun to point at them, I notice Ramone running over. He wasn't in the game, since he has to keep tabs on what's going on if Ryan isn't.

"Pause the game!" he shouts, and I stand up, looking at how panic is dancing across his face.

Slyme looks over at me before we both walk towards a running Ramone. He gets to us, out of breath and covered in live panic.

"Before yuh look–" he starts, but instead of letting him finish I grab the phone.

What I see knocks the life out of my body. I stand still, looking at the phone screen while everybody around us asks what the issue is. My body stays frozen for what seems like two long years, before I feel Ryleigh tugging the phone from my grip.

"J..." her soft voice pulls me from slipping into evil.

"Get back inside the house," I murmur.

"What do–" she starts.

"Guh back inside the fucking house Ryleigh! Everybody!" I sneer.

Months of peace, months! And now this. Nuh know why me think life did ago nice forever.

Somebody ago dead

Everybody ago dead fi wah me just see.

67 | Solemn

RYLEIGH

"Yes that's me," I jump up, walking over to a woman cladded in her white coat. "There has been little to no progress, but we were able to stabilize him... Come with me."

My heart falls while I fight my tears, fearing it will be the last ounce of them for life.

The way mi a cry from **last week** till now is ridiculous. Mi just cyaa believe all of that happened.

One trip, we took one trip together as a team, a family... and now this?

I walk into the cold room, filled with sounds of beeping machines and flashing monitors. Standing at the foot of the bed, I look down at him while picking at my nails.

"He can hear you, mek mi give you some privacy," the words of the doctor meets my ears before the sound of the door closing.

Finding the will, I lift my feet to take me to the side of the bed, just to be closer to him. For every second that passes, I grow more and more cold inside. I can almost feel my empathy evaporating, my once warm heart, becoming pointless. The only job it has now is to keep pumping blood to keep me alive.

Nothing else.

"Training," I hear Slyme's voice behind me.

All him can go run up under him mumma

I hate everybody. Everything.

I look back at Slyme, standing in the doorway with a blank expression, before turning back around to bend and leave a kiss on his forehead.

"I know you can hear me, fight through it..." my hand squeezes his.

• • •

"Run!" Sue shouts.

"Squat! Yesssss! Climb! Yesssss! Climb girl!!! Climb!!!" she continues.

Aye, a wii diss dah lady yah enuh. I'm so tired and if I had known this was what the training would be like me wouldn't promise Jordanne nuttin.

"Ryleigh climb!" she shouts again.

A weh di bloodclawt duh dah lady yah?

"I'm trying!!!!!" I scream, and it must've taken all my energy because as soon as my words fall from my mouth, I'm falling on my ass with them.

Cho fuck!

"Again…" Jordanne's voice comes clear across the field, sounding cold.

Stern…

Poisonous…

Anything but comforting.

I put my pride aside and walk back to the starting point, noticing Jordanne is walking to the same spot. I get there and pick up whatever concoction Sue and mommy made to keep me energized and hydrated for these morning training sessions.

"Love. Wah di problem? You don't want to do it?" Jordanne asks, hovering over my figure.

Mi tyad.

"I do, mi just cyaa make it past the wall," frustration sends my hand up in the air.

"Ignore Mum's voice. She a try give you the same training daddy gave her, but after years of this, mi realize everybody different… and yah prove dat today."

Mi coulda deh a England with Lenard a drink tea and relax enuh.

Girl

A smile pulls onto my face at the thought but is quickly wiped away by the memory of the hospital visit yesterday. I turn to give the obstacle course one last try and feel when Jordanne pulls me in, just to plant a kiss on my forehead.

"Just know after this, a guns, so unless yuh wah jump and run like soldier forever."

I completely forgot that.

I sigh, pull out of his arms and wait for Sue's voice.

"Ready!… Two… Go!"

I take off and God know the doll tyad already. I find myself pushing past the barrels, hopping through the tyres, crawling below the ropes as they get lower and lower, making it through the maze, jumping over random sets of blockades and finally… the wall.

I stop and place my hands on my knees, catching my breath. Sue is already shouting commands, but I decide to tune her out like Jordanne said.

Grabbing the rope, I plant my feet on the wall and push away. Realizing that worked effortlessly, I continue this method straight to the top.

'Push away, plant feet upward, grab rope, pull up rest of body,' I whisper the words to myself while trying to inhale through my nose and out through my mouth.

Then nuh the top this sista gyal?!

Realizing I'm at the top, excitement starts filling my body and I look over to find Jordanne who now looks like a proud father.

My mannn!

Too excited, I lose my balance and slip.

Mi Bumbo

Before I fall completely, I use all the energy I have left to grip the rope and push myself down. Nahgo shame me.

I still have the gun noise, swimming and gas & smoke room left.

Taking a moment to look at my palm that's now red from rope burn and God knows what else, I flash them before looking over at Slyme who's holding the gun– fi bus me fucking ears.

Hesitantly, I jog to him, and without a second thought he starts releasing rounds of gunfire, close enough to waver my hearing, but far enough not to alter my hearing permanently– I hope.

Then afta me cyaa hear a thing right now! Me wah bawl and grab the gun but instead, I scream! Through all that, I can faintly hear Jordanne arguing with Slyme, but I decide to carry on with the course… 'cause me nah climb dah wall deh a next day.

Running off to the pool, built solely for their training, I drop myself in, still unable to hear much.

Mighty Gahd

The water awakens all my aches, with it being ice cold. After a second, all I feel are my limbs going numb. Dipping my head, I swim forward, trying to make it to the end without my lungs giving up.

I get to the end and realize there is no step for me to pull myself up. The single realization sends tears rushing to the forefront of my eyes.

Mi just wah float yah so and dead weh…

"The stick!" Sue's voice comes clear, and I look above to see a sturdy piece of bamboo.

Immediately my senses kick in and I splash water from the pool to soften the ground before jamming the stick into the muddy grass, to help bring myself up.

Thank God for lifting and boxing at the gym, 'cause mi woulda surely fail this rass yah today day.

I get out of the pool and start stripping from the wet clothes, leaving myself in nothing but a biker tights and a camisole. After wringing the excess water from my shirt, I use it to tie around my mouth and nose before jogging to the smoke room, where I can see Surgeon waiting.

Grabbing the goggles from him, I bolt into the room.

Almost there

Almost there…

Almost…

There...

"Two minutes Stevens!" Surgeon shouts.

Two minutes, I think to myself before entering the greenhouse that's a full blown smoke room right now. I stand there for what feels like a minute, only to hear Surgeon say, "Starting clock now."

Take the wheel Fada

I can barely breathe with the wet shirt blocking my airway, but I know if I should remove it, I won't make it to a minute.

Another moment passes before Surgeon says, "20 seconds," and might as well him did shut up, because his voice seems to have triggered my coughing. I'm hacking at this point while grabbing at my throat, tempted to remove the shirt.

"Ten seconds!"

I start moving back to the door, wanting to quit.

"Five!"

Jesus! no drop dung enuh!

"Three!"... "Two!" and before he says one, I'm swinging the door open.

"One!" and that's all I needed to hear for me to step out, dragging the cloth from my nose before falling on the grass– rolling onto my back.

My eyes flutter open to the clouds mocking me.

Mi nah lie me think we did ago dead ina dat

I cough and roll back onto my stomach before I feel hands lifting me and another trying to feed me water.

Me say all now mi a hear doubles. My eyes are buuuuurrrrning, and my lungs are giving up, mi sure.

"Love, drink," Jordanne's voice pulls me from my pain.

The water starts going down my throat, but I'm not sure how.

"Come," he lifts me, "we still affi go support Joshua ting."

I almost cry at the memory that today is Joshua's event. See why you must just deh with the nerd from school.

That's what you did

Okay, deh wid the nerd yuh sure is just a nerd and not the nerd weh almost beat up somebody fi skip yuh in the cafeteria line at school. Me shoulda know from then and there.

● ● ●

BUBBAS

Mi just wake enuh

Sexy Bitch: Yuh gwaan with yourself today mi hear.

Mariah Boo: Yeah girl, hear say you jump through

shit and all kinda things.

Muuch Boo: Lmao Mariah shut up!

Keif Boo: Ya'll ready? Unuh in yah a chat ago weh.

Dutty Foot: Me ready and a take pics already |attachment|

> Lorelle yuh pretty enuh dutty foot. Muah!

Dutty Foot: Mi know ☺

Sexy Bitch: Fi real.

Kelly: Can we focus on getting ready? @ Toni-Anne who no done do her makeup yettttt.

> One ting wid yuh Kelly, yuh ago miserable lmao! ☺

Kelly: And? ☺

Rolling my eyes, I decide not to reply. Mi and her know the little laughing emojis are there to cover the real tone.

Forgetting the conversation altogether, I move to the shower, not forgetting to put my music on. Kartel starts booming through the shower speakers causing me to lose myself in the almost boiling shower.

Moments later, I exit the room to find that Jordanne is still not back.

Like nobody no remember is a day party

I toggle to his contact to shoot him a text.

> How mi a get ready and yuh not even reach back home?

Mr.Sheer: |attachment| I'm downstairs actually. Just park.

> You sent that picture on purpose?
> We not fucking today Drip

Mr.Sheer: And if I take off the durag? Show you the waves?

> WE ARE NOT FUCKING. Mi ago do me face, bye.

Mr.Sheer: I'm coming up. ☺

I hiss and drop the phone, deciding to lock myself in my closet to do my makeup.

• • •

Well what a way that failed.

Jordanne opened my closet door in less than ten seconds and if I told you we were anything but nasty for 20 minutes, I'd be lying.

We're now pulling out and my eyes involuntarily find the guard house to hail Troopa but then I remember he isn't there anymore. This jolts my memory to JJ, causing my mood to sink.

Jordanne notices, because he glances at me before saying, "Ry, just mek we enjoy today."

I take his words with a grain of salt, knowing I'm dying to tell him Muuch is pregnant and ask him why the fuck Slyme likkle play thing and his little play thing a big fren?

Biting back my curiosity, I decide to ask the group what's the ETA, only to find out that everybody is waiting in the parking lot of the event.

Since last week when things went down at the house, security has been amped up to the max. Our shadow guards aren't even shadows anymore, and when we move in a group, it's even more.

Less than forty minutes later, we're pulling up to the venue. Just by looking around, I'm immediately impressed by how organized everything is. A group of guys start directing our car, the two cars before us and the one behind, to the private section for parking and that's where we find the rest of the team.

Jordanne gets out of the car and moves around to open my door. I step out and I can already feel the eyes on me.

This me cyaa badda wid enuh.

I can't remember us ever being this public since being together. The closest to this would be when he posted me on his story, and that was over two years ago. He takes my hand and almost immediately, we are swarmed by security– Slyme at the head of it all.

Dirrrrtyyy man

I can barely get a good look at what's going on but I can hear the mumbles as we come through the entry and while moving through the crowd. The DJ does the usual announcement and before he's done, I realize we're at the risen cabana.

J' pulls me in front of him and we ascend the few steps. This is when I get to look down at the crowd and venue decor properly.

It's so unique… Above the general patrons are umbrellas, jumbled together to shield them from the scorching evening sun. There are two bars, one premium and one for mixed drinks– both sponsored by Appleton.

T' came through…

I look over to the back and realize that's where the food court is– filled with different tents housing all sorts of cuisine.

Know a Sue section that

I look to the opposite of that, where the porta-potties are lined up, along with a station for the girls to sit in the AC room, have their makeup or hair touched up or pick up manual fans and feminine products. I spot my mommy, directing a young lady to her chair. Her doing what she loves in an environment like this brings a smile to my face.

"Yuh good?" Jordanne's voice pulls me from my stare.

"Hand dem still a burn me," I shout over the music, opening my palm to show him the rope burn.

He pulls them to his lips and kisses them both… "Ago order the liquor. When it come keep some ice in your hands."

"Okay," is all I say before turning to stand with my friends.

"Yeah man! 'Cause me think yah itch on pah yuh man wull night!" Mariah laughs, pulling me in.

"Then watch the girl weh just leggo her man," I giggle, slapping her shoulder.

"Me think yuh blind!" Mariah laughs and Lorelle comes and shoves her to the side before pulling me to the couch closer to her.

• • •

"Shots! Shots! Shots!" Keif shouts, holding the Azul bottle above our heads.

Me cyaa take nuttin else enuh

And I want to peeeee!

I duck Keif and move to Muuch, "Follow me go the bathroom nuh please. The rest a dem drunk as fuck."

"Okay!" she shouts over the music.

I tell Jordanne where we're going and he appoints us four shadows. Before I would deem it unnecessary but now? I wouldn't mind if we had eight each. Muuch and I climb down the stairs into the crowd and start moving through the sea of bodies. Just as we're about to step down into the restroom village, I hear a female's voice…

"Cyaa she that…"

My head snaps to where the statement came from but before I can say anything Muuch grabs me.

"No bother wid it," she begs.

Badda wid wah?

I was just going to ask her what she meant.

"Just did wah ask weh she mean by dat," I mumble, rolling my eyes before stepping away to a single potty.

Half the liquor gets out of my system in one go.

Pheeeewww, freedom.

Pulling my shorts up, I raise my foot to press the flush button. When it goes down, I flick the latch from 'occupied' to 'vacant' before exiting to walk straight to the pipes.

When I get there, mi no see Michelle, so I assume she's doing her business in one of the potties as well. While pressing on the pump to get water up the pipe to wash the soap from my hands, I look up to search for Muuch again, but Toya comes into view.

Ryleigh just wash your hands, get Michelle and go

Wash my hands…

Get Michelle…

Go…

I repeat the words to myself right up until I see Muuch exit the potty she was in. I watch her move to the pipes on her side and hear when Toya and two other girls laugh out.

'Wash my hands, get Michelle, go.'

Fuck it.

"A wah the issue Toys-R-Us?!" I shout, walking swiftly to their side.

"Ryleigh," Muuch starts but I wave her off.

"Dem a fuck the top killa and think them bad now," one of Toya's minions laugh out.

"Try mi today," I hiss, grabbing Muuch's hand as she tries to finish washing them. We move off but before we can leave, another one of their friend steps down, making it four of them.

This friend I know…

Then watch likkle Ms.Week Five

"Wah go happen if we try yuh mumma?" she laughs and that's all it takes for me to stop walking to really look to her.

"Mi know yuh gyal?" I sneer, looking her up and down.

"Yuh man know mi babes," she blurts out, sending the group of them into laughter.

"Yuh sure? 'Cause me woulda at least expect yuh fi even loooook like him spit pah yuh, but right now you look like yah lead the line to Red Cross."

Why me really stand up yah so a argue with them gyal yah?

Muuch yanks me away and I can see that our security is peering down at the small commotion.

I hiss! Anyhow a did me and anybody else we fight dem dung ina this.

"Tell di man me miss him big nice hood dung me thro–" before she ends her statement I grab a jumbo sized sanitizer bottle from the entrance and throw it.

Yuh bloodclawt

It slaps her directly in her face.

Not caring about the outcome, I join the guards and Muuch before moving back to the cabana.

• • •

The party is now at its peak and even Jordanne seems a little drunk. Masicka is performing and it literally couldn't be anybody else for the first staging.

Jordanne of course picks up and starts singing along , *"Di 'mount a yute ina di gravin, from dem diss me press dem out."*

The only lyric I know from this song is, "pieces from the puzzle ah life" and that's exactly what I wait to sing. Toni moves over to me, hugging me and singing on the top of her voice.

"Ruub bup bup bup buppp!" Paw shouts, holding his gun finger in the air.

"One Syyyde!" Ruse adds.

Then them happy sah?!

Masicka ends his set with 'King' and J' couldn't be happier. Singing and rocking me in his arms, he pulls his gun and lets off a few rounds.

Then wi nuh must deaf today

Mustttttt.

The vibe of the party slowly changes to the gyal segment and by now I'm on my man, Mariah is on Ruse and Toni is bending Kelly right ova.

Murdaaa!

Lorelle has a spliff in her mouth while watching her cousin Keif dance with Muuch. The vibe is immaculate me cyaa lie, despite wah me and the germs dem gwaan with ina the restroom village.

Somewhere along the way, Rygin King's, 3ZN starts playing and Jordanne starts whispering the lyrics in my ear. His breath is warm and filled with the aroma of marijuana, tickling the deepest parts of my core.

The hairs on the back of my neck fly up as he snakes his hand around my throat. Taking a deep breath, I bring the last of the water I've been drinking this last five minutes to my mouth.

Him definitely gone tonight

I don't normally get to see him like this…

Now I'm upset we didn't take the Porsche, because I'm sure I'll be driving us home tonight.

• • •

Jordanne holds my hand as we leave the party, surrounded by the team. This man still insists on leading me knowing him high and drunk as fuck. We get to the parking lot and he throws me the keys.

"Oh so yuh know?" I ask smiling.

"Neva leff the Taycan a yard fi no reason," he laughs, and I roll my eyes.

One day mi ago rev out dat.

One sweet day...

As I press to start, my mind takes me back to Troopa, Ms.Pat, Stace and JJ. A heavy sigh leaves my lips and what I thought tonight had healed, comes back ten times over. The flashbacks are much less frequent now than they were last week but they don't hurt any less.

"I know... I'm going to fix it," he mumbles, bringing the passenger seat all the way back.

Mind reader

"It's not your fault babe," I mutter while putting the car in drive to pull out behind Slyme.

Dutty nasty man

He chuckles at my effort to ease his mind, tone lacking all humor... and I know that means he doesn't believe my words.

Affi bring in Terry now.

I don't think him a handle it well on his own.

Nah handle it well at all

68 | Limbo?

JORDANNE

Today I'm on the roof watching the sun rise. Couldn't sleep last night– have a million things on my mind.

I've been out here ever since Ry' fell asleep. Anybody woulda swear a she drunk from the party, the way she drop asleep quick.

Sleep has never been easy for me though, so me deven a worry.

Yuh need fi tell her 'bout Rome

I don't...

And if shi find out?

Mi certain mi tell her him in a better place... Hell is by definition a better place than my torture vault.

Taking a long pull from my, fifth spliff? Sixth? I don't know, I watch as the birds move form tree to tree, carrying out their morning chirp. I've always found peace in watching nature. It's such an easy concept. They live to eat, reproduce and carry out their duties. If humans did so simple, life woulda better and I probably wouldn't have this much on my plate.

Swear.

I sit like this for another hour before feeling Ry's presence.

"Good morning," my words ring clear, my tone empty.

"What, you have eyes in the back of your head now?" she mumbles.

Without dragging my eyes from the view, I say, "Connected."

Her footsteps start inching closer, until they come to a stop behind me. Her hands find my shoulders and her lips find my neck... and for the first time since getting home, I relax.

"You didn't sleep," she scolds.

I don't answer.

"Jordanne, you have to sleep, it's been days."

Sleep? If I could, I would... believe mi.

Even cuddled up in her bosom, I still failed to drift off. No amount of weed, liquor, sex, gym or sessions with Terry seems to be helping. Trying not to start an international war, but day by day mah inch closer and closer to dat.

FLASHBACK

"Guh back inside the fucking house Ryleigh! Everybody!" I sneer.

Months of peace, months! And now this. Nuh know why me think life did ago nice forever.

Somebody ago dead

Everybody ago dead fi wah me just see.

"Man dem!" I shout, "Call the subs and mek dem know any and all shipment through Boston and Chicago fi pause."

"But–" Slyme starts.

I turn to look at him, long enough for him to read my eyes. I watch as the fear creeps into his body causing him to tense. In this very moment, me know this nahgo end well. The reaction Slyme just had confirms that I'm not myself anymore.

Took less than twenty seconds for me to feel this way after months of ongoing work.

Feel like two and a half years ago

Sitting down, I replay the video, hoping, praying...

... that all they did was leave a message.

"Drip–" Ramone mutters.

I don't answer.

"Watch the next video."

Sightly tapping my hands on the screen, I slide it to the left. I watch as a team of eight walk into the kitchen, dragging Ms.Pat from around the stove before bringing her to her knees. One of the eight has Troopa, his head covered by a bag and his hands tied up... while the rest seem to be searching every inch of my fucking house. Another one comes into view, holding Stace, before shoving her up against the island.

A cyaa... No him cyaa really a do dat

The anger starts soaring through my veins and I physically have to prevent myself from not spiraling.

If Stace is out there, where is JJ?

"The rest ah the cameras cut out?" I ask Ramone, not shifting my eyes from the phone screen.

"Yeah, only the kitchen and one from the garden them no damage," he explains.

Dead boy dem

My thoughts are answered by Junior running down the stairs, in an innocent attempt to help his mother. Before he can, the guy gun butts him, causing him to fall flat on his back, hitting his head on the tiles.

My body tenses, and the devil within me starts to dance.

Bredda...

Mi did say everybody ago dead just fi the invasion, but this?

My eyes move back and forth with the images showing a masked man trying his best to force himself onto a woman, ina me house dawg. Unuh know how me feel 'bout dat already, whether she a Rome baby madda or not.

Ms.Pat seems to be crying.

Shaking...

Begginggggg for him to stop.

He doesn't, and she makes the mistake of holding onto his leg in an attempt to save Stace from the wicked act, but...

... he shoots her... and the marrow from her brain splashes against the tiles and nearby walls.

My fist curls up into a ball from the sight.

A di woman this weh grow me. When Sue and Robert busy all over the world, she a di one weh make sure me safe, make sure me eat, make sure me go school tidy, help me with homework when she can, go PTA. She did everything.

Ms.Pat killa???

She was to retire at the end of May, only three months ago... and I begged her to stay while Ry' and I searched for someone new.

Ms.Pat???

Something shifts on screen, causing me to refocus.

The others who were searching, run back to the kitchen from the sound of the gunshot, finding the culprit with his pants down– still trying to rip Stace's clothes from her body. A tall guy that seems to be in charge grabs him from behind her, pulling him away. They argue for a moment before the guy in charge shoots Stace, but only in her legs. He walks over to her and whispers something and I watch as she tries to respond but fails.

They drag Troopa outside and pull out, leaving the women and a child lying on the kitchen floor. The video plays on, until I see Stace, dragging herself over to her son, blood smearing the white tiles. She nudges him but he doesn't respond, and my eyes start to darken.

Breathing becomes almost impossible... My hand tightens around the phone...

... and a wave of coldness takes residence within my being as I watch on.

Seconds later a team of my men arrive, pulling the injured out and then disappearing in the distance.

I push the phone back to Ramone who doesn't have to ask what's next.

Mi yard mi ready fi go...

PRESENT DAY

Ry's words pull me back to the present and I pull her down into my lap.

"Have supm fi say to you," my words low while I pull on what's left of my spliff.

She fans at the smoke while sitting up to look down at me.

"Rome dead," the words leave my mouth faster than I anticipated and in a colder tone than I wanted them to.

She doesn't answer but I can see her thoughts in her eyes.

• • •

RYLEIGH

I try to hide the pang of pain weh just reach mi chest as much as possible.

Weh him mean?

Jacen was literally just there... chained up, half dead. Three quarter dead, but still not dead-dead.

"What do y–" I try for clarification.

"Him dead, full stop," his tone has become eerie and my breathing has started to quicken.

Mi no want him think me too worried enuh, but JJ... If he wakes up, he'll wake up without a mother andddd a father? When I got the news that Stace had bled to death, it was enough to throw me into limbo, and now this?

The thought brings me to Ms.Pat and then back to Jacen.

I choke back a whimper.

"Why yuh look so hurt?" Jordanne asks, drilling his 'all seeing' eyes into my skull.

I–

Before I can stop myself I blurt, "Muuch is pregnant!" hoping that will avert the conversation to something else.

His eyes grow narrow, and I know he knows exactly what I'm doing, but I had to try.

At Michelle's expense?

Somebody had to tell him, 'cause him friend a move like school boy.

Wasn't our place, but okay

"Fi who?"

"Liam. Wah kinda question dat??" I hiss, standing in the process.

He doesn't answer, but instead picks up his work phone.

"Muuch no tell him yet!" I whisper-shout.

He looks away from the phone and back to me, "So why exactly yah tell me?"

"He's treating her bad, forcing her to do a threesome with the Toya girl, again..."

He looks away in deep thought but doesn't say a word. He then uses his index finger to tap his knee, scrolling through his mind no doubt.

Ignoring the feeling, I continue, "And me notice the girl friend a yuh woman," I almost hiss, folding my arms.

A smile plays on his lips, before he brings his spliff back to his mouth. The tapping on his knee picks up and just by seeing that, my body grows nervous.

"Yah hide supm?" he cocks his head to the side– eyes narrowed in mild question.

My mind shoots back to Ramone and I whisper a prayer, hoping he didn't say anything.

"Mi look like me a hide supm Drip?"

"Jordanne," he corrects me, "and yes... Reason why mah ask yuh killa."

I hiss and turn to move away, hearing when he takes a sip from his glass.

He knows, he knows, he knows

"Ry?" he calls, tone icy, "mek sure a supm light," he warns.

I wave him off, feigning annoyance, when really I'm about to pass out from fear. 'One foot after the other' I tell myself as a walk down from the roof. I make it downstairs and instead of using the glass doors to the side to enter the kitchen, I walk to the front door, just to avoid the space.

None of us have been back in there for more than a minute.

When I get back to our room, the first thing I do is text Ramone, requesting an encrypted call for tomorrow.

69 | Cards at Play

RYLEIGH

"**M**y condolences girl," Nadifa's tone is holding empathy. I don't answer but offer her a soft smile.

'Cause weh mi fi say? Thanks?

Sigh

I'm finally back at work. I should say in office, since I've been working from home. Dr.Drew told me to take time off but I don't see why. The kitchen gives me wicked flash-backs and since yesterday I haven't been able to be comfortable around Jordanne.

Ramone should be calling any me minute now.

"I'm going back to the office," I mutter.

"Girl you didn't even eat. You've been out here for less than five minutes," she pouts.

She reminds me of Mariah– a less crass version.

The thought of my friends bring a smile to my face and I stand, deciding to call them instead of sitting in the break room, nibbling at this salad with my work bestie.

"I have something to finish and send in Nadz," I lie. She rolls her eyes and pouts.

"Okay, me can help."

"Nadifa!" I laugh out, causing other eyes to turn at us.

"See mi mek yuh laugh gyal," she giggles.

I guess she did.

I'm so closed off to new friends and meeting new people that I judge everybody so harshly when they're probably being genuinely sweet.

Mhmm

Moments later, I'm back in my office with all of 50 minutes left in my lunch hour.

Ramone no plan fi call?

Trying to shift my mind from worry, I ring the group chat, hoping at least two of them are free. Lorelle, Mariah, Toni and Muuch pick up. Keif she probably a sleep midday... and I really didn't call for Kelly.

"Wahpm, your work no have duties and dem ting deh?" Lorelle starts off.

"The girl a sparks, probably done her tasks from 10am," Mariah adds.

"Mah turn unuh down. In a product meeting via zoom," T' whispers.

"Think the girl a dead," Muuch rolls her eyes.

"Like mi cyaa miss unuh??" I retort.

"Weh everybody up to fi the week?" Mariah asks.

"Have some outreach fi look ova," Lorelle goes first, pointing her phone at the pile on her desk.

Then why Digicel still a use hardcopy?

"I don't have much to do since I've been working through the nights while Jordanne haunts the house. Cyaa sleep if God tell him fi sleep."

"Mommy used to drop DPH ina him fruit juice," T' laughs.

We all join in.

Ms.Sue a supm else enuh man

"That can't shake him again," I chuckle before noticing that Michelle is tapping away at her phone.

Bwoyyy…

"Muuch, we call fi talk to you. You no have no class today so how yah tap so?" I query while bringing a piece of lettuce to my mouth.

Mi know nothing ova Law no mek people slap up dem phone suh.

"Taps and Roses the girl go," Mariah laughs.

"Unuh a gwaan like dem no dash weh man problem pah me. Stop act brand new," she rolls her eyes.

"Girl we cyaa fight datttt," Mariah laughs out.

"Weh di girl do a the party wrong though," Lorelle mumbles, forgetting to keep what I shared with her a secret.

Jesus…

I wasn't sure if Muuch wanted anybody to know about the incident at the party, but I had to share my frustration with somebody.

"Which girl?" T' whispers, peering down at her phone that seems to be in her lap.

Lorelle looks at me and I roll my eyes.

Me fi just end the call enuh

"Toya," Muuch mumbles, giving me a knowing look.

"Again?!" Mariah asks, "Gyal yah comin like return of the mummy. Every time me think she dead she rise again."

You know everything Mariah take fi joke? Haha!

"Mariah!" I fake scold her, giggling a little.

"A just di truth," Muuch agrees.

"Yuh tell him 'bout the cocomelon?" Lorelle asks, turning away from her work to focus completely on the call.

Toni also peers down looking for confirmation. Mariah is listening but is also busy fixing her hair.

Michelle sighs… and finally the tapping on her phone quiets.

"I'm not keeping it so I haven't told him ye–"

"Tankkk Ghaddd!" Mariah shouts in praise.

"God nah sleep enuh," Lorelle adds, before turning back to her work.

I take a second to observe Muuch's face. She's good at masking her true feelings but this time it seems genuine.

She alright with her decision then

Good. If she goes through with it, it'll be another secret I have to struggle to keep from such man. If him no see no belly in months, him just affi go think it didn't grow to full term…

Not our secret to tell

I know, but he can literally read through my skull. Mi nah ask, know mi know…

"I know the friend," I mumble, in efforts to change the topic from Michelle's decision.

"From?" Toni questions, finally closing her laptop and giving us her attention.

"Your brother," is all I say.

"Drip can mingle wid some gyal. No joke, yuh man terrible," Mariah laughs.

"When him bad a her man but when him good a yuh brother?" Muuch laughs, pointing her question to Mariah.

"Precisely," Mariah laughs. "Weh Unuh say the girl do?"

"The girl try talk to Muuch mlavve and J' own say she miss him big hood down her thro-" my words are cut off by Nadifa at the door.

I click 'end call' and look over at her.

"Miss I Have Work To Do And Will Be Busy But Is On The Phone Gossiping'… there is a very scary, but sweet looking chunk of chocolate in the front asking to see you," her words fall smooth, eyes filled with lust.

"What's this chocolate's name?" I ask, ignoring the heat filling her cheeks.

"He won't say… Say you shouldn't have any other man visiting so you should know who it is," she explains before adding, "I hope he's your brother and yuh can set me up."

I almost scream out from laughter, but manage to only giggle.

"He's my best friend," I laugh, before telling her to send him in.

Ramone no call we all now enuh

To soothe my anxious mind, I watch her leave before quickly sending a text to Ramone, letting him know not to call until I text again.

"Here he is," Nadifa pushes the door, not taking her eyes off him for a second.

No sah! I laugh internally.

Walking around my desk to meet him, I take the food from his hands.

"Nadifa bought me a salad," I smile, loving how concerned he is that I didn't bring lunch from home today.

"Couldn't have known that, BESTIE," he scoffs.

I laugh out, almost throwing the food, looking around him at Nadifa who is still swooning.

Yeah me man nice

"Nadifa this is Jordanne. Jordanne this is Nadz, my only work friend apart from Richard."

"Richard?" he questions, not acknowledging Nadifa.

"Dr.Drew."

"Call him that then," he squints and I narrow my eyes at him, using my mouth to point at Nadifa.

He turns and says, "Pleasure to meet you Nadifa. Thanks for keeping my wife fed when she refuses to feed herself."

Him really affi leggo the wife talk. The people dem ago talk say me married now

Nadifa looks at me, eyes fullllll of questions.

"Later Nadz," is all I manage to say.

"Nice to meet you Jordanne. Lata lyad gyal," she shouts before leaving.

The smell of the curry tickles my nose. Watch how me ago nasty up the people dem office with dah Indian food yah.

"Mi bring a million napkin, yuh good."

"Stop walk and read mi mind nuh J'," I breathe, watching as he displays a satisfied smile.

I take a seat at my chair and he does the same with my guest chair.

"Cyaa stay long, just did wah make sure yuh eat, so eat," he challenges me.

"I already had the salad," I whine.

"That salad?" he asks, pointing at the full plate of grass.

Yess grass me call it.

Laughing out, I decide to surrender, "Fine"

I spend ten minutes eating what I can, while we talk about soft topics, avoiding anything touchy, especially anything that was mentioned yesterday morning. While I push the last fork of rice to his mouth, he rolls his eyes. I've been alternating the fork between us in efforts to finish the food as quick as possible.

When I look down, the plate is almost empty. Picking at what's left my mind travels to JJ. I neva know me coulda love smaddy bad bruk pikny so.

Honestly.

"You know you can tell me anything right?" his voice soft, luring me into his truth spell.

I know him too well to fall for that shit.

If I tell him what I did, in a millisecond he'll switch from Jordanne to Drip... I can see the headline now, **"Young Girl, Strangled to Death in Her Office by Boyfriend"**

Dat nuh cute.

"I know," I assure him while my fingers find each other, just before the twiddling starts. Almost immediately I notice what I'm doing and in efforts to not give myself up, I start checking beneath my fingernails.

"Yuh ago pay fimi nails enuh, them curry up," I complain.

"I always pay for your nails Love," he smiles, observing my every move.

Grabbing at the mess we made, I start packing everything away. Anything to ease the guilt in my body.

The sound of my door flying open causes me to look up while Jordanne is unaffected.

"Ryleigh you wouldn't belie–" Richard barges in, only stopping at the sight of Jordanne.

"Don't mind mi bossy, I was just about to leave," Jordanne stands.

I move around to hug him. He nuzzles at my neck, squeezes my ass and leaves a kiss on my forehead before saying, "Training is at six."

He then pulls away and walks to the door and before he can exit in peace Richard says, "Nice to meet you Mr?"

"Sheer," Jordanne shares his name but doesn't extend his hand in greeting. Instead, he looks at me and winks before walking out.

I continue packing up all the things we were chewing on for lunch, when Richard speaks again, "Stevens you didn't say you were in a relationship."

Excuse me?

"I didn't know that information was required," my brows go quirking from confusion.

"Not necessarily, but if you're going to have visitors and behave in... that manner," he scoffs, now hugging himself and kissing the air.

"Richard!" I laugh out loud, wayyy too loud.

A now dem ago say unuh close

"Mi just a sayyyy... and yuh man look like him kill people fi less than looking at him wrong."

He does.

"Really? Is it the tattoos?" I take the oblivious route.

"No, his tattoos were barely visible. His aura, the eyes," he explains.

"What a way yuh a look ina me man eye. Mine enuh Richard," I giggle.

"Bun up!!!" he laughs. "Come in here fi whisper and tell yuh say the spot is down to you, Nadifa and three others weh me sure nah get it. So your bestie is now your competition."

"I'm sure when whoever gets it, the other will be fine."

"Just no tell nobody mi tell yuh, especially she," he warns.

"Okay, come outa me space," I laugh.

He exits and I quickly text Ramone again, letting him know I have ten minutes left in my lunch hour.

•••

JORDANNE

"Weh di man really a say to me?" I stare at Slyme in disbelief.

Hombre yah just a add more headache pon weh mi have already.

"Believe mi. Mi tell her dash it weh still."

"An she ago do dat???" I question, knowing the type he's dealing with.

"She no have a choice mi mek dat clear. She can be a single mother if she want. Dah part deh nuh up to me."

Weh di man a say?

"Mi stay far from unuh personal business as much as I can but me cyaa have a man pon me team weh have pikny a road and know... and nah mine it. Waste man style dat bad man."

Slyme just a disappoint me, Jah Jah God.

"If a did yuh get somebody pregnant a road, and dem no dash it weh, yuh woulda able fi face Ryleigh?"

"One... duh question mi 'bout me woman. Two... me is a man weh mek suuuure the abortion sealed and delivered... and why yuh nah use boots with dem caliber girl deh?" I heave a sigh.

"Drip, me love feel–"

"Hear wah, done. Just duh make none a yuh circus float ova into me life, please or else anuh you and Muuch again, a mi and you... fist to fist."

He laughs and shakes off my statement, not realizing how serious I am.

Hmmph

Nah wile him.

I look over at Ry' who is killing the gun training. For a blindy, she on target.

Waving my hands in the air, I signal to Paw to pause. He halts the training and she turns around disappointed.

Me baby...

I chuckle and walk to meet her.

"Time fi mi turn yuh ina sniper," I find her neck, just to whisper.

"Get a room!" Sue shouts from the barrier.

We both laugh and pull away to walk to the hills.

• • •

"Be gentle," I whisper, laying next to her. "Lightly pull the trigger, only when you're ready."

She shifts and steadies her hands. Her breathing? Not so much.

"You're breathing heavy."

"Cause yah whisper ina me earrrsss," she complains.

Cyaa help but laugh. The effect I have on her duh just shut off during these moments.

Affi memba dat

I stand to my feet and step back, giving her room to execute what I taught her.

"Remember the blow back, steady hands an–"

"Okayyy Jordanne," she cuts me off.

Well alright, mek we see then. This anuh show. The kick back on the rifle is wicked.

"Ry," I mutter worried that she's freezing up.

She doesn't answer. A few more seconds pass and nothing.

"Okay if you don't wa–" I start but the blow back from her shot cuts me off. She's laying on a thin flat platform that's now filled with dust from said blowback.

Her hair is now messy and her shirt has risen above her hips a little. I bring the binoculars to my eyes to check her shot.

PERFECT.

A smile appears on my lips and I look down to see her smiling up at me.

"Cyaa kill yuh fi dat. Yah sharpshooter," I chuckle, giving her a hand to help her up.

"So that's it, one shot?"

"Nah, should be more but yuh just mek me dick hard."

I watch as lust rushes to her eyes and she moves her hand down to feel it.

"Rock," she giggles, tipping up to kiss my neck.

"Play with me yerr, might fuck yuh right yah so," making my thoughts clear, I lift her into a straddle.

"Jordanne, let's go home. You too bad."

I laugh knowing it's true.

Using her to hide my erection, we move all the way to the car.

• • •

After two rounds of sex, we're laying down, intertwined, looking at the ceiling. The room is dark and filled with the aftermath of lovemaking.

"I love you," her words pull me closer.

"I love you too Ry'."

Turning to look at her, I move my hands to her nipple, flickering at it just for fun.

"Stop play wid me. I'll fuck you again," she whispers.

"Not a problem," I retort.

No know if she have memory loss, but my max is four rounds… with her.

"Joke mah mek. Leff mi nipple nuh," she brushes my hand away.

My laughter fills the room and I feel when she climbs on top of me.

"Babe?" she asks, laying her ear on my chest, above my heart.

"Yes…" is all I offer.

She stirs a little, heaving a sigh before asking, "Is there anything you wouldn't forgive me for?"

Wah dis now?

"Haven't I forgiven you for being in relationships without me?" I chuckle lightly.

"I'm serious," she mumbles.

"Weh this a come from Love?"

She stirs again and this time, she starts playing with the covers.

She a hide supm

Know that, just a wait fi she tell me because mi no have the time right now to go searching. Hopefully she learnt from the past not to do anything fi compromise the general safety of the family.

Hope

"Just wah know," she continues, her voice sounding meek– almost inaudible.

"Let's see… I can forgive you for anything, except breaking loyalty, be it in our relationship or towards the team."

Her body stiffens for a quick second before she relaxes.

The fuck?

"I forgave you for Emily though," she whispers, "And that was disloyal as fuck."

"And I forgave you for Lenard–"

"Wah?"

"Lena–"

"Jordanne please be for real, I'm being serious," she lifts her head, holding my gaze.

Me serious though, she knew I was coming back. Two years, three years… coulda ten years, she shoulda never go ina no relationship and wid a square at that.

"Jordanne," her voice pulls me back.

"Okay mi get that, but that was in the past, so right now, in this moment… loyalty is important to me," I explain.

"Mhmhhm," she breathes.

"Why are you asking?"

"Just pillow talk," she moves in to kiss me and before I can protest, the girl have me at her will.

Since she's naked, I take the opportunity to slip a finger into her pussy, while holding her steady at the waist, preventing her from moving.

She breaks the kiss to say, "J' I said no mo–"

"No what?" I ask, with a smirk on my face.

Since she wah try distract me with pussy fi try say weh she a hide, let's do that then.

Fair trade

Let's fuck it out of her...

"No what Love?" I ask, now capturing her breasts in my mouth.

The last thing I hear from her is a long moan.

Good... Let's get to work.

70 | Hurt

MUUCH

It's 2am and I can't fucking sleep. The conversation keeps replaying in my head over and over andddd overrr again.

He's sleeping so peaceful, not a worry in this world– breathing like an angel.

The thought has come to me about stopping that breath but surely Drip nahgo mek me live that down... or would he extend Ry's immunity to me?

Sigh.

My feet have been shaking as they do when I can't bring the peace of sleep to myself. Turning for comfort, I spot my phone on the nightstand. I blink a few times before deciding to pick it up, careful not to wake the wicked man side ah mi.

Fucking germs

Scrolling to Instagram and making my way to my DMs, I stop at Toya's chat. A tiny sigh leaves my lips before opening the box again.

Toy_yah: Me know a u tell di man fi mek me dash it weh but just know we a fuck b4 di 3sum! N AFTA bitch! Nah dash weh my seed u brighttt! Crazzzy! U ago tyad a mi cause mi neva look u man.

Dash weh seed?
Toya stop the wishful thinking.
Mi man nah fuck no gyal like
youuuu without condom.

Toy_yah: Dis need crowd
Toy_yah: The man live ina me good ole! A that wid unuh Uptown gyal. Unuh feel nice talkin n clean skin can keep man! Me say me nah dash it weh!

Toy_yah: Period. Point blank. Full stop.
Go bawl now bitch! Haha!

A really just the embarrassment fi me

The way me tell my friends mi and the man do threesome and now look? The gyal a claim belly– While I'm pregnant? I haven't even had a chance to tell him.

My eyes move from my phone to him, and all I can feel is disgust. Trying my best not to wake him, I climb out of bed and move to his personal phone.

The spirit ina me body just say search it

He sleeps with his work phone in his hand or right by his hand, so I couldn't get to that one if I tried.

Couldn't open it either

That too… Ramone have dem phone deh on super lock down.

Tiptoeing, I continue my walk to the bathroom. The door creaks open and he stirs a little, startling me. I steady my movement and wait for him to fall back into his dream-world before stepping into the bathroom and locking the door.

Mi hand dem a shake yuh fuck!

I try the password I've been studying for the past month… but nothing.

How???

I'm almost certain that's the correct code. Each time he would enter his password I would look at a number, deliberately looking away when he gets to the end… and when-ever I got the first three numbers, I wouldn't look until he got to the end.

Took me a month and multiple peeping days but wi bingo

8–5–2–3–7–3, I try again… Still nuttin.

Bumbo! My heart is about to jump from my fucking chest!

Okay knowing him, he might just change the last digit.

We ago block the phone!

8–5–2–3–7–4

The phone opens itself to me and I whisper a thank you to God himself. Wasting not even a single second, I make my way to his WhatsApp. It's coded, so I use the same se-quence of numbers to open it and… Bingo!!!

My fingers move through the app, searching for Toya but no Toya nah come up… only Toni-Anne. I relax, and tell myself to breathe. Starting from the top again, I browse through all the starting statements of each chat carefully, while pacing my breathing.

Seconds later, I open one from 'Blak Bunny'.

You deal wid dah ting deh

Blak Bunny: Bredda don't fuck wid mi brain rn.
Blak Bunny: Me done tell u say mi a keep it.

Cyaa keep it Toya. Me a fwd the money to u. Just deal wid it.

Blak Bunny: **When u did a bldclt fuck out mi ole u neva rmbr say baby can come? If it was that rass gyal u wuda mek she keep it.**

Duh mention mi woman. Yow just do weh mi say cause u no wah mi do it fi u.

Blak Bunny: **Do anything u wah bldclt do. U wah bet me mek di world know say we a fuck b4 the 3sum? Wah bet mi mek she know a style u use bring me ina unuh ting?**
Blak Bunny: **Ano my woman ago lef me.**

Kmt. More while man nuffi deal wid unuh enuh. Just lock chat man. If me check tmmro and dat no do, a it dat.

I quickly read through the conversation and di wave a shame weh lick me.

Jesus...

Before the threesome??? After??? Just like she said... Pregnant, just like she said... and he's not denying it's his so him fuck her raw fi real.

Realllyyyyy????

I notice a tiny pool of tears have gathered on the phone screen. Dat alone mek me even realize I'm crying, to how me zone out and disconnected.

Crying ova a man? MAN???!!!

So wah happen if she deal with it? If she dash it weh dem back at it again?

I think about calling Ryleigh, but I know if I do Jordanne will want to know what's wrong. Throwing out that decision, I call Toni instead... but there's no answer.

I try Mariah... no answer.

I try Lorelle... no answer.

Keif? Not even ring.

Sighing, I pick up the phone and call Ry'... she picks up on the last ring, sounding muffled or is she moaning?

"Sorry if mi a disturb yuh but can you come get me please? Duh ask just please," I plea.

"J' relaxxxx nuh," she hisses before coming back to the line. "Okay me a come in less than five."

"Thank you."

She hangs up and I stand, open the door and walk to the closet. Not caring if he gets up, I grab my bag and throw all my school stuff inside, along with a few pieces of clothes. While zipping the bag shut, I hear his footsteps moving towards the closet.

He walks in and cuts the light on.

"Michelle, why yuh up dem hours y–" his hands move from rubbing his eyes when he finally realizes what I'm doing.

A sarcastic smile presents itself on my face before I decide to reply.

"Yuh know exactly wah mi a do," I grab the bag, throwing it across my shoulders.

I move to exit the closet but he blocks me.

Of course

Refusing to say a next word, I shove his phone to him.

"Yuh go through mi tingz Muuch?" he asks, eyes riddled with panic.

I giggle, and try to move past him again, but thisss time he yanks me from the door, throwing me to the ottoman. My hand moves to protect my tummy before crashing into it.

Mi say a cyaa try dah man yah a try put him hand pah me

I look up at him, to see regret in his eyes. He looks down at his phone and back at me, still not moving from the door. I ease myself up onto the ottoman, just waitingggg for Ry's call.

He says nothing…

I say nothing…

Yuh phone a vibrate

Feeling the vibration coming from my bag, I dip my hand in and pull it out, answering without hesitation.

"We outside," Ry's voice comes clear through the speakers.

"Coming," I respond.

We she say? A must God mek nobody else no answer, 'cause only Drip can mek him let mi outa this house.

"Yuh nah go noweh enuh Michelle!" he starts… and I duh know weh me find strength mlovve but me push weh dat.

Bolting outside the room and down the stairs, I run to the home office to grab my laptop. I can hear his steps behind me, so instead of wasting more time, I grab the laptop, leaving the charger plugged in.

"Michelle! Mi nuh want di girl, yuh know that!" his voice is coming from the stairway.

I don't react.

Fucking lyadddd

Once mi see weh mi need fi see, mi no really need no explanation.

I exit the office and move to the foyer.

"Muuch!... just listen no babe," his voice moves from shouting to a softer tone, "mi no want her, ah swear."

Sound like him a try convince himself more than me. Repeating how much him no want a gyal weh him fuck raw? Please.

"Yah try convince me or yuhself bad man?" I ask, holding no emotion in my tone.

"A just after the threesome ting. Me just... Mi go back a one time behind yuh back."

"Liam STOP TELL LIE. STOPPPP TEK MI FI BLOODCLAWWTTTTTT IDIOT SUCK PUSSY bwoyy!!!" I scream, releasing all my frustration.

He moves to grab me but I bolt outside, slamming the door as I make my exit.

"Michelle weh yuh just call mi?!" he asks, flying the door open to follow me.

I spot Ryleigh's car parked outside the gate and start heading for it.

"SUCK PUSSY!!!" I scream, "Lowe mi mek mi leff. Di gyal done tell mi say unuh a fuck from before! A fool yuh take mi fah Liam. Mek gyal all a laugh ina me face a party! Done it yah so. Now, ina dah moment yah!"

I watch as his eyes change from soft, to hurt, to confusion and finally... cold.

• • •

RYLEIGH

"Open the gate!" I scream at the security, while watching them argue.

The guard is letting me know he only works on Slyme's orders.

"I'm here for herrrr! Open di gate!" I try again.

"Beez open the gate," I hear Jordanne speak before hopping out of my car.

"Boss? Mi neva know a you and I don't know the car," he explains, shakily watching as Jordanne walks up to me.

So it look like me fi only drive his car fi likkle recognition???

Yup

Slyme and Muuch are arguing, LOUDLY... and I can see that it's about to spiral any moment now. The gate finally starts to slide open, so I bolt through it, running to her rescue.

I pull her away while she continues to tell Slyme what she saw in his phone and what Toya apparently told her today, not forgetting to call him every thing ina di book. From suck pussy right back to germs.

Sigh...

Jordanne is unaffected by the drama and is just watching us from the palm tree nearest to the gate.

Man vex from me cut the sex short

"You really do mi this?! How yuh fi breed gyal like dat!?" Muuch cries.

449

Breed who? A cyaa Toya. A joke ting?

The fact jolts the memory of Emily being pregnant by Jordanne, while I was here going to school and not dating anybody– waiting for him.

Yammy-leigh

I shake the memory away and decide to focus on getting Michelle to the car.

"Come nuh Muuch!" I pull her bag from her shoulders.

"Yo she nah go nuh weh!" Slyme hisses, grabbing the bag from me.

Without thinking I move to grab it back as he walks off with it towards the house. He turns and nudges me off him, causing me to slip from the tiled steps to the asphalt.

Murdaaa! Come gwooope!

Then mi can shame sah? A tyad!

"Yessss kill off Ms.Jannette one daugh–" Muuch screams, but before she's done, I watch Jordanne grab Slyme and slam him against the wall.

Jesus now

Muuch comes to my rescue.

"I'm okay," I murmur.

"Gyal yah bleed," she hisses, picking me up while looking at my hands. I have a few scrapes from the asphalt on my fingers and in my palms.

And I just got over the rope burns.

"Pussy!!! Yuh lick yuh fucking head?!" Jordanne's voice transforms into pure venom.

I know what's about to happen, but I don't think Slyme meant to push me to fall. The fucking old Bridget's just nahv no grip!

"Jordanne mi good!" I say, hoping he'll see reason.

"Boss mi neva mea–" Slyme tries but J' isn't having it.

I can see the fear in Slyme's eyes, and I start thinking to myself… I really do not know Drip. Mi neva see Slyme look so yettttt. This cannot be my Jordanne, forcing fear into Slyme's eyes like this.

"Mi tell yuh fi keep yuh fucking circus to yourself enuh bredda! Don't!!!???" he asks, pressing against his throat with the back of his arm.

Slyme nods.

"So whyyyyyy mi woman a get call, ina the middle a we love making, fi come pick up her friend?"

Slyme stays silent. He couldn't have answered if he wanted to…

… And I don't think Jordanne needs him to.

Muuch's eyes find mine and I know what she's thinking. Same thing me a think, 'cause it sound like J' know wah gwaan and mek it happen.

"When you say you like her years ago, weh mi say to you killa?" he starts pulling the back of his arm away from Slyme's throat.

"If mi ready fi sekkle du–"

"Ifffff yuh ready fi sekkle dungggg. So wah dis yah keep up?"

Slyme falls silent again. This time the silence continues for minutes.

Neither me or Muuch shifts.

Jordanne breaks it moments later by hissing and turning to me.

"Car," is all he says… and I take Michelle and head to the car.

Her sobs become louder as we take our seats. Instead of asking her if she's okay, I move my eyes to Jordanne and Slyme. They're having a heated conversation that my ears aren't privy to.

Jordanne takes the bag from Slyme and begins to walk back to the gate. He gets to the car and throws the bag in the back seat next to Michelle. I look outside, to see Slyme watching from the entrance. My eyes move to the rearview mirror, catching Muuch, who is now locked in a stare contest with Slyme.

Jordanne opening the door pulls my attention from them and back to my fingers.

"Yuh good?" J' looks over at me, before putting my car in drive.

"I am," I mumble.

He looks at Muuch and shakes his head before pulling off. I take a deep breath, keeping my attention on the road as we head home.

What a night…

What a month…

What a fucking year…

71 | Layers

RYLEIGH

Michelle has been crying non-stop since we got in. We're in the guest room down-stairs, nearest to the kitchen, and I hate that, but it's where she walked to when we came in.

Sigh...

"Muuch, mi ago give you some privacy okay?" I whisper, trying to stand from the bed.

"... Stay," she croaks, and my heart winces at the sound of her pain.

Mi neva know Slyme woulda cause this. They've been happy for two plus years. She's never complained about him, nor him her.

Or was I just absent from the group, focused on healing myself?

Might be that... but regardless, mi nah expect this from Liam. She really loves him, like love, looovvve and Muuch anuh gyal weh walk and love off people. In fact, I think this is her first time actually being in love because according to her, Steven was simply high school fun.

Dat funny 'cause looking back now, I definitely neva loved Folan... but who coulda tell mi that years ago?

Muuch moves, taking the water bottle from my hand to gulp its contents, probably hoping to calm her cries but...

... it does little to nothing.

"I knew–he–I–" she starts.

"Michelle you don't have to explain anything to me. Process your hurt and when you're ready to talk I'll be right here."

I don't know if my words gave her much comfort because her cries just got worse.

Sigh...

I decide to join her beneath the sheets, pulling her into a hug. Used to do the same for Toni when she had arguments with Joshua, in first year at UWI.

"I could feel it, from the very start. Mi just... mi just neva wah believe," she starts again.

Staying silent, I decide to listen to her release. Her eyes hold so much pain, a hint of confusion and a tip of regret.

Sigh

"When we moved from flirting to a full on relationship, I asked him... Mi ask him enuh, if him have nobody and he kept saying no. I didn't believe so few times me search the phone and see things, but mah say a Slyme, him must did have woman before me or at least people him a fuck... so mi nuh pay it no mind. Mi ju–" her voice breaks.

I take a second to process the new information and she takes that same time to gather herself– biting back tears while wiping those already racing down her cheeks.

Mighty God

"Ryleigh, mi convince myself say him drop alla him gyal dem fimi, to how the bwoy nice and looooving. Yuh see fi yourself, so a nuh mad mi mad."

I nod, knowing it's true.

"And alla this funny because I'm not even angry with him... instead, I'm searching for what was missing in me... I–" she breaks down again, crying and coughing.

My hands move to hug her and I can feel fresh tears forming in my eyes. She has triggered my trauma. Nuttin me hate more than men causing women to question themselves.

"Michelle..." I whisper, fighting my own emotions, "duh say that outa yuh mouth again. It took me a while to learn this but yuh no need male validation. You're enough... and if he can't see that you have to gather yourself and move on. Only sounds easy, I know, but you just have to at a certain point."

"But I love him... and I–" she tries.

"Michelle, sometimes love isn't enough. If you run go back to him now, then he won't fear losing you."

Then hear all me

I said whatttt I said, mi neva say me live by it.

Come to think of it I do... 'cause one thing with me??? Me ago tit for tat. Coulda be the law maker of the galaxy, mi nah play no dolly house with nuh bwoyyy. Afta anuh me twin fi we cyaa separate.

"Ryleigh, what about the baby?" she asks, and I watch as worry fills her eyes. "I have a year and some change left in law school, how–"

My hands find her now trembling hands.

"Relax, I'm here... If you want to have it, we'll be right here. And if not, we'll hold your hand," I speak for the girls and I.

The room falls silent as we both think it through. Knowing her parents, this is going to be an uphill battle.

"Lucky thing me no tell him. I can peacefully make the decision on my own," she breathes.

My mind races back to me blurting her secret to Jordanne. Once again, he will just have to think the pregnancy didn't take.

Girl

I–

"Muuch," I mutter, thinking of telling her… but I don't. She's been through enough for tonight. I'll leave that for another day.

I grab the covers and pull it up to our chests. She releases a sigh, and my fingers find her hair, hoping to give her comfort until she finds sleep.

• • •

A light knock on the door wakes me and I slide from the bed quickly, knowing he'll knock twice if I don't get up. I open the door, rubbing my eyes and yawning from the lack of proper sleep.

"Going to work today?" J' asks, eyes not wavering from my breasts.

Mi cyaa keep up with dah white liver boy yah enuh

Maybe having a side gyal nuh so bad. I would appreciate the help.

"Yeah," I groan, stepping outside to not disturb Muuch.

"Why wouldn't you take the day?" he asks, finally bringing his eyes to mine.

"I don't have any more days," I yawn.

He fans at my breath, and I poke his shoulder. Ruuude!

"Can get some fi yuh enuh," he smirks, cocking his head to the side.

Why him think him run Jamaica?

Cause he doesss

Or is he talking about maternity leave? Mek mi ignore dah thought deh.

"Jordanne," I scoff, my tone slightly reprehensive, "I just want the position, that's all."

"I can get you that too," he smiles, teeth offering more light than the rising sun, peeking through our windows.

"Jordanne, some things I want to get for myself. My career accomplishments a supm me nuh wah yuh touch. You gave me an entire business before I was 20… and I'm grateful, but that's the same business that allowed me to buy a car, buy more properties and all that. So sometimes I feel like all my achievements really belong to you. Don't taint this one please."

I watch him search my eyes, trying to read my mind as usual.

"Alright pastor Stevens, yuh nahfi lecture mi. If a that yuh want then–" he mumbles before throwing his hands up in surrender.

Good, 'cause mi know him will go threaten the people dem weh already no like me.

His lips land on mine while I think, pulling me from anxious thought, towards comfort.

"I'm about to leave," he pulls away before diverting the kiss to my forehead.

I giggle and tighten our embrace, surrendering to the morning kiss storm. It has become a routine with us. He no longer sneaks out in the mornings, trying to not wake me. Since we both haven't been getting any sleep after the incident, I'm normally up before he leaves.

I like it…

If we ever get back to normal, where sleeping is concerned, mi no want it stop. Him have permission fi wake mi from the deepest sleep with them lip deh.

"Stop think 'bout fuck Ry' jeez man," he scoffs, feigning disgust before smiling.

"A who and yuh? Gwaan yah. Right now me tyad a yuh a beat out mi back," I laugh.

He joins and the volume of our voices bring my thoughts to Muuch. My head snaps to the door and he notices.

Kissing me a final time, he says, "Take care of her. See you at training."

So mi cyaa take a day from training, but him wah me miss work?

I groan and move out of his arms and back to the room. Mi can get another hour in bed before getting up for work.

• • •

"I have a question," Mrs.Wellz speaks, raising her hand with a smirk.

Mi have time today

I don't know which part of my presentation she coulda have question fah. It was so clear.

"Has HR cleared your choice of… outfits," her eyes dance across my figure.

I look down at my attire, struggling to find the continuous problem both these people and Jordanne seem to have with my clothes. If a skinnier girl were to wear the clothes, them woulda good, so wah the issue?

Ask her

My eyebrows pull together and I smack my mouth open to say something, but Dr. Drew blocks it.

"That's it for today everybody… Ryleigh stay for a moment," his instructions are spoken clearly.

I look to Nadifa who is now offering me a thumbs up and a wink. Her bubbly attitude brings a genuine smile to my face. As everybody gather their things to leave, I power off the projector before gathering my things as well– waiting for the room to house only myself and Richard.

"So…" he starts, "I think they're leaning to Nadifa, but I have the final say. Do you want it?"

Excuse me? Would that even be legal? Morally correct? What is it with men and wanting to hand me things.

I hiss, internally– frustrated at the thought.

"I'm sure she deserves it just as much as I do Richard," I mumble, disappointment clear in my voice.

He looks at me, searching for something else to say. His eyes linger a little too long at my bosom... and I think to myself, maybe I really should wear a tent to work... or, maybe I imagined that just now.

I probably did.

Shaking the feeling away, I watch as he moves closer to me, "I don't think she does but if you don't want me to intervene, I won't."

Then why him a stare down ina me soul?

"Is that all?" I manage to ask.

He seems to realize the tension created and backs away, putting distance between us, "I was thinking of joining you at lunch again today."

The one day mi mek the man sit down with me and Nadz, now him wah be a part of the crew

I don't know if I like it but, I guess.

"I mean, the break room is public," I breathe, clutching my work files tighter against my chest– leaving no room for wandering eyes.

"Good," he picks up his briefcase.

Maybe me a overthink?

Maybe...

• • •

JORDANNE

I listen as Skulli does the talking. Weeks later and we still don't know who invaded my fucking house. Searched every database ah New York and nuttin. Ramone a start Chicago next, although I doubt that would be the correct state.

Which enemy me or my father create deh so?

I don't fuck with Italian Americans. The Italians from Italy itself are enough to handle.

Skulli's voice pulls me back to reality, "So all shipment through Boston is clear to go again. Nuttin no come up across the East coast so that waterline is safe, fi now."

I watch as they nod in relief.

Man dem a move like them hungry fi shipment more than anybody

"Ramone?" Skulli calls, beckoning him to present on technology.

I pull my glass to my lips, observing the meeting. Ramone looks over at me for confirmation. I didn't have the time for him to brief me on any new information he has found, but since it's only my small circle and a few top leaders, I nod– giving him the go ahead to share.

Him have sense. Him must know what I would pass or not.

"Law," he starts.

"Lawww," they return his greeting.

"Supm came up in the database I just ran. Nahgo say which state but I'm going to say a name," he turns to me and I know what he needs.

I rest my glass down, ready to observe keenly. I'm about to watch who will have a slight shift in mood, focus or even breath control– at whatever name will be called.

A few seconds pass.

"Croc," is the word that falls from his tongue. The person that's having the shift in reaction is me.

Fuckkk...

I quickly mask my confusion and raise my hand, signaling him to stop. He does... and I stand, giving myself time to play it off. For another moment, I watch to see who else might have known that name before now, apart from me and Skulli.

"Man dem know di name?" I ask, searching for a shift anywhere amongst them but I come up empty.

Good

"Back to work then..."

I watch as they disperse, leaving Ramone, Skulli and I standing. Skulli's facial expression says all the things I need to say.

"How him woulda connected to Rome?"

The note that was left plays back to my mind.

Yo mans Rome let us know if he wasn't back in the Ps before a certain time, we wus spose to fuck shit up. Ay see man, my condolences blood. We ain't mean to kill women.

"Chicago," Ramone snaps, pulling me from the memory.

I know he doesn't mean it but he really has to work on not stating the obvious.

Jah Jah.

"Mi know dat yute, but how? When Croc supposed to deh and stay a Venezuela." Skulli asks, making his concern clear.

"Dat mi ago find out," I mutter.

The one thought that comes to my head is my father. That man always has secret after secret. I spent two years uncovering a shitload of them, trying to fix each one– killing people left and right, all while completing my degree.

While Ryleigh deh UWI ago bay party

That anuh the focus right now... If Croc is back, that's going to be a big problem... and if he knows we're together, even worse.

Ry' ago have me head pon a platter fi this shit, all because of Robert.

Man dead and still a cause problems

Jah Know.

72 | Anuh Play Pen

RYLEIGH

It's Saturday morning and mi excited bad-bad. Not because it's the week before my birthday but because today I get to go visit my cousins. They've always been visiting me but mommy would never allow me to visit them often.

Say May Pen nuh safe

As if I didn't live there right up until age eleven? And spent my summers there until I was fifteen.

So the lady behave

Ever since daddy him up and left, she's been extra cautious, for what? I duh know.

As me a talk 'bout men leaving, where is Jordanne? From week the man a dodge mi. My walls are grateful but my heart? Not so much.

"Ry' this too?" Muuch asks, holding up a bug repellent.

I look at her crazy before saying, "Yes girl, batlassss willll kill yuh after five."

"Batlass?" Jordanne's voice bellows down from the balcony into the living area.

I look up at him, wondering why the funny question and the weird expression plastered on his face.

"Yeahhhhh…" I drag, "the little things that sting, smaller than mosquitoes but bites worse."

He scratches his temple while looking at me. A light goes off in his eyes and his lips curl up into a smile, "SAND FLY?!"

"BATLASS!" I shout back. Pretty sure I read somewhere the name is Botlass flies, nevertheless a batlass fimi, bout sand-fly.

I'll leave him to call the little flying demons sandfly though. When one grab him, mi pretty sure a 'batlass' him ago scream out.

"Sand fly the thing name big farrid. You're not in Clarendon yet and I already can't understand you," he laughs, now making his way down the stairs.

"Whatever," I hiss, packing all the things my cousins have asked for.

"What was that? Mi couldn't understand," he laughs, moving to Muuch and I.

He tries to pull me into a hug but I shove him.

"Batlass it name," my mother confirms, coming from outside.

"Definitely sand fly," Sue disagrees, coming in behind her.

Bwoyyyy...

Jordanne's eyes find mine and we both start laughing. Our mother's walk over to us, hugging their child and switching to hug their child-in-law, respectively.

Yuh married?

Might as well.

"Ms.Janette that thing I needed to talk to you about, we can talk in the office before I leave?"

I look between mommy and J', wondering what they have to talk about that's so private. My prying mind will always ruin a surprise. Thinking of my birthday, I don't bother asking.

Moments go by and Muuch and I have finished packing all the things we'll need as if May Pen isn't less than an hour away.

We frighten yes, we are.

It's to be myself, Jordanne, Muuch, Mariah and... Liam, since J' swears up and down he can't leave his righthand while he has minimum security. I suggested Ramone or Skulli but no. At this point him a try force Muuch into a confrontation with him nasty friend.

Hear how me a deal wid him. He was my favorite just last month

And him ago be my favorite again when Muuch moves on or forgives him, not now.

"Ready?" Jordanne's voice startles me. You would think knowing him for years would make him less intimidating but... think again.

"Yup."

He grabs our little goodie bag and the duffel bag that's filled with random things for my family, before exiting the house.

"Mommy me gone," I start my farewell, looking at my mother who's just now making her way from the office with a worried look on her face.

She notices that I notice and quickly replaces it with a smile.

Too late.

"Wah happen?" I start my dig, as she walks over to me.

"Nuttin Ryleigh. Tell your uncle me say send breadfruit fimi," she switches the topic effortlessly.

Hmmm, okay... I guess.

"Okay, I will," I assure her. "Bye Mrs.Teathers," I turn to hug Sue.

"Sue Ryleigh, just Sue," she laughs.

I smile, and walk out of the house, leaving her and my mom to do what they do best– gossip.

When I step outside Jordanne is getting into the GLE, followed by Muuch and Mariah.

Girl reach and no say nuttin

I notice three other cars and shrug. When I hop in, I look at Jordanne.

"This is minimum security?"

"With all that's going on, yes," his answer comes soft and comforting.

Well okay.

Moments later, we're at a Juici Patties drive-thru and I'm excited for a cheese patty.

"I don't know how unuh like Juici Patties, it just tough and shelly," Muuch complains.

"Fi real," J' agrees.

I shoot a wicked glance at him. He catches it and chuckles.

"Only from Spain to Downtown like Tastees. Unuh patty taste bad just like unuh KFC."

"Babe how the KFC get ina it?" Jordanne laughs.

"A true enuh, the KFC them from country well fry," Mariah backs me up.

"And Juici Beef originated in Clarendon so we get the best ones," I gloat.

Jordanne pulls down to the speaker.

"So why yuh nuh wait until we get there to prove your point?" he asks, rolling the window down.

I roll my eyes, "Mi hungry now."

"Hellooo," the girl's voice comes muffled through the speakers.

We spend two minutes putting in our order and another two or five waiting in queue to get to the window. My head is now buried in my phone when I notice the girl from the window is talking to me.

"Long time mi no see yuh browning," she smiles.

Me??? See me?

It takes me a moment to realize it's the girl that was there most evenings at the branch in Liguanea... and look how me avoid dah branch deh with the drive-thru excuse.

I force a smile before saying, "Neva recognize you enuh pretty."

"Yeah goodz, them put mi yah so now. Surprised yuh nah order red peas," she giggles.

Mi bumboclawt

I almost choke on nothing but air. Jordanne looks at me while slowly handing me the orders for everybody.

Jesus mi hottt.

"No man, not today," is my only comeback.

"Okay girl, well yuh know weh mi deh now, so drive yah so when yah do your evening run, I'll set yuh–"

"Thanks!" I cut her off, hoping she'll shut up now.

"Then a when yuh start buy red peas? When you only like Jannette or Sue own?" Mariah asks.

I–

"I like the one from the Liguanea branch," I whisper so low, I myself barely heard.

With my head turnt, I look to see Jordanne's reaction, hoping he hasn't picked anything up. The car goes silent while we pull out, apart from Muuch and Mariah tapping away at their phones.

"Like she see yuh well often, that she remember you outa hundreds of people..." J' breaks the peace.

"Yeah," I mumble, more to myself than him while bringing the patty to my mouth, hoping to have an excuse as to why I can't clearly answer his question the next time he asks.

Forgetting how hot beef is, I wince and do the 'HOOHAHUH' mouth thing.

He doesn't ask anything else, instead he tells me to connect my phone and play what I want.

• • •

We come through the toll leading into the parish and I can feel the excitement bubbling up my throat.

I'm ready to point at everything.

I've convinced them that we need to stop in the town to get liquor for my uncle and him bagga friends– knowing full well we'll go through two smaller towns before getting to my cousins.

As we turn onto the local main, I'm already pointing at where I used to stand to get a taxi while in primary school. My happiness amuses Jordanne and I can see how satisfied he is. Muuch is finally in a better mood and Mariah wants to know all the details, claiming she wants to live here someday, if a so her daughter ago grow happy.

I keep pointing until we get to the bridge. Muuch notices, that the stoplight doesn't work, and there's a truck in the bridge. It amazes her how everybody stops without the lights, allowing the truck to come through before they enter.

Nuff day dem stuck ina dat

"There is another bridge, nuh know why she force we fi drive yah so," Jordanne laughs, tugging a handful of my hair.

"This route is nearer," I snicker, knowing I only wanted to point out things.

A few meters down, I start pointing at the bus park, telling them how people only die in fives there. Then the library, the clock and the infamous Stork Street. I continue my tour until we get to Guinep Tree.

"Weh di guinep tree?" Mariah asks, looking around.

"From mi born mi no see no guinep tree girl, I couldn't tell you," and with that the car fills with laughter.

I watch as Slyme and another guy exits the car and enters the wholesale.

Muuch sighs…

Minutes later they exit with crates of liquor, loading the trunk of the car before us.

We pull out and I start my little tour again. The great house, the acid lake, the bauxite plant… but after that it's nuttin but houses and cane piece mlovve… so I take the time to nap, no longer interested in being a tour guide.

Noise is what pulls me from my sleep and mi just know we a pass through the small town before we get to our destination.

Yup

I prop my head up to look and just as I expected, not a thing no change.

Less than five minutes later we pull up to my old dwelling. All eyes are glued to the four vehicles as they park.

Watch my anxiety kick in, in 3… 2–

I fly my door open, not waiting for Jordanne, when I spot my cousin swinging.

"Big gyal like yuh still a burden the swingah?" I cackle out.

"Cee?!" she hops out, running towards me. I run into her and we scream, like the annoying 21 year old girls we are.

"Mhi nevah know yah coom dung yah ina real life," she laughs. "Pardon my manners. Hi I'm Trisse," she says, holding her hand out to Jordanne who has somehow appeared behind me.

"Hi Trisse, your cousin talk 'bout yuh every time she pass a tree," J' chuckles.

I do, I do, the gyal can climb.

"I'm Mariah and this is Muuch. She nuh always so grumpy, she have man pro–" Mariah starts but Muuch elbows her.

"Ahwuh!" she whimpers.

"Nice to meet you guys, finally," Trisse laughs.

My uncle makes his way out of the house, and I greet him, immediately delivering my mom's message.

• • •

JORDANNE

I watch how happy my woman is… and if I could put this little district in my pocket and gift it to her I would.

Girl bring me go all 'bout within the **past two hours.** I've learnt where she went to church, where she swam, picked plums, drag cane, run box truck, race and most importantly, the wall she sat on every Sunday to eat her ice-cream in her Sunday's best.

I've also come to realize that my childhood was severely lacking. I can't remember doing much more than riding my bicycle or playing my little Nintendo.

We're now on the way to the football field, where apparently most of the community comes on Saturday evenings to watch the local league. All her other cousins, young and old, have gathered with us to walk to the field.

Mi like di experience, I might bring her back more often. I've been to Clarendon to visit the South central team numerous times, but never to this point of the parish.

"A Cee that!?" a male voice asks. My eyes find the body to match and I watch as he throws his boots over his shoulders.

"Kirk?!" she asks, spewing as much confusion as me.

"A mi man," he chuckles.

The fuck funny? This betta be her cousin too.

I don't know what it is but when it comes to her the jealousy is unbearable. I've always wanted her to be mine– emotionally and physically.

Boy Lenard ruin that

Knowing she's been with somebody other than me, sexually, drives me crazy– daily too. And yes, I'm aware I was the one that left her but dat nuh change the fact.

She runs over to the… male and they hug… way too long for me.

They hugged for less than two seconds

Shoulda been zero seconds.

She drags him over to us, "This is Jordanne my boyfriend."

Man… husband, I correct her internally.

"And this is Michelle and Mariah, two of my closest gyals."

"Well everybody, I'm Kirk," he smiles, holding his hand out.

I don't offer him my hands, nor do I offer him any form of welcoming gesture. Mariah picks up and grabs his hand, shaking it, followed by Muuch. Ry' looks at me and shakes her head, before we continue the journey.

We get to the field and I'm surprised to see the crowd of people. Fi a small place, a nuff people deh yah killa.

• • •

The match is heated and in full swing. The score is 1-1 and Ryleigh is screaming louder than I've heard her before… Louder than when my–

Just know she loud right now.

"Kirk act like yuh have bloodclawt sense!" her cousin Trisse shouts from the sidelines.

My team is captured by the game as well. Everybody is, except for Slyme, who has his eyes glued to Michelle that's busy talking to a random guy.

The crowd goes wild all of a sudden and I look up to see that the Kirk person has scored. He runs across the field, pointing to–

Who him a point to? A cyaa mi woman killa.

All my guards' heads turn to me and I find myself shaking it 'NO' instead of nodding 'YES' for them to pull him from the field.

I still don't know if that's her cousin… Almost sure he isn't since she nuh introduce him as dat. I glance over at her. She's clapping and screaming completely oblivious to what's going on behind her.

More time passes and a commotion ensues, causing a few people to run to the field. According to onlookers, somebody is badly injured.

The Kirk male person, runs to the sidelines.

"If dhem cyaa find nobody dem haffi give up di match and wi win," he explains, breathy.

In what world of football, one team nahv somebody fi sub?

I groan.

Paw laughs before saying, "And di match nice enuh yute. If a never work me deh mi join dat."

He gives me an idea…

No, buil

Ignoring my logical thoughts, I start stripping from my shirt, leaving just my merino on.

"Yah go in boss??" Paw chuckles.

I don't answer. Instead, I take my phone from the pocket of my Nike Tech joggers and hand it to Ry'.

She looks up at me confused, "What are yuh doing?"

"Play football. Cyaa mek Kirk team win."

"Kirk's team is our community team," she laughs, "but do you, me ago turn cheerleader," she smiles, before tipping up to kiss me.

Her cousins swoon and start mek some typa mating call noises.

Jah know… Can't remember when last me play ball but, this should be fun.

I walk to the other side where the opposing team is, and offer myself after convincing them of my skills.

Man dem no wah nuh amateur join dem thing at all bad head

Moments later the whistle goes off and I join the sport. Adrenaline rushes through my body and mi cyaa believe mi give up ball years ago. I move through the field, passing the ball to those in white, carefully shifting those in blue with ease. This continues until the score moves to 2-2.

I can hear Ry' shouting from the wrong side of the crowd cheering me on. I chuckle at her tiny voice, straining to get to my ears. Noticing that Kirk has the ball, I decide to tackle him for it.

We put on a show, fighting for the win. Mi affi give him props, him nuh bad but—

I exit my thoughts and deliver a 'salad' swiftly moving to recollect the ball, dribbling to the perfect angle from the goal, before I kick. The Keeper dives in the wrong direction like the worthless fuck he is and the crowd goes wild.

2-3... Beautiful.

I hear my baby screaming and I look to her. She and di man dem alone happy from that side a di field. I extend a point to her and then a half heart with my thumb and index finger.

Cornnyyyy

I laugh at how fun the game has been, the entire day really.

The game goes on for another three minutes before the referee blows it off. I jog back over to them and plop down on the grass.

"Not mi man can do everything ina the world," Ry' laughs, handing me a Gatorade that she claims to have known would come in handy.

Affi give her, her props. She'll be a good mother... If you ask her fi a pain pill right now she have it too.

"Sir mi no appreciate how yuh come mek me team lose enuh," Trisse says, hovering over me– her arms akimbo.

"Yuh team no good man," I chuckle, and she laughs before warning Ry' not to bring me back.

I like her cousins, the family, the vibe. I can understand when she says she misses her old parish now...

Real

73 | Law Abiding

JORDANNE

"Nah say a word without my lawyer enuh so right now alla we time a waste," I sneer.

Dem man yah really feel like me dumb enough fi answer dem question.

I cooperated with them in the initial stages of the investigation. Told them what I wanted to– mostly the truth. With Junior being involved, it makes it a bit harder for the usual plan to take form.

Pay the commissioner... and wait for things to fall in place

Not this time though, with a child involved they continue to disobey orders, pressing my family and I for more information.

"It just seems to me that you're always in the middle of these shootings," the police that's interrogating me asks.

Mr.Wellz...

Pussy

I look at him and refuse to grant him the least bit of my energy.

"Yuh nah answer Mr.Sheer, just like yuh fada eeh?" he smirks.

I use the time to tap my index finger against the desk, giving the room a once over before releasing a heavy sigh. It's a **day before Ry's birthday** and me just wah have a peaceful get away with my woman.

"Years ago, the shooting at your family home took over eight lives. The commissioner dismissed the case, claiming property defense... Didn't seem like that to me or anybody else on the scene."

I raise a brow at his pathetic grab at a floating straw.

He continues, "Now this time around, you leave the country and more lives are lost, a child is in critical care and your house guard is missing."

I start to become annoyed, this time not masking it.

"So tell me Mr.Sheer, do you have enemies we should know about? Because it seems to me that every year or two, we should look out for a mass murder involving you."

I look up at him, holding his gaze before smirking.

Like him wah me add him to the murders so?

Easily…

I hear a small commotion coming from the corridors and I don't have to ask who it is. The door swings open and sure enough Washington comes through.

"Mr.Wellz mi hope yuh nah question my client without me being present," he chuckles sarcastically.

"Just a share some simple observations."

Washington takes a seat next to me while handing me a bottle of water. He flops his briefcase on the table, loosens his tie and pushes the chair away from the desk all while looking at Wellz.

"What's the premise of the interrogation? Has my client not given enough information to aid unuh likkle investigation?" he asks, waving his hand around aimlessly.

I shift in my chair, tempted to answer my phone, that's now going off in my pocket.

Know a Ry'

She alone call so much times back to back.

I look at my watch to see that it's 3:21 in the afternoon. I should be getting her from her nail appointment at Lorelle's place, like I said I would, before taking her to Mum's. Don't know weh she want with her the day before we leave, but mi nah get ina mother and daughter-in-law business.

"In that case, we should be free to go," Washington snaps, grabbing his briefcase and jumping to his feet.

His words and sudden movement bring me from my thoughts. I stand and look at Wellz up and down.

Long time mi wah dash weh dah miserable boy yah.

Smiling faintly at the fun thought, I turn to walk out the door.

Waste a mi fucking time killa

• • •

RYLEIGH

"After him nah answer," I hiss, looking at Toni-Anne, who is now forcing Michelle to go with French tips for her toes.

"I like white!" Muuch complains.

"White toes a fi people who think dem ah Instagram model girl. Just try it nuh," T' fattens her point.

Muuch ignores her, finally turning to me, "Yuh know dem ever busy. Call him again in a minute."

Busy wid wah?

Slyme did busy wid Toya. Jordanne probably busy wid throatgoa–

I shake the thought away, deciding to back up Toni's argument, "Yeah get the French-ies, it just cuter. Everybody has white toes now and once everybody join the French train, the real dolls dem ago switch again to supm new."

"Yup! Just like how a tape-ins now instead of wigs, Tory instead of Bridget's, Hermes if yuh can reach it! Chrome Hearts, Gallery Department and whatever else for the men instead of Polo this and that," Toni adds.

Five hype enuh

"Alright T' we get it," I laugh, "do weh the likkle bossy gyal say Muuch. She know the trends fi real. That's why she so good at Marketing," I giggle, knowing Toni won't give up.

The lady scrubbing my feet, goes a little too hard and I pull back. She says sorry and I offer her a small smile, letting her know it's okay. The door buzzes open and I look to see Lorelle walking in.

"Watch mi gyal dem. Unuh supportive eeh," she laughs, walking over to us while greeting her employees.

"Tell her a French toes a the thing nuh," Toni starts again.

"Toni-Anne, Muuch have her own mind!" Mariah laughs out, finally getting off the phone with Ruse.

"Fine," T' laughs genuinely, "but no complain when unuh a match everybody else," she rolls her eyes.

Just as I'm about to say something else my phone goes off.

Mr.Sheer ❤...

Now him ready fi link me? I roll my eyes, feigning annoyance before sliding to answer. I let it ring almost to the end too.

Cyaa so available.

"Who this?" I answer, unable to hide the prominent happiness in my tone.

"Same man yah dead ova," he chuckles.

"Nah dead ova no bwoy weh cyaa answer dem phone enuh."

"Station me a come from," he lends me new information.

Station???

"Station?" I voice my thoughts.

Thought the commissioner was on the payroll?

Mi really need fi understand everything there is to understand about that side of his life enuh.

"Yes Ryleigh station. The place weh house the most battyman ina uniform, but when I get to you we can talk in person."

Guess it serious.

"Okay," is all I offer.

"You done? Mah get to you in the next 10-15 minutes."

"Good, I'm almost through," I mumble, watching the nail technician work her magic on my toenails.

"Ah, see yuh when me drop a foot. Love you, more than mi own life."

"Love you too J," I smile, pulling my friends' attention.

"LoVE yOU tOo J," Mariah mocks, causing us all to laugh out.

• • •

Moments pass and Lorelle has left to go get something at home and Toni is now leaving to go get Kelly. Mariah has decided to stay here with Muuch and I, since Jordanne is on his way to get us with the intention of dropping by Sue's.

I'm on my phone when the door buzzes open. I don't turn to look who has entered, since I know where all my people are.

"Mi rass," Mariah shrieks lowly, slapping me to gain my attention.

Dah gyal yah man. Me a try find out if dem people yah a carry me orders before we leave tomorrow. Serve me right for waiting until the last minute to order vacation clothes.

I just wasn't in the mood, I'm lowkey afraid to leave the country again after the last time, but Jordanne has assured me that it'll only be us and the shadow guards, nobody from the inner circle, so the house and everybody should be safe.

I don't know how he's back to normal already… and if he isn't, he does a good job of hiding the trauma.

Or him just used to loss?

Maybe…

"Look nuh!" Mariah whispers, shoving her lips in the direction of the receptionist.

I can't see who the person is clearly, since the dry wall is partly blocking the entrance.

"A who?" I ask, locking my phone to drop it in my bag.

"Throatgoat77, live and direct mlavvve."

I almost fall face forward at her comment.

"Who?" Muuch questions.

Week five masah

I watch as Michelle's mood shifts. She try nuh badda with it enuh. Dem gyal yah nuffi change mood.

Dat mi know

I hiss and lead the way to the exit. As we're walking past the tiny entrance into the reception area, Muuch almost slips, while stepping down.

Mi warn unuh 'bout dem zero grip, old slippers yah enuh

She grabs onto the counter and her heavy keychain brushes against likkle Ms.Five's hand. As Michelle is about to apologize, she's cut off by a loud hiss.

"Watch weh yah do nuh big gyal! Suppose yuh did markup me skin!?"

I'm taken aback by her response, 'cause this cannot be real.

"Whuu yah chat to Rent-a-front??" Mariah's voice now loud, dripping in hate.

Week Five stares at Mariah for a moment, before hissing and turning away. I hold Michelle's hand and lead her to the exit where a customer is now holding the door open.

"Thanks," I breathe, while offering the middle-aged woman a soft smile.

I'm trying my best not to be angry. Michelle is still pregnant, with only a week left to come to a decision of whether she wants to keep it or not. Now is not the time for her to stress. The first trimester is fragile, I should know.

That wasn't your fault

Me nuh believe that.

Plus… the last time me fight was when, in high school? When Toni nearly kill Ghale.

"Dem bitch yah no know who dem a ramp round enuh," she picks up.

Alright, a it diss.

Dropping my purse on the floor, I kick my slides off and move to her within a second.

"Aye gyal weh ya–"

I fold my fist as best as I can with the medium length nails and connect it to her throat.

Throat goat yuh say bitch

She grabs at her chest, gasping for air and I use the opportunity to grab her hair, twisting it before slamming her against the counter.

Her wig glue on good though

The receptionist, screams and moves to the back.

"Ry!" Mariah's voice comes clear, but I ignore it.

Week Five is huffing and groaning, but I don't stop. She bigger than me ina body so she fi take lick. Wrapping the hair tighter, I lift her head up, pulling her neck back to look at me.

"Yuh know how long me wah grab yuh gyal?!" I ask, unable to recognize my own voice.

She grabs at my shirt, but I step away. Then shi start swing wild, only hitting the air and a standing vase.

Lorelle must kill me

Look how we a mash up the girl things.

A few of the customers and nail techs are begging us to stop but I can't control my hands. I plant my foot firmly and swing her to the floor. She lands on her side, wincing and cursing. Moving over to her, I grab her firm enough to start delivering blows... but somebody's hand is now on my shoulders.

"Ryleigh get up!" Mariah's voice intercepts my hand on the way to her face. I look up at her for a second.

A second too long...

Pppeoprrrrrrr! The girl flip me!

I land on my back and scurry away before she tries again.

"A weh di bloodclawt! Aye gyal!" Mariah hisses before jumping in.

The door flies open, I don't look up to notice who it is but less than two seconds later I'm fighting again.

Somebody new...

My hands are going wild as this new body fights. Soon enough Mariah has Week Five and I have whoever this is.

Dah person yah strong yuh fuck!

A blow is delivered to my abdomen and I wince before moving my hands from above me to find the area where pain is now shooting.

 I almost give in.

The person grabs me, lifting me to my knees, before they step back. The female tries to grab at my hair, but I duck and use my feet to sweep her from hers. Her body falls and I look at the figure.

Then unuh look pah big bloodclawt Toya she.

Big Leyland, overloaded cane truck, suck cack Toya

The sight of her irritates me and I pounce, deciding not to bend, instead I start to kick.

Ry she pregnant

Woahh... The thought causes me to pause.

I snap my head, trying to find Mariah through the tiny crowd that has formed in Lorelle's nice, clean, upscale beauty bar.

She definitely ago done we

My eyes find Mariah who is busy sweeping the floor with Week Five. Then a cyaa she did a tell mi fi stop.

I'm distracted by Mariah's skills, and Toya tries to stand but her movement prompts me to shove her back to the tiles. She grabs my leg and drags me down with her.

A must a fucking alien baby she a carry. What a way she a partake ina WWE.

The door flies open and I hear a gun cock.

Fuck now

"Ryleigh get the fuck up from the floor," Drip's voice fills the room, causing every person to go still.

No sound…

No movement…

All the AC sound like it stop… Just heavy breathing from those involved in the fight coupled with the scared eyes of onlookers. I'm the only one brave enough to shift… I stand to my feet while moving strands of my hair from my face.

"Weh mi eye dem a see Mell?" Jordanne asks– his body oozing a calm but dangerous aura.

Mell?… Melllll? What a way he didn't know the names of the girls.

"She–" she tries but he uses the gun to signal silence to her.

"That was a rhetorical question," he breathes, and Slyme is now walking in at the end of his words.

This bumbohole

"Yuh put yuh hand pah me woman Toya?!" Jordanne throws the question out.

She doesn't respond… and Mariah slowly walks over to me.

"Answer nuh man. Mi no have all day. Simple yes or no," he urges her, eyes dark, voice cold, smile sadistic.

"Mi come find the two a dem pah Me–"

"Lie dat," Mariah shuts it down.

Drip looks at Mariah and back to Toya. Slyme doesn't move or looks like he cares at all.

"Me sister say a lie, so me ago need a better fucking explanation enuh mi killa."

Toya looks at Mell, who is now shaking.

"Alright mek me ask again, before mi turn unuh ina mesh… Yuh put yuh hand pah me woman Toya?"

Slyme tries to say something, but Drip dares him to try, with a look as readable as the ABC's.

"Yes…" comes Mell's voice, and Toya hisses her teeth at her friend's betrayal.

"Duhh mek me clear the teeth dem from yuh mouth," J's tone now eerie, while he stares at Slyme's plaything.

"Liam, pack up yuh fucking circus. This a di last time me ago say it. Next time anybody breathe 'gainst me woman, youuu and dem ago meet the maker… believe."

Slyme looks to be uneasy, but still manages to grab Toya, while leading Week Fi–Mell or whatever she name, outside.

Jordanne a act like alla this a Slyme fault. Like him neva did a fuck 'round di friend? He looks at me, disappointment stuck on his face. I hiss and roll my eyes, deciding to walk out.

If a neva fi him and him dutty friend this wouldn't happen.

I walk to the car not giving anybody my attention.

Plopping myself in the front seat, with my lips sealed, I buckle my seatbelt as I watch him speak to Liam. Michelle and Mariah join me seconds after that.

When Jordanne gets in the car, I turn my entire body to face the window.

Mi vex yuh fuck!

"Ry?" he tries but I ignore him.

I'm about to be 22 tomorrow, and me just deh pah floor a fight. Wah can go so bredda?

I hear him sigh before pulling out of the plaza's parking lot, to enter the main road.

Mi just know this ago reach Pinkwall enuh. If me nuh sure of nothing, mi sure ah dat.

Fi certain

74 | Decorum

JORDANNE

"Yo di man waste yuh fuck dawg," Paw laughs, directing his lethal words to Slyme. Fi once me cyaa take Slyme side. Everybody know him get special treatment, but this time mi can't extend that.

Out of all the soldiers Dadz had, I only kept a few of the youngest after cleaning up the team– weeding out the bad seeds. Slyme was among the first to be chosen. Why? We basically spent the latter part of our teenage years together. Though he's almost three years older, we did our advanced training in the same time frame.

He grew up in Spanish Town, and Dadz got to him when he was only 16. He treated him as a son and I felt like I gained the big brother I never had.

Still memba how Ramone used to hate di man, because as school over me wah run gah mi yard fi go watch how the man shoot.

Clean…

Effortless…

Nuh target nuh miss… He was good but my father deferred his training, for him to enroll in classes, earning subjects he never had the chance to acquire. Took him a year and by then my father already had me in basic training. With him 17 and myself 15, we were inseparable.

Why it sound like mi in love wid di man?

I chuckle at my own thought.

Differently still, apart from Ramone, Slyme a me bredda fi life. Lately me feel like leff a coated clip ina him but a love same way.

Surgeon can patch him up

"Suck yuh gyal nuh bredda," Slyme hisses, bringing his cup to his lips.

"Watch yah, dat is a compliment bad man," Paw snickers, causing them all to laugh.

I shake my head.

We're at whatever Sue likes to call these things. She really just love cook and have her family all in one place, seeing as she grew up without most of hers.

Slyme, Paw, Ramone, Ruse, Joshua and I are seated beneath the gazebo. Ryan, Surgeon, Skulli and Buckle are off in the distance playing the usual game of dominos. Snoop has been standing guard in place of Troopa and him absolutely hate it. I trusted nobody else that held his rank to do it though. Him just affi understand dat.

"Man dem wid di loose argument man," Surgeon hisses.

"A wah? Yuh nuh suck yuh gyal doc?" Paw counters.

Surgeon hisses again, this time shaking his head.

"Watch yah! That's why me cyaa see yuh wid nuh woman," he continues, almost choking himself with his own laughter. "Yuh nuh do that?" he starts again, looking at Ruse this time.

Ruse raises his eyebrows, before joining in the laughter.

"Unuh done wid dah argument deh," Joshua adds his input.

"Di man weh a live di maddest life a tell we fi stop argument??" Paw is now almost on the ground.

I puff the smoke from my mouth, watching them try to squeeze information from each other. This goes on for some minutes, granting me the time to live in my thoughts.

"Who Michelle? As me say yah wasteman still," Paw shakes his head, now serious while responding to Slyme's complaint about missing Muuch.

"Yuh wah say dat again!??" Slyme jumps up, eyes dazed, looking at Paw.

Everybody else falls silent.

"Di man a move like a lie. How you lose yuh woman to a gyal like Toya? Me and me friend dem fuck it go and come ina high school yute... and den breed har??"

Slyme moves to him and I sigh.

"Yo Slyme, relax," is all I say.

"Yo boss, yuh know you too soft wid him? If a did anybody else break yuh warning we head deliver to we mother long time. Yo the preference real, like mi fi turn wasteman too," Paw curses.

"True dat, 'cause him tell me 'bout Lorelle time and time again," Ramone chips in, lowly making his point.

I chuckle, before standing.

Grabbing them both– Slyme and Paw, by their collars and shoving them apart, I decide to make my thoughts clear.

"Mah tell unuh this... and it go fi everybody. Ryleigh friend dem off limits unless unuh ready fi settle down, 'cause when shit hit the fan it spill ova ina my ting. Liam a big man, him know which consequences him a face. Rest a unuh nuh affi know dat."

Ramone hisses.

"Yuh wah do that again?" my tone now clipped, "mi tell yuh a ting bout Lorelle and yuh vex? Yuh nuh ready fi settle Ramone, me and you know that," I hiss and pick up my glass from where it sits on the gazebo rail before moving down to the lawns.

Tired a dem man yah and the fuckry.

Cyaa wait fi leave tomorrow… if she even still wah go. She hasn't said a word to me since we got here.

• • •

RYLEIGH

After Mariah and I took showers separately, ridding ourselves of the act we committed earlier, we're now in the front yard chilling with everybody else.

My eyes follow him, as he walks to the side lawns with a sour look on his face. Cyaa me him still vex with 'cause me vex first so him lucky.

"Look nuh!" Lorelle says, dragging my attention to her phone.

It's a post on Pinkwall, showing the damage done to her salon.

Jamaicanmateygroupiepinkwall We DRIPing, we dripping.

View all 867 comments:

Lrrle That's not my salon.

User6888 Every month Toya a breed! Mi see her a roundrobin a drink Sunday gone! Kmt.

I hiss, not wanting to think about what we did.

"Yah comment pon it fah?" I look at her, puzzled at this point.

Her eyebrows form a knot before she says, "Girl mi no wah me place get no bad name. Weh unuh do a real fuckry so now me affi a do light damage control."

I'm taken aback by her tone.

Fair enough, we wrong fi real, I can't deny that.

"I'm sorry," I apologize to her for the millionth time. Cyaa believe di gyal dem bring me down to dem level.

"The gyal gwaan the bloodclawt most all now me benn!" Mariah adds, clearly tipsy from the mixed liquor in her hand.

"All now yuh nuh say sorry," Lorelle retorts, snapping her head to face her.

"Mi nah apologize to yuh ova beating nooo gyal weh go after me friend dem. A weh yuh come from?" now raising her voice, she walks over to Lorelle.

"Unuh stop, alla this a my fault. It done and gone just rest it," Muuch adds.

Keif, Kelly and Toni-Anne have been silently watching our encounter, offering no words. A car horn goes off in the distance and I see when Michelle gets up. Snoop signals at Sue and she nods.

What's happening?

Anuh Muuch mother car dat?

My mom and Sue walks over to talk to Mrs.Egar. Michelle gets up and walks to the kitchen. When she's back out, I notice she has the bag we were making fun of her for having earlier today. It's all coming together, as I watch her walk to the car.

Unable to control our feet, both Toni and I jog over to her.

"Weh yahgo? Anuh me yuh fi leave with?" I ask, staring at her bag.

"Yeah, you're to stay here after tomorrow when Ry' gone on her trip, anywhere else might no safe."

She releases a heavy, tired and frustrated sigh.

"Guys please, my flight is in three hours."

Flight???

Flight??????

"Girl flighttt?" I shriek, as low as I can, bearing in mind the mad man dem weh group up under the gazebo.

"You're leaving and yuh never tell we?" Toni pushes.

She sighs again, this time switching the hand that holds the bag.

"Me just need a break, from everything, so me ago clear me head. It's only Florida. I'll be back before you know it," she explains.

I completely understand. There is nothing like a painful breakup, where you still have to see the person daily. The time you take for yourself is important.

I pull her into a hug and Toni joins me. In the distance, I can see that Liam has questions but is deciding to act civilized for once.

Thank God.

"Okay baby girl, call us when you get there," Toni tells her.

We hug her again and this time Mariah, Kelly, Lorelle and Keif walk over to join us.

You can just know when one a we a leave, you no affi say much

Slyme picks up again and I see when he starts lifting himself from the chair. I pull away and slightly nudge Muuch, whispering for her to get in the car. Liam makes it down the gazebo steps but Skulli grabs him before he can cause a scene.

"Later girls!" Mrs.Egar waves while tooting her horn.

We all shout 'later' and she pulls out of the yard.

I have a strong feeling she's not coming back soon. I know what that peace feels like, you might get addicted to loving yourself.

• • •

We're all eating and laughing. It's almost midnight and I haven't seen Jordanne since he got up from the gazebo.

Oh well…

"Ryleigh go fimi charger fimi pleeeeeeaaaase!!!" Toni whines.

Why she no send her woman and lowe me? I said no like five times already.

"Kelly talk to yuh woman nuh. Me no wah go ina the house."

"Why?" Mariah giggles at my reason.

"Me no wah get up from beside her," Kelly whines.

Cause me affi be the resident send-out-gyal

Whatever, me wah take a nap anyways, 'cause mi know dem ago out yah till a morning… and me have a flight to catch, If he still wants to go…

I hiss, rubbing my arms before I step away on my conquest for the well needed charger. Now mounting the all too familiar stairs, I feel for my phone to give me some light. One thing with Sue, her house ago dark and the way my eye dem set up, it's never good for me.

I literally had every chance fi drop in my contacts earlier and didn't. They have been in my eyes all day prior to tonight, me tired ah the feeling man.

Within seconds, I'm shoving T's room door open before moving to where her charger should be. I spot it, unplug it, wrap it around in a loose circle and exit the room.

Wonder if me can throw it down deh, 'cause mi cyaa bother go and come back

Cho.

I decide against it and continue to walk down the hall, to the staircase. As I'm about to step off, a hand covers my mouth. Jumping from fright, I try to flip them.

He chuckles.

I hiss my teeth… Jordanne.

Wonder if Toya lick out mi senses. I didn't smell, hear or feel his presence just now

"Anuh training yuh deh, flip ting deh nahgo work," he whispers just behind my ear. His breath tickles my skin and I melt internally.

"Happy Birthday Love."

Mi cyaa vex in peeeace?

I try to talk but he doesn't shift his hand from my mouth, instead, he leads me to his old room. Pushing the door open, he lightly shoves me in before releasing his hold and locking the doors.

I squint my eyes while looking at him. He ignores me and walks to the balcony. The balcony of memories... I follow suit and watch him sit. Deciding to stay standing, I look at him.

Waiting... just a wait fi the scrutiny.

"Wah that yuh do today?" he breaks the silence.

The words plant themselves on my skin, forcing shame to the forefront of my being.

"A she–"

"Try again," he scoffs.

I–

"Muuch–"

"Try, again," he repeats.

A ring of silence circles us as I try to figure out weh him wah me say.

"I was frustrated," I let out.

"Good. Dat did hard?" he asks.

"What?"

"Not playing the victim," he breathes.

I roll my eyes, and he pulls me down into his lap.

"Now that you finally beat the people dem daughter you good?" he asks.

Am I?

"No..."

"Wah di issue then Love?" he asks, and I think to myself, him can read mi mind any other time but now?

I hiss internally.

"Just feel like one a your roach dem pop up every couple weeks. You know she came at me at the party?"

"Guard dem tell me before you reach back a the section."

I roll my eyes at his confirmation.

We go silent for a while, his hands circling my thighs.

"Ryleigh, mi just want you understand say nobody nuh come before you. Never has and dem neva will. So why you ina fight with girl like that? I don't know," he expresses his grievance.

Continuing he says, "Dem ting deh fuck wid me medz. Me nuh wah me woman name a call ina no form ah drama. Done tell yuh a ting already and is like you nah listen. Dem girl deh no ina your league babe."

Mi know a this him did ago come with enuh... and to be honest I know. Mi just tired fi walk weh now. When dem go low me wah gah hell, 'cause dem think mah push ova.

Deciding not to voice my thoughts, I lean down into him. A second flies past before he starts laughing, causing me to snap my head back up.

"A wah???"

"Supm mi never tell yuh," he manages to get out.

I look at him in confusion.

"Share di joke…"

"Used to dream say mah fuck yuh pah dah balcony ya. When mi say dream me mean every single night– the same dream."

A lie? A so gyal fi mad man

I laugh out while saying, "When dat?" genuinely curious.

"That time I took a semester off, when you just go ina second year," he explains, now snaking his hand up to my breasts.

"Oh…" is all I let out, all laughter now gone from both our lips.

His eyes meet mine and we know what's about to happen.

"Out here?" I ask and he nods, pupils now dilated from raw lust.

"But everybody deh rounda front and–"

"And nuttin just be quiet," he says before capturing a boob into his mouth, while using his free hand to shift my panty.

A moan escapes my lips and I know immediately I won't be quiet.

He plays with my clit for a while before sliding his finger inside. Turning them up into his signature hook to hit my spot, he causes more goo to exit, pooling his jeans. I lull my head back, holding onto the chair and his shoulder. The feeling of him growing beneath me, sends a tingle up my spine.

Focus on your breathing, duh mek di demon boy mek yuh cum ina three seconds

His thumb finds my clit and I revel at the sensation.

Warm mouth over nipple…

Fingers rubbing my G-spot…

Thumb circling my nerve ball… and him wah me be quiet???

A moan escapes my lips again and almost instantly he slips out of me, shoving the same fingers that were just inside me into my mouth, to demand silence.

I–

He lifts me without saying a word, bringing me to the glass balcony to bend me over while lifting my dress to my waist. With his fingers still in my mouth, he uses his free hand to free himself and I feel when he springs out, brushing against my ass cheeks.

He taps it a few times before sinking it into me mercilessly. The thrill of not being able to moan is doing something to me!

He gives me no time to adjust, instead he maintains a steady deep pace.

"Yuh ago learn fi listen?" he asks.

Unable to talk, I try nodding, but he doesn't seem to like that.

A slap finds my ass, forcing me to wince.

Jesussss Chri–

Another two follow, echoing out into the open.

He grabs my neck from behind, bringing me up to face him– inverted. He likes to do this position, knowing he has complete control.

He slows down and leaves a wet kiss on my forehead before asking the question again, "Yuh plan fi obey me?"

Scared of what he'll do next, I try my best to nod. He realizes his fingers are still lodged inside my mouth and slides them out before finding my nipples.

"FuUuccckkkk," is what slides out of my mouth with them.

"Not the answer I'm looking for Ryleigh."

I–

He releases me and pulls out simultaneously. I almost lose my breath at the swift motion, stumbling a little.

"Knees," he commands clearly.

I drop to my knees before looking up. His dick is dripping in my juices and mi affi say this, me is one wet likkle gyal.

I await his instructions…

"Open."

I open…

"Wider."

I go wider…

"Good girl," his tone is raw and my pussy is needy, but if I start to play with my clit he might do something crazy.

My thoughts are interrupted by him entering my mouth. He moans from the feeling, only moving in and out slowlllyy.

Tonight is gonna be a night.

A great night.

75 | With You

RYLEIGH

"Coming now babe," I shout from the bathroom.

It's our fifth day on this mini tour. We're about to leave the BVI, Virgin Gorda to be exact and sail to the USVI of St.Thomas– before heading back home.

We spent the first day in New York, shopping for my clothes because I procrastinated and didn't order my things in time. And yeah, me did affi listen to him lecture me all day about being last minute and blah blah blah.

I've been in the bathroom flooding my stories just fi everybody head hurt them. The usual rule is not to make live location posts so of course I'm posting clips from the previous island– Tortula.

When it uploads, I move to the mirror, just to take moooore clips of myself to post when we leave.

So me walk a so mi look pah me body.

"Ryleigh, me nuh 'fraid fi leff yuh in here enuh killa," Jordanne warns.

But he won't let me stay on my phone when we're together, so weh him expect? Me affi take the clips from now. 'Enjoy the moment'… men always say that, but then they ask for the pictures you took of them, while apparently not enjoying the moment.

I push the door open, smiling when I see that he has my two suitcases, my bag and his duffel, ready to go.

"Think you did ago leff me?" I giggle.

"Yeah, nah leff the things me just buy you though. Did ago sell dem back Downtown," he feigns discipline.

A who and him? 'Bout Downtown

"More while yuh sick me stomach enuh J'," I cackle out.

483

"Think a mine yuh sick? A–"

"Duh finish dah line deh drankro," I laugh, taking my bag from across his body.

"The yacht is waiting, no bother with the slow waltz," he reminds me.

Picking up the pace I walk out of the villa behind him, admiring his built. What a boy nice. Me ago say it every day until the world know. We walk down to the pier and if you think Half-Way-Tree sun hot? Try again.

The captain greets Jordanne before taking the suitcases on board. We then follow him below deck, where he leaves them in our room.

"You guys already know the vessel, if you need anything, my co-captain and I are on the deck."

J' nods, offering him no words.

"Thank you," I smile, before plopping myself down on the bed.

"Hungry?" J' turns to me.

"Why you always think me hungrier than anybody else?" I pout.

He laughs, a little too long and a little too loud for me. "Bredda a you we a talk 'bout enuh– the Ry' that you are now, not the one from high school weh no eat."

Accusations... Mah tell you bwoy.

"Excuse," I roll my eyes while he positions himself on the bed beside me– propping his head up with his hand. He looks at me expectantly for a few seconds before I break.

"Okayyyy, jeeeez. Feed me Drip, feed me," my laughter now loud and raucous.

He chuckles before moving to the platter I didn't notice was there.

"Today's catch them say," he mutters, opening the cloche to look at the lobster, mussels and... sushi I think.

Mi blind enuh, so I can't really see if it is, but last time me try dah raw fish supm deh, let's just say it didn't end well.

"I'll have the lobster tail."

"Well babe, a couldn't the head yuh want," he snickers.

I bite down on my bottom lip, fighting the laughter that's threatening to exit my mouth.

Him nah get no comedic points from me

I watch him roll the cart over and before you know it, we're halfway through the platter.

• • •

It's been less than twenty minutes onboard and we've decided to go lay out on the deck.

"Still no know why yah try carry we go bun up," he complains.

"Come nuh, Vitamin D good fimi."

"Me nuh give you enough ah dat? You wah mo–"

"Nuh touch me," I laugh, flashing his hands from my ass.

Man yah will kill me with hood

Say that like a joke but a real ting.

He grabs me, pulling me into a hug, before squeezing my ass and burying his head in my neck.

I breathe...

"You know sometimes, I think about sharing you..."

He pulls away to search my eyes.

"A weh di fuck mi sister a put ina you head???" he laughs, now shaking his head repeatedly.

I almost scream out from crippling laughter. The way me never even remember T' in a poly is hilarious.

"I think about it fi real, like you need a lotttt of sex and–"

"You literally just beat up somebody weh me dick no see fi almost three years," he smirks, cocking his head to the side.

Okay, points were made.

"Sooooo just have less sex with me then becau–"

"You mad? You have no idea how long mi wah you to myself???" he starts.

Here we goooo...

"Through you and idiot Folan, you and Dalani... Rome... LeNERD," he emphasizes the NERD and I scoff. "I've wanted you for myself for as long as I've known you. Cyaa tell you that enough. Luckily I had to involuntarily wait still 'cause maybe me woulda fuck it up with the bagga woman thing."

And woulddd.

Definitely would

We lay there, looking at the clouds in silence before he speaks his mind again. He's generous with his words today isn't he.

"Pre... just you being with Lenard sexually, bother me brain... sometimes daily," he breathes, bringing his hand behind his head.

Why is he trying to kill the mood? Knowing mi mouth wassy.

"He was the only other person outside of you, and that bother you brain?... Daily??? When youuu left meee?" I turn, taking down my shades to look at him.

"Yo lower you voice... Nah say you shouldn't have, I'm just letting you know it bother me."

"Men," I mumble to myself.

"C'mere," he breathes, pulling me into him when my attitude starts boiling over, "let's not argue, did just a say a ting."

"I get it... but I don't... but I do," I mutter, now wrapping my fingers into his.

"Good 'cause I love you punk, and no, you nahgo get fi share me, so learn fi tek fuck," he laughs out, prompting my laughter– switching the serious moment back to pure and innocent fun.

• • •

We're near to the island of St.Thomas. I know because my phone has signal again. J' is asleep– head in my lap, hand on my ass. I smile at how peaceful he seems, after weeks of haunting the house.

You should tell him you want to move

I do… the house holds bitter memories I don't want to have. Good ones mostly but the incident just rubs me wrong. The kitchen gimi the wickedest level of anxiety and–

Notifications start popping up on my phone, cutting my internal rant. I bring it up to my face to look at it but it's nuttin more than Digicel a tell me 'bout roaming. I go to my feed, looking to see if the picture I took in Gorda posted since we have signal now.

It did.

I toggle to my notifications, hoping to go through them all before dah sir yah wake up and get miserable. While sliding through the usual heart eyes and compliments, I spot a notification from, **Drip_Law.**

This man don't even use Instagram. I swear if him post me tracks me shove him offa dah boat yah.

I click the notification…

Oh, I smile looking at his little boomerang of me on the deck, sipping my glass of champagne while looking out at the bluest waters I've seen to date. He knew it wouldn't post until we were almost at the next island. Me??? Love my man.

Deciding to return the favour, I pop him on my story too, using the only picture I got to sneak of him while we were in New York. Hope I darkened it enough. Know how him stay when it come to the building and the cars.

The yacht comes to a slow sail, before we dock, and his eyes fly open at the sharp and sudden rock.

"We reach," I whisper, watching him stretch and tremble.

"Ready fi go home?"

"Like yesterday," I laugh and he does too.

While throwing my bag on, my phone starts ringing.

Mummy 🖤*…*

"Hello?" I wait for my mom to come in view but nothing.

"Mummy???" I try again, this time grabbing J's attention.

"Hayluh… Ms.Ryleigh," a tiny, weak voice that could only belong to one little human comes through the speakers.

My heart begins to race, "JJ??!"

"Yeh…"

This real? My eyes begin to well with water and I look to Jordanne who is now walking back towards me. Unable to move or say anything, he takes the phone from my hand, and begins to speak on my behalf.

"Big man a you dat?" he chuckles.

"Drip!" JJ shrieks.

"Mr.Sheer fi yuh big head boy," J' laughs.

Well now we know why the pikny no stop walk and call me Ms.Ryleigh

Jordanne pulls me into his arms, rubbing at the small of my back to offer comfort. Just by that tiny gesture, the pace my heart was going finally slows.

"See Ryleigh yah big man," he says to the phone screen, before turning it to me– both our faces now in view.

"Hi JJ, how you feel?" I start with what I want to know first.

"Hungry!" he complains, "I want pizza," his innocence is making this unbearable.

"I'll come get you pizza in a few," I assure him.

"I want it now though," he whines.

This causes me to smile. Still bad bruk I see.

"Give me the phone JJ," I hear my mother's voice.

"You will get pizza soon enough," I pick up Sue's voice in the background too.

"From yesterday him wake, but we never wah disturb unuh. Toni-Anne say unuh a come back tonight so mi say mek mi try me luck."

"How is he for real," I ask my mom.

"Them say he should get rest and he won't be leaving before the week ends."

"That's all?" my concern now speeding through my body.

"That's all them tell me. Sue pull all her strings fi we even in here. Them say they have to speak with direct family or legal guardian."

So where is Ruse?

"Ramone a sort that out as we speak," Jordanne cuts in.

"Okay Danne, when unuh come in… Tell them bye JJ."

"Bye, remember the pizza, pleeeea–" my mother moves the phone away from his pleading voice before saying bye and hanging up.

I look up at Jordanne, who seems to be unaffected as usual. Everything from that day flashes back to my mind. With tears threatening my eyes, I rest my head on his chest before saying… "I want to move…"

"Already on it babe… don't cry," he kisses me at the top of my head, allowing me to be an emotional mess in his arms

76 | Bells

JORDANNE

I've been back in New York since early October and it's now **Christmas day**. If it was up to me, I'd be in Jamaica 24/7 but I can't do everything virtually. Some things I can't outrun forever. One being, all the business meetings that these dinosaurs think have to take place in a boardroom, at a bar or on a golf course... and two being, searching for Croc.

Ruse was sent to infiltrate the Italian Americans, with hopes of gaining access to what Rome's plan was, apart from seeing his son and how the fuck Ryleigh father got involved.

How him even leave Venezuela

A sigh leaves my lips and I move to the window of the penthouse, looking down at the city. The time is around 4am so it's dark out still, and the roads are quieter than usual.

Everybody deh home wid dem family

Except me...

My personal phone goes off and I hesitate before picking it up. Hope anuh Ry' a complain say she miss me again. Me tell her fi leff the waste work and come stay wid me, but nooo... she wah follow dreams.

I hold my phone up to see what the disturbance so early in the morning is about, when I notice a... group chat??? The fuck a gwaan?

<u>SNIPAZZ</u>

<u>Liam:</u> **Yo unuh look pah this |attachment|**

<u>Paw:</u> **A stalk yah stalk the woman dawg?**
Hahaha! pussy watch man dis.

**<u>Liam:</u> Buil nuh yute. Yo me did affi send
everybody at once cause me feel like fly out!
<u>Liam:</u> Who the fuck carry her gone watch game? She
deven like basketball killa.**

<u>Ramone:</u> Man dem a talk bout woman at 4am?!

<u>Paw:</u> Like she line wid gold. Dwfl man gah yuh bed.

**<u>Surgeon:</u> Which battyman mek dah group yah? Me
nah read alla dat, but Muuch look good.**

<u>Paw:</u> Mine di divorcee try fight yuh enuh doc.

DWL!

<u>Surgeon:</u> Lol! Rass

**<u>Liam:</u> Yow kmt everything unuh take fi joke. Me
miss her you fuck.**

Eh Boy Slyme stress from August to December. That's a whole fucking semester. One whole semester him a study one subject, Michelle Egar.

She's not showing, and I mentally check how far along she should be. Four months... Shouldn't start showing that much until around late January.

Slyme ago know fi sure I kept it from him but him just affi go vex. Ryleigh begged me not to say anything to him and as long as Michelle alright then me good wid dat.

And if mi say nuttin, him ago find her and stress her out

Fi sure.

<u>Paw:</u> You life just funny bro, no joke.

<u>Ramone:</u> Drip di ting dem ready.

*Paw changed the subject to *Bowazzz**
*Surgeon changed the subject to *Liam's diary**

<u>Joshua:</u> Yo unuh no sleep and dem ting deh?

<u>Paw:</u> We know yuh need yuh rest enuh Mr.triangle lol!

<u>Joshua:</u> Kmt dwl!

Yo Slyme, you soon get back you woman just
buil and wait. Ramone link up.

<u>Paw:</u> Man love tell ppl fi wait cause him
a wait fi decades fi fiim woman.

SYG!!! Looool! Me always did have my
girl still. Some man blocked from September.

<u>Liam:</u> Watch yah. Mi tell di man a ting and
him a use it fi a come back.

<u>Joshua:</u> Ahaaaa!

<u>Surgeon:</u> Dwfl! Loool!

<u>Paw:</u> So how tf him deh pon her ig? Is a fake page
the man mek? Mine me send yuh go the mix up page enuh yute! Lol!

Ahahaha!

Liam left

<u>Paw:</u> Look weh unuh cause smh.

<u>Ramone:</u> Dwwwll! Fucka.

<u>Joshua:</u> Man create the group and gone star. Me
gone back a my bed.

<u>Paw:</u> The one bed wull di three a unuh?

Pussyclawt dwl! Yo Ramone
link me, the laptop up and running.
Them man yah nahv ntn fi do.

With that I click my phone shut and walk over to my laptop, waiting for Ramone to bring up the camera footage the detective requested. Apparently, they need footage from what took place during the home invasion… four months later.

Dah country deh always a lag

I wait for approximately six minutes before the secured call comes through.

"Yeah check the inbox section, me send everything," Ramone directs.

"Cool," is all I offer.

I tap through, realizing he sent a little more than my old house footage from that day. Dat good still, I haven't looked over the cameras in months anyways, I'll just look at everything– keep my mind off not being home.

"Ahhh me get them," I assure him when he starts looking at me expectantly.

"Me nuh wah hide the ting with Lorelle anymore," he almost whispers, dragging me away from focus.

"Which ting bad man?"

"We been a fuck around since you leave October," he explains, becoming uncomfortable on the screen.

Jah.

"Weh yah say to me is you disobey mi orders?"

What comes next is silence.

"Talk nuh monnn," I push, leaning all the way back into my chair while rubbing my knuckles.

Is like me have a set of high schoolers when it come tuh woman. Liam mek gyal trick him 'bout dem a breed and lose him woman. Joshua ah get jealous ova how much Kelly and Toni-Anne leave him outa things. Surgeon nuh stop fuck off him two nurse... now them hate each other. Ruse wah abort the mission fi come see him woman fi Christmas. My mother run Skulli head...

... And nowwwww, Ramone a tell mi bout Lorelle. Them think a the likkle Love island show this weh Mariah always a watch? Am I a fucking guidance counselor?

"Bredda weh mi say to you bad man? Mi say deh with who you want but when it come to Ry' friend dem, make sure yuh ready fi settle. So if you ready fi settle mi nuh have a problem."

He looks away for a moment, then back to the screen, "Mi ready..."

"So mi nahv no issue, just make sure you do better than Slyme. I might not be as lenient. Unuh fi thank God fi Ryleigh, she mek me nuh stay certain way again."

He nods and I decide to end the call before anything else is added. I lift the laptop and walk back to the window, deciding to look at the complete file.

I pull up the one from Hope Pastures, that's dated back months ago and start browsing.

Everything seems normal so far. I click on a few more and continue to look. I haven't been looking at it keenly because if something was up, Ramone woulda tell mi dat.

While pulling on my spliff, I start to admire the tree swaying in front of the gate. My mind goes to how the trees here are empty now from shedding their leaves for the winter, when I notice something...

... a leaf falls.

Mi sure me see dah leaf deh drop ina the last two videos?

Same position, same shadow casted.

The fuck this?

The time stamps are all between 6 and 8pm.

Mi a start feel uneasy now, because either that leaf re-attach itself after falling every-day or this video was cropped in for something else that's missing. I run the footage again–slower this time… pausing at 7:02pm, where I can clearly pinpoint the leaves on the tree across the street blowing the same.

Not even just the leaf falling this time

Ramone affi think me a fucking idiot. I got into an Ivy League university for a reason.

I pull up the next day… 7:28pm only fi see the same leaf movement, same shadow from the streetlight and everything. I hiss and pull up the following day, from that same week… 8:10pm.

Same thing.

A chuckle leaves my lips.

My mind is telling me to call Ramone and ask him what he's hiding and why him feel him need fi chop up my footage and add a place holder, but the words of my father are telling me not to.

'Let them come to you, don't show your hand too early'

I go through more footage, fast forwarding the tapes to that time of the day, but based on what I can see, the discrepancies seem to have only been during that week. That was the last week of Rome being in the vault.

Weh di fuck the man chop and edit the video for? Without my permission at that. Why?!

• • •

RYLEIGH

"JJ!!!!!" I shout.

Mi nuh know wah this me tek up pon myself enuh. Dis ting is like supm weh wii kill yuh. What a likkle boy fi raise a young gyal blood pressure.

"JJ!!!!!!!!!!!!!!!" I try again.

"Bumboclawt Ryleigh, you nahfi loud so enuh," Toni-Anne whines.

"Sevenla'clack a morning and di lady a scream already," Mariah adds.

"Cocomelon nuh look good pah yuh at all sista gyal," Keif laughs.

"Lie dem a tell," Muuch disagrees from my phone screen.

I've grown closer to Michelle these past few months. Mi nuh know if a trauma bond we trauma bond but she live pah me phone more than J' himself.

She hasn't mentioned her pregnancy, not once since leaving and I haven't asked.

I'm hosting Christmas this year, so I've been up since 4am, getting everything to-gether. Suanne is here, helping me cook and my girls are here helping me set up. My family from May Pen should be here by noon to enjoy Christmas dinner with us, along with the gift exchange.

"I'll go get him. Him probably have the game ina him ears," Sue says, throwing down the mixing bowl before flying up the stairs.

My mom is outside waiting for us to bring him out for her to take him to church with her.

"Why yuh face look so?" Muuch's voice comes through the speakers.

I look up at her and shrug.

"Ryleigh?" she pushes.

Ughhh.

"Mi no wah seem ungrateful but I wanted him here," I mumble.

"Did you tell him that?"

Why me fi tell him me wah spend we first official Christmas together? A Jordanne. Drip Law, sharpshoota, engineer, multiple business owner, draws droppa, mind reader, Jordanne. Mi fi explain such a simple concept?

"Nuh feel like mi need fi do that," I breathe.

"Bu–"

"See him here!" Sue exclaims, demanding my attention.

JJ is in the church suit I left him in, holding his controller. Sue takes it from him and sends him down the stairs. He walks to me forcing a pout.

"What is it?" I ask, holding his chin up.

"I don't want to go," he whines, twisting at his hair.

"Why not? Nana Janette is waiting for you. Yuh wah break your promise to a woman?" I ask.

"No," he shakes his head slowly.

"Good, so grab your snack bag and let's go meet her."

He bolts to the kitchen in pursuit of the bag.

"Walk nuh Junior!" I scream.

"Okay maybe they were right. You scream enuh gyal!" Muuch laughs, and everybody else joins in.

"And unuh know the lady loud from a longer time!" Mariah laughs.

"As a siren me man did say enuh," Toni-Anne joins.

She a call him her man again, they must be on good terms this week.

"Likkle pikny deh ago mad me! Jordanne need fi come home so him can behave, him alone him fraida," I say, waving my hands in surrender.

JJ walks back to me and I take his hand and move to the exit. As I open the door, my mother is facing us.

"Likkle most me cyaa find yuh new place mi pikny!" she laughs, breathing heavy.

"Mummy it's been a week since we've been here, yuh come twice already!" I laugh, taking the bag from JJ and handing it to her.

"Yes but yuh know if anuh me drive, me nahgo remember a weh," she looks down at JJ and smiles. "Come JJ, let's go give the Lord some praise."

He smiles when she takes his hand, offering him a lollipop.

Weh mi tell her 'bout the sweetie?

She seems to pick up on my concern and says, "Him ago alright, one sweetie neva kill a soul."

"Whatever, 'cause a cyaa church yahgo, a must brunch," I giggle, pointing aimlessly at her outfit.

Her knee length, burgundy dress is hugging her body a little too tight while her big church hat is blocking the sun for me, her, JJ and everybody else in St.Andrew. The heels? Six long inches mlovve.

My mother a supm else.

"Byyyye," I bend to give JJ my right cheek.

He pecks it multiple times before telling me bye. I watch them go through the gates and my mind lands on Troopa. I should go visit him soon. Surgeon have him from when and I'm starting to lose faith in his skills. I suggested they transfer him to a hospital but Jordanne say that's a no-no. Surgeon say him got this, and him might wake once the brain swelling go down.

Him can say anything still, but I won't believe until me see results.

Hours later, we're busy singing Christmas carols and taste testing all the dishes. The food is almost done, and I sigh at the fact that me can go bathe and look like Janette daughter now.

I drip the last bit of sorrel in my hand middle before tasting it.

"Bad duh??" Toni asks.

"Yuh deal wid it yes," I laugh, smacking my mouth at how strong the rum is. "Mark that jar so them know a the strong one this. Me nuh wah JJ drink it."

"Him anuh like nine?" she contests.

"And?"

"And me a drink sorrel from mi a 'bout six or seven– rum included," she laughs.

"And now you is a mad gyal, so you see how that went?" I laugh and she shoves me playfully.

"Me ago bathe and look like somebody."

I quickly remove my apron and alight the stairs, moving to the guest bedroom. The new house is very similar to the last– light, airy, with no horrible memories.

As I push my door, I find Lorelle smiling at her phone.

"Think you say you nuh feel good and up yah a sleep from morning girl?" I ask, my face twisted in faux anger.

She quickly ends her phone call and snaps her head to me.

"God know say mi just neva wah cook," she smiles but her eyes hold a hint of guilt.

A who she did a talk to?

As I'm about to ask the question on my mind, a sharp cramp presents itself a few inches below my navel.

"Awuhh!" I shriek.

"A wah do you?" Lorelle perks up, lifting herself from the bed.

I hold my hand up stopping her from moving.

Nuttin to be alarmed about

"Just cramps from the IUD removal, gyno say they should stop after a few days."

"Yeah when me did take out mine, I didn't have much cramps but I had light spotting for like three days."

Hope me nahv dat. Jordanne should be here tomorrow, me can fuck him with cramps but not with no spotting

It's been out for two days now, I should be feeling okay in a few. I've had it since when? May? I planned on having it for a year but me and the pelvic cramps just nahgo work.

And we and a baby at 22 nahgo work either

Mhmmm, I don't know. Maybe if me man did a somebody else, but I feel safe now. Safe in love and finances.

My mind snaps back to the topic of birth control. Regular oral contraceptives make me chubby, nauseous and moody... and the IUD only grants me pelvic pain. When dem ago come up wid supm fi di man dem take instead of we? And not that pill thing they're developing 'cause we know men won't take a thing. They need an injection or supm, that lasts for a year or two.

Dem can breed 365 different women in a year, meanwhile we can only breed once fi the year, twice if you active.

"Mi no get no spotting yet so hopefully not... Me ago bathe," I snap out of my mind to respond to Relle while stepping into the bathroom– deciding not to ask her about her call.

● ● ●

I drag my dress down and leave the room with Lorelle. We walk to the master bedroom to get the rest of the gifts I hid in the closet. I haven't been sleeping here– figured I'd leave that experience for when he got back and could see the house in person.

We grab the wrapped boxes and walk out into the hallway. When we get to the top of the stairs, I hear him.

This cyaa real

Me a hallucinate the man voice now. That nuh look good at all.

It's giving mad gyal.

"Wah else dem say a church?" Jordanne's voice comes clear this time.

No man, if I laugh in yah. Like dem put weed ina the sorrel.

The way this house is set up, you can't see half of the living area from the top of the stairs, so I start to descend and...

My lips decide to abandon my teeth when I see him stooped down in front of Junior, asking him about the sermon.

"Mine yuh jaw tear!" Mariah laughs out.

I giggle out too.

He looks up at me, and JJ runs to me, stopping to walk when Jordanne tells him to. I make it to the end of the steps, before he latches onto my leg, asking if he can open his gifts now.

"No, we open them after dinner... and mi mek you open one this morning already."

"Okay everybody hurry up and eat!" he says, winning an uproar from the family.

"Unuh a joke out mi ting," he adds, causing even more laughter.

JJ runs up the stairs, with his grand aunt Ms.Cherry, right behind him. Jordanne moves to me, taking the boxes I had before planting a kiss on my forehead.

"Think you say you nah come until tomorrow," I whisper, blushing beneath his built.

"You know better," he counters, pulling his bottom lip between his teeth.

That alone warrants throbbing between my legs.

I look up at him... He looks down at me... and my body is reminded that I haven't had him inside me for ten lonnnnng weeks.

He pulls me in, to whisper in my ear, "I missed you, Merry Christmas Love."

Nipple? Stiff.

Skin??? Tingling.

Lungs? Outa breath.

Draws??? Wettttt.

"Rooooom! Roooooooommm!!" Sue laughs and we break away to see her and my mother covering their eyes.

He ignores them, raising a single brow at me as if to take them up on the offer.

"I can't," I shake my head, "I have some spotting," I lie.

He doesn't know about the IUD, and I don't plan on telling him since it's out. Sure me woulda breed if a never fi it. Sure me ago breed soon after this if me no careful. I need to find a birth control that works for me.

"Lucky girl," he smirks, taking my hand while leading us to the gigantic, white decorated Christmas tree.

In this moment I'm happy...

My man is home...

My friends and their families are here.

My extended family will be here soon…

… and the people dem pikny weh mi take ova is well and is enjoying his day so far.

God is good.

All the time

What could go wrong?

77 | Slow Reveal

RYLEIGH

It's Boxing Day, the day Junior is used to seeing both his parents. We've already explained to him with the help of Terry, that his parents aren't here with us and won't ever be. Being an almost nine year old, I didn't think that it would be easy explaining it to him, but I didn't think it would be this hard. There are times when he randomly asks for them, especially her, Stace... and half the time I don't know how else to phrase the answer.

Today is one of those days.

"Mommy not coming back???" he cries, staring directly into my soul.

See all dem supm yah pah me young soul

"I–" I try to say something but choke up.

"Junior, remember we told you she wasn't?" Ms.Cherry tries.

"Yes but it's Christmas."

From what I know, Stace was never a good mom or fit enough to care for him on her own, so while Jacen lived in Chicago, he had him in Ms.Cherry's care half the time, with Ruse there in and out.

Regardless though, him ago miss him mother.

Less of these episodes happened for the little time Ruse was present after the incident. He reminds him of his dad and I don't know the mechanics of it but it works. Now that he's been away and it's just been myself and Ms.Cherry, I think he's having a much harder time understanding that they died.

Cho, I can only do so much.

Jordanne enters the room, catching mine and Ms.Cherry's attention whilst causing JJ to fall quiet before shoving his head into his pillow.

I shrug my shoulders, looking up at J', when I realize he's questioning me with his eyes.

Mi nuh know, him did alright like five minutes ago

Jordanne motions for myself and Ms.Cherry to exit the room and we do so without question.

Me mi love? I've never dealt with raw loss, so mi nuh know weh fi tell the people dem child

Walking downstairs and to the backyard, to find Mariah, I decide to ring Muuch. She picks up before the phone even get fi ring good.

"No man, you couldn't give it some time?" I laugh out.

"Girl me just did ago call yuh! You nahgo believe this."

Judging her enthusiasm, I lower the volume of the phone and instead of going to the back yard, I slip into the kitchen pantry.

Yeah me can eat and listen to drama.

"The man EMAIL mi!!" she starts off.

"Who??? Email? Talk straight nuh man!" I push.

She hisses and stands to close her robe and I'm certain her navel is protruding.

The lady keep her baby enuh

Well, I don't know for sure but–

"Nuh must Liam, which other man yuh know mad so?"

Jordanne, but we move.

I laugh out, grabbing the jar that holds the Oreo cookies.

"Continue," I say, flicking the cap off before shoving one into my mouth.

"Mek mi read it. Hehumm!!!" she clears her throat dramatically. "Michelle, I miss you," she starts off mimicking his voice and I almost scream out..." It's been over four months and I can't do this anymore. You left the house and that was okay, but then you left the country and are yet to say anything to me. You block me pon everything and me sure you know me can find you if I want to right? But me give you peace. Enough is enough, I want you home. Mi love you more than anything or anybody else pah Jah earth Michelle," she ends with a bow.

She unserious yuh fuck

Stifling a laugh, I wipe away my fake tears dramatically.

"Bravo!" I clap.

"Open this! Me know yuh in yah a chat people!" Mariah's voice comes at the door.

"Bitch how yuh so fass?" I giggle, opening the door.

"Stop skin off yuh black teeth dem and gimi one a di Oreo."

I hand her the jar, closing the pantry door after.

"Yeah girl," Michelle continues, "the bwoy wouldn't even say mek him apologize fi put him hand pah me! Or fi set up gyal put ina we bedroom, 'bout love. Love him madaaa!"

"Dirty Liam unuh itch up in yah a talk 'bout?" Mariah says scornfully, looking at me as I hold the phone trying not to laugh too loud.

Dem girl yah a drama. It's never what they say, it's always the tone and face play.

"Mi no wah hear weh him say to you. Fuck dat light skin ass wicked rasta bwoy. Weh meee wah know is if you keep me niece or nephew."

Asking the right questions

Michelle pauses, as if caught off guard. Mariah smirks, grabbing the phone from my hands.

"Yuh keep it enuh. Look pah yuh titti dem!" she adds.

"Gyal tek time! You know me man ears bionic and Slyme deh ina the back yard, can pass yah so at any moment," I whisper-shout, slapping her arms.

As if we nuh tell we man already?

Welllll…

"Mi no wah talk 'bout it," Muuch frowns. "Unuh just affi go wait and see."

She cannotttt trick meee

Mi see the lady navel earlier, but if she no wah say nuttin a her life.

"Ry?!"

Fuckkk.

I grab my phone from Mariah, whispering bye to Muuch, before ending the call.

"A wah do yuh gyal? Yuh ago fraida Danne forever?" Mariah laughs.

A she a get the punishment fuck dem or a me?

I roll my eyes at her, before opening the door, stepping out to him just entering the kitchen, with JJ behind him happier than a puppy. Mariah steps out beside me, holding the Oreo jar still.

"Unuh look so suspect?" he says, raising a brow.

"Yuh woman did a chat to your friend ex-wife."

One thing 'bout dah group yah, the mouth dem leaky.

"Michelle good?" he averts his eyes from scrutinizing Mariah's grip on the container, to me.

"Yeah she alright," is all I say, before Junior is tugging at Mariah's waist, asking for an Oreo.

"Likkle boy, yuh think a Ryleigh this. Go learn yuh timetable," she sneers, scraping him from her waist.

Jordanne laughs out at her statement, and I playfully roll my eyes.

Not everybody knowing him nuh listen to me

When J' sobers up, he walks over to me, pulling me into his hold. We both watch as Mariah finally softens to JJ's pleas.

"Alright, come my… step-stolen nephew based on Danne… or is it just nephew-in-law since a Ruse real nephew?" she questions herself. "Come let's leave before your dolly house parents do supm nasty with us here."

Jordanne chuckles, before planting a kiss on my lips.

When he pulls away, he asks, "Yuh ready?"

"Ago start get ready now yes," I offer, running my hands down his chest.

"Mean if you ready fi everything that's about to happen?" he clarifies.

Am I?

In my head everybody already knows who we are and the relationship we have. To-night will just confirm the words of wagging tongues. We have a charity event for the foundation granted in his father's name. The Robert Sheer Foundation- 'For Underprivi-leged Teens'.

I like it... Coined when we weren't together, but I kept up with it every step of the way, every article and every video clip from both years.

"I don't think I am, but mi nahgo can avoid events like this forever so," I mumble.

"That nuh sound good. Know you no like put things out there, so if you want us to stay we can."

He knows we can't

"We can't, now sshhhh, before me change mi mind fi real," I mutter.

"Duh take the whole day and a half fi ready enuh mamas," he warns and I roll my eyes, knowing it's about to take three days in his time.

Moments have passed and by now I'm fully dressed and ready, but on the phone going back and forth with Ramone.

"Weh yuh mean Ramone?" I whisper, barely audible to my own ears.

My heart is almost through my fucking mouth.

"Me say the man ask me fi talk. So naturally me go ova the footage I sent fi mek sure ano dat him wah talk 'bout, only fi realize I fucked up. The cropped in version has repet-itive movements."

Weh him mean???

"Weh yuh mean!? Listen nuh, me coulda tell him enuh and you tell me 'NO', say you woulda take care of it," tears prick my eyes, but if I ruin my makeup J' will notice.

The blood, the blood, the blood.

"If anything, me take the blame still. Me did ina rush, I thought I cropped in different times of the day but a just the same time, same leaf falling, same shadow, wind movement everything. There is no way him no notice."

I try to speak but my words are caught in my throat.

Yuh ago mek di man take the blame fi we fuckry?

I can't. No way.

"Yuh can't do that, him ago kill you," I whisper, now peeking through the tainted glass door of my closet, "and I know him, him ago wah see what you replaced."

"True, but you weren't in the videos enuh, remember that... Just your prints showed up in the time frame of the gate opening magically each evening," I hear him sigh... and so do I...

... Because why me so fool? Even if they didn't see me, they would see the gates open slightly and investigate either way.

"Babe, you ready?" I hear Drip's voice enter our room.

I almost throw the phone but instead I hang up and take a few deep breaths, calming my nervous system as best as possible.

"Ryleigh??" he tries again.

"In here," I finally answer.

The door to the walk-in closet swings open and my fingers find each other.

"What's wrong?"

"I–" I try to get my words out but me scared fi Ramone. I'm not the only one in the situation this time.

"I'm nervous," I breathe.

Well at least that's honest

"Nahfi nervous babe, you just have to be pretty and you master that already," he smirks, moving to close the gap between us.

A just the way mi ago pass out any minute now

Then how bad is it that I fed Jacen? It's not like I released him.

"You're in your head, I can see it. C'mere," he pulls me into his arms while I try to keep my face away from his suit, so as not to soil it with my makeup.

"Woulda fuck the nerves outa you but you say shop lock, so mahgo make yuh take a shot," he adds.

I almost protest but I'm scared my words will end up just being the truth. Unuh know mi cyaa take the pressure.

I nod, offering him a small smile before he gently pulls us away.

• • •

Moments later we're in his home office with my head tilted as he pours the oldest, harshest shot of whiskey down my throat.

Hatttt! Tonsil dem roast off.

I cough when it hits my chest, screwing and fanning.

"Next 30 minutes you won't give a fuck about who's at the event," he chuckles.

We'll see...

He walks over to his desk, bending to quickly type something. I watch him look through whatever he's looking through while waiting for the liquor to kick in.

Twenty minutes go by... I think, before he's done and ready to leave. We walk out of the office to everybody that was here for Christmas dinner yesterday. Tell me why the people dem a cheer and offer coos and smiles.

It's giving prom or ball, as I call it.

Sue, Skulli and mommy are all dressed and ready to go. Toni-Anne and Mariah opted out this year, blaming aches and pain but mi know ah 'cause it boring dem no wah come.

"Eh man clean up nice enuh," Joshua laughs.

"Not even a tattoo in sight," Kelly adds, smiling.

"So we dweet," J' smiles, before getting serious. "Slyme, when me come back mi wah talk to you and Ramone so don't leave."

"Cool," Slyme replies all while tapping away at his phone– probably a bother Michelle.

That is the least of our worries right now. Yuh no hear di man?

I did, but if me think 'bout it me faint ina this bumbo.

After a few minutes, we say our goodbyes and move out to the cars. He's taking the Taycan. I haven't seen this baby in months. Wait, why are my thoughts all over the place??? The liquor cannot be that stronggggg. It's been like 30 minutes, right?

"You good?" J' asks, looking over at me from the driver's seat.

"Yup…" I trail off.

Alright, I'm definitely feeling it

"Okay, so tell me… why were you on the phone with Ramone earlier?" his tone is now serious but not cold.

Bumboclawt

I start coughing uncontrollably causing water to spring to my eyes.

He turns to look at me, handing me a mini bottle of water before bringing the engine to life. I unscrew it, and take as many sips as possible, hoping a fucking excuse would pop up in my brain.

Nothing…

He gets distracted by the cars lining up to pull out in front of us and those that are supposed to be behind us. This gives me a little more time… not enough because all now me cyaa think of nuttin.

Suddenly I remember Ramone coming to me about Lorelle, while I was with Lenard. I think about it carefully but realize that nahgo work– that's just throwing Ramone under the bus. I know Jordanne doesn't like when his team mixes with my friends romantically.

Another moment of silence passes…

He shifts, taking his gun from the glove compartment, leaning back and resting it in his waist.

My eyes follow his every move…

"Nah answer? Him a hide supm from me enuh, and if him a try rope you in, talk from early," he warns, now wrapping the steering.

The AC on? 'Cause me really a sweat to pussyclawt.

My face turns up in question as I try to figure out how him know. Did he hear the conversation or what???

"Yah wonder how me know? As me say me no trust him, so I've been watching who the secured calls go out to from his end. Mah think 'bout fi go further back through the list go see who else him mek dem to."

Then him nahgo seeeeee me in deh couple more time!!!???

Fada be a fence

My thoughts are going crazy, jumping from one reality to the next. The alcohol in my blood is making it really hard for me to focus. Must be the strongest whiskey pah God land.

Okayyyy here we go. Me might as well talk.

"I–"

"Know what, you see the meeting later, be present… speak then. No want weh you tell me 'bout him, throw off the night," he expresses, now driving out of the yard, while bringing the radio's volume to its maximum.

'Bout him? It's about me!

Me just wah evaporate right now!

Masicka's Darkest Times is now shaking the car as he sings the lyrics.

"Me see di snake you know man nah live blinddd," he bobs his head, speeding down our street.

I swallow…

Weh mi say mi wah do? Evaporate from yah so.

God? If you're there…

78 | Slow Reveal Part TWO

RYLEIGH

"She's not this nice to me at work," I whisper to Jordanne.

Mrs.Wellz has been cheesing at me ever since I came in on his arms.

"Her husband is the detective that won't drop the case," he says through his teeth, smiling at the cameras flashing in our faces.

I will not get used to this.

I shift in my seat, feeling a bit out of place and uncomfortable.

More alcohol?

Yeah, that's it.

Lifting my champagne glass, I chug it. Mommy snaps her head to me, giving 'the look'.

Mi a me own big woman

I think about rolling my eyes at her but the past trauma of her slapping me when I was younger, prevents it. Grabbing Jordanne's arm, I scoot my chair closer to him. Don't ask me why, I couldn't tell you.

Feel like yahgo lose him?

Ignoring my subconscious, I whisper my next thought to him, "Sue is such a natural at this."

He chuckles, "Mum know how fi play the game. Years now Dadz have her a smile up with the one percent."

Will I eventually be like that?

Girl we a make it pass tonight?

I have a plan...

Let's hear it

I'm gonna initiate se–

Wrap it up. That's dumb

"You good?" Jordanne asks for the hundred-millionth time.

"Yeah, just uneasy 'bout th–" I'm cut off by the host.

"… as the founder himself will now grace us with his wise words."

Jordanne stands, while the crowd claps. He moves to the stage commanding the large room and everybody in it.

The teenage girls don't care to hide their blush and whispers amongst each other, while the teenage boys seem to be looking at their idol.

He gets to the podium and knocks the mic.

"Talkaphone on?" he starts and the crowd chuckles in unison. "I don't speak much each year, unuh know that."

"We do," a random voice in the back shouts.

"Like she want a talkaphone fi herself," he smiles at whoever that was… "But seriously, on previous occasions, I would pull back from speaking much because I wasn't in the correct space mentally. You know a lot of people look at me and think, him grow up privileged and went to the best schools, got an Ivy League degree, businesses… the prettiest woman in the room," he pauses, "mommy you're a close second," he laughs, and so does the crowd.

Sue holds her hands up in surrender, "I'll pass my crown onto my daughter-in-law without a fight."

Poor ting, no know me nah have that title by a morning

"Good sportsmanship," he laughs, looking at his mom, "as I was saying… the lifestyle that everybody sees, didn't reflect my mental health. I was forced to take on a lot as a teen and I know now that it was too much. Before my father's passing, I never once thought I'd be shoved into leading an empire just weeks before my 16th birthday. I never spoke to anyone about it, because I thought it weak… emasculating if you will. The younger me would use different outlets to free my mind from the pressure. Weed, alcohol, women… you get the gist… I say all that to say, privilege comes in all forms. Mine came as financial stability but was lacking in many other areas. So today I want to implore the teens in the audience to not dwell on the privilege they lack, but to focus on what they do have… Some of you might have the privilege of both parents or the privilege to go to school freely without worry, while others might just have the privilege of being here tonight, rubbing shoulders with the people who are responsible for the work force in this country… Again, don't dwell on what you lack, focus on what you have and the latter will come eventually… Big up unuh self and to the people with the overflow of money," he points to our section and behind it.

"I'm looking through the books in the morning and mi judgmental bad," he chuckles and the crowd roars.

Judgemental…

Judgement…

Murdaaa, nerves ago kill me

I take another glass of champagne and try to sip slowly this time.

Apart from being nervous, I'm really proud of him. He really has been battling his grief and emotions for as long as I've known him. And even though I might have added to his stress… well, not on purpose, never is… Okay maybe a little… not this time though.

I've lost my chain of thought.

I'm so tipsy

He exits the stage, shaking a bunch of hands on his walk back. When he sits, he plants a kiss on my cheek, winning himself my smile.

My emotions are all over the place, my thoughts too, and I just want to tell him. I've tried when Ramone found it… and he talked me out of it… and I've tried again before we got here and J' didn't want to hear it.

Sigh… It's eating me up.

• • •

We're mingling now after another hour of persons presenting. I watch as Jordanne keeps looking at his watch as if eager to get home.

No sah we need fi drunk from now, now

Agreeing with my mind I move to the bar, while J' chit chats with an Asian guy and his wife– can't remember their names.

"Can I have a shot of your best whiskey and a Moscow mule, extra vodka please," I ask as low as I can, considering the music in the back.

Nuh wah nobody hear my order.

The bartender looks at me, then to Jordanne.

"He'll be okay with it," I smile, offering him some assurance.

He hesitates but then moves to make my request, regardless. When he delivers, I quickly take the shot, making sure there aren't much eyes on me.

Di supm bittttaaaa

Ughhh, I screw my face at the wicked taste, before picking up my cocktail and turning to walk ba–

"Isn't that a little much Ms.Stevens?" Mrs.Wellz asks, flashing her million dollar smile at me.

I offer her my best smile too. Two can play this game.

"Soooo you and Mr.Sheer huh?"

I keep the straw in my mouth, hoping to avoid her question, 'cause like the man nuh just say me a him woman.

I roll my eyes slightly, I think.

"How long's it been?" she squeezes in another question.

"Longer than I can remember," I give her the answer she's looking for. I've learnt to not say we've been together since this past April, because he doesn't like to hear it.

Man wah me say since 6ᵗʰ form

"Oh," is all she says and I swear I pick up on a hint of jealousy?

"So when you say longer than you can remember, how far back do you mea–"

"Listen Mrs.Wellz, you're my co-worker, nothing more. I don't feel comfortable having this 21 questions conversation with you," I sneer, before grabbing the length of my dress and walking back over to J'.

Bright. She must want her husband job, ova yah a interrogate me 'bout me man

I get to Jordanne and we do a few more rounds of talking with other couples that are seemingly interested in the cause, as well as other business adventures.

The night drags on and I must've gone through five different shots and four glasses of cocktail– mixing my brown and white liquor, hoping to fuck him like I never have before, and then have a wicked hang over tomorrow, delaying the dreadful meeting.

Mi nuh see no other way fi get outa this.

In this moment, we're heading home and to say I'm nervous would be an understatement.

"They love you," he smiles, keeping his eyes on the road.

Of course they do. For the second half of the night I was tipsy as fuck, chatting it up and delivering jokes.

"Yeah man, liquor talk enuh," I giggle before realizing I'm a bit louder than usual.

He chuckles before saying, "Don't worry, there is not much more of those here. The rest takes place in Manhattan mostly, but the way you no like come ah you yard a foreign."

"Your yard," I correct him, "and you know it's because of work."

"Work, work, work. Wah work supm else but–"

"I'm fine," I quickly say, shutting down the spotting excuse I lied about. I haven't felt a cramp in hours, could be the alcohol but who cares.

IUD out and IUD removal pain gone…

He glances between me and the road a few times, before asking, "Really???"

I nod, biting down on my lips while squeezing my legs together. I really am horny. Shit came out of nowhere, following my last cocktail.

He smiles, flashing his perfectly aligned white teeth just before licking his lips.

The lips I want between my legs…

Now focused on my mission, I lift the console between us and retrieve the sanitizer. We don't have long before we get home and me wah be a–

"Yah do?" he asks, snapping his head at my hand.

I ignore his sudden concern and carefully cleanse my hand, putting extra focus on my thumb, middle and index finger.

Dropping the small bottle to my feet, I scoot out, grabbing the hem of my dress before pulling it up.

"Ry'… fuck yah do?" he breathes.

He knows exactly what I'm doing.

I offer no answer, instead I bring my seat allllll… the way… back. Shifting slightly to face him, I slide the seamless fabric that is my panty from the clump between my legs.

I watch him grab his phone, quickly dialing somebody. He holds it to his ear for a moment or two.

"Law… Make sure me house clear please… That affi go gwaan a morning killa… Yeah… JJ can stay a Mumz and the rest ah family can stay ina her guest house… Bad man do dat before me drop in… Less than 15 minutes away… Cool," he hangs up, and clicks the phone shut.

Now circling my clit, I decide to set the moans I was holding onto during the call free. I can feel my juices, making their way to his leather seats. Another moan leaves my lips and I insert my middle finger into my needy center.

He glances at me and I smirk.

"Always do this. Girl spiteful yuh fuck," the second half of his statement geared more towards himself than to me.

"MmmMm," I moan, now picking up the pace.

We come to a stoplight, and he actually stops this time, since the road is still a bit busy. I take the opportunity to slide my fingers out, to display my clear, gooey juices. Rubbing the liquid between my thumb, index and middle finger, I smile… before pulling it apart, showing off just how gooey it is.

A sigh leaves his lips before he says, "Years later and mi still no know weh mi ago do with you."

He tries to touch me for himself, but I swat his hand away.

Nothing turns him on more than restriction.

The light switches to green and I watch his lips curl up into a mischievous smile before taking off.

• • •

JORDANNE

She's fucking me like she owe me supm killa…

"Ohhhh Myyy G–Jor!" she screams.

Mhmm, love hear her like this.

I have her feet held in the air by the hollow of her knees, pushed back to her chest, while I sink my dick in and out.

Pulling out to the tip, I give her a moment to recover before slamming back in. I've been doing this for the past two minutes, waiting for her internal hose to spring free.

"Jordannnnneeee!!!!!"

Love when she scream mi name…

Love when she moan mi name…

Love when she cry me na–

"Ah Uhhh," she continues to fight it.

Girl stubborn from birth. Jah Jah

I bend, finding her ear, all while still giving her the slow, hard thrusts. While lingering at her ear, I start to notice how her pussy is clenching just from me being this close to her neck. I use her reaction to my advantage and start leaving wet kisses along her neck before moving back to her ear…

"If," I thrust.

"You," I thrust again.

"Don't," another thrust.

"Cum," … thrust.

"For," … thrust.

"Me," … thrust.

"I'm," … thrust.

"Going to," … thrust.

"Punish," … thrust.

"Y–" before I can finish the last word she starts shaking. Pussy grabbing me into my favourite paradise.

I continue the strokes at the same pace, pulling her to the peak of her orgasm. I can see that she wants to say something, but nahv the words or di strength.

She nahfi say nuttin still, I know her body– her mind

I pull out to the tip and slam back into her. This time her eyes roll back while her hands search for the sheets to grab– rooting herself to earth like she always does and…

… There it is. Yeah man, it dat…

Her internal hose is cut free and I move my hold from the hollow of her knees to her ankles, just to watch the view of her spraying my dick.

Fucking best

Best bloodclawt pussy.

The water doesn't stop and neither do I.

Wait…

Fuckkkkkk, mi wah buss

No…

No, no…

I slide out to stop the feeling, using my shaft to slap her clit while watching her shiver.

"J you keep doing that to yourself, it's been like 40 minutes," she takes a deep breath.

Hour and some change, but who's counting? I just want to savor the feeling. She's climaxed endless times before that one just now and mi love that. I love… her.

Deciding to give myself the gift of an orgasm I flip her over.

One yah me cyaa pull from, so

She assumes the perfect position… ass up, perfect arch, head down, legs a good width apart. I smirk, knowing what her aim is. My eyes start moving around the room, searching for my pre-roll. I spot it on the nightstand, grab it and quickly light it before taking puffs– while moving back to her.

"Jordanne wah yah d–"

"Ssshhh," I shut her up with a merciless thrust, pausing to hear her scream circulate the room.

Good…

I stay still, taking more puffs, while slapping her ass. Me just love watch it jiggle. The slaps seem to stimulate her and I feel a fresh set of gooeyness coat my length.

Bloodclawwwwwwttttttt

A weird sound leaves my lips, and my toes separate to ground my feet. I hear her giggle before she starts throwing it back.

Fuckkkk!

Mek she have her way mi give up.

●●●

RYLEIGH

I start throwing it back and the sounds of him crashing in and out of me turns me on even more. He slaps my ass again and the pain quickly turns to pleasure, granting him more of my juices.

"Ry'… fuckkkkkkk," he grunts.

Yeah, I love this. I love him…

I start forcing it back more when he grabs me, pulling me off the bed and walks me to the glass doors that lead to our balcony– dick still inside. The view isn't like the one from Sue's or the one from our old house. Our room is more towards the back and so I can see the city lights a good distance away, instead of our street.

I realize he doesn't want to go outside, instead he presses me up against the glass, my breath condensing and causing a smudge. I clap my palms open against it to keep a good stance while he prepares himself to take control.

The feel of him sliding out slowly while holding my waist in place before sinking himself back into me– balls deep, sends me to HEAVEN.

"Jordanne!!! Please!!!"

"Please??? Nuh fuck yuh fi weeks now Love. No pleading," he counters.

"I–" I try to get my words out but he picks up the pace.

"Fuck you mean please?" he mutters to himself and I know he's nearing his climax. It's when he talks the most.

His hands move from my waist to my breast and throat, pulling me to press against his chest.

Him favourite ting dis fi do

I feel his breath on my ear and it sends shock waves not just down my spine but throughout my entire body. No way him ago mek me cum againnnnn…

"Jor–"

"I love you," he whispers and just like that, I start falling apart, jerking through my orgasm as he finds his– squeezing my throat as he moves through it.

I can almost feel him fill me.

His hand moves from my throat and joins the other that's holding my breasts. Before I can move, I feel him leaving multiple kisses at the back of my neck and on my shoulders.

Through heavy breathing I say, "I love you Jordanne… beyond and above all else."

He rests his head atop mine and I can already feel the tears welling in my eyes, knowing tomorrow I'll have to explain myself to him.

79 | Revelation

JORDANNE

"**I**na the next five minutes," is what I say to Slyme. I've instructed him and Ramone to find themselves at the entrance of my home office, before I do.

The sun threatening to burst through the black-out curtains and the sound of Ryleigh brushing her teeth gives a wholesome vibe.

Much better feeling than the penthouse.

I roll out of bed and walk to the bathroom, joining her. I move to the toilet, releasing my bladder, while she complains about me being disgusting with no shame. While washing my hands, I grab my toothbrush from the holder at my sink and move to hers, deciding to torment her.

"Weh yahgo?" she barely gets her words out, mouth filled with toothpaste foam.

"Wah mi cyaa brush my teeth at your sink?" I question, feigning ignorance.

"Nooo," she groans, shoving me back to mine.

"Buil nuh, yours me wah use this morning."

She bends to spit and I slap her ass. She's in nothing but a white T-shirt and I take the opportunity to guide my fingers to her entrance. She jumps, grabbing my hand away before turning around.

"Stop nuh J'."

"Mi supposed to get my fill for the weeks I missed though," my tone now whiney while I wet my toothbrush.

She mumbles something while leaving but I don't hear.

She can gwaan enuh. Affi get dat.

Less than ten minutes later, we're heading to the office. We make it to the foot of the stairs to see Ramone and Slyme waiting in the living area. A look sweeps Ramone's face... A look I don't understand, coming from him.

Well mek we find out nuh

We will.

"Morning," Ryleigh offers them both a greeting

I don't. Can feel me head a go already.

We all walk to the office and I enter the code, releasing the double doors. Stepping in with Ry' just behind me, I move to the curtains, closing them, before taking a seat around my desk.

Ryleigh is already playing with her fingers.

Hope she know she no affi fraida Ramone.

I point to the two chairs before me, signaling both men to sit. Ry' moves to the chaise nearest to the bar before sitting down, keeping her focus on us all.

"Before me start ask questions, everybody know how me feel bout loyalty?"

• • •

RYLEIGH

"Before me start ask questions, everybody know how me feel bout loyalty?" he asks and I can already hear the tone of his voice changing.

No longer the playful Jordanne he was mere minutes ago...

He's becoming hi–

"And unuh know how me feel 'bout lies???" he adds, keeping his focus on the men before him. The two men he trusts the most.

Sigh.

They nod in unison.

"Cool, cool. So what section of my footage is missing?" he turns to Ramone.

Slyme looks at Ramone confused, almost as confused as I would be if I didn't know what was going on.

"Jordanne I–" Ramone starts.

"Boss," Jordanne lowly corrects him. So low and lethal, I almost missed it. His eyes darken at Ramone's choice of words and I watch his index finger as it begins tapping his desk.

Him a get vex.

"Boss... th-the video yuh get was wrong. Did a practice crop and paste, like I usually do... You just get the wrong version."

"You need practice, since when???" he snaps, leaning all the way back into his chair.

Suicide, suicide ah my only option right now

"Always been a practice still, neva stop," Ramone counters, he seems to be getting angry as well.

Jordanne laughs and I mean really laugh.

Slyme looks at me and I shrug.

Still no like him but if anything, a him affi go save mi

J' rises from his chair and walks over to a safe, camouflaged into the wall. He retrieves the shiniest Glock I've ever seen, along with a silver revolver. He walks back to his desk and rests the revolver on a stack of papers.

"My father loved this gun," he turns to Slyme, holding up the Glock proudly... "You know that already though," he smiles.

Liam nods, face still riddled by confusion.

"Him only ever use it as his concealed weapon. Nuh have nuh duppy pon it. You know why?" he now looks at Ramone.

"No," Ramone breathes.

"Because... him did have a team weh him think him coulda trust. Neva affi pull in public, so his licensed gun still brand fucking new... You can believe that?" he laughs but there is not even a trace of humor in his voice.

He pauses his sinister laughter, to ask Ramone, "Mi say if you believe dat?!"

I jump, startled by the sudden raise of his voice.

"Believe man," Ramone mutters.

My chest starts rising rapidly and if you frighten me again right now, me piss up. No amount of years knowing Jordanne nahgo save mi.

None...

None at all.

"So why the fuck yah call mi woman?" he points at me, "on an encrypted line without my knowledge bad man?"

"Bloodclawtttt..." Slyme whispers, looking back and forth between Ramone and I.

Ramone looks speechless. He couldn't have known that Jordanne found out about the latest call. Normally he doesn't go through those phone logs to check. All of that responsibility falls on Ramone himself.

The log should've been deleted. It's just giving sloppy at this point.

And him woulda retrieve the log too idiot

True... I'm guilty of forgetting how smart he is sometimes–

"Yah take too long fi answer," now cocking the gun he says has never been used to kill.

Slyme realizes how serious he is and intervenes, saying, "Boss... mek him explain."

"Liam, yah the next one. I put you as next in command and you so fucking busy a run down pussy from the most waste gyal ina the island, dat you mek bay things a slide, right in front your eyes," his words fill the room, spewing nothing but venom.

Me ago dead.

God please.

Somebody call mi mother.

"Weh di fucking original video??!!" Jordanne shouts.

That's definitely Drip

I look at both my palms, trying to locate the pipe that's been set loose, because the way dem a SWEATTTT.

"Boss mi–" Ramone tries but Jordanne is already walking around the desk to him.

"Mi–" Ramone looks at me.

"Duh look pon her. Mi say weh the bloodclawt video deh bad man? Or you wah me retrieve it myself?" he laughs, now pressing the nozzle to Ramone's temple.

"Drip!" Slyme warns, keeping his hands above his head.

My breathing is ragged and I can even hear my heartbeat.

My vision is leaving...

Sas Crise, Mighty Gahd of Daniel. Why me woulda take up gun man? Good, good gyal pikny like me? Fada...

"Three!" Drip's voice comes clear

"Two!" he continues.

"Drip weh di fuck bredda?!" Slyme tries again.

I–

God...

"OKKKKKAYYYYYY!!!" I scream, "It was me, a mi. It wasss meeee!!!"

Ramone releases his breath and Jordanne looks to me.

"Duh lie fi him Ry," he breathes.

"I'm not!" I start, "I was sneaking into the safe house, fe-feeding Jacen and-and uh... Ramone saw my prints in the logs and the gates being slightly opened on the tapes and deleted the footage... along with the log of my prints. Him call me yesterday fi mek me know him see a glitch in the footage, but he already sent it to you while you were in New York."

I release my breath, now noticing the feeling of tears on my cheeks. Slyme's eyes are wide from shock, Ramone looks relieved but worried at the same time and Jordanne?

Jordanne is heartbroken...

His eyes dance from confusion while the room falls silent for more than ten minutes. Sit down right now and set ah ten minute timer on your phone... and just see how awful that is.

"Who you say you feed Ry?" his voice now low, consumed with pain and disbelief.

My fingers find each other.

Sigh.

"Jacen... I was bringing him soup and water, for a week, maybe a week and a half. I was just concerned abo–"

"Yuh did know this???" he points at Slyme

"No," is all he answers with.

"Leave the room," Drip continues.

They both attempt to leave.

"Nuh you me boss," he says, directing Ramone to stay.

Meanwhile I can't control my fucking tears.

As if reading my mind Jordanne says, "Dry yuh fucking crocodile tears and come to me."

And di lady foot dem nah work?

I really don't think they are, but mi nah disobey Drip… Jordanne maybe… Him? No.

I stand and my feet start moving to the desk. Hesitant to take a seat, I stay standing just before him. Instead of moving back to his chair, he takes a seat atop his desk, using the gun to scratch his head in confusion.

"Mek mi put this together," he starts off, wildly waving the Glock between Ramone and I.

"You… mi woman… love a mi fucking life and after life possibly… get up outa the house weh me buy fi you… sneak go way a the safe house weh mi trust you enough to grant you access to… Sneakkkk in, avoid most of the cameras, somehowww get ina me vault without me noticing, which means you spin the numbers back to what they were each day you reach… go in, feed a man weh tryyyy kill me, countless times. A man weh try take you from me? Feed him fi wah Ryleigh???"

"Because I–"

"Keep yuh fucking explanation!" he shouts.

… And dah shout deh? lacedddd with hate.

He turns to look at Ramone, "And youuu, weh mi know from K1, know alla this and try cover it upppp?"

Ramone doesn't answer, learning from my mistake I assume.

Jordanne folds his arm, now shaking the loaded, already cocked gun, in thought.

We all stay there for what seems like a millennia before he springs to his feet, grabbing me by my throat, gun against my skull.

"Leave the room Ramone," the voice that comes out of his mouth is one like no other.

Deep…

Sadistic…

Venomous…

Cold…

Sinister… Everything bredda.

Ramone doesn't protest, he couldn't if he wanted to. My eyes follow him as he leaves the room, shaking his head.

"Lock it," Drip commands, knowing once the door is pulled shut, none of them can open it from outside in time to save me.

"Look at me," he breathes, tightening the grip he has around my neck.

My eyes move from the door, to meet his.

He presses the gun further into my skull before whispering, "Yuh gyal, Yah born wicked."

"Jordanne I–"

"Shut up! Before mi pull the fucking trigga!"

I squirm, collecting my words and locking them in a part of my brain they'll be unable to escape.

"My father was right about women. Unuh ah just distraction and a vessel to bear fruits of our name," he hisses. "You deh wid me enemy!!! And then even after me telllllll you wah him and Mase dem plan you say duh kill him. Me spare him life... him come back againnn and DM yuh and you hide it, only fi him pop up fi try do supm AGAIN and yuh wah feed him???"

"Weh yah try prove??!! Say yuh have the best heart ina the world??? Or say no matter wah yuh do, you untouchable to me?"

He pauses, as if waiting for me to answer... but I can't. I can barely breathe. He releases me roughly and I stumble to the ground.

"Ansahhhh me!"

"I'm sorry, I tried to tell you," I try.

"Nahhhhhh, nuh come with dat. When you wah tell me anything else you find a time and a way bad man," he seethes.

Mi ah beg yuh no say nuttin else mama

I take my mind's advice and keep quiet.

When he realizes I'm without words, he stoops to my level, using the gun to bring my chin up, forcing eye contact.

"Yuh me a talk to enuh killa," he continues.

"Just kill me," I sob, my words breaking.

He laughs, this time holding actual humor.

"You think me ago kill you??? Nahhhhhh Ry', none a datttt," he smiles, not a smile to celebrate... "You ago stay here and watch me become the person I try to hide from you daily. Yuh no know everything, but you know enough to not be able to leave. You begged for ittt, to be in on this side of my life. So now dat yuh can't leave, you ago watch me fuck as much gyal as mi like, leave as mi like, come in as mi like... just live life as mi like... You ago go work and come back home... and if me even dream say yuh have a man me kill dat and mek yuh feed him to mi dog dem," he hisses his teeth loudly before standing.

His words cut deeeeppppp... and my tears start rolling again.

"Since you love Rome so much, go dig him up and mek him save yuh and your mother from yuh wicked daddy," he uses the gun to tap against his leg, before exiting the room.

Daddy??? Which daddy?

80 | Dust Settles-J

THREE MONTHS LATER

JORDANNE

I can't seem to find my footing, or forgive myself... because how was I that blind? Too much shit slipped right before my eyes. Too many times I saw that she was hiding something and didn't dig for answers.

Tuh much time bad head.

So now me leff fi question myself... I can't let her leave and I almost don't want her to stay. Not because I want to live without her but because I know she'll be just as unhappy as my mother was years ago.

Took twelve long weeks for my anger to dissipate... Twelve long, painful weeks for the dust to settle, for me to see that what I've been doing, still doing, is no more than a harmful cycle, picked up from the man that everybody told me to follow suit.

Even after death, he plagues my existence.

Fuck!

"Are we supposed to stay today?" a soft voice pulls me from my thoughts.

Bloodclawt, forget dem even deh yah

Without offering a verbal answer, I shake my head no.

Them know dem can't stay on any occasion, so me nuh understand the fuckry question today.

Blowing the smoke from my mouth I signal to the door. One of the girls hiss at my action and I raise a brow at her. The other yanks her out of the room while I sit up to make myself a drink.

I look at the bottle confused. Why it empty killa?

Why yuh need it at 6am?

Mi affi explain dat?

I don't usually stay at this apartment but last night I chose to. Last night I missed her a little more than usual and so if I could change the environment… maybe I'd forget the love I can't seem to shake. Everywhere else reminds me of her one way or another. Whether it being her helping Mum to decorate it or her simply overseeing the books.

So here I am, at an apartment I bought on impulse last week.

Jah…

No way she do mi alla that and I'm still trying to figure out what I did for her to do that. Was she not comfortable with my lifestyle? Mi dat hard fi deal wid? Why me woman 'fraid fi tell me simple things weh might bother her?

Woman?

Friend?

Hostage at this point bredda.

"Yo the guard dem carry dem gone enuh, drink?" come's Liam's voice at the doorway, holding a fresh bottle of Henny.

Might as well

I walk over to him, taking one of the two glasses and the bottle. Pouring myself a drink, I start to realize two a we ina the worse boat. As the two man dem weh basically responsible fi the island, two woman nuffi have we so skull.

I chuckle at the thought and Slyme looks at me as if he understands.

"Yeah man, we fuck up," he laughs.

"Cheers to dat den," I raise my glass.

Just wait till him figure out him woman pregnant, me nuh have no more drinking buddy, so I might as well make use of the time.

"You know your situation no need fi be like this though right?" he starts.

Not this again.

"No start," I mumble, taking a seat in the chair at the foot of the bed. He stays standing, refusing to ever sit anywhere in the rooms I use, claiming him nuh know weh me and the girl dem do in yah.

"Fi real… you can go home to your woman, mine disappear and somebody… YOU, decide say me nuffi find her myself."

"Yo just trust me, you'll see her soon enough," I mumble.

"Yah say that fi months now," he counters.

"Have faith," I pull the glass to my mouth.

He hisses, chugs his drink and exits the room.

Man nuh like hear dat enuh.

Putting the glass down, I re-light my spliff, getting ready to drown my thoughts. I sit there, leaned all the way back for some minutes before I drift into thought.

FLASHBACK

"Mi deh yah so first though!" Ryleigh complained, glaring at the older guy trying to cut in-front her in the cafeteria line.

"Move mi nuh," the guy seethed.

In less than a second, she was pulling on his shirt, defending her spot in the queue.

"Aye gyal, weh yah do?" he grabbed her, as if to fight her for her own spot.

"Bad man, the girl say fi liff," Jordanne intervened, bringing his coconut water to his mouth, a mixture of authority and nonchalance radiating from his built.

Both parties involved in the small tussle turned to look at him.

Although he seemed to be younger than the guy trying to bully Ryleigh, he commanded immediate respect, and the guy moved his hand from her tunic.

"Ahh Danne," was all the older guy said, before walking away in surrender.

This puzzled Ryleigh, causing her to forget about getting back in line. Jordanne walked over to her, taking her hand before bringing her to the empty hall entrance just before you enter the cafeteria.

She didn't protest, nor did she feel uncomfortable.

Crazyyy, she thought. His dominance was intriguing.

At almost 16 years old herself, she thought, 'Why dah likkle boy yah think him a smaddy?'

He opened the side door that she didn't once think led to the kitchen. He pulled her inside and the instant heat caused her to bat her eye lids.

"Sheer how much time me say nuh come in yah 'cause yuh nahv no hair net!?" the chubby lady scolded him.

He smiled, "Easy no Ms.Sandra. Give her wah she want fimi please."

Sandra gave Ryleigh a soft smile before asking what she wanted.

"Cinnamon roll... and cheese.," Ry' whispered.

Jordanne looked her up and down before doubling over in laughter.

"She's a part of the cult," Sandra laughed, moving to get what she asked for from the front, since she didn't want actual cooked food.

At their high school, cinnamon roll and cheese was a staple and so was a cheese patty with a spice bun instead of a cocoa bread.

"You fi eat supm heavier," Jordanne suggested, now standing before her.

He was intrigued by how shy she was all of a sudden, as if she wasn't about to fight with a 6th former.

"I don't eat much," she shrugged.

"Mi see dat," he laughed, poking at her collar bones.

She laughed out, swatting his hand from her.

Sandra came back with her order, an added bottle of coconut water and a small foam cup.

"Red peas," she said.

Jordanne nodded, taking everything from Sandra's hands except for the small cup. Ryleigh took that from Sandra and Jordanne took Ry's hand before leading her outside. They walked out towards the tables, where she could now see her boyfriend walking out of the dorm.

She stopped walking, "Maybe you should give me those," she suggested while pointing at her 'food' in his hands.

"Why?" he asked, stopping to search her eyes.

She looked to her boyfriend now nearing where they stood.

Jordanne chuckled in, disapproval?

*For a moment it seemed as if they knew each other for years before this moment. They both knew **of** each other, yes. Her that he was somebody with wealthy parents and a little too much privilege for her liking... and him that she was the girlfriend that the striker from the school's team didn't deserve.*

He handed her, her lunch order, just in time for Folan to walk up to them.

"Why you never wait pah me?" he asked, looking at her in annoyance.

She shrugged, causing Jordanne to chuckle.

"Supm funny?" Folan asked him, now looking him up and down.

Jordanne gave him none of his words but all of his eyes.

"Yo Danne!" Dalani called from a distance, now watching the intense stare off.

Jordanne snapped out of it and smiled at Ryleigh.

Turning to Dalani who was hanging onto Ghale, he said, "Mah farwud dawg."

He took a few steps backwards, keeping his eyes focused on Ryleigh, before turning to climb the steps to where his friend was.

Folan took Ryleigh's hand, leading her away. She looked back for a moment, catching Jordanne still staring, while his friend tried to tell him something.

They smiled at each other, before getting back to their separate lives.

'Nuh like dah boy deh,' he thought to himself, before walking off to find Emily.

PRESENT DAY

"Bad man!" Skulli's voice grabs me from my thoughts.

I groan at his presence.

"Get up yute, and get you shit together. Everyday cyaa be the same thing!"

How the fuck him know say a yah so me deh??? Mmmchtt!

"Me cyaa keep run things fi yuh. People ah ask fi you bad head," he continues. "You and Slyme can't continue."

Quit me wah quit, I hiss internally. But how do I quit my life?

Change your name and go live a Costa Rica?

Without me wom–

Without Ryleigh?

Why not?

Mmmcht.

"Nuh ina the mood Skulli."

"Drip mine me affi puff up yuh chest two time. Get up," he grabs me to my feet. "We a leff," he scolds.

Moments later we're pulling into the yard. Skulli parks, and waits for me to exit. I hesitate, knowing that she's here at this hour, since it's a weekend. She's probably even up by now to get JJ ready to go to Ms.Cherry's.

I fly the car door open and step out and Paul doesn't wait another second before leaving.

Jah know?

I walk to the side of the house, and towards the back, moving to the guest house, where I've been staying. Just as I thought, she's on the balcony, singing, horribly... while Junior lathers his face in a slice of pineapple. She notices that I'm looking, and I see her mood physically change.

"Good morning," I greet them both.

"Good morninggg!" Junior shouts, waving his pine at me.

Ryleigh though... no answer.

Instead, she hisses, takes the pine from Junior's hands and pulls herself and him away from the balcony. She slides the door shut, causing me to sigh, before walking off.

Haha! You deserve dat me boss

True...

81|Dust Settles-R

RYLEIGH

"**E**at the pine slower nuh JJ," boy yah a behave like me no feed him often. He completely ignores me, picking up another piece before he's done chewing the one he just shoved into his mouth.

My God, him need fi turn nine like tomorrow, and then ten, and then eleven, so I can rest my nerves, throat and energy.

The shuffle from my phone goes to a song that I've been singing everyday now. I sing it so much that sometimes Junior joins in.

"Made you check your bullishit at the door," I sing, looking at the city view across the hills. Jhene knew what she was writing when she put the pen down for this.

My singing is disturbed by the sound of a car pulling in. If ano Toni, is her brother, this early. Ignoring it, I continue to kill the lyrics.

In the middle of my grammy winning, heartfelt performance, here comes Jordanne waltzing in at 7am. When anuh 4am, a 5am... or 6am, sometimes it's even 24 hours in passing. Once it was two full days, but as anuh my problem anymore.

When it first started, he used to come in at like 1am, drowning in the smell of women, weed and alcohol. I would watch him drag himself to the guest bedroom downstairs, sleeping there and getting up to leave again in the mornings before I leave for work.

Used to bother me, but not anymore.

If he wants to live that life then him can do that. The childish tit for tat games are no longer appealing to me. I still love him, I do... love duh just get up and shut off but, I've learnt to let him be and not allow him to drag me down the whirlpool with him.

Cause we all know when I retaliate I'm the bad person right?

Right.

To be stuck in a situation like this where I can't figure out my next step is probably the only thing resting on my mind right now.

"Good Morning…"

But a weh di bloodclawt this?

Junior waves his pineapple and extends a good morning to the man downstairs, looking up from the back lawns. I hiss at his audacity, and grab JJ's hand, pulling him behind me into the house.

Fuck him feel this be??? MMMCHT!

"Can I go to him?" Junior asks, now running from me towards the pool table.

A heavy sigh leaves my lips.

Jesus a tyadddd.

Then a cyaa me this at 22, stuck living with somebody that I can't even tolerate, while co-parenting a child I just met three years ago, that belongs to neither of us.

I pull out my phone to text him.

Junior wants to spend time with you.

Almost immediately he replies.

The Warden: Gimi like 20 minutes.

Cool

The Warden: Can we talk today?

**Everything you need to know about his
schedule, I've already told you. Nothing
has changed. Just have him back to me
by 8:00 'cause Ms.Cherry and Mariah
a come get him around that time.**

**The Warden: Yah act like we no live
on the same property.**
The Warden: I'm talking about Us.

What's happening in the U.S?

The Warden: ☺ yahgo stop?

**Just confused, you haven't said
anything about 'us' since last year.**

The Warden: I want to now.

**And I wanted to back then, I don't want to
now… JJ will be with you in 25 minutes.**

With that I click my phone shut and move to the kitchen.

• • •

"Me say girl, I don't know which gyal stress him last night, him come 'bout talk this morning. Me pass dah stage deh mlovve."

Muuch laughs, shoving a piece of carrot into a jar of peanut butter.

"Lawd, pregnancy cravings disgust me," I shudder, screwing my face at the phone screen.

"Gwaan till a your time," she jokes.

"Please stop. Wah fi breed me? Me middle finger???" I ask, wiggling my finger around.

She stands to cover the peanut butter and I get a glimpse of her tummy– round and cute.

"Pregnancy fit you enuh Michelle," I coo.

"Then me no know… Take it in 'cause a one and done," she laughs, mouth going around in circles, seemingly enjoying the nasty carrot and peanut butter combo.

LAWD.

"Mi a plan fi tell Liam," her next words shock me.

Mi rass, more trouble ina dah prison place yah now.

"Well me know the day did ago come and him must a wonder why you stay so long."

"Lucky thing me a citizen, because me couldn't come back after no six months, the torment weh woulda cova me life," she shakes her head.

I smile, thinking of the torment weh wrap up mine right now. My mother's contact flashes across the screen.

"Lata Michelle, mummy a call me."

"Okay mi gyal. Netflix date tonight?"

"Wouldn't miss it fi the world," I giggle, ending her call to pick up mommy's.

"Mummy?" I answer, hearing a loud Beres Hammond song in her background.

"Where are you?" she asks, shouting above the music.

"I'm home, I'm always home mummy. Me miss you, you coming to see me today or what?"

"Yes a that me call you 'bout. I can't come this Saturday, yuh mother have a date," she giggles.

Date?! For as long as I've known myself, it's always been me and my mother. Wah this pah me now? Wah kinda cherry revival she a try?

"Okay, I guess I'll sit and look at the walls," I whine, hoping for her to change her mind.

"Likkle girl, you have man enuh. As a young girl you nuffi itch up ina house with your mother every Saturday evening so."

Wellllll... now would be a good time fi mek unuh know say, mommy duh know nuttin waah gwaan. I've only told her Jordanne has been busy these past couple of weeks, which gives me the freedom to see her more... and that because of what happened last year, I don't really like to be out that much on my own unless it's with Toni and dem.

Who we a lie fi protect exactly?

My dignity...

"Okay young foot, enjoy your date. I'm gonna go get Junior and have him wait for Ms.Cherry. Love you, lata."

"Love you too me one seed, lata," she says, making kissing sounds through the speakers.

Affi my mother to rass.

I slide from the bed and decide to neaten it before leaving to go find JJ and such man downstairs. Grabbing the cushion, I was playing with while on both calls, I fluff it before moving it to the head of the bed.

"Ry?" Jordanne's voice startles me.

Cho bumboclawt man.

• • •

JORDANNE

I watch as she grabs a cushion, putting it back in place. My eyes roam her body, bringing nothing but lust to the forefront of my brain.

Jah know...

She has her hair out today– messy but cute. The tights and camisole she's wearing hugs every single curve perfectly. My eyes stay lingering on her ass, longer than it has in weeks, but I quickly shake the feeling away.

Wonder if she know she can sleep in our bedroom? She really nuh affi in yah so...

"Ry?" I find myself involuntarily saying her name.

The sound of my voice causes her to tense, and her eyes almost roll outa her fucking head. I almost laugh at how much I annoy her, but I don't.

"What is it?" she asks, now pulling the tights down her thighs.

As if dem can go no further

I don't answer, all my focus now belongs to my eyes, that are busy sweeping her body again.

"Where is JJ?" she speaks again.

Oh yes JJ, that's what I'm here for.

Yute haha!

"Him ina the car," is all I say, forgetting to tell her why.

She looks at me and her lips form a hard, straight line.

"Why? Yah drop him ova Mariah dem?" she asks, almost bursting with annoyance.

I find it cute, how angry she is with me... A smirk finds its way to my face before the words I want to say leave my mouth.

"Taking him to the Stewarts them fair and–"

"No," she bitterly scoffs, cutting me off.

Sigh...

"Why not?" I ask, already knowing the answer.

"How long we ago keep this up? We're not married. Why do I have to keep going to these events with you?"

Because I want us to?

"Because we went public... like newspaper article public," I try.

"Stop eh fuckry a me ears big man. If I can't leave the team then fine. Hire me to run the books, to control the real estate, to do something... and go 'bout your life. Go public with somebody else. We nuh married, I'm not tied to you in any way, shape or form."

Cut up

Yuh fuck.

I stand there looking at her for a few seconds, trying not to get angry or force her to do what she doesn't want to.

"I never said you couldn't leave the team... You can't leave... me."

Her eyes squint into tiny holes of confusion before she says, "All you muss mad."

Thought that was a known fact?

"Yah come or not?" I ask again, hoping she changed her mind.

"No–"

"Cool..." my answers comes soft, but cold... and with that I turn to walk out of her room.

• • •

RYLEIGH

I'm halfway through the tub of grapenut ice-cream when my phone goes off.

Then a who this now? Like mah run a hotline today.

Sexy Bitch...

I slide at the screen to answer her, "Toni-Anne?"

"Why yuh no deh yah? Ah just me, you man and bay pikny," she starts her whining.

Yes unuh hear her right. Man is what she said because she also doesn't know what went down. The only people that know are Muuch because I told her and Lorelle because Ramone had to explain to her why he was sent on the mission to accompany Ruse.

He wasn't needed, Jordanne just unbearably annoying and spiteful.

"Mi no feel good," is the only excuse I can come up with.

"Yah breed?! You know me think yah mule gyal," Mariah's head pops into the screen of the phone.

"Excuse me???"

"Yes, mule, 'cause the way you fuck nuff and all now yuh cyaa bree–" T' grabs the phone from her.

"It's a kid's event Mariah! Jeeeezzz," I hear her scolding her in the background before her face appears on screen again.

"Yah breed fi true?" Toni laughs, raising her eyebrows at me.

"Yuh see how rumour start though? Me say me no feel good. How it reach yah so?" I bring another spoon full of the ice-cream to my mouth, before I sight a text come in from Jordanne. I toggle to it...

**The Warden: |attachment| Just look how you
fake son do mi face killa.**

**The real subject of this picture
is why yuh in a coat?**

**The Warden: JJ wanted to wear his version and
wanted me to match him ☺**

I smile at how cute that was of him. Matching the likkle bad bruk boy and letting him paint his face.

If only...

"A who the lady a smile wid?" Mariah interjects, shoving her head back in view.

"Danne. See him right deh so a stare pon him phone too," T' explains.

The smile instantly leaves my face. I hiss loudly, closing his chat before digging my spoon back into the tub.

Cause me no born a yam grung, ah cane me know grow a Clarendon

"Mi nah smile wid nobody," I mumble, rolling my eyes. "A night. Unuh nah gah unuh yard?"

"Girl a now it just ago nice. From day the pikny dem a run up and down, ah our time fi go pon the rides now," Mariah shrieks in excitement.

"Alright, enjoy unuh self. Me ago done watch Franklin."

"Snowfall?" Toni laughs out

"Franklin me say and a dat me a stick to, bye," I cackle out before hanging up.

• • •

"Ry," a deep but hushed masculine voice finds its way into my dreams.

"MmhMm?" is all I offer.

"Ryleigh," the voice continues.

Bumboclawt man. A wah kinda nightmare thi–

I feel hands against my skin and I fly up, rubbing my eyes, trying to pry them open simultaneously.

Of course…

I hiss and plop myself back down onto my pillows, trying to ignore Jordanne who is now trying to get into bed with me.

A weh di–

"Jordanne, you smell like alcohol and weed. Duh try come ina me bed with the fuckry please," I ask, mustering up as much energy as I can.

Literally just shut me eye enuh man. It has to be no later than 2:30am judging by where my playlist is right now.

"Mi woman me come fi sleep wid still," he mutters, grabbing the comforter from me.

"Are you drunk?!"

"Well… mi nuh necessarily sober," he chuckles, mimicking the action of pulling a spliff.

Alright here we go… I can't remember him being like this since his dad passed… so I sit up, just looking at him.

"So if mi take off the clothes, can I come?"

I find myself nodding… I guess me affi change my sheets again tomorrow. Ughhh!

He drags his white T over his head, leaving just his merino. He then unzips his jeans, kicking it off before throwing it on the couch at the foot of the bed. He then moves around to the emptier side of the bed and crawls beneath my sheets.

"Who drove you home?" I ask, confused.

He never ever gets this drunk or high. Never know it still possible the way me see him drink and smoke endlessly without any effects.

"Skulli," is all he whispers, before planting his head in my bosom and throwing his hand across my abdomen.

"Neva say we coulda get cozy," I whisper… but he snuggles into me even more.

"Wah'pn tonight, couldn't find no girl fi carry home?"

"You ever see me with no girl?" he mumbles, words falling out hoarse.

I don't have to, I know.

Idiot dah boy yah take mi fah but as me a play the long game

An eerie silence fills the room for what feels like days– longgg, cold days.

"I'm sorry," he whispers, squeezing my side.

"Weeks and 'bout 26 girls too late suga," I heave, proud of the random number I chose to throw out.

Another couple seconds of silence passes before he starts again, "Why yuh mek mi find out like dat?"

"You're not the easiest person to talk to Jorda–"

"Bullshit," he counters.

I shove his head from me. Mi nah argue wid no boy enuh.

"Fuck yah do?" he looks at me confused.

"Yuh never even mek me explain after the fact. You just go back go slip ina yuh dutty ways," I hiss.

"Bredda a weeks pah top a weeks mah ask you weh yah hide and you no say nuttin. Like you nah understand weh you do. Is like you clueless bad man."

I hiss again, ignoring his rant.

"Yo, if somebody did a your rival, and me go talk to dem just outa spite fi it bun you, then that same person try kill you, twice, you woulda wah me take care of them? Maybe me mad 'cause me cyaa understand. So me need you fi explain," he looks directly at me, searching for a genuine explanation.

"I was not feeding him because I cared about him Jordanne. Just neva want him dead. You kept saying he refused to eat from unuh in fear of poison... I know what it's like to be without your father in the younger years. As much as yours was missing, you still had him in the earlier days... and see now, both parents gone and I have to bring up a child I didn't ask for."

"You don't have to do anything you don't wa–" he interrupts me.

"Duh tell me that because Ruse gone how long and when he's here he's at work half the time and Mariah nah keep nobody pikny."

Cho

"Yuh logics dem based pon emotions. You were trying to keep the man that wanted me dead, alive... Me just cyaa forgive you fi dat... but I can't turn the fucking love off!" he raises his voice...

... And I raise my eyebrows.

We sit there in another spell of silence before he's nuzzling into me again.

And me emotional?

I'm not where I was weeks ago when everything just happened. If we had this conversation earlier, I would think about staying but right now? Mi nahgo do it. Call it weh you want, mi nahgo live ina dah cycle yah. Every time me upset him, him ago turn to weed, liquor and pussy weh anuh mine? Fuck that.

"Jordanne... what is it that you want from me?" I mumble.

I feel him breathe before saying... "I want you to just choose me... for once."

His words, catch me off-guard.

I–

I stir, now fighting the urge to comfort him. Why would he even think that anybody else was above him? That's not the truth.

I try to think of words to say but come up with zero. Sigh...

After moments of us just breathing, my hands find his head. That's the only level of comfort I can give him in this moment. Have I not chosen him each and every time? In every situation it's always him no matter how much I try to fight it at first.

My breasts begin to feel wet and I know–

Nah, he can't be...

Is he?

Instead of trying to figure out if those are tears or not, I snuggle into him a bit more, making myself comfortable. We stay like this for a few more minutes before drifting off to sleep.

• • •

The feel of heat against my skin pulls me from my sleep and I realize it's probably way beyond the early morning. By the look and feel of the room I know it's way past 9am for sure.

What a way you sleep weh

Right?

Noticing that Jordanne isn't in bed, I stretch over to my phone to check the time, when I see a text from him. Tapping on the screen to open his chat, I stare at the message.

<u>The Warden:</u> What I said last night stands. I am actually, truly sorry. You however don't sound like you are. You gave me a reason for doing what you did, instead of a simple apology. If I should take my emotions out of this and be objective, it a lead me fi think you woulda do supm like that again. And if you do, you might not live to tell the tale. Until you come to me with a sincere and genuine apology, this ago continue.

<u>The Warden:</u> Junior will be here at 4.

I keep reading the text over and over again, wondering what changed between last night and now.

Man sober

Instead of replying, I roll out of bed, deciding to go start my breakfast.

Fuck dat.

82 | Old Butterflies

RYLEIGH

"Why you ask that?" I ask T' while turning the plantains, careful not to take my eyes from the pot– 'cause as you look weh dat bun up.

"Because why would I have to bring breakfast for just him? Normally a fi both or none," she explains.

"Maybe him just did want him madda cooking this morning?" I suggest, not even convincing the paint on the walls.

Toni releases a long hiss, "Aside from the fact that we've drifted apart, wah else coulda give you a reason fi think mi ago believe that?"

I shrug, now taking the plantains from the oil, to drop them on a plate lined with napkins.

"He's never in the guest houses... not this one, not ours, none. So why hi–"

"Toni rest it nuh. Do I really have to spell it out?" I roll my eyes before slapping the freshly fried plantain in my loaded egg sandwich.

T' moves around the island, picks up the fork and starts eating the slices of plantain left on the flat plate.

"Weh you do?" she asks, still trying to drag the information from me.

Why a me affi do supm?

I look at her while taking another bite into my sandwich. She raises a single brow at me in anticipation.

"Just know we no good," is all I offer.

"To the point where him nah stay ina the house?" she whisper-shouts.

Unuh know dah girl yah ago send mi go mad house though?

"Yes Toni-Anne," I nod, "to the point weh him ina the guest house."

Her eyes find mine, as her mouth circles, going to work on the plantain dem weh me neva plan fi share.

"Okay but unuh did a talk yesterday..." she narrows her eyes at me.

I laugh out, "You know me nuh know how your woman and man manage you. Nuttin no miss you?"

Or her brother. Like dem trained fi sieve out the bullshit

"Yeah we did a text, about JJ, that's it," I counter, pressing my lips together, trying to avoid a smile.

She rolls her eyes.

"You definitely think yah talk to the rest a yuh friends. This is not that," she points between us.

I bring the glass of orange juice to my mouth while watching her watch me.

She nahgo let up enuh

"I did supm he won't forgive me for. Try explain myself months ago, him neva wah hear until–"

"Months?" she squirms, "him vex with yuh fi months... and nuh come stress mi fi talk to you? Yeah you fucked up huh," she laughs.

Not a thing nuh funny enuh.

"Gweh nuh gyal," I giggle, "until last night, he had me explain and then woke up and just gone back ina him shell."

Her face forms a look of confusion, "Duh sound like him," she breathes.

I shrug, bringing the last piece of sandwich to my mouth.

"Thank youuuu," T' grabs it from my hand. I try to grab it back but she swats my hand away.

If mi neva love dah girl yah esi

"Did you apologize for whatever you did? You know how him stay bout da–"

Mmchttt!

For the past thirty minutes my brain has been replaying the text he sent, forcing me to think about my actions. Do I need to apologize? Mi just feel like, he should know I'm sorry. Thinking I would do anything at all to intentionally cause him pain is ludicrous if you ask me.

"Mi come off selfish to you?" the question leaves my mouth without being filtered through my 'what's okay to say/ask' net.

She takes my glass and start to fill it with more orange juice.

"You wah me be honest or you want me to butter you up like the rest a group?"

I playfully roll my eyes at her statement, "Honesty, please, thanks."

"You are... Couple that up with being vengeful and a recovering people pleaser? Yeah you annoying sometimes," she starts.

Mi rass. Now wait one minnnuttte!

"Yuh more give off a people pleasing vibe these last a days though… but it gets tricky because the people you hold closest, you kinda treat the worst. Kinda like… yuh expect us to know you love us?" she brings the cup to her mouth.

"Nuh know if yah get me? You know how real best friends don't really have pictures together, but regular friends have a lot? 'Cause the bff's know weh dem stand but you might need to show the regular friends them important too?"

I try to say something, but she holds her hand up to silence me.

Okay…

"Take me for example, we almost never speak or hang out that much, but when push comes to shove you're there… and I know my place, so these days it no bother me, but it used to."

I see.

She continues to read me, "… so if yah do the same thing to you man, duh expect him fi be good wid it. A yuh man now, not your friend, so he should FEEL like it's him above everything else, at all times. Whatever you did, be it trying to be petty or just doing something you think you have to do at the cost of him being angry, just apologize 'cause me can tell yuh right now him nah mek yuh go noweh."

"Mmhmm," is all I say.

She ate us up

Nyammm.

"Neva coulda understand unuh. Everybody else can see say unuh literally mek fi each other, except you guys. So maybe work on showing each other that, 'cause the rest of us know for sure," she breathes, before taking the final sip from the glass.

She then gets up from the stool, corks the bottle and places the orange juice back inside the refrigerator.

"And that'll be $225 USD Ms.Stevens. Same time again next week?"

I laugh out, hissing my teeth loudly.

"Come outa me place and go itch up under you gyal and man."

"About thatttt," she squirms, now looking at her phone, before walking over to show me a text thread.

We spend the next two hours talking about her, Joshua and Kelly. She lets herself out at 1pm and I take myself upstairs to try to find a book to read.

• • •

My phone pulls me from my nap.

Grabbing it before opening my eyes, I turn to rid myself of multiple cushions, while my eyes flutter open– trying to gather the words on the screen.

<u>The Warden</u>: You're about to be here alone. Ago

get JJ, Sue say him beat up somebody son.

I look at the time it was sent and map it against the current time.
Two minutes ago…

                    I'm coming, cause yahgo rough him up.

**<u>The Warden:</u> And you coming ago
stop dat how?**

                         -_- Sir.

<u>The Warden:</u> I'm downstairs, drop if yah drop killa.

I hiss and roll out of the bed, not caring to turn the AC off or anything else that's been running. I make my way down the stairs, grab my keys, my purse and pop a gum in my mouth. Walking by the entrance mirror, I look at my hair in disgust.

I have to do better.

Still not caring too much, I ruffle it with my fingers, to raise the side that's been flattened by unruly sleep movements.

As mi open the door, I can see Jordanne hopping into the Range. I quickly walk over, opening the door to the passenger side before hopping in. The immediate tension in the car is thicker than Diamond from Taboo, and mi hate that fimi self.

Uhmmmm…

"Who him fight?" I ask, trying to cut it.

"Nuh know. Them carry him go to Sue people dem a Spain, so more than likely somebody from the yard."

Sue people dem, as if Sue's family isn't his family too

Spain??? Yah tell mi say mah gah Spanish Town right now? Stay so??

"Think him ova Sue why yuh neva s–"

"Yuh ask before you volunteer fi farwud?" he counters, keeping his eyes focused on driving through the gates.

I don't answer.

"Good," he mumbles, before speeding off. I grab my seatbelt and buckle it, frightened by the sudden acceleration, while he brings the volume of the music up.

Halfway through the journey, we're singing along to all the songs like there was no tension before.

"Glock 45 front seat a eh Bimma," he picks up Bayka's lyrics.

"So mi go to work a yuh three fimi dinner," I pick it up too.

We continue singing like this, song after song. If anything, music has always been his escape and more so mine since lately. The playlist shifts from violent songs, landing flat on a Drake.

He skips it…

Amen. That would have ruined the mood. What comes next is an afrobeats song. The rhythm? Nice…

Nice bad.

The lyrics??? I don't like the words I can understand. I look at the radio screen to see that it's a song by Ruger called Girlfriend.

"I know what I'm doing is sooo wrong," J' continues singing.

Turning my head, I cock it to the side, observing how much he's enjoying it.

We know the man no sing weh him cyaa relate to don't?

Right.

I shake my head and lowly hiss. He seems to catch it and starts to smile while tapping on the steering and continuing the lyrics. Ignoring him, I roll my seat back and decide to scroll through my phone.

"A wah yuh no like dah one yah?" he asks, tone wrapped in amusement.

I ignore him to continue scrolling through my phone. Why we cyaa reach all now? As soon as the words leave my mouth, I notice we're turning into a lane. Almost immediately, a car appears in front of and behind us, and I know them to be the shadow guards.

We turn on another street, narrower than the last. He takes it slowly, driving as calm as possible. We roll past shops, bars, and corners filled with knowing eyes. A few of the men try to hail the cars and each time they do Jordanne responds with a honk of the horn.

We make it all the way to a dead end where a nice house is. Too nice to be in these parts, if you need a proper description and or comparison.

He stops in the street instead of parking to the side and I watch as the men exit the vehicles before and behind us. The cars stay running so I know the drivers of each are staying put. Of the six men that exit, two of them walk to either sides of the Range, to guard his vehicle or me, whichever.

"Stay inside," J' mumbles, while flying his door open.

"But–" I try.

"Stay ina the car Ryleigh."

No sah, if anuh prison this den a weh?

Rolling my eyes, since that's all I can do, I watch as he opens the lock box outside the gate of the property and places his hand inside. The gates slide open and two of the remaining four guards walk in, leaving the other two positioned outside.

I'm always in awe of how well trained they seem. Neva see dem look confused or outa place yet.

It takes him twenty minutes to walk back out with JJ hanging onto his hand. I glimpse Sue saying something to him, but he dismisses her.

She waves at the car, knowing I'm inside it and I roll the window down to put my hand out, waving back.

Jordanne gets to the car, opening the back door for Junior to climb in. When he gets in, J' straps him in, closes the door and hops back into the driver's seat. We wait for all the guards to get back into their respective vehicles before the cars all make a 'K' turn to exit the lane.

Snapping my head to the back seat, I decide to ask Junior why he did what he did but then change my mind and ask both of them instead.

"Nobody no plan fi tell me what happened?" I cut through the deafening silence.

"Boy say mi look like girl with my hair," JJ blurts out.

Watch yah. His response causes me to laugh lightly. I look over at Jordanne who is biting back his laughter too.

"So unuh fight because him say you look like girl?" I ask, for more clarification.

"Yeh," is all he says, staring at me nonchalantly.

"You talk to him?" I direct my question to Jordanne.

"Wah dideh fi talk 'bout?" he asks, keeping his eyes on the road.

Think the man a come yah come instill discipline ina the likkle boy. I could've been cooking right now.

"Weh you mean?"

"Anuh him start it Ry," he breathes, handing me his phone to find music.

Mek breeze blow you go ina the messages

Girl listen me nuh, me wah keep on the little weight weh me have yah now, 'bout message. I don't want to see what he's doing. I prefer draw all kinda conclusions a morning time.

"Still no say him must be violent," I mutter, scrolling to find something JJ can listen to... and bwoiiii what a challenge. It's strictly slack songs, gun songs, choppa so– Oh, here's one. Not clean but I feel like being petty. Just a tinyyyy bit. I click on it, knowing he'll turn it off before JJ can listen.

IQ featuring Stefflon Don – Bun Fi Bun.

Before I can start singing though, JJ is already on in. Both our heads snap back to look at him in slight confusion.

Haha! Unuh cyaa raise no pikny good ina dis

I blame social media.

He continues to sing, and my eyes find Jordanne's. We look at each other for a few seconds before laughing out, realllly laughing out. I point at the road, signaling for him to keep his eyes on it. He smiles and turns his head dramatically, acting extra attentive before he says...

"See weh you cause. Yah corrupt the man."

"Think you woulda skip it," my laughter subsides while my smile stays put.

"Put me did ago put you outa me car 'bout bun fi bun," he hisses playfully.

My laughter picks up again, even more this time. Says the man weh not even did wah me exit the car while ago.

• • •

Now back in Kingston, the cars that were shadowing, are no longer here, or if they are, they aren't as close as before. We're slowly driving down Constant Spring Road heading to Twin Gates, where Jordanne has to pick up something apparently.

We get there and I watch him collect a small bag from a tall, skinny, dark skin guy with long plaits in his hair.

Me just know a weed the boy take we off route fi collect, nah ask.

He gets back into the car, and the smell confirms it.

"Yah judge me?" he asks, dropping the bag in the console between us, before looking at me with a smile and a wicked wink.

I roll my eyes and bite down on my lips, trying to hide my threatening smirk.

Stay Focus!

Ignoring him, I turn to JJ who is fully engrossed in his iPad. AirPods in and on maximum volume, since I can hear the game from where I sit.

I grab the tablet from him, "Weh you wah fi eat?"

He whines about the game before shrugging in confusion.

"Tell her weh yuh wah fi eat bad man. We no have all evening," Jordanne butts in, while pulling out of the plaza.

"Pizza," he answers quickly.

Hellll to the nooo.

"Pick supm else," I scold him.

"Yuh ask him wah him want though," J' starts.

"And mi say him fi pick supm else," I counter.

He shakes his head, keeping his eyes on the road and on all taxi men.

"Wendy's," JJ tries again and I smile, handing him the iPad, before giving him a Hi-5. Me know mi train him good.

"A plan ting?" Jordanne asks, chuckling at our actions.

• • •

It's now some time after 6pm. JJ is somewhere in his playroom, probably shouting at whichever group of kids are online with him, while Jordanne and I are downstairs around the kitchen island.

We fell back into the silence that was present prior to us leaving– the tension thick and the emotions high. I bring my sandwich to my mouth and watch as he chomps down into his garden salad.

Before I can think about it, I ask, "Do you feel like I intentionally do things to hurt you?"

He pauses his chewing, looks up at me and quirks a brow.

"You don't?" he asks, tone laced in slight annoyance.

"I don't…"

"Cool" he shrugs, now continuing to eat.

Sigh… Well this is going to be harder than I thought.

"I would never d–"

His work phone goes off and he holds a finger in the air, signaling me to wait. I fall silent, bringing the bottle of water to my mouth while watching him walk to his office. Whatever courage I had just now is beginning to diminish. I decide to take more bites of the sandwich, all while scrolling through my phone to distract myself.

Moments later he walks back to the kitchen.

"Mahgo liff," is all he says.

Why? I think it, but I don't ask. The look on his face says he doesn't have time to explain and I'm sure the look on my face is asking for an explanation. An explanation I'm probably not entitled to anymore.

"Work," he mutters, in an attempt to soothe my thoughts.

Well a must work, but what at work that he's rushing out on a Sunday evening?

Anuh our business again

I get that but–

But nothing

I quiet my thoughts, as I watch him walk to the hall and towards the front door. When he gets to the door, he looks back at me before exiting. His mouth moves to say something, but his phone goes off again. He answers it, forgetting his initial planned action, and walks out of the house.

I sit there sipping away at my water, bringing a fry to my mouth in between. His engine roars to life, confirming his departure. I hear the sound of the gate slide open… then the 'Lata honk' that he extends to Snoop before leaving.

That used to be Troopa's honk. Hope him wake soon

… And finally, the sound of the gates coming to a close.

Dat a dat

I guess.

Grabbing the paper my burger was wrapped in, I throw it out. I then move back to his side of the island to pick up what's left of his salad before bringing it to the refrigerator for safe keeping.

As I'm about to spray the countertop and wipe it clean, my mother's number comes across my phone screen while it vibrates.

Mummy ♥...

"Mommy, you remember you one seed," I giggle.

"We need to talk. I'm on my way over there now," she says, sounding frantic.

A wah this now?

"Why yuh sound like that? Yuh good?"

"Yeah, I'll be there in twenty minutes," is all she says before hanging up.

Bringing the phone from my ears, I look at it in confusion before shrugging and actually wiping the countertop.

Maybe she just well wah tell we who she go pah date with yesterday?

Maybe...

Nuh think so though, she sounds too shaken up.

83 | Clearer & Clearer

JORDANNE

"**W**eh mi tell yuh say Slyme?" I ask, reeling from anger.

"Drip, me cyaa do it no longer, mi need fi see her," he says, words breaking.

If dah man yah shed tears pah me byrd today Jah Jah God

"Bro yuh know the code, duh step past it, simple. Months now yah test mi. If me say relax and trust a ting, then wah the problem?"

"A deven 'bout me seeing her anymore, just did wah she deh yah... wid everything weh 'bout fi pop off," he explains.

I shake my head, stepping on the brake as I move into traffic.

"And yuh no feel she safe outside the country?"

"No, that's all mah try say," he sighs.

"Anuh dat alone yah say. You wah see her fi you own selfish reasons, but me did a think 'bout fi bring her back in for a month till things calm down fi real. Have couple guards pon her but she safer ina my place– Big Apple or Jamaica," I share my thoughts.

"Yuh see pre..."

Mhmhmm.

"No joke. Dat a dat still. Yuh reach the safe house?" I query, wanting to end the call. I have another call to make before I get there.

"Mhmm mah wonder if a walk yah walk. All now me cyaa see you drop a foot like yuh no hear your boy say ah emergency," he chuckles.

My boy.

Ramone... Man dem cyaa stand each other fi 3/4 a the year.

"Yuh nah no style man," I chuckle, "him done show me a ting so you can liff offa me line wid the gyal shade."

"Man yah? You know say day by day me hate yuh likkle more," he laughs.

"Hate yuh side gyal weh nearly gi yuh 'air-baby'," I release a hearty laugh.

"Yuh bruk vibes. Come offa me phone yute," he hisses, seemingly annoyed.

Ah just eh truth.

No joke.

"Dat is it," is all I say before hanging up.

What a man fi bus ears, Jah Jah.

Now to the real issue… I glance down at my phone, and back to the road, trying to find her number. Should be somewhere here– if she no change it. Doubt that still, she woulda find some way of making sure I knew.

I scroll the the contacts, landing on her alias. Tapping on the number, I press the call icon, putting the phone on speaker before averting my attention fully to the road. Fi a Sunday evening, the road busy as fuck.

"Fancy hearing from you young Sheer," her voice immediately annoys me.

"Cut the bullshit, why you husband nah drop the case?"

"He's been a little, ambitious these days," she giggles, sounding a little too happy to hear from me.

I shake my head in disbelief. If wicked was a form of woman, it'd be Tonya Wellz. Her mother used to be around the house when I was younger, not sure of the reason, probably working for Robert, but she used to bring Tonya with her. Tonya is five years my senior and so when I was 12/13 she was 17/18.

Let me just say from now, she was my first intimate partner, if you even can call it that. I was too young and excited at the time to realize that she was no good. Long story short, by the time I was 15, Mumz found out and both her and her mother weren't allowed within miles of the house. I didn't see her again until Dadz' funeral a year later. Too caught up in grief, I didn't speak to her nor did I reach out after such.

Found out she was married to di detective boy during my two years of darkness. What was I doing with her to find out?

HaHa!

So each time Ry' complains about her, I think about why… because she clearly nahv no reason fi stress me woman.

No reason?

None. It couldn't be because of me, she must have sense.

"… So I've been trying to pry but… are you listening to me?" she asks and I just now realize how much I tuned her out.

Jah.

"Yeah man mi hear you," I lie.

"But don't worry he won't find anything to act on his behavior."

"Cool," I say before attempting to hang up.

"Duh hang up Drip," she almost shouts.

She know me no linger pah call.

I chuckle, "What is it Tonya?"

"I miss you..." she whispers.

Siiiclawttt, as a married woman enuh

"Tonya one a dem day yah you affi change yerr?"

"That day is not today," she giggles.

Women.

"Just get you man fi drop the case. Know yuh nuh wah be a widow and dem ting deh, so do dat fimi," I explain as clear as I can before hanging up.

• • •

I listen as murmurs spread among the men in the safe house. Ramone, just ended the well needed update call from Chicago and needless to say everybody is now on edge.

Fucking Croc.

The only piece of the puzzle I can't seem to put together is how he evaded our radar. There is no way di man coulda leff the post in Venezuela and Gabriel dem nuh notice. Then to end up in Chicago? Mingling with the same Italians Rome was mingling with for years.

Why?

Him neva seem fi want him family when he had them, so wah di purpose now?

Money?

Title?

Nuttin nah connect, but at least now I know enough to make the first move.

"Man dem just affi buil back, watch unuh points card and await further orders... Shipment nah stop, nuttin nah get interrupted 'cause dat ago mek it seem like we deh pon guard and we no need dem fi know that," Skulli speaks to the group.

They all express some form of agreement.

I lean further back into my chair, wondering if Ms.Janette has already told Ryleigh what she needed to.

Me? Nah face her until she at least get out round one of the anger

If it was up to me I would've told her from the discovery anyways, but I decided to respect her mother's wishes, not knowing something like this would ever fucking happen.

"Yo yah handle the ting?" Slyme whispers, interrupting my thoughts.

Him cyaa serious?

Michelle have me friend a way killa.

"Ago make you do dat yourself. Doubt me can leave Ry' tonight. You can take the jet... and Liam, justtttttt pick her up. Me give her the details already. Duh argue with her, duh do none ah dat. On Sue's life and Ryleigh own, me carry you head go leff ah Spain clock if you disobey me yerr dat?"

He looks at me confused.

Him soon know man

"Nah argue wid her, ago too happy fi see her anyways," he stands while dapping me up.

Happy? Mek we see nuh.

Skulli looks over at me, and I know he's asking if I have anything to add. Me no do the talking unless I absolutely need to, so no. I shake my head 'NO' and watch as he dismisses them.

"Lawww," they all hum in unison before dispersing.

Skulli walks over to me and takes a seat in the chair next to mine, previously occupied by Slyme.

"Yah send him alone?" he asks, eyes following Slyme as he exits.

"Mhmmhm," is all I offer.

"You sure 'bout dat?" he questions.

I chuckle. Questioning my decisions at a time like this won't end well for anyone, but mi get why him concerned. Slyme been a move without him head lately, and I understand. The love a yuh life can do that to you– Skulli of all persons fi understand.

Almost lose him real head fi Mum

"Him good man. If him wah disobey my orders and fuck up nuttin, him know the consequences," I breathe.

Now standing, I slap my pockets for my keys. My hands find it in my left pocket and I dap up Skulli before exiting. As I leave the house, to enter the car, I switch my personal phone on. As soon as the screen lights up and all the apps load, a string of missed calls from Ms.Janette, Lorelle and Toni-Anne pop up.

Yeah man, mi know

I hiss and turn the car out of the parking lot, sinking the gas pedal to get home to her.

And she deven apologize

Think she did a try do that earlier… and was absolutely uncomfortable. I find myself smiling, thinking about giving her a hard time when she actually does apologize.

… But for now, let's see how she's handling the news about her father being on the island…

… and me knowing about it.

84 | Rock

Warning (DV/MD/CA Triggers)

RYLEIGH

I can feel my my brain fighting to understand what she's saying, struggling to let the memories I've suppressed for years push free.

My body is rooted still…

Heavy breathing, chills, dry mouth, confusion…

More confusion.

I know I'm here, I'm present, in this body, right now… yes.

Am I?

You are

"Ryleigh? Do you need your pills?" somebody that's not my mom asks.

Pills?

Pillllls? What pills?

My right hand finds my right thigh and I start to dig into it with my nails. Feel something, you're okay.

You're okay… You're present, in this body, your bod–

"I think we should bring her to her room."

Is that Toni-Anne? Did she not leave like a few minutes ago, hours ago?

Breathe

Breathe, yes I should breathe. How do we do that again?

In through the nose, out through the mouth

I try to follow my subconscious' instructions but fail. My chest? It's tightening. Weh di rass do me? My nails dig deeper into my flesh, trying to figure out if this is a lucid dream or not.

Clinical dissociation. Remember?

Disassociation?

No, we are way past that point. Dissociation… slight difference

Somebody's hand is shoving something into my mouth and somebody else is trying to get my nails out of my thighs. The cold fingers bring my lips together after adding water to the mix. This annoys me and I try to move but can't.

Almost instantly two fingers move to clamp my nostrils.

What now? Wah dem expect me fi d–

My thoughts are cut off by a bitter taste in my mouth.

Wah really a gwaan???

I want to spit it out but I have to choose between breathing and swallowing apparently. So I swallow, whatever dat was.

Yeah, mi need fi figure out what's going on.

"Is like she not even present in her body," that's Toni's voice for sure.

Love ah mi life enuh. Then dah dream yah feel soooo real.

It's not a dream Ryleigh

"It happens. She supposed to good if we can get her fi sleep."

Lorelle??!

Mi gyal! Literal heart string

Can we focus???

"Iffff we can get her if sleep," mummy that.

Mummy…

Mommy?

Mo–

FLASHBACK

"Mommy!!!!!!" Ryleigh screamed for her mother, while watching the man she called daddy drag her down the stairs head first.

"Shut up!!!!!!!" her father screamed at her while finally coming to the end of the stairs, hands wrapped tightly in her mother's curls.

Six year old Ryleigh continued to scream for her mother, knowing she was in danger, hoping somebody would release her precious mother from his tight grip. Janette's pupils were dilated as she laid there on the floor with Mark's knee now pressed up against her skull.

"Tell yuh duh call mi a work!!!! And weh yuh do? Call mi a work same way," his voice enveloped their small living room, bringing in cold chills of fear from outside to settle on both child and mother.

"Mi neva have the phone Mark! She wanted to hear from her father that's all. She just a learn fi dial."

"So yuh no have control ova yuh own pikny Jannette???" he shouted, words dripping in pure hate for the woman crippled beneath his knee.

The volume of Ryleigh's cries picked up and angered Mark even more. He eased his knee out of Janette's neck and moved towards their young fear-stricken daughter.

"Touch her again and mi call Sue!!" Janette screamed the words with the last bit of energy she had. When they landed, she winced in pain.

Her daughter cried even more from the action but at least it led Mark to stop, no longer going after his own child, but instead, focusing on delivering deadly blows to his wife.

"Mommmmmyyyy," young Ryleigh bawled, wiping the tears from her eyes with one hand, while the hand that held her stuffed toy, digged at the skin on her thighs.

"Weh yuh just say?!" Mark's question brought an eerie feeling to the room.

Janette turned her head fully to her daughter and mouthed for her to 'HIDE' before repeating the words she said to her husband. Ryleigh hesitated in fear of what her father would do to her mother, but when her father's umpteenth blow connected to Janette's back, Janette screamed for her to run!

This time she listened...

She ran to the washroom and hid herself in the open front dryer. Noticing that if her father were to open the dryer, he would immediately notice her, she carefully climbed out and grabbed the bunch of towels just like her mother told her to that morning.

Climbing back into the dryer, she placed a few to the front and wrapped herself and her teddy bear in the next.

Earlier that day Janette had tried her best to explain to her that if anything were to happen, her cell phone would be in the stuffed animal and she should press the call button twice and wait for somebody to answer the line. Mark had called the morning of, seething with anger about the fact that Janette allowed his daughter to pick up her phone to call him while he was at work.

Ryleigh recited her mother's instructions lowly, and unzipped the teddy bear where she found the phone, hidden inside. She pressed the green call button and it opened up a list of names, some she knew and some she didn't.

She pressed the button again and saw that it was doing something... calling somebody?

She placed the phone to her ears, waiting for a saviour...

Somebody...

Anybody...

"Janette wah gwaan girl?"

.... the line stayed silent. Ryleigh no longer knew what to do.

"Janette???" Sue's voice came clear across the speakers, riddled in confusion.

"Da-da-daddy is beating her... Mommy sehh he's undercover... Policeman... I'm in ... dryer."

"J' leave your sister ALONE!!!" Sue screamed before coming back to the line. "Mi nah hear you good baby, speak up."

Ryleigh started crying in fear that the saviour from the phone couldn't hear her and her mother would die before anything.

"DADDY IS UNDER– UNDER COVER POLICEMAN... BE-BEATING MOMMY ON THE STAIRS!" she shouted.

Sue flew to her feet at the new information. Keeping the phone line open, she grabbed both her children, leading them from the kitchen that was swarmed in her cooking, to the living area. She wasn't supposed to interrupt Robert in his office, but today she would have to. She walked over to the office, pushing the door open to a busy Robert tapping away at his desktop.

Not caring, she started to spill, "Yuh new worker undacova, and out fi kill off Janette and the likkle girl."

Robert glanced up from the monitor to meet her eyes.

"Speak properly Suanne. Who's what and do what?"

Sue hissed at his consistent battle with her 'lower class lingo', as he called it. She never understood why he would bring her from Spanish Town, only to try to change the root of who she is.

"Robert mi nahv time fi this. The child is on the phone now."

Ryleigh was still in the dryer, listening and breathing as quietly as she possibly could.

But that wasn't enough...

The dryer door swung open and just like that, her father was dragging her out by both feet. She held onto the phone, screaming and slapping him as he threw her over his shoulder. When she saw that her mother was laying still on the floor– zero movement, she thought her dead and decided to sink her changing teeth into her father's shoulder.

The pain of the tiny bite startled him and he threw her straight into the thick T.V. The child was wickedly sprawled out against the T.V for a millisecond, before crashing to her feet.

An instant unbearable pain shot through both her legs. Ryleigh screamed at the unfamiliar feeling, but not once did she loosen the grip she had on her mother's phone.

As Mark began to walk over to her, a male voice came through the speakers. He looked down and finally noticed his daughter was holding a phone.

He grabbed the phone from her and held it to his ear...

Ryleigh could not move either of her legs, now twisted in a weird way she didn't understand. She decided to ignore them to look at her mother.

Janette was unconscious but still alive, while Ryleigh earned two broken legs, neither issue known to her at the time.

"Lie she a tell Boss... The mother no wah me discipline the child! So she will say anything," Mark lied, in fear for his life.

"Stay weh you deh. South Central man dem already supposed to a lock off all exits from your place... and Mark... pray to God anuh lie yah lie to me," Robert's instructions came clear, leaving no room for Mark to protest.

PRESENT DAY

There is now a warm feeling bubbling against my skin. Comfort, I like that.

Girl you're in the tub

Tub??? How we reach yah so?

"Yuh good?" Jordanne's voice brings me right back to reality.

I laugh at the the fact that only him woulda ask such a fuckry question in the midst of an episode like this.

"How long?" I ask, looking up at him, sitting across from me in the freestanding tub.

"Your mother said forty five minutes before I got here and since I got here? Another ten minutes maybe?"

An hour???

We both fall silent, staring at each other.

So all the memories my brain locked away so neat and tight, are now here to stay. Not only that, but the new information mommy just kindly shared earlier. My father never left on his own terms, he was forced to, by Robert.

World tinnnnyyyy

Sue and mommy met through their husbands at the time and became friends. They stopped being close a year after the incident with daddy... or Mark me fi call him 'cause he's definitely no parent.

They revived they're friendship once we moved here for my schooling. Funny, 'cause the first time I brought J' over she shook his hand like she nuh know her friend son.

A yourrr mada enuh

Couldn't nobody else own.

Apparently, Mark is somehow back in Jamaica and has made contact with mommy about wanting an official divorce so he can move on with his life... but we know dat anuh true. Him can easily change him name and carry on with life, or just... not get married again?

"Ry?" Jordanne calls, splashing the water against my skin, "duh slip back into it."

"I won't," I mutter.

I should apologize, that was the last order on my brain before alla this shit. I sink down further into the water, bringing my feet atop his thighs...

"I'm sorry," I start.

"You should be," he counters, not giving me a chance to even start my monologue.

I raise a brow at him and he squints his eyes into a line.

"Anywaysss," I roll my eyes, pulling myself closer to face him directly. "I'm sorry for making you feel like you're number two... You've never been and I don't think you'll ever be–"

"Feel like it mi killa," he butts in.

"You ago buil?" I snap. Why mi feel like him a interrupt me on purpose?

He smirks, before lifting his hands in surrender.

"Fi real though. You've never been, not when I was with my ex in high school, not when I was playing with yah little friend, not when youuuu lefttt me for going out because you tek picture with woman weh you end up deh wid in the long ru–"

Girl

I stop myself, realizing I'm being emotional within the apology, and this isn't about me and my feelings... but him and his.

"...... Forget the last part of that sentence," I whisper, and he smiles– enjoying how hard this seems to be for me. He knows I don't know how to express my feelings, neither do I like to apologize.

"You were never second while I was healing for those two years either. If you came back during that process, I'm almost sure I would've dropped the therapy for you... without question. And you were certainly not second with Lenard... You're not second to my friends or to my career. It just feel crazy to me because the way I feel about you, is unrealistic, borderline unsafe even... and to think you have no clue of that is mind boggling to me... I'm sorry for making you feel that way... Most of all I'm sorry for not telling you about the miscarriage the moment it happened years ago..." I sigh, before shifting slightly.

"With the Rome situation, I honestly, truly just never wah JJ fatherless. Mi and the world coulda see say Stace never did ago be wah steady mother– RIP to her same way, so if he had at least his father– bad as him be, in my mind, that would be one less boy child falling to statistic... Feeding him was wrong, yes I know and I'm sorry... Constantly causing issues within the camp because of my actions, I'm sorry... I hope you know that nah ever happen again. I duh even wah know the next half of the business like that," I shrug.

He looks at me quizzically before smiling.

"You nahv a choice, you affi learn that side fully... C'mere," he pulls me closer, while angling my body away from him– allowing my back and head to rest on his chest, while his arms snake around my waist, keeping me safe.

"If I'm being honest, the only time I thought I was second was in high school. I think for the rest of the time I just held onto that and used it to punish or judge you for the decisions you made along the way. I've apologized before but mek mi mek it clear again... I'm sorry for the Emily thing, for proving your point with Lizz, for the other countless girls in between that–"

"A million gyal! And yuh cyaa even manage one bloodclawt me," the comedic reference leaves my lips before I can stop it.

"Second time yah say dat. Yuh see me wid girl Ryleigh?" he genuinely asks and I almost choke from laughter.

"A just supm from the media Jordanne, jeeeez," I shrug, still giggling lowly.

He brings a handful of water and soap to splash against my face.

"... I'm sorry for expecting you to know how life is on this side when you weren't raised that way. Sorry fi try force you fi bend to my will after fucking up. Your retaliation scheme dem always extreme but most of the time if you think 'bout it, the fault is mine... Anything me leff out just know say me sorry... and I love you more than my life. Woulda give it up in a heartbeat fi see you happy."

I bring my head back into the nook of his neck before planting a kiss there. We sit in comfortable silence for another 10-15 minutes before I break it.

"I had an IUD since last May. Took it out days before you came back last year," I breathe and feel when his body tenses... and then relaxes.

"You know yuh wicked though? Whole time me think mah shoot blank," he chuckles and I laugh out, holding back nothing.

"Mi nuh sorry. You did wah shoot up the womb club daily."

"Since we're being honest, Rome didn't die from bleeding out because of negligence. I killed him. Mi nuh sorry either."

My heartbeat picks up.

I think I kinda knew... because if he doesn't want somebody to die on his watch, it won't happen.

"And mi wicked? Yuh dust the man and a raise him son? Who ago tell him when him older?" I ask, now twisting my fingers into his, while his free hand finds my left nipple.

"I'll figure that out when the time comes," he replies, tone empty.

"You know our parents knew each other from before? Mommy just a mek me know today," I add, trying to change the sudden mood shift caused by the last statement.

"So she tell me weeks ago, when me bring up your father," he responds.

"Why didn't you say something about him?" I ask, genuinely wanting to know fi real.

"Neva know he was your father until like three years ago. When I found out me go to your mother first and she say she needed time to tell you. None of us knew he would be brave enough to try to come back."

Fair enough

"She told you everything... about what happened when I was younger?" I pry.

"Yeah," is all he offers, and mi can feel the fresh and sudden anger radiating from his body.

"Release the anger Jordanne, his time will come," I squeeze our right palms into a fist.

"Me him time ago come from. You never tell me the man almost kill you mother and bruk you two foot dem at once... at six years old? Nuh know how or why me fada woulda mek somebody like dat live," his words fall around the room, laced in vengeance.

I try not to remember it myself, because what a time that was.

Just by always trying to suppress that part of my life, I've suppressed whatever brain chemical I need to express feelings. I'm not sure how the people-pleasing came into play, but mi sure it has something to do with it as well.

I shift into him more before saying, "It's okay, I'm okay and she's okay... and mi like me twist up foot dem. They healed this way for a reason," I giggle, trying to make a joke to lighten the mood but he doesn't find it funny.

A heavy sigh leaves my lips...

"Jordanne, on a serious note, don't go into anything seeking vengeance for anybody hurting me. When you do, it no end well, for more than just the person who deserves it," I explain my thoughts. "That was forever ago. If him come back and a cause problems, then handle that, in and of itself... okay?"

He exhales, loudly.

"Mek we see," are the words that leave his mouth.

Another wave of silence goes by.

Two? Maybe five minutes pass before he says, "Yuh know you friend a mad out mi righthand?"

"Him deserve it," I counter, silently cheesing.

He laughs, splashing the soapy water in my face again, "Man ago kill me when him see Michelle wid belly."

"Who say she kept it?" I ask.

"You think I don't have eyes on her?" he releases a chuckle, feigning disappointment.

I duh know why it surprise me, mmcht.

We sit there for more minutes, just allowing the water to soak up our mistakes, while turning us into soggy lumps of flesh.

• • •

"Girl duh frighten mi so again!!!" Toni hugs me, latching onto my body as if I was missing or died and came back.

"No enuh! Back awayyyy from my gyal wid yuh fish ways T'," Jordanne basically digs her off me.

Lorelle doubles over in laughter while Toni rolls her eyes.

"Danne she nuh belong to only you enuh," Toni retorts.

"Annuh dat she tell me just now. Ask her if me nuh been ah top the charts," he laughs and she slaps his shoulder.

Funny, if only he knew she's the one who got me to verbalize my feelings.

I giggle at the thought.

"No fi real, when we look ina you eyes earlier, we swear you gone enuh. If a never fi aunty Janette we knock you out and drop you off a Bellevue girl," Lorelle explains while cackling.

I join in.

I can laugh now, but going through a dissociative episode is very lonely and scary. The confusion is crippling... You're just there, stuck inside your body, not remembering how to function.

"Where is JJ?" I ask nobody specifically.

"Sue," they all reply in unison.

Oh.

My mother comes out of the kitchen with food for everybody on two separate trays. Brown stewed fish and plain white rice with broccoli on the side. Jordanne, JJ and I normally eat around the kitchen island but since we're all here, we might as well use the dining table.

We all take our seats and are getting ready to dig in.

"Excuse me? Prayer!" mommy cuts us, "Jordanne, pray ova your table," she announces her demand.

Toni snickers and I think J' kicks her from beneath the table. I shake my head at their actions. Sometimes I forget we're all just a bunch ah force ripe 22 year olds.

The prayer starts and ends after two solid minutes.

As I watch everybody dig into their food, a smile creeps across my face.

There is absolutely nothing like peace

Nuttin at all...

85 | Yellow Roses

MUUCH

Packing what I can without overworking myself, I look at the time on my wall clock. 8:35pm...

As it so happens, Ryleigh man say it's safer for me to be in Jamaica for a few weeks. Hopefully whatever is going on, gets taken care of so I can fly back before my due date. The cut off time for traveling internationally while being pregnant is between 25-34 weeks, so I'm a little worried.

What a lucky thing you breed fi good man

Gooooddd???!!!

Anuh jet a come fi we? Yah worry 'bout commercial flight rules

Dat nahv nuttin fi do wid Liam himself and if it were his, him still wouldn't fall under the 'good man' umbrella... I try to quiet my conflicted mind.

But you've been thinking about him?

Yeah, because me feel a time him know. Now that mi ago home, let's hope it'll be easier to break the news since the evidence deh right in front me.

Grabbing the last of the things I need, I exit the bathroom before leaving the bedroom to walk out into the passage. A sudden sound of crumpling paper... or plastic, makes its way to my ears. I stop in my tracks, knowing that nothing should be making that pro-longed noise.

Maybe a the breeze from outside a blow supm

Nuh know, but me nahgo find out. Mi anuh the mad girl dem from show weh wah find out weh the sound a come from.

I move quietly, slipping into the tiny storage closet in the passageway that houses all my cleaning supplies. I hate the smell of them from mi start breed till now.

Especially the Pinesol.

Standing as quiet as I can, I pull my phone out and text Ry'

Ask yuh man if he sent somebody to the house?

**FarridBoo: Think you suppose to just wait on the
driver and go board the jet yourself but I'll ask.**

I wait for like a minute, not wanting to alarm them, because I know how Drip is. Him ago wah check the cameras and surround the house and all kinda supm, when a goodly just breeze a blow some kind of paper weh me no remember 'bout fi real.

I watch the screen, noticing that she's typing her reply.

**FarridBoo: He's checking your front porch cameras.(Di
boy nuh answer if somebody did fi accompany you
from the house or not)**

How mi know him ago draw it outa proportion so?

More than three minutes go by and the smell of the Pinesol becomes unbearable. Noticing that the crumpling stopped for more than two minutes, I convince myself it was nothing, before exiting the tiny closet. As I enter the living area, my eyes connect to his.

Liam…

MMMMMMCCHHHTTTTT, I hiss internally. Mi cyaa trust Ry' and her man enuh!

My eyes move back and forth between him and the bouquet of yellow roses he's holding… and his eyes move back and forth between me and my plump stomach.

My phone vibrates and I look at it, breaking our stare.

FarridBoo: A Slyme. I did NOT know, swear.

**Cyaa trust red gyal enuh… (but
why di sir have roses? me tell
nobody me wah start nuh garden??)**

**FarridBoo: Murdaaaa! Michelle keep me
outa it!!! mi no able yuh man push mi dung again!**

**Murdaaa!!! DWFL an him look angryyyy
enuh! lucky ting me a breed cause like him
love push dung gyal!**

**<u>FarridBoo:</u> Ahaaa! Yuh sick stomach!!
I'll see you when you're here. 🖤**

I attempt to reply to her last text but Liam speaks.

"So yuh no see mi?"

I look up at him… frown, and turn to walk back to the bathroom, now remembering I left my makeup kit there somewhere. Walking down the hall, I hear the paper crumpling again. 'Twas the paper used to wrap the roses, so I know he's about to be on my tail.

Seconds later I'm in the bathroom trying to remember where I left the kit.

Pregnancy brain real enuh man

I can remember packing everything into the kit but I can't remember where I put it. I hiss from frustration, before hearing footsteps approaching.

"Muuch, please tell mi say a gain you gain weight ina yuh belly alone."

I giggle a little, unable to stop myself from enjoying his obvious disbelief.

"Yuh know how foreign food stay already…" I answer, almost ripping through my cheeks with my teeth, trying to bite back the laughter that's threatening to spring free.

The bathroom goes silent, and I stop rummaging through the cabinets to turn, checking if he left.

He hasn't … He's just standing there with the dumbest expression… Locs pulled into a knot, lips absolutely scrumptious… the veins in his big ha–

Focus gyal! Focus!

I snap out of it, turn back around and suddenly remember the kit was already packed. Shaking my head at how foggy my brain has been lately, I say a prayer to God, asking him to send my memory back when I give birth, please.

"Michelle," Liam's deep, commanding voice echoes in the bathroom.

Yuh know how wicked hormones are when your pregnant??? Well mine dem wickedaa than Ryleigh before therapy. I have to be fighting not to jump him right now.

"Liam," I reply, now cocking my head to the side in confusion.

"Wah dat in front yuh Michelle?" he asks again, now moving closer to me, eyes set on my stomach.

I shrug, "Food…"

He hisses and comes to a stop directly before me– hovering over my built. I look up at him, challenging his stare.

"Yuh breed fi man up yah Michelle?!" he raises his voice.

"Breed fi man before me come up yah. A wah? Yuh no breed somebody too? Wasn't that the game? We tie now," I smile up at him.

His eyes darken and I watch as he moves through multiple different emotions.

Deciding to test my luck, I egg him on a little more, "Oh? Yuh did wah win the game? Me nuh like lo–"

"Betta yuh lock chat. Who yuh breed fah? When? Ho–"

Then mi nuh think mi fi lock chat?

"How that concern you bookie? We no have airport fi go?" I try to move past him in an effort to leave the bathroom.

"Muuch, mah ask you one last time," he seethes.

Murddaaaa! The boy a red up enuh! Me fi stop?

"Is what happen? You only like see when gyal a breed fi yuh? Everybody else sekkle pah yuh chest?"

"Nobody nah breed fi me Michelle. If ah Toya yah try bring up, that anuh wah scheduled event right now."

Oh?

Wellll…

"Sorry to hear but I think it's time for us to leave. Wah reach home before Ry' go sleep."

Ry' done tell mi say di gyal nah carry no belly from when. Him lucky, she shoulda breed fi real and giim a nice jacket.

"And you know we nah leff until you tell mi wah dis? Who the fuck you breed fah Michelle?" he asks, in a calm, soft tone– toooo calm and soft for my liking.

I try to move past him again but he continues to block the door.

"Talk 'cause me affi empty me clip ina whoever did brave enough," he chuckles, still in disbelief.

I hiss and roll my eyes for the millionth time in the last five to ten minutes.

"And you know a long time mi wah yuh kill yuhself. Move outa mi way?!" I push at his chest.

Wheewwww! Him chesttttt.

Just memba di boy carry gyal ina yuh bed yerr?

"Weh dat mean?" he asks, looking down at me.

"A when you get slow Liam?" my question holding nothing but blatant annoyance and bitterness.

Man yah better move outa me way before me ring him boss

He looks at me, eyes searching for confirmation. I watch as he struggles to accept the the truth. Mhmmhmm, breed me, stress me and nuh get fi deh yah fi the pregnancy. Yuppp, what a 'great' man.

"School?" he asks.

Ohhh? we concerned about school nowww?

"Took time off. Couldn't manage law with everything crumbling around me…"

He sighs while stepping away from the door, his demeanor oozing defeat.

Good.

I walk out of the bathroom and head to the living area where my suitcases are. My eyes find the yellow roses and a small smile presents itself on my face. At least him know me. He knows I love yellow roses.

Sigh.

Mi say di man push him hood ina Toya enuh, and she laugh after you fi weeks

The painful memory jerks my body into anger and before you know it, I'm throwing the roses into the bin next to the island. As I lift my foot from the pedal and the lid drops to a close, I hear him speak.

"No know if me fi angry or sad 'bout alla dis," he waves his hand around.

"Maybe help me bring the luggage to the car so me can gah me yard?" I sneer.

He shakes his head while waltzing to the suitcases.

Mhmhm, be useful

Moments later we're both sitting in the car in complete silence. His eyes are stuck on the running road ahead of us. I shift at the uncomfortable silence settled between us, just trying to gain some sort of comfort.

We sit there like this until we get to the airport. Nothing is said, nothing at all. We stay silent right up to standing before the aircraft.

As I'm about to climb the air-stair, he stops me in order to go first, before taking my hand to help me climb them carefully. The gesture pulls at my heart yes, but I remind myself that, that's the bare minimum.

And we nah settle fi that, no time

We make it inside, get seated and buckle up before taking off.

• • •

RYLEIGH

"Wah time dem fi reach? mi have work a morning enuh."

"No you don't," Jordanne corrects me, before going back to his work phone.

Well, mi really deh a the point weh mi nah question him. Next thing you know mi go work and Mark dideh a wait.

"Well see 'cause mi nahv no man weh run people head," Lorelle laughs, "me a cut before 11:30 if dem no come. I actually have work."

"Mi nuh have a thing fi do other than post some makeup content," Mariah adds, rubbing the back of her arms.

We're all seated in my living room, waiting to see Michelle come through the doors as Jordanne said she would. Toni-Anne, Keif, and even Kelly are all here. We all miss her and me specifically want to rub on her belly.

I'm not sure the rest of the girls know how she's been doing this past month, but since we talk almost every other day, I know what to expect.

Apart from that time last year when Mariah grabbed my phone and took over our conversation in the pantry, I don't know of another time that she's spoken to her outside of the group chat. She wants to keep her pregnancy to herself– stress free and without any unnecessary news of Liam or Toya. And we know how hard that can be to avoid in a group of girlfriends.

"Them outside," is all Jordanne says, before standing to walk to his office.

Mariah is the first to run to the door. We all follow, just as excited. When the door opens, we watch the car drive around, stopping at the nearest point to the door.

Less walking for her

Slyme exits the car and we all roll our eyes simultaneously. Everybody hate di man right now and I don't know when that will change.

He walks around to her door, opens it and helps her out.

"A wah unuh never see a breeding bad bitch before?" she asks, looking at how we're all 'shook'.

Her tone alone gathers laughter from us all before we start moving down to hug her– releasing tiny screams and fake sobs.

"Come, come, mek we go in. Me wah see yuh belly," Mariah starts.

"A wah do dah frighten gyal yah?" Toni laughs out, shoving Mariah.

"From wah day she outa hand enuh," Keif giggles, moving in front of Kelly who is staring at Michelle in complete awe.

How Kelly look like she wah baby so? Mek mi mind me business deh yah.

"Come girl, me set up you room," I say, pulling her from everybody.

"I'm gonna be staying with mommy," Michelle corrects me.

"Really? That's not what Jorda–" I stop myself.

Yuh know wah, dem can sort that out tomorrow or whenever. She probably no wah deh nuh weh weh Slyme ago have too much free access to.

We enter the house and I notice that Liam has left her suitcases in a corner by the stairs and is now walking to Jordanne's office.

"Slyme," Jordanne's voice bellows from the room.

"Mah farwud Drip," Liam answers, continuing his quick stroll.

The girls and I make it to the room and before you know it, we're all chatting it up.

"Mah tell you girl, I don't know if me ever ago wah go through the buss crotches process. I want the child but the buss front can stay," Lorelle adds her thoughts on bringing a child into this crazy world.

"And the stretch marks!" Mariah shrieks.

"A not even the stretch marks, a the loose belly skin weh you get after me fraida," Keif frowns, grabbing onto the skin of her belly as if she has it already.

"Afta yuh nahv no man!" Mariah laughs out before Keif joins her parade.

"It mah say. She skip couple steps well," Toni-Anne giggles.

"Babies are so cute though. I want a few," Kelly adds… and we all look at her.

A few? Then fi a rainbow girl she prime yuh fuck.

"Then a who ago breed you mumma?" Mariah asks, breaking the short silence.

"Joshua," she answers without hesitation.

"No the fuck he won't," T' mumbles, not low enough, so we all catch it.

"Anywayyyysss chiiile. Wah 'bout you Ry, 'cause we know your body nuh like contraceptives and your man live ina you hole," Lorelle asks, mocking the movement of sex with her fingers.

I pause for a little, just to think about it. I know I want kids, but now?

"She nahv a choice she affi gi me bredda him heir," Toni laughs and everybody in the room joins her, except Kelly.

Bwoiii I hope dem stop argue because when they're good, they're really good. Reallllyyy good.

When we all sober up from laughing, I speak.

"Whatever, when me ready me ready. A my body and mi man sweet, he knows that," I smile, barely believing it myself.

"Then yuh believe dat?" Mariah laughs out causing me to slap her.

"Unuh think me fi go back to Liam?" Michelle's question cuts all laughter.

A weh di? Then a weh this come from?

Nobody extends an answer…

Mi feel him fi suffer fi seven more months but that a just me

"I think so," Keif is the first to answer.

"Me too," Kelly adds.

"It's up to you, only you know your relationship and your heart," Toni gives the most political answer.

"Wellll me duh think so. A me did affi fight di gyal so ELLL to the bloodclawt nooo," Mariah swings her raw thoughts at Muuch.

Muuch seems to be taken aback by her words.

"Mi never ask no gyal fi fight fimi," Michelle counters, words wrapped in attitude.

"Oh?" Mariah pulls back, "go deh wid him then. I hope yuh get bun all round. A next bun ina yuh oven when it free up, bun Easter Monday, bun Christmas, bun every day a di week," Mariah hisses.

"Yah gwaan like a mi alone get bun ina dis bumbo," Muuch argues, staring at Mariah who is now rolling her eyes.

"Unuh stop," I try.

They don't.

"Yuh get bun, yuh get bun, wulla bloodclawt unuh get bun," and I don't know if it's the hormones but Michelle seems to be extra angry.

"Mariah yuh moooouthhhhhhh," Toni whisper-shouts, now dragging her from the bed.

"Apologize Mariah," I turn to her.

"Mi nah apologize. Me fight fi di girl and she a come bou–"

"Yes yuh fight and mash up mi place and no say sorry all now," Lorelle jumps in.

But unuh a see this???

"Unuh come fi bloodclawt gang me???" Mariah asks, now laughing and tugging away from Toni-Anne. "Must 'cause me no born and grow Uptown. Move unuh pussyclawt! Go back to him, him just ago dweet again... And leggo mi hand Toni and go wul on pah yuh man! 'Cause him wah baby and yuh so called woman ready and willing fi give him."

Toni-Anne releases her hand, staring at her in what seems to be shock, anger and hurt...

Rass now, mi baby secret deh a road

"And yuh coolie gyal! Yuh know Ramone have him woman a foreign and yuh no stop hide and giggle wid him pah phone. Go say sorry to di gyal and no stop wid me," Mariah scoffs while pointing at Lorelle.

Alright it a get outa hand now.

I grab her as she continues to talk before pulling her from the room.

"Weh di bumboclawt do yuh gyal?" I ask, pushing her towards the kitchen.

"Mi know yuh did ago pick up fi dem. Mi a the loud ghetto one right?! All me say is me no think she fi deh back wid him 'cause him ago do the same thing and me feel it 'cause a me did fight, not she. She ago say she never ask me fi fight," her words break before they turn into soft sobs.

No sahhh, hormones dash weh ina the air or supm?

"Mariah yah act like me grow Uptown either. Sometimes a just yuh delivery girl, not what you say," I pull her into a hug.

"Mi no fit in but that good. The day pon the balcony before you wake dem say a me yuh follow go deh wid Rome, and a mi yuh follow go the party weh daddy get shot... Two a we fight ina Lorelle salon and she keep on a say a mi mash up her place," she breathes, before starting again. "All now Toni never open her mouth and call mi her sister... Might as well me deven come round unuh."

Wheeewww, if me coulda pay fi everybody therapy I would.

We can...

Oh, right.

I smile internally at the thought of my bank accounts.

"Mariah, I apologized to 'Relle right after everything. Maybe she just wah hear it outa yuh mouth... I can't say why T' no call you sister, you woulda affi work that through with her but you can't force somebody to see you as you see them," I give my thoughts. "Things weh people say to you in confidence shouldn't be thrown back at them when you angry though, no matter wah."

She stays silent for a while.

"Yuh know mi no stay so. Me might run joke here and there 'bout things weh everybody know yes. Blurt it out on purpose and laugh, just fi jokes, but just now… that wasn't my character. Me just fed up. It's like a me a the black sheep."

As I'm about to say something, Jordanne calls my name.

"Ryleigh," his voice comes calm and clear.

Neva coulda understand how him do that. No shouting, but I can hear his calls clearly from anywhere in the house.

"Mah come," I shout in answer.

"Use my 'get vex room' to sleep tonight… and just take you mind offa everything and everybody," I pull her into one last hug.

After pulling away, I turn and walk to the office speedily.

Look how as Michelle come back ah argument– same thing she a try avoid. Me know she must wah go back. A now she ago wah stay with her mother.

Fi sure.

Sigh…

86 | Wheew!

RYLEIGH

"You act like yuh neva get breast fed as a baby," I whine, trying to force his head from my breasts.

He completely ignores me.

"Jordanne," I try again.

He looks up at me for a moment, then back to my boobs.

"Unuh hear somebody?" he poses the question to the two sacks of fat sitting on my chest.

I slap him lightly, causing him to laugh, before he settles in them again.

"Mah try talk to you fi real babe," I mumble.

Jordanne groans wickedly, before pulling himself up to lay beside me. I watch him look at his work phone before snuggling up beside me to dedicate his full attention.

"Bus ears now," he mumbles, staring at me.

I hiss and roll my eyes, preparing myself to complain about my friends– as if he doesn't have much more things to worry about.

"Nobody nah 'gree with nobody again, I swear. This person no wah that person know this, next person want apology, next person nah give it. Just arguments and tension as if alla we anuh basically family?" I start off, voice covered in concern.

I duh know wah do my friends, them nah 'friend' like one time.

"Mhmhm," is all he hums.

"So weh me fi do? Me stuck ina the middle, because me get one person point but like I understand everybody too…"

His hand begins to move beneath the covers. I watch to see how far he'll bring it while continuing the spew of frustration. He lands it on my inner thigh and my breath hitches.

"J' ... a serious supm mah tell you," I whine even more.

I watch as he ignores me, nodding as if he's listening to anything I'm saying, so I decide to test my theory.

"And then Porsha started dating the other girl's husband and now dem married," my tongue changes to the events of my favourite reality series.

"Yeah?" he asks, faking concern.

Mi rass.

"And Pam ate the rat... and the rat ate the cat. I am a girl, see my bag here."

"Jah Jah," he shakes his head, his hand now trying to shift my bed shorts.

Alright, mek we see supm.

"So... Lenard said tha–"

"Who?!" he stops, looking up at me with quirked brows of confusion and another emotion I can't read.

I giggle and try to move his hand from my entrance.

"Mi know yuh woulda hear dat. Me a try tell yuh supm but you nah listen," I release a sharp sigh and turn over, pulling the covers to my head– just to exaggerate the hurt.

He laughs heartily before dragging the covers from me.

"Okay, mah listen fi real this time," he whispers, bringing me into his hold.

A so man fi smell good

"Mariah and Muuch kick off, Lorelle somehow end up in deh, T' a try calm down everybody and catch bay stray. Bay things."

"That's why everybody still downstairs? Them nahv no yard and dem ting deh?" he asks, in all seriousness.

I giggle before slapping him with a cushion.

"If it make yuh feel any better, my team nuh mek no sense right now either, but as mi say earlier, Ramone a touch back tomorrow so I'll have a meeting with everybody. The family lines a get crossed ova into the business and mi no really deh pon dat if everybody cyaa be good."

I shift, letting his words simmer. Me cyaa keep not a meeting wid my friend dem, fi dem go fight? Because it look like everybody been a carry all types ah feelings fi every body while mi just clueless.

As usual

A few minutes of comfortable silence pass before my fingers creep to his chest. The index finger creates abstract art as my mind tries to figure out why Mariah would snap like that earlier. She's usually defending us, not tearing us down.

"Continue do dat and me ago fuck you into tomorrow," Jordanne's voice brings me from my thoughts.

Yeeeessssss

Noooooo

Yesss

No?

Yes?

Yes.

"Who said that's not what I want?" I whisper under my breath, still circling his chest.

He grabs my hand and flips himself landing just above me. Holding my stare, he searches my eyes for genuine confirmation. The stare starts pulling me in and when I break it, he chuckles.

No way he's this intimidating after years...

Both his hands are to either side of me, propping him up, which makes it even worse.

"Neva say we must have a session with Terry before we cova up the issues with sex?" he asks, knowingggggg I know what I said.

Fuck the session

I somehow find the courage to meet his stare again and my brain stops thinking. It's like when you open the exam booklet and you all of a sudden forget everything you studied– so mi feel bredda.

The man havvvveee me.

"When's the session again?" I ask, trying to seem interested in anything other than him fucking me senseless.

He smirks, before moving down to my ear, whispering, "Next week."

My breathing picks up, my already throbbing clit is about to have a stroke and my nipples are trying to find a way out of my night top.

"Session," he pecks my neck, "or sex?"

Fada God?

Session or sex...

Se–

He moves closer down, allowing me to feel his erection pressing into my thighs. All of ah sudden, I can't find my words, me really affi go find out if a tie di boy tie me.

"Ry'?" he asks, now bringing the kisses from my neck to the top of my breast... then to my nipple, where he lingers.

The trail continues along my stomach...

... to my navel, where he stops, to look up at me.

I hold his gaze.

The only thing my body allows me to do is nod, and like a light switch, he dips down again, kissing my inner thighs.

He's teasinnnggg me.

I'm way too impatient for this. I can already feel how wet my panties are. Regardless of my impatience, I decide to let him be, focusing on my breathing and the sweet kisses of pleasure he's leaving around my center.

His hands find my legs before he slowly pushes them back towards me, never halting the kisses. I take a long deep breath, trying to anticipa–

"Hmhm," my breath is cut by a moan escaping my lips, when he shifts both the tiny shorts and the panty, leaving me exposed.

My eyes find him, watching as his eyes linger between my thighs.

Wehm a look pon?

Me fi know?

He stares between my legs for another millisecond before turning and sliding out of the bed.

A weh di?

Feeling too exposed, I bring my legs together, but the rubbing brings even more pleasure, leaving me agitated.

I watch as he walks into the closet… my closet. Why not his?

Reeling in need, I hoist my hips and pull off the tiny pieces of cloth that threaten to block the impending pleasure from my body. Not satisfied enough with just those two, I start to take my top off.

"Where is it?" J asks, sounding frustrated.

I pull the top off before looking over at him while he exits my closet.

"What?"

"Yuh likkle bullet thing," he asks in a hurried tone.

"Jordanne, people downstairs a sleep and how you know mi have bu–"

"Can put dem out right now. Weht deh?"

I shut up, knowing he would most definitely put out everybody just fi do weh him want– no shame about it either. Pointing to his closet, I smile when his eyebrows furrow in confusion.

"Duh ask. Above the jewelry section," I giggle and he chuckles before moving off.

Less than ten seconds later he's back between my legs, after pulling me to the edge of the bed– both of us without any piece of clothing on. The bullet buzzes to life and mi feel like me ago cum already. He gently places it on my clit sending a wave of shudders down my limbs. My back involuntarily arches from the bed, while my toes and hands are gripping at the sheets.

Siiiclawttt

For a good 45 seconds I lose track of what's happening. My brain to body transmitter just stop work until…

Until he–

"Fuckkkkkkkkk," I moan at his sudden but slow entrance– no prep, no likkle warning.

He stays quiet and still… not a single movement while looking down at me– not shifting the bullet for a second.

"Jor–" I try, but he increases the speed of the pretty pink toy, lifting it lightly before gently resting it directly on my nerve ball again.

I jerk forward at the evil action and he... chuckles.

My walls start convulsing. It's been no longer than two minutes leaving me to wonder what he's trying to do to me. He reaches down with his free hand to wrap his fingers around my throat, before bringing me up to face him...

... still not stroking, but just the feel of his dick inside is enough to drive me crazy.

I–

Wheeew!

His eyes find mine, and I notice how dark they are, how eerie but at the same time sexy. My chest rises and falls while our breathing and the hum of the vibrator are the only sounds filling the room currently. I look down between us, trying to focus on not watering the bed before him even start stroke it.

"You ago cum like this," his words bring my eyes back to him.

Me confused, like this? Wah him mean?

He nods as if reading my mind.

The grip around my throat?

His voice?

The look of raw need in his eyes?

The vibrator on my clit?

His dick lodged inside?

Mi nuh know a which one but I'm definitely going to cum like thi–

"Ohhh mmmyyy–Oh my G–" I breathe. "Fuckkk Jordanne! Mi cyaa manage!!!" I start trying to grab at the hand that's holding the vibrator but he tightens the grip he has around my throat.

"Duh try dat again," he speaks clearly, and before his words can settle, I'm shaking from my orgasm.

Shaaaakinnnggg!!!

My eyes start getting foggy, filled by tears of unbearable pleasure.

I–I– Mi ago dead ina this bumbo!

The feeling of his breath finds my ear, "Good girl," is what he whispers.

"J," I barely get the word out.

"Love?"

I have absolutely no words to share. Just a check if a dream mah dream or not... He moves me back down while I'm still riding out my orgasm and at this point I've lost all sense of time and space... and mi nuh know when or how, but he starts his stroking.

Finally

Hand still around my throat...

Vibrator still on my clit...

Never left

VIBRATOR STILL ON MY CLIT!!!

My body jolts from the realization and I can already feel the new developing climax.

"Jordanne please!"

"You wah keep the pussy from me again?" he groans.

No, I share my answer internally and it causes him to start thrusting harder.

"Yahgo keep mi pussy from me again Ryleigh?" he repeats, now panting.

"N- No," is all my body allows me to say.

Happy with my reply, he releases the grip he had on my neck, and uses the same hand to scoop me up, flipping us around, so that he's now seated while I straddle him– dick still inside.

He moves the bullet from my clit and I release a breath mi deven know mi did a hold.

Pheewww!

I place my hand on his chest, pushing him to lay back, before finding the nook of his neck. He holds me firmly before pulling us up to the pillows. When we're settled, he slaps my ass and the sound echoes throughout the room– bouncing our sex memory from wall to wall. I start to kiss his neck, and from there my lips find his lips before they lock.

Jordanne trails his right hand from my ass cheek, all the way up my spine before hooking his fingers into my hair and pulling it slightly. The gesture of dominance forces a moan from my lips into his mouth, and he slaps my other ass cheek with his left hand. I try my best to steady my pace, but the pleasure is sooooo unbearable, I just... mi just wah melt weh ina the boy.

I continue to ride him, tip to root, not breaking our kiss for a second, not even to breathe. The occasional slaps that he delivers to my ass, tugging of my hair, mixed with his low, throaty groans are pulling my second orgasm to the forefront.

*And his first... *

His breathing picks up and I already know what that means. I pull away from our kiss and his hand moves from my hair. Sitting up, I lean back to find his balls. With my right hand, I start caressing them gently, trying to bring him to his peak.

"Ry'... fuckkk, buil," he groans, inhaling sharply.

I smile a little while bringing my hands back around to his chest to start riding him again. He holds onto both my hands, pulling me back into a kiss. I scoot up to my feet and start slamming it down on him. He moans into my mouth, but I don't allow him to break the kiss.

Somewhere along the way our fingers become intertwined– one of mine between each of his.

I feel when he begins to stiffen and that alone prompts me to start riding just the tip... And just... like... that, he becomes undone, withering away beneath me. Watching him lose control throws me over the edge and my climax enters the chat too. He releases my hands and I finally pull away from his lips, to rest my head at the crook of his neck.

Wheeeewwww…

"You affi stop mad me Ry," he breathes.

"I love you too Jordanne," I breathe back.

His hands find my spine before he starts sweeping his fingers up and down my tired flesh while trying to steady his breathing.

I want to stay like this forever…

The thought prompts me to snuggle into him even more– dick still inside… As I said, I want to stay like this forever…

… and ever.

87 | Family not Friends

JORDANNE

Aphone keeps going off, not sure who's phone, but mi hope anuh mine. Tyad yuh fuck.

Fuck tyad a weee

Haha!

After doing all that last night, mi nuh know if me wah do nuttin today, honestly. But, the day off thing anuh part of my life unfortunately.

The phone in question keeps going off and I try my best to ignore it, snuggling more into Ry'. She shifts, and groans at the sound of the vibration shaking the nightstand.

"Babe answer the phone nuh, too tired fi the noise," she whines, in the groggiest, yet softest voice.

A reminiscent smile causes my lips to turn up, as I remember having her all across the room... and it's a big fucking room.

Both walk in closets

Yup.

And the master bathroom

Mhmm.

Not the balcony though

Nahhh, she fight out that.

"Jordanne pick up your phooooone," this time her request comes with light taps to get my attention.

I heave a sigh, knowing if anuh work a some kinda family issue. All depends on which phone it is that's vibrating.

"Okay miserable," I smirk, slapping her ass before turning to grab both phones.

I look down at the one going off.
Mmmcht, me affi exit dah thing yah killa. The man dem wild yuh fuck.

LIAM'S DIARY

<u>Paw:</u> Bro G, mi know Muuch nuh lef yahsu,
so round lol. Slyme yuh breed di girl and she run weh yute?

<u>Surgeon:</u> Haha! A real ting?

<u>Paw:</u> Mi downstairs a wait pon Drip fi start the
so called family meeting ting weh him decide fi text
people bout 3am, and a Muuch that me see a eat up
her fruits. Belly round ahaa!

<u>Joshua:</u> Yo di man deven ina the group dwfl! Fuck
unuh a do yo?

<u>Ramone:</u> Unuh good?

<u>Paw:</u> Mr.Ghost a yuh dat!? Think Drip send yuh
weh fi life bad head.

<u>Ruse:</u> Man dem nuh up to date? Mission
done, we get enough info.

<u>Paw:</u> Di man slow yuh fuck. Like yuh tattoo out
yuh senses. Know dat killa, man cyaa pick up humour
since him go foreign?

Joshua added Liam to the group

<u>Paw:</u> Scary movie 3, welcome back *hugs*

<u>Liam:</u> Man dem add me back fah?

Yow unuh buil offa the chatting. Mah
swing to the office ina like half hour.

<u>Paw:</u> Ah we downstairs. Mi fi let in
anybody else? Cause me notice your yard

572

turn Pegasus dwl! Feel like Slyme fi wait out
ina the yard still. Nah open the door.

Ramone: I third that motion lol!

Surgeon: Man skip the placement after first dwfl!

Joshua: Dwfl!

Paw: Joshua me know you love the third thing
enuh. Isosceles lol!

Dwl!

Liam: None a unuh no breed nuh gyal so relax -_-

Paw: And if we do dat she nahgo run weh fi
months lol! Boss yuh nah come down? Tell the
First Lady fi set u free.

Lol! Take me outa dah ting yah.

Paw: Yah spend too much time wid your boy
enuh, yah move slow. U know u can exit right?

Liam: Cyaa me yah call 'your boy'

Paw: ^^^ Unuh see weh mi a say though loooool!

Ramone: Bbc loooololol!

Joshua: DWFL! ☺! ☺! ☺ !

Ruse: Dwllll! Lol!

Paw: All the man emojis set to three. Joshua dedicated yf.

I set my fingers to type again but Ry' grabs the phone away.
"See, now yah laugh and a wake mi up," her sleepy demeanor makes me proud.
Beat out
Yuh fuck! Ahaha!
"Yuh nah gimmi a yute?" I ask, pulling her into my arms.

"Way how you gwaan last night, you might get alla dem at once," she giggles, rubbing her eyes.

My blindy.

I snake my hands around her, pulling my phone away without cause for an alarm. Nothing is in my personal phone but somehow, the vibe a say take it from her still.

And we nah do nuttin

Anymore… Just no wah the vibe pull up.

I start to rub her thighs, admiring all the evidence left from the countless slaps I delivered a few hours ago. My eyes move from my artwork, up to her neck, while she uses her phone as a mirror.

Jah Jah.

"Dat sweet yuh?" she asks, now rubbing at the love bites.

I don't offer her an answer, just straight teeth.

She fi go back a work tomorrow, under heavy guard of course. She wii have supm fi show her co-workers– explain why she did missing from the office today.

I chuckle to myself, unable to hide the override of happiness moving through my being.

"C'mere," I mutter, lifting her over and on top of me.

"Jordanne, nuh badda wid it. Mi good fi the rest a year," she plops her head down onto my chest.

I grab her ass, remembering how mi buss the first time last night. My dick stirs, but then a knock presents itself at our door.

"Ms.Ryleigh?"

JJ… Bumboclawt man.

Her head shoots up at the sound of his voice and I hiss.

So this is what it'll be like if we have a child. Nahgo have her for myself. The thought forces me to make a mental note of hiring a nanny for Junior.

Ms.Cherry is right there

Lady have her own life.

Ryleigh lifts herself from me, without any signs of hesitation. I watch as she drags her robe on, tying it, while walking to let in the little culprit. The door pulls open and he stands there, looking at me from around her hips. I chuckle at how scared he seems to be of me– certain times.

Nuh understand it at all bad man.

She looks back at me, then to him, before shaking her head and leading him out and down the halls.

Mmmcht. Man gone wid mi woman. Ultimate cockblocker mi have a live ina me house.

• • •

KEIF

First time mah step foot in yah so. Nuh sure why we a part of the meeting but mek we see. I'm one to do more observing than talking so I don't even think I'll be needed. Nevertheless, Ry' say me fi come since I'm probably the one with the least bias.

Lorelle and I are cousins, yes... but me split justice how it fi split all the time.

"Man dem, this anuh wah work meeting per se, 'cause as unuh can see the woman dem deh yah too," Drip speaks, commanding the room.

Nuh sure how Ryleigh sleep beside him nightly. Man just gimmi a cold, evil vibe

From high school days him serious. I don't think he's that way with her though. From what I can see, he's a different person when she's present, or when they're on good terms rather.

Ryleigh releases a big yawn and our eyes meet, making four. I look at her knowingly and she giggles, blushing in embarrassment. Yeah man, betta mi did go home ina the late night. The amount a screaming me hear– cyaa recover all now.

In the room is Ramone, who's standing nearest to the exit. He would usually be standing with Danne but who knows? Maybe when you go pon a mission too long you change. Beside him is Ruse and in Ruse's arms is Mariah. She look vex, but the way she gwaan yesterday neva too call fah.

On the chair beside them sits Michelle, chomping down on... raw tomatoes and butter??? Or mustard? Some yellow condiment, ah duh know. Slyme is off the right of her, standing the closest to Drip who is seated on his desk, with Ryleigh slumped down behind it in his chair.

The girl look tirrrreddd.

It's the hickeys for meee

Mightyyy! Me count three.

Toni and Joshua are on the other side of Danne's desk, standing as if they're business partners and not actual lovers. Kelly comes next, seated on an ottoman next to the small in-house bar. In between her and I is Lorelle, standing annoyed because she had work today, but didn't leave last night because it was too late, much like the rest of us.

The circle ends with Surgeon and Paw, who seem to be just as confused as I am, about why us girls are here.

"So mi woman nuh happy... and unuh know from experience how that go already," Danne speaks again, capturing the room's attention.

I actually admire how much he loves her... When God?

"Bay uncalled for problems deh amongst everybody and it a start spill ova into actual business," he continues.

Slyme tries to say something, but Drip gives him a look, that I wouldn't want even mi mate get from we man.

Which man dat Keif?

The one mi make up. Work wid me.

Danne looks away and continues his starting remarks.

"So weh we ago do is, fix it right now by way of communicatio–" Ryleigh giggles at his statement. She did it lowly but the room is super quiet so it comes off loud.

He slowly turns to look at her... and she holds her hand up in mock surrender. See how she no seem fazed? If a me, me faint weh.

"Yeah, so since everybody wah cuss and fight and hate each other, mi deh yah fi mek unuh know it no make sense, 'cause everybody knows jussstttt a little too much to leave. So mah need unuh fi fix up, starting wid di man dem. Say unuh problem wid whoever and mek we see if it can solve today... Days dem after this ago long and murderous, so start talk fimi please."

I take a quick look around the room. Nobody speaks or seems to want to go first. My head snaps back to Ry' who is now eating a vine of grapes.

Live life fi me and yuh yah girl

"Ramone," Drip decides to choose who should speak first. The tone he just used to speak Ramone's name comes lethal, almost as if he's the enemy and not his oldest friend in the room.

My eyes avert to Ramone just in time to see him shake his head before saying, "Just feel like nuttin weh me do no fully appreciated."

"That's it?" Drip asks.

Ramone becomes a little agitated but shakes it off when Drip's eyes become narrow. "Like me know you before everybody and is like me get the most wicked consequences more while."

"Probably 'cause you deserve it," Slyme mutters lowly.

Michelle looks up and around at him, before hissing her teeth.

"Noted," is all Danne mutters in response to Ramone.

"Me no done. Mi do a thing weh wrong and you pull mi from yuh side, send me in a situation where at any moment I could've died. Mi nuh rate da–"

Drip chuckles, without humour, "Woulda rather me kill you? 'Cause that was the next option."

Low gasps, including mine, spread throughout the room. The only persons that seem to not be surprised are Slyme and Ryleigh. I look over to Lorelle... She nuh seem surprised either, so a wah him coulda do so?

Ramone smiles but not from happiness. He then shakes his head and nods as if saying 'Cool, cool'.

"Ruse," Drip says next.

"Nahv no issue with nobody per se. Just a mek everybody know mi girl no happy either," he stares down at her. Mariah shifts her weight before snuggling into him more.

"Noted… Paw, Surgeon?" Danne asks, almost smiling.

The man mood change almost in ah instant. Wasn't he just about to snap on Ramone?

Paw and Surgeon turn to look at each other before doubling over into laughter.

"We good enuh," Paw says, now trying to sober up.

"Yeah, weh him say… and before you ask, me stop mingle wid the nurse dem."

Whore…

Danne chuckles, shaking his head, while moving to the bar. "Joshua?" he mutters, now pouring himself a drink.

"Nahv no issues."

"You sure?" Toni turns to look at her man.

He looks at her with pleading eyes. Danne turns to observe the encounter.

"T', wah the issue?" he asks, now walking back to his desk.

Toni releases a heavy sigh, looks at Mariah and then to Ryleigh. Ry' offers her comforting eyes and she steps away from Joshua, readying herself to say her piece.

"Two a dem ready fi have baby," she points between Kelly and Joshua, "and I'm not. Nuh sure how that affect the man dem but that's my issue."

Paw let's out a laugh, like him did a struggle fi keep it in. His laugh is so contagious mi almost wah join in but me know mi place masah.

"It affect the unit. Me ago need everybody in the coming days, so me no wah nobody a do nuttin petty while things start move into play. Work that out as best as possible or put it pon the back burner until we get to Croc," Drip explains.

T' nods and steps back, closer to the desk than to Joshua himself.

"Sis," Danne goes again, bringing the glass to his lips, while he looks towards Mariah.

Her face is buried in Ruse's chest so she misses the gesture.

"Mariah?" he tries again.

She lifts her head and turns to face him, "No have no issues with a soul," she waves him off.

"But you look like yuh stressed out more than anybody else," he counters, now chuckling.

Mariah sighs, "Me done express me feelings last night. Nuh have no more fight ina me. Everybody treat me like the outcast. Dat a just dat."

Danne's demeanor softens, for the second time since we've been in here playing Dr.Phil.

"Yuh mean by dat?" he asks, looking at her genuinely puzzled.

So yah tell mi say Ry' no say nuttin to him last night? Strictly fuck keep up deh?

"Mean weh me say. From me likkle daddy a run down unuh mother. Never yet get fi meet mine, I've always been here– whether me did live wid unuh or not. But that a just that, it's fine. The thing is me always get blamed fi shit. Ask dem weh dem say to me the day after daddy got shot," she says, shooting eye daggers at Muuch.

Michelle rolls her eyes.

"But did we lie though?" Toni-Anne chips in.

"Lorelle was just as much a part of the decision as mi!" she shouts, "Just as Ryleigh was just as much a part of the fighting in the salon as me," she lowers her tone with the second statement.

"But she apologized, you didn't," Lorelle breaks in.

"And I won't! 'Cause me no sorry. Ask me fi buy back yuh things weh you claim me mash up but me no sorry me put me hand pah dah gyal deh ina yuh place. All if Michelle wah go back ten times ten, I woulda beat them gyal deh again right now," she seethes.

Ruse pulls her from stepping further, forcing her back into his hold. Danne now has his fingers laced together, observing them.

"Yeah and a so you nahgo sorry fi air out everybody business," T' whispers.

"What was that, sISteR?" she holds up air quotes as she says the last word.

"Yuh hear her," Lorelle adds.

Mariah hisses and throws her hands up in surrender, "Mahgo just stay to myself, forget it."

Danne observes the room for a while longer before he speaks.

"Everybody a worry 'bout her tone, and apologies but unuh a disregard how she feel, probably a feel this way fi years," he explains, in an understanding tone.

"Can I say something?" I ask, wiggling my index finger around.

The entire room is now looking at me.

And this is why mi no talk bredda

"So… I think the problem is everybody have dem own life now and them own feelings. In high school and university, we might have not understood our feelings completely and brush dem aside but with time, that just ago mek it worse and I think a that reach Mariah," I pause to look at Toni-Anne. "You don't treat her like a sister fi real, or a best friend even, not sure why bu–"

"I just duh see her as a sister. My mother cheated with her father. How that mek her mi sista?" she's asking me genuinely.

I mean dem married now, so?

"T'," Danne's voice comes like a warning to his sister. I look between them, wondering if I should've kept my mouth shut.

• • •

RYLEIGH

I look at Toni surprised. Mi know she have up her mother fi nuff things but I didn't know Mariah was a part of the issue.

"Yuh cyaa say dat T', like a she mek dem do weh dem do," J' counters.

"Okay?... and mi say me no see her as a sister that's all. Unuh ago force eh dung pah me??? She's a great friend, deh so it stop."

Woahhh

"Hear wah, unuh affi hash it out, whether it be with Mum and Paul or just unuh, but as me say mi no want nobody ina disagreement for the coming days. Need everybody thinking as one," his tone holding no nonsense.

"Slyme... The whole room know your issue by now. Me done talk to you last night, so me ago grant you and Michelle some privacy fi unuh decide wah unuh wah do."

"Nuh bother mek she run weh again," Paw laughs.

Forget him even deh yah.

Jordanne takes my hand and leads us out, followed by everybody else except the... couple? Mi deven know dem a wah right now.

We ascend the stairs, and I start thinking about the long warm shower I'm about to take to finally relax my body.

"Go get ready," J' pulls me in to whisper, as we make it to the top of the staircase.

"Why? Mi tired, bad bad bad," I whine.

He chuckles, "I want to take you out, before the bagga fuckry start."

"Oh, okay," I mutter.

He looks down at me, "What is it?"

My fingers find each other before I mumble, "I'm nervous about it."

Pulling me in, he places a kiss on my forehead before whispering, "Yah forget who you deh wid too often now. Nuh nerves nahfi ina it, yuh ago good."

I pull back to look up at him... and in this very moment, I realize... I don't have to be worried. I've never had to and won't ever have to. He's always going to be there for me... as a friend, as my man and as my husband, if that happens.

"Yuh know mi in love wid yuh likkle boy?"

"And treat mi so?" he laughs, lifting me suddenly to throw me across his shoulder.

I shriek at his actions.

"Mi want a quickie," he mutters.

Sas Crise... Prefer when we anuh friend enuh.

Yuh gwaan, unuh love out like

Love right out.

88 | 9-5 Woes

RYLEIGH

"Apart time you work enuh girl so me nah listen to your promise," Nadz laughs, while complaining about me leaving her here with these people.

I laugh out, bringing the fork to my mouth.

"Yuh bright 'bout part time. Weh you deh when work a kill me a me yard?" I laugh, "I had a family emergency man. I told Mr.Man I couldn't come in yesterday."

Not that I need to explain, but Nadz is the only person I get along with genuinely in my department.

"Girl I get it. If it was me I woulda milk it all week long," she adds, taking a sip of her juice.

Nah, it's good to get out of the house. Jordanne woulda fuck me to death if I stayed the entire week. Mi nah ask yuh, know mi know.

"Today dem a announce who will join the Reserve Managers enuh. Mi nervous yuh fret," she brings her voice down.

She looks nervous too. Me on the other hand? I'm okay. If I get it, I get it and if I don't, I'll try again. My plate is starting to run out of space and if I were to get this promotion, I wouldn't be able to work from home as much as I'm able to now. The work for reserves is more hands on and certain information cannot leave the company's system.

Cyaa go bring home much work.

With JJ, my friends and dem issues, the books for Sheer Holdings, my properties, my father lingering around and Jordanne's sex drive, mi woulda must dead.

Mi is just one girl.

One likkle lady. A tyad

"Lunch?" Dr.Drew takes a seat beside us, before we approve. Nadifa looks up at me and I her, before we shrug.

Richard has been having lunch with us once per week almost every week and we still haven't gotten used to it. Nuh sure if him nahv no friend but having lunch with your boss gets annoying. We cyaa get fi talk 'bout who a stress we, and who a cock we up so and suh.

Mmmcht... And look how me finally have a story fi tell, after weeks of listening to Nadifa's situationship stories.

"Richard yuh no see big people a talk?" I ask, looking at him in disapproval.

"Me nuh blind like you enuh Stevens, me see unuh. If unuh no wah me here today just say that..." he trails off, holding his chest to feign hurt.

Nadifa and I laugh out, bringing multiple sets of eyes to our table.

Them stuck up sah

"Yes gwaan. We can't talk 'bout nuttin when yuh deh yah, and me no see her yesterday," Nadz adds.

I giggle at her audacity while watching him grab his things to leave, but Nadifa pulls him back down.

"A joke boss, sit down."

Bringing my aloe water bottle to my lips, I watch how playful they are. Then what a way dem close? Then again, people would say me and him close too so.

"Unuh ready fi the announcement?" he asks.

"You see weh Nadz a say? Who tell you we wah talk 'bout work at lunch?" I ask, now bringing the bottle from my mouth.

"Right, me wah talk 'bout such man," Nadifa blushes, now using her teeth to rip the paper from a chocolate bar.

Richard's body tenses for a quick second, but I catch it. Mi man woulda proud of how observant I've become.

For certain

He slightly shrugs and opens the wrapper holding his sandwich, before asking, "Which man dat?"

Almost immediately Nadifa responds with a, "Yuh wouldn't know him."

Then unuh a see this? I don't know if me always a misread him but... Mi nuh know yah man.

"Soon come back," I say before standing. Mi a come go bathroom 'cause them two yah need privacy.

None of the two reply and I take the opportunity to slip away. As I move out of the break room and into the hall, I give my phone some attention.

Mi need fi find a good excuse to leave early today.

That's why dem nah promote we enuh

You right, I giggle to myself at the blunt thought.

Opening the bathroom door, I quickly start unzipping my pants, even before closing the door behind me. I snap my head around at the realization and snap the locks shut. A few minutes later I'm finished and looking at myself in the mirror. My hair is in a low sleek bun with minimal untamed 'baby-hairs'.

It really grow back nice enuh

Can't wait till it's at its full length so me can breeze the tape-ins.

A knock comes at the door, startling me. Looking at it confused, I decide to wrap up my self admiration tour, to see who the fuck so bright. Mi sure other bathrooms available and dem see the occupied sign.

I release the lock and pull the door open, only fi buck dutty Wellz she. Ughh!

"You were taking forever. I need to use it," she starts, already annoying me.

"Okay? Are there not any others available?" I ask, stepping out to grant her access.

"I like this one," she flashes the fakest smile of this century.

MMCHTT.

Mek me go back to the break room yah.

"Didn't know people got attached to bathrooms," I murmur more to myself than to her.

"I get attached to a lot of things. Some I don't want to let go," she snickers.

Ohhhkayyyy?

I ignore her, making my way back to the break room. We only have like two minutes left in the lunch hour and immediately after this should be the meeting about the position– so mi nahv time fi mad people.

When I get to the break room, Nadz and Richard seem to be arguing lowly. I clear my throat, in an effort to get them to notice my presence. They notice, and both look up at the same time. Dr.Drew offers me a small smile before standing and leaving briskly.

I plop down on the chair I was seated on earlier, staring at Nadz.

"Nuh tell me say Dr.Drew is such man," I ask her, unable to hold my inkling suspicions to myself.

She blushes.

Me rasssss, but Nadifa nuh easy.

"He is," she breathes while watching him walk away, "and he's not happy I told you about it, although me swear up and down you nuh know a him."

I look at her puzzled. She try nuh draw me ina the bangarang enuh.

I'm almost certain he made small advances at me before he knew about J'… or were they imaginary? That day in the offi–

"So yeah, mek we go back a work," she cuts into my thoughts, while grabbing her things to leave.

I turn, aiming to look around because of the sudden change in her tone. When I look around fully, I see that Richard is walking back to us.

Oh?

"Can I speak with you before the meeting?" he asks.

Unsure of who he's referring to, I go ahead and assume it's Nadz.

My eyes find hers.

"You Stevens," he almost whispers.

Then a weh mi do Fada?

I stand and watch as Nadz ignores us, well him. He walks off and I follow suit. We make it to his office but not before I see Wellz bringing her phone down, before scurrying away down the halls.

"Have a seat," Richard commands.

I take the chair in front of his desk while he sits on the desk instead of in his chair.

"Weh she tell you say?"

"Who?" I ask, pretending to be confused.

"Duh act smart Stevens. If H.R eva fi find ou–"

"She nuh tell me nuttin, but based on your reaction right now, I'm assuming you're such man?"

He shifts a bit, peering down at me. Why mi feel like a principal office me deh?

"Just promise me you'll be quiet about it," he asks, with pleading eyes.

Then who me woulda tell? Wah this pah me?

We a tell Jordanne as sooooon as him pull up

Ahaha! True dat.

I bring my hands to my lips and mimic the action of zipping them shut. He laughs and I watch as his body moves from tense to relaxed.

"Mi a leave early today," I let out, because I might as well say it and done.

He looks at me before bringing his eyebrows together, "Yuh know that's why you no get the–"

He seems to realize what he's about to say and I watch as regret settles on his facial features.

"Weh you say?"

"Stevens, mi neva mean fi–"

"What does me not being here and being chummy-buddy-buddy wid everybody affi do with my work ethic?" I ask, now standing to my feet. "Last time me check working from home is just as hard as working in office– harder if you have a child."

And a man wid the whitest liver

"You have a child?" he asks, his eyes widened.

Call it so.

"That's not the point," I retort, now visibly getting upset. "Who got it?"

I knowwww, I know I said I couldn't handle it right now, but stillll.

"Cyaa tell yuh dat Stevens," he dismisses my question.

Oh? Alright, my yard me ago. Somebody shoulda tell me BOJ a patty shop. Not tooting my own horn here, but nobody numbers nuh better than mine. I guess that's how corporate is? It's not only about the work is it? Yuh affi kiss likkle ass.

"I'm leaving," I mumble, while unlocking my phone to tell my man I'm about to be off.

I'm about to leave work, still ago can pick me up personally?

BD🖤: Yeah, gimi like 5-10 mins.

BD🖤: You wah stop home or go straight?

We can go straight.

He doesn't reply and I make to exit Dr.Drew's office, but he grabs my hand.

I pull away.

"Yuh mad?" I turn asking.

"Since you want to act this way about it, Nadz got it," he barely gets the words out.

Then nuh that him shoulda start wid. She alone fi get it over me...

Wait one second, a hope anuh because–

"See you're already thinking about it that way. Nuttin like dat. Her numbers are second only to yours and she's here much more than you– mingling with those who voted, so it had to be her. I still have the final say... I would shift against all the votes and be under scrutiny if you said outright, right now, in this moment, that you wanted it," his eyes hold a glint of an emotion that I can't read or pin to this moment.

Nuh sorry fimi. Anything me get, I want it fair and square. Plus I love this for my girl. Now I have to be in the meeting to support her.

What a way the sir willing fi shift the promotion from him 'situationship' to we

Right?

Weird as hell but okay.

His office door pushes open and Mrs.Wellz' head comes around it, "Am I interrupting a lover's quarrel?" she smirks.

Thiiisssss bitch

I hiss lowly before walking towards her as she stands in the exit.

"Meeting has started," is all she says, smiling at us while standing aside so we can pass by her.

• • •

Twenty minutes later, I'm hugging Nadifa as she sobs on my shoulders. Happy sobs, that she couldn't express in the boardroom seconds ago.

"Mi proud ah you so till," I whisper, rocking her back and forth.

"Mi affi leave," I mutter, pulling away from our hug. I just know Jordanne has been outside a say me give him di wrong timing.

"Now?" Nadifa asks, "work deven done," she giggles.

"Girl you know how my thing go already," I laugh out and she joins in.

We both walk off– her wiping her tears and me fixing my pants so J' doesn't complain about my work outfit, for the trillionth time.

Nadifa walks me to my office to grab my things and we both walk to the main exit. I share my farewell while stepping out of the building before turning my head back, to search the parking lot.

Would you believe what my eyes spot?!

The Taycan. Haha!

Jordanne is leaning against it. I also notice the hundred million shadow guards pretending to not look suspicious, while they roam around.

Him really send six man a work wid me daily and the same six to pick me up

Madness.

I spot Ramone as he exits the car, seeming to be moving towards mine.

"Taycan you go? On a regular Tuesday afternoon?" I shriek, asking J' the obvious from a distance.

"Yeah gyal!" Nadifa's little voice comes from the doors at the entrance. I turn around to look at her while giggling like a fucking child.

"Give Ramone your keys," Jordanne commands, "Cyaa believe me a say this but, take the driver's seat."

Mi pussyclawttttt!

I break out in excitement and a happy dance. Looking back at Nadifa we both dance in excitement. She knows how long me wah step ina itttt!

"Hell mussi freeze ova," I smile after sobering up while running around to take the driver's seat before him change him mind.

"Fi sure," Jordanne sighs, looking nervous.

We get inside and settle down.

"Please babe, nuh mek mi regret it," he begs while looking at me.

Hihihi step ina it gyalll!

"Duh fret, a you teach mi fi drive so if I do a bad job that's on you."

He shakes his head while dragging his seatbelt on– bracing for what? I duh know.

"Which one a the brake?" I joke, just to get under his skin.

"Ryleigh buil," he chuckles, keeping his eyes glued to my every movement.

I giggle before putting it in drive, slowly bringing us out of the parking lot. When we're to enter the street, I step a little too hard on the gas pedal, propelling us both forward.

"No! Stop and get the fuck out," he raises his voice.

I giggle, knowing I did that on purpose.

"Too late!" I snicker, sending us smoothly down the short stretch, before we come into moving traffic.

Wait till me touch the tollllll!!!

Him nahgo put me back ina it haha! And dat's why mah make use of this one time to the fullest.

89 | Just Before

JORDANNE

Ry' a tell mi supm 'bout the coworker girl but mi cyaa bloodclawt focus! She literally a tear down the toll, following Slyme's speed.

"Babe, if me affi tell yuh fi slow down again mahgo–"

"Yahgo wah? Jump outa the moving car???" she glimpses at me.

"Keep your eyes pon the road!" my voice comes out louder than I intended it to.

Jah Jah God.

Affi get her, her own. Heart ago fail me at this rate

She takes a corner with too much speed and I'm almost sure if she gave any less brake, we would scrape the concrete barrier that separates the highway.

"Ryleigh! Bredda yuh nah come back ina me car! Not even as a passenger, swear!" I sneer, trying to control my nerves.

She ago crash me car yo.

Love is a serious thing enuh, because nobody at all cya–

She speeds up even more, pulling me from my thoughts. I look up to see that Slyme has created a gap before us.

"Duh follow him, just go easy nuh babe," beg mah beg her at this point.

She giggles.

I love her little laugh…

Focus yute, she still a speed

"You're such a pussy," she continues to find this funny. "Since yuh no wah listen the work mix up. Mah try tell yuh me no get the promotion because Nadz and Richard a jook."

She nuh get it because I asked him… nicely… not to give it to her…

What? I want her home.

Hmhmm nicely?

Nicest way possible.

Instead of indulging her, I tear my eyes from the road ahead of us to call Liam. Her hand moves from the wheel to try to pick up her phone– aiming to skip the songs I assume.

"Use the fucking buttons on the steering!" I swat her hands away, forcing them back to the wheel.

Jah know.

She starts laughing uncontrollably.

"Babe jeeeeezzzz. If I keep skipping, it ago play similar songs. Mi wah listen my playlist," she explains.

Mi nuh give a fuck! Feel like me head ago explode.

We start going over the the transverse rumble strips and just by the sound of it, dem nah slow down a ting killa. I sigh, out loud before bringing my phone to my ears. Slyme picks up on the second ring.

"Slow down fimi 'cause Ry' a gwaan like we nahgo ever stop fi me wul her and bruk her neck," I breathe.

At the end of my request, laughing starts coming from his car.

Man dem think a gimmicks?

I watch as he slows down, allowing his car and mine to fall in line. He brings his windows down and Ry' does the same, both now going at a decent speed.

"Yuh serious boss? We deven ago fast," he laughs.

"Dat mah say," Ry' butts in.

"Yo just do weh me say," I speak clearly, bringing the windows up from my side.

Ryleigh looks over at me, now realizing how serious I've gotten. A smile makes its way to her face. It stays a smile for no more than a second before she's screaming from laughter.

I avert my eyes back to the road, ignoring her. Mah dead fi just reach bad head.

"So mi cyaa play the genre me wah hear right now?" she asks, but I don't answer.

Just wait mon. Hope she no ask mi fi slow down later.

"Aaawww, baby daddy yuh vex fi real?" she asks, exaggerating her sad voice.

Vex yuh fuck

Observing her new pace, I finally relax– now comfortable with the speed.

"Mii skip it fi you," I mumble, picking up her phone to find whatever song she wants... and in this moment, I can feel the stress leaving my body, enough to remind me that I love her.

"Yuh wah listen?" I ask, keeping my head in her phone.

"You know me password?"

I do, but she nahfi know that. I also have never looked… Nuh see why when me can read her so good.

" 3 3 7 4 7 7," she says clearly.

 I type it in and the phone opens up to me.

"Wah dat spell?" she asks in a proud tone.

The memory of the keyboard pops up in my head and I think for a second before realizing.

I start laughing.

"Might mek you drive go home, just fi dat," I offer, through the spell of laughter.

* D D R I P P *

She continues to laugh before saying, "Not us being corny as hellll."

I shake my head, before repeating my prior question.

"More than Happy, Alkaline," she mutters, taking glimpses at me.

Playing with fire I see.

"Yuh too horny fi your age enuh Love," I chuckle

I watch as her face screws, "The pot must not speak to the kettle Mr.Sir,"

'Mr.Sir' I chuckle to myself.

Women.

Pulling up the song, I click it and lean back, finally comfortable enough to take my eyes from the road. She starts singing word for word, while I think about smoking in the car. Nuh know if it worth it but–

My thoughts are cut and my decision is made by my favorite part of the song being seconds away. Fuck it, wah di point if I can't enjoy the car to the fullest.

"Dem back shot yah duh good fimi heartttt," we both chip in at the very same time.

My eyes find her and we both laugh out. I bring my window down, releasing the smoke before taking a few more puffs and deciding to enjoy the ride down.

"Obsessed wid yuh, aye gyal yuh cya go home," she decides to sing along to more lyrics.

I know exactly what she's alluding to but mi no do nuttin other than look at her and chuckle, before pulling on my spliff again. I release the smoke and decide to join in. We continue like this until we're there.

A just our style that, from eva since.

Mhmhm.

• • •

RYLEIGH

"This is a surprise for real for real. Normally my birthday is celebrated like a two or three weeks late, so mi kinda happy unuh decide fi do it on the actual day," Mariah continues.

We all got here some time before her for the surprise– reminds me of that time in high school. We always celebrated her birthday in April, since we waited on the Easter holidays. We had school every year except last year...

Think we took that for granted though, so much so that on the actual day, we would low-key neglect her.

She's about to continue but Jordanne takes the mic.

The shade alone in that one sentence was enough for him I guess

Haha!

She looks over at me and I blow her a kiss. Unlike the last time we were all here, our parents aren't with us. It's just us and like a million and one guards.

When J' ends his rant about everybody having to get along, I pick my bag up and enter the villa.

"Watch memories," I mumble to myself.

Most of the furniture have been upgraded but it's by far the same. "No way we were 17 'bout we deh a villa a drink and party," I laugh to myself while climbing the stairs.

Moments later, I'm back downstairs where the party is picking up. The shots are going around but to how me have work a morning, let me not even. I watch Mariah take two back to back and I decide to move to her, since I just passed Ruse in the living area Facetiming JJ.

"Yuh good?" I ask her.

"Weh yuh think?" she asks, looking up at me.

She try no stop wid me 'cause a class fi class if it come to that.

I stare at her blankly...

"Mi good man," she mutters.

Good.

"Happy birthday. Hope you know alla we love you, regardless of what might be going on right now," I pull her into a hug.

"I guess," she gives me a small smile.

Feel it fi her enuh, I really do. Cyaa imagine if mommy did in love with a man while growing up, and I had to be at that person's home 24/7... only fi them get married and after years the kids no accept me. Well kid, 'cause Jordanne good wid her. Toni want a beating.

My eyes take the thought and start to search the small group. I find her standing with Kelly– both of them watching as Joshua selects the music.

"Soon come," I shout above the music to Mariah.

She nods, bringing a cup with mixed drinks to her lips.

Enjoy yuh birthday yah girl, drunk fi me and you.

Waltzing over to Toni, I rub my hands against the back of my arm. Fi a early spring night, it's chilly as shit.

"Can borrow yuh?" I ask, not waiting for the answer. I pull her to me and we walk to the side of the house.

"You say happy birthday?" I ask, staring straight into her eyes.

"Alla we say happy birthday when she walked in," she retorts.

Be fucking for real

The look on my face must've spelled out my thoughts 'cause Toni opens her mouth to speak again, "Yeah mi text her this morning. We talk likkle after that too. Let's just say it cyaa fix without mommy and Paul."

Mhmmm. Point taken.

"Okay, well why you itch up one side wid Kelly. A wah so?"

"She nah leff Joshua side so me nah leff," she answers, revealing her jealousy.

"Correct me if I'm wrong but anuh you bring in Kelly?" I ask, bewildered by her previous words. "How she a take step now?"

T' shrugs seeminly agitated.

"I… uhhh, kinda maybe, cheated, on them?" she whispers.

Weh she say? Mighty God of Daniel, a wah dead weh ina dis. I try to hold it in, like reallllllly try, but Toni starts laughing first.

"Hihihihahaha AHHH! Ahahaha murdaaaaaa!" I let out, and mi sure mi louder than the music.

"Stop nuh man!" she slaps me while trying to cover my mouth.

"Yah tell mi say two different genitals cyaa satisfy yuh likkle gyal?"

Ah weaaaakkkkkkkkkkkkk!!! Tears start springing to my eyes.

"Yuh nuh take nuttin serious enuh," she laughs, trying her best to keep me quiet.

"Fada God. Mi cyaa manage. Lucky thing Mariah never know that," I whisper, still crying from laughter.

"Yuh fuck!" she laughs out, louder than me this time.

"Cyaa keep you clit ina yuh draws?" I ask causing us both to hit the silent laugh.

You know? The one where you're dyyyyying from raw laughter and hitting each other but there's no sound coming from your mouth? That one!

We come up for air, but then we look at each other and start laughing again.

Jesus a tyaaddddd!

"Gyal stop nuh," she slaps me.

Okkkkkkaaayyy. Phewww! Wow. A long time me no laugh so.

"Come, mi pretty sure Joshua will choose you ova her any day. You nahfi fight fi no spot and if you're tired of the poly, just let him know. Which man you know in his position, making the money he is, a refuse pikny? Probably a just that. Just tell him you genuinely nuh ready."

"That's the thing, me nuh know if me ever ago ready," she says, in a serious tone before we fall silent, just looking at each other.

Welpppp, I duh know rasta… I duh know.

"Might as well you come drink and party then," I say, throwing my hands up.

"Might as well yes," she agrees and we both walk back to the lawns.

• • •

MUUCH

Everybody is on the lawns, having the time of their lives while mi deh yah a rest me foot. Cyaa wait fi drop mi gem and go back outside.

Weh yuh mean? Yuh affi stay in and feed it

You're killing the dream.

Keif and Lorelle just brought me food and T' and Ry' are supposed to get me something to drink– water or coconut water preferably.

"Baby madddaaaa!" Paw walks in, now putting his spliff out.

"You alone me see inside enuh. Snap mi. Me have a few girls weh me need fi feed," he chuckles.

I laugh out.

"Wulla a unuh a di same thing," I scold.

He holds his heart as if in pain, "Noooo Muuch, no compare mi to your boy. Mah good yute," he laughs handing me his phone.

I take it and stand.

"Wait mah drag on my jacket, affi hide the tatts. Is a nice Christian girl mah par wid yah now," he chuckles.

I laugh out again. A which pastor daughter Paw a stress out yah now man.

After taking the picture, I look at it before handing it to him. The boy look decent fi real enuh. Right height and dark skin with waves. God go with whichever girl him a whisper lies to.

"Respect baby madaa," he says before helping me to sit and leaving after such.

I avert my attention back outside. Everybody is dancing, drinking, singing, smoking or eating. My eyes fleet to the bar area and I spot Liam. Mmmchttt, drankro.

My mood shifts and I pick up my phone to continue texting.

• • •

RYLEIGH

You know me man into dah song yah too muchhhh?

"Have mi gun in har face and shah suck off eh G," Jordanne sings while pulling me into his arms.

One thing wid Bayka, him song dem ago touch the crowd, worst if dem drunk… and my friends are definitely drunk as fuckkk. To the point where Mariah is singing along with T', while she has Lorelle bent over. One ting dem ago do a wine pon each other and ignore dem man under liquor.

I shake my head before smiling at the sight.

Jordanne reaches out and pulls me in before whispering a line of the song in my ear. His voice turns my insides into mush. Pure, mushhhh. The control this man has over my body is ridiculous.

Ramone pops a bottle of champagne and Joshua mixes the song into Kraff's- CalmC. He starts singing while spraying the champagne and in that same instant, Paw laughs, walking back from inside the house whilst pulling his jacket back off.

My friends walk over before pulling me from J's grip and just by how dem ah move, mi know them fully drunk.

"Sing!" both Mariah and T' shout in unison, causing myself, Keif and Lorelle to laugh.

We continue singing and vibing, lyric for lyric for minutes on end. Happy so till! Finally my friends feel like them a 'friend' the right way again.

Until dem sober

Until…

I turn to look at the guys and Jordanne smiles at me, releasing the smoke from his mouth. T' has her hands at her crotch mimicking the movement to match the lyrics of the song being played currently… and the laugh session from earlier comes to mind, jolting me into uncontrollable laughter… again!

Joshua plays song after song afterrrrr song, and we sing and gwaan to each and every one– enjoying Mariah's birthday like it's for everybody.

● ● ●

Now on our way back to Kingston, at 1:22am. Jordanne, myself, Slyme, Michelle and a shitload of the shadow guards, are speeding down the toll. When him a drive him can speed though, unuh notice?

World nuh level killa.

"Have supm fi say," J' mutters, and I look up realizing the exit toll booth is coming up just before of us.

"Go ahead," I yawn, searching for the card we took when we entered. He slows all the way down, carefully going over the speed bump before settling into the lane.

"Have a flight tomorrow, well today," he mumbles, turning his head to look at me.

Huh???

Flight go where???

"What? Jordanne nuh bother stress me right now," I hiss, trying to complete the transaction.

"Real medz. Need you fi understand and take care of things. It's only gonna be until the plan is complete."

I look at him dumbfounded. He didn't say anything like this while explaining things. Dah man yah man?

"You never say you weren't going to be in the country. You say you just weren't gonna be in Kingston," I snap.

I can't do it if he's not here. Mi ago nervous and do supm wrong.

"I have to go... and me know you wouldn't agree or want me to leave if I said this earlier," he breathes.

Cut me fi cut up him passport, but him woulda get one by a morning

"Jordanne–" I try.

"Ry' it's the same thing. You'll be in charge and won't be able to reach me. Nobody will, except for Ramone and he's only to call if I say call. The only change is that you thought I was going to be in Hanover but I'm not, same plan," he explains, now taking my hand into his.

Me nuh want him touch me enuh.

Mi tell nobody me can call shots? Wahm to Skulli? Slyme? Paw? Anybody at this point... Sue herself can do it. I don't voice my thoughts though, because we've already been over it. How him so sure me nahgo fuck it up?

"Stop getting into your own head. You ago good, anuh nobody else father. I don't trust anybody enough to see it through, to make sure every single thing falls into place. Man dem know fi nuh mek nuttin happen to you so them will listen and your friends will listen to you more than anybody else I could leave in charge... Cool?"

Mmkkayyyy, I duh know.

"Okay..." I murmur.

He brings my hand to his lips to kiss it, while slowly driving. I slump back into my seat, allowing a million different scenarios to run through my brain.

Mark...

Croc...

Stress...

90 | 'On your Mark...'

RYLEIGH

"You sure you can't stay?" I mumble, snuggling into him. I don't know if I can do this shit fi real. Mi no used to dem supm yah.

I'm pulled back to reality by him rubbing on my thighs and kissing my forehead.

"Long as you do exactly weh mi say, you ago good," he groans.

I should let him sleep. We haven't slept since we got in. We showered, I gave him a massage and we've been talking ever since then. Mi must sleep pon the people dem work a morning, but who cares, after them nuh promote the doll.

Sigh.

"Skulli, Ramone, Slyme and Mum alone know most of it. Talk to them and only them, not even your mother."

I nod, knowing how hard that might be... She ago worried.

"Ry, nobody else, cool?" he repeats, wanting to hear the words from my mouth.

"Yeah, heard you," I whisper.

He pulls me in again and if we move any closer to each other we might merge. I fall into my thoughts and before you know it, we fall into sleep.

Five minutes later here comes my alarm.

Girl it's been four hours

Four hours, five minutes, same thing.

J's still deep in sleep with his arms across my stomach, just below my breasts. I bring his hand up to move out of bed, but he shakes my hand away to grab my waist and pull me back in.

Swear him a sleep.

"Yahgo?" he mumbles, voice groggy, still looking fully asleep.

"Work…"

"Work? Soon burn down dat," is all he says before lifting his arm, granting me freedom to slide out of bed.

Yeah, burn down the central bank, sure.

All wah gwaan, I've never been able to stop him from working. He works almost all day, every single day of the week.

Emails…

Contracts…

Business calls… This, that and the third. Whether he does it from the home office or leave to go on sight or abroad, a work same way.

I look back at him before leaving the room. He's sprawled out on his stomach now, with the comforter up to his waist. My lips turn up into a smile caused by satisfaction. I'm happy we're finally happy and on the same page. No more sneaky shit, no more unnecessary secrets.

I turn on my heels and exit the room quietly, making my way to being the villain in JJ's morning routine. I get to his room and push the door open.

"Junior?" I whisper-shout while making my way to his bed.

From when we tell him fi pick up him clothes?

From last week.

"Junior get up!" I stop whispering, now annoyed at how many pieces of clothing I can feel brushing against my ankles.

My feet carry me straight to the windows to drag the curtains open.

He groans.

"Get up, Ms.Cherry soon come up here."

JJ drags the sheet above his head before releasing a short hiss. Me done learn weh me fi learn a school already enuh, so him can gwaan.

"Like you wah me call Drip," I mumble.

The sheets suddenly roll down his body and I watch him drag himself out of bed.

"Good morning," he mutters, looking up at me.

"Morning big head. Your uncle supposed to bring you today," I murmur… If him mek it back from Ochi already.

"Can I go with you instead?" he peers up at me, asking his question.

I don't think me have the time or the energy to deal with the parents at drop off.

"Why don't you like to go with him?" I stoop to his level.

Somehow, he always has an excuse as to why him no wah stay with him uncle or do things with him anymore. He doesn't answer my query, but his face becomes solemn.

"… Looks like daddy."

I– Uhmmm.

I stoop there dumbfounded while he looks at me.

"You can come with me," I whisper, barely getting my words out. Something within me tells me to plant a kiss on his forehead, and that's what I do, before I hear his door open.

"Junior breakfast is downsta–" Ms.Cherry saunters in. "Oh hi pretty girl, breakfast is there for you too if you want. I made enough for the house… Junior come, mi affi run go Mobay today. Nuh waste mi morning likkle bwoy."

He moves on her command.

Then a when him ago move pon my command?

• • •

"Cyaa believe yuh nuh ina me department no more, my gosh," I whine, while Nadz and I pack our things to leave work. She spent the day in my office today since her new area isn't even ready, but they had the audacity to put someone in her old space.

Patty shop enuh, mi tell unuh.

"Girl yah gwaan like a leff mah leff the company," she giggles at my constant complaining.

Might as well a did leave she a leave, the way me nahgo see her as often.

"You wah go out later?" she asks, as we exit my office, waltzing down the hallway.

I think about the fact that I want to accompany Jordanne to the airport and then, maybe I can invite all the girls out. On second thought, me nuh want she meet the girls and realize dem mad.

"Weh yuh wah go?" I ask.

"I don't know, Tacbar?" she suggests.

"If I get back from what I have to do, sure," I agree.

"So we a 'outside-of-work-fren' now?" she asks excitedly.

I stop, feigning shock and a world-shattering heartbreak before I say, "Then this whole time I was nuttin more than a work bestie?"

She laughs out, pulling the attention of those leaving along with us. We continue walking until we're out the doors. I press my keys when we're no less than a foot away from my car, and the doors click open. Nadz and I get in simultaneously, releasing a breath when we finally hit the seats. I'm supposed to pick up JJ today and since Nadz lives a little way from his school, I offered her a ride.

We pull out and she notices the shadow cars taking their place at different points on the road.

"Why them sandwich you so girl? From we leff Downtown. Yuh no notice!?" she asks, while looking back and forth.

I giggle.

How do I explain this?

"Them nah sandwich mi man," is all I offer, and I can feel her staring at me for a moment before she drops the question.

Turning onto Ardenne Road, I slowly roll to a stop, knowing JJ will run out to the car when he sees it.

So said, so done.

He lifts himself in, while greeting me, panting and sounding overly happy.

"You don't see somebody else?" I ask, waiting for him to acknowledge Nadifa.

"I didn't... Good evening new lady," he adds, while forcing his backpack from his shoulders.

I giggle at the name he gave her.

"Evening handsome," Nadifa's reply comes soft and nurturing. She looks at me and I can see the multitude of questions in her eyes.

"Don't ask," I laugh, now wrapping my steering to spin and leave.

Before I exit onto Hope Road, a call comes in interrupting my '90s souls playlist.

BD ❤*...*

I don't hesitate to press the answer button.

"Baby da–"

"Why yah go that route?" his voice blocks the end of my statement.

"Dropping off Nadz," I grant him a soft answer. The coldness from his voice changes the mood in the car, causing both my passengers to seem uncomfortable.

"Dat good. Just randomly check the tra–" he holds back, "just randomly checked your location," he explains, fixing his words to match the fact that Nadifa's present.

Mhmmhm, me know him on edge about leaving me here alone while him go figure out things in Venezuela and then Chicago.

"Come home, before you drop her off. Can do that?"

I look at Nadz, whose head is glued to her phone, trying her best to not seem as if she's hearing our conversation.

"You late fi nuttin Nadz?"

She shakes her head and with that I signal to the guard cars about my route change.

● ● ●

We pull up to the house and Snoop lets us in. I glance at Nadz just in time to see her mouth agape. Haha! Bay question fimmi likkle more enuh.

I pull in and park, to see Jordanne walking out of the house, tucking his gun into his waist.

Another question for her to ask

Junior lets himself out and runs to him. Jordanne stoops and throws him up and over his shoulder. Nadz? She sidung just a watch the scene.

I open my door and step out, to find out what he could've wanted that was so important.

"Why you mek me stop here?"

He ignores me, grabbing me with his free arm before pulling me into a kiss.

"Nassssttttyy," JJ snickers from his shoulder.

"Affi carry him to Mum and I'm about to leave right now. Couldn't wait pah you fi come offa you Uber shift," he chuckles.

"And yuh just alright with a new person coming here?" I pull away.

He chuckles again, lowly, while bringing JJ to his feet. Junior bolts off into the house and I bring my eyes back to meet J's.

"Yuh funny you know that?" he continues to chuckle while looking at me. Bringing his hands to brush my cheeks, he adds, "If you think I don't have a file on every single person you work with daily, then yuh still no know me."

I–

Well I mean.

"Oh–kayyy," I jokinly scoff, "Ago drop her off and come back come shower and nap before you go airport. 8:30 you say?"

"Yup. Mah leave Mum 'round 6:30 ish dem time deh," he pulls me back in, to kiss my hairline, causing my cheeks to become flushed I'm sure.

He then releases me before waving to the car. Nadifa waves back slowly, as if a load of confusion is resting on her frame.

"She look so shakey?" he laughs, while I turn to walk back to the car.

"She duh know one fuck," I laugh out, making my way down the pavement.

I fly the car door and hop in, ready for her inevitable question and answer session.

"Giiiiiiiirlllll, what the fuck?" she starts, causing me to almost scream out.

"Yuh nuh know the half," I smile. Ignoring her stares, I pick up my phone to call Mariah.

Maybe she want another night out, without everybody else being there to remind her of her hurt. I'm sooooo tired, but I can't put off Nadifa anymore, plus I want to get the Mark thing over with.

• • •

Now on my way from the airport, I watch as Ramone turns off route, heading home. He honks at me and I return the action, continuing my route to pick up Nadifa. Mariah made it known that she would be late since Ruse and her are just getting in from St.Ann.

I get to Nadifa's moments later and only a few minutes after that, we're seated at Tacbar getting handed menus to look at.

Forty minutes after such, this is what she's saying, "Glad mi come see this."

She's laughing while Mariah expresses how much she hates content creation these days.

"Cyaa tell when last me vlog nuttin. Mi tired ah it so till. A just like selling front. Me is a prostitute to the company them."

Nadz and I are at the brink of tears at this point.

"Unuh a laugh? My hairline whore out. Wig after wig, outfit after outfit, me tired man," she wipes away her non-existent tears.

"Yah supm else enuh girl," I laugh, focusing on our surroundings.

Looking down at my phone, I decide to check the time– 9:53pm. I miss him already. He would be texting me right now, threatening me with starting whichever series without me, if I don't get home in time.

It's been less than two hours

And?

My phone vibrates, showcasing an unfamiliar number across the screen.

+876-567-9876...

I quickly excuse myself from the table, moving to a quiet enough area that grants some level of privacy. I take a deep breath before answering the call...

Holding the phone to my ear, I await his voice.

"Daughta," he starts, sounding exactly like he did when I was younger.

Exactly like he does in every nightmare.

Every daydream...

Every episode...

I take another deep breath, "Mark," I murmur into the phone.

"Haha. Yah me daughter fi a reason enuh. Know you did ago come through," he hoarsely chuckles.

I shift my weight to the less dominant foot while my free hand finds my thighs, digging through the thin dress fabric and into my skin.

"If I do what you want, will you drop everything?" I get straight to the point.

He laughs, a little too long for me. My anger begins to boil and my nails go sinking deeper into my flesh, trying to prevent my mind from slipping.

"Of course bunny. You carry out your part and mi will handle mine."

I think about it for a few seconds, before saying, "Okay... I'll do it."

"Beautiful. We can meet up for the details so that I ca–"

"Nah meet up with no man," I shut his idea down immediately. Something has snapped within me, and I can't pinpoint what it is.

The level of anger surging through my body is starting to worry me. I'm beginning to feel cold, literally.

"I'll reach out to you from a secured line, where you can speak less vaguely about what you want. If it's not done that way, he'll find out before anything is set into play," I explain.

Realizing the grip I have on the phone is too tight, I try to breathe slowly, relaxing my limbs.

"Look at you. Yah really mi daughta enuh. Like father like dau–" before he's able to end his little proud parade, I hang up the phone.

The hand that was digging at my thighs, find its way to the hand holding my phone and I squeeze my eyes shut, trying to stay calm.

"You alright?" Mariah's voice startles me.

She looks at me in confusion.

"I'm okay, the taco them come?" I ask, trying to shift both the topic and the mood.

"No you're not, but alright, since yuh wah pretend. No dem nuh come, like dem wah hungry twist we tripe ina this," she complains, waving her hands around.

I offer her a small smile, before we walk back to the table where Nadz is still sitting, drinking a glass of, I don't know what.

"Rum head gyal yah man?" I giggle, looking at her mysterious glass.

"Girl me affi liquored up fi later tonight."

"Pon a regular Wednesday night? Yuh nuh easy," I laugh out, knowing I'm about to order something to drink too.

"Live life yah fren!" Mariah laughs, now bringing her glass to her mouth. "Alla we a big people!"

"Affi do weh we affi dooo!" both Nadz and I finish her statement, giggling like school girls.

We continue chatting it up while making small jokes for upwards of an hour. Mariah and I have been listening to Nadz complain about her 'such man', while dropping the vaguest stories about our own lives. Don't get us wrong, Nadifa is cool but it takes a certain amount of time for me or any of us to feel comfortable enough to share certain things, especially with the lifestyle we live.

Another 30 minutes roll by and by now, Nadifa is asking us to take pictures of her. I have refused because she's drunk and I know who she wah send them to. Fun and jokes aside, an office romance is cute and all, but when you ago send raw evidence of it? No.

Mi nuh know yah, maybe them a plan fi declare the relationship to HR still, but if not, sending pictures is just asking for problems. Wah happen when such man get vex and say a she did a look him off?

Mariah stands and grants her, her wish. She cheers when a couple pictures are taken. Mariah hands her the phone happily before falling back to her chair.

• • •

We're now all walking to where I parked, shadow guards on our heels as per usual. I find my keys before opening the car for us all to get in.

"Come friendddd!!!" Nadifa blurts out of nowhere.

"Ah memba we nuh fuck out!!!" Mariah adds.

It takes me less than a second to realize that they're mimicking the Tiktok video and I join in too.

"Ah we nuh suck out!!!" I add, now giggling uncontrollably.

"Ah we batty duh touch!!!" we basically scream in unison, causing one of the guards to look at us, quickly looking away when his eyes meet mine.

"Some gyal batty touchhhhh!!!" we say in unison again, doubling over in raw laughter this time.

No way we're the new adults? Merccyyyy. Then how JJ fi listen to me?

Before we all can enter my car, a honk of a horn on the opposite side of the road pulls our attention.

"He came!" Nadifa shrieks, staring at the black Benz parked, seemingly awaiting her.

I try to read the plates, but I don't have my contacts in tonight, and my glasses are in my car's center console.

"A yuh such man that?" Mariah asks, as we both observe Nadifa's newly found shyness.

"Yeah," she confirms, now offering us both hugs.

Mi no like carry people places and then them no leave with me enuh

Riggghttt…

"Girl, mek him know if anything do you him wings can get clipped," I jokingly warn.

Nadifa stops to look at me. She seems to have taken my statement seriously, probably because of all she's seen today.

"Girl gwaan. Enjoy yourself fi me and you and nuh bother call out a morning!" I save the mood, giving her a light shove.

She giggles, and I watch her cross the street safely before hopping into the car. Richard pulls off before flashing us a farewell.

Watch BOJ couple

Murdaaa!

Mariah and I take our seats in my car and before you know it, we're on our way home.

"Mi can stay a yuh house tonight?" she asks, over my lowly playing music.

I look at her in slight confusion, "Sure? When since yuh affi ask that?"

"Duh start," she shrugs, "Ruse say him a deal with supm and me just nuh wah ina the place alone."

I know exactly weh him a do.

As di man second in command enuh

Fi two weeks haha! Relax.

"Nuh need fi explain girl," I laugh. "Coulda live there fi all I care. Probably wouldn't even see you fi days to how the place big and complicated."

"Mi woulda hear yuh though!" she laughs out.

I laugh out too, loud enough to send us into more laughter. You know mi ago stop mek noise though? Yeah man, me ago practice.

We get to the house and I watch as the guards leave as soon as Snoop lets us in. We both get inside, and I bid her goodnight almost immediately. 'Cause if me follow her we chat and laugh until a morning and I have to be up for work.

Minutes later, I'm out of the shower and wrapped in my robe.

Ouuu I can sleep naked without worrying about J's dick finding its way inside me. Feeling happy about the fact, I crawl into bed and snuggle up into the sheets, while finding my phone. I toggle to his chat, only to see that he has already texted me.

BD♥: Here, Remember every day that I love you.

After this if you need me just link Ramone.

BD♥: Mi know you reach home, reply so I can sleep

in peace.

> **I went straight to the shower and**
> **I know what to do. I Love you**
> **Mr.Sheer ♥. Miss you already ⊗**

BD♥: More than mi own life Mrs.Sheer.

I think about stretching the conversation but I don't, knowing he must be tired as hell. Staring at the screen while smiling for a few more minutes, I roll over and start thinking about the first time he said two words to me.

'You fi eat supm heavier'. The memory brings a smile to my face. Since the very day he defended me in the cafeteria line, I've been under his spell. Fighting it for years yes, sure... but still never being able to break free regardless.

Pulling his pillow, that holds his scent, closer to me– since I don't have him to cuddle, I start thinking about all the other good times we've shared, before drifting off into dreamland.

91 | Conform or Go

TONI-ANNE

"Even so T', you can't hold that over her head."

What's mommy saying right now? Who said I was holding anything over Mariah?

I simply just don't see her as my sibling and I can't say I'll pretend.

Ever...

How am I all of a sudden the bad guy? A mi air out everybody business? Me nuh understand dem people yah. The relationship with my mother has always been fragile. I'm a daddy's girl but that's beside the point. Point is, I love Mariah, I do, but calling her my sister? Nope.

"I'm not holding a thing ova her head though. I simply said I don't see her as a sister. Why nobody nah tell her weh she do wrong?" I ask, now looking at her.

"I already said I was wrong and I was frustrated," she breathes.

Well...

So why it nuh done deh so?

I slump back into the chair folding my arms, displaying my irritation.

"So then what's the issue? Because I don't have a problem with her. That night in the room I was telling her to apologize to Muuch," I explain for the millionth time.

Ughh! Me wah gah me yard enuh.

"Yuh treat mi a way from we younger though Toni-Anne," Mariah starts again.

I look at her and then to mommy.

I'm pretty sure that wasn't the case.

"How so?" mommy asks, directing her question to Mariah, who's now playing with the hem of her shirt.

The room falls silent for a moment, while she searches for her answer.

"Just the little things... I can't pinpoint everything because I've always brushed them off... Like she would make it a point to clear up to strangers that we weren't all siblings when we went out in the early days or, when she came to 6th form, she made it a point to everybody. Like a years me and Danne ago high school without her and everything did good. She never even have interest ina we before dat. So much so that she didn't even know Ryleigh was the best friend he would complain about every evening. She had her own life, until she came..."

"Other day supm tick me off too. Like we're all at the Stewart's fair thing right and she a tell Ry' a only she, Danne and bay pikny deh deh– asking her why she neva come? Like me invisible. If me never push my head in the phone... Cho, mi nuh know. She does things like that and dem small, yes but them add up and–"

"Idiot gyal, when mi tell people say we anuh siblings a protect mah protect you half the time!" I sneer.

But a wah do dah girl yah?

"Who yah call idiot? Dutty fuck ou–" she pauses, "You know wah? Mi tired ah this," she folds her arms and slides down in her chair. "Nuh wah talk 'bout it no more, we can just no deal."

Mhmmhm, 'cause if she did end dah sentence deh me send it back down her throat.

Sue is just sitting there observing each of us keenly. Moments pass before anybody makes a move or speaks a word.

"Toni-Anne, did we not speak about the issues you had with me?" mommy asks.

I roll my eyes, because of course she nah take my side.

"Likkle gyal, mine me collect couple a you teeth dem yerr? Ansa the question," she snaps, allowing her original accent to pierce through her 'uppity' demeanor.

For a moment I'm surprised but in truth and in fact, I know where my mom is from. I know who she was before 'all this'. She's never kept it a secret so...

"Mummy, as usual mi nah expect yuh fi take my side, but me honestly neva do her nuttin. Maybe she think me a be cold to her over the years, and maybe I was, but that night with Muuch, I was just trying to stop her from saying too much or doing too much and di girl ago say back weh mi tell her in secret. Even if me did wah consider you my sister now, I won't. Ole fridge!"

MMMCHT.

"Toni, your TOOOONE. Take time fi understand each other's point of view becau–" Sue speaks but is cut off by Mariah making a comeback.

"Couldn't fill dat spot 'cause Ry' have that," she mumbles, but I hear every word.

How the fuck Ry' reach ina it???

"Wah?" I ask, looking at her, while Sue is saying something that neither of us are interested in right now.

"Yuh love di gyal!" she stands, "more than a friend or sister too!"

A small laugh leaves my lips… and before I can stop myself, I move to her and my fist connects to her mouth. The next thing I feel is Sue dragging me outside the library.

Bitch!

• • •

RYLEIGH

"That's what he told me to do," I explain to Paul, who is confused about me watching and listening in on the meeting instead of being there.

Jordanne wants me to make my presence unknown, so that when Skulli announces I'm to take the lead for the next two weeks, whoever has something to say, he'll know. I'm not worried about those from the family, I'm more worried about all the other subdons that might not like to see a young… woman… handing out orders.

Heavy on the woman

"Probably wah know who ago screw. Smart," he mutters.

Don't? Mi man nuh ease up in that department.

I almost giggle, but a serious times masah.

"Yeah… " I trail off, giving away as little as I can.

"Alright, Ramone show you how fi power it up?" he asks, pointing to all the devices in Ramone's office.

You know Skulli think me a six?

Think everybody a still baby yes

I laugh softly before answering, "Yeahhhh?"

"Cool," he chuckles, grabbing his hair into a top knot before walking out of the office and out of the basement altogether.

I watch him enter the elevator before disappearing. By now my fingers are already moving to power up the monitor and all the mics. Sliding the headset over my head and to my ears, I focus on the screen while bringing a grape to my mouth.

I watch as Paul moves to the front of the crowd of men, who have been lingering and awaiting the daily meeting. My eyes find Slyme who is standing closest to the exit, instead of to the front where he usually is with J'.

He's to leave to join Drip soon, but him and Michelle have ah doctor's appointment.

Co-parent them say enuh

I search the screen to find Paw, just a small distance to the left of Paul, while Ramone is to the far right of him. The men settle when Skulli raises his hand to command quietness.

His lips are moving but… But afta mi cyaa hear nuttin!

Check the mic again!

I do as my mind suggests and realize the settings are on mute. I quickly change it, allowing the sound of his voice to rush through the headset.

"Good?" Paul's voice comes clear.

"Lawww," the men all say at once.

Not yuh mek we miss the first statement

"Sas Crise, be quiet. Not today please," I mumble to my overactive inner monologue. Nerves ago kill mi today.

"Few changes ago gwaan while the boss is away a handle some business," he speaks again.

Oh you no miss nothing it seems

Be QUIET!

I sit there trying to quiet my mind enough in order to listen and observe everybody's body language all at once. And mek me tell you, being a blindy is not helping. My glasses can only do so much and no more.

"For two weeks the person he shared his plan with, will be the one in charge until he's back," Paul speaks clearly, lacing his fingers together while observing them.

Small mumbles travel through the back of the crowd but nothing outside of the usual, it seems.

He waits until they calm down before he continues, "That person is Ryleigh," this time his hands find his pockets, as he observes the crowd.

I swiftly shift my eyes from him to the group of men.

"Him woman?" a voice comes from the back-right, near to the exit. The person's tone reeks of confusion and disapproval.

Hmm yah so it start enuh

I rock back into the chair while zooming in, trying to place his face. His features fall unrecognizable, and I shrug.

"Same one," Slyme butts in, staring at the guy. "You have an issue?"

Watch me old friend! If him coulda keep him dick ina him pants we woulda good enuh man.

Focus

The guy doesn't answer but somebody else does, "Weh she know 'bout owah side a di ting?" his question is directed to Skulli.

"She know enough bad head. Unless you think Drip nah make the right decision?" Paul snickers.

Paw joins in, humorlessly laughing.

Me never ask fi none a this enuh, so them can relax.

"Nah question him, just a say, we cyaa take orders from somebody weh only claim to the top is pussy."

Murdaaaa!

Shaaaaaaaaaaaame!!!

I can't help myself, a small amount of giggles start falling from my mouth.

Slyme looks at Paw, Paw looks at Skulli and Skulli looks at Ramone before they all look back at the guy. He seems unaffected by the sudden wave of coldness creeping through the room. Even through the monitors, I can clearly see how thick the tension got in just a few seconds.

"Mi agree wid him enuh," the guy who posed the first question rejoins the conversation.

Two enuh.

Two grown ass men a complain 'bout little ole me.

"Can tell yuh weh mah hear?" Slyme speaks up, now walking to the front. Buckle takes his position near to the exit.

"Tell we," Ramone, Skulli and Paw reply in unison as if rehearsed.

"Sound to me like him nuh trust Drip," Slyme laughs.

"Sound so to me too," Paw smiles.

Slyme gets to the front and takes Ramone's position. Ramone then moves to a tiny set of cables to the side.

Seconds later, his voice comes through the headset, startling me.

A weh di?

" Wah yuh wah we do with him?" he repeats himself, since I was zoned out when he asked first.

It takes my brain less than a second to remember what to do if something like this were to actually happen.

My index finger moves to the button for my mic.

"Bring them to me," is all I say, and my words must've bellowed throughout the room upstairs because everybody seems to be in shock.

Ramone nods and Slyme smiles proudly.

Me on the other hand??? Nervous so till. Who told Jordanne I was Bonnie?

I bring the headset from my ears and to the desk. Sliding the chair back, I stand to my feet and exit Ramone's office to move to Jordanne's. Just as I take a seat, the elevator door dings open. Footsteps and mumbling make their way to me.

"Just a serious question mi did a ask still," a male voice seeps beneath the door, landing on my ears. I recognize the voice to be that of the first guy.

"Nuh need fi the chatting now still," I hear Paw, almost laughing.

The door opens and I look up to greet them.

"Hi gentlemen," I smile, watching as the first guy's eyes meet mine.

Yeah man, me know me did fi know him from somewhere. Jerome's son. Supposed to be in charge of Clarendon now.

Literally like two or three years younger than me, and a try throw questions at my credibility?

Paw and Slyme releases them both, while I sit there observing them– head to toe.

"What seems to be the problem?" I ask, now tapping my fingernails against the hard wood of the desk.

Mi wah know if it's really my gender. Having a pussy cannot be causing men to be up in a bunch like this.

Certain that's what it is

If so, that's pathetic.

92 | Bienvenido a Venezuela

JORDANNE

The smell of the unfamiliar air tickles my nostril. The view from the small porch is calming and the sounds of the nearby birds, bring me a new sense of peace.

But we nuh deh yah fi dat...

Not at all killa

We deh yah fi figure out who mi affi kill and how.

I bring the cigar to my lips, watching the van drive towards me. The dust from the dirt road gathers, forming a yellow cloud behind the wheels, with each meter covered. There are two other identical vehicles coming from the opposite direction. They all come to a slow, before lining up to make their way to the house.

All three vehicles get to the front yard, parking strategically so that the one that Gabriel occupies stays in the center.

The first time I was here, with my father, they did the same routine.

"Don't let the multiple vans intimidate you son. It's all a tactic," the memory of his words pull at my heart.

Bad as he was, mi did rate mi old man.

Rest in peace, elder Sheer

When Gabriel exits his designated vehicle, I stand to my feet while putting the cigar out in the ashtray beside the porch chair. Stepping down to the small pavement, I extend my right hand. Gabriel takes it and hands me a firm grip.

"Nice tuu finally meet chu mi amigo!" he's the first to speak, looking above his dark shades– getting a proper memory of my face I'm assuming.

"Likewise," is all I offer.

I collect my right hand from his and we both move into the house, walking straight to the tiny antique office. I take a seat at the chair closest to the window. Knowing I'll need the view to keep me calm, if I can't get answers to my questions.

Gabriel's little chunky figure, lands a seat next to mine while two of his men stand by his side.

Man dem can relax 'cause if anything even look like it ah go wrong, my snipers are outside, with clean shots. Yeah the window view was never to calm my nerves via view... It calms it by way of reassurance– protection.

A couldn't fi look pah bush, enough bush deh Jamaica, Ry's parish to be exact. I wonder how she's doing right n–

"So young Sheer, what'iz the prublem? Why come all da way here? To Benezuala? En-encryp-encrypted call wasna good enough?" I want to smile at his accent but decide not to.

I probably sound the same way to him when I speak Spanish.

"Te sigo diciendo que hablo español con fluidez Gabriel, no necesito inglés," I breathe, keeping my eyes met with his.

("I keep telling you that I'm fluent in Spanish Gabriel, no need for English.")

He chuckles, looking up at his men, before looking back at me.

"You Spanish es, iiisss, how do you say?... formal... tuu formal for Benezuala mi amigo," he chuckles, "and I want tuh practice my inglés."

Man broken English harder fi understand than him just speaking Spanish bredda.

Swear

I find the bottle of Santa Teresa and pour myself a still glass, before bringing it to my mouth.

"Te sigo diciendo que hablo español, no necesito que me hables en inglés... Informal enough for you?" I ask, finally bringing the glass to my lips.

("I keep telling you that I speak Spanish, I don't need you to speak to me in English.")

"Sí sí," he chuckles, "but English for me. Help a friend. Why-why, you are here Sheer?"

Deciding to get straight to the point, I ask what I need to know, "How is Croc in my country?"

I watch as the jovial spirit he sported falls from his being and is replaced by confusion. Unsure if it's genuine confusion or not, I bring the glass to my lips again, watching his every move.

"Croc?" he asks, seeking confirmation.

I nod.

"Yes, Mark Stevens," I answer clearly.

"No, no my friend. Croc esss been dead, for years, killed him myself."

"Well yuh neva kill him good mi genna," I murmur, cocking my head to the side.

"Qué?" he asks, struggling to translate the patois.

"You didn't kill him Gabriel, he's been in the U.S," I sneer, now placing my glass back to the small table.

Why him woulda try kill him anyways? Things keep getting more interesting by the minute.

One of his men pulls at his waist and in no time a red dot appears on each of their foreheads. Gabriel slowly raises his hand, signaling to his guys to relax.

"I tau we were good my friend. Snipuurz?" he asks, referring to the snipers.

Mah lose mi patience now bad man. Nahv the fucking time fi the run around.

"Who gave the order to kill him?" I ask, a question I didn't think I would have to ask today.

Gabriel looks at me in shock, confusion, amusement even.

"You, mi amigo," he says.

Me??!!!

Jah Jah God.

"Why would I do that Gabriel?" I ask as calm as possible.

I wouldn't kill Ry's father, without giving her a chance of reconciliation.

"Sí, Mrs.Sheer said you–"

Gabriel continues to talk but my brain is now spinning loose from the mention of my mother. Cyaa show the confusion, affi stay grounded.

Mum? The fuck a gwaan?

I cut into his rambling, "So how did he make it to Chicago last year? If you're claiming to have killed him? Explain that to me?"

"Look at deh body myself my friend. My most trusted guy right here handled it."

Hahaha! I see.

Soon as the man say dat me lose all faith ina him. You wah supm done right? You do it yourself.

Most trusted guy?

"Well Gabriel, this guy didn't complete the job, because I'm 100% certain he's alive and well, otherwise I wouldn't be here now, would I?" I smirk.

Gabriel turns to his, 'trusted guy' and before I can blink, di man pull gun pon him boss.

A chuckle leaves my lips.

Jah know mi short friend

Gabriel seems to be confused and stressed, unable to think. The second guy pulls his weapon, pointing it at the Judas in the room, granting Gabriel more time to... think? Wehm have fi think 'bout? Mmmcht.

Deal wid it fiim

I bring the glass to my lips, holding it there for more than five seconds before shifting form the window. Less than a millisecond after me shifting, the glass shatters and Gabriel's 'most trusted guy' falls to the floor with a clean cut shot to his forehead.

Beautiful...

"My friend what wuz dah?!" he turns, staring at me.

Man accent ago mek mi laugh ina serious times.

"I don't have the time for you to investigate," I breathe while stepping over the lifeless body.

Me have a flight to Chicago in less than two hours.

•••

SLYME

The car ride to Michelle's OBGYN is silent. Siiiiiiiilent.

My thoughts bring me back to the meeting earlier and mi can't wait fi tell Drip how him woman behave.

"Girl deh a supm else," I chuckle to myself– cold.

"Wah sweet yuh?" Michelle asks.

Oh? She a deal wid me now?

"Nuttin," is the word that rolls off my tongue.

Mi nahfi look pon her fi know she roll her eyes just now. Know mi woma– Know mi, baby mada?

Jah know.

The ride falls silent again before we turn into the business center. I park the closest I can find to where she says the office should be. Shutting the car off, I hop out and walk to her side, releasing her door before taking her hand to help her out.

Groans of discomfort leaves her lips while she finds her feet. When she does, she hands me her bag, brings her right hand to her back and starts waltzing to the office.

We enter the waiting area and she moves to the receptionist.

Me coulda do that still, she nahfi a walk up and down so.

We stand there a while before the receptionist looks up at us both, "Liam and–"

"She knows you?" Michelle asks, staring at me, huffing.

I almost laugh out, but I know not to.

"Michelle anuh you add mi name to the appointment?" I breathe, finding her eyes.

She rolls them, before saying, "Mhmhhm"

Jah Jah God.

The receptionist looks between us both, waiting to regain our attention.

"Michelle and Liam Burkett?"

"Egar," she corrects her.

"Burkett," I say, flashing my best smile at the receptionist.

She look like she already tired a we

She sighs, as if reading my thoughts.

"You guys can have a seat to the side, they'll call you in soon."

"Thank you," I nod, before walking off.

Michelle is already halfway to the chairs. Miserable yuh fuck.

I get to the chairs and try to sit beside her but she slaps her hand onto the open chair, signaling for me to hand her, her bag. Following her command, I place the bag on the chair next to her. I then attempt to take the next seat beside her but she pushes it away.

"Michelle, yuh cyaa handle the people dem furniture so," I whisper, now looking at the receptionist, whose eyes are planted in our direction.

Dat mah talk 'bout, I shake my head.

"Just cyaa stomach you Liam, please," her words do more to hurt me, than they do to annoy me.

Nodding my head while pressing my lips into a flat line, I take the seat next-over, burying my head into my phone aimlessly to pass the time. A few minutes later, a nurse makes her way to us, repeating my surname. I look up and nod before standing.

"Are you the mama?" she asks Michelle.

"Yes, last name is Egar though," she corrects her and the nurse writes something on her notepad.

The name she a correct

Might bruk her finger them, mmmchtt.

Quieting my intrusive thoughts, I move to Michelle, helping her to stand while taking her bag.

"You have all your information from the visits abroad?" I ask, out of genuine concern.

She pauses to look at me for a second before saying, "No, mi use them boil soup."

I chuckle, walking closely aside her into the examination room. We get there and the doctor greets us.

"Hi my name is Dr.Graham," the middle aged lady introduces herself.

Before we get to greet her, she says, "Mom and dad right?" pointing between us for confirmation.

We both nod in silence.

"Okay, I have all your previous results here," she says, tapping away on her laptop. "Mommy, you can have a seat on the bed," she points, "And daddy, you can have a seat in the chair next to her."

We both do as we're told without hesitation.

"It says here, mommy's iron is low. Have you been taking your iron supplements religiously?" she poses the question to Michelle.

Michelle shrugs, "I try to, they make me sick."

My eyes find hers, holding questions and slight anger.

"I understand that, but try your best to take them every day. Baby will need it and you will need it more when the time comes. Did you guys check for sickle cell?"

"Yes," – Michelle.

"No," – Liam.

Nuh take no test. Just find out she pregnant, sigh.

The doctor looks between us while Michelle plays with her dress.

"Mommy and daddy weren't in agreement for the first half of the pregnancy?" Dr.Graham asks… and if dah woman yah keep on call we mommy and daddy mahgo mad.

"I took mine abroad, since I wasn't here and… he didn't know…" Michelle breaks the short silence that was threatening to engulf the small room.

"That's fine, I'll have the nurse take a sample after this," she adds, comforting Michelle.

I don't say a word but inside mi ben bredda.

"Okay… This is going to be cold, though I'm sure you know that already. We're going to check to see if everything is okay with baby. Do you guys want to know the gender?"

"No," – Michelle

"Yes," – Liam

We both look at each other, before laughing. We off the ball yuh fuck.

"Why not?" I ask Michelle, while watching the doctor rub a gooey substance on her tummy, before she uses the probe to start observing.

"What does it matter Liam?" she asks, keeping her eyes on the monitor.

My eyes find it too and within seconds of Dr.Graham pressing the probe against Michelle's tummy, I hear the heartbeat.

"Heartbeat is strong," Dr.Graham smiles, now pointing at the monitor and saying a bunch of things that my ears fail to register.

Only ting mah listen right now is the heartbeat.

Cyaa believe me lose mi relationship ova fuckry yute.

"Look like yuh enuh Liam," Michelle laughs out.

I look at her confused.

"Dawkkk," she giggles out.

I laugh out, "Yuh nahv nuh mannaz. A style ting?" I find myself standing to place a kiss on her forehead before I can stop myself.

She looks at me after the action is completed. Hear disss now, just listen.

I stand still, awaiting her remarks.

"Yuh love woman suh Slyme?" she giggles.

Really? Better than weh mi did a expect… so I use the opportunity to plant more kisses on her forehead.

"Doctor tell the bobo dread fi come offa me!" she whines, still giggling.

Eeeh? Nuh know when she ago allow this again, mah take full advantage.

• • •

RYLEIGH

"Weh you mean by you lick the girl T'?" now driving home, I'm shocked by the news.

"She piss me off. I don't know when mi hand reach her mouth Ry," she explains, tone holding regret.

Fada God dem ago gimmi grey hair.

"So what happened exactly? You keep on a say she piss you off, but yuh never lick her 'bout Joshua dem so what now?" I question.

Joshua dem?

Kelly dem? Whatever. Mi no have time fi this. Me have everything weh Jordanne supposed to have on his mind, on mine right now.

Soft life me fi a live enuh. Wah dis the boy gimmi?

The line stays silent for a while but I can hear her breathing.

"Toni-Anne?" I try to get her to speak.

Fada mi tired, I want to go home, take a nice, long, warm shower and chuck off ina me bed.

"She mention you..." she murmurs.

"Weh she say 'bout me? Everybody know my business anyways so anuh li–"

"Ryleigh... She mentioned you," she cuts me off.

I sit there puzzled for approximately three seconds before I put two and two together. Think a mi alone the likkle girl tell, and look how me hold on pon her secret like life itself.

"You told her?" I ask, and even I can hear the confusion within my own voice.

"You alone me ever tell that. That was years ago, so mi nuh know why she woulda say that outa her mouth now?" she mumbles in frustration.

Mhmmhm. Nahv a clue miself yah.

"T' me coulda swear we agreed that you mistook those... feelings, as being more than platonic because you did just a figure out yourself?" I say, seeking clarification.

Cause mi know the lady couldn't have no real feelings, afta she no crazzzyyy

"And that's exactly what they were, but her saying it today just piss me off" she hisses over the line.

It wouldn't bother me, if it was me, and me know what is what... but everybody different, I guess.

"I get that. Try to understand her point of view though. At this point she probably just a poke you back, mi nuh know but unuh need fi make up. All Lorelle tired ah it. We wah back we friend group and you know Michelle wul grudge looong, so unuh need fi make up first so she can follow," I laugh, trying to lighten the mood.

"Mi nuh know, I'll try again. Maybe with just mi and her, so nobody no intervene or so," she adds.

Good...

"Okay come offa me phone, me soon reach home. Mi tired and just wah go sleep from early," I whine.

Then thank God, JJ deh a Sue

Toni hisses and I laugh out.

"Gwaan yerr, if a did Michelle you stay pon the phone," she mocks.

"That's why di people dem think you want mi. Come offa mi phone triangle queen!" I laugh out. She screams out and I know to hang up before we start laughing uncontrollably without an end.

As I'm about to pull in, Mark's number flashes across my phone screen.

+876-567-9876...

I know not to answer it when I'm home, so I click my phone shut and beckon to Snoop to open the gates.

"Snoop, you no plan fi switch from night shift to day shift nuh time?" I smile.

"Wah switch from security fully enuh Ry," he starts.

Awww, mi feel bad fi him enuh. Jordanne nuh easy, from when him fi seek out a security until Troopa wake, all now.

If he wakes up

Right? God nah sleep still, him ago wake.

"Yahfi talk to you boss," I shout, now almost fully through the gates.

"Yuh alone dem man deh listen Ry," he chuckles, bringing the gates to a close.

I just might, Snoop too talented fi be gate guard.

That's exactly why he is, after what happened

True.

I get out the car and enter the house, releasing my keys into the entry basket and kicking my shoes off, before making my way up the stairs. Midway up, I hear some shuffling. Stopping immediately, my hands move to the railing while moving back down just a few steps, to where I know a small pistol is perfectly camouflaged.

My hands brush it and I struggle a little before pulling it from under the handrail. Tipping lightly, I creep to the top of the staircase and move slowly to the master bedroom where the noise seems to be coming from.

Cocking the gun, I slowly push the door open, stepping back to see who is inside.

Nobody...

Maybe me mad? Or just overly tired… Sighing, I lower the pistol before placing it down safely.

"Yuh think a Law and Order this?" his voice comes clear.

"Jordanne?"

"Love…"

Know mi nah hallucinate thisssss time! I turn around and spring into his arms.

He chuckles.

"How are you here?" I ask, excitement now shutting off my brain.

"Come fi live ina yuh ho–" he tries.

"Jordanne please," I giggle, shoving my head into his neck.

Smellllssss soooo gooood

"I can't stay long. I have to be in Chicago by tomorrow morning. You, Snoop and Skulli alone know mi deh yah," he explains.

He continues to speak but I'm already thinking about what I want him to do to me.

"Stop look pah me so. Go bathe, and take yuh frownzy self offa me," he smirks, biting down onto his bottom lip.

I slap him, now laughing like a hyena, before he lowers me and I find my feet. Fastest me ever run gah the shower.

I don't know how the stocking no slip me. Mi not even pull up the door before stripping.

The sound of him laughing at my antics makes its way to my ears, but me nuh business. The boy have mi head reeeealllly going.

No shame to mi game.

None

93 | Still...

RYLEIGH

"What's wrong with your knuckles?" J' asks in a calm but still concerned tone. Think him woulda know, the way I can't blink without him knowing these days.

I bring my hands up to observe them. Him nahgo like the answer, at all.

"Nuttin," I try, knowing he won't accept that.

"Okay," he breathes before moving to pick up his phone.

Rass

"Okay yuh nahfi call nobody," I laugh, while throwing my legs across his waist.

His eyes find mine, staring directly into my thoughts. I look away and back to him a few times before I find what I think is the best answer.

"Boxing," I let out.

"You always box. Nuttin never do you knuckles yet," with this, his eyes squint into skepticism.

Uggghhhh! Alright here we go.

"Just challenge one a di subdons earlier, weh say my only claim to the top is pussy. So I brought him to the training field and we fist it ou–"

"Wah?" he asks, cutting me off.

See weh mah tell yuh? A still boxing if you ask me, or anybody else. Just boxing without the glove, the gym... and the punching bag

"Who exactly?" Jordanne adds to his question while my fingers find his chest.

"Jerome's son, you know, from Clarendon and somebody else, I think from St.Thomas," I explain as vaguely as I possibly can.

Out of nowhere, he drags me onto him fully, now looking into my eyes.

"Talk clear Love," his words are hoarse and his eyes have become darker– darker than they usually are.

"No need fi worry, them good now," I giggle at the memory of me being swift enough to evade any hits, but quick enough to land them freely.

"Ryleigh, speak. Mi nuh have di time fi the run arou–"

"Okayyyy," I roll my eyes, bringing my head down to his chest for more comfort. "I know you said to just pull them down from command for whichever parish they're in charge of if them try disrespect me, butttt…"

"But?" he asks.

"But I just feel like weh dem say did too disrespectful, especially the one from St.Thomas. So mi did just affi prove a quick point and see the point proven. He wanted to cause a scene so me give everybody a production," I shrug before lifting my head slightly to look at him.

Cyaa read him expression.

"Ryleigh, if a did anybody else you would've had a few bruises, yuh know dat right?"

I giggle knowingly.

"I know, after me nuh mad. I know how him grow, from prep school days till now. Now that I proved my point me can walk in peace," I breathe, bringing my head back down to his chest.

His chest rises and falls, a few times before he starts stroking my hair.

"Wah dem say nuh wrong still," he chuckles.

I fling my head up to find him biting back his laughter. Staring at him in disbelief, I try to slide from atop him. He grips me tightly, restricting my movement.

"Yuh pussy good fi real though Ry'. Ting have mi a way fi years," he laughs out.

"Why you so brawling?" I ask, feigning disgust.

"Naturally… Fun and joke aside, that's not why I left you in charge. You're probably the only person that knows me well enough to know what I would do, if there's a case where unuh can't reach me and a decision needs to be made on spot."

I take a moment to recognize the reasoning behind his decision.

"Who say mi know you?" I ask, my voice hushed.

"You act like you don't, but you do," he murmurs, bringing his fingers down my spine. "Years me watch you a do the only things you knew would get my attention, so duh even play fool wid mi right now."

I giggle, turning my head to the left, still on his chest. Well, it took him long enough…

"And duh challenge none a the man dem again, you might start problems within the camp. Do weh mi tell you fi do and weh mi tell yuh fi do only."

Okay babbyyy

"Okay Drip," I say deliberately, cause who him a run orders pon?

We lay there in silence for some time, before we both drift off into sleep.

• • •

Following Day

MARIAH

"No because if me nuh lick her back me nuh name Mariah Leanne Teathers, swear to yuh," I seethe at the thought of how the girl nearly damage me money maker face.

Nuttin nuh hurrrtttttttttttttt mi so!

All because me say weh me observe. All she did was confirm it, 'cause if a did lie it wouldn't burn her so.

"Mariah, change you mood before them reach," Ryleigh pleads, now turning into the supermarket parking lot.

MMCHT! She always deh pah some kumbaya shit. I was okay with just speaking to her, everybody else can walk out ina traffic.

"Mariah," she tries again, now fully parked and releasing her seat belt.

A wah tell Danne she out yah with him Taycan, but the people dem say mi a old fridge. I laugh at the thought while flying the door, to lift myself out of the low car.

"BEASSSSSTTTTT," a set of guys shriek as we walk away from it.

Ryleigh ignores them, heading straight inside. She's becoming more and more like Jordanne by the day.

A so him nuh see people, unless he should

I pick up the pace in efforts to get to her side. Weh the lady a run leff me fah?

"Girl how yah move so speedy?" I ask when I'm finally by her side.

"You think me have all evening, a dat a your problem," she retorts.

Nobody never tell her take out the man car, now we affi a run in and out quick before him check the tracker or nuttin.

Moments pass and the other girls are here with us, walking the aisles. The tension is thiccckkk and the silence is deafening. Ry' keeps trying to make small jokes to break the ice but none of us are having it. By the looks of it Michelle wants to get off her feet, Toni and Lorelle want to be anywhere else but here and Keif is just picking up all the things she wants since Ry' is paying.

Why we no say supm?

Me???!!! Afta anuh me lick meself.

We come to the snack aisle and I get excited to pick up every single thing me need. This me come fah, mi nuh business weh them have fi say, honestly.

We all start grabbing what we want just before we hear Ry' let out a shocked, muffled scream.

We all look up, to look to her.

'LENARD' she mouths.

Mercyyyyyyy!

"Unuh mek we gah the next aisle then come back," she whispers, making a U-turn with the cart.

We all turn and begin to scurry away but...

"Wait a minute, Ryleigh?" the tall guy, holding a clean British accent, mixed with faint patois, rings her name.

I watch as she slowly turns around to face him. He walks up to our small group, as if excited to see an old high school friend.

"Know a you me spot," he speaks, smiling from ear to ear.

Hmhmm, better laugh less before me brother find yuh

"Hi... Len," Ry' greets him nervously.

Nervousness is required in this situation. The guy, Len? Lenard or whatever him name turns to greet us all.

"She never want me meet her friends back then, so it's nice to see you guys now," he offers us all a genuine smile.

Watch nice man

We all nod, cautiously, knowing Ry' must be super uncomfortable, seen as her man nahv no sense. Two things she a do wrong now, a talk to man and bring out the Taycan— to a supermarket run at that.

Ry' is refusing to say words, instead she looks like she wants to up and leave.

Len averts his attention from us and back to her before whispering, "You look beaut– se– ... cu–... You look nice," he finally finds an appropriate word and mi almost scream out ina this.

"Thank you?" Ry' offers, her words sharp and emotionless.

Nuh know how him nah pick that up, or maybe he doesn't want to. I would save her, but this is tooooo entertaining. Toooo gooddddd.

"How have you been?" he asks, trying to carry the conversation all on his own.

"Good," is all her lips offer while her eyes look at everything except him.

He cocks his head to the side while observing her. I see when the light finally comes on in his brain and he realizes she doesn't want to chit-chat.

"Okay well, carry on. It's nice to see you again plum," he smiles while his eyes linger on her for a few extra seconds before he walks away.

Watch plummmmm

When he leaves the aisle, Ry' releases a heavy breath.

"Unuh couldn't butt in???" she says, evidently disappointed in our actions.

We all start laughing, and I mean lauuuuughing.

"Mi did wah save you but mah say this nice and funny bad, bad, bad," I explain.

"Bad, bad, bad!" Toni agrees with me, and everybody pauses to look at us.

The pause lasts for a good four seconds before we're all laughing again. Toni picks up a jumbo sized pack of Oreo and offers it to me.

With a curtsy, she hands them over, "My peace offering..."

I look at her, and back to everybody staring at us. Cho! Why me cyaa keep malice?!

Grabbing the pack from her and throwing it into the trolley, I decide to speak, "Yuh lucky me cyaa keep malice enuh gyal. Mi nahv no peace offering but I'm sorry as well, for airing out yo–"

"Hoooorayyyyy!!!" Ry' exclaims, "Unuh no bother say nuttin else, leave it at that," she adds before dragging me away.

She knoooowww me woulda add weh me sorry fah enuh

Damn right.

I'm still upset but for now, mek we just mek peace reign, I guess.

We move down the aisles, all picking up more snacks to bring the cart to its max.

"Yuh nuh see the cart full, no take up nuttin else Keif!" Lorelle smacks her cousin jokingly.

"Me will carry them ina me hand," Keif laughs.

"Take up what you want Keif, nuh mek the girl rule you," Ry' laughs, struggling to push the cart that she's telling her to add more to.

"Alright, remind me nuffi try save you pocket again," Lorelle adds.

"When yuh fi save me just now, yuh stand up a entertain yourself, move nuh," Ry' counters jokingly.

• • •

We make it back to Ry's place and are already knee deep into rewatching Bridgerton from the very first season.

"I want a Duke soooo bad," Keif squeals.

I hope she knows men aren't what they're cracked up to be enuh. I know firssst hand. Nuh get me wrong, Ruse is the best but he's still stressfulllllll.

"Deh yah want a Duke myself," Toni trails off, grabbing everybody's attention.

Watch greedy

But mi nah open my mouth tonight.

Smile and nod, Smile, and nodddd.

I watch as Ryleigh squints her eyes at her, while T' seems to assure her it's 'okay' with her body language.

"Then yuh nuh have a Duke anddddd a Duchess lady?!" Lorelle asks, almost damaging my eardrums.

The room falls silent, except for the sound of the series playing in the back.

"I... them vex wid me in a way," T' starts.

Mek me cork my ears 'cause we nuh wah hear say me leak nobody business.

"Girl???" Michelle says, bringing the bag of chips to her mouth.

Toni looks as if she's unsure she wants to share the details. Mi nuh wrong her, the way we've been fighting as a group lately? You never know.

"I mighhhtttttt have... cheated," she blurts out.

Mighty Gahdddddd, somebody come look at this

Look pah this! And look good.

"Weh she say?" Lorelle looks to Ryleigh, who seems as if she isn't shocked.

Of course she knew before us, she's so easy and comfortable to talk to. I think we all go to her first, with anything we feel we'll be judged for, 'cause the lady nah look pah you noooo different.

"Say she give her couple bun, yuh deaf?" Keif whispers, trying to quiet Lorelle.

"No because me hear she say *might*," Lorelle adds.

"That me say yes, because Joshua say we did deh pah 'break' and mi really think a done it did done. Just remember me and Josh a come from high school. A yearrrsssss dat... and Kelly was a nice little addition, but we were slipping back into being more like friends instead of lovers."

Cyaa relate. Ruse and I are strictly lovers. So much so that I wish we had more of that friendly banter.

"Cheating upset me enuh but not when my friends do it," Muuch laughs out. "Afta unuh cyaa wrong. A must him do yuh supm," she continues, "or them do yuh supm, in this case."

"Dat mi know!" I blurt out, agreeing with her.

No a fi real. Then how my friends fi wrong? Yuh crazy?

"So wah exactly push you to that point?" Lorelle asks, "because, being the person that they cheat with is kinda weird."

Everybody averts their eyes to her, then to me.

Mhmmhmm... mah tell you bwoiiii.

Shouldn't blurt out that secret. Of everything I've said, I'm mostly sorry about handling her that way.

So apologize

I will, to each of them on my own time, just nuh wah ruin the vibe right now.

"Nuttin really," T' starts and her answer pulls me from my thoughts. "Just text a girl me know from high schoo–"

"Our high school?" Keif asks, fully enthralled by the story.

Ryleigh smacks her. Ry' really turn ina her man enuh. Not a word she no say until it necessary these days. A so me wah somebody turn me ina dem mini me, but Ruse only like full me up with him wet mini me's.

"No, my high school, before 6th form. Know her from Andr–"

"Then nuh that yuh fi say long time!" I cut her off, laughing loudly.

Mi know the girl dem from deh school deh will break up anyyyyyy happy home. Nah ask Crise and me nah ask twice!

"Then unuh ago mek me tell the story or wah?" she asks, now falling into more comfort, seeming to realize that we're not about to judge her.

"Anyways, we used to text, after graduation. Nuttin intimate just, you know... Long story short, she did university abroad, so we never really keep up with each other, apart from the usual IG likes, etcetera."

Lorelle opens a bag of Doritos, breaking the silence and focus everybody had going.

"Sorry," she whispers, bringing a chip to her lips, "continue mlovve."

I look over at Ryleigh, who is smiling at her phone from ear to ear. All when the man deh seas away, him a give her giggles. Danne cut from the best husband fabric, mi sure. Love that fi dem... From him complaining about the girl in the class next to ours weh him 'fraid fi tek on, to her complaining about him 'taking her on' too much these days.

"... and that just happen," T' shrugs.

Then a weh me miss?

"Say that again?" I whisper, since everybody's face is on the floor.

"Me say when she came back to live here, we–" she mimics scissoring with her fingers, "and we did again earlier this year but Kelly found out and tell Joshua."

A dutty gyal, Kelly that is.

"Mek me be the first fi say my spirit nuh take that girl," Keif murmurs.

Ryleigh nods, and I don't know if it's to her phone or in agreement with Keif.

"Why she woulda do that?" I ask, staring at Toni, "From weh me see, you and her did closer than her and Joshua."

"Probably out of hurt," Ryleigh adds, before tapping away at her phone again.

"Yeah," Toni agrees, "I think she feel it more than Josh. Like if it was with a man him woulda definitely leff me but because it's a woman, him kinda no see it as a threat?" she explains.

I bring my lips into a straight line... Poly dem say sah...

"So yeah, that's why I keep saying might, because Joshua barely business but Kelly just a stir up things. Now she wah breed 'cause she know him ago agree, when in truth and in fact him only want the child from me so..."

"Poly unuh say sahh," my thoughts slip from my mouth before I can stop them.

"Poly unuh get," Muuch adds, giggling at my statement.

Thank God, swear them did ago nyam off mi head.

Sigh... They don't hate you Mariah

Sure feels like it sometimes.

I hear when Ryleigh clicks her phone shut and drops it on the side table at the handle of the couch.

"Which girl have me gyal head a way?" she's now interested in our conversation.

Toni smiles at her… That smile is how I know. She smile with her like how you smile with your first ever crush. A cyaaaa me alone see it?

"And you know you probably know her though," Toni adds.

"How would I kno–"

BAM *BAM* *BAM*

There's a rowdy knock at the front door. Ryleigh springs to her feet, moving swiftly to the sound.

"Like Snoop nuh know fi use the intercom again," she complains, dragging the shorts from her ass.

Seconds later I hear both her and Snoop mumbling at the door. Toni and I look at each other before jumping up to go see what's wrong. When we get to the door, we are met with an angry, annoyed and worried Snoop. As if I was blind before, I just start to notice the blue lights flashing at the gates.

"Fi do?" Snoop turns to Ryleigh, asking. "Them have a warrant enuh."

Police…

Warrant…

Jail…

Floor sleeping…

Jail food… Those are the words that start dancing across my mind. Mi nuh ready fi gah no prison enuh! Me nuh do nuttin, no… but me very, very, verrrry close to people who have done a mighty lot.

I look at Toni, before I look to Ryleigh who seems to be confused and worried. The sound of the other girls' footsteps, meet my ears.

"Then nuh police?" Muuch asks, shock now taking residence on her face.

We all stand there for a while, waiting for Ry' to make a decision. I mean ah her house, so…

"Let them in, if you say them have a warrant," is all she says before running towards Jordanne's office.

Mi nervousssssss

Bad…

Bad, Bad, Baddd.

94 | Null

RYLEIGH

I expected them to come, but not this early.

Digging through Jordanne's desk, I desperately try to find the deed.

Duh fuck it up

Now is really not the time for my subconscious to be annoying...

Deven have on mi glasses!

My fingers quickly slip through the files, only coming to a stop when I recognize the paper. Yes! I pull it out and slide the desk drawer shut, before running back to the front door. By now the officers are approaching the entrance.

I take a quick glance around the room, observing the shock, fear and slight anger lingering on all their faces– my friends that is. I notice that Kelly has made it from upstairs. She didn't want to join us at the supermarket or for Bridgerton but she's joining us for the blue lights.

Don't talk to nobody, don't explain yourself, just do the do' the memory of J's words cloak my hippocampus.

Sigh...

Do Not Have A Panic Attack.

Just relaxxxxx

I watch as Mr.Wellz leads a team up towards the front porch. Snoop looks at me with a million questions twinkling in his eyes, but I have already turned off that side of me. The side where I have to explain or grant comfort to anybody. The focus is now on protecting Jordanne, like he's always done for me.

"Good night, we–" Mr.Wellz starts his statement but I cut him off.

"May I read the warrant Mr.Wellz?" I ask peering down at him from the entrance steps.

He smirks with confidence, handing me the signed sheet. I take it and start to read.

Blah, Blah, Blah... Blah... *the premises and all parts therein, including all rooms, safes, storage areas, containers, surrounding grounds, trash areas, garages and outbuildings assigned to the residence of Jordanne Robert Sheer.*

Which idiot write this? A small smile pulls on my face as I find the first loophole. I continue to read the list, carefully.

For all the vehicles parked at or near the premises which can be identified as being associated with this location by keys, documents or statements. (Inside and all parts thereof)
And for the person known as Jordanne Robert Sheer who is believed to reside at the above residence.

I continue to read but Mr.Wellz decides to interrupt me.

"Satisfied?" is what I hear him ask.

My mind is busy finding all the loopholes I was told to seek out. Raising my index finger to silence him, I continue to read.

Toni-Anne presents herself beside me.

"You good?" her words find their way into my thoughts.

I don't answer. In this moment it's just me, the warrant and my man's words.

"Mr.Wellz," are the words that leave my mouth next.

"Ms.Stevens?" he offers, tone condescending.

"The probable cause is that YOU believe, based on information given, that items of illegality are being held here?" I ask clearly.

The tiny smile he had on his face has now been replaced by slight shock and annoyance.

Good

"Correct," he breathes.

"It also says you're to search the property of Jordanne Sheer?" I add my second question to the mix.

"Correct Ms.Stevens."

"At lot number 14?" I add, and he seems to finally realize what I'm doing.

I watch as he looks to the police who seems to be next in command on this search team and then back to me.

"Correct," he repeats for confirmation.

Well me have news fi him.

"The particularities aren't holding up, but I think you figured that out already by my questions," I speak clearly, loud enough for all parties to hear but low enough not to seem affected.

He tries to say something but I continue, "Firstly, the property does not belong to Mr.Sheer, not even partly," I explain, now waving the deed and all other title and tax documents in the air. "Secondly, the address is incorrect, we've acquired the lots to the left and right–"

I'm cut off by him hissing.

I can hear Toni's giggles from behind me and the mumbling amongst the group further behind her. I take the opportunity to hand the warrant back to him. He takes it and browses through before slamming it into the hold of his colleague.

He then hisses lowly, exuding disappointment, before I watch his eyes brighten.

"If you have nothing to hide, why are you refusing entry?"

"If you have so much to find, why didn't you do proper research and present a solid search warrant?" I smile.

He smiles back, holding zero humour I might add.

"I like you Ms.Stevens. Do not let the Sheers drag you down with them," he retorts.

Mind games

Poor ting. Not a soul in this world can manipulate me. I always do what I want, good or bad.

"Trust me, I'm a big girl," I continue smiling softly.

He moves closer to me, "Then you wouldn't mind coming in for questioning?"

"With my lawyer present, sure," I counter.

He chuckles before saying, "I'll be back Ms.Stevens... Ms.Sheer," he grunts, nodding off to Toni-Anne.

I watch as they leave the premises, and as they do, my mind returns to me. The fun loving mind, the worried mind, the one filled with anxiety and second thoughts. It's like you have to become somebody else to handle all this 24/7.

Compartmentalization at it's peak

"Girl, what the actual fuck?" T' shrieks lowly, now staring at me.

I shrug, wanting to tell her every single detail but I can't. I have to go call Mr. Washington to send someone from his team. They'll more than likely be back with proper cause to question a good number of us.

"Okay so you can't tell mi, mi get dat," she adds and we both walk back to the group.

"Girl wah just keep? Mi heart fly ina me throat 'bout six time!" Mariah is the first to speak.

"Mi say, mi nuh built fi this at all," Kelly adds, rubbing her temples while Keif and Lorelle nod in agreement.

Mmmchtt.

"Then leave," T' mumbles, only audible to me but I think it was directed solely to Kelly.

"Weh Michelle?" I ask, looking around.

I watch as everybody else just seems to notice she's missing. My feet decide to take me inside and straight to the living area.

"Muuch!!??" I shout.

No answer…

I think nothing of it. She probably a pee, the way her bladder set up right now.

"Probably gone a bathroom," Lorelle suggests and I nod in agreement.

"So nobody is gonna speak about what just happened?" Kelly asks, as we all take the exact spots we were in just before the commotion.

I look up at her deciding to say something, but I don't… something inside me is telling me fi just lowe her. Too much is going on in the group right now.

"You knew what type of family you were getting into," T' speaks up.

Lawd Jesus

"I didn't and by the time I did, I already loved you," Kelly explains, in the clearest tone I've heard her use since we met.

Stern, Assertive…

I watch as everybody looks between her and T'.

"Not now Kelly," Toni murmurs.

"No, mek it be now, everything is shared amongst the group at one point or another anyways," she lowers her voice but her point is still clear.

Toni rolls her eyes and pulls out her phone to start tapping away at what seems like nothing in particular.

"Yah ignore me? Yuh know mi ago leff you and Joshua though?" she adds, now desperate to get T's attention.

Toni-Anne looks up and smirks, cocking her head to the side, before saying, "Kelly just relax."

She and her brother mirror each other to the point weh mi affi wonder if them sure them anuh twin. Sue really named them Jordanne and Toni-Anne fi a reason enuh.

"Relax?" she snaps, moving to grab T's phone from her hands, "Absolutely nothing I do gets your attention, to the point where you cheated and you only cared about what Joshua would think. Mi a wah to you?"

Lorelle snorts trying to hold her laugh in. I duh know wah Keif a tell her but mi certain them a make some kind of triangle joke outa this. Mi might no like Kelly most times, but when they were good they were so loving, to the point mi used to wonder if Joshua really alright with it.

T' slides down in the couch, releasing a deep sigh before running her hands through her hair. A moment of silence passes over the room before she finally speaks.

"You wah do this now? In front of everybody?" she asks, staring at Kelly who looks as if she's now intimidated by T'.

You know what? Mek me liff up and give them some privacy.

"Mi ago look fi Michelle," I whisper, trying to lift myself from the couch.

Go easy cause you know we dizzy from morning

Yeah, I need to find out what that's about, but me just no have the time. Ginger tea affi go work a miracle.

"No stay, 'cause if you leave she might follow behind you. It's what she does."

Not thisssss againnnnnn. UGHHHH, mi so fucking tired of this narrative.

I hiss before fully standing up from the couch.

"Listen… Mariah, Muuch and T' just made up. The group is fragile as fuck right now. Duh drag yuh relationship problems into the mix please, I'm mentally tired. I speak for everybody when I say, keep it between you and Toni," my rant is dripping in slight hate.

Mmmcht.

"Amen," Mariah and Lorelle whisper in unison.

Kelly laughs before saying, "You blind ina real life, but yuh cyaa thissssss blind Ryleigh."

Gyal yah ago mek me floor her before the night end

Why am I so irritated? Did I eat?

Mah tell you from morning we nuh feel right but yah ignore mi

"Toni talk to Kelly, she obviously need some typa closure for what you did," I offer, trying to get my emotionally unavailable best friend to show her girlfriend some type of love.

Where is Muuch bredda?

I start walking to the direction of the back room, knowing that's where she's comfortable. Two full steps aren't made before Kelly says what she shouldn't.

"Unlessss mi mad. Unuh used to ina things or wah because," she snaps.

But a weh di mumma pussyclawt

After me never know me front a fi di family?

T' finally props herself up from the sofa, walking straight towards Kelly. She grabs her and yanks her off towards the kitchen. I think to intervene but mi just cyaa badda. More while mi feel fi go live off-grid with Jordanne, honest to God.

Making my way to the back room, I ignore the faint cramps dancing below my navel.

"Michelle?"

"Muuuuuuch?"

I can hear faint movement inside the room, so I know she's inside. Pushing the door softly, I slowly enter. The lights in the room are off, but the lamp is on and her movement around the bathroom cannot be missed.

"Muuch, why yuh one in yah and we a call and you nah answer girl?" I ask lowly.

She still doesn't respond but based on the increase in sound, I know her movement has picked up pace. I move to the switch and cut the lights on, before walking in.

"Mi can come?" I try again.

Why she nah answer me?

"Muuch weh yah d–" as I push the bathroom door open my eyes find exactly what she's doing.

I pause... filled with sheer shock.

Jesus I can't take anotherrrrrr thing on my plate.

She continues to wipe for a second before looking up at me. Her eyes are blood red and her tears are flowing freely. I shake my head rapidly back and forth trying not to believe what the logical part of my brain is telling me.

I can't seem to move, the similarity of this trauma is about to shut me down.

"Mariah!!!" I scream.

"Lorelle!!!" I scream again, with what seems to be the last breath I have.

My limbs start working when Michelle's sobs turn into loud cries. She's rapidly wiping the tiles, somewhat unconscious to the fact that no matter how many times she wipes... the bleeding won't stop.

"Michelle... Michelle, Michelle, stopp, stop," I try to grab the towel from her tight grip. "We have to go to the hospital now, right nowww."

She doesn't answer, instead she grabs another towel, continuing her wipe fest.

I–

"Michelle!" I try again.

Mi wiii bax dah gyal yah back to reality enuh

How long she round yah a bleed?!

I grab the new towel away from her and try to pull her up, but fail.

"I can't do anything right Ry'... I didn't finish law school, I can't keep a man faithful, ready fi take back the same man and see now, I can't bring my own baby into the world safely."

As if on cue, my brain switches from emotions to logics.

"Bleeding happens, and mi no wah hear nuttin bout Liam. Try to help me, help you stand."

She ignores me.

Multiple footsteps enter the room and small whimpers mixed with tiny screams follow.

"Unuh help me lift her up. I don't think she a think straight right now," I turn to them.

Mariah moves to my side, followed by Keif while Lorelle takes the opportunity to start calling whoever. We all manage to bring her to her feet and out of the restroom.

I don't know what to do... My mind has all of a sudden become blurry.

"Let her put on a maternity pad," Keif suggests.

My mind snaps back into thinking clearly at her suggestion.

"Wi nuh have time fi dat, just grab towels and go start the van, now," I counter Keif and instruct Lorelle simultaneously.

Michelle seems to snap back into her mind and starts wailing.

Sigh.

Lorelle throws the phone to me and I find that Sue is on the line.

"Hello?" her voice comes clear.

"Sue? The bleeding isn't heavy but it's constant," I start.

"Look who's quick on thinking. I'll meet you guys at the hospital. I'm going to call her mother," she adds.

Mi deven know how fi get to Slyme, or J' for that matter. I'm not compromising their mission when I'm left in charge.

And a mi man life... Slyme's life too if I try to call at the wrong time.

Really fi deh England a drink tea, mi stressssssssssss

My thoughts are interrupted when I realize we've made it to the foot of the staircase. We move through the hall and outside to the car, where I can see Lorelle laying towels in the backseat. I glance behind me at the trail of blood tracing our journey before sighing.

'God, duh mek she lose her baby. That has to be the worst feeling in the world, and to be this far along has to hurt ten times over. Lay your hands on her Lord, grant her healing and protection. If the baby should come early keep them both safe and healthy throughout the process. Guide your angels to her and–'

My silent prayer is cut short by Michelle screaming, as we put her to lay inside the car.

God please, beg mah beg at this point.

I hop into the passenger seat while Lorelle buckles up and speeds out of the property. Mariah and the rest fall behind us, and I notice when the shadow guards fall in line as well. Looking down at my top, I notice that it has small blood stains... and it takes me everything in my power to fight the feeling of blaming myself for my miscarriage yearsss ago.

• • •

TONI-ANNE

Our conversation was cut short by Ry' screaming for help and now we're in the car behind them rushing to the hospital. Mi nuh wah sound cruel but, pheeew! Because I didn't want to have that conversation at all. I can't open up to Kelly. Mi can shower her with gifts, we can go out, laugh, have sex, surface level things... but opening up to another human being? Mi nuh know 'bout that.

We pull into the hospital and the first person I sight is my mother, rushing towards us with a team of nurses behind her. I exit the car and watch as they rush Muuch inside with Ry' and Mariah directly behind them while the rest of us follow.

I know she won't lose her baby, mi have a strong feeling and my intuitions are almost always correct.

• • •

Hours have flown by and by now we're all waiting to hear what went down behind those doors. It's some time past 3am and at this point I'm getting a little worried.

Kelly is snuggled up in my arms, while Mariah, Keif and Lorelle are sprawled out on each other. Mommy, Ms.Janette and Mrs.Egar are pacing the room, while Ry' is sitting alone, staring into what seems to be a black hole.

Sigh, hope she good.

The doors fly open and the doctor from earlier presents herself.

"Family for Ms.Egar?" she asks clearly, voice commanding the room.

Mrs.Egar runs over and we all stand to join.

Good news, let it be good news please. Pleeeease.

"Both her and the baby are fine–" the doctor starts without hesitation.

"Ohh Jesus. God you alone," Ry' blurts out.

I giggle, because this girl is such an old country granny sometimes.

A the way she say it haha

"Her placenta was covering her cervix. When that happens, and the womb contracts or the cervix slightly starts to open, it causes bleeding that can be severe. Nothing to be alarmed about now since you guys acted quickly, but we suggest she takes it easy for the rest of the weeks before she's full term," she explains.

"Can we see her?" Mrs.Egar asks with pleading eyes.

"She is resting now, but I'll have a nurse let you know when she's awake and ready to take visitors," the doctor explains.

Mrs.Egar nods in understanding.

"I suggest you guys go home, get some rest and come back?" she adds.

Nobody moves though or even takes the suggestion. One thing 'bout we, we might cuss and fight but we're going to be right here through whatever, whenever.

Ry' is the first to move.

"Where is the bathroom again?" she asks... everybody?

"Down the hall first left and second right," Mariah directs her.

I watch as she bolts to the direction of the bathroom. Dem gyal yah cyaa hold dem bladder enuh...

• • •

RYLEIGH

Here we go again, Mi really need fi stop eat fuckry when J's not here. Bagga pizza and KFC ago kill me off.

Shoving the bathroom door open, I try to make it to the stall but...

I grab the vanity and start hurling my insides into the sink. Look how mah violate the people dem bathroom Fada God.

I take a deep breath before gripping the granite for support.

"You okay?" Lorelle's voice creeps into the room.

Then mi look okay?

Duh say that out loud.

"No," is what exits my mouth, just before another round of belly juice start flying out of the hole on my face.

"Jesus Ryleigh. Weh yuh nyam so?" she giggles.

I giggle too, mouth nasty as ever. I don't know, but whatever it is a kill me off right now.

"Mine yah breed enuh. Only breeding gyal me see vomit after 4 ina morning."

I didn't even think of that. Lorelle try nuh come with her fuckry. I wave her off, since the strength I have doesn't allow words from my mouth.

Mercy, and if a true?

It's not…

"Mah go get you some water," she says while exiting.

I grip the granite tighter, fighting the urge to slide down to the floor, to give my knees a break.

Her statement starts dancing through my mind.

No because, it's highly, highly, highlyyyyy possible.

I start to shake my head at the thought, while rinsing my mouth and washing away the vomit from the sink.

Aint no way.

95|Null Part TWO

RYLEIGH

"Yes Ms.Stevens I'll handle it," Hally's voice comes clear through my phone's speakers.

Good, because I haven't gotten any sleep and I'm about to pass out any minute now. Ina real life, me deven eat. I can't keep the food down. Sure it's a stomach bug.

Bug yah call the man seed?

Be quiet, I'm not pregnant.

Hally has been managing my properties since I was gifted the complex by J' years ago. Sue recommended her and she's been doing a mighty good job. The problem now is, I have been adding more and more properties outside of just the complex and she now needs help managing them all. The complex alone has 25 modern apartments, so just managing that alone is work in and of itself, let alone everything else.

"Boss?" Hally calls when the line is silent for too long.

"I'm here... If the complex is fully occupied, I'll clear out my old apartment. Just have the guys renovate it within budget and you can give it to the new property manager. You need the help, I understand," I grant her as much assurance as I possibly can.

"Thank you... and for the villas in Treasure Beach?" she questions.

I can't remember the point of topic surrounding those. Mi cyaa remember one thing. I'm just, TIRED.

So tired...

My office door swings open to Nadifa standing in the frame. She looks at me quizzically before saying, "Yuh look so? You look like them just turn you ina vampire."

Her words register but I don't answer.

I realize there is another call coming in on my phone though. Holding the cell from my ears, I notice that it's Junior's school.

Sigh

"Hally, can I call you back? I'll decide on what to do about the villas being double booked. Ensure you send me the payroll for my staff, I want to look it over while confirming Mr.Sheer's staff."

"No problem, I'll email it to you now," she says, and without any formal end to our conversation, I hang up the call and accept the incoming.

I take a deep breath before answering.

"Hi good day–"

"Ms.Stevens?" the voice asks for name confirmation and I look up in time to see Nadifa closing my door before moving towards my desk.

I beckon for her to sit.

"Yes, this is she…" I trail off, waiting for whatever news could've caused them to call me midday.

"I'm sorry, we know you must be at work. We tried calling the first number on file but got no answer. Jacen has been in another fight, this time the child has a broken nose and needless to say, the parents are really angry, so we need you to come in."

MMMMCHTTTT!

I look at Nadifa who is staring at me, concerned.

"The opposing child has already been taken to seek medical care?" my question falls flat and I can feel the level of irritation bubbling over within me.

"No–"

"Then how do you know it's broken?" I cut her off.

And if it is, why him nuh deh hospital? Them ago sit down and wait till me reach up there?

Empathy Ry'. You nah show no empathy

Mi nahv that right now. My patience is thinnnn.

"Ms.Stevens–" the person tries to continue.

"I'll be there in 30 to 45 minutes," I scoff before hanging up.

My body immediately releases a breath, and I fall back into my chair, bringing a piece of bread that I've been munching on all morning to my mouth.

"What's up with you?" Nadifa asks.

Silence, can I please get some silence?

Silence from my thoughts…

Silence from my friends…

Silence from my coworkers…

"Stevens?" she tries again but by this, I'm bringing my head down to the desk.

"Wake me up in like five minutes and I'll answer all your questions," I murmur while yawning.

I don't hear her reply, but I feel her light hands patting my shoulder, offering comfort. Mere seconds later I drift off into sleep.

• • •

"Don't wake her up JJ," a female's voice jolts me from my nap.

Napppp???!!!

"Ms.Ryleigh?" another voice whispers.

What's this dream about?

"Ms.Ryleigh?" Junior starts tugging at my arm, that's set on my desk to cushion my head, and that's when I realize I'm not dreaming.

Wait? Then Nadz really never wake me???

I prop my head up and my eyes fly open. The sight of Mariah standing with her arms folded makes me smile. My eyes move beyond her to see Nadifa giggling. Ignoring them both, I pull Junior into my lap. He immediately starts babbling.

"I didn't mean to, they pushed me. Mi push back," he's explaining while looking directly into my eyes.

This little boy is going to be something else.

"How did the nose get broken?" I direct my question to Mariah more than to JJ.

"Not a thing no do the little boy nose. It was bleeding but the nurse say it's not broken. The mother was on top of her voice but the father wanted to leave, so I told them if they are to bring him to a private doctor for a second opinion, we'll cover the bill. Dat a dat."

I shake my head, before looking back at JJ.

"You have to stop the fighting. You fight ova Sue and this is your second fight at school. What's the problem?" I put him to stand.

He says nothing.

"Junior, mah ask yuh wah di problem?" I repeat clearly.

When me say me patience thin it thin– even for him.

"Them just keep ah say things mi nuh like," he mumbles.

I don't counter, instead I wait for him to continue.

"… always mi hair or the way I say certain things," he explains.

"You can't put your hands on people for what they say Junior, you know that right?" I ask, searching his features for confirmation– because me really hope him know.

"Them first though," he retorts.

Two wrongs nuh mek a right.

Haha! That statement coming from me is a little crazy isn't it? I find humour in the moment and have to hide my smile.

"Regardless Junior, next time just report it and if the teachers won't listen you tell me or Ms.Cherry first, we will handle it. Mi nah say you must stand up and allow them to hit you but try your hardest to walk away... okay?" I breathe, bringing his head up from hanging low.

He stays silent.

"Okayyyyyyyy Jacen Stillen Junior???"

"Okay Ms.Ryleigh," he offers while slowly looking up at me.

"Good."

Looking at the two other adults in the room, I roll my eyes.

"Mah bring him to Sue dem. Nadifa say you sick and a dead," Mariah speaks.

I look at Nadz, who now has her hand in the air signaling surrender.

"Mi just tired. Memba we up from when with Muuch. You alone go get sleep enuh," I remind her.

I watch her try to say something but stop herself before she does. If one more somebody call down baby pah me today.

Mariah walks over to my desk while I bring myself to my feet. I walk half the way around before she pulls me into her arms.

"Mi nuh do the mushy thing often but you look like shit. Eat and take a pregnancy test. Maybe give sleep a chance?" she suggests in a soft tone.

I smile.

Fiiiiiiiiiine...

"I'll eat and sleep for sure," I answer, pulling back. "Nadifa, weh you even get dah girl yah number?"

Nadifa laughs, "Not your memory gone too. Anuh we go out other day?"

"Yeah but me never know number exchange keep. Unuh tight man," I smile.

"Yuh jealous?" Nadifa asks.

Kinda... Mi no like mix or share my friends.

"Me a come gah me yard, 'bout jealous," I smile even more.

I don't know why me come here come sleep down the people them work, what a shame.

• • •

5:45pm

"Yuh good," Jordanne asks.

Nope.

I'm actually a mess and I want you to come home. Don't know if me can pull this off, while handling everybody and overseeing everything. I'm not eating, mi nah sleep, I have stomach flu... just bay things.

"I'm okay," despite all the things running through my mind, all I can do is grin at the face on my screen.

Wheeew, now how in the world mi think him coulda just be my friend? I laugh at the thought.

"Wah sweet you Ry?" he asks, raising a brow at me.

You...

"You," I voice my thoughts. "You don't plan to come home?" I ask, batting my lashes.

"Sooner than you think Love," he speaks. "Why you look tired?"

Here we go.

"I told you we were up with Michelle and then I went home for like an hour, then straight to work–" I try to explain but...

"Nahh yuh look sick, tired sick, and not tired from staying up. Talk to me."

No sah, mi tired fi dah man yah read out mi life daily, ahaha!

My internal laugh turns into an external smile.

"Nuttin serious. I haven't been sleeping a lot so there's that, coupled with me just not cooking since you're not here, so mi eat out most nights, and then from managing your team, to your books, to my books, right back to my job... it a get heavy."

A moment of silence passes.

"Ryleigh, what's been added that you haven't been doing before?" he asks.

I take a moment to think...

"Managing your team?" I answer.

He chuckles, "Babe, you go two meetings. Mah be serious, weh you wah stop do, 'cause making decisions fi the man dem for two weeks, isn't what's making you sick. Yahgo affi give up the books, your job or Junior."

No enuh, nope.

"Nuh think a none a that if mah be honest. I've been vo–"

I pause my statement when I hear somebody speaking to him in the background. Listening as they murmur, I wait for him to come back in view.

"Love, mahfi liff, but I'll be home. See say yuh miss me and a dead weh. Just so life go sometimes, you nahfi miss me till yah fade weh... Jah Jah," he smiles, causing me to cackle.

"Okay J' whateverrrrr... I love you, remember that," I speak clearly.

He stands, bringing the laptop screen to his face

"More than mi own life Ry'.... but you know that already."

Coulda bawl...

This minute we angry, next minute we sad, mmcht

We linger on the call for another five to ten seconds before ending it. My spirit has been lifted and I start to think about calling T'... so I carry out my thought by dialing her number.

• • •

We're now on our way to visit Michelle with a shitload of food, since she keeps complaining about the hospital cuisine.

"Mi did alright fi drive enuh," I whine to T' who is now speeding down the small stretch of empty road heading towards traffic.

She offers me a glance, rolls her eyes and looks back to the road.

"Please nuh piss me off. You look half dead, you nah drive and kill off yourself fi Danne come yah come kill off everybody," she retorts.

Wellll…

"Girl cyaa vomit in peace and everybody no drag it outa proportion?" I ask, feigning ignorance to the fact that I look ill for real.

T' ignores me and turns the volume of the music up. I laugh out at her blatant disrespect before shaking my head.

No manners she nuh have.

She picks up speed and before we're able to bend the corner onto Hope Road, flashing blue lights and sirens disrupt us. We're being pulled over.

It this

T' comes to a stop and we both look at each other, knowing it's not just a traffic stop. We both knew Wellz was coming back with cause for questioning, we just didn't know exactly when. I glance at the side mirror, only to see three different police vehicles.

Okay Mark, go overboard if you want to

I wait for them to walk to the vehicle, trying not to blurt everything out to Toni right this moment. The scrutiny that I'm about to get from her is going be crazyyyy. My breathing picks up but I decide to switch that side of my brain off for the moment. It's the only way I'm going to get through this.

A knock comes at the window.

T' rolls both front windows down, granting the officers access to the vehicle.

"All four," an officer says and she rolls the back windows down.

"Goodnight!" T' offers with an attitude, since we've yet to have any greeting thrown our way.

My focus is on her side of the car, but a voice pulls me to my side of the car.

"Daughter," Mark's voice annoys me and I try to keep it together.

T' looks over at me confused.

Fada

"Mark," I mutter, offering him a low response.

Why him woulda show him face? And ago call mi daughter pah top ah it? Cyaa wait fi put a bu–

"Step outa the vehicle fimi nuh please," Mr. Wellz' voice comes clear.

Cyaa miss the heavy tongue man

"Nobody no say why unuh stop we," T' hisses, looking directly at Wellz.

"Mek dem stay man, this isn't a traffic stop or a routine check. We need both of you to drive behind us to the station for questioning. You can do it this way or you can refuse and be arrested and taken there, your choice," Mark speaks.

I sigh, before T' looks at me and I her.

I watch as the shadow cars drive back and forth but I'm unable to signal anything to them. T' starts explaining her rights to Wellz but he's not having it. My eyes find Mark who is cheesing, before I signal to the cars that they may leave.

"Toni," I mutter under my breath.

She averts her attention from Wellz to me.

"Just mek we go. Resisting arrest nahgo cute," I try to make light of the situation.

She hisses, before rolling her windows up and I nod to Mark who then nods to Wellz.

"Mi nuh know wah you up to, but mek sure a supm sensible yerr?" she breathes, her tone laced in skepticism.

I swallow my words before they're able to come out. We watch as the police vehicles pull out before us. T' slowly drives behind them and my fingers find each other, in an effort to calm my racing nerves.

96 | The Windy City

JORDANNE

"**S**he ago good bredda," I speak.

"So them a say yes, but me uncomfortable boss," Slyme expresses as we hop into the truck.

We both start dragging our gear on, and while pulling the vest over my chest, I start thinking of what to say to him. Mi need him head clear and him mind focused today of all days… but not even mi no know if mi coulda pull that off, if the roles were reversed.

Fi sure mi woulda gone home

My mind searches itself, trying to find something, anything to offer him comfort. The man just reach and already Michelle had a complication.

"Slyme, if Mum never 100% certain she was okay, mi woulda send you home myself but she is… Mi understand the level of worry and if yuh wah leave right now I'll allow it. Your decision, not mine."

He pauses for a few seconds.

"Cyaa mek you do this alone. Only chance this we have fi finally clean up yuh fada mess," he breathes. "If this nuh do now me nuh know fi sure say she ago safe, anything can happen with the AIs."

No lies, them unpredictable.

I nod, to honour his choice, but he hisses before pulling me into a hug.

"Just know if me dead, mah haunt yuh daily," he laughs out.

I find myself chuckling at that. Man yah was a definite fish ina him past life.

No joke

"Yuh haunt me daily wid yuh choices skull," I retort, causing us both to laugh out.

"On a serious note though Drip, know mi love yuh like a brother. From you father take me in, to this day. Woulda do anything fi yuh, so if things go left when we drop a the warehouse, mi need you fi know that... and mi need you fi take care of Miche–"

"Killa stop the chatting, nuttin nah go left," I try to lighten the mood, knowing there's a 50/50 chance of that happening fi real. This isn't Jamaica and he knows.

Me just no need my emotions right now. Cyaa go in there thinking about how it miiiight turn out. I need to think about how I want it to turn out.

"You know a serious medz mah pre enuh Drip, but..." he trails off, understanding my decision to not prolong this type of conversation.

He's never been one to fear death but now that he's about to have his own family, it might be enough to have him thinking differently.

The truck starts moving and we both hang onto the barrels that are strapped down, preventing movement. The ride to the warehouse is bumpy and silent. Silence, I think caused by both of us being consumed by our thoughts.

Miles go by before the truck comes to a stop and as soon as it does, all I can hear are voices. The voice of... the security?

Yeah, a that yes

... Doing the usual check before we enter. The truck is supposed to be delivering product to the Italians, under the usual disguise of dough delivery. The driver is one of my guys from New York, hired months ago when Ruse came undercover to get familiar with the family and become trusted– so our entry could go as smooth as possible.

Tedious planning, but it was the only way

According to him, Ruse, Ramone and all my endless research, this is the only time of the month I'll be able to catch them all at once.

Father...

Sons...

Soldiers...

Plugs...

The entire ring.

Slyme and I have decided to take the ground while my men from New York are strategically placed all over and around the property.

"Same things in the back? I don't gotta spot check right?" the guard's voice from outside pulls me from my thoughts.

"Yeah son, how many times have I been here for the past couple months? Same old same old. Look if you wanna, I'm not the one wasting the boss' time," my driver counters.

Good cover

I hear when the side of the truck is slapped, signaling entry. Slyme releases a sigh before removing his hand from his waist.

I look at him and mouth, 'Trigga happy'.

He mouths back, 'Fuck you', and we both chuckle lowly as the truck starts moving again– slowly this time.

Taking my position at the door, I await the opening. The truck comes to even more of a slow and my eyes find Slyme again, who now seems to be executing his usual prayer.

• • •

SLYME

"… Amen," I whisper, leaving my eyes closed for a few more seconds– allowing the darkness to consume me.

That fails.

I can't easily switch. Mi mind fixated pon Michelle right now.

The sound of the door opens and before I can aim and press, Drip ends the life of the first Italian American. I pause, to look at him… Mi affi look pon him, the way the man quick.

He shrugs.

"Wah? Mi ready fi go home to mi woman," is all he says before hopping out of the truck, immediately ridding himself of the thin overall, set to cover our gears if the back was to be searched.

I chuckle and follow suit, hearing when his voice comes up in my earpiece. I pause to listen.

"Man dem, if a bullet graze me, pray say it coated with poison and me end up dead. 'cause mah end the life weh responsible fi the perimeter weh it happen ina. Dat good?"

Nobody shares an answer.

"Dat good?!" Drip repeats himself.

Dat nuh good. Man affi a repeat himself already? Them ago learn still. A them first live mission with him.

"Understood boss," a choir of voices come through the earpiece, causing me to chuckle lightly.

What I sight next is a guy running from the north of the truck.

"Tito?!" he screams, stopping when he sees us. "You guys can't be back here," he commands.

I smile and start to unzip the *dough company's* overall.

"Yeah?" Drip's voice comes out in slight humour.

Dead boy that now

Before my thought settles properly, the sound of his body hitting the floor creates music. I step out of the overall, and the sound of rapid gunfire catches my attention next. Almost immediately 'bout 16 man surround we– men from our team mi fi say.

I look to Drip who doesn't flinch. Tell mi weh di man a do?

Smooooooke di man a smoke– mid gunfire.

Jah Jah God...

"Boss you know yuh fi buil though?" I chuckle into the earpiece, as hearing each other under heavy gunfire will always prove futile.

"If mahgo dead, mahgo dead high enuh Slyme," he chuckles back.

Well if a that a the vibe.

The circle closes in as we move to the warehouse. More rapid fire goes off and I can't tell you from where exactly but I'm certain they're all aimed at us.

"Boss, directly in front of your huddle," comes a voice from the earpiece.

"Speak what it is. Nah open the circle fi vague details blood," Drip responds.

Only thing leff fi the man do a hiss him teeth

The team from New York is highly skilled but they don't fully understand his cues. They aren't as seamless as the Jamaicans are when it comes to understanding his move-ments... and we know di man lack patience.

"Matteo, 12 O'clock," the voice comes again.

"Open the circle," Drip commands– voice holding zero emotions.

Cold...

Empty...

Meanwhile mi still cyaa slip into that form. My mind still stuck pon Michelle.

I peer up to see four men move to the side, allowing Matteo a view. Drip steps for-ward, pulling his spliff as if we no ina the middle a battle. Nonetheless, I follow his lead, staying by his right hand.

The wind and sound of a bullet flies past, too close for my liking. I pinpoint the shooter in less than a second, bring the scope to my eyes and press. Nahfi wait fi him drop for confirmation either, mi know dat dead.

Matteo shakes his head at my action.

"Boys, what happened to smoothing things over by talking?" he asks.

Drip doesn't respond, instead he continues to pull on his spliff.

A chuckle leaves my lips, finding his action hilarious. We all stand there for a few more seconds, until he seems to be satisfied. The spliff is thrown to the ground and he uses his boot to crush it.

"Boys?" is the first thing that leaves his mouth. "Matteo where's your father?"

"Papa is... occupied right no–" but before the words exit his mouth, Drip's hand finds his throat, bringing the skinny Italian up to his tippy toes.

A crowd of red beams start taking over his body but he doesn't release him.

"Fuck you daddy deh? Stop waste mi time yute," he sneers.

Nuh think him realize the son cyaa talk if him basically a strangle him...

Mi watch him release him finger dem from the man neck and in less than a second di youth drop a grung. This cyaa be the son dem say fi take ova everything? Nuh wonder them did a train Rome. Yute yah waste.

"Gentlemen, gentlemen, my son doesn't know common etiquette," an old shakey voice comes from the way of the warehouse.

Hope him know we neva come yah fi talk, di man deh way past that.

More men from our team begin to storm the grounds. I'm guessing the Italians have realized how unprepared they are compared to us, which is why him come 'bout 'talk'. Cyaa storm the man house when him deh pon vacation and expect nuttin less than this.

The old man walks out into the open... and like I said, Drip doesn't want to talk. He gives the signal and before you know it, the old man's body is flat on the floor.

With this realization, the gunfire goes wild from their side.

Siiiiclawttttt!

I start jogging towards the warehouse, only a few footsteps behind Drip. Releasing a few rounds as I move across the open, I pick up the pace just before making it into the warehouse.

"Mi wah the exact pussyhole weh did a try rape woman ina me place," Drip's voice falls lethal.

"Fuck we ago find him Drip?" I ask, genuinely confused.

He doesn't answer.

I watch him search every crevice, every corner– killing everybody he finds hiding.

All a that good and well but wah ah mek me worry right now are the echoes of shots outside that aren't dying down.

"Ramone say him always deh a the monthly meeting, him deh yah," he finally extends an answer to me– after minutes.

Fiiim bwoy, so mek we see

Ten more lonnnnnng minutes fly by and none of the faces we've sent to hell matches that of the guy on video. We come to an enclosed section of the warehouse, seeming to be an office? Nuh know but it pre so.

"Drip? It worth it?" I ask but the look he extends me, confirm seh mi shouldn't even ask that.

Sudden movement is heard inside and a smile creeps unto his face.

I shake my head at his antics.

The door opens on the first turn, revealing that whoever is inside just entered the hiding spot and had no time to close the door. I step in, ensuring there aren't any surprises. Drip follows and ...

Jah Know? I shake my head at the sight. Here we have di pussyhole himself, curled up in a corner– gun in hand.

Dem people yah cyaa be the Italians the man a warn me 'bout fi months now.

"Yo I'll shoot if you come closer!" the corner victim screams.

"Wouldn't expect yuh fi do nuttin else bad man," Drip counters.

I laugh, out loud too. Cyaa believe this shit.

He tries to move away but I grab him, taking his gun from his hand before using it to floor him. Jordanne brings a knife from his boot– a Cold Steel Recon 1, if we a be specific.

A beauty

He flicks it open and moves to the victim on the ground. Without hesitation he starts to play in his face with the blade.

The big man a put up a fight but, Drip nuh like that.

He steps back and looks at me… and I know exactly what to do. I point and squeeze, releasing bullets into his shoulders and knees.

 Dat fi keep him still.

"Nuh understand how yuh wah tryyyy rape woman and gun butt pikny, but yuh fraida knife? Come on man," Drip teases.

"Bruh I barely understand what you're saying," the man trembles.

"Relax man, yahgo understand in a minute."

I watch as he brings a tiny medical flask from his pocket before pouring it along the blade.

Venom

Mhmhhmm, it same one yes. The man sinister.

My area is shooting… clean shots, merciless kills, immaculate missions and observations. Drip though? Naturally evil. Naturally sinister… No trouble fi him torture you in any creative way him feel like.

The scream of the male victim jolts me from my thoughts just in time to see that he's carving something into his face.

R…

A…

P…

I…

S…

T…

The venom must be taking effect because the screams coming from this big man a supm fi mek anybody wonder.

"The burn you feel is the poison making its way through your circulatory system. To every vein, every artery. Moments from now it ago stop your heart," Drip adds.

I keep my attention between them and the door, ensuring no surprise guest enters. Drip steps back, seemingly dissatisfied with his… art.

Man take a moment fi analyze the carvings and then stoop again. This time slitting the sides of the man's mouth, widening his smile straight up to his ears.

Bro turn the man ina the Joka to pussyclawt

Ina real life killa.

"So di man smile ina me camera enuh Slyme," he chuckles before standing up, now proud of his work.

Jah Jah God.

Him deserve it still

"Boss, we have an issue," a voice presents itself in the earpiece.

"Speak," Drip responds.

"There is another set of men entering the premi–" but before he finishes his statement, we hear a thud and some running.

We start making our way to the warehouse exit, stopping in our tracks when we come to have a good enough view of what's happening.

Drip looks over at me, "Remember the Italians I warned you about all month?"

"Mhmm?"

He stares in the open before saying, "Well they're here… and now the real chaos starts."

The fuck?

If me couldn't slip into darkness before, me affi do it now. Nah dead leff me woman and pikny.

Not today.

●●●

RYLEIGH

We enter the station from not the front entrance, but some kinda side entrance. Toni-Anne is just beside me, taking a note of everything and everyone. We get to the waiting area, positioned just before the holding area and I've come to the realization that they picked up everybody.

Mariah, Joshua, Ryan.

Kelly, Keif, Lorelle.

Ms.Cherry… Nadifffffffaaaa???? That's crazy.

And wait, Lenarddddd?

Man yah coming like a recurring boil

Is that? Haha! Not Goose! Mi poor taxi driver.

Surprised me no see Emily and Ghale. Then again, I duh know wah J' do wid dem.

Shaking my head, I chuckle at the line up. They really picked up everybody they think will talk– persons they think they can intimidate.

As my eyes meet each of them, a small smirk creeps across my face. Len and Nadz don't know enough and the rest know not to speak.

"Terry," Toni whispers the name of our therapist.

Terry?

My eyes meet hers and she looks petrified. She wasn't a part of the plan so the sight of her sends me into slight panic. This woman better take Jordanne threats and that NDA serious. Me sure death no better than prison.

I squint my eyes at her, trying to read her mood, but all I'm able to pull from her is panic.

By the looks of it, they're going to question us separately… and I already know it's going to be a long dreadful night. Lucky thing Michelle deh hospital. Not another stress the baby mother cyaa manage right now.

97|Parallel Shifts

RYLEIGH

As I guessed, we're all being interrogated separately. It's been hours of them trying to pry information but I'm not saying a thing without the lawyers.

And when dem come, mi still nah say shit

"Can I have a cup of tea?" I pose my question to Wellz, just to tick him off.

By the looks of it, he's tired of the run around. Good fi him 'cause mi tired ah it too. Might just stop fight the vomit and let eh go in yah.

"We have coffee," his response rubs me wrong.

Him can no bother. No want him poison the doll.

We're so paranoid right now it's crazy

Better safe than sorry dem say, although it would somewhat be satisfying for him to harm me in any way, so I can watch Drip pick him apart.

The light in the room is too bright. Bright light pull confession? 'Cause what's the point? The entire station reeks of weed by the way.

The irony...

A sour mixture of food, bleach, testosterone, lies and a whole lot of ego is in the air too. My sense of smell is heightened for some reason. Nuh know wah gwaan deh so, but mi–

"Cee, I never wanted this life for you or Janette, I'm here to fix it. I'm the reason you guys got involved with them in the first place. Robert anuh good man and so mi sure him son cyaa be a good ma–"

"Mark stop the yapping and duh call mi dat," I seethe.

Him a workkk mi patience

I refocus, trying to keep all my emotions in check– since it's the only way mi can carry this out seamlessly.

"Listen… Mark, please duh mention my mother or Jordanne. Ask your questions and carry on," I hiss.

Wellz looks at Mark and they both chuckle.

Hope dem a laugh when it boil down.

I really hope it's funny to them then.

• • •

LENARD

"So what exactly do you know about them?" the guy that has a very weird resemblance of Ryleigh asks for the umpteenth time.

"Nuttin," I mutter.

I know everything, but I like to watch the Jamaicans try to take down what's bigger than them. I can't remember where I recognize this guy's face from, other than him looking like her.

Me just cyaa place it.

"From what we know, they picked you up after a flight last year, just around this time actually," the other guy, Wellz, throws in.

Mmmcht, pathetic if yuh ask mi enuh.

"Can't recall," I murmur.

I remember every single detail from that day, and every day after that while I did my research.

"Why yah protect dem? We got a call from a number traced back to one of your addresses. The person reported reckless driving and suspicious activity connected to a Porsche Tayc–"

"Bredren, I'm a real estate and tech guy. I own multiple addresses, so you point void right deh so, and you couldn't trace no call back to me unless I wanted you to. Believe dat," my words spew anger.

I really fucked up that night. I wasn't thinking… Jealously can do that, but mi cover me tracks– very good too. By the research I've done, I know better than to go against this family or at least with Jamaican law enforcement because them nuh know di half.

• • •

TONI-ANNE

"Uncertain about why unuh bring me. Me of all persons?" I laugh, as both Wellz and Mark struggle for my attention.

Over the years I've learnt to find things out on my own since I'm the 'girl' of the family and I always have to be 'protected' or left in the dark somewhat. So now me already know half a wah gwaan if I'm putting it together correctly.

Whatever Drip told Ryleigh to do, she's been doing it perfectly. She hasn't uttered a word to me, not to her mother, not to Lorelle… nobody.

Love that

"Your boyfriend could be charged. You're willing to let him go down for something your family caused?"

I chuckle and tap the desk, trying to not get angry at the mention of Joshua suffering in any way, shape or form.

"Drop the sweet talk gentlemen. You underestimate me and it's fine, I'm used to that, but don't insult my intelligence too… dat just disrespectful. Yuh no need my words to arrest Joshua. You need hisss words or mine, to arrest my brother. Do me a favour and save alla we time. Maybe retake unuh detective course 'cause right now it's giving 'Hardy Boys'… 'Nancy Drew'… 'Sherlock Holmes'…… waste."

I hear Ryleigh's father chuckle and watch as Wellz gets visibly angry.

"Sick and tyad a dah family yah!" Wellz almost screams.

Then imagine weeeee?

I giggle at how emotional this big man is.

Sick stomach.

• • •

JOSHUA

I stare at them and they stare at me…

Wah do dem old bredda yah? And why dah man yah have Ryleigh farrid?

"Are you going to answer the question?" the Ryleigh-face man asks.

I say nothing. Mi no open my mouth from mi step foot in yah so bredda. Our lawyers are unavailable. On every night ah the year them present, but tonight them off grid? Joke ting.

"Yuh wah you woman go jail bwoyii?"

Depends on which one…

I kid, I kidddd hahaha!

Kelly can spend a night still, she a stress out T' and T' a stress out meee.

I look up at the big man shouting at me. Fi likkle information? You woulda think Danne fuck him gyal. How him wah bring dung di man so?

… Commissioner must no know 'bout this, because me certain him deh pon payroll. I know dat fi sure 'cause every time me try get a permit fi keep nuttin, Toni-Anne reminds me of such.

"Yuh nah answer?!" he repeats.

Like him no see? Answer what? Dem man yah bro?

Man dem a host a senior citizens clown fest ina government station tuh pussyclawt.

I chuckle at my own thought, 'cause this really cannot be real life right now.

$$\bullet\ \bullet\ \bullet$$

MARIAH

"Sir nuh stop wid mi, stop wid you barber. Line up deh look like KFC line– chakka chakka," I hiss.

Me too hungry fi the bagga questions.

"We understand you're Paul's daught–"

"Yes big up mi clean father, couldn't nobody else daughter. A wah?" I play the hand they gave me.

"We understand he was involved in a shooting years ago in Hanover?" the taller guy asks.

Man yah look like Ry? Or me a turn Toni and a imagine her face pah everybody?

"I have no knowledge of that event Mr.Look Like Mi Friend," my words connect and he chuckles.

The other guy moves closer to me, bringing his face inches away from mine before whispering, "If you help us, we can help you find your mother," he suggests.

The desperation oozing from this man is crazzzyyy

I blink rapidly, before I say, "Mi nahv no madda but yuh know weh mi have?" I ask while blinking still.

He doesn't answer but holds my blinky stare.

"… Gum… winterfreshhhh," I continue.

He pulls back and his colleague chuckles.

$$\bullet\ \bullet\ \bullet$$

TERRY

"I haven't a clue of the subject you gentlemen are referring to. I would gladly be of any assistance where I can, granted I knew," I smile.

Nerrrrrves! Nerves! Nerves!

In all my years, I've never been involved in anything like this. I'm a couple's therapist for God's sake!

The threat I was issued by Mr.Sheer keeps replaying in my mind. Not a word will come out of my mouth tonight. Just being here in the station is giving me the creeps. I need them to know I won't say anything.

From what these gentlemen are saying, there seems to be no grounds for an arrest and so they're grasping at straws.

Well mi nahgo be the metal straw in a pack of paper straws, sorry

"Okay, for some reason I believe you. That will be all for tonight…"

Upon exiting the room I see that a police woman is bringing Ms.Stevens around. The look on her face isn't pleasant. Apart from her looking weirdly ill, she has skepticism plastered on her features as well.

Hope she no think because mi come out quick me talk enuh

I offer her a small smile, but she ignores my efforts.

• • •

RYLEIGH

Why she come out so early?! Mi say if Terry sayyyyy nuttin!

My stomach becomes upset and I chalk it up to the nerves that come with the worry of her speaking on whatever was shared.

Gir–

Be Quiet.

Before I enter the interrogation room again, my phone lights up.

BD♥: Happy Anniversary.

I smile at my cell, just giggling at how sweet and considerate my man issss.

Yah smile fah?

Waaaaaaiiiiiitttt… Wait!

Wait, Wait, Waaaiiiittttttttt!!! He said he wouldn't text unle–

"This way Ms.Stevens," the female officer directs me to the room.

I get to the entrance and I can feel the panic taking me over. He's not supposed to text… Him cyaa serious. My eyes meet Mark's and somehow, I find the will to say…

"Daddy can I go to the bathroom, please?" my plea almost inaudible.

Ughh

My fingers find my thigh while my chest is starting to tighten. He looks at me for a while before a look of satisfaction washes his being.

"Bring in somebody else, let her use the restroom," he speaks in my favour.

Gullible

I don't waste a seconddddd, I'm already down the hall and to the bathroom.

I can't text back but I know what to do… so I toggle to settings and do everything Ramone taught me to. Standing against the stall for a few minutes, I carry out each step before my personal phone transforms into an encrypted device.

With that done, I start to dial…

• • •

JORDANNE

"Remember the Italians I warned you about all month?" I ask Slyme.

"Mhmm," is all he offers as an answer.

I stare in the open before saying, "Well they're here and now the real chaos starts."

I watch as he tries to refocus. From we reach mi know him head no deh pon him body and I can't even blame him.

Man fi deh home

My eyes are focused, watching as the Italians move in rapidly, wiping out most of my men. Jah Jah God.

I look to Slyme while he stares at me awaiting instructions. The only thing my brain brings me to do, is to pull my phone out. Today is quite different from what it was last year. Last year I finally had her to myself.

The memory of that week brings a small smile to my lips.

Like yuh no see wah happen round yuh killa

Death, mi seeit man.

Ignoring my chatty mind, my fingers go typing.

Happy Anniversary.

Sent…

I click out of her chat and nod to Slyme. He turns and we both start moving to the roof. The warehouse is now being riddled with bullets and I can physically feel when my emotions exit my being.

• • •

DRIP

Sight.

Focus.

Move faster killa! Supm a hold yuh back?

Too much gears

Fuck the gears thennnn.

I stop and start to release myself from the ammunition and hindering gears. The mask goes first, followed by the bandolier.

"Drip!?" I can hear Slyme's voice.

My hands signal for him to continue to the roof without me. Continuing the removal of all things unnecessary, I tap my earpiece to speak.

"Man dem?!"

"Boss?" a clear but calm voice comes across, and I can hear the gunfire and chaos from his angle.

"Gimi a head count," I speak back.

A moment passes and I use the opportunity to start climbing the shakey stairs behind Slyme.

The voice comes back in, "50 to 60 closing in all at once. Two exit trucks, two or three at different aerial points."

"And our count?"

"15 to 20 on foot including you and Slyme, 12 at aerial points still, no exit truck. They just bombed that, but the speed boat is still on the pier," he explains.

I chuckle, finding actual humour in the fact that I might die today.

Fuckkkk!!!

"Slyme!?" I shout making my way onto the roof.

The chilly Chicago air hits me, now that I don't have all that shit on.

"Drip!" his voice comes clear, and my body follows it to a tiny rise in the wall.

I peer down at my small team on the ground, making their way to our boat that's been lingering on the pier. Man dem nah miss a targettttt... If I should ever merge the technical skills of the New York team with the authentic gel and flow of the Jamaican team? Chef's kiss.

My thoughts are interrupted by the roof door flying open.

Alrightttt...

I look to Slyme who is already firing.

Good.

The moment mi take fi look pon the man though, a bullet flies too close to me.

Focus!

My eyes find the shooter and I point and squeeze before dipping back behind the wall space. We fire back and forth for what seems like forever before both Slyme and I have no more rounds to spare.

The roof goes quiet...

My breathing goes quiet...

I took down a lotttt of the men trying to make it to us but I don't think it was all.

"We affi mek it off the roof," Slyme suggests.

No shit.

Ignoring him I move from behind the wall area, sliding to the bodies that lay nearest to us. I start to remove their weapons just before shots start flying over my head.

Bloodclawt, dem man yah nuh rest?! If me mek it outa this shit me a string up Croc myself. I look to where I left Slyme, waiting for him to look over at me. He does and I signal to him, pointing at the fire escape.

I give him another hand signal, reassuring him that I'll cover him while he moves. He has to make it to the boat even if I don't... Him have a family fi get back to.

Using my fingers I start to count down.

Three!

Two!

One! And as soon as mi index finger drop, di man take off– and the shots follow his every move.

Man a mooooove through them enuh

I start firing back, giving him as much cover as I can, before moving off myself... buttt out of nowhere I start hearing an automatic rifle going off.

Close to us, too close! Dem man yah really nuh rest a bumboclawttt.

I look to Slyme, just in time to see him fall to the ground...

Wah just happen?

I immediately start moving to him, ignoring the flying metals.

"Slyme!!??" I get to him and drop to my knees.

Man a bleed ooouuutttt already!? For the first time since my father died, my body fills with panic– full paniccccc! I look to see that a couple of the bullets have hit his protection vest, but one has entered his shoulder. While lifting him to find the exit wound, he starts coughing.

"Jorda–" he tries, but I ignore him, trying to pinpoint the wound. "Jordanne," he tries again.

Cyaa find no fucking exit killa!

More rounds of gunfire start going off and I can't think of firing back.

Bredda!

Fuckkkkkkkkk!!!

"Jordanne..." he whispers, choking on his own spit, while I start ripping fabric from his shirt to tie it around his arm, in an attempt to stop the bleeding.

"J..." this time he tugs at the hem of my shirt and the motion pulls at something within me.

• • •

JORDANNE

"J..." this time he tugs at the hem of my shirt.

I look down at him, eyes barely open, short heavy breathing... while I tie the knot around the wound as tight as I can.

Bleeding affi stop

"Liam, just buil. The bleeding ago slow," I offer.

He takes a very deep breath and smacks his lips open, "Duh mek she name the baby after me," he barely chuckles and I can almost feel the tears spring to the front of my eyes.

Jah Jah

"Yuh ago name the baby yourself bad head," with this, I get off my knees to sit, pulling him into my arms to keep his head up.

He's getting cold… Everything ah happen tooooo fast!

More gunfire starts going off but right now, mi deven care. I close my eyes, trying to center my thoughts in efforts to find a way to save my brother.

Breathe, stay calm

"Arrrrrrrriiiibbbbaaaaa!!!" the all too well Venezuelan accent lands on my ear.

Fucking Gabriel!

The sound of a chopper I didn't realize before becomes louder and louder. The wind from the blades causes the dust on the roof to pick up. The light from the chopper is now shining clearly on us while he speaks from his megaphone.

"Young Sheer, ah toldjuh nuh to fuck wit deh Italians, now I'm in America. Jhu know dayy don't like ahhh, us Spanish people in this countrehh."

I smile at his theatrics. The English is getting better.

Better careful before them shoot that shit outa the sky

No joke.

Seconds go by before the chopper lands safely on the roof. Two men run towards us, immediately lifting Slyme to the aircraft. Gabriel looks up at me before shaking his head.

I don't say a word…

"Vamanos!" he says loudly enough, pulling me to the chopper.

We make it there and lift off. I look to the ground, watching as my team is being rescued by my Venezuelan alliance.

It's good to not burn every bridge…

Great not to

• • •

RYLEIGH

"Everybody good wid dat?" I ask the men.

I stilllllllllll haven't slept, but here I am catching the team up on what happened at the station earlier.

"So this happens when?" a subdon throws out his question.

"Tomorrow evening, based on what he agreed to," I answer politely, not releasing an ounce of the irritation that's been riding me this past week.

"And yuh trust him?" another subdon asks.

Before I can answer Paw does...

"Yuh like question her bad man?" he snickers. "If she say a so, ah so. Wah hard ina dat?"

I shake my head, 'cause wah really hard ina that fi real? How much more point me affi prove?

"Duh pay dem no mind. Drip had a hard time getting everybody to bend to his will when Robert died too," Skulli's words grant me some comfort.

I sigh...

"Anybody else have any concerns?" my voice comes out weaker than I'd like it to, but at this point mi deven business.

I just want this to be over with. Mi nuh hear from mi man houuursss now– the usual, since he left... but that text was the signal for me to set Gabriel on his way to the warehouse, so mi need fi know if him good.

Now too

Nobody answers my question, so I guess dem good wid wah me say. I release a sigh and turn to walk away before I hear Skulli say...

"Lawww."

"Lawwwww," they all repeat, and I realize I probably should've said that.

Nahv time fi dat though

I don't, I'm way too miserable ina me own skin right now.

Swear

Moments later, I get home and by now I'm finally getting out of the shower. I had a big bowl of chicken soup that mommy insisted I eat before she left with Sue and JJ. I dry myself, throw my hair in a bonnet and drag his shirt on. Now curled up in the bed sheets, I realize I'm still unable to sleep. How mi fi sleep and I don't know what's going on with J'?

My personal phone has now become my 'work phone' and I now have a new personal cell, that Ryan was able to get all my data back on.

Ramone really a morph him into himself. That's crazyyy

I peer down at the phone to see that it's minutes past 5am and I know now that I won't make it out of bed tomorrow for nothinggggg or anybody other than J'.

Sigh...

My phone flashes and I perk up to look at it. It's not him, but it's still good news.

<u>Surgeon:</u> Troopa is awake. Barely functioning but awake with good enough memory.

Stop the liiiiessssss!

Mi swear him woulda never wake! Eight long months!

**Tell him I'll see him tomorrow!!! Mi
never have no faith ina u enuh David! Lol
you save me big friend life though!**

<u>**Surgeon:**</u> **Mi know man! Drip tell mi weekly
say yuh want him move haha!**

I laugh out at the statement all while hugging up against Jordanne's pillow. Such good news! Hopefully it's enough to send me to sleep.
We really need it
If something happened to Jordanne I would know by now right?
Right???

98 | Cessation

RYLEIGH

My phone is goiiiiing offff!
I willlll cryyyy enuh! Jordanne better living 'cause I CAN'T DO THIS SHIT another dayyyyyyy!

Throwing the sheet from over my head while using my hands to search for the phone, I take a deep breath before bringing it to my ears.

"Mhmm?" I don't know who it is...

Or what time it is

The male voice laughs at my obvious disregard and that's when I pick up.

Pawww.

"Ryleigh yuh cannot be the boss and a sleep till after 10 a morning mi G."

I groan.

After 10 him say? I should sleep till after 10 tomorrow.

"What is it Xavier?" my query falls bluntly.

"Yuh man gi yuh me government Ry?!" he laughs out and I can hear that he's driving with his windows down.

I start laughing at how he asked the question.

"Paw yuh think a play-play books me go over weekly up here?" I giggle, now turning from my stomach and onto my back.

I listen to him laugh just before arguing with somebody that cut him off. And just like that, he's now threatening to end the person's life on this good Sabbath morning.

Mercyyy

He continues to argue while my mind drifts off into the world of food.

Yuh know weh we fi eat right now?

What?

Ice, the one from the fridge dem weh no self defrost

Laaaawddd what???

I'm telling you, that's what we feel for

"Since him a tell yuh my government mahgo tell yuh wah him call yuh," Paw's voice chips back onto the line nice and jovial, as if he wasn't just threatening somebody's life.

"Hmm? Wah dat?" I ask, overly curious to hear.

He laughs out, loudly. To the point where I have to bring the phone from my ears.

"Mi nah tell yuh, but mi know when him drop a foot yuh nah stop till him tell you," he continues his laughter.

I giggle, knowing it's the whole truth. Mi wah know wah him a walk a call me behind my back fi real.

"You call me fi chat out my morning Xavier?" I ask, suddenly remembering he called for a reason.

"Nuttin too serious, just a check in 'bout the thing lata today. Skulli want a meeting before but mah tell him that no necessary since you cover everything last night into this morning. So mah call fi mek sure yuh no mek him change your mind 'cause mah go way a Mobay and come back."

Now weh him ago Mobay go do on a day like today?

"Dat alright with you boss lady?" he teases.

"Come offa mi phone Paw. You wake me up fi ask bout Mobay?" I laugh and before he ends the conversation, I end the call before pulling the sheets back over my head to continue my hibernation.

• • •

JORDANNE

I haven't said a word since getting on the chopper last night.

Now on the jet heading home, I look to my left where Liam should be seated. Pulling in air through my nostrils and releasing it the same way, I try to find my calm. He's the only one apart from Trisse that knows what I planned on doing later tonight... and mi just nah do it without him– cyaa do it without him.

World ina shambles bredda.

Jah Jah

"Mr.Sheer this is your captain speaking, we're on our final descend. Please stay seated and buckled in for the next fifteen minutes. We should arrive 1:33pm local time."

The usual...

I haven't replaced my phone. I have no will to. Just wah go home to me woman.

Still affi deal wid Croc

Croc affi deal wid meeee. If I lose my brother because of this shit? Everybody affi go say goodbye to my sweet side.

Mhhmm, believe.

• • •

Minutes later I'm walking towards Paw.

"Boss! Kingston airport nah work??!" I don't offer him an answer.

He realizes the mood I'm in and quickly hops back into the Range. When we're both inside and buckled, he pulls off.

"Wah talk 'bout it?" is the next thing he asks.

I still offer no reply, no explanation.

He accepts the answer by switching on the music. Chronixx is his choice and I welcome it, seeking to soothe my thoughts.

The three and a half hour ride to Kingston is wordless but tension free. Regardless of the fact that Liam got hurt, the mission wasn't a fail… and we affi give God thanks fi that.

The lessons learnt…

… And the bridges burnt.

And the bridge that saved us

• • •

RYLEIGH

"The questioning not going your way is your fault," I speak into the phone while turning into the pharmacy's parking lot.

Can never find no parking ova yah so

"Girl dem come park up just fi buy name brand coffee and go weh back," I hiss, while circling the lot.

"Nobody answered anything substantial," Mark's annoying voice shifts me from being miserably chirpy to just being annoyed again.

"Listen mi nuh, I made sure that everybody was available. Our lawyers weren't present by coincidence, you got lucky there. I can't do your job for you Mark Stevens."

Ramone looks to me and I him.

I shrug… because I don't know how else fi draw him out for the recording. Mi done say his full name and everything.

"I need more," Mark continues.

MMMCHTT.

"But why!?" I snap, stopping just as I watch a parking spot being freed from the shackles of a Honda Fit.

No shade with it

"Ryleigh, I just want my old life back. I need to prove to the bigger heads dem say I didn't get caught up and failed my mission years ago. I want my family back and most of all mi wah dah family deh pay fi weh dem do to we."

Weeeeee???!!!

I open my mouth to argue but Ramone signals for me to calm down. Taking the deepest breath my lungs allow, I press my lips into a line before continuing the conversation.

"And you willing fi plant evidence and intimidate witnesses to get to that point Mark?"

"Yes!" he raises his voice.

There he is… the Mark I remember– the angry, sorry excuse of a man.

Sperm donor if yuh ask mi

The line goes silent and Ramone nods.

Without hesitation I say, "Well alright mi don. Just be at the address in Hope Pastures later. I'm about to handle something so bye," and of course he tries to say something, but I hang up.

Weird how me still a execute the last leg of the plan and mi no hear nuttin from Drip. But nobody else seems to be worried, so I guess. I know how him operate more while, but I'll still be worried if we can't touch base. Him affi fix dat up fimmi. I will panic every… single… time.

"You sure after you hang up so him ago show up later?" Ramone asks.

I snap my head to look over at him, "Man deh will do anything fi see mommy."

We both chuckle at my reasoning.

A just the truth. He swears she's still his wife. The man delusional.

I fly the car door open and hop out to enter the pharmacy. Ramone and I get to the medicine aisle and I start searching for multi-Vitamins– 'cause a girl is tired.

Get the damn test

Ignoring my subconscious, I pick up the vitamins and a few other things I don't need, before cashing and walking out happily

● ● ●

I just came from the hospital, brought Muuch some food and gave her the rundown of yesterday. She's in good spirits and mi love that fi her. In this moment though, I'm about to call Sue and question her about Jordanne, because what the fuck!?

Moving towards his office, I start dialing her number.

No answer…

I normally sit there in the evenings, this way I can multitask.

Watch Netflix and browse the books

I enter the code and push the door open, not thinking anything of it, but what I see startles me.

A weh di?

Mark is tied up facing me directly, back turned to J's desk.

What did I miss?

I stand rooted in my spot, quickly observing my surroundings. The office is dark and we already know I'm blind, so none of that is helping. My eyes struggle around the room before his voice pulls me from my search.

"Love…"

Chilllllllllsssssss. Raw chills from my man being home!

My lips turn up into a smile and for a moment I forget the man tied up before me. The pace of my breathing picks up and I can almost feel when he moves to me.

Jesusssahhh!

He starts leaving small kisses along the side of my neck while pulling me into his hold from behind, but I get distracted by Mark's mumbles and rocking of the chair.

J' ignores him completely.

"How've you been?" his voice falls low, deep, sinister, but loving all at once.

Mhm! My mannn, my maannn.

"Okay. You?" I barely get out.

"Not good," he responds almost immediately. "So, I've been asking Croc some questions but him nah comply. I must commend him on protecting your name. All now him no mention you."

A lie? Haha!

No but Drip really come home come change the entire plan fi have the man ina me house? I just know he's not in a good mood if he's done this. Something definitely went wrong.

His hands find the light switch and the perfectly placed light bars start shining bright, revealing the room.

"You were asking him questions, with his mouth gagged?" I let out a small giggle.

"No enuh. Gag dat when him start gimmi a headache. We been a do the 'yes or no' since then," and with that he walks over to Mark, pulling what seems to be crumpled paper from his mouth.

Mark coughs and flutters around a bit before he looks up at us to speak.

"Ryleigh don't mek dah boy yah manipulate you. Spitting image of his father in more ways than one!" he seethes, voice dripping in venom.

Cooyah? Hear the man weh fling mi ina the TV.

I look at Jordanne for a second, before he shrugs, causing us both to erupt in laughter. No 'cause why this so funny?

When we sober up, he speaks to me with his eyes, giving me the go ahead to say and ask what I want. I take the opportunity to move closer to Mark while J' moves away.

"Mark, there is no way you think after doing everything yuh did to my mother and I, you were gonna come back into our lives just so?"

He tries to say something, but I don't want to hear it.

"I might've been six at the time, but I have a fantastic memory box," I smile, knocking my forehead.

Nuh big fi nothing

I continue, "so just imagine my surprise when you tried to get me to go against Jordanne, for some stupid vendetta yuh have 'gainst him father. For supm youuuuu caused on yourself?"

I shake my head before looking to Jordanne who is now lighting his spliff. My fists form a fold and before J' realizes what I'm about to do, I bring my knuckles to Mark's face.

Awuhh!

Stepping back, I flash my hands, realizing I might've hit him too hard... 'cause me hand a hatttt mi! Instantly.

I look over to J' whose eyes are widened from shock but still holding a hint of amusement. He smirks before clapping lightly at my performance.

"Fuckkk," Mark winces in pain, as if it just registered.

J' and I both turn to look at him... There's blood now dripping from both nostrils and that's enough comedy for Jordanne and I. We start laughing again, only this time we can't pinpoint the reason... From me flashing my hands, to Mark with a bloody nose, to him really thinking his plan would work.

"Ry' anuh boxing class enuh. Need your finger dem fi stay pretty Love," Jordanne finally releases his thoughts.

Walking over to him, I whisper, "Do whatever you want with him. I thought I would want some level of reconciliation, but I don't feel a thing..."

He holds my chin up before saying... "You don't look well Ry'... I'll be up in less than thirty minutes," he almost whispers and I tip up to kiss his lips before turning away.

"Ryleigh!" Mark tries, but I don't look back.

Instead, I make my way out the office and towards the stairs. I can hear his muffles all the way up the staircase, yet still I don't budge... I feel... nothing.

Nothing at all.

• • •

It's now a few minutes after 1am and we've been cuddled up for the past two hours. He doesn't seem to want to have sex and I find it strange.

"What's wrong? You haven't been saying much or doing much," I ask, peering down at his head in my lap, while I chomp on the crushed ice that he got from God knows where.

The room falls silent for a few minutes.

"Liam got shot in his arm and lost a lot of blood. Think him neva woulda mek it but he did, after hours of surgery last night… only fi them say he might not have full range of motion in his left hand."

That no sound bad to me, considering the mission they went o–

"That's his dominant hand, the hand he uses to shoot, the hand he would use to hold his child, to feed him or her, to teach him or her how to write… Know mi shoulda just mek him come back home."

I heave a sigh.

It's giving high school J' and I don't like that for him– for us.

"Already know yuh ago say don't blame yourself bu–"

"You absolutely should blame yourself. You ignored your instincts, you never do that. What was it this time?" I ask.

A moment of silence washes the room again.

"Couldn't tell you," he mumbles.

With that, I pull him closer into me. Without words, I comfort him into the night until he's able to fall asleep.

Mere moments later, I fall asleep too.

● ● ●

<u>ONE WEEK LATER</u>

JORDANNE

"Yo mah tell unuh the man bawl fimi!" Slyme ah tell a wayyyyy, wayyy different version of the truth about last week.

I hiss and bring my spliff to my mouth.

"Jordanne yuh deh a foreign a bawl fi man?!" Ry' shoves at me, giggling at the lies being spread.

Jah know?

"Ryleigh, allll mah try get the man attention. Memba ah dead mah dead weh enuh. The man a cry and a dress wound. Mah try giim a message fi give Michelle and nothing bredda, bay tears."

"Yuh know me believe though!" Paw is already on the floor.

Nuttin no so funny still.

Everybody is here at Mum's, except Michelle who still has another day in the hospital. Slyme came home today after multiple rounds of surgery in the U.S. The doctors say that if he consistently does physical therapy, he should regain full motion in the affected hand.

Jah alone yute

Nah tell you.

"Hello," Ry' answers her phone. "Trisse me send you go enjoy the spa yourselffff... Me tell yuh say my nails wah do?...... Yuh know yuh renk little girl?...... Just say you want me company ina Town...... Okay mah come jeeeez," she hangs up before finding me.

I smile... Apart from her being partly ill for the past week, she's been happy, and we know that mek me happy. I'm a simple man.

"Mah come with you," Toni-Anne props herself up and they both move off to alight the stairs.

Watching them disappear up the staircase, I bring my phone out to text Lorelle.

Accurate? |attachment|

<u>Lorelle:</u> **Accurate as fuckkkk! Looove it!**

Good, that's all I need to know...

Less than fifteen minutes later T' comes rushing down the steps.

"Danne," she waves me over and I move to her with nothing but questions in my eyes.

"She no wah go again, so you go convince her. I did my best but she miserable as fuck," Toni whines.

I chuckle before shoving her out of the way. "Cyaa leave unuh in charge a nuttin," I laugh.

"FUck you Danne," T' laughs just before slapping me upside the head.

• • •

TONI-ANNE

I've been in the car for almost twenty minutes bredda. Trisse is complaining that we won't make it in time and all now me cyaa see Ry' a come outa Sue house.

My phone vibrates and I look to see who it is this time.

<u>KellyBabe:</u> **Where are you?**

Mommy dem.

<u>KellyBabe:</u> **Okay, what's the dress code you say?**

As if you're going to brunch babe.

<u>KellyBabe:</u> **Got it** 🖤

🖤

I really need to talk to her fi real. She deserves at least that after years.

Looking at the time, I see that it's almost three already. Hissing, I exit the car and move to the side of the house, towards Danne's old room, to figure out what's taking him

669

so long to convince her to come with us... and sure enough, there they are on the balcony, tied up in each other.

He's holding her in a protective embrace. Her head on his chest while his arms cloak her, acting as her shield from whatever is going on with her today– or any other day.

Instead of disturbing them, I turn to walk back to the car.

Mek mi give them another ten

'Cause why was that soooo sweet?

• • •

RYLEIGH

But mi no know why Nadz nah answer her phone?!

"Mek we go look fi Michelle then. Feel bad say we ago out and she nah come, unuh coulda wait until tomorrow enuh," I kick off my umpteenth complaint of the day.

"Ry' she couldn't come tomorrow either, she still affi rest," T' counters.

"Yes and we affi reach weh we ago before sunset!" Trisse adds.

Wah so special 'bout sunset?

We're at my house arguing about what I should wear. I think if we ago all the way a Stony Hill, I should wear something comfortable? Or warm at least? While battling my decision, I feel when T' yanks me from my closet, holding me firm enough to bring me to my bed.

"Ryleigh stop be stubborn. Your cousin is here for the first time in a long time. Just be a good host and carry her weh she wah go. Yuh cyaa selfish all the days a yuh life."

Murdaaaa! Dah girl yah ago eat me up alllll the time.

I giggle at the realization.

Looking up at Trisse, I mumble the word, "Fiiiine," before getting up to get ready.

Almost an hour later, we're pulling into a very nice property. Lushhhhhhh landscape, birds chirping, fresh breeze... Neva know Kingston had it within her.

St.Andrew

"This is nooooiiiice," I let out.

"Noooooiiiice bad, bad, bad!!" Trisse adds.

"Like it too," Toni adds, not looking up from her phone.

Fi somebody weh did well wah come, she's been on her phone a lot.

We walk to the entrance where we're not greeted by the way. What type of horrible customer service dem start off wid? Trisse lucky mi love her and the place cute.

We come through what seems to be a wine cellar or cooler... and I immediately think of taking a picture. Can't tell when last I did such.

"Toni," I mutter in the softest voice I can find.

She looks at me and rolls her eyes.

"Oh my Godddd, okay hurry uppp and don't be picky."

"What's the rush? We reach already," I smile.

We stand there taking pictures for less than three minutes.

"Okay look. Me take like a million," she hands me the phone before walking off, leaving me standing with Trisse.

Perfect! I think while looking at them. Now I can take the heels off.

I stoop to try and loosen the straps but Trisse yanks me up.

"No, come, take them off when we sit down Cee," she pleads.

Ughhh!

"Jeeez alright. The food here better be from heaven, the way how unuh a behave," I counter.

She smiles, holding my hand while leading me through the house? Villa? Restaurant with zero guests?

What a way she a walk like she come here before

I think to ask her but before I can, I hear the sound of… Is that a harp playing???

Fancy restaurant

It takes me a moment to realize the song playing is Adele's - Make You Feel My Love. I pause to ensure my ears are working. Trisse continues walking to push the huge double doors open. They open to the back lawns of the property and…

I–

I can't move…

Both doors stay open and my mother walks towards me, handing me a white rose.

"Hi mi baby! You're okay… Walk with me," her words bring me back to reality.

My breathing picks up and I'm suddenly able to move my legs. We move down the path as the sweet sounds of the harp continue playing.

Mi hearrrrttttt

Everybody I know is here, lined up with white roses for me to… collect???

Jesus, we ago cry?

Sue hands me the second rose… followed by Mariah, then Paul.

My hands shakily collect them from each person…

Lorelle, Ramone, Keif, Paw, Kelly, Joshua, Ryan, Ms.Cherry, Ruse, Snoop, Buckle, my uncle and most of the family from Clarendon.

Nadz??? I hug her a little excitedly, still in shock, but excited to see her. Now me know why she never did a answer!

Kirk?!!! Oh my God nobody nuh missing haha!

I love this.

I continue down the path, to see… Michelle and Liam. This is where I can't hold my tears back. I move to Michelle and we hug, rocking each other without saying words. My hands find her tummy in the process, and I whisper a prayer thanking God for keeping her safe enough to be here.

I feel somebody pulling me away and I turn to look...

Troopa?!

It's been a week since he's been up. He looks very, very slim, weak and still a bit pale, but was still able to be here.

My tears start flowing again as I hug him tightly.

"Alright Ry' mind the crutch turn ova with me and you," he laughs lightly, and I do too through the sobbing.

This is too much. I– I don't have the words.

I make my way to the entrance of a rose made path, filled with... I'm not sure how many white roses. Reallll white roses. At the end of the aisle, are candles on a platform overlooking the city and the sunset.

The sunset

Jordanne...

Jordanne is standing at the end of it all... waiting for me to make it to him.

I begin my walk down, holding all the roses I've collected close to my heart. I shakily make it down the rose aisle and he takes my hand, helping me to the platform, before planting a soft kiss on my forehead.

I know what's about to happen but it's like I'm still dreaming!

The harp stops playing and he moves with me to the center of the platform. My eyes begin to water again...

These pictures are going to be soooo ugly!

I watch through my blurry eyes as J' gets on one knee...

Fada God

JJ brings him a case, bigger than what a ring case should be before running back down to Sue.

He looks up at me and smiles...

"Hi..." he starts.

My words fail me but I'm sure my eyes have answered.

"I'm not a man of many words, but I've never once failed to find them when it comes to expressing my feelings to you..."

Me feel faintish...

Keep it together!

"... Spoke my first words to you almost eight years ago and since then, all yuh do a stress mi out bredda."

I laugh out, but my tears are still flowing.

"... For each day I've known you, a rose is present here today. On your birthday years ago, I told you that one of these days I'd make you my wife... I never say what I don't mean."

Deven sing it!

I giggle, not knowing what else to do.

"... So without making this speech too long and boring," I watch him open the case, revealing three different rings.

All the same cut...

Same clarity...

Same size... but different precious metals.

"Ryleigh Stacia Stevens, you're already my wife, have always been, but will you please make it official???"

I stand there for like three seconds just taking it all in...

A random bird moves across the setting above us and that's what pulls me back.

Meeting his sincere eyes, I whisper the word, "Yes," while bringing him up from his knees.

I pick the ring I like and he slides it onto my ring finger. The entire lawn erupts in cheer and in this moment all I can feel is bliss.

I'm a fiancé? Fiancé!!!

"They're all yours. We did our best narrowing it down but we couldn't pick between rose gold, silver or just gold."

My mannnnn, my mannnnn.

Words still fail me and all I can think of doing, is kissing him.

I grab his head, while tipping up to plant a kiss on his lips. He deepens it and we stay like this for what seems like forever before I notice the harp playing again while everybody is surrounding us.

"Dat is itttttttt Drip!" Slyme's voice pulls us to reality.

"Drip almightyyyy!!!" Paw shouts, walking over to us.

His friends surround him and my friends surround me.

"Yeah gyal blind mi!!!" Mariah squeals.

"It's so youuuu! Cute, simple cut, but still enough to show status! Love it!" Kelly adds and I hug her.

I embrace everybody before walking over to T'.

"You coulda just say supm enuh!" I laugh bringing her into a hug.

"Seet clear a mi yuh want Danne murda," she laughs back, shoving my shoulder and we fall into easy banter.

Minutes pass while everybody is catching up and mingling. We stand there talking for a while and eating the finger food being offered by the waiters, before J' comes and sweeps me away.

"Love, we have to leave."

So quick? I look at him but decide not to protest.

After saying all my goodbyes, I hug my mom and Junior before entering the Taycan. The shadow guards line up like they normally do, and we drive off to wherever or whatever else he has planned.

• • •

JORDANNE

"Jorddddaaaaannneee!!!" she screams.

I smile before slapping her ass. Pussy yah just nah change killa.

I hold her waist steady, forcing her to keep still while I slam upward inside her.

"J, I'm gonna–"

Cum, yeah I know. I can feel her walls convulsing. Listening to what she's saying, I bring her down into a kiss, while slowing my strokes. My left hand finds her ass cheeks while she's busy moaning into my mouth.

Fuckkkk... Love dah girl yah 'till me fool killa.

"Mhmhm," she moans into my mouth again, but I won't allow her to break the kiss.

Her fingers find mine, interlocking before we squeeze them. Almost certain we did this exact thing before, and I don't know how she no breed.

The tightening of her walls around my dick starts to suck the orgasm out of me.

Second one for the night

The feeling forces me to break the kiss and she looks directly into my eyes before smiling. Jah Jah.

I feel my toes curl up, trying to ground my spirit into my body.

Siiiiclawt yo

A second or two flashes by before I realize that she's now cumming on my dick. The gooey feel slipping along my length confirms it and that's enough to bring me over the edge.

"Fuckkkkk!!!" the words leave my lips instead of staying in my mind.

My chest rises and falls as I come down from my high, with her sprawled out atop me. Instead of getting up, I let her stay like this for a few minutes. She seems tired– been tired all week, since I've been back actually.

• • •

I watch how happy she is. How much she loves the ring. How much she loved the proposal...

A tiny smile creeps up on my lips.

While she's busy taking a million videos of her new piece of jewelry, I start to think maybe our journey was meant to be. The way she fought against her feelings for years, di way we couldn't get it right. Every single thing that happened, prepared us for this moment. She's probably the only person that understood me back than and still does now.

Love her more than life itself

"C'mere," the words leave my lips before I can stop them.

She tries to say something, but I ignore it. She know weh mi want.

I bring her atop me, before slapping her ass.

Fiancé, wife. I could get used to that being official.

"Stop nuh J'. Which nickname you have fimi?" she snaps her head up to look at me.

I laugh out immediately!

"Which nickname Ry?" I ask back, feigning ignorance.

"Duh try deny it. Me get it from good source. What is it???" she stares at me and I know she won't give up... so me might as well just tell her...

I chuckle before saying, "ICE..."

"What???" she looks confused.

I laugh out again.

"Jorda–" she tries.

"Mi alone know why me call you that still," I offer.

"Why?"

"Just the way the pussy only melt fimi," and almost immediately we get caught in a laughing fit.

"Murdaaa! Yuh know you nuh sensible?" she cackles out.

"That was in high school though. In recent years you've grown into the name, in a different type ah way... doing and accepting my lifestyle like it's normal..." I trail off while watching her stare at me– eyes filled with love and admiration.

"And if you wake up and wah be a clown tomorrow, I would live that lifestyle with you," she giggles.

 "Yah mi likkle clown already though," I barely get out through the choking laughter.

She hisses, "Mine me dissss yuh."

I look up to realize she's serious. Her mood swings have been crazy lately.

"You switch moods like yah breed enuh," I jokingly mutter.

She looks at me as if holding something back. I stare at her, just trying to read her mind.

"Ry?..."

• • •

A SHIFT TO THE VERY FAR FUTURE

MR.SHEER

"So did you guys get married?!"

I look to see if Ryleigh's back to help me tell dem rugrat yah the rest of the story, of how she got her name– the *birds and the bees* version of it of course. Any weekend dem deh yah, we tell dem a piece… and more while whoever stop by fi me or Ry, get fi drop in fi dem side ah things too.

"Ask you grandmother when she come back from the kitchen nuh."

"We wanna knowwww."

I bring my ring finger up involuntarily, rubbing against the tattoo. Hmmph, aye sahh.

"Who wants pudding?!" Ry's voice comes around the corner and onto the back porch with us.

The kids all jump up at once. *"Me!"*

"Mee!"

"Mi."

"Meeee!"

Jah know? The noise killa, the noise man.

"One at a time," she says softly as they bomb rush her for the slices of pudding.

She clears the tray and takes a seat beside me, resting her head on my shoulders.

"Them wah know if we got married, as if we anuh them grandparents," I chuckle.

She giggles, that sweet giggle that she's had all her life.

"Next week we'll bring them on another rollercoaster," she whispers, and I watch as she too rubs at the small tattoo behind her ring finger.

A moment of silence passes before she breaks it.

"I can't believe that's how we were back then…" she trails off before meeting my eyes.

I do nothing but hold her stare.

"We were in love weren't we? Just two kids, dangerously in love," her words tug on every string in my heart.

I bring my hand up to her cheeks, before placing a kiss on her forehead. I couldn't have done life with anybody else. Love her more than my own life itself.

No joke.

We sit for another hour, watching the children play, as I give her comfort in my hold. Our story should be written, don't you think?

Unuh woulda give the people dem headache

True dat, I chuckle to myself, before bringing my cigar to my mouth.

•END•

BONUS | Pre-Natal

SHIFT BACK TO THE PRESENT
(Night of Engagement)

RYLEIGH

"You made me that way though," I whisper, still using my thumb to rub at the band of my ring.

He looks at me holding agreement in his eyes, before he looks back at the counter.

"It's only been like thirty seconds, relax," my words leave my mouth in a nervous giggle.

J' looks back at me, before pulling me into his arms.

"Tell yuh fi be selfish, not to me, to everybody else bad head," he breathes.

Squinting in confusion, I push back to look at his face before saying, "Sir, yuh tell me fi do weh me want, leff di boy and go see what it's like. Clear as day yuh said… yOU PUt EvERybODy AbOVe YOUrseLF, yOu NEeD fI bE sELfIsH."

A chuckle leaves his lips, followed by hearty laughter.

"Ry' if me did know the advice woulda affect me, you wouldn't get a word from the killa."

Mmmcht, selfish.

"Yah supm else," I mutter before glimpsing at the counter.

A moment of silence fills the room before we're both looking at the counter impatiently.

Nerves must kill me tonight

Right, because why me all feel like me ago have diarrhea.

Are we ready?

With him? I was ready at 17...

"Ready?" Jordanne asks, now stroking my hair while searching my eyes.

I release a heavy sigh, step back from his arms and walk to the counter.

He follows.

We waited tooooo long to check

I was waiting for him... I want to do everything with him, from this point right up until I–

My thoughts are cut off by him flipping them over.

"Yuh so impatient Jordanne?!" I shriek, swatting his hands away from the first stick.

He smiles, holding his hands up in mock surrender, with a smirk on his face that denotes nothing but pride.

"Do yuh ting," he says between small chuckles.

Moving to the first pregnancy test, I flip it over to see a **||**.

I have never seen thicker lines in my life... That mean me far along or a the same thing? The second stick shows the same **||** while the third shows a **+**.

I look to J' who is now biting back laughter. What the fuck funny in a time like this?

My breathing picks up and I flip the fourth stick.

PREGNANT.

Fada God.

"Yuh need fi see more Ry?" Jordanne's words fall on deaf ears, because I'm already flipping the last stick.

PREGNANT.

Me mada, I really am pregnant...

I–

Wait, maybe I need to take one more but that would be an odd number... and I don't like the odd numbers. So I need two more, but I don't like the shape of the number 8, it gives BBL... So I need four more and I–

"Love?" Jordanne's voice breaks my mini panic attack. I feel his arms lift me to the countertop before his hands find my chin, bringing my face to meet his stare.

My eyes start to get foggy from the sudden whirlwind of emotions. Maybe mi no ready? What if I lose this one too? And if I'm not a good mother?

Then watch how me breed fi gunman. God if you nuh bu–

Wait how far along am I??? When last me see period and dem ting deh?

"Ryleigh," his voice breaks my inner monologue again, before I feel him wiping my tears.

"What happens if I lose this one too?" the cold words leave my lips before I can stop them.

I watch as his face softens even more than it already has. His eyes move from pure pride and concern to a protective glare.

"Nah happen Love. Yuh affi stop blame yourself fi dat. Certain things just can't happen before them time and back then, was just not the right time," he breathes, now holding my face between his palms.

"And how do we know now is?" I ask, blinking back fresh tears.

He sighs, using his thumb to wipe the ones that have flown loose.

"Can just feel it," is all he says before showering me with a million tiny kisses.

I–

I start to giggle.

"Mi and me friend dem breed out eeh," again, an unfiltered set of words leave my mouth.

He doesn't seem to hear, or care.

Well thank God, because unuh know me cyaa keep no secret with him less than six feet away from me.

"Unuh breed out fi real mon," he laughs, before lifting me, bridal style.

I'm still on the high from my fresh engagement. I can't say I've ever been happier... ever. Affi share the moment with somebody. We get to the bed and he lays me down gentlyyyyy.

Yeah it start.

"Why yah treat me like phone without the case?" I ask, genuinely.

His eyes fall into a squint, "Not a finger yuh nah lift fi nine months. Call di boss boy from now," and I watch as his lips curl up into a smirk.

Him dream come true

"Jordanne, don't start becau–"

"Nuh argument nuh inna it," he blocks my protest.

I hiss, deciding to ignore him and use my efforts to call Toni. Mi and him knowww mi nah listen that– 'bout no finger nah lift.

She picks up on the very first ring.

"Sista-in-REAL LAW," she laughs out sounding tipsy.

"I technically shouldn't tell anybody until after 12 weeks or at least my first visit but,"

"Woahhh wait deh?" she lets out causing me to almost cackle. "That sound melon like enuh Ryleigh," she picks up.

Melon yes.

"The 'coco' type of melon yes," are the last words I say before we fall off into deep chatting.

The man really set two trap and the two a dem ketch me.

Three even, because that dick is a trap in and of itself.

•••

MUUCH

I sit, observing the view and appreciating the natural brush of the wind. Everybody else is drinking and having a nice time.

People dem engage and gone and nobody no ready fi go home, except me. I'm still so sleepy and weak. Bringing the tiny plate of mixed fruit to my lap, I look over at Toni, who has promised to take me home once she's sobered up... but she's been on the phone for the past 15 or so minutes.

"Yuh good?" Liam's voice breaks my desperate stare.

Ughhh, not now.

I don't answer, instead I take the time to put a piece of mango in my mouth. The sound of him sighing pulls my attention and I feel when he moves closer.

"Michelle, how many times can I say I'm sorry?" he takes a seat on the chair in front of me.

If a never one thing me cut the sling and mek him hand drop enuh. Unfortunately, that one thing is love and it ah prevent me from 'crashing out'.

"Mi accept yuh apology Liam. The access to me however affi limited."

"Why?" he asks almost immediately.

Sour locs boy yah essi man. Wah him mean by why?

"Slyme, yuh no think you put me through enough?"

He pulls back for a second as if searching for an appropriate response.

"Michelle... I don't have an excuse, mi nahv no explanation, no form of made up justification. I was simply stupid and wrong. I'm sorry. I want you, I've only ever wanted you, from the boss 'send-off' party, until this day. I–"

"Is it bad that I would prefer some form of explanation?" I ask him, finally meeting his gaze. "Mi happy say yah take accountability and so on but, I need to know why, otherwise to me, you just got up and decided to cheat... What is it about her?"

"Mi know you love dark skin, thick women, but what else was it? Why you bring her ina we bed? Every time mi think 'bout it me feel nauseous. It just nah add up Liam and you can't blame me for taking this time for myself," I trail off.

He stays silent, eyes dancing left and right.

Yeah I can be cordial but me nuh know if me can take him back... and just look how him almost go kill himself last week? Just careless overall.

"Michelle," he closes his eyes before releasing a heavy sigh, "what I did was disrespectful and careless. Being who I am sometimes a just the ego, other times a just 'cause me think me a settle too early–"

"Weh yuh me–"

"Mek mi finish Michelle," he breathes, and I stay silent. "Last week when my life was up for grabs, the only person I wanted to see was you. Only person mi did wah mek sure govan, was you and our child. Gimmi a chance fi just be the man I know I can be for you and the baby... Mi nah force yuh into anything right now. Take as much time as you want but know mi ago deh yah a wait. Mi no wah be no co-parent, I want a real family like the one I didn't get to experience as a child. Promise yuh the ball will never drop again. You're really the only girl mi ever love more than myself, more than anything else..."

After two years of trying to get him to express how exactly him feel 'bout me in words? Wow. Nuh get mi wrong, him always show it but to put it in words... and sound genuine? Wait, why me feel like mah let him off too easy if me accept this?

Do what makes youuuu happy. Nuttin else no matter

I don't know.

"I don't know Liam," I mutter.

"Jah Jah," he exhales.

We stare at each other for short of a minute before Toni-Anne intervenes.

"Sorry, but me ready," she whispers, causing us both to look at her, "that's if you still a come with me?" she adds.

Liam looks at me pleading with his eyes, no doubt hoping for me to tell her no.

I...

... don't know.

"Yeah, mek we leave, mi tired," I mumble, before standing.

He stands to help me up and I accept the gesture. Me really love the man enuh, I just can't handle another round ah heartbreak. Duh know if I would survive it. Either me ago kill him and go jail or simply slice off him hood.

I'm being honest.

Toni and I walk towards the pathway to leave, and I can feel him staring at me. Before I take the step that will allow me to disappear, I turn to look back at him. His eyes are still on me, holding nothing but regret.

Sigh...

I bring my focus back to leaving, allowing myself not to feel guilty about my choice. If we're to come back together we will, but for now, I don't want to force it. The wound is still fresh to me– almost as if I'm stuck in the past.

So mi need more time, I just do.

Epilogue| Pre-Nuptials

<u>June 17th</u>
(Same Year)

RYLEIGH

"Yuh feel better?" I look down at my phone while curling my hair. Michelle is four weeks postpartum and with the C-section she had, recovery has been... weird? Sometime shi good and other times it's hard. She's been home with Liam and her mother since she left the hospital. Marley decided to make his entrance a week and a half before his due date, so they've been staying wi–

"Me good. Still can't come tonight though," she basically whispers in a tone holding regret.

Cocomelon woes

Then nuh me that come January...

"That good. Still can't believe T' got everything together in less than **two months**. The lady a just the best event planner out right now."

"Yuh fi watch her enuh, 'cause you know your simple and hers different," Michelle laughs out.

I join her in the fit, now wrapping the curling iron around the last clump of hair. Marley's loud cry breaks through my phone's speakers and Michelle picks him up in one swift move.

"Girl me affi go change him, ago link you back later 'cause me a deh-deh pon FaceTime," she giggles.

"Yeah girl mek me charge up me phone, me a carry yuh pon it. Send the cute picture," I giggle lowly.

"Yuh nuh forget nuttin?" she laughs.

"No send the picture Muuch, yuh just vex 'cause mi nice, clean nephew take him daddy entire face and complexion," my words fall out in a snort.

"Damn right, after me nearly dead a bake him–"

"Yuh did hate Slyme too much, that couldn't skip you," my statement jolts us both into laughter.

"Weh yuh say? Come offa me phone, me just send it. Lata," she breathes, moving away from the phone before hanging up.

The picture comes to my phone and I pull it up.

Marley is in Liam's arms, staring at both their reflections in the mirror. Him look like Muuch to me, minus his complexion. The gyal just paranoid. I start spinning the phone to angle it where I can see the 'super twin' resemblance she a mad out 'bout.

Nuh know, it look like a good mix to me.

Exhaling I take a final look at my hair and makeup. Cannot wait for the bachelorette shenanigans or "bridal shower" as weh J' want me call it.

Boss say wi neva did a no bACheloREtte

See now my thoughts have become Jordanne's repetitive words. Di way the boy down me neck fi the past couple weeks.

Jesus, I cannot breathe… but I love it. Love it bad and woulda mad if the treatment changed.

I lay the last curl down my back before picking up my phone to text the 'headmistress' of all things "Sheer Wedding".

Ready, finally.

<u>Sexy Bitch:</u> Finally! Omw, less than five so mek sure yuh nah lie.

Me say mi readyyy. Lmao cho.

Clicking out of the chat, I stand, deciding to walk out of my closet, out the room and downstairs where I know J' is. Before I can make it down the stairs, his aura wraps itself around me.

Intimidating, yet protective and fun loving.

Can't explain his presence to you. It's all consuming in a good way.

"You're showing," his words bring me from my thoughts.

I'm not.

"I'm not, yah imagine," I scoff before smiling.

No because him swear mah show from the morning after the tests. Bwoy yah a supm else.

"If me say it enough, it ago happen though. That's why you fat up now, every day mi sing pon it. Manifestation the youngin' dem a call it now."

"Jordanne, I'll show regardless so you nah manifest a ting."

He cackles, before pulling me into his arms.

A kiss finds my forehead before he whispers, "I love you… Duh mek me affi kill nobody tonight, please."

I–

"Ago just be us J'… until we merge with you guys I think."

"Good," is all he gets to say before T' is honking.

Madda miserable reach.

Soon as the words leave my mind, my phone starts going off and of course it's her.

Refusing to release me, Jordanne tightens the hug, running his hands down from the hollow of my back to just below my ass cheek… lingering long enough to squeeze it before sending his tongue circling around my mouth.

Wettttt… instantly

We made a stupid promise to not have sex for the two weeks leading up to our wedding day. Worse ting me ever come up wid.

"Mhm," I moan into his mouth, while slightly pulling away. If me follow him none a we nuh go noweh, believe dat.

He pulls away breathless, peering down at me.

Lust, love? Whatever it is that his eyes hold is raw, sending my clit into chaos.

Bwoiii me sorry fi dah baby yah. Ago can swim well-well good the way we might water him/her

I giggle at my own thought, breaking the intensity.

"Whatever you say to yourself just now, don't repeat it to me."

"Why not?" I ask smiling.

"Bay fuckry yuh chat from yuh breed, no joke." he chuckles.

"Whatever," I wave him off, now walking towards the door. "I'll see you when we merge."

"Might see me before that," he mumbles but I ignore it.

Pussy will be the death of Sue's son, fi sure

● ● ●

"I looooved it!!" I say hugging Toni-Anne.

The bridal shower part of the night has come to an end and I've decided to show her gratitude.

Decor? Perfect.

Food? Immaculate.

Giftsssssssss??? Oh God man, mi love mi gyal dem bad to bad. From Van Cleef necklaces to Cartier bracelets right back to things as simple as clearing my Amazon cart.

Love it here!

Bad bad.

"Them a come yah so or we a meet dem?" Mariah asks, directing her question to T'.

"Them outside already," Toni answers before pushing the door open, leading us out to the hotel's lobby.

While ambling out the lobby, dreaming of taking the heels off my feet, I spot the group of men waiting for us in the parking lot. My eyes dance to Jordanne who is now leaning on an unfamiliar AMG. He notices me and drops his spliff before rubbing it into the asphalt while fanning away the smoke.

I smile, at how overly caring he is. I cyaa tell when last him smoke 'round mi or has allowed anyone else to. My lips start to curl up into a smile as I move closer to him. When I get there, he spins me around allowing my back to face him before pulling me in and finding my ear.

"Ting go?" he asks, now bringing his hands to rub my tummy.

"Good, got a lot of gifts," my smile widens while I wave my wrist around to show the Van Cleef bracelet.

He chuckles before whispering in my ear, "Baby gift dem deh Love."

"Excuse, anuh everybody 'meech' out to your level. Some a we just 'mee' and still a wait pon the 'ch' fi drop on,"

He laughs out and I mean really laugh.

"Tell yuh fi stop chat fuckry bredda," he manages to blurt out. "C'mere."

I watch him reach into his pocket, retrieving a key, before waving it above my head.

Afta him no like drive wid me?

"Yuh want me to drive? Not 'cause me cyaa drink unuh ago turn mi in the designated driver allll the ti–"

Before I can finish my statement, he cups my mouth, forcing me to fall silent.

"Your car babe," is all he says.

My eyes fly open and he removes his hand from my mouth.

"Jordanne I–" my words fail me and I watch him cock his head to the side while smiling.

Him cyaa serious.

Not knowing what to do, I take the key from him while turning to look over to the group. These days as long as he's here, I forget everybody else.

All consuming

"Good pussss!!!" Mariah shouts from the front of Ruse's Audi.

Only she hahah!

I wave the keys in the air when I notice everybody's been watching.

J' grabs it from my hands while I attempt to move to the driver's side.

"Still a drive," he says.

"Jordanne, a breed mah breed enuh, mi nuh disabled," I protest.

He ignores me while hopping into the car.

Crazy. Him coulda cock me up all ova the house and the yard but I can't drive myself places now? Humph.

I get into the car and start huffing. My mood swings have gotten rampant, and I can feel one coming on.

"Aye, don't start, just couldn't live with myself if anything do you when I could've just done it for you myself," he explains.

His little explanation simmers my brewing rage, replacing it with appreciation.

And horniness

The hormones are wwwwicked. How come me couldn't be one ah the pregnant girl dem weh lose dem sex drive? Mine trippled!

• • •

Moments later, we're all at the private lounge having the time of our lives. Of course tonight it's just us– the bridesmaids and groomsmen along with a few other close friends of us both.

"Bredda mi have church a morning before the wedding. Why unuh think a joke?" Paw shouts to Ramone above the music.

"Because everything yuh take fi joke bredda!" Ramone responds while cackling.

"A serious ting! Mahfi liff, yuh wah the girl put we pon fasting fi two weeks if me miss early service? Watch it mek mi tell the boss," he shoves Ramone to the side while making his way to J' who's now seated just behind me.

I stop listening to them and start vibing to the music. Lorelle joins me and we start going back and forth with the lyrics like we usually do.

"Me touch it!" Toni jumps in, bringing the bottle of champagne to her lips.

"Cuz fuck it!" Mariah adds, giggling wayyyy toooo much.

"And mi think all Pryce him fuck it!" Kelly jumps in, surprising us all.

Weh she stay know Alkaline lyrics?

"Toni bruk yuh out!!!" Keif laughs out at Kelly's actions, while bringing the bottle to Mariah's lips but she finds a way to turn it down neatly.

Her eyes find mine and I offer her a small encouraging smile.

We party for another 30 minutes before I start feeling weary. Taking a seat beside my man, I lay my head on his shoulders. He shifts me up and onto his lap, before his hands find my tummy– the usual these days.

I feel when his breath hit my ear, singing the lyrics to the current Alkaline.

"Why you woulda wah stay away? When you know say nobody no fuck you like me?" he sings in one breath while his hand finds its way below my dress.

Ummm...

My breathing picks up and I can feel the hairs on the back of my neck stand at attention. He kisses the side of my neck before continuing...

"Me ah yuh landlord and mi possessive a mi property," his other hand finds my neck and... mi deven know.

His voice...

His touch...

His smelllll...

Mi ready

Now, now too.

Unable to fight the feeling anymore, I lull my head back and whisper to him, "Ready fi leave."

Whole night me avoid him, only fi come get some rest and just like that, I'm ready for him to do whatever he wants to me. I feel him smile against my ear before lifting me to stand and before I know it, we're on our way out– without me having a chance to tell the girls bye.

• • •

We pull in, park, and within seconds we're already inside the house. Following his lead, we move from the foyer to the back porch.

The sound of the calm night, slow winds and simple insects are now clashing with the sounds of our heavy breathing, lip smacking and tiny tumbles over the porch furniture while we strip each other.

Jordanne's hand rakes its way through my hair before he tightens his grip, forcing me to look up at him. The night wind brushes my nipples, causing them to stand firm between us.

He holds our stare, eyes dancing slightly in the moonlight... As usual, before I can filter my thoughts in his presence, my words leak.

"I don't want you to make love to me," the chosen words shock even me.

His eyes form squints of confusion before he asks, "Don't?"

Yes don't. I want him to fu–

"Yes, I want you to fuck me... with your mind closed to anything else."

Want him fuck me as Drip

Right, but how do I explain to him that I think he has a split personality without ruining the moment.

"I love you. Cyaa fuck you without the love," he breathes and I look down between us at his dick pokes into my belly button.

The curve...

The length...

The girth...

The veins...

The smooth pink head, dripping pre-cum. My hand reaches out to stroke it, before my thumb starts circling the fluid around the tip. While doing this, I start thinking to myself... he slips in and out of fucking me as Drip from time to time, but it's never from start to finish. Somewhere along the ride we always end up making love.

That one time before him leff we though

Let's not talk about that...

"Cyaa do it Ry," his words slide out mixed with moans while he further tightens the grip he has on my hair.

"It's what I want... tonight," I whisper, gathering as much emotions in my eyes for him to see that it'll make me happy.

"Yah supm else," are his last words before he chuckles, lifting me in one swift motion.

While wrapping my legs around him, I notice we're moving to the lawns.

Outside?!

Well we own the lots to the left and right, who ago see?

"If mi lose meself," he starts.

"You won't," I cut him off.

Five more steps and I'm being lowered against the pool's bar. The pool itself has been covered for the night so I know that's not his plan. He looks at me for a few seconds before bringing his hands to my face to sweep the hair behind my ears.

Can see say him a fight the decision. I guess he's worried about our seed... but it'll survive.

His thumb pries my mouth open before he slips it inside, pulling down on my lip.

"No words," he mumbles.

Okay.

"No fighting."

Okay.

"No control, on your part."

Now, I don't know about that.

He seems to realize my concern, "Control belongs to me Ry."

I–

Okay...

I nod, signaling my agreement. His lips curl up in a sinister smirk and I'm almost sure his eyes have changed shape and colour.

"Knees," his command comes out serious.

Nahfi tell mi twice.

I fall to my knees at the command. His thumb doesn't leave my mouth and him having it there is causing saliva to gather and–

My thoughts are chopped by him using his free hand to twirl my hair into a tight wrap around his palm.

Hmm

I take a very deep breath just before he slides his thumb from my mouth, replacing it with his hard length. It goes straight to the back of my throat and I breathe deeper to try to take it all in.

Mission failed…

He pulls it all the way out in a swift motion before staring down at me. I look up at him with slight confusion.

"Everything," he words, almost inaudible.

Yuh know me shoulda leave di man alone. My throat only deep when mi vex enuh

Without giving me time to catch another breath, he re-enters my mouth. This time forcing it ALL in, causing me to choke a little–

We choked alottt

Whatever, mi choke… and this seems to make him happy. Realizing that he's pleased, I relax into the moment and allow him to fuck my face, keeping my eyes locked with his. As he thrusts in and out of my mouth– moaning and grunting, my eyes begin to spring water, but not as much as the pool forming between my legs.

My pussy is aching!

He pulls out completely and uses his dick to slap me on my cheeks.

Above my nose…

My forehead…

Just everywhere on my face…

The actions excite me and my hands involuntarily move out to touch him.

"Keep them at your side," he groans almost immediately.

Anything di boy say a it me a work wid

They fall back to my side on command before he re-enters my mouth. He starts off slow and deep, landing way beyond the start of my tongue each time, before he starts giving me short thrusts, only allowing himself in partly.

"Fuccckkk," he moans.

The moan has triggered something in me. Supm weh mek mi wah take control but, I can't. His breathing picks up and his hands tighten even more in my hair.

He mumbles a group of words that I can't recognize before he forces himself out, releasing my hair and stepping back. I lick my lips and use my tongue to push at my cheeks, trying to rid them of the sudden tiredness.

"Up," he orders, with a raspy voice, motioning for me to stand against the marble countertop.

I do, and he lifts me, laying me on the cold surface, before sending my legs in the opposite direction of each other. The chill from the night brushes against my clit and sends electricity up my spine– forcing me into an arch.

I feel when his finger finds my nerve ball, granting it pleasure.

Feel like me ago cum already

All the juices that came rushing down my pussy, from him slamming into my mouth earlier, are being used as lubricant… and it's going to killlllll me.

"Mhmmhm," a moan escapes my lips and my eyes shoot up at him. Not sure if moans are allowed… I–

My thoughts are cut by him forcing himself inside me.

Jeeeeeeeeeeeeeeeeeezzzzz

My pussy welcomes her oldest friend, gripping it with love, need and greed. I can feel how much my walls are sucking him in while he–

"Jordannnnne!!!"

"No words."

But–

I–

I take a deep breath and start fighting back the urge to scream his name as he lifts my feet onto his shoulders. Di man nah leave an inchhhh of thrust behind. Every entry has every inch.

Every…

Single…

Inch…

"Jor–" I bite back my words, reeling away beneath him.

Deciding to focus on something else, I look to the heavens. Mi affi start count the stars if me ago keep my mouth shut. His hands find the hollow behind my knees, bending my legs back and towards me, before he pulls… almosstttt out– leaving the tip in.

His eyes find mine, and I watch as a sinister smirk creeps onto his face before he starts to sink it again. I know he finds it amusing– the way I'm fighting not being able to speak.

When he sinks it and I grab for the sheets that aren't there, he chuckles.

He then releases my legs, pulls out fully this time and uses his dick to beat my clit. My chest rises so high, so quickly, I mistake it for near death.

Before you know it, he's grabbing me by my neck, pulling me up to meet his eyes. We stare at each other for less than a second before he scoops me up and to my feet, turning me around, before shoving my head down against the cold surface.

Repetitive slaps find my ass and I don't know if me can hold a next scream to pussy-clawt.

Just as I thought, the moment he re-enters me, is the very moment I'm screaming. I feel my hair grabbed and my body yanked up against his chest.

"Nah be obedient?" is his question.

I don't answer...

He forces my head all the way up, back and over to look at him– inverted.

"Be a good girl," and with that his strokes pick up again.

This time they're single handedly taking me to God himself.

Mercyyyy!

I– can't

I can't, mi cyaa–

Bumboclawt.

Unable to keep my thoughts and feelings in check, my orgasm springs free. Instead of my usual screams following it like they always do... pleasure filled tears follow.

My breathing is heavy, rapid and uneven.

"Good girl," the sound of his raw words are enough to add even more pleasure to my high.

Praise kink

Mhmmm.

Mere seconds later, I'm being lifted to hover above his dick. My arms are wrapped tightly around his neck and my legs are cooped up into his arms. Less than a millisecond later I'm being pulled down onto his length.

Sigh.

I don't know another feeling better than this. The way he fills me up every single time, hitting the right spots every single time, being one with my pussy and mind, every single time.

I just love it.

Now filled with his thick shaft, I tighten the hold I have around his neck and he uses that as a signal to start going in and out... Root, to tip.

Slowly first...

... then the pace picks up. He finds his rhythm and keeps it for some time. Time weh mi cyaa count 'cause I barely know what the fuck is going on right now. A feeling shoots through my body causing me to lull my head back while my eyes find the stars.

A whimper leaves my lips but he doesn't seem to care.

His pace has become uneven, and the slamming between his body and mine have increased in volume.

Suddenly I'm being lowered to my feet. I watch as he strokes his dick and I already know what to do. Falling to my knees, with my hands at my sides, I wait for him to release in my mouth...

... but he doesn't...

Tonight… on this night… the night before our wedding… he paints my face off-white. The warm feeling mixed with his low groans hands me a sense of satisfaction I've never felt before.

EVER.

I mean–

Pheew! No sah. Yah tell me say I have a degradation kink too?

I slowly pry my eyes open to look up at him.

Holding his hand out, he helps me up to my feet before saying… "You're prettier with our kids on your face," while smiling down at me.

Hahah! You knowww whatttt

I smile back, not knowing if I'm permitted to talk or not.

"Fuck done Ry, you can talk," he laughs out as if reading my mind.

"Mi tired," is all that leaves my lips.

"Yeah? Lowest flame of me fucking without love that though. I'll show you another level after the baby."

Mi nuh badda want eh. I like my words and my control… and me throat a hurt me.

Do you really?

Sometimes…

"It's 2:17am. We shouldn't even be with each other on our wedding day or the night before," I mumble, now touching at the wet kids all over my face.

He chuckles while leading me into the house and towards the shower.

"Our marriage, our rules," he retorts.

True.

We get to the shower downstairs, and I stand while he wipes the semen from my face with a warm face rag, before he walks off to turn the shower on.

I watch all his movements, admiring even the simplest one.

I can't believe I'm getting married to my best friend, love of my entire life, with a mini 'us' in my womb, only a few hours from now.

Who would've thought?

Right? Who would have.

Epilogue| Nuptials

RYLEIGH

I stir in my sleep to the feel of the AC being too cold and blowing too heavy. The only thing I remember is being laid here to sleep by J.

And then he left early this morning

Yeah, that happened too…

I grab my phone, fearing that I've overslept.

I haven't though, cause the time showing on my phone is 9:45am.

I've never made a better decision than that of choosing a dusk to night wedding. It eliminates the rush and anxiety that comes with recovering from the week of activities prior. Normally the first order of duty is to roll over, kiss Jordanne, make him breakfast and start my day, but today is not a day like that, or even close.

TODAY WE GET MARRIED.

I toggle to T's chat after ordering my thoughts.

<u>Sexy Bitch:</u> Be at the venue for hair and makeup by 1pm. Relle a come get yuh 'cause J say pregnant gyal nuffi drive lol! Your dress and everything else are already here. (Keif say bleach catch her black dress and I need everybody to follow dress code, so me a carry her come raid your closet) Call when you wake, likkle Ms.fuck out. Luv u.

Fuck out yes haha!

I duh like this gyal enuh man ahaha!

Okay, Okay and Okay. Tell you brother

fi nyam me out.

<u>Sexy Bitch</u>: Yuh no tired a dat?!

That's so inappropriate omg, lol! A
yuh family enuh.

<u>Sexy Bitch</u>: Come offa me phone please. I have
Maid-of-Honour duties to tend to thank you.

I giggle at her last statement before rolling out of bed. The first place I end up is in the bathroom. When that routine is done, I head downstairs, to the company of my mother and Suanne lingering in my kitchen.

"Mi pikny!" my mother squeals, walking over to me. "You feel good? Morning sickness? You tired? Yuh hungry? Yuh–"

"Mommy, mi alright. I just came to eat before mi get ready fi leave," I offer her some comfort for her unwarranted worry.

"Okay. Look over the prayer orders… and sista Sherol is asking if her daughter can come along with her."

"Mommy the wedding is private, anybody who nuh deh pon the list come last week, can't be on it again," I respond.

"No but she can take weh him name deh space, Kirk."

Kirk?

"Why Kirk nah come?" I ask, words holding genuine confusion.

"Say him no sure," she answers just before looking at Sue.

I look between them both.

"Not sure is not confirmation, but let T' know, a she responsible fi everything. Me just a make demands and enjoy life," I shrug before moving to the fridge to get to the only thing I can keep down in the mornings.

Raw carrots…

Imagine. Well at least me know the baby wuhh blind like her mother

"You want me to make you something with the carrots?" Sue asks.

I look over to her, watching as she stirs something that seems to be a sauce for later. From what I know, most of the dishes have already been prepped and ready to be cooked– since 3am this morning. Not sure why she's making this sauce here.

"Hope yuh no mind me a use yuh kitchen. Nuh know if you can manage the garlic smell but my kitchen is packed and the industrial kitchen's stove just cut out this morning," she explains.

Aaaw, her worrying about boundaries is kinda sweet

"That's fine, I prefer to eat it raw and I actually like the smell of garlic, a just the cleaning products nah work out fimi," I reassure her.

She smiles and continues to stir.

Deciding to move to the living area, I plop myself down on the couch, chomping on the cold, diced carrots while going through my phone. In an hour or two, I won't be able to look at or reply to anything, so might as well.

After going through my messages and emails, I move to Instagram to rewatch my stories and those of my friends. The first one I click pulls a smile to face. It's a cute video of us, the girls, raising our glasses, but my glass evidently only has water.

Cheesing at the content, I move to something Lorelle tagged me in.

No we gwaan wid we self man. Somebody tell me why Ryan a throw up money and random gang signs.

"Send me this," I type to reply to her. I want all the memories from this weekend.

The next notification I get to is Mariah's– sending in all the videos she took. I click the first one and immediately start to cackle out, on top of my voice– pulling the attention of my mother and Suanne.

I quiet down, before struggling to my feet with one destination on my mind– my bed. My very cozy bed.

• • •

While pulling into the venue, I look at the time before looking at Lorelle.

1:45pm, Toni must kill we but she shoulda say 12. She know we never on time yet... Yes, even for my own wedding. Afta it can't start without me.

Soon as my thought ends, her contact name comes flashing across my phone screen. I look at Lorelle who shakes her head at me before shrugging. I slide to answer the call, knowing I'm about to get it.

"Hello–"

"A yuh a married or me!? Where are you???" she sounds so annoyed.

Murdaa!

"I'm parking baby. I overslept, don't be ma–" before my sentence ends, she hisses and hangs up.

Lorelle comes to a park at the back of the venue and I take a moment to reel it all in. I'm really about to sign away my life.

My phone vibrates and I look at it to see that it's Toni again.

<u>Sexy Bitch:</u> **This simple enough fi you?**
<u>Sexy Bitch:</u> **|attachment|**

> **It issss. Criiiiies.**

<u>Sexy Bitch:</u> **Duh ever open yuh mouth and tell nbdy**
say me no love you. The stressss lol.
<u>Sexy Bitch:</u> **And you said I can do what I want with the**
reception as long as it's black so mi no wah hear "It's too much"

**likkle from this. Bye! I'm going into hair and makeup. Look over
the guest list so you know who RSVPed and who not to
expect from now. I don't want you to have any
surprises cause mi know yuh emotional, so get the
feelings out from before your face start. Thankyouuu!
<u>Sexy Bitch:</u> Oh everybody's in hair/makeup. If you
need us we'll be below your suite.**

**You coulda say alla this on the
call dwl! But I LOVE YOU and
I appreciate it T' muah!**

With that, I exit the vehicle and we make our way to my suite. The atmosphere is busy of course, with more than 20 different workers having already 'zoomed' past Lorelle and I while we make our way inside.

Today is going to be a busy day.

• • •

"I don't want a lot of blush please," I voice my opinion as the makeup artist does another swab.

Me already red

"Trust the process, that's what I thought too," Mariah's voice counters my request.

I have her in my suite before my reveal, to protect her from dodging all the shots I'm sure the girls are taking right now.

"Promise you, I won't have you looking like a clown," the makeup artiste smiles down at me while offering her reassurance.

Mi no know… I duh know much 'bout makeup but I know I hate the super pink blush.

So bad

I offer her a soft smile as she continues to enhance my features.

Before you know it, both my hair and makeup are done and I'm moisturizing my skin while getting ready to put my robe on for the pictures. As I'm rubbing the cream down past my knee, over my leg and to my chalky feet, my phone vibrates. I've been ignoring it all afternoon, but the unfamiliar username catches my eye.

"Me ago tell them say fi come out for the pictures now," Mariah says, grabbing my attention away from the phone.

When she leaves the room, it becomes just me… Me, my thoughts and the message from who I think it is.

I decide to accept the message request, read… and reply.

You're getting married

**? Whoever this is, state ur claim b4
things go left.**

Haha! Easy Leigh.

**Mr. Holmes. Yes I am. What's
It to u?**

**To the man u say me nuffi worry bout lol
Anyways me just fwd fi give u closure. I'm sorry
for trying 2 force u into sex. Sorry fi alla the stress
wid di bun ting. We were young and shouldn't ina no
rship from so early.**

**Just a mek yuh know me happy fi u and I hope yah
mek the right choice.**

**I gave myself closure years ago
but thank u? And I am... Enjoy ur day.**

**1st love just know mi deh yah if u
need me. Hv a great wedding and marriage.**

The words seem genuine but they always do. Ever since that last month of second form, up until lower 6th his words have always seemed 'genuine'… but they never were. Not even once.

Then why the devil send him soldier pon a day like this? Knowing me affi tell J'

And if me tell him it'll ruin his mood and if I don't tell him, he'll ruin my windpipe… and not in the way I like.

"Readddaaayyyyyyy!!!" the girls barge into the suite all dressed up in their green silk pajamas, brandishing faux fur at the wrist and ankles of each set.

"Unuh cuuuute!" I say admiring each of them. "Help mi get the robe on."

T' and Lorelle step forward first, holding each end of the long white robe. My arms find their way into the sleeves and the robe falls beautifully over my green corset lingerie.

"Your appreciation gifts are there," I say, pointing to the couch at the foot of the bed.

Lorelle is the first to move off, "Mi knowwww this ago nice!" she squeals.

I got each of them:

– Dior sandals in their favourite colours for later tonight when our feet are bruised from the heels.

– Customized 'Thank-You' bracelets with my wedding date and their names engraved.

– Body butter, body scrub and their favourite fragrances.

– Shares in their favourite companies.

Picked that up from Jordanne, those dividends at the end of each year add up nicely.

– And finally, a handwritten 'Thank-You' card to each of them, for being with me on this day and all the days leading up to this moment.

The room is now filled with 'oouuhs' and 'aaaws', as they move through the gift bags.

"You really personalized each one? Like the different colours, the different fragrances, the shares, everything," Trisse lets out. "Mi wah move come a Town 'cause my friend dem down so nah cut nuh dash!"

"Mine unuh mek me cut buss out enuh," Muuch giggles.

Her and Trisse's statement brings laughter ringing throughout the suite. Mariah walks over to me and pulls me into a big, tight hug.

"I love you so much Ry," she breathes.

"No cry enuh, 'cause we nah beat the breeding allegations if you do that now," I whisper, holding faint humour in my tone.

She pulls back before smiling at me.

"Photographer deh yah, unuh come, we a take pictures in the other room that's not a mess and then in the garden downstairs before we change and leave," T' starts her orders.

Twenty five minutes later, we're still taking pictures in the room and moving a specific way for videos.

Me a get weary and hungry though

True. Affi eat after this and get a touch up before I get into my gown.

Heavy repetitive knocks come landing on the suite door, causing us all to snap our heads in its direction.

"A Ramone. Unuh decent? Mi need Toni-Anne," he speaks clearly.

T' shrugs unknowingly while making her way to the door. She exits, and all I can hear from them after that is mumbling. Through all this, the photographer has continued taking random videos of me while I look through the balcony doors, holding the champagne glass filled with apple juice.

Every few seconds I bring it to my mouth.

On the last sip, T' swings the door open with her eyes dazed and panic written all over her face.

Wahmp'n now?

She swallows before moving to me, beckoning for everybody to leave us... When they do, she tells me to sit down.

Then a who dead? Mi just talk to mommy so a coul–

"Nobody can find Danne," she trails off.

"Which Danne?!" I ask, blinking in confusion.

She looks at me, holding pity in her eyes.

"Toni-Anne, which Danne?"

"Jordanne Ry'. Ramone nor anybody else has seen him since 'round 2:30 and it's 3:30 now. Him affi get ready before 6 and Ramone say him barber deven line him up yet so we–"

I start to giggle nervously...

Jordanne no wah me deliver a headshot between him eye dem.

"Take it off," I suddenly say, referring to my robe.

She looks at me puzzled.

Like she deaf

"Take it off T', please," I try again, while trying to get myself out of the robe and the lingerie in one go.

"The start time is at 6, we still have two hours to find him."

"Just take it offffffffff," I whisper-shout, and this time she starts to help me.

When she's done, I grab my lounge set, pulling the pants up and dragging the top over my head, careful enough to not ruin my hair or makeup.

Offering her zero explanation, I leave.

I leave the suite, ignoring everybody's questions... and the villa, walking briskly through all the worker and the venue itself, with wondering eyes shooting at me– especially those of the shadow guards.

I beckon to them not to follow, knowing that they'll try.

Fifteen minutes later, I'm in the KFC drive-through, ordering a Zinger combo with some wings and a shitload of corn.

When I get to the window, I pay, collect and speed off.

• • •

JORDANNE

"I'm getting married to her today..." I manage to get out after standing here for the past 30 minutes or so.

"My fear is I won't be able to control everything when it comes to her. You know, like you weren't able to with Mum? And mi nuh want a repeat of what you guys had," I breathe, now feeling more comfortable.

Lighting my spliff, I take the first pull, followed by two more before I speak again.

"Know mi love her, it's not a question of that... but she do supm else to me. I lose my head and my cool around her, and mi nuh know if that good or bad."

"Wish yuh did deh yah fi gimi some advice. Know you see say me fulfill yuh dream wid the team and everything. Now I want to fulfill my dream of having a happy, healthy family... and love life. Neva see dat before."

Apart from wid Skulli and Mum now

Them nuh have the family aspect though.

I stand silent in the mausoleum for another ten minutes before I hear **her** voice.

"Jordanne…"

If nobody else couldn't find me…

A smile presents itself on my face.

Turning to look at her, I drop the spliff, crushing it before she starts walking over.

"KFC?" I ask, looking at the bag in her hands.

"Wings for you, Zinger for me and like a million corn if I can't eat the Zinger," she explains.

I love her…

Moving to take the bag from her hands, I place a kiss on her forehead.

"How yuh reach? Ramone couldn't track your car?" her questions start.

I move her to sit on the iron bench made for family members when they want to have extended visits. The family plot holds my grandfather, his wife… and a few more family members, but my father is the only one who wanted a mausoleum.

Man extra even in death

No joke.

"Taxi," I breathe, offering her an answer.

"Taxi?!" she asks glaring at me, before taking a seat.

"Taxi," I repeat, handing her the Zinger and one of the two bottles of coconut water.

"Hmm… and if I were to ever consider taking a taxi…" she points out.

"Dat different," is all I say before we start eating.

Minutes or maybe a full hour goes by and by now we're laughing… loud, tear filled laughter, while we retrace things from the past. She show mi a one DM the balla boy send her but me can deal wid him later. Today mi just wah mek her happy. All the stupid questions and worry I had earlier have been washed away just by her actions, her presence… her smile.

The killa cyaa get up outa dah love yah, years now

Years…

I chuckle at my own thought.

The sound of angry footsteps stomping towards the grave pulls both our attention– directing both our heads and eyes to the entrance.

Toni…

"Anuh unuh fi a get married?! Listen to bloodclawt mi! Mi nah waste me weeeeeks of work fi unuh deh a cemetery a giggle and nyam KFC! Get up!!!" she screams.

Jah Jah she ago blow a fuse

Ry' leans over to me, before whispering in my ear, "She ago blow a fuse."

I laugh out at how she read my exact thought and it throws both of us into a fit of laughter.

"Ramone tracked Ry's car and me watch unuh in this same spot fi how long bredda! Ah almost 6! Unuh a married or not!?"

"Easy nuh baby sis," I stand to hug her.

The hug lasts for a good few seconds before I pull away.

"We are, mi just come fi talk to daddy and time get weh," with that she huffs and storms out.

I hold Ry's hand and we exit together, moving out to the open cemetery. Ramone is standing out here of course, staring at us while shaking his head.

"Yuh coulda tell mi enuh. Kinda best man yuh think me be?!" he frowns.

"Neva plan fi come Ramone, you know that go already," I counter while dapping him up.

"Dat good. Mek me get yuh back, yahfi line up and get ready before 7:30. Wedding move from starting at dusk to starting afta 7, like Prime Time news," he chuckles.

I look over to Ry' who is about to enter her car with T'. I lift my hand to blow her a kiss, when I realize the tiny bump she has, is definitely showing.

Keep on a tell her she a show but she nah listen.

• • •

KEIF

Kelly, Moya and I are entering the venue since we're not a part of the bridal party. Moya is David's... date? Mi no sure if dem serious masah, but a first me see him with a girl fi more than three weeks straight.

"This is soooo nice! and the fact that the guests are in black while the decor is white!" Kelly beams, looking around.

One thing wid her, she ago act like she no used to nuttin.

"It is," is all I say while taking it all in.

We get to the entrance where I can see the welcome sign. It's painted white wood, swinging from painted white metal.

Welcome to the Wedding of
Jordanne & Ryleigh
#SheerMyHeart

I smile at the hashtag, making a mental note of it for all my posts tomorrow. Looking around I start to observe how much the lights make the decor much more magical since the sun has just ended its shift.

Breath taking...

Toni has free standing chandeliers on the grass, forming somewhat of a canopy above the acrylic aisle. At their base are white roses– Ry's favourite. All the guest chairs are white as well, set against the most clean cut, lush, green lawn. The altar? My gosh the altar has four separate columns, all decorated in white roses from roof to base.

Truly the definition of subtle extravagance.

We move to the next set up before the seats, where the ushers are handing out masks if we should need any, along with insect spray, should there be any mosquitoes looming around for fresh blood… and tiny bottles of sanitizer, should we need to cleanse our hands before feasting later on.

As if alla we nahgo deh bathroom a re-titivate soon

Mi walk right ova to him, mek him spray me dung same way still. No red bump to the girl chocolate skin.

We then move to take our seats, second row, behind the immediate family. On the chairs are gift bags holding tiny battery fans, the program for the night's event order, candles with their names and wedding date atop the cover, engraved glass mugs and … cash.

I laugh out loud when I spot it, knowing a must Drip gift this.

The fan, mugs and candle are definitely Ryleigh's idea, while the USD has to be from lazy Danne.

I'll take it

As everybody opens their bags and realize the content, shock followed by gratitude sweeps the lawn as hushed mumbles.

"This real?!" Moya blurts out, causing a group of eyes to find us.

Lawd Jesus, a next one weh nuh used to nuttin

"Gimi if yuh no believe, mi will believe fi yuh," Kelly counters.

… And her statement makes me laugh. Nobody else but Toni woman.

The saxophonist starts his session, and we all fall quiet for the next three minutes, waiting for what the officiant will have to say.

Seconds later, the music stops and his blabbering starts.

"We all know what we're here for. I want to thank each and every guest for–" I zone out, wishing I had my phone but they were taken on entry, to be returned at cocktail hour.

Moments later the saxophonist picks up another song while Sue and Paul make their way down the aisle, waving and smiling at the guests. We all fall quiet as they take their seats at the very front.

Before I know it, the lawn goes silent again just before the band starts playing the instrumental to Masicka's - Different Type, while the back-up singers chime in with certain 'adlibs' and lines every now and again.

Jordanne…

Jordanne walks out sharp as fuck with the darkest shades I've ever seen, pointing and smiling at everybody. His jacket is a crisp white, while his pants are a clean and deep black. Ferragamo on his feet and as his belt, Audemars Piguet on his wrist.

Sharppppp.

He daps up Ryan who has an aisle seat before he extends his finger to his God son Marley, who is being held by Ms.Cherry. Marley is literally the only baby that was allowed here, only because he's quiet and Muuch is unable to be apart from him.

Mother right outtt

He continues his performance, now dapping up Skulli before planting endless kisses on the back of Sue's palm. The crowd giggles at his antics while he takes his place on the altar. The song picks up and the groomsmen start walking out.

Ramone the best man, followed by Liam, Xavier, Joshua and David… all rocking dark shades and pretty white smiles. Their suits are beige, accented with light green under-shirts and matching pocket squares. Their boutonnières fall just below that and mi affi say, di boy dem clean and nooiiice bad to bad.

"Watch mi mannnnnn," Moya lets out, pointing at David as he blows a kiss to her.

Love really ina the air… time fimi cork me big nose.

After the commotion from their procession, the band switches to a calmer song, while Ramone dabs away light sweat from Jordanne's forehead.

The sound of the piano is clean and I watch as the lead singer takes her place, positioning the mic to her comfort. It takes less than five seconds for me to realize the song is Kina Grannis' version of Can't Help Falling in Love.

Aye mine mi bawl!

The girls start to walk out, while the saxophonist smoothly joins the pianist, just before the silky smooth voice of the lead singer comes in.

"Is that the actual singer?!" Kelly asks.

… And it takes me a few blinks to recognize her, but it is! Mi rass, mi shock! A mi no used to nuttin now haha!

"I think so enuh," I play off my excitement.

"She same one. No sah issa production," Moya adds and we all giggle silently before switching our attention back to the ladies.

Michelle is leading the line, walking as if she wasn't just cut open weeks ago, followed by Lorelle, Mariah, Trisse and finally Toni. They're all in different styles of the same color green dress, except for T'… hers is a lighter green, distinguishing her role. Each dress is floor length, some with slits, some without, some with sleeves and some without.

Mere seconds later, JJ is walking down the aisle holding the flower girl's hand. He too has shades on while holding a briefcase I assume houses the rings. The little girl is Sue's niece, I think from her brother, who is somehow still getting young kids at his age.

They get to the altar and part ways. JJ goes to the guys and the pretty little girl goes to the girls. The officiant signals for us to stand without interrupting the live music. We all get to our feet, waiting for Ry' to make her entrance.

"Shalllll I stayyyy? Would it beeee a sinnn? If I can't help, falling in loooove withhhh youuuu," Kinna sings, effortlessly while Ry' makes her entrance with her mother on her arm…

… And just the sight of it causes my skin to populate with goosebumps.

I take her in. Her hair has perfect Hollywood curls, laying in a side part. Her dress is simple… a heavenly white, thick satin, strapless, A-line, with a long slit between the pleats. The showstopper though is her veil… It's somehow plain but still shimmering silver as the lights catch it in the night. It falls beautifully, covering her face, abdomen and the Calla Lilies that make up her bouquet.

Beautiful

I might cry fi real and nuttin no start yetttt.

She makes her way down the aisle, while her veil is still more than seven feet behind her. I look to Jordanne who now has his shades off, looking as if Ry' is the only person out here with him.

This affi be the first time me see him look nervous… His index finger does not leave his thumb, as they hug to relieve the nerves I assume.

Or fight the tears

Ry' gets to the altar and before she steps up, the officiant asks who hands her away and Ms.Janette responds, leaving her in the hands of J'.

I watch her whisper something to him, and they giggle before he visibly relaxes.

His safe haven fi real

● ● ●

"You may now kiss your bride."

Without hesitation, Jordanne takes Ryleigh into his arms, solidifying the marriage with the horniest kiss me eva see ina me life.

Me cyaa stand dem ahahah!

"Dat is ittttt!" Paw cheers and everybody else follows with the cheering.

I look down at the program to see what's next…

Opening Remarks

Prayer/Sermon

Exch. of Vows

Exch. of Rings

Couple's Introduction

Sand and Signing Ceremony

Cocktails (1 hour)

Reception

I can't wait to see what the reception is like.

And mi cyaa wait fi the cocktail food and pictures

The main dish mi cyaa wait fah. Mi know Sue and her team step ina dat!

Less than 20 minutes later I'm shoving the last veggie spring roll in my mouth before running my hands down the acrylic seating chart.

Table three... that's my table. I step off to the entryway and I cannot believe my eyes... The entryway itself is lit from its roof and down to the sides by fairy lights, glistening in the dark, against the reflective acrylic flooring. The reception area is black with nothing but translucent thick glass tables and chairs, arched free standing chandeliers, candles on each table and I don't even have to describe anything else. Just know, Toni did her big one.

As soon as we exit the entryway the ushers direct us to a photobooth that we should use to snap pictures that'll be printed immediately for us to add to the guest album before signing it. Moya, Kelly and I all go in together, snapping away before we exit, collecting the pictures and adding them to the album while signing.

'Love you good ole. Congrats to you and yuh mad man'

-xoxo Keif

Is what I sign below my picture before moving to find my table.

Table three, table threeee...

Oh, there.

Toni really outdid her fucking self! I just have to say it again. Me??? love this bad.

• • •

"Deh a di top fi a minute!!!" the groomsmen entrance song has the audience in an uproar.

The clean version yesss, but are we singing the clean version? Nope!

Ahaha! The vibe is immaculate!

Paw picks up on the next line while dancing and raising his glass.

Man a drink from the cocktail kick off... and still

"Shoot out every tools out mi a bring it," Jordanne joins while his friends and the crowd hype him up.

A Masicka song woulda affi be dem entrance again. They come to the end of their time before standing to the side, waiting for the ladies. The song then mixes into Natasha Bedingfield's - Love Like This.

The bridal gang enters with their routine– Ry' at the center of it all. The girls dance around her while she sings to J' with the widest smile on her face. I watch him wipe away fake tears before moving to her.

"We were cool back in high school ooouu I really liked you, must've been your attitude," she lip syncs.

They continue right up until the chorus, before the mix moves to Fine Whine by Alkaline. Only them... Love say dem find a new Alkaline song fi shout after each other though.

• • •

JORDANNE

"Lady mine yuh stitch dem!" Ry' shouts to Michelle who is wrapped in Liam's arms, rocking from side to side.

Love dat, love dat

I look to my left to see Mum and Skulli looking the same. To the right, my sister is all over Joshua while Kelly cheers them on. Beside them, we have Mariah who is in Ruse's lap, grinding. Paw? Paw tek off him shirt, have it ova him shoulder and a try tell the DJ wah fi play.

David is explaining something to the girl he's dating. Cyaa remember her name...

Ms. Janette, Ry's uncle, Ryan, JJ, Ms.Cherry, Trisse, Troopa, Snoop, Buckle, Nadifa, Hally, di boss boy and... Kirk, are all learning a random dance move from Keif– on the beat of a whining song of all things.

Jah Jah, a sample dem.

I feel when Ry' pulls me in, bringing my focus solely to her.

"I love you Mr.Sheer," she whispers in my ear, tightening her hug.

She nahfi tell me, I can see and feel it...

"More than mi own life Mrs.Sheer," I respond, bringing my hand down to her ass.

Her reception dress is crazy sexy.

Killa, fix up you thoughts

Why? She's mine.

"Mrs.Sheer," she giggles, looking down at her ring.

Suddenly the DJ mixes into Make Me Feel by Kalado.

"Ayeeee long time mi no hear dah song yah!" Ry' announces, and like the Power Rangers, her friends group up, moving over to us, while she bends over.

Jah know

"Pull up dat, pull up dat! Wifey ago give the boss a whine," Paw's voice overpowers the music and commotion.

I laugh out!

One set a wildings dem enuh killa.

"See how she bend ova with the arch!? Then yuh no must breed!" Mariah shouts.

She woulda get pregnant on her back, laying still same way. The arch nahv nuttin fi do with it.

I smile at my thought.

The song starts over and immediately she starts whining, with the raw lyrics ringing throughout the night air. I start moving with her and the next ting mi feel ah Ramone, handing me a glass of whiskey, before popping my collar.

"Eassssyyyyyyyy!" Skulli shouts from across the dance floor.

To think earlier we were slow dancing to Adele's One and Only mixed with Burna Boy's Onyeka after being prayed for, for 20 long minutes… to now watching mi woman transform into a full time Taboo worker.

Life funny yuh fuck

The thought makes me happy and I start slapping her ass while shi shake it.

"Murdaaaa slap up dattttt!!!" Mariah screams, and that I do.

That I definitely do…

• • •

Everybody has left to walk down to the lawns, to watch the fireworks. We're the only ones left in the reception area after hours of games, drinking, dancing and just creating raw memories.

Her head is rested on my shoulders, as we complete our last slow dance, surrounded by nothing but the reception decor, the annoying videographer and the overbearing photographer.

"Jor?" her tiny voice creeps out.

"Love?" I respond.

"We really did it," she continues– voice breaking.

Jah know…

"We did," is all I can offer, pulling her closer into me.

"I think I more than love you," she adds.

Same feeling mi have. Cyaa explain it, not in words at least.

Pulling away slightly, I look down at her. Her eyes are now glossy from the tears she's fighting back.

"I've been way past that point, years now…" I trail off, and with that, our lips find each other.

The fireworks go off, and so does the flash from the cameras… but in this moment, it's just us… not the fancy decor…

Not the sound of the fireworks…

Not the cheers from everybody watching it from the lawns…

Just my Love and I… wrapped in each other, as our souls become one.

•UNTIL NEXT TIME•

BOOK II?